Kidnapping the Classics

Book 2 of the Mari Fable Mysteries

Emily Fluke

Also by Emily Fluke

To my son, who asked me for a snack approximately 7,521 times while I wrote this.

Somehow, I still finished.

Prologue

D~~ear Journal,~~
I don't need to address the notebook formally. Also, why am I talking to myself? You'd think I'd be a better writer after years of journalism. Anyway, per Kai's suggestion, I'm dealing with my stress by writing. We'll see if it works. . .

Approximately one week ago, I came into possession of a magical hood. Is magical the right word? Hood of immortality? No, the invisible hood that senses my intention. Oh, I've got it: The Hood that Haunts Me.

Any chance at a normal life vanished the moment I stole the hood from The Keeper of Stories, AKA Scarlet. I tried to give it back but Scarlet doesn't have the aura anymore. It is nothing more than fabric in her hands now. I guess she is no longer The Little Cloak Girl. She's a woman about several centuries old but looks more like an actress in her twenties who plays a teen on TV.

At least, this stupid hood will keep me looking young. I think.

What I know from the former Keeper so far:

1. If I take the hood off, more stories spill over into the real world and join the cycle in the next century. Except not all stories. Note: investigate this later.

2. *Stories didn't spill over into our world when the hood transferred from Scarlet to me. Why? Who knows. Well, Scarlet knows because apparently when stories cross over, the earth shakes. Yes, literally shakes. And people think it's because San Francisco is on a fault line. . .*
3. *The hood makes it possible for me to see the story aura around the people who have become characters.*
4. *Without the hood, Scarlet has lost all power.*
5. *I suck at portal creation. I can't do it at all despite Scarlet's efforts to teach me. She says I don't "want it enough".*

In fact, I suck at all things classic literature and the responsibilities of The Keeper of Stories. At least I'm not Red Riding Hood anymore.
I need a nap.

Chapter 1

Something Wicked This Way Comes

(1 year and 5 months later)

Crimson liquid dripped over the keyboard and my screen blinked until it faded to black. Of course, the red drink skipped my hood and stained the carpet, the coffee table, and the white pants I swore I wouldn't wear until Wendy graduated.

"Cursed sippy cups," I said. For a moment, I allowed myself to grieve the murder of the article I'd woken up early to finish writing.

My laptop sizzled. It *actually* sizzled as the Kool-aid reached its murderous fingers inside the computer and pulled out its beating heart. *Okay, dramatic much?* I swiped my hands over my face and ignored the reflection of raccoon eyes from the black screen on my lap.

I've got to get some sleep. Any day another, possibly dangerous fairy tale character could land, and, as the one with the hood, I'd need to figure out what to do with them. Plus, the whole missing persons case my boss expected me to investigate stunk of something fictional. *Fictional come to life, that is.*

I shook my head and snapped the lid back on the sippy cup after it'd already done its damage. The screen on my watch lit up and buzzed that I had exactly five minutes to get out the door and get to work on time. Wendy scooted herself across the rug to tug on my pant leg and beg for more juice. Instead of wallowing over the hours of work I'd lost, I stood and stripped myself of the white pants that looked like I'd just lost a battle with yet another wolf-turned-serial-killer.

But that fight happened over a year ago now and only a few benign fictional characters had popped up around San Francisco. That I knew of.

My daughter reached a grabby hand toward me, and I scooped her up. The TV blared with another jingle from a family-friendly show that bored me to tears, but I liked the background noise. Plus, the sitcoms helped me avoid that inevitable mom-guilt about watching anything too serious in front of a child. Not that I had time to sit and binge steamy medical dramas, anyway.

I flicked the TV off and carried Wendy on my hip to the kitchen.

"Whoa," my husband said as he emerged from the bedroom. We crossed paths in the kitchen and Kai grinned at my pant-less legs. "You should have told me you were feeling frisky before I got all dressed up."

Final testing must have arrived at his school because he wore a pullover sweater and the pants he called his 'fancy jeans'. Kai insisted that dressing nicely encouraged his students to work harder and hold themselves to a higher standard. Despite the warming June weather, he always wore long-sleeves while passing out the history exams that would determine the high schoolers' final grades before graduation.

"Wendy's sippy cup exploded," I said as I tossed the plastic into the sink. It demonstrated my explanation when the lip popped off again. Red juice dotted white porcelain in what looked like blood splatter around the sink.

At least that's what it looked like to me, but Kai would say I'd seen too many crime scenes. And he'd be right. But was it *too many* or *not enough*? The city's people suffered murders, attacks, and all the crap in between and, as an investigative journalist, I swore to inform the public about how to keep themselves safe.

Kai took Wendy, lifting her from my hip, and gave her a nuzzle kiss with his nose bumping against hers. The cuddles left her beaming. I couldn't help but snake my arms around my husband for a quick hug that melted into a few kisses of our own non-nuzzle-style.

"Ebenezer Scrooge," I cursed as I pulled away from him. I missed him. Busy days parenting, actively avoiding anything to do with classic fairy tales, and investigating the missing persons case, deprived me of my husband. And Kai, with his sexy pullover sweater and ruffled brown hair, was the only one who could knock me off my tight schedule.

My planner seemed to scream at me as it lay splayed open on the counter next to the diaper bag. Colorful scribbles covered the boxes that showed each day of the month. Looking at it caused my chest to tighten. I needed to stay on task because it was the only way I knew how to survive.

"Will you pack her snacks for daycare while I change?" I asked, breathless from both our long kisses and the edge of a panic attack that my planner incited.

Kai nodded and started whistling a Taylor Swift song that he claimed he only knew because of his students. My wrist buzzed again. The digital clock sent an alarm that I should be out the door, down the condo staircase, and on Main Street headed to Ruby Slippers daycare this second.

My stomach growled to announce that I'd neglected it in my quest to finish the article before work. That same article that was now lost inside a burnt laptop since my planner didn't allow me an extra second to send the document to my work email.

I didn't bother clicking on the light in our closet and grabbed the first pair of pants off the floor. I tripped and struggled into the legs and wondered why I didn't wear slacks more often—they were roomier and rather comfy. Despite the ease of the slip-on pants, I'd never been graceful. I stumbled into the wall, hopping on one foot.

I bounced out of the closet while wriggling my other foot through the pant leg and thanked my lucky stars that this dang hood had molded itself to my body, becoming weightless and invisible. It was a far cry from the heavy, velvety fabric that Scarlet had handed me during that fateful day back on Cygnus Island. The day went down in history, my history, as the day I overcame the wolf and twisted the end of my fairy tale.

The red hood didn't tangle between my legs, get wet in the shower, nor was it even noticeable during mine and Kai's sexy times. It simply didn't seem to exist, and the further time passed since the wolf's attack, the more it felt that whole fairy tale fiasco, full of magic and death and supernatural beings never happened at all. At least that was what I pretended.

When I emerged from the bedroom, the red numbers on the microwave stared me down as if to say 'you're late, you're late for a very important date!'. I scrambled around the kitchen, shoving my lunch into the diaper bag. Then I snatched Wendy from Kai's arms despite his protests and offers to take her to the daycare.

"No, this is my routine," I said. "Every day I call my mom on the walk to daycare. Then I drop Wendy off with a twenty-second nose-nuzzle kiss and remind the daycare that she's allergic to peanuts. I swear they'll forget." I recited the schedule, though Kai knew it as well as I did.

"I'm glad you and your mom have become so close over the last year," he said, his gaze on the dishes he washed. I whirled like a tornado from the kitchen to the front door, where I shoved my feet into flats without looking. "But don't forget you're a kick-butt mom on your own and you don't need to double-check with her!" My husband called after me. I was already out of the house and marching down the corridor of condominium doors.

Tala and Mr. Geppetto, two separate neighbors that had gotten rather cozy lately, nodded their good mornings to me as I hurried down the staircase. They held identical, disposable coffee cups and plastered themselves to the stair railing to let me pass. I wore the bulky diaper bag hanging off one shoulder, balanced Wendy on the opposite hip, and had my bookbag slung across my chest. Thankfully, the bookbag was considerably lighter today without the laptop weighing it down.

Tala tilted her head at me and said something that I didn't hear.

Though my neighbors were like the grandparents I had never had, I didn't have time to stop and chat today. My stomach turned at the thought of how far off-schedule that spill had thrown me. Not to mention the lost article. Such was the life of a mother. And an investigative journalist. Plus The Keeper… I shook my head to knock the thought from my mind and focus on making up for the lost time.

I barreled down the stairs and hauled up Main Street with Wendy bouncing on my hip. Though I usually sang the alphabet to my daughter during the first half of the twelve-minute hike to daycare, I forced myself to sacrifice that part of the schedule today. I called my mom early. The free time on my walk between daycare and the office was already filled with a plan to rehearse a confession. My boss wouldn't be happy about the lost article.

With my cell phone pinched against my shoulder and Wendy yanking on strands of hair that had escaped from my messy bun, I felt pulled in two directions. A cool bay breeze cut through the summer sun and swept through my roomy slacks. I shivered and cursed at the other line. My mom's phone continued to ring, and I prayed nothing serious had happened. More likely she was in the shower or had left her phone on silent.

Still, the paranoia she instilled in me would resurface every now and again. Mom lived like she was on the run.

Speaking of running, my breath ran out and my chest tightened as I climbed the sidewalk up San Francisco's urban hills. Ruby Slippers daycare came into view down the street. Relief mixed with sadness twisted in my mind. I needed a break from parenting, but leaving Wendy at the daycare routinely broke my heart.

"Are you in danger?" Mom's voice came on the other line as the rhythmic ringing finally cut short.

"No. What?" I asked. "Can't you answer the phone like a normal human?"

"What if I don't want to be a normal human?" Mom said. I couldn't argue with that one. As much as I loved my schedules, I admired my mom's spontaneity from afar. Very far.

"Speaking of a normal human," I said while hefting Wendy up

higher until she nearly crushed my ribcage. "Wendy still won't talk or walk and the child development book says she should show signs of both by now."

"Didn't she say the words dog and dad?" Mom asked, reminding me of the rare occasion when Wendy would cry for Kai instead of reaching for him. She'd only said dog once, and I didn't encourage that one since she'd pulled her *Little Red Riding Hood* board book off of the shelf and pointed to the wolf. I didn't want to think about fairy tales when I was drowning in motherhood and trying to keep up with the missing persons case at work.

"That was almost a month ago now," I said.

"She'll get there. Not everything happens on a timeline," Mom said. "Ease up a bit and learn to be flexible."

"I'm plenty flexible," I muttered. "I go to yoga every week." Of course, every week was more like once a month, and yoga usually meant a Saturday coffee run in stretchy pants. But who could blame me?

Classic stories found me even while at the gym. One minute I'm tipping over in Tree Pose, and the next I'm watching the story glow land on my yoga instructor, Liz Bennet. It came with a soft but sudden change over her and I stared at the poor instructor with my mouth agape. The pink glow pulsed around Liz like a heartbeat from a living story. Scarlet had said it's my duty to make sure the classic stories played out as written, but I wanted to avoid all Keeper responsibilities until Wendy was in school, or graduated… or retired. Jane Austen's *Pride and Prejudice* would just have to wait.

"You know what I meant," Mom said.

Wendy tugged at my hair. I used my free hand to rummage in the diaper bag for a toy to replace my poorly dyed strands in her fist. Another gust of salty air blew up from the pier on the opposite side of the neighborhood. Goosebumps prickled my legs, and they almost felt bare.

A shadow cast over me and I stopped short. The goosebumps spread from my legs to my stomach and crawled up my spine. My eyes trailed up the giant body that stood on the sidewalk in front of me and blocked my path. The phone slipped from between my cheek and shoulder and clattered to the cement. Goodbye to another screen I'd probably broken in less than two hours.

"Bad," Wendy babbled.

The man stood twice my height and folded his thick arms across his chest. He glared down at me with eyes as dark as pits. Not to mention, the smell coming from his pits…

"What?" I asked. My mouth dropped open, and I snapped my head to Wendy as her words finally registered in my brain.

"Bad," she said again. She raised her tiny finger toward the man and then curled it back toward her face to chew on.

His features looked vaguely familiar, the same way I'd recognize an actor in a movie that I'd seen briefly in another show. Instead of squiggly 'Pig Pen' lines coming from his body odor, a faint glow surrounded the man like that of the morning sunrise. It was almost pretty, but ominous too, like I hadn't gotten enough rest before a long day.

The story aura.

"Ebenezer Scrooge," I cursed under my breath. I didn't have time for this. I didn't want this red hood, or the extra responsibility, or even the immortality that I refused to acknowledge.

Of course, the man went right for the spot the red hood exposed, my neck. His meaty fingers gripped my throat and panic surged through me.

Wendy repeated her word loud and clear with the touch of a squeal. "Bad!"

My crushed windpipe ached and my lungs burned with lack of air, but what disturbed me the most was the possibility of the man grabbing Wendy.

"You will not stop her, Keeper," he said with breath so bad I thought I'd curl up like a dead spider. One glance at my daughter gave me a rush of adrenaline and I kneed the man in the groin. He didn't react in pain as I expected. Instead, he only appeared startled, as if the kick had awakened him. He released the chokehold and stumbled back.

I was suddenly aware of how bare the street was. Everyone had already scurried off to their jobs or school on this late Monday morning. Nobody saw the attack. How did my attacker know I'd be here in the first place?

The man gawked at me with his mouth open and a speckle of drool on his lip. I cringed, frozen between wanting to scream, kick him again, or ask him what he meant and how he knew I was The Keeper.

Before I could decide, he backed away and bonked his head on Ruby Slippers' sign. He hurried for the shelter of an alleyway. When he turned, I caught the sight of something odd. Red lines criss crossed up along the side of his neck, along his jaw, and around his collarbone. The thread was stitched to hold his flesh together.

"Frankenstein?" I whispered.

Please, no. I have enough crap in my life already.

And here I thought I was the only one with a weird red thing. At that moment, I wanted to throw the hood off and run down the alleyway in the opposite direction. As if I could escape my role as The Keeper.

"Frankenstein's monster," a voice said behind me. I straightened and whirled around to see fiery red hair and another figure with arms folded across their chest.

Scarlet raised her eyebrows as she stared at my legs.

"What?" I asked while I tried to gather my thoughts.

"It's a common misconception. Frankenstein is the doctor. The monster doesn't have a name," she said. The former Keeper's judgmental gaze pierced through me. Scarlet nodded toward my legs again. "I thought I was finally getting the hang of modern fashion, but I'm wondering if I have a misconception of my own."

I glanced down to see that I'd replaced my white work pants, not with slacks, but penguin-covered pajama pants.

The day defeated me, so I sighed and let my shoulders slump. I couldn't avoid it any longer. I was late, failing as a mom, and the story aura had found me.

Wendy wiggled and squirmed in my arms, reaching for 'auntie Let-Let' as we had called her when Scarlet had slept on our couch. Since losing her immortality and passing the role of The Keeper onto me, Scarlet was learning how to live a normal life. She had stayed with Kai and me while trying to get on her feet and assimilate into society. It was a slow and sometimes hilarious upward climb as she learned things like Uber instead of her long-gone ability to teleport between doors.

"How is my favorite little Bug Rat?" Scarlet cooed and reached to pull Wendy from my hip. The weight on my shoulders didn't lift.

"Bug Rat?" I asked.

"I heard it on a play on the television," Scarlet said with a shrug. "The adult character called a child character a Bug Rat."

"I think you mean Rugrat," I explained. "And just call it a TV show. It's not a play."

Scarlet rolled her eyes. At least she'd gotten that modern gesture down just right. I resisted the urge to roll my own eyes. When Scarlet shed the hood, she shed all responsibility and threw herself into a lazy study of twenty-first-century society. She watched too many sitcoms, yet still confused or forgot simple modern phrases and words like TV.

"Okay, sure," she said without stifling a scoff. "Like you're doing much better. *Frankenstein*." Scarlet mocked me while she nuzzled Wendy's nose and laughed. "Frankenstein!" she said again since Wendy seemed entertained by the word.

"I get it, Frankenstein is not the monster," I said. "Do you want to tell me what he's doing here and why he attacked me?"

Scarlet shrugged again. "I'm not The Keeper anymore."

"Uh-huh," I said. I folded my arms, then suddenly felt uncomfortable, as if I'd turned into the monster myself. I unfolded and let my hands dangle at my sides, though the diaper bag nearly slipped off my shoulder. "And you're just here to say hi, right?" I knew better.

Scarlet offered a cringing smile.

"The story aura is back," she said. I stiffened.

"I thought you weren't The Keeper anymore. How could you know?"

She straightened the little green bow in Wendy's tiny ponytail. It stuck straight up from her head like a unicorn horn. My daughter babbled nonsensical words that Scarlet pretended to understand. It seemed Wendy had a story of her own to share. We just didn't understand it yet. I'd smile at my daughter's pure, innocent joy if I wasn't stressed about her developmental timeline.

Finally, Scarlet met my gaze and answered the question that hung in the air between us. Was that tension or the lingering stench of Frankenstein's monster?

"I don't know," she said. "I'm not sure. But I was The Keeper for centuries, Mari. I dedicated my existence to finding story characters. I know fairy tales inside and out. And even though some characters are tricky to identify, like you were, I can feel it in my bones. I saw the television reports of the missing people. Something big is about to happen."

My stomach curdled. *My case.* I'd been hoping, praying even, that my investigation didn't tangle with fairy tales.

"What does that have to do with stories?" I asked. My voice came out in a squeak.

Scarlet planted a big kiss on Wendy's cheek and handed her back to me. I braced myself for what she was about to say. The former Keeper's nose crinkled, and she looked like an apologetic rabbit at the same time as my wrist buzzed with another alarm.

You're late for an important date—AKA a meeting with your boss.

"What is it?" I prodded, finally tapping the 'off' button on my alarm rather than snooze. I was late, I'd have to accept it.

Instead of telling me directly, Scarlet always worked in riddles. I believed it was a combination of not knowing how to communicate like a normal person and the fact that she was still close to the story cycle but couldn't quite identify any without the hood. *The magical, stupid, horrific hood.*

Scarlet gave me a small smile. "Do you know how many fairy tales involve kidnapping?"

The list of stories ran through my brain, each with its own color. I noted Rapunzel in gold and Hansel and Gretel in black. Avoidance would no longer be an option. And here I thought, destroying my laptop was what would flip my day upside down.

"A lot," I said with a grimace.

If people were kidnapped because story characters spilled over into our world, my entire case would turn upside down, inside out, and backward.

Chapter 2

All That Glitters Isn't Gold

Ruby Slippers daycare wouldn't need to worry about Wendy's peanut allergy today. I refused to let Wendy out of my sight with Frankenstein running amok in the city. *Excuse me—Frankenstein's monster.* Even more reason to keep my daughter close. And why did I recognize him? Couldn't a woman live her life without someone stalking her to Starbucks or work? Apparently not, especially not me.

I marched past the colorful door to the daycare. Bay Side Media's office building came into view as I crested the hill. Though the rest of the walk was downhill, I huffed the entire way with Wendy in my aching arm. Scarlet trailed behind me, gabbing about Mary Shelley. She claimed Doctor Frankenstein's story would soon come to a deadly end if his monster was already out and about.

I'd never read the book, but I gathered from Scarlet's tone that I'd need to brush up on my SparkNotes if I wanted to twist the ending the way I did with Red Riding Hood.

A throb pulsed in my temple and I grit my teeth at the spark of a headache. I stopped and whirled around to beg Scarlet to speak slower and quieter.

"You've garnered much luck this past year with little fairy tales to seal. But even you cannot deny this one," she said with a nod toward the alley where the monster had disappeared. Red curls tossed across her smooth freckled face. Scarlet would be a dang TikTok star if she knew how to use technology.

"Doesn't Frankenstein die in the book?" I asked. "That would leave no chance of an immortal monster at the end of his story, right?" My breath ran out by the end of the sentence. Maybe I needed to attend the yoga classes I'd signed up for rather than ditching them for Starbucks. Wendy tried to stick her fingers into my mouth as I talked, but I pulled my head away.

"Frankenstein dies, the *monster*, however…" she pursed her lips and shrugged. "He might need a little encouragement to off himself."

"Look, Scarlet," I said with a sigh. I wore the stupid hood and I'd stopped a crazed serial killer-turned werewolf. Wasn't that enough? "I can't."

"Can't what?" She quirked her head, not understanding my response.

"Do this Keeper thing," I said. The diaper bag fell to the sidewalk. I glanced up at the tall building toward the window of my boss's office. "People are missing and it's my job to report on it. What happened to your job?"

Scarlet bared a row of white teeth and I knew she'd lost yet another job. Flipping burgers was a hard position to accept after centuries of hunting fictional villains and cutting them down before they could ensure an eternity of evil existence. Except, of course, that wasn't what she did. We were so *different*. Scarlet only cared about the story ending correctly which meant she ensured even the stories with sad endings played out.

I shivered. She wasn't The Keeper of stories anymore. I didn't need to be creeped out by it. But who could blame me? A giant creature with other people's body parts had just held me in a Mortal Kombat chokehold in front of my toddler's daycare. Creeped out was *all* I could be.

"Ending monsters is more important than anything else," Scarlet said with a lift of her chin. Her confidence on the subject was blatant, like a slap across the face.

I raised my eyebrow and hefted Wendy higher on my hip. "Say that again, but look at my daughter this time."

Scarlet rolled her eyes. It tempted me to tell her they'd get stuck like that. But as clueless as she was about modern society, Scarlet wasn't dumb and she wouldn't fall for tricks.

"I'm not great with subtlety," she said. "But I assume you're suggesting that your family is a higher priority than other people's families?" She folded her arms and stuck out one leg, matching the perfect mean-girl position. Despite her history, Scarlet wasn't cruel or mean, just painfully honest. A realist.

I snorted. A realist who ended fairy tales for a living. *I guess that makes sense.*

"That's not what I meant, and you know it," I said. After turning, I yanked on the door to the office building. Inside, a hollow hallway led to doors and elevators. The bottom floor housed an insurance company and mortgage lending office.

Scarlet glanced inside and back at me. Her scoff turned into a laugh. "What's the word that describes when something is terribly dull?"

Boring. But I didn't give her the satisfaction. Instead, I marched into the building and into my boring life that was anything but. Hadn't she ever seen my day planner? A girl needs free time to get bored and 'free time' wasn't on my radar.

I heard my stalker, AKA Scarlet, stomp inside after me like a kid having a tantrum. The muscles in my arm strained and shook under Wendy's weight. I bumped the elevator button with my free hip and stepped back to wait for the ding.

"You need to come with me," Scarlet said. The elevator doors bumped and slid open.

I stepped into the metal cube meant to take me to the top floor where I'd pretend Bay Side Media and Wendy were my only responsibilities.

A sudden sickening moment of déjà vu assaulted me. The memory struck me fast and my throat dried and tightened—the second time that morning I nearly choked. Scarlet, or Redhead as I once called her, sparked a memory about the first time I'd ridden in an elevator with The Keeper of Stories. Except for this time, I hadn't lost my daughter, and I wore the hood despite my efforts to ignore its responsibilities. I refused to acknowledge the immortality I'd gained and what that would mean decades from now when Kai and Wendy grew old without me.

A sob filled my throat in a painful lump that made breathing impossible.

Scarlet squeezed in before the doors sealed shut, her stubbornness finally giving. "The stories have to play out correctly or the people will be stuck in the cycle again," she said as she stood beside me. But instead of turning to face out toward the elevator door, she faced the wall. It would unsettle me if I didn't know she was just clueless about normal behaviors. I'd forgotten she did the same thing the first time I'd ridden an elevator with her. "What if Frankenstein's monster gets on one of those flying canisters and his story can't play out without Doctor Frankenstein there to stop him?"

"Flying canisters?" I asked since I couldn't identify this one. The door's bell dinged and opened to the sixth floor, where dozens of windows left the area blindingly bright. Bay Side Media owned the whole floor, which meant we stepped right into the bustling office rather than a dim hallway. My coworkers sat tapping away at their computers which was a painful reminder I'd ruined mine an hour ago. At least I still had my office desktop.

"The point," Scarlet said with a huff, "is that the monster will keep on living and wreaking havoc and no amount of weapons or canister crashes can end him. Not with the story protection."

A couple of close-by coworkers quirked their heads at me as they saw my parade of chaos. The parade included but was not limited to my late arrival in penguin pants, a lady in mismatched clothes trailing me, and a toddler on my hip.

I offered a curt smile and dumped both the diaper bag and laptop bag to the floor of my cubicle. Wendy wiggled to get down and Scarlet made herself at home by taking a seat on top of my desk. Despite the distraction of the paper calendar on the wall with its schedule of witness interviews, research meetings, and deadlines, my brain was stuck on the stupid flying canisters.

Wendy crawled to the laptop bag and pulled a cube of sticky notes from the front pocket, which she promptly ripped apart and tossed around the tiny space like colorful confetti. I pinched the bridge of my nose and sighed. An epiphany about Scarlet's flying canisters cut my frustration short.

"Oh, airplanes!" I said as I palmed my forehead.

"Yes," Scarlet said. She picked up a small mirror off of my desk and checked her teeth. After returning it to its place, she stared me down. "So, are you going to let the monster travel around killing people, or will you help him find the end of the story? He kills himself at the end of *Frankenstein.*"

I flopped in the desk chair and it released a series of cracking sounds under my exhausted collapse. "You really expect me to guide a person–"

"Monster."

"Monster-person," I half-heartedly agreed, "to commit suicide?"

Scarlet shrugged and chewed on her cheek. The gnawing created a sunken look on her face that had me worried. How was she faring in the real world? I shook my head. *I don't have time to dive into that right now.*

The smell of stale food wafted into my cubicle. Elsie's reheated egg bowl had definitely exploded in the microwave again.

"It's the way the author wrote his story, not you," Scarlet said. Wendy inch-wormed to Scarlet's short-heeled Mary Janes and gripped her ankle. Using Scarlet's leg, Wendy pulled herself to standing, but her behind still waggled around like a cheerful dog. The unsteady dance showed me she didn't plan to do any walking. Not without encouragement, anyway.

I leaned forward, ignoring the cracking sound from the chair, and waved for Wendy to walk toward me. She promptly dropped to her knees and crawled for my hand. My chest tightened again. Each worry seemed to stack directly on top of my ribcage like bricks rising one by one to create a wall. Throw Humpty Dumpty on top and it was the perfect image of how I felt—crushed by the weight of looming fairy tale responsibilities. Not to mention motherhood, my job, trying to drink enough water, keeping up with friendships, and sleeping. *What is sleep?*

"So?" Scarlet prodded. "Isn't this whole investigation gig meant to protect people?"

I furrowed my brow, but not in concern, for once. Impressed, I smiled and nodded at Scarlet. "You learned new slang."

She shrugged again while pulling a lock of her curls straight. It popped out from between her thumb and forefinger and bounced back toward her skull. "The people on the screen help."

"TV shows," I said to clarify. "They're just TV shows. And yes, I investigate and write articles about attacks in the city to inform people how to protect themselves. Speaking of which, I have a missing persons case I need to focus on." My computer booted up with a whir of the fans. The screen blinked to life as I mentally prepared myself to rewrite the article I'd lost that morning.

"They're probably missing because there's a monster on the loose," she muttered.

I closed my eyes and took a slow breath before rage built up. Scarlet knew how to push my buttons. Sometimes it felt I was raising a teenager rather than friends with a twenty-four-year-old. Despite our nearly decade age difference, we'd learned to get along well enough over the past year and I almost missed her presence in our house since she'd secured a roommate situation with a few college girls.

"I speak the truth," she said as she hopped off the desk and scooped Wendy up. "Now, I'll take care of this one while you take care of that one." She pointed to my computer, which I had programmed to open to the news.

Young Man disappears off Pier 99, Second Missing Without a Trace in Two Weeks.

I grimaced. She was right. As much as I didn't want to worry about fairy tales, this case could involve the monster. But I had no proof either way. It could be a good old-fashioned serial killer who dumped bodies into the ocean off the piers, not the creature from Mary Shelley's imagination. It was fifty-fifty.

"You look like you've seen a ghost," Scarlet said with a laugh. "It gets easier."

"Does it?" I asked, and my frown deepened with a bitter taste on my tongue. I interviewed killers, I didn't hunt them. Until the wolf, that is. I shook away the memory of Jameson's open, unseeing eyes. Everyone at Bay Side Media acted shocked for about a week after the murderous rampage was revealed. We had suspected foul play from him, just not *that* foul. So our boss, Pam, forced us to move on by sending us right back to work and scrubbing Jameson's cubicle clean of his memory.

Scarlet offered a smile. "You're going to pay me for this, right?" She hiked Wendy up higher on her side.

I rolled my eyes and nodded. "But don't leave the building." I tapped the computer mouse and booted up a blank document.

"You still don't trust me?" she pouted while Wendy tugged on Scarlet's necklace. I'd never noticed the locket back when Scarlet wore the hood. But in modern clothes with lower necklines, the silver chain was exposed and the tiny jar on the end that held a small, curled piece of paper glinted against the office's overhead fluorescents.

I glanced up from the necklace to her freckled face. "You stalked me and tried to lure me to my death less than two years ago, Scarlet."

"Yes… But you understand why and that I only wanted to protect people as much as you. Sometimes that takes tough decisions like sacrificing characters to end the stories and cut down monsters before they loop back into the cycle."

My stomach soured. I couldn't blame Elsie's egg explosion this time. Could I really lead this monster, this person, to his death? I helped get killers off the street, but that was the extent of my involvement.

When I didn't respond, Scarlet patted my shoulder with her free hand and stooped to pick up the diaper bag.

"I'm going to find out what insurance means," she said in a bright tone and bounded off toward the elevator.

One brick seemed to lift from my chest and I could breathe easier. The blank document called to me and I knew I needed to dive into the zone and type up my research to reset my brain. With Scarlet gone, I could ignore fairy tale shenanigans and rewrite the article to get it on Pam's desk before lunch. Plus, hopefully, I'd still make my meeting with Detective Wilhelm. We planned to walk the piers and question employees at nearby shops and restaurants if they saw anything on the night the first guy had vanished. Detective Wilhelm only agreed under the belief that the public preferred talking with pretty young women. His words. I didn't feel young these days.

The keyboard clicked under my fingers, and the words flew out of me. The meticulous note-taking on colored Post-its, and inside my handwritten notebook, helped the details stay inside my brain. Losing my laptop didn't take the information I'd gathered because I always had backups for theories. Maybe I'd need to do the same for the articles I wrote.

Travis Young was last seen on June 2nd by his girlfriend. She called Travis a thrill-seeker and explained he enjoyed breaking and entering abandoned buildings. He had planned to climb the walls on Cygnus Island and spend the night in what he believed to be the abandoned Alcatraz prison, despite the proof that Cygnus Island had since been taken under the care of a religious organization that called themselves a monarchy.

I paused and rubbed the bridge of my nose. My grandmother and father were on that island somewhere, supposedly part of the 'religious organization,' or cult, or whatever it was. Investigating their business was the last thing I wanted to do. But this story would launch Bay Side Media upward in the news world if I could snag the truth behind it. I needed to separate my personal involvement and find out what happened to Travis Young before other innocent people vanished.

"Your babysitter is hot," Elsie said. I nearly jumped out of my chair, startled, but turned to face her. She stirred her steaming tea, then sipped it once she seemed satisfied the liquid had cooled. It took a moment for my brain to catch up.

"Do you mean Scarlet?" I asked as I pointed toward the elevator.

Elsie nodded with a wry grin.

"I doubt your wife would appreciate that you're daydreaming about another woman," I said.

"She appreciates beauty, too. It doesn't hurt anything."

"Well, Scarlet is not my babysitter." I swiveled back toward the computer and typed the last sentence, then clicked the print button. The printer beneath my desk roared to life and spit out the two-page rough draft. I snapped a staple on top and stood. With a curt smile, I pushed past Elsie.

"You've been different for a while now," she said and took another slurp of tea.

Different? I stopped and furrowed my brow.

"This is more than the stress of mom-life and working in a big city," she said. "Trust me, I'd know." Elsie pulled her phone from her pocket and waved it around to show me the picture of her and her wife's family of five kids.

"What do you mean?" I asked.

"You're grumpy, which is normal," she said as she pulled at a stray strand of her blonde hair that had caught on her lip. "But you avoid everybody. We used to be friends, you know? We'd hang out and get cocktails after work. Now you just stomp around with a scowl when anyone gets in your way. It's time you get out of your head and patch up your social life before you go insane."

I didn't have an argument. If I let anyone get close to me, I'd spill the beans about the story cycle, the hood, and that technically, *I'd* killed Jameson a year and a half ago. My organization and note-taking had morphed into rigid scheduling and obsessive routine to further cement myself in reality and as far away from fairy tales as I could.

"You barely even crack jokes anymore," Elsie added. "Unless your outfit is supposed to be a joke." She nodded toward my penguin pants.

Yikes. Had I really become that boring? I made a quick note in my mind's eye to throw on the extra skirt I had tucked in my desk drawer before meeting with Detective Wilhelm. More boring. The plain black skirt with my simple shirt would match the dark mood that I carried around. Anything exciting felt too dangerous after Jameson's attack. It left my life in a rut of paranoia.

"Screw that," I said aloud. Elsie raised her eyebrows. "Not at you. I mean, you're right." I'd refused to let the fate of the story determine my life before. Why was I letting fear of the hood's responsibilities control me now?

"Can you get a babysitter?" I asked, meeting Elsie's gaze.

"Can it be your babysitter?"

I gave her a *look,* and she shrugged sheepishly.

"Let's go out tonight," I said. "I want to go to a restaurant instead of ordering in. Let's get drinks and do the whole thing in heels in the city."

Elsie grinned. She loved a good party night despite what her family life would have you believe. She could switch from mom-mode to trivia game genius in the blink of an eye. "I'm so in," she said.

I didn't feel like hiding anymore. Though cocktails on Main Street didn't exactly mean I'd faced what'd happened with the wolf. At least it was outside of my planner's schedule and it was spontaneous.

Chapter 3

The Game Is Afoot

I did it. After months of burying myself in motherhood, going to bed early, and wearing sensible mom-clothes (AKA sweats when I wasn't at work), I went out on the town. Elsie harassed me endlessly when I'd ordered warm milk instead of a cocktail and left before Wendy's bedtime.

The next morning, I pounded a cup of coffee to stop the throbbing in my head. Thankfully, I didn't exacerbate my stress around Frankenstein's monster with a hangover. I dropped several cubes of ice into the bitter beverage and sipped. My reflection in the microwave stared back at me with raccoon eyes. The way I cupped the glass of coffee with both hands resembled a squirrel nibbling on a nut. Forget werewolves and Goldilocks' talking bears. I was a mythical creature all on my own —a mixture of mother, trash panda, and investigator.

The mishmash parts of other beings haunted me. I needed to track down Frankenstein's monster before he could do any damage. Could I really lead him to his death? And if I helped the story play out, didn't that mean Doctor Frankenstein would die too? So far, I had no proof that the monster was hurting anyone or anything other than my own neck.

I gingerly touched my collarbone and shook my head at the reflection. The microwave beeped an alarm, and I nearly jumped out of my skin. At least I knew Doctor Frankenstein was out there somewhere and could patch me back together if need be.

The red numbers blinked on the timer and Kai emerged from the small porch that jutted from the side of our condo over Main street. He huffed and puffed and wiped at the sweat on his forehead with the bottom of his T-shirt. Wendy crawled over the threshold of the sliding glass door to follow him.

"You're awake," he said with another gasp of breath. Kai swiped a water bottle from the tall counter that split the living room and kitchen into two separate spaces and chugged. "Do you have a headache?" He furrowed his brows at me.

I relaxed my face from pinching and let my shoulders fall. "Yeah, I think I have to do something about Frankenstein."

"It's a good thing I've been working out," Kai said after another gulp of water. He nodded toward the porch where we stored our treadmill. My mom had bought it for me after Jameson's attack. The equipment came with her insistence that I needed to exercise in the safety of my house rather than run through Pioneer Park. But Mom is more cautious—borderline paranoid—than I ever wanted to be.

At least Kai liked the treadmill.

"The problem is that I have no proof the monster has hurt anyone," I said. "So far, the missing persons case doesn't show any foul play. Detective Wilhelm believes the missing people skipped town. Travis Young and a local mechanic disappeared within the same week."

My husband took a breath after downing half of the water bottle. The liquid sloshed as he set it back down and leaned against the counter.

"What about the pile of hair they found on Pier 99? I thought it matched the mechanic's DNA," Kai said. He reminded me of the only solid piece of evidence that showed the first missing person did, indeed, vanish.

"It does but—" I shook my head. "Hair isn't enough to indicate that the mechanic was in danger or had gotten hurt." The detective had insisted the discarded locks of hair only proved his theory. He believed the mechanic was ditching town with a new style to hide his identity. I didn't have a strong case to argue otherwise, though it didn't sound right that he'd cut his hair and leave it on the pier.

"Does Wilhelm have reason to believe they were running away from something?" Kai asked, always the yin to my yang, the storm to my brain. He knew the right questions to get me forming new theories.

"He does," I said. "He found that the mechanic had racked up major debt and likely dipped out of the city. Plus, the guy didn't have any relatives or friends I could question. The station had to use a sketch artist with one of the mechanic's customers since we didn't find any updated pictures of him, either."

Kai pursed his lips and considered this. The detective and I had scoured Pier 99 for people who might have seen something, but the most we ended with was a street performer who claimed he'd seen a very bright light. Wilhelm chalked it up to the guy's need for dramatic flair while I jotted the note down.

Is this bright light the same as the story aura? I'd seen it before, the glow around my yoga teacher, showing she was Elizabeth Bennet from Jane Austen's classic romance *Pride and Prejudice*, but I wouldn't call it bright–just a vague glow to the person, like I was looking at them through tinted glasses.

The cold coffee sent chills down my arms as I took another drink. But the bitter, strong taste kept me alert and my mind sharp. My eyes trailed from the dark beverage to the living room where Wendy pulled herself to stand. Using the couch to balance, she lifted her foot.

"Look!" I yelled. After slamming my cup down on the counter, I hurried into the living room. My legs tucked underneath me as I plopped into crisscross applesauce and beckoned for Wendy to walk toward me. "Come on, Sweets, you can do it."

Wendy's butt wagged back and forth like a happy puppy and her pudgy foot inched forward. She reached for the coffee table that we'd taped washcloths around to avoid toddler-sized injuries. I held my breath as she released her hold on the couch and bent the other knee ready to stomp her tiny foot down in her first real step. If she started walking now, maybe, just maybe, I'd stop feeling the guilt of being a distracted and busy mother.

Kai crouched beside her and let her wrap her hand around his finger.

"What're you doing?" I asked, annoyed. "She's learning to walk by herself."

"She just needs a little help. It's no big deal," he said as he pulled Wendy along. She stomped her feet, confident with his hold, and squealed happily. After several steps, she tumbled into my lap and turned around to get comfortable. Kai handed her his water bottle to play with.

"She's behind the developmental stages according to the parenting book," I said as I pinched the bridge of my nose. The headache threatened to return with a small twinge in the center of my eyebrows. "I haven't been helping her enough."

"Wendy is fine," Kai said. At the mention of her name, Wendy looked up at him and beamed. "She's perfect, see?"

The sigh built up inside me. I didn't want Wendy to sense my stress and mistake it for frustration at her rather than disappointment in myself. I pointed to the parenting book on the coffee table that my planner had buried, as well as my broken laptop, the stained pants from yesterday, and the TV remote.

"The chart says that she should run by now," I said. "Run, Kai. Run."

"I heard you," he said with a shrug. "I don't think life follows a schedule as intensely as you do these days. Especially not kids' lives. And don't tell me she's not strong. Has she pinched you yet? She's in a pinching phase and it hurts."

"I know. The daycare told me she learned it from another little kid."

After Wendy crawled from my lap and scooted herself across the rug, I dropped my head into my hands. She yanked board books off the shelf underneath the TV and started looking at the brightly colored pictures.

"She's not talking either," I said with a groan. Kai took another swig of his water bottle that Wendy had discarded on the floor for more interesting toys. He sat on the corner of the coffee table and leaned forward to pull my hands from my face.

"Watch this," he said. "Do you want a drink?" The water in his bottle sloshed back and forth as he shook it. "Wednesday!"

"She'll never remember her real name if you keep calling her by nicknames," I said. Except she proved me wrong. Wendy ignored him until he called her by her real name.

"Water?" he asked.

"Juice," she said.

"See? She talks." Kai smiled proudly and stood to fetch the princess a sippy cup of juice. Though I'm impressed with everything my daughter does, I was worried. I wasn't convinced that a word here and there proved Wendy was on track, or that I was a sufficient mother. The coffee soured in my stomach and I stood to track down a mini bagel or something appropriate for a morning meal.

Water roared through the pipes, indicating that Kai had fired up a shower as part of his post-workout routine. I appreciated he followed a basic routine despite it being the weekend. The expected soothed me.

Always expect the unexpected. Psh, right.

I rolled my eyes at the memory of the article I'd written after Jameson's death a year and a half ago. My coworker had turned into a wolf and tried to eat me, so it wasn't a memory I wanted to keep close and treasure. But I'd learned a lot from the experience and, with the story aura glowing faintly around the monster and my yoga teacher, I was happy to have dealt with a fairy tale before.

I peeled a too-ripe banana and headed for the coffee table to dig out my planner. In between all the color-coded chaos, I penciled more notes for today.

Wendy is closer to walking. How should I be helping?

The pink pen ran dry. I capped it anyway and switched to orange to squeeze one more note between my record of Wendy's development and the plans we'd scheduled with our friends for a game night. *Ask Scarlet if she can deal with Frankenstein's monster.*

I knew she couldn't take the hood back, but why couldn't she lead the monster along in the story instead of me? The most important things for me to focus on right now were Wendy and the missing persons case. Besides, Scarlet knew what she was doing. She'd completed fairy tales for hundreds of years by leading the people who became characters to their story's endings. And to top it all off, I had a job. She didn't.

When I flipped the planner shut, the edge of the paper sliced into my thumb. Kai was the superstitious one, but I couldn't help taking this as a sign.

I'm The Keeper now. It's my job. But I didn't even trust myself to make the right choice on Wendy's daycare, much less make the call whether to lead someone to their death—monster or not.

"Mama," Wendy said as she held her juice cup up.

"No, Honey, don't cheer for Mama. Mama doesn't know what in the wonderland she's supposed to do." I sighed and slouched. If Kai could hear me, he'd be chiding me for second-guessing myself. But he couldn't, and that was exactly why I pulled my phone from my fleece pajama pocket and dialed my mom. Once I heard the shower curtain slide shut, I knew I could call her and fret over Wendy's development without my husband insisting I worried too much.

The other line rang several times until Mom's gentle voice greeted me. The sound of it would soothe me. We'd grown close since Wendy's birth and I longed for her advice.

"What is it?" Mom asked after a curt hello.

"Are you okay?" I answered with a question since she didn't sound normal. A long sigh blew into the phone and I stood to pace. It was her job as my mom to comfort me about my motherhood, right? Except I knew the expectation wasn't fair. She had her own life chasing after eligible bachelors until she felt they no longer afforded her protection.

"I didn't sleep well last night," she said. I paced in front of the window overlooking Main Street and started absent-mindedly picking up toys. The pointed end of a doll's brush stabbed the soft spot of my foot and I yelped.

"Are you safe?" Mom said it so loud I had to pull the phone off of my ear.

"I just stepped on a toy," I said.

"You let me know if anything happens, okay?" she asked. I cleared my throat and agreed cautiously. Mom was paranoid, sure, but her frantic voice and startling words went beyond her regular look-over-the-shoulder behavior. "Promise me."

"I promise."

"Good," she said with a breath. "That's good. What did you call for?"

"Wendy took some steps today, but she still held onto the couch," I said with a glance between the coffee table I was clearing and Wendy. She'd emptied the shelf of books and sat in the pile with open fairy tales surrounding her. "Should I take a leave of absence from work? It'd be a terrible time. I'm in the middle of this missing persons case, but I can't help wondering if Wendy would be on track if I focused on only her."

Mom let out a weird laugh that was somewhere between relief and amusement. "What would you do to help her walk? A watched pot never boils."

"What does that mean?" I asked.

"What does who mean?" Her voice cracked.

I furrowed my brows and looked at the phone. "Are you listening?" After returning the phone to my shoulder, I scooped the pile of junk on the coffee table into my arms and carried it to the bedroom, where I dumped it on the dresser. During a second trip, I stacked toys in a basket and dragged them next to the crib-turned-toddler-bed in the room that was once my office. I'd traded corkboards tacked with evidence and crime scene photographs for bunny pictures and princess quotes.

We chatted about Wendy for a few more minutes but mom kept pausing, distracted by something else. Maybe she was preparing for an afternoon date or Dad had tried to reach out to her again. That always riled her up and sent her in a spiral of paranoia.

"Take it easy, Mari," Mom said, dialing back into the conversation. "Maybe stay in for the next few days. Don't go out—"

"Never walk alone," I finished the quote for her. "I know. Kai and I have plans at home tonight."

Mom spoke in muffled tones and then a man said something. I could have sworn I heard the crash of waves and the rippling sound of wind rushing into the phone's receiver.

"Are you taking a walk on the pier?" I asked.

"I have to run," she said. "Be safe."

The line clicked, and I was left with my mouth hanging open, about to ask what had distracted her. I'd paused in the middle of the kitchen with a tied trash bag in hand. With my free hand, I pulled the phone from between my shoulder and ear and plopped it on the counter. Kai emerged with the fresh scent of mint and lime from his shampoo.

He looped his arms around me and pulled me into him, trash bag and all. But I wiggled away, remembering my schedule that didn't account for hugging time.

"We have three hours to clean the house, then I have two to rewrite a better version of the article I lost yesterday," I said. "After that, I plan to spend thirty minutes reading to Wendy. By the time I'm done, we'll need to cook dinner. Esmeralda and Jake are coming over at six."

Kai took me by the shoulders and breathed in a long, exaggerated breath in from his nose and out through his mouth. He continued until I finally relented and repeated the process with him.

"We've got this," he said. His gaze shifted to Wendy in the living room where she used the shelf to pull herself up. While standing, she could reach the top of the TV stand and yanked the controllers from our gaming system down. "You've got this."

He didn't need to elaborate. Kai knew I'd called my mom and asked about the development, not because he'd heard me, but because he knew me better than I knew myself these days. I hated to admit it, but the hood had changed me. If only I could control every second of my life, maybe, just maybe, I could escape the hood and all that came with it.

I nodded, and he enveloped me with a hug. As much as I wanted to melt into him, I quickly wiggled out, because the clock kept on ticking, chipping away the day.

"I know I can't see it or feel it," Kai said. "So it's easy for me to forget sometimes, but the hood was made for you."

The string around my neck hung loosely over my collarbone and brushed lightly against my skin. It was the only part of the hood I felt or noticed. If I pulled the string and removed the hood, it would materialize and conform itself to the next wearer. At least that was my theory, considering that had happened when it went from Scarlet to me back on Cygnus Island all those months ago.

"How can you say that?" I asked without frustration or bite. My voice was curious but strained, ready to argue, but I didn't know where to start. "I should focus on my daughter and my career and our marriage, not a bunch of old stories."

Kai smirked. "Because I know you. Remember our first date when you told me why you became an investigative journalist? You wanted to bring the story to the people so they could stay safe."

I nodded and swallowed a lump in my throat. Our spontaneous trash bag hug had grown unexpectedly emotional.

"The rest of the world lives in darkness to the story cycle," he said. He'd used my own words.

The victim's families get to know the details from the police. But the rest of us have to live in darkness. I'd said it many times because I believed information and knowledge could save lives.

"I'll get to it," I promised. It came out quieter and more exasperated than I intended, like saving lives by stopping monsters was just another task scheduled in my planner.

Kai nodded, satisfied with my answer for now. He'd reminded me who I really was. Or once was. *Who am I now? I know what Scarlet would say.* But I had enough titles—mom, wife, daughter, investigator, friend—I didn't need to tack on 'The Keeper of Stories' too.

The stench from the trash bag stung my nose. I hurried out the front door and down the cement staircase. My watch beeped with a reminder of the amount of time left before our friends arrived.

The salty air from the bay blew up into the city, clearing out the afternoon pollution. The cool breeze did wonders for my stress, but I didn't have a second to spare for enjoyment. I took several large gulps of the fresh air after tossing the bag into the large dump then climbed the first flight of stairs.

A glaring bright light caught my eye like the glint of the sun off of a piece of jewelry or mirror. I finished my climb to our floor and looked out over the parking lot. On the other side of our building, we faced the street where big buildings blocked our view of anything but cement and windows. But in the back, on this side, we overlooked the parking lot and Pioneer Park in the distance. Beyond that, were the piers. And today, the piers seemed to emanate from the vibrance of the sun itself.

The rippling, pulsing rainbow ignited something inside me. The thundering in my rib cage left me shaky and tense.

I squinted and shot my hand to my forehead to block the light. It did nothing, but it didn't matter because as fast as the glow had flashed, it vanished.

The story aura isn't bright. This isn't a fairy tale. Nope. Nope. Nope. My heart pounded. I spun and jogged down the hall, slamming the front door behind me.

I could say no as much as I wanted. It didn't deny the fact that I'd just seen the story aura—no dozens of different story auras—coming from the direction of Cygnus Island.

Chapter 4

Even at the Turning of the Tide

The rest of the afternoon was a whirlwind of checkmarks from my Saturday to-do list. I didn't know what to make of the island auras but I'd wait to speak with Scarlet about it later. Before I knew it, a knock rapped at our door, and Kai welcomed our newest and closest friends, Esmeralda and Jacob.

Esme complained her babysitter had upped her rate, and Jake laughed with Kai over a joke about the last time we'd played Settlers of Catan. We'd rolled for the robber seven times in a row, which meant we spent half the game attacking one another and the competition got heated.

After stuffing ourselves with fried rice and orange chicken from takeout boxes, we laid out the game board on the coffee table and chatted about work and kids. I'd attempted homemade egg rolls, but they came out soggy and I didn't give myself time to make mistakes. Thankfully, I knew my way around all the mobile food apps. I'd deleted the one with the delivery dude who mentioned Pinocchio. For now.

"So," Esme said. She glanced at her husband, or her roommate, rather. They'd been best friends and married for trade purposes. He'd wanted to please his dying mother, and she'd wanted a child. Thus their pact was born. "Jake has decided to go back to law school."

"How exciting!" I said.

Kai rolled the dice to see which player would go first in the game. I arranged the colorful tiles to create the board but it didn't stay that way long. Wendy walked around the coffee table, holding onto the edge to reach each piece and pull them down one by one. The tile representing rocks went flying across the room. She grabbed the tile with the sheep pasture and waved it around like a flag.

"Esme insisted she supports me while I finish my degree," Jake said.

Esmeralda rolled her long, dark hair into a bunch and flicked it over her shoulder. She'd wear it tied in a tight, sensible bun while on patrol, but let it free for this evening. "I owe him after he put me through the academy."

"Will you be close by?" Kai asked after popping the corner of a fortune cookie into his mouth. The crunch caught Wendy's eye. Wispy pigtails swayed to the side as her head snapped toward Kai's chewing. She dropped to the floor and crawled as fast as her rug-burn knees could take her (another reason she needed to learn to walk ASAP). Using the couch to pull herself up, Wendy reached a grabby hand toward the rest of the cookie and repeated her version of the word 'snack'.

Jake shook his head. "Out of state," he said. "But I'll video call for game nights. You can't get rid of me that easily. One of these days, I'm winning the longest road." He picked up the two-point card that showed he'd earned an achievement in the game.

"I have a new strategy," Kai said as he pointed at the stack of game cards. "And if that doesn't work, it'll be easier to cheat when you're playing from Zoom."

None of that mattered because Esmeralda was undefeated in the game and we didn't stand a chance. I chomped into another potsticker for a mouthful of deep-fried goodness and reached for a bag of game supplies from the box.

"I'll miss in-person game nights for the food," Jake said between bites of fried rice.

"No more procrastinating," Esme said. She wagged her finger at him.

"I won't," he said. "I wish I could have finished it when I planned, but life doesn't always follow a timeline."

"It definitely doesn't," my husband agreed with a glance at me.

After downing the rest of Kai's dessert, Wendy dispersed the game tiles across the room like a toddler hurricane who tore through the world of Catan. It took several minutes, but we replaced the game board and played a round of lively competition. Esmeralda celebrated her win with a cheer that Wendy copied with a squeal of her own. The excitement was hushed as a loud knock came from the door.

While Kai scooped up Wendy and carried her to the changing table in the next room, I answered the door. The pounding echoed several more times.

The frantic knocking had me tripping over shoes by the entry and yanking on the door. Our elderly neighbors could be in trouble, or maybe Scarlet had found a way to take the hood back. I'd gladly give back the immortality that came with it and let Scarlet go on her merry way.

I gripped the knob and swung the door open. Instead of red hair, my mother's unusually bright face greeted me.

"Hello," she said. Though she often dropped by unannounced, it didn't always come with a smile this big.

"Hi," I said, moving out of the way to let her in. "We're just playing games. Do you want to join?"

My mom marched into the living room and took Kai's empty spot on the couch. Greetings passed around and once everyone had updated everyone else on how they were feeling, Mom clasped her hands in her lap.

I plopped down in my usual spot. As hard as I'd tried as a kid, I couldn't match my mother's poise and grace. She perched on the edge of the cushion while I sank into it with a slouch and a sigh. Since becoming an adult, I'd given up the impossible feat and chose comfort over perfection.

"Gramma Sammy!" Kai said as he emerged from Wendy's room. In one hand, he carried a wrapped diaper that smelled like death and our daughter in the other. She looked like perfection herself as she twisted in his arms to greet her grandma with a beaming smile.

Tiny hands reached for Gramma Sammy and my mother took her into her lap while the rest of us wrinkled our noses. I waved Kai to hurry and take the bombed diaper outside before we all fainted from the stink.

"I'm glad you're here," I said. "Esme says that Wendy is fine not walking yet, but I want you to watch how she drops to her knees right before she takes a step. I'm worried there's something wrong with her legs."

When I tried to pull Wendy from her arms, my mom hugged her tighter. "You should listen to Esmeralda. There's nothing wrong with Wendy."

At the mention of her name, my daughter squealed and looked around at each of us. The attention only made her smile bigger and throw her head side-to-side, sending her wispy pigtails dancing back and forth like swaying tree branches.

"I told you," Esme said with mock anger. She crossed one leg over the other and folded her arms to drive the point home. Still, nobody could comfort me about all things motherhood other than, well, my mother.

Wendy demonstrated her lack of walking with a fast crawl that wore the knees of her pants thin. She followed Esme and Jake to the door as they said goodbye. Once the hugs and farewells had died down and our friends had left, I dug in the plastic bags for more fortune cookies and sat on the floor.

The fortune cookie left sprinkled crumbs on my lap as I cracked it open. I held one piece out to bribe Wendy from the front door toward me. Kai turned after closing the door and raised his eyebrows.

"Do you see what she does to our daughter?" he joked with a shake of his head. Despite his disagreement, he stooped to help Wendy to her feet.

My breath hitched while she swayed back and forth and lifted her foot to take a step. The moment of suspense left us all silent and staring at Wendy. She noticed the attention and promptly dropped to her knees to crawl to Gramma Sammy. Apparently, Grandma's cuddles beat cookie treats in Wendy's book of favorites.

I dropped my head into my hands and groaned. "This is my fault, isn't it?"

It may have taken a list of reasons from my mother, but I calmed down and accepted that she was right. For now. I hadn't failed as a parent yet, and I had my mom's comforting words to confirm that. Kai had tried the same words before, but it didn't land the same since he was as new at parenting as I was.

"Now that we've cleared that up, I wanted to give you some news," Mom said. Wendy scooted to the edge of Mom's lap and reached for a chopstick from the styrofoam plate on the coffee table. The drum solo that followed seemed to introduce my mom's news with a suspenseful and rhythmic tap.

"Hey, she could be in a band," Kai said as he scooped the game board contents into the box at the other end of the coffee table.

Mom shot him a glare for interrupting her announcement. News with my mother came often. It didn't surprise me to have her drop by to say she'd broken up with her on and off boyfriend Edward or gone on a date with her plastic surgeon. Sometimes her announcements were a warning that we'd need to get used to her newly sculpted nose or expanded lips.

"I've decided I'm going to divorce your father once and for all," she said with a slight nod of her head. The courage it must have taken for her to say it after all these years awed me. I wanted nothing more than for her to be happy, but she always felt tied to him, or that she owed him, or something else I didn't understand at all.

"That's good!" I said. "Right?" The dull, sullen expression on her face didn't match the tone she'd said it in or the bright atmosphere she'd brought when she'd arrived.

Her throat rippled with a slow swallow, and she nodded. "Yes, but Johnson refuses to share the message and your father doesn't believe in technology." Her tiny nostrils expanded as she sucked in a deep breath. "So I'll have to see him."

A heaviness dropped to the pit of my stomach for two reasons. I knew how much discomfort my mother felt at the idea of seeing my father and when she was on edge; I was bound to join her, though I never gave in to paranoia. And last but not least, this meant she was going to Cygnus Island.

"I'm going to take the papers to him and demand that he sign," she said with a slight breathlessness, seemingly before her courage ran out.

"I'm happy for you," I lied.

"If I didn't know you so well, I might believe you," she said. "You look like you've seen a ghost."

Spoiler alert. It's your ghost if I can't deal with whatever monsters and villains these new stories might bring. I didn't like that she planned to walk into the heart of the intense rippling colors. I wasn't ready to twist the horrific ending of one fairy tale, much less many.

"I think I ate too many egg rolls," I said as I rubbed my stomach and forced a smile. Kai tilted his head at me with an expression on his face that repeated my mother's question. *What's* really *wrong?*

I tugged at the string on the hood that hung like a ribbon necklace, the only part of the garment that others could see. Kai's gaze trailed to my collarbone and, after a moment of registration, his face paled as white as the wall Scarlet had once used to create a portal. It seemed everything would remind me of the nagging bright light that haunted me from the island where my father lived. And where my mother intended to visit.

"I'm leaving tomorrow," Mom said.

"I'll go with you." Why did I say that? I didn't want to run into the thick of a thousand stories. Okay, ten or twelve stories. . .

"Absolutely not," she said. "You're too busy as it is. This is my choice." A far-off look steamed over her eyes with faint wetness. "Besides," she said while rubbing her palm over her bare shoulder and arm. "I want to go. I need to see what I left behind when I ran away all those years ago. It feels like a part of me is still there. Something is missing." Her hand curled into a fist and she absentmindedly pulled it into her chest with her eyes still glazed.

"Like what?" I asked with a glance at Kai, then back at Mom. *You will not stop her, Keeper.* The monster's words came back to me. He couldn't have known my mother planned to go to the island, right? Would that make Mom a character in *Frankenstein*? I quickly snapped my gaze away from her. For a second, I thought I saw a glow surrounding my mother, but I refused to believe it. How likely was it that both myself and my mom were fairy tale characters?

"I don't know how to explain it," she said. Once she blinked, she finally looked at me. "Have you ever felt that something you owned had become a part of you?" It was a question, but she didn't expect an answer. The room fell into silence except for the faded tapping of Wendy's drumming as she nodded off in Mom's lap.

The string at my neck felt tight like it'd dug into my skin. It reminded me of a noose and I gasped for breath though nothing about the hood had physically changed. The string still hung loosely, comfortably, and I couldn't feel the fabric of the hood at all. But just like the glow on the island, it existed all the same.

I'd ignored the glow on my yoga teacher because nobody dies in *Pride and Prejudice*. They'd live out their story and return to mortality without ever knowing it had forced them to follow the fate of the story. I'd even ignored Frankenstein's monster because I had no proof he'd hurt anyone, yet.

But I couldn't ignore the dozens of colors all mashed together from Cygnus Island now that my mom planned a dangerous visit. And if I didn't have the fairy tales to worry about, I had dead bodies to deal with. Both of the missing persons were last seen near the island. It seemed they were all wrapped together in a messy, tangled bunch; the stories, my case, and my mother's plan.

I tugged my finger from the string, but it wouldn't budge. The hood had sensed my desire to rip it off, and the string seemed to wound itself tighter against my skin. After hundreds of years of guiding and empowering Scarlet, the hood only worked on me now. I needed to make a plan to safely navigate the stories on the island before they could hurt my mom. And I needed Scarlet's help to do it.

Spoiler alert, I have no idea what I'm doing.

Chapter 5

In the Twinkling of an Eye

Light streamed in through our bedroom window. I cursed at Kai for not closing the curtains all the way as I threw up my arm to block the light. The clock on my nightstand displayed it was half-past four in the morning. The red numbers glared at me. *Get up now, you have so much to do.*

I almost threw my robe over the clock but pulled it over my arms instead. Once I waddled to the window, I noticed the curtain was in place, fully covering the window, but it didn't block the light.

The stark white faded to a dim yellow and vanished. I shook my head, took a trip to the restroom, and returned to bed. When I woke again, Sunday felt doable. The clock read seven, and I heard Wendy calling for Mama from her room.

My Sunday schedule included helping Kai with his lesson plans for the week, interviewing Travis Young's girlfriend, and taking Wendy to the park where she could watch other kids walk and hopefully try it herself.

By the end of the day, I was beaten and no further on the missing persons investigation, or my confidence as a mother. But I had one more item on the to-do list that I'd squeezed into the tiny white box on my planner last night. *Meet with Scarlet.*

My heart cracked a little to leave Wendy. I'd hoped to read a book to her at bedtime, but she waved and, for the third time only, put two words together.

"Bye Mama." Her tiny hand slapped over her mouth and then shot out again. She repeated the farewell of blowing kisses until Kai stepped back inside our condo and I headed down the staircase. Normally, I'd take her with me—I didn't have time to *not* multitask— But Scarlet requested we get together at a bar and, even though I wasn't Mother of the Year for leaving Wendy in the first place, I was smart enough not to bring my toddler there.

The early evening carried a slight chill from the coast, but I went without a jacket since summer promised it wouldn't get too much colder. Laughter and conversation echoed from the outdoor patio at The Drunken Elf bar. Twinkling fairy lights decorated the overhang on the patio, giving the place a whimsical, innocent vibe. It was exactly the type of place Scarlet would pick.

I stepped inside to see her waving at me from the bar top. Literally, on the *top* of the bar's counter. She sat perched on the edge where she leaned over and filled her glass from the soda fountain. The bartender shouted at her to get off, but she finished filling the glass before moving. She leaped down and waved again, so vigorously I thought her hand might fly off her wrist.

I forced a smile and almost ducked behind a large man. Despite my gut reaction to hide, I wasn't ashamed of helping Scarlet learn how to live like a mortal in the twenty-first century. It just took some getting used to, and a lot of explanation.

The smell of pretzels sent my stomach groaning, a reminder that I'd forgone dinner in order to squeeze more time at the park with Wendy. Plus, I'd skipped Pioneer Park and walked all the way to the playground on Soup Cracker Street. I'd accepted the terrible memories there, but it felt weird to see my child play near the site of multiple murders.

"Mari!" Scarlet squealed. She sipped her soda, then threw her arms around me, leaning her full body weight into me. The stinging smell of vodka blasted in my face from her breath and I was startled. My sweet, innocent, monster-hunting little friend who'd tried to lead me to my death was drunk for the very first time.

"Hi Scarlet," I said as I plopped down on the barstool. The bartender took my order–a virgin Shirley Temple, and I turned to my friend. Her cheeks shaded the same blood red as her hair.

"Call me Scar," she said. "I've been watching all the fake people's movies from that big magical place. I like the name even though he's a villain and a lion and I'm human and mortal." Scarlet leaned back in her chair and almost tipped over. "I'm mortal. I'm going to die some-day. We all are!" Her voice grew louder with each choppy word.

Several people turned to look at us and Scarlet responded by holding her vodka soda in the air. She hiccuped.

"Okay, you need to simmer down," I said. The bartender slid me the drink and a bowl of extra cherries. "Us mortals have always known we're going to die someday. It might be new to you, but announcing it is a little weird."

Scarlet downed the vodka soda and slammed it on the wooden counter. "Another!"

"No. No!" I said, realizing she'd ordered more alcohol. "How are you even paying for this?"

She waved at a man sitting several seats down at the bar. The man returned our gaze complete with a creeper smile.

"Definitely not, nope," I said. "That's not happening." When the bartender returned with another vodka soda for Scarlet, I told him to put her tab on my card. "And you don't need this." I slid the drink away from her.

"Then you drink it," she said, flopping her head into one hand as she leaned on the counter. The TV behind her head finished a commer-cial and returned to a baseball game. The group at the table behind us cheered.

"You're boring right now," she said.

I flinched. The word struck me like a slap to the face. Routine wasn't boring, but perhaps, *my* level of routine was a problem. I'd give her that.

"Where'd you even learn that word?" I asked with a frown and took a sip from the vodka soda. Maybe I needed to let go a little. But control felt so *good.*

"From you, remember?" she said.

"I mean before that."

The shine on her lips brightened as she licked them and looked at me. "I learned it from the actors," she said, pointing at the TV.

"Those are athletes, but I get what you mean," I said.

"So have you seen the fake people's movies?" she asked as she tried to sneak the drink back. I grabbed it and took another sip. Alcohol burned my throat, and I found my fingers had trailed to my neck where Frankenstein's monster had grabbed me.

"Cartoons?" I said. "Yes, we already talked about this, and that Magical Place is called Disneyland. Maybe I'll take you and Wendy when she's older."

Scarlet slammed her palm against the countertop. My Shirley Temple splashed out of the cup and the creeper two seats down snapped his head to look at us.

"I am four hundred and seventy-one years old—" A hiccup interrupted her. "And you're talking to me like I'm a child!"

I took another swig of her drink and rubbed my temples. "What'd I say about simmering?"

"I don't even know what that means," Scarlet said with her hands flying out to the sides. If anybody had walked by, she'd have clothes-lined them. "Am I supposed to boil like water?" A gasp escaped her, and she slapped her palm against her chest. "Do you want me to die like the frog in the pot myth?"

"What? No." I leaned in closer and lowered my voice. "Wait, is that myth part of the story cycle?"

Scarlet responded with a giggle. Red flushed her cheeks, and the laugh turned into a full-blown giggle attack. A pitcher on the TV tossed the ball, and the batter hit a home run. The crowd in the bar went wild, effectively covering up my friend's crazy-sounding laughter.

I sipped again; the vodka stinging my tongue. "Are you coherent enough to help me figure this out or not?"

"Figure what out?" Scarlet stopped laughing and her face turned serious in an instant. She sputtered one more giggle, then took a huge breath and looked at me straight. The sudden focus and seriousness in her eyes startled me. "Are we going after Frankenstein's monster?"

Even drunk, she didn't mistake the doctor for the monster. Scarlet knew the stories like my body knew how to breathe. She could recite them better than I could my schedule, the same schedule I'd followed every day for a year and a half. Or tried to follow, as much as I could with a toddler.

"We? Never mind," I said as I shook my head. "My mom is going to the island where I killed the wolf. I saw the aura there."

"Really?" She snapped her head to look at me, her curls bouncing about her face. The man several seats down poked his head forward to eye her until I gave him a death glare and he returned his attention to the beer in his hand.

"I don't know," I said, backtracking. "Can the fairy tales ever cross over with one another?" With another swallow, I'd almost finished Scarlet's drink. Hopefully, it'd save her from a big, bad hangover.

Scarlet nodded, considering this, but stayed silent. Her lip curled in and she chewed. It was a new habit she'd adopted since becoming mortal. With mortality—or rather, without the hood—came quirks: wrinkles, blackheads, scars, and habits. And the inability to hold down a job, apparently.

"It is possible," she said. The hiccup that followed betrayed her attempt at soberness. I should have worried she would not give me the right advice, but I trusted her knowledge on the story cycle, even while inebriated. "Why do you ask?"

I shrugged and snuck a glance at the bartender. Before diving into the next topic, I wanted to order a double shot of tequila. Maybe after downing the liquid courage, I could admit what I couldn't bring myself to say aloud.

A crapload of stories has spilled over into our world. And my mom is headed straight for them.

"You mentioned fairy tales with kidnapping in the story as a suggestion for the missing persons case. I'm wondering if Frankenstein's monster is responsible for the death of Travis Young. What if it is two stories mixed?"

Scarlet gnawed on her bottom lip. "Interesting theory," she said.

The group behind us cheered again, and she twisted her head to look at the TV. After a moment of intently watching the fast-food commercial, she turned back to me. The leftover liquid at the bottom of the glass swirled as I readied to down the rest of it. It didn't make it to my lips before I set the cup back on the counter and met her gaze.

"How did you know the story aura was back?" I asked, referring to her statement from the other day. She didn't have the hood anymore, so her claim to know didn't make sense.

The creeper two seats down stood and said something about how we should 'smile more' and then sauntered off into the bathroom. I grimaced just to spite him.

Scarlet shrugged. "I can't know for sure, but I've been following stories for hundreds of years. I guess I just feel 't upon my bones."

"Excuse me?"

"It's a quote from Shakespeare," she said.

I finished the vodka soda and my head spun a little. Becoming a mother gave me super strength when I needed it but it did a number on my alcohol tolerance. Mostly because I hadn't drunk a drop since the day Kai and I started trying for pregnancy years ago.

"Ebenezer Scrooge," I cursed. "Don't tell me Romeo and Juliet are real."

"Maybe," she said nonchalantly. "But not all of Shakespeare's works are part of the story cycle. I don't know why. It's something I have always meant to research. But I never had the time in between hunting wolves and making sure Snow White's second mother danced in red shoes until she died."

I frowned and suddenly wanted to pull Wendy's enrollment from Ruby Slippers daycare. Scarlet waved for another drink. Once the bartender slid it over, I stole it. Again. The curve of her pouting lips didn't deter me. I had a toddler, for goodness sake.

"So miss Bones," I started. I knew Scarlet would get the reference to my favorite TV show. After living with us for several months, I'd forced her to watch it with me, considering her bed was our couch and the only TV we had was in the living room. "What makes the story aura stronger than ever?"

"There is a great load of stories all starting at once," she said. "At least that's my theory."

"So what do I do?" I said. Our voices had grown loud to accommodate for the boisterous group behind us and I glanced at the bartender, hoping he couldn't hear our crazy conversation. He moved closer, slapping a wet washcloth on the counter then he swirled it around to clean up the splashes from my Shirley Temple.

"This is new to me, too. Usually, I had a little time in between stories considering they're spread out over a hundred years. But they don't follow a timeline." She sighed. "If I were still immortal, this wouldn't be so absolutely daunting."

The bartender shifted his gaze to us and raised his eyebrows. I asked him to close the tab so Scarlet couldn't order anymore and hoped he assumed she was drunk-talking. If he dug into our conversation, I doubted he'd like what he found. Unless he believed us, in which case he could be a greedy sort of fellow who would vie to become a story character and loop in the cycle.

"I believe we should try to find some characters," Scarlet said thoughtfully. "You need to want to see the story aura, and we could start a list of those we identify. Let's even color-code it. I know you like lists. It will be just like one of your investigations, except there's no dead body."

"Not yet," I mumbled, knowing how violent those old fairy tales could be.

The bartender popped the receipt into a clean cup and slid it toward us. Though dizzy, I caught it and totaled it with a tip. Upon seeing the several hundred next to the dollar sign on the bill, I forced myself to finish the last vodka soda. I downed the burning liquid, then popped the glass back on the counter.

Scarlet cheered my chugging and the group at the table behind us shot us a glare. The TV announced the red and white team's victory, which meant the other had lost. Apparently, their favorite didn't fare well, and they'd mistaken my friend's cheer as one for the opposing team.

"Are you ready to hunt some people?" Scarlet asked with a wry grin.

The bartender's eyes bulged, nearly popping out and rolling down the counter.

"Kidding," I said. "She's kidding. That's what she calls it when we order an Uber ride," I said. He only raised his brows in response while I guided Scarlet off the chair, dizzy and unbalanced myself.

We stumbled out of the bar, leaving the crowd of grumpy fans to wallow in their whiskies and sour beers. The chilly night air didn't sober me as much as I'd hoped. The smell of salt filled my nose, and it felt like home, which comforted me but didn't sober me up. For once, the thought of going on a story aura scavenger hunt sounded fun. It could have been the alcohol or the fact that this distracted me from my mother's plan, but I'd let go. *I did it.*

With a huge breath of the sea air and city pollution, I grinned and closed my eyes.

"Mari," Scarlet snapped. "Let's go."

My eyes popped open, and I scanned the street. No glow or colorful haze surrounded the pedestrians that milled about the nightlife downtown. Scarlet linked her arm in mine and we walked in support of one another as we climbed the hilly San Francisco streets.

This is a waste of time. Not to mention dangerous. My brain nagged. *Don't go out.* My mom's caution came back to me, but the effect of the drinks pushed away my rational mind and I enjoyed the night.

I squinted and tried to see the glow around the strangers we passed. "I don't see any characters."

Scarlet scoffed. "You didn't see the story aura at the island until last night, either, and it could have been there for a long time. You aren't seeing what you don't want to see."

I opened my mouth to argue but promptly clamped it shut again. I had no comeback. Instead, I prompted her to help me. "So, how will we find characters?"

"We ask people!" She beamed and skipped ahead, un-linking her hold on me and letting me fall behind. Something about mortality really brought out the immaturity in her, and while it bothered me when I tried to hold a schedule, I liked it tonight. Tonight, when my brain was fuzzy, and I'd convinced myself I'd let go of my obsessive need for control.

"Hi," Scarlet said to a man who stood at the end of an alley. Two restaurant buildings butted up to one another but not close enough to block the small walkway that led through to another street. The man shouted into his phone. Once Scarlet stepped closer, he covered the receiving end and furrowed his brows at her.

"I can see your future," she said with gusto, like a kid in a poorly executed magic show.

What in the wonderland is she doing? This is ridiculous. I should have been at home, scheduling interviews with more of Travis Young's friends or calling Detective Wilhelm to ask if he'd secured more information. Or maybe if I put everything I had into an argument, I could convince my mom not to go to Cygnus Island. *Yeah, right.* Nothing tethered my mother's free spirit, except, apparently, whatever she'd left behind when she walked out on Dad.

"Like a psychic?" the man asked.

Scarlet glanced at me, then back at the man. Hair whipped across her face from the sudden movement. "Yes, a psychic."

"Good," he said. "Then why don't you tell my girlfriend that I'm not cheating?" He yelled the last part into the phone.

"If you tell me something first," Scarlet said. "Does your girlfriend like water a lot? Or maybe she's accusing you of infidelity as an excuse to end your companionship because you stole something of hers and she's feeling trapped?"

"Excuse me?" The man spat in Scarlet's face, but she didn't back down. A screeching sound came from the man's phone. I could only assume the person from the phone was asking if Scarlet was his mistress.

Maybe I should have worried about the situation more and pulled us out, but the distraction left me standing with my arms limp at my sides. Something about Scarlet's question rubbed me the wrong way.

The man straightened and gave his full attention to Scarlet. "Hey, are you legit? Could you tell me if I get fired for, you know?"

Scarlet raised her brows. *Ebenezer Scrooge. . . it's working. He thinks she's telling the truth.*

"Do you have anything, Partner?" Scarlet asked, looking at me.

I shook my head and shrugged.

"You get fired," she said before walking away. The guy watched her with his mouth agape. I slipped past and hurried to lead the way down the alley. In the secluded area, we discussed our game plan.

"Okay," I said. "This time we're FBI agents." The alley came to an abrupt end on a busy sidewalk in front of a pawnshop and a convenience store. Across the street, a line of people stood waiting to get into a club that boomed with a beat only younger people dance to.

I pointed to the women sitting at a table in front of a twenty-four-hour cafe. "We'll ask those two ladies if they've ever gotten pregnant while in a coma."

"That's so icky!"

"Like Little Briar Rose?" I said, reminding Scarlet how disturbing true fairy tales were. "The sleeping beauty?"

Scarlet reluctantly nodded and sighed. "I suppose. Mortality has made me so squeamish now. It's been over a hundred years since I've dealt with the sleeping princess."

Once the pedestrian light turned green, we marched across the street and up to the two women. I popped out my wallet and flashed my driver's license like a badge before they scrutinized it. "I'm agent Mama and this is Red." I winced, realizing that my mind wasn't as sharp as the liquid courage made me want to believe. *Agent Mama?*

But the women were curious, if nothing else, and answered our questions. Despite Scarlet's giggling, we made it through without them questioning our professional status. After thanking them, we moved away from the headache-inducing beat of the club's blasting music. At one time, I might have enjoyed a place like that. Maybe. Tonight, I only wanted to go home and snuggle with my husband while our daughter snored peacefully in the next room. Though I had to admit, the fairy tale investigation had me intrigued. I wanted to see the plan through and determine if interviewing strangers could help me find characters. Maybe I could streamline the story cycle process and assign each fairy tale to a schedule then tackle them in a timely manner.

"Okay, wait," I said. The cool breeze finally started to sober me. "We're going about this wrong. We can't just ask about one or two fairy tales because that will take forever and I have a mattress with my name on it." Not to mention Kai would be worried if I stayed out later than expected. I *never* stayed anywhere later than expected these days unless it involved work. "Let's interview people like I do for investigations and then see what story they might fit into."

"Perfect," she said. The tap of her short heels hit the cement with confidence and I was left catching up to hear what she was saying. "That means you won't be avoiding the aura anymore and you'll be able to see it." With a glance back at me, she smiled. "But don't call me Red and this time I want to be a talent scout. I saw it on TV."

The dizziness lifted slightly as we picked up our walking pace.

"I don't know if you should learn everything about the real world from shows…" I said as I followed her past a music shop that had closed for the evening. A small crowd stood outside a steak and surf restaurant, waiting for their party to be called for seating. A family of four sat on the bench while a couple stood leaning against the side of the building.

We exchanged a nod of knowing agreement and stepped up to the couple. Channeling my best Sam and Dean Winchester impressions, I stood tall and pretended to be a Hollywood talent scout with all the confidence in the world. Of course, it was fake, but I enjoyed it while it lasted.

"I'm—" I froze. I'd never needed to lie before. Instead, I'd march up to witnesses of a crime and introduce myself before diving into an interview. But this was new. And if my parenting of Wendy proved anything, it was that I sucked at new things.

"Talent scouts," Scarlet finished for me.

"Yes." I swallowed the lump in my throat and smiled. "I'm Rapunzel." *Nope, nope, abort mission. Rapunzel? Who says that?* "You know how authors have pen names? Talent scouts sometimes go by—"

Before I could embarrass myself, Scarlet interrupted. "We see potential in you two to become stars in our new acting motion picture."

I cringed. Scarlet sounded like a talent scout from the 1930s. It was my turn to save her. "We're scouting for a new reality show. It's about…" I glanced around for ideas but only saw some gum on the sidewalk, a blinking street lamp, and a trail of businesspeople leaving the restaurant. So I dug something out of the recesses of my brain. "It's about fairytale romances and will follow your life as a couple."

"We're already married," the woman said, showing her wedding ring.

"Perfect!" Scarlet said. "So tell me a little about yourselves. Do you have a stepdaughter? Or was your husband cursed with an overly hairy body and loneliness before you fell for him? Maybe he found you by returning your lost shoe?"

We're drowning. I should have been worried, or maybe pulled Scarlet from the potential embarrassment. But the woman laughed and nodded.

"He was definitely lonely before we met and I made him shave that unruly beard of his," she said. The husband laughed in agreement, then kissed his wife's hand. I squinted and tilted my head, but nothing glowed around them, not even after they almost fit into the role of Villenueve's *Beauty and the Beast.*

"Is she okay?" the woman asked with her finger pointed at me. I snapped my head up and offered an awkward smile.

"Oh, I know that look." Scarlet clucked her tongue. "Yes, she has decided you're not fit for the role." With a curt smile, she spun away from the couple and offered a polite farewell. "Good day."

Scarlet linked her arm in mine and dragged me away from the restaurant. The smell of red meat faded as we hiked up the hill and away from the all-you-can-eat steak and surf.

"Did you see the aura?" she asked.

"Nothing," I said. "But I wouldn't even if they had been Beauty and the Beast. If they're already married, that means their story would be done, right?"

"Not quite," Scarlet said. "Remember, modern society is trickier than staying true to the stories. Sometimes the stepdaughter is an actual daughter or the wife of the mother's son. We don't know if that woman was trapped under the beast's spell. He could have had a body full of hair under that leather jacket."

"Look, Scarlet," I said as I pulled away from her and stopped under the blinking streetlamp. "It's late."

The sobering reality that tomorrow was Monday morning, and I had my daughter at home in need of a goodnight kiss, sent me wanting to strip from the hood and forget fairy tales forever. Not that the feeling was unusual for me. I never intended to inherit this supernatural hunt when I stole the hood and killed the wolf.

"We can't stop now," she said. The desperate protest in her voice almost convinced me, but the swimming drunkenness in her eyes reminded me how stupid our little adventure had been. Bouncing about the city streets late at night and being inebriated without a designated driver or sober friend put us at risk of the murders and attacks I reported on every day.

"I'm going to call you an Uber," I said.

"No." Scarlet stood her ground, folding her arms and raising an eyebrow. "You can give up if you'd like, but I won't."

Tipsy or not, she was whip-smart, and I knew I wouldn't convince her without logic and facts. "We still have alcohol in our systems and this isn't working. It will take us forever to find story characters like this."

Scarlet turned her head away from me. "When will you take the story cycle seriously?"

I sighed and fiddled with the string around my neck. The red twined around my finger so tightly it cut off circulation. I released and let it unravel. The light above us finally winked out, and we were left in a dark spot on the sidewalk, and I wasn't in my sharpest mind, so self-defense was out of the question if someone jumped us.

I pulled out my cell phone and tapped Kai's contact picture. The picture where I'd held my hands over his eyes during the first look at our wedding lit up brighter as it dialed his phone number. My husband's goofy grin in the memory calmed me. Scarlet refused to listen to me, but she might just let Kai drive her home. Since he had no story, no hood, and no claim to the cycle, Scarlet argued with him less. If only a little.

The plan worked, and she didn't even scoff when our SUV pulled up to the sidewalk. Of course, Scarlet's shivering in the nighttime breeze probably did half the work of convincing her to climb into the car.

Exhaustion left her zoned out in the backseat and the car ride when smoother than I'd expected. All three of us stayed quiet while the city's noises came through the windows in muffled honks and shouts.

After dropping Scarlet off at her apartment, I turned to Kai. I asked if Tala had minded staying at our condo with Wendy while he left.

"Thankfully, I caught her just as Mr. Geppetto was leaving her house, so I didn't interrupt anything," Kai said. He flicked the blinker on and turned down Soup Cracker Street to take the shortcut home.

"They're getting cozy these days, aren't they?" I said, snuggling into the front seat as the liquor wore off and exhaustion set in. I let my head rest against the cool window.

"Yeah, but I don't think Mr. Geppetto sees Tala the way she does him. He's still processing his daughter's and wife's deaths. You can't blame him for not wanting a relationship right now. He just needs companionship."

I nodded as my eyelids drooped. The warm car combined with the steady motion lulled me until a flash of light sent my heart rate soaring. I jolted up in the seat and grabbed the door to brace for impact.

"Whoa!" Kai said as he used one hand to shield his eyes.

The flash didn't come from the headlights of an oncoming car. We stopped at a red light. The brightness faded and, behind it, was Pier 99. In my sleepiness, I hadn't realized we were still several minutes from home.

"You saw that?" I asked, my heart threatening to pound out of my chest.

"Yeah." he breathed.

"So it can't be the story aura," I said. "Because how are you seeing it? And the man Detective Wilhelm and I interviewed saw it too."

But the story aura was clear. I couldn't deny the familiarity of the glow and the pull I felt toward the bay, past Pier 99, and toward Cygnus Island itself. Somehow, Kai and the others could see the aura. It didn't make sense.

"It's so strong." I squinted. The pure white brightness melted into a base yellow with other colors. *Other colors?* Greens and reds and blues rippled through the light like a doggone rainbow of fairy tale aura. "Pull over."

"What is it?" Kai asked as he obliged and eased the car into park next to the sidewalk.

"The colors. They're stories. . . so many stories," I said, breathless. The window hummed as I rolled it down and a blast of salty air hit me in the face. "I've never seen the aura in a rainbow like that before. This isn't like Scarlet explained. What if she got it wrong and they're new stories from when I took the hood from her?"

"I don't know what to tell you," he said.

My breath shuddered as I tried to gather my thoughts. "If they're new stories… how can I close them? I wouldn't know how they end."

Kai said something about never-ending and about how some stories live on with open conclusions. I assumed he related it back to history somehow, knowing him, but I didn't hear. Exhaustion, awe, and most of all, fear overcame me.

The colors rippled and pulsed but didn't wane. The only way for me to snag a moment's reprieve from the brightness was to close my eyes and sit within my own darkness.

Chapter 6

An Ill Favored Thing, but Mine Own

Mom's answering machine ended my call. I'd called her as part of my workday routine but I refused to give in to worry when she didn't answer. The sunny morning lifted my spirits and I allowed myself to bask in the feel of it as I walked.

With caffeine in my veins and the start of the workweek, I moved with a skip in my step. The light of day made everything feel easier. Wendy didn't cry when I dropped her off at Ruby Slipper's daycare. Plus, I'd matched my clothes, and I was running exactly three minutes early. Kai and I even had time to squeeze some special loving in this morning while Wendy overslept.

I swung open the door to the office building and beckoned Elsie inside first. As I followed her to the elevator, my phone buzzed, but it wasn't Mom.

"Rowan," Detective Wilhelm said when I answered.

"Wilhelm," I returned the exchange of last names. The bump of the elevator doors sliding open made me press my phone tighter against my ear. Multitasking allowed me to dig into my bag with my free hand, step into the elevator, and speak with the detective while preparing to take notes.

"Did you get my message about the interview with Travis Young's girlfriend?" I asked.

The elevator dinged and carried us up while I shuffled through my notes and balanced the phone between my shoulder and my ear.

"Sure did," he said. He'd listen to me now, even share information, because I offered free police work and his department had tightened the purse strings. But that didn't stop him from talking to me in a condescending tone. "The message was something about how Travis had told his girl he'd seen a large man stalking the piers, right? She'd said it was a couple of weeks before he went missing."

"Correct," I confirmed. The elevator stopped to let someone else off on the floor beneath Bay Side Media's office. I swayed back and forth to the elevator music with my planner in hand and all. The mini dance move reminded me more of my old self.

Elsie shook her head at me, but I didn't care. I'd finally gotten a tiny lead on the case *and* it could involve Frankenstein's monster. I'd refused to acknowledge the connection before, hoping Scarlet would tell me what to do to get rid of the hood's responsibilities. But after the ripple of colors last night, I couldn't hide in darkness any longer. And maybe I wouldn't have to throw myself headfirst into the hood's hunt and I could do what I do best, investigate with my resources and the detective's help, then arrest the monster. That'd solve all my problems. An arrest would keep him from killing people while I figured out what to do with the ending of Mary Shelley's famous horror.

Detective Wilhelm blew a sigh into the phone that sounded like the rush of wind or a loud crash of waves. "Someone definitely stalked him," he said. "Because Travis Young was murdered."

My heart skipped a beat, thumping in double-time to catch up. *No, that means the monster may have already killed.* Guilt twisted in my stomach, the lingering coffee flavor soured on my tongue, and my breakfast bagel threatened to upend.

The elevator came to a jolting halt, and I stumbled against the wall. Elsie marched into the office, but my feet refused to move. One step and I might hurl liquid chunks of guilt all over the elevator.

"Rowan. Are you there?" Detective Wilhelm asked.

This is all wrong. I messed up. I'm too late.

"I think the girlfriend lied about what Travis saw, not to mention a load of other stuff," the detective continued, not caring if I listened or not. I knew the feeling, working the case out loud always helped organize my thoughts. Then came the color-coded note-taking for me anyway. "She has a history of violence. We have documentation showing that the chick has beaten up a bunch of her past boyfriend's female friends. The records were in another state, and it took forever to get the stuff sent electronically. These stupid rural law enforcement stations are so unorganized."

I let Detective Wilhelm ramble while the elevator carried me back down to the first floor. Physically and personally, I'd hit rock bottom. *How could I let this happen?*

"Did you hear me, Rowan?" The detective asked. The one-second pause didn't give me a chance to respond. Detective Wilhelm wanted to be right, not heard. "The girlfriend is the suspect. She lied to you. This man she spoke of sounds like a deflection. I bet she wanted to pin the murder on another boyfriend or a pimp. Are you listening?"

I finally took a full breath, and my throat released its squeeze. My mouth ran dry with a sandpaper tongue, but I responded.

"I heard you."

"Women always believe other women and I'm not taking an argument on this because this situation proves it. This is how she tricked you. But it's not only men who are violent," he said. I wanted to come back with a snide remark about how he finally afforded women *some* equality in assuming that we're strong enough to kill, but my thoughts were already too tangled.

Okay, it's not the monster. It was the girlfriend. Maybe.

I'd spoken with her. The girlfriend's behavior didn't match any of the other murderers I'd interviewed and the thought sat like a rock in my stomach. Several people piled into the elevator, but I pushed my way out just before the doors slid shut.

"So, is it a closed case?" I asked, marching out of the building.

A rush of air blasted my loose hair into my face as I pushed through the door. A pedestrian glanced at me, then did a double-take. I likely looked ready to puke or punch somebody, most likely myself.

"Most of Travis's body washed up on the island early this morning," Detective Wilhelm said. "I haven't gotten the report back from Reese yet, but preliminary observation hints at strangling."

Strangled. I scribbled in orange in my notebook as I took a seat on the curb of the sidewalk and pinched my phone against my shoulder. My cloth organizer slipped from beneath my arm and I laid on the cement beside me, displaying an array of colored pens. The rainbow shades sent me a flashback from last night.

"What do you mean by most of his body?" I asked as I capped the orange pen and slid it back into the cylindrical pocket.

The detective coughed to clear his throat. "He's missing his hands."

Oh no.

"He's what?" My fingers shot to my throat. I dabbed at the bruise left by Frankenstein's monster. Did the creature want to remove my head the way he'd taken Travis Young's hands?

"The girlfriend cut off his hands," he said as easily as ordering a tuna sandwich for lunch. Detective Wilhelm's nonchalance showed he'd solved the case. In the past, he wouldn't bother to explain the details to me. I'd have to hunt those down myself. But we'd almost become partners against crime and he'd take the time to relay the extra information that confirmed his suspicions. Or so I'd thought. He stayed silent.

I shook my head, selected a red pen, and crossed out the word I'd just written.

"This can't be right," I said. "She isn't even five feet tall."

"You're trying to poke holes in my case, like always." The detective groaned. "It's common for murderers to cut the victim's body into pieces to hide it."

"Then why didn't she finish the job and chop off his feet or ears?" I challenged. A woman stared at me as she passed by, her brows pinched and face twisted in concern. I offered a smile that only sent her hurrying away faster.

"Maybe she chopped off his hands because he touched another woman," he said. "Girls like this are nutty."

Detective Wilhelm leaned further into his judgments and prejudices. He'd evolved, temporarily. But when the police department had lost three good officers to maternity leave, the detective let the stress get to him and he blamed all women everywhere for his station's overwhelmed status. I resisted stooping to his level and judging him for it. If I knew anything about stress and overwhelm, it was that it made me grumpy too.

I stood and paced again, walking back and forth along the sidewalk.

"Do you honestly believe the girlfriend and her brother followed Travis to Cygnus Island and strangled him?" I asked. The words sounded skeptical on their own, but my tone came out as desperate. I wanted the detective to be right. No monster involved. Other than the murderous girlfriend, of course.

"You know, I didn't have to share this information with you. But out of the goodness of my heart, I figured I'd save you time from wasteful interviews. It's open and shut, Rowan. The girl needs to be taken off the streets before she hurts anyone else. The problem is, I can't find her. I'm pretty sure her brother is helping her hide."

"What about the mechanic?" I asked. "He's still missing, isn't he?"

"Henry?" Detective Wilhelm said.

"Yes." I'd forgotten his name. We didn't have a photograph of him, only the sketched portrait from the police department, and I struggled to keep it in my memory.

"He was an off-the-grid kind of guy. Henry's probably avoiding the tax evasion or something," he said. "These cases don't crossover. Don't invent a connection so that you can write a juicy story for your gossip column."

I resisted the urge to curse at him and pulled out the facts instead. "Are you forgetting both men disappeared around Cygnus Island at the same time of night and only days apart from one another? What about the piles of Henry's hair that were found?"

"So he cut his hair. What does that have to do with Young's case?" Detective Wilhelm asked.

A paper cup rolled across the sidewalk after my foot accidentally kicked it. I stooped to pick up the litter and throw it in the nearest trash can. "I think this needs a deeper look," I said. "They might not be related, but if there's a chance they are, don't you want to know?"

"Fine, Rowan," he said with a snort. "Go ahead. Run to the island and waste your time. I'll be busy arresting the murderer while you dabble in nonexistent drama."

Go to the island? Though he'd suggested it as a joke, the idea wasn't bad. The thought was horrific as The Keeper, considering the dozens of auras that nearly blinded me, but not bad as an investigator who knew the island had something to do with the missing persons case. The stench of old food wafted from the public trash can, and I shuffled the few steps back to my spot where I'd set out my pen case.

"And if I find anything, will you join me out there?" I asked, hoping he'd back me up.

"Not a chance—" He started with a scoff that signaled he was ready to argue. My phone beeped with another call and interrupted him. I returned the red and orange pens to their respective places and told Detective Wilhelm to hold. Whether I agreed with his conclusion on the case or not, I needed to work over the information with him.

The sharp edges of Mom's face appeared on my screen. Plastic surgeries had changed her naturally graceful, curved features, but they made her happy, at least temporarily. I tapped the green button and answered with a hello and 'why didn't you answer this morning?'

"Mari?" Mom asked.

"Can you hear me?" I asked, raising my voice when a loud truck zoomed by. It left a trail of exhaust in my face. Pollution was the least of my worries.

Mom spoke in a strained voice, pitchy and breathless. "I'm with your father."

Oh no. This can't be good. Dear Old Dad was stalker material. He loved Mom a little too much, and she'd been running from the suffocation since I was a little kid.

"What's going on?" I asked. A car honked at another and I used my free hand to pinch my other ear closed. I stood and paced along the sidewalk. At least I could check off my steps on the to-do list in my planner.

"I've brought divorce papers for him to sign," she said.

"That's great, Mom," I cheered her on, knowing how free and happy this would make her. She'd never had the guts before. Something must have finally given. "Is he cooperating?"

"Mari, this place—" she cut off. At first, I thought the connection had dropped, but I caught the sound of a man's voice in the background. Not unlike on my last call with her.

"I've been here for two days trying to convince Heath to sign," she said. "But he won't see me."

For a guy obsessed with my mother, I expected him to at least want to visit with her. I continued pacing, staying close to my pack of pens on the sidewalk.

"We had this place all wrong," she said, her voice quiet now, almost a whisper. "It isn't a religious organization and they're not just here to preserve the ecology of the island." Mom gasped and her words spilled out twice as fast. "Heath won't let me leave."

"That's long enough," a deep voice bellowed in the background. I recognized the pitch from a man I'd heard before, but couldn't put my finger on who it belonged to. A shudder ran through me at the thought of Jameson, but I knew he was dead. I knew that. Right? *Yes, you saw his body.*

Still, the voice nagged at me with a sense of impending doom.

"Mom?"

Shuffling. A button beeped. More shuffling.

"Is this the Fable girl?" a man's voice spoke into the phone.

"Where's my mom?" I asked.

"Schwanna is well taken care of," he said.

"Johnson?" I stopped pacing when I placed his voice. I hadn't seen the man since his intrusive visits during the Red Riding Hood investigation. But I remembered the heavy way he spoke like he was the human version of a Basset Hound, slow and tired. "Let my mother leave."

"Nobody is stopping her," he said and followed it with a wheezing cough. "If she can figure out how to leave, she's welcome to. But the king has died."

A king? Dad?

Johnson seemed to read my thoughts. "Your grandfather, I suppose he was. He's passed on, which means Heath must take his place on the throne. We're a small community, but strong and we respect our royalty. Heath doesn't exactly want me escorting his queen off the premises. That'd look real bad right before a coronation, don't you think?"

"They're getting divorced. My mom does not belong to him," I snapped. Two business people in suits glanced my way as they passed by. I didn't bother offering them a smile.

"We expect Schwanna to stand by her king—"

"She doesn't live there!" I gritted my teeth.

"And as such," he said, my outburst unable to deter him. "He will not be divorcing the queen. She must stay here." His voice came out in a growl.

"But you said—"

Click. *Ebenezer Scrooge!*

"This can't be happening."

A woman and her poodle both gave me the stink eye as they paraded past. Did I say that out loud?

After a dozen unanswered calls to my mom's cell, I dropped into a crouch and selected the red pen. I shuffled through my notebook and flipped to the last page, not caring if the pages wrinkled and bent. Later I'd care, but I didn't have the time or brain space for it now.

The monster is in the city.

The missing persons case: did the monster kill Travis Young or is D Wilhelm right? What about Henry the mechanic?

Mom is stuck on Cygnus Island, where Travis Young's body was found. Most of it, anyway. Plus, Henry went missing off Pier 99, where the only dock has a ferry that goes to the island.

The island was the source of the multiple-story glow.

My breath hitched. I had to face the stupid, crazy stories-come-life.

HOME DIDN'T SOOTHE me as much as I'd hoped. Without Wendy and Kai, it felt cold and too quiet. The imprint on the couch left from my butt welcomed me, at least. It looked comfy and cozy and inviting, feelings I needed but couldn't let distract me right now. I didn't plop like I normally would on a day off from work, and I didn't schedule relaxation or do any fun research.

Instead, I perched on the edge of the cushion, outside my comfortable, worn spot, and arranged Post-It notes across the Coffee Table of Evidence. It'd been a while since I called the old, now Sharpie-stained hunk of wood at the center of our living room my evidence board. Not since before Scarlet, when the coffee table had become her nightstand. I rang Mom another dozen, or thirty, or fifty times. I'd lost count. The machine always answered.

When my watch buzzed, I jumped for my phone, hoping to see Mom's picture on the screen. But it only blinked with the time I'd scheduled a lunch break between writing at the office. After clicking it off, I dropped my head in my hands. I'd told my boss I needed to meet with Detective Wilhelm. That lie might come back to bite me on the butt, especially since the detective never allowed me to get away with anything. But it'd have to work for now.

Peering between my fingers, I confirmed what I already knew. None of the 'evidence' I gathered matched in a cohesive or logical way.

- *Cygnus Island is a monarchy.*
- *Dad is the king.*
- *Dad-King is keeping Mom as his queen.*

- *How come she can't leave?*

The last note bothered me the most. It sent my heart thumping and head spinning. I took a sip of water, but my mouth stayed dry. If I rode a ferry to the island and marched into the so-called kingdom of Cygnus, would I be trapped, too? As an investigator, I had to consider the best possible way to approach the situation. I wanted to save my mother, not get lost with her.

You will not stop her, Keeper. Stupid monster and his stupid voice echoed in my head like the haunt of a song that gets stuck in your memory and refuses to let go. Maybe the monster was on Mom's side and he knew I couldn't stop her from getting the divorce.

I sighed and leaned back into the cushion, letting my eyelids fall. My brain appreciated the opportunity to shut everything else out—the mess on the counter, Wendy's pile of books, and the smell of the full diaper pail emanating from the bathroom.

Mom didn't ask me to save her, but I couldn't leave her there either.

My eyes shot open, and I straightened. Why didn't I think of it before? I was an investigator, for goodness sake. Fairy tales filled the pile of books on the floor in front of the TV shelf. I dropped to my knees and scooted across the rug, eyes on the pile.

For once, I didn't mind the mess. I shuffled through the books, laying out each one so I could see the covers. Goldilocks stared back at me. As did a cartoon version of Red herself, along with Rapunzel, Sleeping Beauty, and the mermaid who sacrificed her voice for a man. *Ew.*

None of them struck a chord in my brain, but I liked the idea. I knew little about my father, but I knew more of his life than I did the strangers we harassed last night. If he had a story, I'd identify it and be able to see the aura.

Or did I just want to blame the story cycle for my father's awful behavior? It didn't seem too far-fetched to loop my father and the people of Cygnus Island into the missing persons case, which also connected to kidnapping. Though I couldn't claim my mother was exactly kidnapped. She'd gone to the island of her own free will, right?

My stomach answered with an angry groan, reminding me I'd skipped lunch. I snagged my phone from the coffee table and started scrolling through Wikipedia's page of fairy tales on hopes one would jump out and bite me in the nose. With my phone in one hand, and a knife full of peanut butter in the other, I researched while lunching. The sandwich never made it to a fully formed PB&J since I ate it in pieces and licked the jelly off the butter knife. I preferred less cleanup.

For the first time in a long time, I lost track of the day. The hours passed while I paced around the Coffee Table of Evidence, circling the colorful notecards like a vulture does its meal. I clicked on every fairy tale link and scanned the plots to find something that sounded like my dad's obsession with Mom. But the words eventually all blurred together on the screen and I couldn't remember which story was which. Too many involved kidnapping, trapping, or imprisonment in the form of curses. My organized brain descended into chaos with every hour that I spent studying stories. This wasn't evidence, and I wasn't an English professor or literature buff. I solved *crimes*, not fairy tale conflicts about distressed princesses.

The lock clicked on the front door and the greatest sight in the world emerged. Kai carried Wendy in one arm and his backpack in the other. I'd tried to convince him that backpacks were for the students, not the teachers, but he preferred it over tote bags or a snobby-looking briefcase. He needed something to carry the papers he brought home to grade.

I scooped my daughter into my arms, smelling her sticky toddler scent of crayons and that powdery remnant from diapers. She popped a loud kiss on my cheek and started petting my hair like I was one of her dolls. With the other hand, she drove a monster truck toy over the mountain of my shoulder and up the side of my neck. The ridged wheels pressed into the faint but tender bruise the monster's fingers had left on my throat.

"I'm so happy to see you," I said, returning her kiss. Kai snuck in with one of his own, then set to work in the kitchen. Cooking boxed pasta meant we ate far too much sodium, but it saved us money since we didn't order food.

After the meal and a quick snuggle with Wendy, I brought the case to Kai. We worked well as a team, and I hoped he'd offer a different perspective. Of course, I already knew what he'd say.

"You need to go to Cygnus Island."

I swallowed the lump in my throat and adjusted my position on the couch to face him. "Mom likes to take care of herself. She'd kill me if I showed up and risked myself to get her out."

"Oh, I know. Trust me," he said. "I know how scary your mom can be, but you've been running from the story cycle for over a year now—"

"I'm not running," I said with a shake of my head. My hands absently twined the hood's string around my thumb. The knot never unraveled or loosened unless I willed it. The hood itself bent to my intent, which was the only reason I'd tolerated it so far. Okay, that *and* the fact that if I took it off, I may or may not cause more fictional monsters to spill over into our world.

"You know what you told me when you finally went from being an interning journalist to a full-time investigator?" Kai asked. He looked at me straight, refusing to let me look away and pretend this was different. Stories weren't cases. It felt different. *I* felt unqualified. "You said you never wanted to be on the run like your mother. You were going to hunt people down, people that are just like your father, and force them to stop acting crazy. Now's your chance."

"I'm not. . . No," I said with another slight shake of my head. Even I couldn't ignore my denial any longer. But my mother is an independent sort of woman, despite how much I may have wanted to help her. "Mom's always begged me to stay out of their marriage."

"That's not the point and you know it." Kai leaned over and unzipped his backpack. He pulled the final essays from the classes this semester and plopped them on the only free corner of the coffee table. The action gave me space to think for a moment. Kai didn't start grading even though he uncapped a red pen, the one that floated around the bottom of his backpack, but somehow never got lost.

He handed it to me with the unspoken suggestion that I'd feel better if I took notes on the situation. The look on my face must have clued him in because my husband tossed the pen on the coffee table and pulled me into him. I laid my head in the crook of his neck and tucked my legs into my stomach. The comforting position would have lulled me to sleep if my mind would shut up.

Eventually, the silence got to me. My buzzing brain never liked the quiet. I sucked in a deep breath and sat up.

"You saw the colors in that light," I said. Kai nodded.

The statement sent my mind into a twist of theories that I needed to voice to unravel and understand. I picked up his discarded red pen and hovered the point over a blank, sticky note. The theory threads tangled with one another and my thoughts disappeared into one liquified goop like the ingredients of a smoothie after the blender did its work. The pen fell from my hand, uncapped and all, with a clatter against the wooden table.

Tears overwhelmed me in a sudden rush of emotion. "I can't do it, Kai."

He was right. I'd been running, I'd been living the life I vowed to stand and face. But killing Jameson had broken me, and the only string holding me back together wasn't the red one on the hood. I depended upon schedules to keep me moving like a robot or a rat in a race. I wasn't *living*. But hunting villains was no life either.

"I can't kill another person," I said. "I'm not a hunter or a Keeper, or whatever. What if Jameson never would have resorted to murder if the story didn't determine his fate? How is that fair?" Even rescuing the uncapped pen couldn't make me feel better right now. I stared at it laying inches from the cap that'd save it from a dry death.

"You know the story found the right person," he said. "Jameson was already a violent guy."

"And when I killed him, it was self-defense. But this is different." I rubbed my palm over my face. "I'm supposed to lead this monster to his death like in *Frankenstein*, but he just looked like a man. Large and stinky and aggressive. You know, not all that different from Detective Wilhelm."

Kai laughed and leaned forward to cap the pen. Or so I'd thought. Instead, he pulled me into him again, and that was it for me and my emotions. Memories flooded me from the night I lured the wolf. I watched the beast pounce on Kai, lunge for my daughter, and ultimately eat me. I'd bottled up the thought of the inside of the wolf's stomach for over a year. What if I couldn't twist the ending of other tales? How could I live with myself if I couldn't stop the prince from sexually assaulting Sleeping Beauty?

An exasperated rush of breath escaped my lips. I gasped for more air, but my breathing shuddered like a toddler unsuccessfully trying to calm her tantrum. Tears streamed down my face. "I can't, I can't," I repeated. I finally let go, *really* let go, of my emotions anyway. Last night was a practice run, a fake with booze and lowered inhibitions. Tonight, I cried.

After the tear fest, I used Kai's shirt to dry my eyes. He produced a napkin for my nose from his backpack, which reminded me of Mary Poppins' bag.

"Do you feel better?" he asked.

"No, but I have an idea," I said. The barest hint of a smile twitched on my lips. Ideas, theories, answers, or solutions excited me just enough to put a plug in the water faucet that was my eyeballs. My tears dried on my cheeks as I scooted to the edge of the couch and slid off to balance on my knees in front of the coffee table. I rearranged the sticky notes in one long line.

Dad is the king. This message sat at the top of the Post It tower. As a king, that meant he was once a prince. But which one?

"I'll get the tea," Kai said. Thankfully, he returned with a steaming mug of hot bean water full of caffeine instead. He knew me too well. "So what'd you uncover?"

"What you said that got me thinking. I don't know my father very well. But if he's part of a story—a prince no less—then I'm willing to bet my mom is a character too. And I've spent a good hour or two on the phone with her every day for the past year. I know her inside and out. I think."

Kai nodded, his lips turned down in exaggerated consideration. "That's a good strategy. Not even I could have come up with that."

I lofted a pillow at him, but he caught it like a football, absorbing the blow into his torso.

"Ah, there's the Mari I know." He beamed. The square screen on my wrist buzzed with a bedtime alarm. If I wanted a full six hours, I needed to obey the plan I'd set for myself. Instead, I tapped the silent button on the alert and froze at Kai's look. He had both eyebrows raised.

"You haven't missed a task on the schedule in months," he said.

"Yeah, well, the story cycle doesn't follow a schedule." I stole Scarlet's words. "Besides, I'm not going into the office tomorrow."

A smirk curled onto Kai's face. With the mess of his hair, the shadow of a coming beard, and the sleeves of his button-down shirt rolled up, my breath caught. A twinge of sadness struck me as I realized he wouldn't be going on this job with me. He had finals this week, and he loved his job as much as I loved mine. I couldn't ask him to leave.

"I'm going to Cygnus Island and I'm getting my mom back."

"Please don't finish the phrase," Kai said as he sat next to me. I tilted my head, unsure of his meaning. "You know 'if it's the last thing I do'?"

I laughed without joy but threw in a shrug to prove to myself how relaxed I felt about the plan. "Let's hope not."

"Cheers to that," Kai said. He knocked his glass of Dr. Pepper against my mug. I snuggled into him and made mental plans for the small trip. In yellow, I pictured the list of items I'd need to pack for the day away from the city. For orange, I filed away thoughts of parenting while on-the-go. With the black pen, I added notes about the missing persons case and a quick speech for my boss about why I'd be out of the office and on Cygnus Island for this research.

Finally, in red, I mulled over fairy tales that matched my mother's life.

Chapter 7

Now Is the Winter of Our Discontent

Scarlet downed a full cup of coffee and gave her body a little shake. Wrinkles bunched the skin on her nose as she twisted her face into a frown. She stared at the empty cup on my counter while I rushed around behind her, beside her, and reaching across her for a sippy cup by the sink.

"Is it supposed to taste like that?" she asked. The pop of her tongue smacking from the roof of her mouth was louder than Wendy's repeating 'Mama, Mama' from the other room.

"Yes," I said. "Have you really never drank coffee? It's not like you were an alien from another planet all this time."

"I feel like I should take offense to that. Should I take offense to that?"

I shrugged, too busy to worry about Scarlet's lack of normal experiences. Wendy's clothes, wipes, snacks, and toys spilled out of the overstuffed diaper bag. I shoved my notebook, a fresh block of Post Its, and the colored pen organizer in the flat side pouch.

"Besides," Scarlet said. "When I ate and drank as The Keeper, it was for sustenance. I didn't have time to enjoy the pleasures of cooking and baking between hunting. Especially not after I'd left the hood off for so long." She shuddered again, but this time, the bitter beverage wasn't to blame.

I punched the wipes deeper into the bag and dropped my water bottle on top. It would have to work. *Almost ready.* I turned and crouched to Wendy's level, zipping her little sweater since I knew how windy the weather got off the coast of San Francisco. The sun shined, but I had no idea what it was like inside the walls on Cygnus Island. Would we be inside the giant compound-looking building most of the time?

"Are you positive bringing Wendy is the right call?" Scarlet asked. She turned and leaned her back against the counter. With her arms folded, she looked down at us. "I know I don't have offspring, but I seem to remember you were vehemently angry with me for suggesting you put your daughter in danger of luring out the wolf. Wasn't that just a year ago?"

I looped tiny hair bands over my thumb and pulled half of Wendy's thin hair into a pigtail. Biting the hairband, I pulled it off my finger with my teeth and secured it against her head, then repeated the process on the other side. She'd taken after Kai with hair the color of nutmeg and a slightly sweet attitude. Wendy tugged away from me and yanked out one pigtail. Before I could redo the style, she threw the hairband into the air and used the cabinet to help her scoot-walk from the kitchen to the living room. *Slightly* sweet.

"A year, right?" Scarlet prodded.

I sighed and let my shoulders slump. Wasn't I feeling positive about this plan just last night? When I looked up to respond to Scarlet, the diaper bag had tipped. A waterfall of wipes, toys, and other junk rained down on me, one bonk on the head at a time. My crouch turned into a flop on my butt as I leaned against the counter.

"Yikes," Scarlet said. "So, are you sure you don't want to leave Wendy home?"

"I'll leave *you* home at this rate," I said. I pulled the bag from the edge of the counter and split the opening wide enough to use my arm and shove all the escaped items back inside. Once I stood, I flicked my chin-length hair out of my face and met her gaze. "I'm not leaving

Wendy behind in a city where there's a monster running around who seems to know my schedule. Does he know where we live too? Or her daycare?"

"What about Kai?" she challenged while pouring herself another mug of cold coffee left in the coffeemaker. After swishing it around, she gulped and made another disgusted face.

The bag pulled heavily on my shoulder, so I yanked the giant water bottle and tucked it under my arm. Maybe Frankenstein could sew a third arm on my body to carry Wendy. Once I found him and interrogated him over the whereabouts of his monster.

"Why didn't this dumb hood come with pockets?" I asked, tugging at the hood's fabric that only materialized when I reached for it. Somehow, it knew my intention, that I wanted to touch it. Pockets appeared on the inside of the thin, red fabric. They lined the seam in small squares like the pockets on a polo shirt. "Whoa. I didn't know it could do that."

Scarlet shrugged. "I preferred the gorgeous velvet myself."

I popped my house keys into the pocket and the fabric faded from my hand. Scarlet sputtered into snorting laughter.

"What?"

"Go look in the mirror."

The keys floated about my body while the hood stayed invisible. I rolled my eyes, emptied the pocket, and looped the ring of a keychain around my thumb. With my free hand, I knelt to scoop Wendy and headed for the door.

The clock on the wall ran two minutes ahead so I confirmed the time and synched my watch. It'd taken half the night, but I'd also filled the calendar on the watch with an itinerary. I tapped the screen and pulled up the electronic list.

- *Identify Mom's story.*
- *Use it against Johnson to rescue her.*
- *Find out if new stories exist in the cycle and where they came from.*
- *Scour Cygnus Island for clues on the missing persons case.*

- *Get out.*
- *Ask Mom to help me teach Wendy how to walk.*
- *Celebrate with Cheesecake Factory (if I find the answer to the missing persons).*

Detective Wilhelm thought he'd solved Travis Young's murder, but what about the mechanic who'd disappeared a week before? I knew better.

"You never answered my question." Scarlet interrupted my thoughts. She stood at the door's threshold, where I'd trapped her from creating a portal and dashing away less than two years ago. So much had changed since then and yet I felt like I went backward, stuck in time, unable to pass go and collect two hundred dollars worth of under-standing the hood.

"Kai has a job that he can't miss," I said. "But that's not something you would understand."

Scarlet scoffed and dug the toe of her shoe into the ground as she leaned against the door frame. She reminded me of a scolded teenager with her arms crossed and eyes rolling.

"He can't take her to school with him and I'm not comfortable leaving her at the daycare after the monster found us right outside it." I hefted the diaper bag higher onto my shoulder and pushed past Scarlet. She reluctantly leaned away from the door so I could shut and lock it.

"And what am I? Chopped liver?"

I flashed her a confused look while fumbling with my key in the door.

"I heard it on TV."

"Should have known," I mumbled. The early morning sun blinded me when we reached the end of the outdoor hall and started down the staircase. "Besides, how can I trust you won't go on your own hunt for characters with Wendy in tow? You don't have the hood."

"The hood isn't a weapon," she said.

"Isn't it though?" It was my turn to challenge. "Because of this, I'm led to innocent people who I have to guide through violent stories."

Scarlet took the diaper bag off my shoulder and helped with the weight of my cargo. She trailed me through the parking lot to the cover spot where I left our SUV.

"I wish I could help," she said, her voice quiet. Once I heaved Wendy up into the car seat, Scarlet handed me the diaper bag I'd tucked behind the passenger seat. I dug out a snack cup and plopped it into my toddler's lap before spinning around to see another pouting face.

"You're welcome to come with me," I said. "But I can't keep paying your rent when your jobs fall through."

Scarlet's frown deepened. After double-checking Wendy's seat buckles, I shut the door and walked around to the driver's side. The hundred-pound redheaded puppy dog followed behind.

"How can I help you?" I paused before climbing into my seat.

The pout on her face had formed into a pinched, pained expression. Just like a puppy, she was lost. "I'm useless," she said. "You saw me last night. I couldn't find the characters. I'm mortal and there's no purpose in my life. Plus, taking people's orders is boring, Mari. They're so boring."

I laughed without humor. "The hood has dictated your life for so long. I know it feels directionless and confusing right now, but you'll learn to have goals and decide for yourself. You'll learn what you want, and what you like, and *who* you like."

Scarlet's eyebrows raised at that, and a smirk twitched onto her face. "I'm partial to a man on the vampire show I watched yesterday. He's immortal like—" her shoulders dropped. After centuries of immortality, I supposed it was difficult to let go of the concept and embrace mortal life.

"Those are characters anyway," I said. "You need to meet real people."

"Characters are real." She blinked, and I swore I could hear it like the tinking of cartoon eyes.

"That's not—never mind." I shook my head. "You're welcome to come with me. But I think making friends and finding a hobby is the right call for you." A twinge in my stomach told me I needed to beg her to come. *Please help me.* But it wasn't what was best for my friend. And since I'd stolen the hood, I felt responsible for her ability to assimilate into mortality.

I struggled to take a cleansing breath. The crushing weight of responsibility added another brick to the stack.

"Good luck," she said as she launched into me with a sudden and overwhelming hug. Her curls suffocated me, but I returned the hold and wondered how long it had been since someone hugged Scarlet. I pulled her in a little tighter.

The drive to Pier 99 took longer than expected, with the road construction starting on Soup Cracker Street. I paid the parking meter in the lot and displayed a day-use ticket in the windshield. The sea wind had picked up this morning and whipped my hair around like a tornado of dark brown. It poked my eyes and stuck to my lips and, by the time I climbed onto the ferry, I looked like the girl from The Ring. At least, my monstrous appearance cleared a path through the people.

The ferry ran twice a day and only stopped at the island if a passenger requested it. Most people were content to leave the so-called religious organization alone, believing that they took care of the land, preserving the original history of Alcatraz prison. But others enjoyed the small rocky beach because it provided an escape from the hustle and bustle of San Francisco's big city.

I found a seat in the middle of the boat, as far away from the railing as I could. Wendy didn't walk, much less climb, but I wanted to take precautions and avoid the possibility of my toddler tipping over the railing and into the frigid ocean water. I shuddered at the thought and redirected my attention to the notebook in my hand. Wendy enjoyed her chocolate graham crackers and a juice box, which gave me approximately ninety seconds to work on my theories.

A prickle crawled up the back of my neck and I whipped my head to see if anyone was watching me. A couple busied themselves observing the water and a vacationing family posed for a picture with the island in the distant background. Everyone else buried themselves in conversation. I watched the family enjoy a bout of laughter. The elderly man and woman in the group—grandparents, I assumed—posed for a picture with a young boy and girl in their arms. The grandmother kissed the top of the boy's head and he tugged on her arm as toddlers do.

A pang of sadness struck me. It took a full minute before I realized the source. Wendy wouldn't have her Gramma Sammy anymore if I failed to bring her back. Mom had gone by Sammy, shirking the name Schwanna since I was a kid and she'd happily adopted the role of Gramma. I let myself fume at Johnson, or my father, or whoever was holding her captive, before I returned to the notebook. Anger was easier than sadness.

The satisfying *shick* of peeling a Post It from the fresh cube delighted me. I arranged blank notes on the page and began writing.

Father = prince (now king).

   Mother said she never loved him but refused to say why she married him.

I gnawed on the back of the pen and tried to think of my mother's characteristics. Of course, a story character didn't always match the person the aura had landed on. With my short, dark hair, and thicker, muscular body, I looked nothing like the pale, young Red Riding Hood.

I wrote what I knew about Mom, anyway.

Graceful. Paranoid. Always on the run and searching for something better. Easily attracts men. Addicted to changing her appearance and the concept of freedom.

After switching which color of pen I used, I lined up a row of sticky notes. Wendy giggled in the seat beside me. I snapped my head up to see her waving a teddy bear-shaped graham cracker. When I followed her gaze, I only saw the couple at the railing—the only people in Wendy's immediate eyesight who weren't staring at their phone like a zombie. But they weren't waving at my daughter either.

They stood with their backs turned and heads pointed down toward the water.

Weird. I returned to the note-taking and started with the title of the list that I felt accurately matched my mother's life.

Stories about kidnapping:

Rapunzel. Except Mom loved her mother, and they looked nearly identical before Mom's plastic surgeries.

Hansel and Gretel. Mom doesn't have a brother and there's no prince in this story.

Swan Maiden. Mom loves the ballet. Or is that Swan Lake? Either way, there's a sketchy man in the story–Dad?

Beauty and the Beast. This is the closest fit. Mom is beautiful. Dad could have been the beast.

What if she's the woman from Rumplestiltskin and Dad was the king?

~~Snow White?~~

I crossed out Snow White, then highlighted it, wanting the reminder to return to it later. One of these days I would track down the woman who killed Sophia, a victim from one of my old cases, and hid her inside a glass case in a museum. The woman was a villain stuck in the story cycle, immortal in the loop, since Snow White had died and the story didn't play out correctly. But all records of her existence were scrubbed, and she'd likely fled the country. It was a problem for another time.

Underneath Snow White, I added *Frankenstein* in case the monster's murders counted as kidnappings.

My temples throbbed, and I regretted I'd let Scarlet force down the last of the coffee. I needed an extra dose of caffeine to get me through this day. Wendy pointed and babbled something nonsensical. Had she said the word bad again?

I slapped the notebook shut and pulled her into my lap. The fine hairs on the back of my neck rose like a cat sensing a fight. Frankenstein's creation couldn't be on this boat. The space was too small to miss the monstrous figure. He'd have nowhere to hide amongst normal, five to six-foot humans.

Wendy reached for my notebook and ripped the sticky notes off the page. She tossed them into the air like colorful confetti and, for a moment, a horrible flashback sent a slice of fear through my heart. The colors of the story aura had overwhelmed me. Was I absolutely insane for heading into the heart of them to retrieve my mother?

I couldn't overthink it. I had a strategy to get my mom away from Dad and investigation was my middle name. Besides, not all stories are violent. The *Pride and Prejudices* of the bunch didn't need my attention.

A sticky note floated down like a feather in front of me and landed on my arm. I snapped back to reality and grabbed Wendy's hand before she could destroy the rest of my notes. After settling her back into the seat, I gathered the Post Its and shoved them inside the notebook. I'd deal with the mess later.

The prickly sense of someone watching me tickled me again. I whipped my head around, but everyone stood, readying to leave, and blocked my view. I straightened from a crouch and lifted Wendy with me. My carrying arm seemed to double in muscle with every monthly milestone she gained.

The passengers moved to the edge of the boat to survey the view of the island. Only the couple from the railing and another straggler or two followed me off the ferry. They remained on the beach, sitting on rocks or taking pictures for social media while I set to hike up to the wall.

Only halfway up, my arm ached from carrying Wendy. We took a break on a rock. Wendy happily picked at the moss growing on the rock while I caught my breath and stared at the looming cement wall. It matched the building behind it, gray, plain, ominous. Nothing about the compound looked like a kingdom from the outside. But of course, my idea of kingdoms came from movies and fantasy books where the castle has glittering spires and magic-wielding princesses.

The thought of my possible princess heritage passed as quickly as it came. I didn't want that tie to my father and I'd already lived a fairy tale, I didn't need to become a princess too.

Even halfway, I couldn't hear the people down below anymore. The crash of waves against the rocks drowned them out and tall shrubbery partially blocked my view.

"Hi," Wendy said.

"What?" I crouched, my heart pounding. Did I miss another word? She'd never said hi before!

"Hi, you." Wendy pointed a chunky finger at a pile of rocks.

Two words strung together? I refrained from bursting into full-blown cheerleader mode. I scooped her up into a hug and we continued up the craggy hill.

My fingers trailed along the cement wall while I bounced Wendy on my other side, repeating her words.

"Hi, you," I said.

Wendy wasn't amused. She broke our shared gaze and looked behind us. But it wasn't until she released her grip on my arm and waved that I stopped and spun around.

The shadow of a figure moved behind a tree. My heart thumped in rhythm with the whipping wind.

"Who's there?" I shouted, like the idiot in a classic horror movie. But instead of heading toward the stalker, I felt the comforting lump of a small pocketknife in my pants pocket. The diaper bag slipped from my shoulder and landed with a thump on the ground, startling me into a gasp.

"Hi," Wendy said again.

I dragged the pocketknife out and flicked the blade from its closed position. With Wendy in my arms, I couldn't get ready to self defend, but I didn't want to set her down. The wind moves the branches, revealing a slice of pale flesh.

I stepped forward, blade out, and beckoned the stalker to step into the open. "Why are you following me?" My voice didn't come out as confident as I'd hoped. It couldn't with the shake of my body and my heart racing so fast my breath couldn't catch up.

The figure squealed like a Guinea pig and leaped from the bush. "Don't stab me!"

In a flash of red, I identified my stalker. "What're you doing here, Scarlet?"

She dropped her shield of arms. Her green sweatshirt matched the leaves and shrubs around us. "I know you said I should find a betrothed and—"

"I said to make friends."

The red curls bounced about her face as she shook her head. "I want to help with the stories."

"Okay." I flicked the knife into its stored position and tucked it back into my pocket. "Why didn't you just say that? Why creep around and hide behind a tree?" Intense relief flooded me, more than I expected. The sight of Scarlet's face helped ease the tightness in my chest. Sure, it was wonderful that I didn't have a dangerous stalker, but my relief went beyond that.

Pink flushed her cheeks. "It's shameful."

"What is?"

"That I cannot support myself. You're right, I should pay for my home and food. But I just want my old life back."

I swallowed. The wind carried our voices and tossed our hair. Wendy repeated her new word, greeting Scarlet.

"I know you can manage this on your own and that you don't need me but—"

"No," I said, interrupting her. With a shake of my head, I said it again. "I can't do this on my own." With the source of my relief identified, I let my lungs fill with salty air. "Plus, I'm already running two and a half minutes behind the schedule I'd planned for today and I need to stick to it or else. . ." my voice trailed away when I spotted the grimace on Scarlet's face. Pain laced her features with the slight downward curve of her lips and lost eyes.

"I'm sorry," she said.

"No, I'm glad you're here." I glanced at the towering wall of cement and back at my redheaded stalker. "Do you have any idea how to get inside?"

Scarlet smirked. Even the mischievous expression looked flattering on her. If anyone could snag a sparkling romantic vampire, it was Scar. Perhaps, I shouldn't have told her they're not real. What did I know?

The roles reversed, with me following in her wake. Gratitude joined with relief in slowing my heart when Scarlet offered to carry Wendy. We hiked past a familiar sight. Blood no longer stained the area since leaves had grown anew and the bay's rainfall washed the rocks regularly, but I knew the spot. I felt the lingering sense of fear and death where I'd cut through Jameson's stomach months ago.

I hurried past it, forcing myself to look away. Crime scenes rarely bothered me, but I'd never been the victim who'd killed someone in self-defense either. It scarred me and the hood was a constant ominous companion, reminding me of what I'd done to survive—and could I do it again?

Yes. If danger had found my mother, I'd bring the fight.

We stopped, and I figured we'd reached the opposite end of the island. I'd never seen this side before, but I wasn't one for joy rides on ferries either. The wall looked the same, giant, gray, and solid.

Scarlet set Wendy down where she stood, holding Scarlet's leg for balance. Wendy reached for the wall and, once she'd confirmed it would keep her upright, she used it to shuffle her feet forward.

Scarlet's fingers brushed against the cement and only then did I notice the tiny engravings. "I'd seen the story aura here before," she explained, without taking her eyes off the tiny markings. "When I lured you here to find the wolf. The wall had a faint glow. When you were speaking with police officers, I found these markings. But I could no longer see the glow, of course, because you had the hood. Do you see it?"

I stepped closer, but instead of focusing on light and color; I read the words.

Has a blade of jagged cut,
Keeps the quickest hand out shut,
Goes in darkness. Wears a ring.
One is quiet, many sing.

Wendy flopped on her butt and picked at something on the wall. I crouched and noticed a thin cut in the cement. How in the wonderland did my mother get inside? Was this more proof that she was a story character?

"It's a door," I said.

Scarlet clucked her tongue. "No, a door doesn't have a jagged cut."

"It's not the answer. I mean, there's a door hidden here." My brain jumped to a scene with a hobbit and a wizard and I briefly wondered if Mordor was real too. I filed the thought away to ask Scarlet another time. Before I worried about which stories existed, I needed to investigate what made the stories classics. "Friend," I blurted.

Scarlet arched her eyebrow at me. Maybe I didn't need to worry about *Lord of the Rings* in the story cycle.

I shrugged. "At least I'm trying."

"A key!" she shrieked.

Despite the rush of wind, I heard every scrape and scratch of cement against cement. I snatched Wendy away from the wall as it shifted. An entire rectangular block, large enough to fit the monster, vanished. The frame of the makeshift door glowed with a deep, royal blue. My breath hitched. Scarlet and I exchanged looks of utter shock, both of us silent.

"That's killer," she repeated Kai's words from when I'd become The Keeper. I shot her a glare. "I'm serious. Someone else is using the gift of the hood to trap people inside a wall. That can't be good."

"How though?" I breathed, my voice barely above a whisper.

"Let's find out." Scarlet waved for me to enter the door. Or was this a portal? Did it materialize with the purpose of taking The Keeper to a place with the story aura?

A chill ran through me as I took the first step inside. Everything felt wrong like my body had lost its natural heat and my major organs had traded places.

I immediately put my palm on Wendy's cheek and forehead. She felt normal, smiling even. Scarlet didn't look bothered either as she emerged through the wall. My father's family had transformed Alcatraz prison into a sorry attempt at a kingdom.

Fairy lights lined the inside of the walls, casting a strange manipulation of depth perception. Their faint twinkle, reflecting the sun, drew my eye away from the gray cement, almost like it didn't exist at all. A massive mural depicting a man on a throne and a woman with a crown covered the side of the main building. To our right stood the old homes of civilians. Prison guards' families once took residence on the island. The apartment building had transformed with murals and paint, tapestries hung in the windows, and more twinkling lights adorned the edge of the roof. The prison dwarfed an older-looking building behind it. Both lay ahead, beckoning us to investigate.

The taller trees swayed in the wind, but the wall blocked the rush of air that streamed up from the coast. I spun to see the wall solid, without the blue glow of the door or even a hint that it had ever existed.

And since I didn't seem to receive the gift of portal creation along with the hood, we found ourselves in the same situation as my mother. The situation I swore I'd avoid by using strategy and organized preparation. We were trapped.

Chapter 8

Off With Her Head

The old style of Scarlet's dress would have been a perfect fit for Cygnus Island. A few women wore corseted dresses, strung so tightly I worried they'd faint like the damsel in Pirates of the Caribbean and fall with a splash in San Francisco's bay. Of course, they'd have to do the impossible and scale the wall first.

I marveled at the clothing and their intricately braided hair. They shared my expression of curiosity and confusion. What might have once been a giant landing pad for aircraft had been crumpled into small chunks. The cement had cracked into bite-sized pieces, now overgrown with plants, and it created a cobblestone effect that aided in the historic atmosphere. I could have sworn the portal door took us to the unknown–an alternate history version of Alcatraz.

Instead, I recognized pieces of modernity that proved my theory wrong. One woman wore a watch, not with a screen and text messages like mine, but it was definitely from this century. A man had paused his weed whacker to shield his eyes from the sun and stare at us as we passed by. He fired up the engine again and returned to cut the weeds at the edge of a fenced garden.

"Hi." Wendy waved to everyone we passed. Children played a

game of catch with a bright red ball but paused long enough to return her wave.

"What's your plan?" Scarlet asked. My moment of awe and interest shattered as her words brought me back to the issue. My mom needed me to stay sharp, to treat this like any other investigation.

"I assume she's somewhere inside the prison," I said. We continued toward the largest building.

"And you think we'll just be able to find her?"

I considered the hundreds of cells that had once housed violent criminals. It would take us more than a day to search the prison, and if they held her somewhere else, we'd need a week to scour the island.

"We'll find my father," I said. " But we need to be careful about how we approach the subject. I don't trust him or his people."

Scarlet noticed my body tilting under Wendy's weight, and she pulled the toddler from my arms. I used the opportunity to dig out my notebook and shuffle through the pile of Post Its. With my voice low, I read my theories to Scarlet, hoping she'd simply know the answer and we could check that off the to-do list. Knowing the fairy tale could help us find my mom, identify Dad's motives, and use the plot of the story to our advantage. If he was the beast, I'd tell Mom to pretend to love him, just for one day, and then break the curse. He'd *have* to let her go then.

But where would the beast keep his beauty? I pulled one of the prison's giant doors open.

The inside of the building almost confirmed my suspicions, and I expected a talking teacup to greet me. Though I knew the actual story wasn't about songs and cute dishes.

I didn't know what the real Alcatraz prison had looked like, but I'd bet that this wasn't it. We stepped into a large entry with a glittering chandelier and a crystal clear floor that reflected the illumination from above, sending thousands of speckled lights around the room. Was it a trick of light or from the story aura? What about the portal magic that we'd thought only belonged to Scarlet when she was The Keeper?

The lack of windows kept the interior chilly. My breath escaped me in white puffs. Did the Snow Queen fairy tale involve kidnapping? I wracked my mind, but the brainstorming came to a quick halt when a woman greeted us. One short, older woman in this giant place. She used a cane but walked with plenty of speed.

Mrs. Potts? I shook my head and silently scolded myself for letting Scarlet's recent obsession with the Magical Place's movies get to me. I swore I saw the story aura change colors around the woman. Pale pinks and greens and yellows lit her up like an Easter egg, but when I blinked again, it had vanished and I realized I only imagined it. Maybe I'd let the island's glow get to me, not to mention the shocking appearance of a doggone portal.

The wrinkles around the woman's eyes folded together as she pinched her brow and frowned. "I assume you're California law enforcement who has not been made privy to our arrangement?"

Scarlet and I exchanged glances. I knew we shared the same thought. *Pretend to be FBI agents?* But Scarlet hiked Wendy up higher on her hip and I understood that wouldn't work this time.

The woman's eyes narrowed as she surveyed me.

"She's a director," Scarlet said. "I'm the producer. And this is one of our youngest actresses. Nepotism." She winked and nodded toward me. *Another word you learned from TV?*

The woman's grimace deepened. "This is your child?"

I nodded, but before I could speak, Scarlet dug us further into the lie. "We'd like to use this site for an upcoming film."

I shot her a look.

"I watched a documentary on the making of movies," Scarlet whispered from behind me.

"This land belongs to Cygnus," the woman said. "We follow a strict set of rules around here and expect to be unbothered." Her voice had the clarity and sharpness of a blade.

"Cygnus?" I asked.

"Like a church, but we consider it a kingdom," she explained as she stretched her arm to welcome us inside. "I can forgive the trespass if you didn't know, but this is our sacred land. Once you've had a drink of water, I'd ask that you leave." Her dark eyes shifted between me and Scarlet but landed on Wendy. "Immediately."

"Can we speak with the king first?" Scarlet asked.

The woman arched her eyebrow, but only afforded Scarlet a quick glance. Her gaze settled on Wendy again.

I closed my eyes for as long as I dared, drawing out a blink. When I opened them again, I focused on the woman. She wore a section of her salt and pepper hair cut short, like mine. The longer section was curled in a braid on the top of her head. I wanted to see the story aura, so if she had it, I'd see it. Right? Right. I blinked as several faint colors dusted the woman's frame.

She must be part of Mom's fairy tale. Which meant I didn't trust her.

"The king is dead," she said with a twitch of her lip. She refused to take her eyes off of Wendy, so I shifted to block Scarlet and the woman's view of my daughter.

I wasn't above punching an older lady if she threatened my loved ones. I folded my arms and straightened. "We'll compensate you for the use of the island. Our film will explore the prison that was once active here. I suggest you accept our offer before competing directors vie for the idea and you find yourself overtaken by Hollywood's most persistent people."

The woman didn't react, but the slight twitch of her mouth betrayed her and I had to resist the urge to say *a-hah!* Scarlet nudged my back with her elbow, a gesture to communicate that she was impressed I'd fallen in line with the lie so easily. She'd forgotten I knew how to talk to people—especially guilty people. And if I recognized anything in this woman's eyes, it was a secret.

"So this film, tell me more," she said as she started walking. It was a manipulation tactic to put her back in the position of power and force us to follow in her wake. I'd used it before on a man I'd known killed his wife. He was stone cold until I refused to acknowledge his fake displays of grief and walked away from him. He'd followed, nearly begging for information on the case. Which I'd later confirmed was because he needed to know what the police knew, to keep his name clear. I hated to admit that Detective Wilhelm had taught me that trick.

"As expected," I said fluidly. How could I relate this back to fairy tales? "Your citizens are welcome to play as extras."

"Why would we want to do that?" she asked. The *thwack* of her cane echoed in the entry. We followed her into a large room that may have once been a visiting area for inmates and their families. But the memory of Alcatraz prison was wiped and replaced with something I only expected to see in fantasy movies. Once we stepped inside, I realized this room was an addition. It did not match the concrete slabs stacked on one another like the prison. This wasn't the visiting area, but an addition built with wood with handcrafted beams above and benches carved to match. It exuded an old-fashioned simplicity that matched with the people's clothing.

Rows of benches faced one end of the room like a chapel. At the head sat a throne, not a pulpit. Although I felt I'd stepped into another world, my journalist's heart pumped with joy. I'd love to write a report on this place. But if they were truly a respectable religious organization with no threat to their members or anyone else, it was my job to afford them privacy just as much as it was to expose killers. I was in the business of knowledge for protection, not shock value and entertainment.

Though, for now, this woman believed we belonged to Hollywood.

"Why wouldn't you?" I retorted, playing the part of a cocky director. "We'll pay, the actors will have fame, and it's all for a good cause."

"Oh?" she said, though she didn't sound impressed.

"To remember history," I explained.

"Not everybody wants fame, dear." She took a seat in the chair beside the throne, her knees cracking as she relaxed. "Some of us just want to live a long life." She'd placed herself physically higher than us, but I felt I'd held my ground. We weren't kicked out yet.

The woman rubbed her hands over her face and sighed. "And you say there are other directors who want to come here?"

I glanced at Scarlet, then nodded. "This is a highly sought-after concept right now. I suspect others in our industry will swarm the island soon. If. . ." I trailed off. It was another tactic I'd used in interviews. In the past, I'd sat down with a serial killer to get inside her mind and the only way I could get her to talk was to give her partial sentences and make her want more from me. Kai called it manipulation, but it was nothing more than a simple understanding of psychology.

The woman raised her brows, waiting. She wouldn't give that easily. I rubbed my palm with my thumb, hoping to come up with another idea. I'd gotten a serial killer to talk using this tactic, but not this woman? A shiver stole down my back as the woman's unblinking gaze looked through me.

I felt I'd accidentally stumbled into a staring contest.

Scarlet set Wendy down on a bench and popped up from behind me. "So, are we filming? Because our little actress is getting fussy."

"I assume you landed here in a helicopter," the woman said.

I resisted the urge to glance at Scarlet and held my stare. The woman blinked first, and I almost pumped my fist up in a victory cheer.

"There is no shortage of transportation like ours in Hollywood," I said, confident I'd won the power in our tug-of-war.

Finally, her flat expression changed. The wrinkles on her lips smoothed as her mouth expanded in a tight, fake smile. "Alright. You have one day for your… film." The woman's eyes bore into me and it seemed she could read my thoughts.

"Thank you," I said with a nod. Wendy used the seat of a bench to walk along until she came to the end. She reached her free hand toward my leg, the other still balancing her with a hold on the bench. She let go and paused as if to say 'look, Ma, no hands!' This wasn't the opportune time for her first step, but I needed to remember what Kai had said. I knew children didn't live on the same timetable as adults. Still, I silently cheered for her to take that first step when I needed to focus on the situation at hand.

Wendy swayed and tilted forward. Before face-planting on the cold ground, she stretched her arms and used my pant leg to hang on.

"On your way now," the woman said.

"You didn't tell us your name," Scarlet said. "I'm Scar and this is Mar."

I mentally facepalmed at the silliness of our rhyming names. The woman's thin lips returned to a flat line.

"You won't be here long enough for us to exchange names," she said. "And be sure to keep our members out of your film."

"We're here for the history," I said. "Are any of the prison cells here still intact?" I asked, looking around, then landing my eyes on her again. "And are they still used for anything?"

The woman's lips curled into a deep frown, but not without the hint of a tremble. She averted her eyes from my gaze. "No more questions."

My internal interviewer's voice screamed at me.

This unnamed woman definitely *has something to hide.*

I itched to pull out my notebook and record her behaviors, gestures, appearance–anything that could help me learn a little more about her. But I didn't need to because a faint blue aura surrounded her and my breath hitched.

Scarlet snapped her head to look at me. Without speaking, I knew she could tell what I'd seen. Worlds collided. Here I had Wendy, and I continued being a mother while also a daughter in search of her parent, and the one with the hood–expected to deal with the fairy tales.

"The buildings are off-limits," the woman said, adding more to my full plate. "If you follow my rules, we will not have a problem."

Footsteps echoed from the entry and a man burst into the room. He panted and dropped his hands to his knees to catch his breath. The woman stood, forgetting her cane. I glanced between them as he sputtered something between gasps.

"Tricia," he said with a cough. "She's dead. Someone slit her throat."

"Ebenezer Scrooge," I said under my breath. Fairytales plus parenting and now a murder? Bile rose in my throat. That was how I knew I'd gotten older. Instead of parties or junk food causing my stomach to get sick and my head to hurt, the thought of an upended schedule nearly upended my breakfast.

The woman grimaced but didn't react with shock as most people do when a murder was announced. I narrowed my eyes and watched as she leaned on her cane to stand. The movement was slow and deliberate and the thwack of her cane against the hard flooring sent echoes around the room. I suspected she'd used the sound to garner attention and respect before.

It didn't work this time. Scarlet and Wendy didn't notice the woman. Instead, they stared at the messenger man with bugged eyes and a sheen of sweat across his forehead.

"Who could have hurt our dear Tricia?" The woman said.

"She died right in front of the castle," the messenger said as he wiped his brow.

This sparked a response on the woman's pinched, wrinkled face. Her lips parted and her hand quivered as she brought it to her chest.

Scarlet gasped in an appropriate surprise, though I suspected her interest came more from a morbid curiosity than sadness. She was no stranger to death, after all. And neither was I. Though I'd only investigated murders up until the day I'd committed one myself. I shuddered at the memory of the wolf. The memory left me feeling icky but inspired to help.

I mentally added *investigate another murder* to my itinerary below *rescue my mom* and above *buy more diapers*.

It was a good thing I'd learned how to multitask.

Chapter 9

Stiffen the Sinews

The messenger man helped the unnamed woman down from her small throne and she leaned on him as they hurried for the door. She quickly traded his help for the cane and instructed him to escort us out of the building.

Usually, I focused on the mystery behind a killing. I enjoyed every bit of the process, interviewing loved ones, taking notes, arranging evidence, writing the article, and even dealing with Detective Wilhelm wasn't so bad anymore. This murder almost gave me an excuse to ignore the story cycle, for now.

The icky feeling of selfishness turned my stomach. My job and my instincts said to help with the murder. I needed to bring this woman's killer to justice, comfort her loved ones, and tell the others how to keep themselves and their families safe from another similar incident. But that didn't excuse me from dealing with stories.

"Queen Fable," the messenger man said as he held the door open for the unnamed woman to pass through. She hadn't wanted to exchange names with us, but I'd suspected I'd learn it soon enough.

Queen Fable. A little shiver stole down my back as I stared at the back of my grandmother's head. This woman was related to me. She'd once been part of *Little Red Riding Hood* and maybe that explained why I saw a flash of story aura around her. Though Scarlet made it vehemently clear that the glow only existed when the story landed and vanished as soon as the plot ended.

The man ushered us through the entry and into the crowd outside. The people of Cygnus had gathered in front of the prison—or castle—depending on how you looked at it.

Gasps echoed through the crowd as everyone huddled in a circle around the body. The victim lay sprawled with her neck contorted in the wrong direction. Open, unseeing eyes stared at the entrance.

I'd seen dead bodies before but Tricia died with a look of sheer horror on her face. The lifelessness in her gaze didn't bother me because it was nothing compared to the white glow that surrounded her. The glow forced me to squint as I observed the victim's body. She looked like an angel or spirit with a white story aura.

Though she'd been to a crime scene before, I kept Wendy angled away from the bloody scene. I wasn't about to add to my stack of mistakes as a mother.

Someone gripped my bicep. I yelped, instinctively yanking away.

"Come on," Scarlet whispered. She nodded toward the castle's open door behind us.

A woman wailed in the crowd.

"Did she fall?" another woman asked.

"She was killed," the messenger man announced.

The people of Cygnus bowed their heads when she spoke. I glanced over the small crowd and noticed the gesture was a silent form of respect.

Scarlet slipped away, heading for the door. I tore my eyes from the dead body and forced myself to follow her.

"Let's go!" Scarlet said, waving me over. She had no trouble with deceit, sneaking, and trickery, which came in handy at a time like this.

"Ebenezer Scrooge," I cursed, and dragged myself away from the crowd. At the door, I stole a glance back at the victim. The white glow gave her an ethereal look that reminded me of an angel. *Which character are you?*

"I saw the aura," I said as I followed Scarlet.

"I know," she said with a nod toward Queen Fable. "Around her?"

"No. Yes, but no. I meant the dead woman."

Scarlet stopped so suddenly I bumped into her back. She spun around, her eyes searching the floor. "That's not possible. Unless her death was written."

"This is too much. We have to find my mom first." I pushed past her and started up a staircase. Dozens of doors lined a long hallway. I opened one by one but found identical rooms in each.

"If we identify which story this is, we'll find her faster," Scarlet said.

"So a queen, a king, and a woman with a sliced neck," I said. Saying the evidence aloud helped me remember it. Or as Scarlet would prefer I called it, the plot pieces.

"It could be from many stories," she said. "We need more information."

That word was music to my ears, peanut butter to my jelly, Watson to my Sherlock. If I could throw myself into an investigation to save my mother, I'd feel one hundred times more confident we'd succeed. But life came with twists that I couldn't control. Plus, another dead body on Cygnus Island meant Detective Wilhelm would have to acknowledge the island's involvement in our case. When I'd set out on this quest, I intended to find my mother but I didn't expect to get to the missing persons case this quickly. Maybe with this unfortunate event, I'd actually get answers about Henry, Travis, and this woman's murderer.

We stumbled through the prison, opening doors and inspecting each room. The layout had changed so much from what I'd seen in pictures of Alcatraz. Nothing resembled a cell or prison cafeteria. Instead, the building matched its role as a castle with an open area of shining floors that reminded me of a ballroom, a massive kitchen, and dozens of bedrooms that looked untouched.

"There's no one here," I said, exasperated. Carrying Wendy exhausted my arms, and we came up empty with no clues or leads. How did the pieces fit? This puzzle was a thousand parts of mismatched colors and we'd barely connected one corner. I couldn't even guess at the picture or what our next step should be.

The echo of a voice stopped me short. Scarlet and I backed into the ballroom and out of sight, but not before I caught sight of the aura. An array of colors surrounded the man. A man I recognized.

"Dad?" I whispered.

"Dada, Dada!" Wendy squealed and whipped her head around. Her pudgy cheeks rolled into a pout when Kai didn't appear to answer her call. My heart ached as I tried to stay focused. Scarlet shushed Wendy, but it didn't matter. This was just the man we needed.

Evidence rarely finds the investigator. But the unicorn occurrence had happened to me once before when a victim's fiance had bumped into me at Wal-Mart and unknowingly given me information on a live case.

I stepped out of the ballroom and froze. "Mom."

My father held my mother's arm, and Johnson gripped the other. They all stopped to stare at me. It was Johnson's dropped jaw that first drew my eye. He looked the same in a cracked leather jacket and less-than-hygienic appearance, but he didn't seem to share the same thought. His eyes dropped to my chest and, though my shirt wasn't remotely low cut, I wished I'd worn a turtleneck.

"Mari." my mother breathed. Her look of shock melted into anger and then fear. "Don't listen to them," she said. "I didn't do it."

"Mari?" my father said, looking me up and down with only a glance to my right. Scarlet had emerged from the room and stood beside me.

"To the dungeon, Heath," Johnson growled, finally breaking his creeper's gaze on what I assumed was my breasts. He craned his neck to look at my father, then tugged on my mom's arm. The stench of cigarette smoke emanated from his cracked leather jacket.

The bird pendant my mother always wore around her neck caught the light of the chandelier and flashed in my eye. I blinked and tried to focus on her again, finally seeing a blue glow. It didn't feel right to enjoy the minor victory–to know I could control sight of the story aura

now and that my suspicions were confirmed. Mom was a story character. Now I only needed to determine which one.

Johnson shoved her forward, and she yelped.

"Stop," I demanded. Johnson only snorted and I couldn't blame
him. I claimed no authority here and nothing about me holding an
adorable child and a sagging diaper bag looked threatening. "You're
hurting her." I resorted to desperation at the pained look on Mom's
face. If I didn't hold Wendy, I'd insert myself between them and use a
self-defense move or two to twist Johnson's hold off of my mother. I
didn't regret keeping Wendy from the city with the monster, but it took
everything I had not to march forward and kick the man in the groin.

"She should have thought of that before she killed Tricia," he
snapped.

"What?" I asked.

"I didn't do it," she wailed.

"Heath?" Johnson looked at my father. Sandy brown hair fell into
his face as he hung his head and cast his eyes to the floor. Age treated
him well. His smooth skin and lean body were fit for a younger man. I
recognized him quickly because he'd changed little since I last saw
him at seven years old. My brain finally caught up with the accusation.

Mom can't kill a fly.

"Take her to holding," he said with a nod at Johnson to drag her
away. My father released Mom's arm and squeezed his eyes shut.

"We have to call the police," I said as my rational mind caught up
with the situation. "I'm calling the police." I shoved my hand into my
pant's pocket and started dialing.

"Heath," Johnson growled.

"It doesn't matter," my father said. "They never come."

My phone finally picked up service after a moment of the wheel
spinning in search of connection. The line trilled with several long
rings.

"They'll come for a murder," I said.

"They haven't before," Heath insisted. "They didn't come when
we'd first suspected foul play on my father's life. And he was the *king*.
The city's law enforcement is far too busy to worry about us."

The other line rang, and a man at the station answered with a cheerful greeting. I relayed the information anyway. The man agreed to send an officer. *One* officer, that they could spare, which meant it could take days.

Johnson grew tired of waiting. Before I could hang up, his thick fingers dug into the flesh on my mom's arm and he forcefully directed her toward the door at the far end of the room.

"Wait, stop!" I shifted Wendy into Scarlet's arms and ran after them, pushing past my father. Johnson pulled Mom to the back of the building, the area we hadn't gotten to explore yet. Above, doors surrounded us, overlooking the open space that caught the sound of our voices and echoed.

I grabbed a handful of leather and tried to stop Johnson. Mom looked back, her brow furrowed and expression pinched. With a small shake of her head, I released the hunk of Johnson's jacket from my fist.

"It's a trap," she said, barely above a whisper. Her hand found mine and squeezed. "You can't solve my way out of it. Leave this be."

"Enough," Johnson said. He pulled her away with a grunt and pushed her through a door to a long hall. They stepped into another long hall with a door at the end. A small square with thick bars provided the only window between the hall and the darkness beyond–solitary confinement.

The door slammed shut behind them and I froze before spinning around to face my father. Scarlet looked between us, but it was Wendy who broke the silence. Toddlers have a way of dissipating any tension with one word. Usually, it was the romantic tension between Kai and me that she magically made vanish with a scream for Mama or a babbled word that only vaguely sounded like 'poop' when her diaper was full. This time, the tension didn't drop so easily.

"Nack," she said. "Nack."

My daughter wanted a snack. Heath wanted his queen. And my mother was wanted for murder.

I just wanted to get the hell off of Cygnus Island, throw the hood into the bay, and return to investigating crimes that had nothing to do with my family.

"Nack!" Wendy said louder, aggressively persistent as only toddlers could be.

I hurried to scoop her into my arms. My father finally looked up. His face twisted with shame, but he didn't shy away from my gaze.

"I wish we weren't meeting again like this," he said.

"My mom didn't kill anyone," I said, confident this didn't need an investigation.

Without a response, Heath dug into his pocket and produced a folded paper. *San Francisco County Court* was typed on the top in bold letters. Blood had stained the page, covering the legal jargon in droplets and a third of the bottom of the paper.

The muscles in his throat rippled with a hard swallow, and he offered me the document. I took the crisp paper, but it lagged in the heavy corner where it appeared someone had used it to wipe a weapon clean. My mom's elegant signature remained clean, free of red, while the spot where my father would sign had a distinct red line through it. The blood almost underlined my mother's name, highlighting her guilt. It was the name she hated but never had the courage to change, *Schwanna Fable*.

"Heath," I said.

"I'm sorry," he stopped me. "You must address me as Prince Fable here. Until I become king. It is our custom."

"No," I said. "And this isn't proof of anything." I held the floppy paper up and shoved it back into his hands.

"Please understand this isn't what I want," he said. Tears filled his eyes, and he huffed, his hot breath expelling a white puff of air. "I love Schwanna more than anything. As the future queen of Cygnus, she will be pardoned once Tricia is properly grieved, and she'll be free to roam the entire castle."

I scoffed. "Free to roam? So trapped inside this building, you mean?"

"It is better than the alternative."

"My mother came here to divorce you, and I'm going to make sure that happens."

Heath laid his hands on my shoulder. "We could be a proper family again."

My heart skipped a beat. I never needed my dad around. Mom was more than enough, plus she raised me to be independent and I regretted nothing about my childhood. Still, that didn't mean I hadn't wanted a father to walk me down the aisle at my wedding, or a granddad for Wendy to do puzzles with at Thanksgiving dinner.

Wendy reached up and put her pudgy fingers on his arm. For a moment, it seemed we were one messed up little family. Mom had been thrown into this castle's equivalent of a dungeon, and after over twenty-five years, I'd spoken to my father again.

But the fantasy vanished when Heath jumped back and shook his arm. He let out an awkward chuckle, and I realized Wendy had pinched him.

I stifled a sudden laugh by biting my lip. Sobering, I fixed my eyes on the rippling colors that surrounded him. My father was bound to a story where it seemed he'd kidnapped my mother in order to convince her to stay married to him. Sickness twisted my stomach and my tongue tasted bitter.

"Nack," Wendy said again. I wanted to agree. A salty goldfish cracker or gummy fruit might keep the bile at bay.

But it wasn't just my father's possessive, aggressive tendencies that made me sick. Or even that he'd resorted to framing my mother for murder to keep her here. The contents of my stomach pushed up in my throat and threatened to spew all over good old Dad's shiny shoes because of how much I'd wanted to lean into him and let us become what he'd said. For a moment. I swallowed the emotion.

"Nack," Wendy said again.

We'll never be the family you're trying to force.

With the thought tucked away, I focused on what I do best instead. "I'm going to prove my mother's innocence, and then you're going to sign these papers." I tapped the blood-stained document in his hand. "Now tell me where I can get my daughter a doggone snack around here because I only brought enough for one day and we aren't leaving without my mother."

The *prince* raised his bushy eyebrows, glancing between Scarlet and I.

Scarlet only shrugged.

"You can stay but she—"

"Is my babysitter," I interrupted him. Out of the corner of my eye, I saw Scarlet's jaw drop. She folded her arms and pursed her lips. I'd get a mouthful about that later, though I didn't know why since she'd offered to babysit Wendy plenty of times. But I knew that look and that look meant she didn't like what I'd said. "And we'll need rooms to stay in too."

Heath sighed and scrubbed at his scratchy, short facial hair with his palm. The mealy sound of it reminded me of Detective Wilhelm. I straightened to stand as tall as possible, though my father towered over me. That he reminded me of the most misogynistic detective I knew should have been the first red flag. But Heath also shared the speckled freckles under his eyes and the slight auburn in his hair when the light hit it just right, as Wendy did. I'd hoped she'd take after me or Kai with nearly black hair or that it would stay nutmeg, but the hint of red was clearer now that I stood in front of my father and saw the resemblance.

"You can take any room you'd like," he said, clearing his throat. "The queen will not allow you to stay for long if you will not become part of our community. We're a private people."

"Understood." I nodded. I'd worked under plenty of deadlines before and this was proof my schedules were necessary. Once we got food in Wendy's belly, I'd sit down and map out each step we'd take to bringing the actual killer to justice. "How long do we have?"

The door to my left slammed with a clang so loud that Wendy slapped her hands over her ears. Johnson had the gall to step into our conversation.

"You're letting them stay here?" He looked at Heath.

"She's my daughter, Johnson."

I could have sworn something sparkled in Johnson's eye, but his frown didn't turn upside down. Thankfully, he backed off and I could breathe fresh air again.

"I heard," Johnson said.

"Nack!" Wendy squealed now, desperate for the food she requested so eloquently.

"The kitchen is stocked," Heath said with the flick of his chin toward the room behind him. "You'll find food there."

"Thank you," I said, bending to pick up the diaper bag. Scarlet stepped forward and grabbed it from my hand. She shrugged and muttered something about being my babysitter with an air of annoyance in her voice. Did she finally learn how to use sarcasm correctly?

"I'm happy you're here," Heath said with his eyes fixed on me.

What would I say to that? I came for my mother, not him. I pushed past my father and marched toward the kitchen.

"I'll be starting my investigation immediately," I said. If nothing else, I wanted to remind him why I was staying here. And it wasn't for him or his skewed view of our family.

IF WENDY WOULDN'T EAT vegetables covered in cheese or peanut butter at home, she certainly wouldn't accept the plain, fresh items from the Cygnus Island gardens. So much for the portal door. I was convinced of the magic of this place when Wendy proved me wrong.

A loud crack split when she bit down on the carrot and crunched. She held it in her fist and ate from the larger end first, happily munching away.

"I can't believe it," I mumbled.

"Agreed," Scarlet said as she sat down at the giant table next to me. The chair groaned as she pulled herself toward the table. Twenty-five chairs fit along each side, with one at each end, but only two or three ever got used based on the fingerprints in the wood polish. My brain dived into full investigator mode with a side salad of motherhood drama when Wendy started asking for juice.

I stood and rummaged through the cabinets and the icebox that opened at the top. It reminded me of the ice machines in hotel lobbies, but it came with a pick to chip at a giant block inside rather than cubes.

"I believed they were going to send us away," she said.

"I was talking about Wendy," I said. "I'm surprised she's not screaming for G-O-L-D-F-I-S-H."

Scarlet wrinkled her nose and mouthed the letters to herself. "She eats fish that are gold?"

"Nack! Nack! Nack!" Wendy squealed. The carrot went flying across the room, landing in front of the closed door. I palmed my face and sighed.

"You weren't supposed to say it."

After scouring the rest of the cabinets, I gave up my search and returned to the table. Wendy wriggled in her chair until she slipped down to the floor. The blue cloth that ran down the middle of the table and over the long sides slid to one side as she used it to help herself stand.

"Are they expensive?" Scarlet whispered.

"It's not actual gold," I said. "It's a cracker."

Small, high windows lined the kitchen like crown molding and let in a dim amount of natural light. Candles flickered from the center of the table with wax dripping down their long stems and gathered in piles of gray at the bottom. The effect further convinced me we'd stepped inside the Beast's castle. And with Mom locked in a dungeon, I almost wanted to call her Beauty.

I plopped my elbows on the table and leaned over the notebook. The blank page stared back at me. With the fairy tales, I had a few theories. For the murder, I'd follow my process—a process I couldn't start until my child ate something. "Where do you think they keep their records around here?"

Scarlet shook her head. "I don't have a clue. I can't even get past the aura being multiple colors. For hundreds of years, I hunted stories and their villains and I never saw more than one color on a character."

"That's not important right now."

"Not important?" She squealed almost as high-pitched as a terrible two-year-old. Which Wendy wasn't, of course. After all, she was only twenty months old. "Remember the plan? First, we identify the story, then we get ahead of them because we know how it ends."

"That was before we had a dead body on our hands and my mother in solitary confinement for murder."

"You can't ignore the story cycle," she said, refusing to let me off the hook. The hood's string tickled my collarbone, but I resisted tearing it off and throwing it across the table at her. I rubbed the heels of my palms into my eyes and groaned.

"Solving the murder comes first," I said. "We don't need to find my mom anymore. We know where she is and we already know the two steps to free her, clear her name, and force my father to sign the divorce papers."

I ran a black pen down the middle of the blank pages to create two columns, then added dots for bullet points. Each of my investigations started with the same process: organization. I needed Wendy to eat so we could get back to the scene of the crime ASAP.

"Right," she said with a cluck of her tongue. I was almost impressed at the inflection that hinted she finally understood sarcasm. "The same paper that has a story character's blood all over it who shouldn't have been able to die in the first place."

"Unless it was her story to die," I interjected. "Maybe she was Mina from Dracula or something."

"Mina recovers after Dracula's death ends the curse," she said. "It is necessary you do more research on the original endings of the classics."

"I have enough on my plate right now, Scarlet," I said. With each bullet point, I added the steps to my process.

- *Visit crime scene.*
- *Find witnesses and take statements.*
- *Speak with the victim's loved ones.*
- *Check in with Reese, Medical Examiner?*

I crossed out the name of the M.E. I knew since he wouldn't be part of a Cygnus Island investigation and added a question mark at the end. Did this 'kingdom' have any sort of law enforcement or crime researchers? I'd bet I wouldn't like the answer. It seemed Johnson himself was my father's henchman and their version of the law, considering how he'd been the one to lock my mother away.

Wendy finally gave up tugging on my pants and crawled for the discarded carrot. I stood to stop her from eating food off the floor. The five-second rule had long passed. I crouched to scoop her up before her fingers could wrap around the orange vegetable.

A crack split through the air and a shadow cast over us. The carrot broke in two under the heel of a heavy brown boot covered in mud and grease. I looked up to see Johnson towering over us in the doorway. The shadow of his body blocked the natural light from the high windows. I stood, trying not to grunt under the weight of lifting Wendy with me. After this, I swore I'd stop skipping Saturday morning yoga for coffee runs. Though I didn't know what I'd do if Liz-the-instructor asked me for dating advice again. It was like she could sniff out my Keeper power and wanted me to help her find Mr. Darcy ASAP. Maybe I'd use the treadmill on our porch instead.

Johnson lifted his leg to see the carrot before meeting my gaze and opening his mouth. "I overheard you asking about our records."

I stiffened, though I should have known they'd be eavesdropping on us in their own castle. "It's part of my investigation process, yes. I'd like to know the facts about Tricia, along with what her loved ones will say about her."

"Don't tell Queen Fable I told you this," he said.

"You'll find information about the people who live here in the library," he finished with a nod of his head in the general direction toward the opposite end of the island from where we'd entered. "It's the building behind the castle."

I narrowed my eyes and lifted Wendy higher on my hip. When she wiggled to get down, I backed up and set her in the chair. Scarlet fetched a fresh carrot from a bowl on the flat counter. It lasted all of ten seconds before it became the second vegetable to take flight and land in front of Johnson's boots with a thump.

"Why are you helping me?"

Johnson looked up from the carrot and folded his arms. A puff of his unpleasant scent wafted my way. I refrained from coughing.

"You're a Fable," he said. "I am a loyal servant of Queen and Prince Fable."

"But you're going behind the queen's butt," Scarlet said.

"Back," I corrected, shooting a glance her way. "The phrase is 'going behind someone's back'." She'd slid another carrot within Wendy's reach. Instead of throwing this one, Wendy entertained herself by rolling it into the table runner to make a cloth and vegetable burrito.

"I'd prefer that my future queen not be a murderer," he said. "As of right now, Schwanna is the only suspect. If you can wipe her guilt with proof, we'd have a happier kingdom."

Nothing about Johnson looked happy. Something about his offset clothes that didn't match the old-fashioned style of the other Cygnus citizens made him more ominous. When I met him in San Francisco, he only seemed like another dude with a poor sense of hygiene and a nicotine problem. Here, he had the power to throw the prince's wife into the dungeon.

"You'll want to go tonight when it's not busy," he said. "And look carefully, our information is not out in the open like you people in the city do. We value privacy."

"Fine," I said without the added expression of gratitude. Though I was thankful for the tip and I couldn't argue with the assessment of city people, or even modern-day people. We might have shared too much on social media nowadays. At least that was how it could look to the untrained eye. I, however, appreciated information like the articles I wrote for the public's safety and shared truths I enjoyed on parenting blogs. Not that a grump like Johnson would ever understand such things.

He offered a curt nod and I could have sworn a puff of dirt fell out of his muddy brown hair before he disappeared back out the door. Didn't the queen take any pride in her servant's appearance? I shook off the unimportant thought and turned to Scarlet.

"I need to get to the crime scene."

"I'll watch Wendy," she said. "I'm just the babysitter, after all."

"When are you going to get over that?" I asked.

"Never." She stood and marched toward the counter, grabbing a knife and slicing off the end of a crusted loaf of bread. It sent a snowfall of crumbs to the floor around her feet. Once satisfied, she cut another piece and brought it to the table. Wendy chomped into it. "See? We'll be fine."

"I brought her here to spend more time with her."

"What happened to the island being safer than the city with Frankenstein's monster?" she quipped.

I frowned.

"Let go a little," she said. "I can make sure she doesn't starve while you inspect someone's blood or whatever it is you do at a crime scene."

I scoffed and snatched my planner and the cloth pen organizer. "That's real rich coming from the chick who wrote notes in people's blood."

"I've changed," she said. "And besides, I was swamped with stories to seal. I didn't have me to help me. And don't call me a baby hen again. I'm Scar, a lioness."

"Chick is a common phrase for women." Though I almost gagged saying it. I'd picked up the word from Detective Wilhelm and didn't realize I'd even been using it until Scarlet pointed it out. *Blech.*

"Off you go," she said. "Get the mystery solved so we can focus on what's really important here." At the wave of her hand, I started for the door but double-backed to drop a kiss on the top of Wendy's head.

"You mean rescuing my mother?"

"If that's part of the story," the *lioness* answered with a smile that bared her teeth.

I rolled my eyes and tucked the planner under my arm.

Off I go. Her words echoed in my head. I didn't like her waving me away and trying to force the story junk but I welcomed the break. It gave my arms a break not carrying Wendy with me. Plus, I didn't need to expose my toddler to the dead body again.

My footsteps echoed through the massive space. I hurried to the door, eager to dive into what I do best. My fingers found the hood's string and twined it around my thumb as I walked.

I pushed through the double doors and shielded my eyes from the light. The natural glow of the sun soothed me. It wasn't story aura, and I wasn't in the dark. I knew how to solve a murder, which meant I knew how to save my mom and get the hell off this island.

Chapter 10

Thereby Hangs a Tale

I'd smelled death before. It was the unique stench of old meat left out on the counter too long because I'd asked Kai to put the groceries away and he'd gotten distracted by the History channel. Morgues covered the smell with refrigeration and embalming, but the immediate decomposition at the crime scene came with plenty of odor.

The people of Cygnus had dealt with it differently, and the hay they sprinkled over Tricia's body partially masked the smell. The proximity of the sea helped with the constant breeze and saltwater scent. It created a barn-by-the-sea effect that almost made me forget this was a dead body and that I stood in the middle of a small graveyard.

Tricia lay on a pyre made of crisp wood and dried hay. Three blue lily petals covered her eyes in neatly arranged columns. The sticky substance was applied to her eyes to keep the flowers intact against the rush of the wind, though the walls blocked most of its intensity.

If they intended to hold her funeral tonight, I'd need to hurry my crude examination of her body. With any luck, even just a sliver, the cop from the city would arrive before the people of Cygnus burned Tricia and any physical evidence of the murder that could still be on her.

Though I didn't have any professional training, I'd seen Reese and other medical examiners inspect victims on site before. Tricia had been moved from the crime scene, but other than the cleanup of the blood, and the minor points of decoration, her body looked relatively the same.

I twined the string of the hood around my thumb until it tangled. I continued fiddling with it while I used my free hand to pick pieces of hay away from her neck. The cut was deep. It hinted that the attack came from someone stronger than my graceful wisp of a mother.

I continued wrapping the string around my thumb while ignoring the white glow around the body. How could she still show as a story character after her death? I filed the thought away to question Scarlet with later. If nothing else, it would cull her persistence and pressure regarding the story cycle.

My finger traced above the wound, following the angle as it tilted up. Her killer was taller than her and by the looks of it, Tricia could have played for the WNBA, or maybe just high school basketball. I wasn't an expert judge of height since I came in right at 'boring' AKA average five feet and seven inches. Nobody ever complimented my long legs or envied that I could shop in the kid's section and save a few bucks, because I fit into neither of those roles.

This killer is the opposite of my mother. Large and in charge. I wanted to fit Frankenstein's monster into the role of the suspect but nothing else about this killing matched Travis Young or Henry's death.

I went to reach for the planner tucked under my arm, but the thumb of my opposite hand was still tangled in the hood's string. After a few tugs, it tightened, and I scrambled to pull my finger out before it turned into a tourniquet and cut off my circulation. The doggone string was the only part of the hood that didn't conform to what the wearer wanted. It hung there looking like a thin, eternal necklace of red ribbon.

I finally broke free and felt a rush of relief mixed with adrenaline as I took notes. Note-taking would always gave me a hit of dopamine. But notes at a crime scene where I intended to bring a killer to justice? That brought me buckets full of the feel-good hormone.

- *Strong enough to cut deep.*
- *Victim was taken by surprise or it was someone she trusted.*
- *Suspect taller than six feet?*

That matched both my father and Johnson's height.

The wind snagged yellow straw and tore them away from the pyre, revealing a bruise on Tricia's left arm. The hay scattered across the graveyard, teetering on the edge of tombstones and speckling the grass like a cow's confetti. I pulled out my cell and snapped pictures of both the bruise and the cut. Then I scribbled a terrible doodle of one stick figure standing behind a shorter stick figure, gripping her arm and using their free hand to slice into her neck.

I'd hoped the drawing would jog more thoughts than that the killer was right-handed, especially considering my mother was also dominant on her right side.

The wind picked up and scattered straw over my shoes. I reached out and pinched a flower petal between my thumb and forefingers to press it into the sticky substance before another gust could carry it away.

"Who killed you?" I whispered to the still body. The wind tossed hair into her face and the strands stuck to the jelly substance on the petals, and I took care to fix it.

"The real question is why." A man's voice shattered my private investigation. I spun around to see my father approaching. His white tunic billowed in the breeze and sandy hair tossed about. He looked like an older, Great Value brand of the dude in a historical romance.

"*Prince* Fable," I greeted him with an air of sarcasm. Dad or not, I just couldn't bring myself to respect him after tossing my mother into a dark cell and practically throwing away the key. I'd never been fond of him. Even as a child, I recognized possessiveness differs from love. But to this day—today, in fact—hadn't he claimed he loved Schwanna?

"We're not in the castle," he said. "You may call me father."

"No thanks," I said, returning my focus to the victim.

"You could be a princess, you know."

I had to bite my lip to keep from laughing. The statement caught me by surprise and yet fit with Heath's personality perfectly. He took himself too seriously. I didn't judge their way of life, but my father went overboard on the royal titles. And maybe he used it as a manipulation tactic. The more he said it, the more people respected him or worshipped him or obeyed his rules.

"Thanks, but I have enough hats to wear already," I said. I continued my notes, adding a quick description of Tricia's clothes so I could ask potential witnesses about it later.

"Hats?"

Not you too. "It's a phrase."

He laughed. "I'm aware of that. I'm not an alien from an alternate universe. We choose this way of life because it's simpler and keeps a tight-knit community. The bustle of the city and too much technology distract us from our true purpose of human connection."

I furrowed my brow and fixated on what he'd said. "A tightknit community. . ."

"Yes, we enjoy knowing one another on a deeper level. We migrated from the rural areas of Arizona and settled on this island after the heat became too unbearable without the luxury of modern air conditioning."

"Interesting," I said. "And you've grown up in this community?"

He nodded, hair falling into his face. "I did but I took time away from it to live in society when I met your mother. We visited here some but being here made her sad."

Interesting times two. Did Heath actually care for Mom's feelings?

"My father raised me to take his place," he said, "though he died sooner than any of us thought. Until I'm crowned, my mother reigns. She controls the community, everyone's jobs and our laws. She holds temporary power until my official coronation, which we've been preparing for this past month. My mother wants everything to be perfect, so we have delayed it several times." He chuckled and shook his head. "Sometimes I think she's let the power go to her head and doesn't want to give it up."

The knowing wink he flashed to me sickened me once he tied it with a comment that reminded me of Detective Wilhelm. "You women always want what you can't have."

Barf. Sexist much?

I forced a smile to appease him for the moment and slip away. "I have to get to interviewing," I said. "But thanks for the history lesson." This time, my gratitude was honest. Any information about their lives helped me understand the case better. And without Kai, I didn't have a history buff friend to research documents I'd fall asleep reading. The staler parts of history bored me unless directly related to my investigation. Kai would always be my perfect opposite.

I filed a mental note, imagining the words in pink. *Call Kai and ask him to research the history of the Cygnus people in Arizona. And to tell him you love him.*

It'd be my first night not sleeping next to his psychopath-socks-to-bed-wearing self, since the night Detective Wilhelm arrested me for murder. And now it came full circle with my mother. Another case, another Fable framed.

I sighed. Heath's mention of their small community gave me new ideas on how to approach my discussions with civilians. In a place this small, somebody must have seen who came near Tricia. And I suspected the community was close enough that more than one person would have known her plans for the day and how they might have differed from her routine.

The ideas didn't diverge too far from my regular interviews, but I suspected they'd have different results since everybody knew everybody here. In the city, many people never even met their neighbors.

Heath directed me where to go to speak with Tricia's family. On my way, I stopped to chat with two people gardening, another who was busy delivering dried beans to the castle, and a group of women sitting on benches outside the apartments and repairing clothes.

While I climbed the apartment staircase, I pulled out several colors of pens. I scribbled the bits I'd learned on the top of the Post It cube and tore the paper off, sticking it inside my notebook.

In gray, I recorded facts about Tricia herself.

A spitfire. Argumentative. Stong-willed. Inspiring. Funny. Lost her mind.

I tacked little shapes next to each description to remind myself who'd said what. Even within the sewing club, they'd shared contrasting views. Some didn't like Tricia's outspoken personality, others admired her courage to break the rules.

The cap clicked into the pink pen and I traded it for green, recording the pieces people saw leading up to her death.

Holding a book. Went to speak with Queen Fable. Worried look on her face.

A woman in a plain beige dress with strings to tighten around her waist smiled at me as we passed on the stairs.

"Hi," I said, hoping she'd stop. "Did you know Tricia Day?"

She nodded but pinched her face in concern. A line creased between her eyebrows and she broke our gaze.

"I'm looking into her death," I said. "Would you mind answering a few questions?"

The woman only stared out over the island, one hand resting on the railing.

"Okay," I started. "Did you cross paths with Tricia today?"

"I did," she said, her eyes still searching the view of rock and shrubs and the garden in the distance by the castle.

"How did she seem to you? Did she act scared or unusual in any way?" I asked.

"Tricia looked like she'd gotten into a fight with a hornet's nest or fallen down a hill," she said with a small scoff. "But I wouldn't call that unusual for Tricia. Did you know she served in the castle until Queen Fable had to release her for spying on the royal family's privacy?" The woman looked at me now, her blue eyes fierce and unblinking. Those with the strongest opinions about the victims often revealed the most information.

I hurried to scribble as much of her reaction and words as I could while maintaining the conversation.

"She claimed they couldn't be trusted. We all loved King Fable. He'd have died to protect his people."

A twinge of jealousy popped up in the back of my mind. This stranger knew my grandfather better than I ever could. And if what she claims was true, he was a good man.

"But Tricia kept babbling on about how the Fables had a secret that could hurt us."

"How recently did she say that?" I asked while underlining the word *secret*.

"Yesterday." She lowered her voice and took one step up, closer to me. With a glance around, she leaned. "Tricia and I weren't exactly close, but we served in the castle together as designers. We'd prep the kitchen for celebrations or decorate the great room for balls. Tricia swore someone tried to poison her at the Queen's birthday speech. She was out sick after that for four days."

"What was the speech about?"

The woman startled and straightened. She busied her hands with smoothing her thin slip of a skirt. I noted her obvious discomfort, wondering if the speech was some sort of secret or maybe this woman disagreed with what Queen Fable had said.

"The queen spoke in honor of King Fable's accomplishments." Tears pricked her eyes, and she swiped at her nose.

Grief, not discomfort. This woman had nothing to hide, and she didn't look taller than Tricia.

"He moved us from Arizona. We've taken to the sea well with fishing and plants that couldn't grow in the desert."

As fascinating as it was, I needed to steer the conversation back to who'd murdered Tricia.

"Do you believe someone tried to poison her?"

She sniffled. "Everyone here is close. There are no secrets in our community."

I nodded and added a little triangle above my underlined word, noting to approach the subject with caution when I continued the interviews.

"Who do you think killed Tricia?" I asked. I'd saved the question for last, hoping the bit of shock from my bluntness would cause anyone skirting the truth to slip up.

"Everybody says it was the future queen." She twirled the ribbon from her corset in her fingers and I absentmindedly did the same with the string of the hood. "But I think it's just as likely that one of the townspeople saw Tricia's behavior as treasonous and took it upon themself to protect the royal family."

I nodded, still twisting the string, then letting it unravel before I wrapped it again.

"I get the feeling Schwanna doesn't want to be the prince's wife."

It was my turn to be shocked. I expected my father to keep that under wraps and had assumed he only used Johnson because he didn't want people to know. "Why do you say that?"

"She kept saying that she wouldn't be here long. I, I think it's possible. . ." she trailed off and took a breath. "I can't help but wonder if his wife knows something about the future king that we don't."

A sharp pain stabbed through my temples and I squeezed my eyes shut. When I opened them, a muddy, beige glow dusted the woman's head, shoulders, and arms like she'd become radioactive in the time it took me to blink.

She mistook my dropped jaw and stare for shock at her potentially treasonous slip.

"I trust King Fable," she hurried to say, words tripping over one another. "He's a good man. He works alongside us just like his father did."

Did the story aura just land on her in front of my own eyes? And why? I swallowed a lump in my throat. Fairy tales added another layer of confusion and research and nuance that I didn't have the expertise for.

"I don't know why someone wouldn't want to be his queen," she said. "I cannot fathom a reason."

I held back a snort, knowing how obnoxiously my father had

treated his wife during their whole marriage. But here he was, a prince, soon to be king, and a champion at supporting their old-fashioned way of life. We exchanged names, and I concluded the interview, eager to speak with the victim's family. I thanked Vivian for her honesty and turned to continue up the stairs.

After speaking with Tricia's mother and brother, I returned to the castle. During the walk back, I took care to record the routine of the people. According to the sewing club women, each member of the community had a specific job that they carried out each day. They'd claimed it would be painfully obvious if anyone had abandoned their post. All one hundred and ninety-one people who lived on Cygnus Island respected their positions and wouldn't dare skip their daily jobs of gardening, sewing, cooking, cleaning, etc—except Tricia. That left only the two royals themselves, Johnson who seemed to come and go as he pleased with no specific chore other than to serve at the whims of the Fables, and Vivian who had been late to decorate Tricia's body with the flowers according to Tricia's mother.

I hiked the staircase up to the cells-turned-bedrooms and found Scarlet and Wendy laying on a bed in the first room. Wendy's body splayed like a starfish, taking up most of the giant bed while Scarlet had curled into the fetal position at the edge of the mattress. I knew the position all too well from the many early mornings when Wendy would crawl into our bed and nearly kicked Kai and me to the floor. Sometimes Kai gave up and took his pillow to the opposite end of the bed, letting Wendy lay across his legs while I clung to the edge.

The quiet gave me a moment to think and survey my notes.

Secret:

- *Is Heath killing women who want to be with him?*
- *This doesn't match with Tricia's distaste for the royal family.*
- *It* does *match with Vivian's obvious interest in Heath.*

I didn't know if I was ready to accept my father as a full-blown murderer. But where had he been when Tricia died? I pulled a blue pen and wrote a new theory.

Is Frankenstein's monster involved? It didn't make sense. I knew killers stuck to a pattern and his pattern was murdering men, at night, and removing body parts. With a black pen, I crossed out the note about the monster and moved on.

The blue pen ran dry, so I licked the end and dabbed it on the paper again to jumpstart the flow of ink. The light on my phone brightened on the bed beside me. Kai's name appeared on the screen with a message with a dozen exclamation marks that said he'd found an online version of the Settlers of Catan game. I smiled and picked up the phone, but another thought occurred to me. Settlers of Catan is all about choosing the right resources and preparing ahead. Maybe King Fable, Heath's father, hated Mom and had planned ahead, hiring a hitman to frame her. But the theory fell flat since Mom hadn't told anyone that she intended to go to Cygnus Island except me. *The timing is all wrong.*

Wendy stirred. I glanced up from the notebook to see Scarlet squinting at me. Her red hair was mussed and tangled and she wiped spit from the corner of her mouth.

"Good morning," I said. "Have you been napping the whole time I was gone?"

Scarlet yawned and shook her head. She smoothed down the frizz from her curls before diving into a list of foods they dined on before their nap. "Try the jelly biscuits. Wendy had five of them."

"So this is a sugar crash," I said, hoping those biscuits weren't too big and that Wendy would eat regular, non-sweet foods again after the bottomless plate of treats she'd enjoyed.

Scarlet ignored my comment. She smacked her lips and dropped her legs to the floor, careful not to disturb the sleeping toddler. "So is it Beauty and the Beast?"

I shrugged. "I'm more concerned with the murder suspect right now."

Scarlet rolled her eyes and stood with a stretch. When she sauntered over to the sink and mirror, I returned to my notes.

- *The queen is hiding something.*
- *But if she didn't like her daughter-in-law, why not kill her instead of Tricia?*

Plus, she couldn't have killed Tricia, she was with us at the time—unless she had a hunter like the one who promised a certain queen he'd bring back the fairest one of all's lungs and liver for her to eat. . .

"Could there be two Snow Whites in one cycle?" I asked, capping the green pen and trading it for purple.

"No," Scarlet said. "Speaking of Snow White, will you ever take the time to track the evil queen down?"

"I have enough kings and queens to deal with right now."

"She's a murderer. You'd think finding her would be your priority." Scarlet said, referring to the case I'd solved years ago on a poor woman named Sophia. Her mother-in-law had poisoned her with tainted water and hid her in a glass case inside the museum they'd both worked for. Since the story had ended incorrectly, with Snow White's death instead of the evil woman's, the woman had been thrown back into the loop. The story aura would protect her until The Keeper could hunt her down.

"I've tried, Scar. That woman erased herself from existence. I can't find her on any database anywhere. I don't even know where to begin because her son has vanished too and the men who worked with her at the Portland museum have no clue what happened to them."

"You'll learn to follow the story aura easier," she said as she pulled on her wrinkled sweatshirt. Modern clothes still didn't look quite right on Scarlet.

"I'll get to that. One thing at a time," I said. I pointed to my note-book and readied the end of my purple pen against the page.

- *Was Johnson protecting the royal family from something Tricia knew?*

This was the easiest to believe. I wanted it to be true after how roughly he'd handled my mother. What about Vivian herself?

- *Vivian admires Heath.*
- *She wasn't Tricia's biggest fan.*
- *Is this a 'kill two birds with one stone' situation by framing Heath's wife and getting rid of Tricia?*
- *But she didn't act guilty and wasn't tall enough.*

I sighed and closed the notebook. These theories wouldn't get me anywhere without more information. I needed records on these people. Criminal pasts could help narrow the field. Even knowledge as simple as who had the likeliest access to the murder weapon could send me searching in the right direction.

I jotted down a list of different blades, from kitchen knives to the metal blades in a weed whacker. Even sewing scissors could be split open to be used as a weapon if sharpened enough.

"We need to go to the library," I said. "Hopefully they keep records of the citizen's jobs and if they have any history of violence."

"That doesn't seem like something that would be in a library," Scarlet said. She scooped Wendy off the bed after Wendy had woken with an enormous yawn. My daughter begged for another 'nack' and I wondered if she was in the middle of a growth spurt. With her tiny hands holding to the blanket draped over the bed, she side-stepped toward me.

"Come on," I said, reaching for her. "You can let go."

Wendy released one hand, and I resisted the urge to clap. I smiled and waved for her to walk toward me. "I believe in you."

"I wish you believed in me," Scarlet mumbled.

"Okay, Santa Claus." I shook my head.

"I'm serious," she said, pulling her curls to one side of her head. "I'm telling you that if we find the fairy tale, we'll get your mom out faster and seal a story at the same time."

"That's only if I can twist it into my mom's favor," I said. "Wait, is Santa Claus real too?"

Scarlet only smirked. "I'm just the babysitter. What do I know?"

Before I could retort, I snapped my attention to Wendy, who'd picked up the pace. She walked along the bed, stomping bare feet. The blanket bunched at the end of the bed. Wendy took two shuffling steps toward me without letting go of the blanket. I beckoned her, but stubborn toddlerhood meant she did the opposite. Wendy stood still, yanking the blanket off the mattress and waving it around until she plopped down in the middle of it.

"Even I don't know all the characters," she said. "I once thought Romeo and Juliet were real only to discover that Shakespeare's most popular play wasn't part of the story cycle."

"How do you know?"

"I don't for sure. They could still be out there, somewhere." She waved toward the door as if Romeo and Juliet stood outside it. "But I searched for seventy years for a story like theirs and nothing ever came up."

"Nobody killed themselves for love in seven decades?" I asked, incredulous.

"It's not that simple. They'd need to poison themselves in the right order with Juliet waking to find Romeo dead after she faked her own —" Scarlet dragged her finger across her neck and made a cracking sound out of the corner of her mouth to pantomime death.

"Tasteless," I said. "Considering my mom just got framed for slitting someone's throat."

Scarlet licked her lips. "Incorrect," she said. "I can still taste the rosemary from that crust of bread."

"Never mind." I shook my head and stood. Wendy reached for me to carry her. Instead, I offered my hand, and she used it to pull herself up. She walked beside me out the door until we got to the stairs. It was an improvement since the last time I'd spoken with my mom about her development. Before, Wendy would only hold our hands and walk three or four steps. Maybe all of my encouragement had helped. I mentally marked it as one minor achievement for the day.

"Let's go," I said, calling back to Scarlet, who twirled in front of a mirror. I'd run out of theories, inspected the body, and conducted interviews. I needed the facts to see the bigger picture.

"Not until we get a few more of those jelly biscuits," Scarlet said.

She broke off from our march toward the entry to swerve into the kitchen.

When she caught up with us at the entry, Wendy happily grabbed at the biscuit Scarlet had offered for me to try.

I enjoyed a small bite of the sweet preserves stuffed inside a crusty, flakey bread before my daughter devoured the rest of it.

It's fine. I don't have an appetite when I'm investigating. Though I knew the thought was a lie, and Kai would call me out on the many times I'd texted him from a crime scene to bring home Cheesecake Factory or orange chicken takeout.

But Kai wasn't here, and we'd be spending the night on the island, far away from my favorite restaurants.

Chapter 11

A Wild Goose Chase

The sun hung so low in the sky that the wall surrounding Cygnus blocked most of its light. The shadowed walkway felt more ominous knowing a woman had died here only hours before.

The island had fallen quiet, possibly in respect for Tricia's passing. People gathered in front of the mural on the castle's wall and in each of their hands was a single unlit candle.

Scarlet and I took a detour to check out the crowd. They stood in a rough line, waiting to say goodbye in front of the pyre. A man stood beside the body with a torch, ready to burn Tricia's physical existence away. On the other side stood Johnson, Heath, and Queen Fable.

A loud crunching sound broke the silence, and I cringed. Wendy munched on a bag of pretzels from the diaper bag. I was grateful the wind carried most of the sound in the direction away from the funeral. I'd rationed out her favorite snacks, hoping we'd only be here for today and tomorrow. Tomorrow she'd get the Goldfish.

The procession shifted forward upon the queen's signal. She dipped her head and crossed her hands. One by one the line scooted up as the people tapped their candle into the torch and touched it against the hay and pyre to ignite or add to the fire.

I took the opportunity to observe my suspects, but Heath, Johnson,

127

and the queen showed no emotion. I spotted Vivian's braid in the crowd but couldn't see her face. Noting whatever I saw served no true purpose until I could connect facts with observations to thread the narrative and understand the bigger picture.

"Time to get to the library," I said, keeping my voice quiet with respect. Scarlet stooped to pick up Wendy and follow me.

The walk to the building behind the castle took longer than I expected. Though tiny compared with the city, the island was bigger than I realized. Approximately two hundred and fifty people lived here and now I understood how. They lived in tight quarters, but comfortably.

The double doors on the library matched the castle, though they were much smaller. These doors didn't need to welcome royal giants, as it seemed the castle expected. I wondered how much of the original buildings remained intact. The prison's added wooden room and the shift from cells to bedrooms must have changed so much of its original atmosphere, though it remained as cold as I imagined the prison would have been.

Hopefully, the library wasn't as icy. I tugged on the door, but it didn't budge.

"It's locked," I said.

"Try the other one," Scarlet said.

I readied to yank as hard as I could on the other door, expecting it to be locked, too. It wasn't, and I stumbled backward, smacking my tailbone on the hard, damp earth.

Scarlet didn't bother tempering her laughter. "Now that's how you go behind someone's butt."

"Ha-ha," I said, though her prank impressed me. I'd underestimated how much Scarlet had absorbed from the real world. Her inaccurate use of slang and confusion with technology often made me forget she was a quick learner when she wanted to be.

I got to my feet and wiped the dirt and mud from my pants. Scarlet had already disappeared inside with Wendy in tow. I followed them and saw Wendy immediately go for a shelf. Her fingers gripped the smooth wood that was built into the wall.

The building looked smaller on the inside and I figured it was the illusion of the towering, dark shelves. From floor to ceiling, the bookshelves covered every inch of the library's walls. The lack of desks, tables, and chairs forced all of my focus on the books themselves. This wasn't an inviting place to sit and read, rather a storage room for hundreds of thousands of stories.

I shivered even though the door clicked shut behind us and blocked the evening breeze. My heart thumped out of rhythm before kicking back into a pattern after the uneasy palpitation. The smell of books might soothe Kai, but I was a nerd for lists, evidence boards, and clues written on sticky notes. Not to mention the thousands of stories the books contained reminded me of the hood bound to my neck, holding me to a responsibility I wasn't equipped to handle.

Scarlet trailed her finger along the bookshelf while Wendy reached to pull the books down. I squatted to scoop Wendy away from the mess of books on the floor I saw in my immediate future. My legs protested in a stark reminder that I'd lost a few muscles in my desperate attempt to stay on a schedule, a schedule far too full to worry about my health. I grimaced at the thought but brushed it away because I didn't have the time.

"I've never heard of these stories," Scarlet said. "What is *Eve of Anarchy?*"

I shrugged. "No idea. But some of these are classics." A lump gathered in my throat at the word. I forced it down and plucked *Wuthering Heights* off the shelf. After fanning through the pages to ensure the book was, indeed, Emily Bronte's gothic romance, I tucked it back on the shelf between two titles I'd never seen before.

One book stopped me short. Right there on the spine was my name, well, my maiden name. Under the title, it read *V. Fable.*

I yanked the book from the shelf and paused. Small curls decorated the corners of the simple hardbound cover and the title was a shiny yellow over a green background.

Life Alone. The author must have been one of my ancestors. The spine cracked as I pulled the book open and scanned the pages.

Only the first eleven pages were filled. The story started with someone looking for romance, but based on the title, they'd never find their beloved. Whoever V. Fable was, they'd never finished their idea, or journal entry, or whatever this book was.

I sighed and put the book back on the shelf. "These don't look like records. How is this supposed to help?"

Scarlet didn't answer. She'd frozen in the middle of the room where a skylight sent a beam of moonlight into the center. I furrowed my brow and watched her extend her arms out to either side, then trail a pointing finger around the room, slowly rotating her feet.

"What are you doing?" I asked.

She shushed me and continued. I didn't have time to play games since Wendy yanked a pile of books down. The awful *shick* of pages tearing caused me to jump. I hurried to her side, swiping the books from her hand before she could rip out another page from a text on Greek mythology. The book slid back onto the shelf with ease between Roman mythology and a study on ancient Egypt.

A wave of dizziness washed over me and I silently chided myself for not having a crust of that bread or packing a snack for myself. We'd need to hit up the kitchen before returning to our room tonight.

I balanced Wendy on my right hip and continued my search around the room, hoping to spot a book titled "Cygnus Records," or "Documentation". Anything about their history, beliefs, criminal activity, traditions, or memberships gained and or removed could aid in my investigation.

"You're in my way," Scarlet said in a sharp tone. She walked back to the shelf beside me and yanked on a thin book. Much like the door, it didn't budge. After a huff and a puff, Scarlet failed again. She gave up pulling and pushed the book back onto the shelf. It triggered a loud thump inside the wall and the clink and churn of gears shifted until silence fell and we exchanged bug-eyed expressions.

"What in the wonderland?" I asked as I shuffled to stand next to her and stare at the book. Shel Silverstein's *A Light in the Attic* wasn't what it appeared. Instead of a bound copy of poems and drawings, the 'book' was a block of wood, carved and painted to look like the cover. The block was attached to the shelf and slid on a thin track in and out.

"It was sticking out," Scarlet said. "I noticed it was the only book not pushed all the way into place. When I tried to pull it out, the skylight opened all the way."

"I didn't see that," I said while rubbing my temple. My head ached and stomach protested with a roiling sound.

"Are you okay?" she asked.

I nodded and closed my eyes for a moment. "Blood sugar drop."

"Your blood needs a cookie?"

The silly question made me laugh, which sent another throb through my head. "No, it means I need to eat. I'm hungry. Maybe I'll have Kai bring home some old anatomy and biology books from the school for you to learn from."

"I know a lot," she said. She stood a little straighter, though Scarlet had already walked with perfect posture.

Wendy babbled a word that closely resembled 'cookie' and reached grabby hands toward Scarlet.

"So after I pulled it out, and the skylight opened, I stood in the light because I thought I might see something," she said as she returned to the mystery of the mechanism.

I pulled my phone from my pocket and clicked a toddler app that enticed children to catch virtual bugs with letters on them in alphabetical order. Guilt would get me later when I'd have to face the fact that I stuck my kid in front of a screen to get work done. I didn't have the mental capacity to worry about it now and Wendy squealed in delight at the sight of the brightly colored ladybugs and bumblebees on the screen.

I set her down with the game and stood where the moonlight had shone. "Pull it back out," I instructed Scarlet.

"Yes, princess," she said with a scoff.

"Sorry," I said. "Curiosity got the cat. Will you please pull it back out? I want to know what happened inside the wall."

"You said the phrase wrong. The metaphorical cat gets killed by curiosity, according to William Shakespeare in *Much Ado About Nothing*."

I blinked at her and licked my lips, losing patience. Our brains approached everything so differently, but we needed to work as a team since I had the investigation experience and she knew the stories.

Scarlet shifted the block out of the shelf again and the mechanism whirred. The skylight opened, sending a beam like a pillar of bluish light into the center of the library. I stepped sideways to stand in the circle. My investigator's mind did its own clicking and whirring as the gears spun clues.

The book, titled *A Light in the Attic*, opened to light at the highest point of the building. Did a book with a key in the title give us information on where to find locked documents? Or perhaps a book about maps would show us where to go for the secrets of Cygnus Island. I recalled Johnson telling us to look for the records carefully.

The dizziness waned, and my heart thumped again with an offbeat palpitation. This time, eagerness and newfound energy sparked the physical reaction, but the throbbing in my head didn't cease. I stepped from the circle of light and tried to focus on the books' titles. Letters blurred together, twisting and turning like I was Alice—lost in a confusing world.

I squeezed my eyes shut and pinched the bridge of my nose. The bugs on the phone game buzzed and read the letter aloud in a squeaky voice when Wendy 'caught' them by smashing her finger against the screen.

"And you still believe if we find these records you'll solve the woman's murder that easily?" Scarlet asked.

I resisted snapping at her for her lack of support in my plan. It wasn't her fault that my head pounded and my mother was tossed in a dungeon. Plus, this place seemed to work against me, making it as difficult as possible to access members' records. For a moment, I wanted to throw in the towel–or the hood–and insist that Scarlet solve this mystery using fairy tales. But she'd tried. She'd desperately tried to see the story aura again and predict the next tales. It never worked, and I knew the hood had molded itself to me.

"Mari?" she said.

"That's how I've always closed cases before," I answered. "The detectives and I work with evidence and information on the suspects to narrow the search."

Scarlet grimaced and tucked a curl behind her ear. "But you don't have that information, nor am I a detective. I'm just a babysitter."

I ignored her quip. "We're getting the records right now," I said, returning to skimming the book titles. "And once we do, I'll confirm my list of suspects and hopefully be able to cross out a name or two to hone our investigation."

But the question still nagged at me. Why would Johnson lead us here if it contained information on him and he was guilty? Was that enough to cross him off the list now? Was he trying to slip a clue to me? Did he know something about Heath but feared the repercussions of treason against the future king?

I filed the thought away in orange, the color I'd assigned to plausible theory for this case.

My finger didn't catch a speck of dust as I trailed it along the shelf. The library was well-used, clearly, but not all the books looked as worn as the others. The titles mentioned witches and queens and hunts, and I occasionally came across a book I'd read or heard of like *Persuasion* and *The Grapes of Wrath*. I wasn't as well-read on the older stories as I'd like, but I knew someone who was and he didn't obsess over which characters existed or not.

My heart flickered, sending a twinge of emotion into my chest. I wanted to return home to Kai tonight and mull over the evidence together. He'd pull his knowledge of history into the case and I'd organize the facts. If it weren't for the arrest, my night spent in jail under the accusation of a gruesome murder, I wouldn't be as desperate for the comfort of my couch. Now my mom suffered the same fears, wondering if she'd be in prison for life—or at least trapped in this castle.

Book after book blurred in my vision, the titles all melting together in my tired brain until one caught my eye on the shelf just above my head. My breath hitched, catching on the lump in my throat. I grabbed for the identical copy of *Doors to the Unknown* with its small crack in the spine through the work 'unknown' and where the green wore to white on the edges.

On my tiptoes, I pulled the book out, but it wouldn't come down. *Doors to the Unknown* would remain unknown to these people because the copy, though identical in how it looked, wasn't a book at all. The block slid along its track in the shelf, a track I could hear but not see unless I could locate a stool.

The wall clunked with metal, crunching against metal until it silenced.

I spun around. "What happened?"

Scarlet's giant eyes blinked at me. "Nothing. Nothing other than the sound." Her arms hung at her side and she offered a slight shrug. Was she feeling useless again? I needed to assign her a task, so she didn't dwell on what she couldn't do. And maybe I'd solve this murder without cutting through a wolf's stomach. I shivered at the memory and instantly shoved it away.

"Was this sticking out before?" I asked. Another book—or block—jutted from the shelf on the opposite side of the room from Shel Silverstein's poetry. I hurried across the polished wood flooring and froze in front of the third mechanism.

"Ebenezer Scrooge." I breathed a curse that Scarlet must have heard. The heat of her body came up behind me and I sensed her tension at the sight of the book.

Little Red Riding Hood Across the World:
A Study of Twisted Tales.

"Maybe it's simply a quincy-dinner," Scarlet said.

I pinched my brow and rolled my eyes to the left, trying to piece together her minced word. "A coincidence?"

"That's what I said." She edged around me and reached for the book. It slid off the shelf with ease and presented real pages with illustrations and chapters.

"I don't believe in coincidences," I said as I stared at the book. She fanned through the pages. The snarling, blood-covered canines struck me first. Scarlet stopped at the picture of the wolf, the book falling open in her palms. The black-and-white image matched Jameson's face when he was the wolf, right down to the tuft of fur missing on the right side of his jaw that had snagged on a branch in Pioneer Park.

"You don't believe?" Scarlet prodded. Her finger landed on the picture, tracing the familiar features of the man I'd killed. AKA the wolf who'd hunted me. All the fear and confusion and relief rushed back to me and I wanted to run to my mother to apologize for ignoring whatever story from which she belonged. But she didn't know the story cycle. I did. Not believing wasn't an option anymore. I needed to want this so I could see the glow around my mother and find the character who'd framed her once and for all.

A slice of pain cut across my forehead. The pulse of my heart throbbed behind my eyes as light burst into the room. The skylight didn't shine any brighter, nor did a lamp flick on. I resisted the urge to clap or call for Google's Alexa to turn off the light. But this wasn't technology. Hundreds of thousands of books glowed in blazing reds and brilliant yellows. There were as many shades of colors as there were books. The light grew more and more intense until I squeezed my eyes shut.

The thin skin of my eyelids couldn't shadow the story aura. The stories forced their way into my mind. I swayed and shot my hand out, reaching for Scarlet. I heard her gasp but blinded, dizzy, and weak, my knees buckled before I could grip her arm.

I came to on the floor. The hardwood dug into the bone on my hip and shoulder, but a soft fabric cushioned my head. My shoulder popped as I moved from the fetal position to sitting with my legs crossed. Scarlet's sweatshirt lay in a bundle where my head had been and smelled faintly of the detergent I used mixed with the salty scent of sweat. I made a quick mental note to teach Scarlet how to do laundry.

Across the room, Wendy squealed and took a tentative step toward Scarlet. She held onto the shelf until Scarlet peeled her chubby fingers from the smooth wood and guided my toddler's steps in a little circle.

"I believe in you." Scarlet knelt and tickled Wendy's tummy until my daughter giggled and plopped on her behind. Wendy noticed me awake and crawled across the room, wearing holes in the knees of her stretchy blue pants.

The pitch of her happy squeals should have hurt my head, but all pain from the light had vanished. Only a faint glow of varying colors remained around the books. Without the brightness, I could now distinguish between books and identify that only some stories exuded the aura and the range of colors wasn't as wide as I'd thought.

I scooped Wendy into my lap, and she threw her little arms around my stomach. She babbled 'Mama' while sinking into me, and I knew it was long past her bedtime. Wendy took after her dad that way. The later it became, the more cuddles she wanted.

The moon illuminated the room better now that the last rays of the sun had disappeared. Scarlet stood and folded her arms.

"Do you believe now?" she asked. The slight curl of her lip and the arch of her brow said what she didn't. *I told you so.*

I nodded but closed my eyes. "I'm afraid to say it."

"What changed?"

"I guess I wanted to see it," I said. After peeking one eye open and ensuring it was safe, I opened both. "This doesn't mean I'm going to stop my murder investigation."

Scarlet shook the curls from her face and pulled a copy of *Beauty and the Beast* from the shelf. The book covered her face, and it reminded me of an artistic shot from the reading community on social media sites. Kai's students had introduced him to the community when he'd asked them if anyone still read the classics after I'd become The Keeper.

"But you're going to let me be your partner now?" Scarlet asked, dancing the book in front of her face. "Not just the babysitter?"

"Of course," I said. I adjusted Wendy from my torso, to hold her higher against my body as I stood and lifted her with me. "We'll use everything. The stories, the aura, the interviews, and records and evidence. Speaking of which. . ." I pointed to the mechanism that had pushed *Little Red Riding Hood* from its place on the shelf.

Scarlet shrugged. "I couldn't figure it out."

"Okay." I nodded. "Will you search the room for any other stories that could involve kidnapping, forced marriage, or framing someone for murder while I work on finding the records?"

"Nack," Wendy demanded.

"Maybe we'll solve the mystery of where to find dinner first, then come back?" I said.

Scarlet agreed. I stooped to pick up her sweatshirt and toss it to her. We replaced the blocks and watched the skylight roll shut. Darkness fell. The only light came from the faint illumination from the screen on my phone.

"I'll freshen up on Victor Frankenstein too, for when we return to San Fran and the missing persons case," she said.

"No," I said as we followed the flashlight on my phone toward the door. "We'll get my mom out and then I'm back to using police resources to solve future cases."

"But the monster–"

"Is a human too," I said. "And I have to follow the law, Scar. I can't go killing people off of a hunch." But even as I said it a yellow glow caught my eye. It shined brighter than the rest of the books on the bottom shelf at the corner of the room.

Scarlet sighed and mumbled something, but I didn't hear it. The glow burned more intensely, and I blinked until I could focus on where it'd come from.

Mary Shelley's *Frankenstein* had been pulled from the organized rows of books. It sat across the tops of the other books, laying sideways. A scrap of paper hung out from the top like a bookmark.

I swerved from my path toward the door and walked to the corner. The scrap of paper slipped easily from between the pages. I expected Scarlet to protest since I'd redirected the flashlight on my phone to the paper in my hands instead of lighting the way.

But she'd already reached the door, twisted the handle, and yanked it open. Over her shoulder, I spotted what stopped her in her tracks.

Talk about doors to the unknown.

A man stood outside the library, blocking her from exiting. Another, in a matching black shirt, jogged up behind him with heavy chains in his hands. They clanked against one another as he handed one set to the man in my way.

"You've broken Cygnus law," the first man spat. In reaction, I shoved the scrap of paper into my pant's pocket. "No one is allowed entry into the library without permission from the king."

"The king is dead," Scarlet said. I cringed as her announcement triggered a deeper grimace on the man's face.

"Exactly," he said. "So I know you broke in here without permission."

"It was unlocked—" I said, but Wendy's scream interrupted me as the second man stepped up and ripped her from my arms.

My heart pounded in my throat and I shoved past the first man to reach for my daughter. He stopped me short and tossed the heavy chains over my wrists, knocking the phone from my hand. It landed on its corner; the screen shattering and blinking to black.

I pushed against him, giving myself enough space to use a self-defense kick I'd learned in a class. But it was no use. The weight of the chains threw me off balance and my mind couldn't focus on anything but Wendy's cries.

The first man prodded Scarlet forward and away from the library, while he turned and locked it. I followed the second man who carried my child. Wendy reached over his shoulder for me, her face pinched and wet with tears as she screamed.

"I need to speak with Heath," I said.

The man didn't slow or offer a response beyond a curt nod of his head. But he didn't agree with my demand.

My father stood in front of the castle, face twisted with an emotion I couldn't place. Anger burned in my chest. *What did you do?*

I wouldn't get to ask him tonight. He disappeared inside the castle before we reached him and was nowhere to be seen once we got inside. The men—or guards, as my brain assigned a role to them—led us to the last cell left in the building.

Chapter 12

In a Pickle

Solitary confinement isn't so solitary when you share the space with your hangry toddler, scared mother, and obnoxiously persistent stalker-turned-friend-turned-temporary-partner. One guard left us with a bowl of apples and pears, but Wendy refused anything with juice that wasn't wrapped in a colorful box and had a straw sticking out the top. Instead of having the *nack,* she threw herself onto the floor and kicked her way into a full-blown tantrum.

My mother swooped in to help, comforting Wendy. She bit the skin off the pear and gave the inside to Wendy until my daughter finally relented and tried the fruit. It reminded me of a bird feeding her nest of babies. Mom was harsh but loving when she raised me, not Mother of the Year considering how distant she could be, but far better on the parenting front than I could claim. My attempts to calm Wendy left us both in tears while I begged her to stop crying and Wendy only got more frustrated that I couldn't read her mind. If only I knew what to do like Gramma Sammy.

I sighed and leaned my back against the wall. This wasn't the time for self-pity over my parenting failures. As much as I wanted to be the one to ease my daughter's tornado of hungry and confused emotions, I was grateful for Mom's help. I slid down the wall and sat on the floor, ready to dive into theories now that toddler screams didn't freeze my brain.

But Mom wouldn't talk tonight. She insisted Wendy knew what was best for all of us and that a good night's sleep would better prepare us for theories tomorrow. The small bed barely fit my mother and Wendy, but they curled together on the mattress with a thin blanket. If someone told me I'd fall asleep on freezing concrete, I wouldn't believe them. A lot of things came true I didn't want to believe. The impossibly long day had my muscles sinking into the rough floor and my mind drifting into unconsciousness.

When I woke, I didn't know if the night had ended, and morning began. Maybe we'd slept through to the afternoon. Mom sat on the bed, raking her fingers through Wendy's tangled hair while Wendy munched on fresh bread. The clang of the door shutting had roused me, and I assumed our food delivery had just left. But Johnson was no DoorDash, and this wasn't home.

I pulled myself up and scooted to lean against the wall. Brain fog slowly lifted as sleep melted away and theories filled my mind.

If Johnson had wanted to help us, why leave the library unlocked but not warn us we needed to leave before the guards found us? My mind assigned the chain-carrying men as some type of guard of law enforcement for the island. And what were they protecting at the library?

What information about the royal family had Johnson intended to lead us to?

Scarlet paced back and forth with the sweatshirt's sleeves tied around her neck and the rest of the fabric draped down her back like a makeshift version of the hood. She jutted each finger out one at a time as though counting something.

With Wendy quiet now, calmly munching on a bite of pear, Mom looked up and gave me a tight-lipped smile.

"What happened?" she asked.

"It's a long story." I flinched at that word. *Which character are you?* The faint blue glow moved like water as it traced my mother's graceful movements. *Water.* I filed the thought away, hoping I'd remember to add it to my list once I got my notebook back from the guards. If I got it back. If we ever got out.

Think Mari. I tapped my temple. "Use your noodle," I whispered one of Kai's phrases to myself.

"Why did you come here?" Gramma Sammy asked. I looked up to meet my mother's sharp gaze. Stiff brows balanced in arches over her eyes like two tiny wings on an otherwise changed face. Her appearance had changed so much since I was a child. Mom chased plastic surgery almost as hard as her husband chased her. I could never guess what look she sought.

"Never walk alone," I answered with a phrase of her own.

Mom broke our gaze with a quick turn of her head. Her chocolate hair had been bleached, but a glimpse of roots darkened her scalp.

"You're the one who taught me that, Mom," I said. "I will not let you do this alone. You came here to divorce Heath, but you knew he wouldn't go for it."

She huffed but turned to look at me again. "I didn't expect him to lock me up."

"Didn't you?" Scarlet interjected. The pacing stopped, and she stared at my mother.

"Why is your friend here? And Wendy?" Mom asked, ignoring Scarlet.

"Scarlet is helping me and I couldn't leave Wendy in San Francisco with—" I paused. My mother might believe in human monsters, but not the Frankenstein kind. "Like I said, it's a long story."

"We're partners." Scarlet beamed at me from behind Mom. Did Scarlet want to keep working together after we escaped this new version of Alcatraz? If she could curb the fairy tale pressure, I'd consider taking her on as an investigative assistant. She certainly had the guts.

As if she could hear my thoughts, Scarlet stood a little taller.

"Yes," I agreed, then fixed my eyes on Mom. "Can you tell me everything you know about the accusation against you?" If only I had my set of colored pens with me. I'd noted my mother's information in blue to match the glow. That nod to the fairy tale would have to satisfy

Scarlet for now. I'd promised my partner that I believed and would consider the classics in this investigation. I didn't intend to break any promises. And maybe, just maybe, the story would give me insight into my father and what he intended by throwing us into a dungeon.

The cell felt several degrees colder than the hall and the rest of the castle. Our breaths puffed in front of us and Wendy cuddled closer against Mom's body after the heat from her tantrum dissipated. I wanted to pace with Scarlet to keep from shivering, but exhaustion settled over me like Kai's weighted blanket. I loved when that thing got wrapped between my legs and I woke all cozy and snuggled like a burrito after Kai got up on Saturday mornings to run on the treadmill.

Mom hugged Wendy to share her warmth and then sighed out of her nose. "When I asked your father for the divorce, he refused. He promised that I'd love being his queen and requested that I stay and try it. I told him I was not interested, but he insisted."

"How did you get inside the walls?" I asked. I felt Scarlet's gaze shift to me. Did Mom know more about the story aura and the hood and The Keeper than I thought? Which was nothing, of course, unless I'd accidentally butt-dialed her while discussing it with Kai or Scarlet.

The only wrinkle left on my mom's Botoxed face appeared between her eyebrows. "There was a door open on the far side."

Scarlet and I exchanged glances.

"Is that not how you arrived?" Mom asked.

"The door wasn't exactly open when we got here," I said. "Did you try leaving after you refused Heath's offer?"

The soft snores of Wendy dozing filled the pause between us. She'd fallen asleep curled in her grandma's lap and the scene only fueled my fire to free my mother from this place and her marriage. It was nearing Wendy's naptime and the little fruit in her belly must have satisfied her enough to make sleep possible.

"I looked for the door again," my mom said. "But I got turned around and Johnson helped me find my way back to the castle." The island was small. She wouldn't have needed help. I knew that was my mother's gentle way of referring to Heath's possessiveness through his leather-jacketed lackey.

"Besides," she continued, looking down at Wendy and smoothing back my daughter's messy hair. "I don't want to leave without his signature."

I nodded, my chest tight and voice apologetic that I didn't save her yet. "Do you think Heath framed you to keep you here?"

My mom's eyes remained fixed on Wendy, but her throat rippled with a swallow. "I don't want to believe your father is capable of murder."

"Mom." I stood and walked over to her. After taking a seat next to her and draping my arm around her shoulders, I hoped she'd meet my gaze. "There are a lot of things I don't want to believe, either."

The tapping footsteps behind us ceased, and I felt Scarlet's eyes on my back. I glanced sideways.

"Every case I solve comes with a shock in one way or another. It's never easy to accept that people we thought we knew have secrets."

"Secrets. . ." my mother's voice trailed off. The wrinkle appeared between her brow again and her eyes searched the gray concrete floor until she looked at me. "To tell you truth," she said. "I've always felt like something is missing in my life and when I got to the island, it was like I came close to whatever was missing."

I resisted breaking my concentration on my mother to exchange a look with Scarlet.

What were you missing?

The list of fairy tales I'd outlined popped into my mind's eye. Scarlet would be proud. Which one of those included a character in search of something? Or maybe something stolen?

"They have strict rules here," Mom continued. "I don't want you wrapped up in all of this. Work your investigator's magic and get yourselves out of here and off this island."

"Mom—"

"Mari Elise Fable, you promise me you will take your daughter and friend home as soon as that door opens." Mom's voice was firm but not unkind.

"No," I said.

Mom scoffed and white air puffed out in front of her and over

Wendy like a tiny cloud. Speaking of clouds, my mother's head was in them. I wanted to ground her with a reminder that she didn't need to protect me. Investigating was my job.

"I appreciate your concern," I said, giving her shoulders a squeeze then letting her go. "But this is what I do. I cannot leave until I solve Tricia's murder or until an officer or detective I called from San Francisco arrives and takes over the investigation."

Mom gnawed on her bottom lip. With her, silence meant agreement. She spent years quiet about my father's attempts to reach out. It wasn't until she finally wanted to end their marriage that she responded to one of his attempts and followed Johnson's directions to Heath's home.

"Besides," I said, repeating her phrasing. "I don't want to leave without my daughter's Gramma Sammy."

Mom's mouth twitched, and I almost spotted a smile. "That's another thing you need to promise me," she said. "Trust your choices as a parent."

"Yeah, I'll get there." I'd deal with that later. For now, my child slept peacefully and my case needed narrowing.

I questioned Mom about Heath until I felt confident she didn't know his whereabouts during the time of Tricia's death. The victim couldn't have been dead more than a few minutes before someone stumbled upon her right in front of the castle. Though I had none of my normal resources to solve this murder, I appreciated that the small location narrowed my search.

Scarlet finally quit pacing after wearing herself out and took a seat on the floor beside us. The heavy circles under Mom's eyes told me that even a few hours in this cell had exhausted her. Or maybe she was ready to give up and give in to remain Heath's wife forever.

Absolutely not. Not if I have a say in this. My mom deserved the freedom to choose her future, and I'd fight for that future as hard as I did when I believed Wendy was sealed to the fate of Little Red Riding Hood's story.

"Do you know a woman named Vivian?" I asked, ignoring the groaning in my stomach. When did I last eat? It seemed weeks ago that

I was at home, downing a bowl of apple cinnamon oatmeal and coffee with too much cream. I'd only had pieces of bread or fruit since we'd been on the island and it must have been close to half-past eight when they'd arrested us in front of the library. Wendy had eaten an armful of jelly biscuits stolen from the kitchen by Scarlet, plus the bag of Goldfish, but I'd only had a bite.

"She's a decorator." Mom nodded. "She and the woman who died had checked in with Heath when I was presenting him with the divorce papers. But she couldn't have killed Tricia."

"Why is that?" I quirked my head.

"Because she was with me when we heard the scream."

"What the fork?" Scarlet said.

I glanced over to see her head in her hands while her elbows rested on her knees in the crisscross applesauce position. She looked genuinely fascinated by my mother's admission.

"What?" Scarlet asked. "I heard the phrase on a show about a good place you go when you die."

I furrowed my brow, which prompted her to explain further.

Scarlet shrugged. "I have to know now that I'm mortal."

"Pardon?" my mom interjected.

I shook my head and returned to the massive piece of evidence my mother had just dropped. "Vivian was with you when Tricia died?"

"We were both in the kitchen waiting to speak with Heath. About very different things, of course."

"And you said Heath was nowhere to be seen?" I asked.

"I said I didn't see him," she clarified. "It was after Johnson returned with me to the castle. I intended to ask your father if we'd make a trade. I'd stay for his coronation if he'd then sign the papers and escort me off this island. The decorator wanted to speak with him regarding the candles for the ceremony."

"So she's your alibi," I said, perking up. "This is it. You should be free to go."

Mom shook her head and released a breath of misty air. "I heard her speaking with Johnson before she came into the kitchen. I can't be sure she saw me since I was sitting at the far end of the table. She entered with him, and he chipped off a block of ice for her drink, as is customary for those serving in the castle."

I remembered the length of the massive dining table and accepted the plausibility of this. "It's already freezing in this place. Who'd want a cold drink?"

"They come from the deserts of Arizona," Mom said. "They don't seem to get chilled easily."

I wanted to ask more about when she'd met my father. What other customs did she know about them? How long had she spent in this religious…cult? Monarchy? I didn't know what to call it. But my mom was a private person and now wasn't the time. We'd have plenty of opportunities after I solved the case and we returned home to San Francisco.

I couldn't wait to have a meal in front of the TV and return to my routine where I could check in with a call to my happy and safe mother every morning during my walk to work. We'd discuss Wendy's development or lack thereof and Mom would say I hadn't totally failed as a parent. Not yet, anyway.

The lock outside the door dropped with a clunk. We startled and looked at the cell's heavy, rusty door. The conversation had kept us so engaged that none of us noticed the footsteps coming from the hall until they were right outside the door. The lock clanked and the door creaked as it opened.

My father stepped inside the cell. The twist in his lips and worried eyes combined into an apologetic expression.

"I'm pardoning you and your friend from trespassing in the library," he said in a gruff voice. He coughed and cleared potential embarrassment before forcing out a genuine apology. "I'm sorry for the way the guards treated you. I didn't know Johnson suggested you enjoy a visit to the library. Once I spoke with him, I determined he was confused about your access. Since you're a Fable, he granted you passage, but the queen did not approve it."

"I don't understand," I said. I stood and wiped the dirt from the cell's floor off of my pants. Mom followed suit after I lifted Wendy from her lap and rested my daughter's face between the base of my neck and my shoulder. Wendy grumbled in her sleep, but her eyes stayed closed and she snuggled into me.

"The queen is displeased with Johnson's misunderstanding and he'll be punished accordingly," Heath said.

Johnson definitely wants us to know something without Heath finding out. I tried to picture the words in a specific color, to cement them into my brain files until I could record it in my notebook, but without food and the impossibly long day, my mind refused to work.

"So you can pardon my mom too," I said, marching up to him. The faint scent of garlic wafted from his breath and vampire books flashed in my mind. *Wait, that's the other way around.* The garlic bread proved he wasn't Dracula and my mom couldn't be the woman the character stalked and fed on in the novel.

Heath glanced between us and shook his head. He opened his mouth, but I cut him off before the garlic stench assaulted me.

"You know she didn't hurt anyone," I said. I held his gaze, using the easiest interview tactic I could think of. If he looked away, I claimed the power in the conversation. "Just pardon her."

"For another day, I am the prince," he said. "Queen Fable is the only one with the power to pardon a crime as grievous as this. She holds most of the control until my coronation."

"Fine," I snapped. "Then I'm going to keep tearing this place apart until I find the actual murderer."

Heath finally broke our gaze. Strands of sandy hair fell into his tanned face. Either I'd age amazingly or my father paid a bag of gold to plastic surgeons, too. Maybe Heath and my mom had more in common than I'd thought. He looked down the long hall and lifted his arm to beckon me out the door.

And I'm going to prove you're more than just possessive. A moment of grief struck me. This was my father, and yet I was determined to see him as the murderer. But who else?

My mother provided an alibi for Vivian and Johnson while Scarlet and I were with the queen when it happened. The rest of the island's inhabitants were accounted for at their respective jobs. That left Heath.

I shot my mom a confident look, trying to erase the twinge of sadness from my tightened lips. "You'll be out of here soon."

My stomach groaned again, but I ignored it. I'd lost my appetite, though dinner had long passed, and I skipped the second bread delivery. I wanted Mom and Wendy to have as many pieces of the warm slices as they could eat. The pit in my stomach wasn't from hunger, anyway.

It was time to accept the possibility that my father was the murderer. What did Tricia know about Heath? And was it dangerous that he had my mother here under lock and key?

I chewed on my cheek and nodded for my father to step out of the cell before me. If nothing else, I took comfort because I had eyes on the suspect and I wouldn't let him smooth-talk his way to innocence.

Chapter 13

Truth Will Out

After four jelly biscuits, I was convinced I'd shape-shifted *into* a jelly biscuit. I pulled my high-waisted pants up over my stomach so the waistband didn't restrict my dinner intake. The roasted turkey leg, buttered corn, and fresh boysenberries didn't help. What could I say? Food fueled my investigations. If only I had Kai by my side and my butt in my favorite spot on the couch.

Instead of the Coffee Table of Evidence, I made do with the giant dining table in the kitchen. The castle settled into silence as the night wore on. My father, Johnson, and the queen were nowhere to be seen, long retired to their rooms, I suspected. Wendy snoozed in Scarlet's arms while Scarlet's head dipped, then bobbed back up each time I mumbled another theory aloud.

Colorful sticky notes covered the polished oak, and I'd shoved the table runner and candles aside to arrange the evidence in matching columns. I folded the Post-It notes with Johnson's name and information, as well as Vivian's in half. I never tossed theories, though I'd ruled them out as the murderer.

I sipped steaming orange tea from a porcelain cup. My hand lingered on the warm cup to keep the chill of the castle at bay.

Heath's name sat at the top of a column with a row of multicolored Post Its beneath it.

- *Motivation: To hide something. Bonus–to keep Schwanna here.*
- *Alibi: None. I accounted for everyone else inside these walls.*
- *Behavior: Pardons us but refuses to let Schwanna go. Inconsistent. Is it to keep the suspicion on her and off of him?*
- *Access to the murder weapon: Blades are abundant in the castle from kitchen knives to gardening tools*

Another sip of team warmed my throat and chest. Wendy's soft snores sparked a smile on my face. It felt good to know she was here with me instead of in the city where a monster ran rampant. I worried for Kai, but he knew to watch out for Frankenstein's creation. Marriage to an investigative journalist came in handy.

The only two columns not folded over contained my father's name and my grandmother's, which I'd learned was Delores. Despite the fact that she was with us at the time of Tricia's death, I didn't like how nonchalantly she'd reacted. The thought of coming from a family of murderers only dragged me back to the horrible memory of slicing Jameson's stomach open. I'd saved my life, but it didn't mean I enjoyed taking someone else's life. Of course, he *was* a serial killing wolf.

The sticky back of a purple Post It clung to my finger. I folded Delores's notes over, closing her as a suspect. Her reaction to the murder unsettled me but it wasn't enough to consider her a suspect. I rubbed my eyes and sat back in the chair. My back screamed at me for hunching over the table, and my brain sloshed with a blur of evidence.

Next on the to-do list, I needed to speak with Johnson, go through Tricia's belongings if her family would let me, and question my father.

The blue sticky note with his name fluttered from Scarlet's breath.

She blew a curl from her face and straightened in the chair, careful not to move Wendy's curled position. My daughter snuggled into Scarlet's stomach with her knees tucked into her chest and head down like a cat.

I didn't bother to hide my investigation. If my father came in and saw his name on a note, he'd know I meant business. Thanks to the hood, he couldn't hurt me, and I wasn't worried about Wendy. Scarlet was terrible at knowing when to stop giving a toddler sugar, but after hunting villains for centuries, I knew she'd kick anyone's butt that threatened her or Wendy.

"Bedtime?" Scarlet mumbled. Hair caught in her thick eyelashes and created a curtain effect on the sides of her face. She blinked, and it seemed she'd closed the curtains for a good night's sleep as the hair tugged further over her face.

"Bedtime." I agreed, nodding. I carefully peeled each sticky note from the wood and arranged them inside my notebook. The screen on my watch read a quarter past three in the morning and the service bars still showed empty. Without Wi-Fi for my watch or a working phone, I couldn't make a call and say goodnight to Kai for the second night in a row. Had he called today or last night and worried? I wouldn't receive any messages on the watch until we reached Wi-Fi again, either. He knew I could lose myself in an investigation, but we also kept tabs on one another for safety purposes. My husband likely notified the police station about my missing status by now, especially knowing what kind of case I'd left to investigate.

I climbed the stairs, dragging my heavy limbs behind Scarlet. We sank into separate beds, with Wendy sharing mine. With my body curled on the edge, my toddler enjoyed the space and splayed her body out as far as her arms and legs could reach. The soft mattress pulled me into a sleep that my mind wanted to fight.

I need to solve this and get Mom out.

Not to mention I'd need to return to the office with information on the missing persons case. As much as I tried to connect my investigations on the island with the two men who vanished near Pier 99, I couldn't find a thread. Even the murders didn't match up.

Dreamless sleep left me rested and ready to tackle my father. And I meant that only metaphorically if he cooperated with my questioning.

The next morning involved a battle that ended in a score of bruises. Wendy flailed and kicked at the mention of a bath. Before she even hit the warm, soapy water, she threw herself into a tantrum. No amount of complaints would convince me not to wash the exploded diaper residue off her back and legs. Plus, I overpacked, but two days left me low on supplies and if I didn't bust my mom out of the dungeon before tomorrow, I'd have a serious diaper shortage.

More water ended up soaking me and the floor than cleaning Wendy. I pulled her from the tub and found a clean cloth by the sink to dry her with. Battle over. Score: Wendy, 1. Me, 0. Soaked and shivering without a change of clothes, I carried my daughter down the stairs and into the kitchen. We skipped the jelly biscuits and opted for bananas and bread.

After breakfast, I found my father in the ballroom, instructing Vivian how to arrange the tables. It was my understanding that the kingdom would enjoy a feast after Heath's coronation while I'd be enjoying my ferry ride home with my friend, my daughter, and my mother by my side.

When Heath agreed to have a little chat with me, he insisted we sit in the throne room. It wasn't until we arrived I realized he wanted the upper ground. Literally. Heath settled into the throne but stood at my insistence that he share the bench with me. Eye-level and proximity helped my interviews. The psychology of him placing himself physically higher than me could aid his boldness in lies.

To my surprise, my father cooperated quickly. He smiled, looking delighted that I'd invited him to come and sit beside us.

I bounced Wendy in my lap while she tapped on the screen of my watch. A whining. We sat on the bench in the front row of the throne room and faced my father. With my notebook folded open so I could hold it in one hand, I dove into the first question.

"Where were you when Tricia died?"

Heath crossed one leg over the other and met my gaze. "Can we talk like family? I'd love to invite you to stay and run the kingdom with your mother and me."

Barf. My mother would run if she heard him talking like that. At least until her trade with him ended. Schwanna was a woman who kept her promises, but she'd hate every second of her lack of freedom.

Still, emotion fluttered in my chest when he called us family. How many times had I dreamed of this moment as a child? I'd thought his constant communication with my mother meant he loved us. When I matured, I learned that possessiveness didn't equal love. But knowledge didn't erase my desire for a friendly father.

"Tricia?" I prodded.

Heath nodded, dropping his eyes to his lap. "In my bed chambers. I'm not the speaker my father was." He sighed. "He could command a crowd while I must spend a great deal of time practicing my speech for the coronation. How I wish you'd had the chance to meet the man. You remind me of him, verbally tough and focused, but gentle with people."

Ha! Proof he didn't know me. I'd gutted a serial killer to save mine and my daughter's life and I'd do it again for my mother's freedom. My heart fluttered, but not from emotion. The thought shocked me, coming from the recesses of my mind. I'd avoided the memory of killing my stalker, disappointed that I didn't follow my normal procedure to use strategy over suspects rather than brute force. Plus, it didn't feel *true* when I reported on Jameson's death, which went against everything I believed as a journalist.

Maybe I had what it takes to be The Keeper after all.

"Mari, sit with me at dinner tonight, will you?" Heath asked. The invitation shook me from thoughts of fairy tales and dropped me back into the investigation. "The entire kingdom will be inside the castle for my coronation, and I'd be proud to introduce them to my daughter. What is your favorite food? I'll have the cooks match it."

I didn't give him the satisfaction. Coronation or not, he wouldn't get out of my interview. Plus, he wouldn't have my favorite food because this wasn't a Cheesecake Factory.

"Can anyone corroborate your location at the time of Tricia's death?" I asked.

"I'm getting the feeling that you suspect me," he said, with brows furrowed. My father spoke smoothly, and I wondered if I'd inherited that skill from him. The regular interview tactics didn't work on him as well as I'd hoped.

"You know Schwanna didn't kill anyone," I said. "What would her motive be?"

Heath opened his mouth with a shake of his head, searching for something to say. I didn't let him answer.

"Who do you believe murdered Tricia?" I asked.

A sigh blew from his nose, and he nodded slowly. "I haven't wanted to think about it," he admitted. His eyes softened, though the lack of wrinkles still struck me as odd for his age. "I hope to carry my father's legacy as I enter the role of king, but I've already lost so much respect by allowing one of our own to get hurt. How could this have happened as soon as I'm about to be crowned?" Pain flashed in his eye. The faint glow of multicolors rippled around him.

After countless interviews with liars, killers, and plenty of those telling the truth–I knew the signs. Dear Ol' Dad here had some guilt, but his pain was honest. The slight bounce of his leg told me everything I needed to know.

My father was hiding something. But it wasn't Tricia's murder.

Mentally, I folded the sticky note with his name on it. Physically, I slumped.

Wendy shook the sock puppet Scarlet crafted for her. Scarlet's intentions were in the right place, but now I walked around with one sweaty foot in my low-cut boots.

"Thank you," I said. I stood and offered Heath a forced smile before guiding Wendy to the door with her hand in mine. She'd picked up the pace and learned to walk quicker with the help of someone else, but refused to keep going if I let go.

"Mari." Heath stood and turned to me. "How about that dinner?"

I stooped to pick up Wendy, eager to hurry and find Johnson. What did he have to hide about the Fables if not a murder plot? And what did Tricia know that ended up with her dead on the castle's steps?

"I have a lot of research left," I said. The door between the throne room and the spacious hall past the entry creaked when I pushed it open. Wendy babbled, making her sock puppet say something I couldn't understand.

"Wait," Heath said.

I paused and spun to meet his gaze again. *A confession?*

But my father's eyes looked hopeful rather than humble. "Will you speak with Schwanna–" his throat rippled with a thick swallow. "Will you tell your mother I trust she meant no harm and that I look forward to when we can start our lives together?"

I blinked and left him alone in the room. The door swung shut behind me. He knew Mom didn't want this marriage or a life with him. He wasn't a man who gave up easily. Maybe I took after him in that way. Because I didn't plan to tell my mother anything of the sort.

Of course, she meant no harm because she did *no harm.*

The thought nagged me. Everyone had an alibi except Mom. As much as I hated to admit it, Heath wore his emotions on his face and he worried for his people, including Tricia. My mom, in her quest for freedom and privacy, nobody could corroborate her location at the time of the victim's death, which meant nobody would believe me when I'd tell them she was innocent.

I marched from the throne room to get an early lunch and plan the day. After I'd wasted the morning in search of Johnson, I longed for my schedule. Cygnus Island had thrown me from the comfort of planning and knowing my next move each day. I clung harder to Wendy's development. Everything I did here felt like the wrong choice. Even one look at the library had earned me hard eyes from the guard posted outside. A schedule would fix all that, right?

Wendy napped with Scarlet in our room after a late lunch. I had to put a cap on the number of jelly biscuits I'd allow my toddler to get a sugar high on. She'd stuffed two into her mouth before I could take them from her reach. Though I believe it was the following tantrum that caused her to crash into a longer nap than usual than the treats themselves.

My boots squeaked against the newly polished floors. I marched for the front door, past a man scrubbing the ground until it shined so clearly my reflection stared back at me.

The outdoor air did me good. My brain needed to clear and find a new way to attack this case, and I needed to do it fast. With my father's coronation tonight, I was running out of time. Once he became king, he'd pardon Mom, and she'd feel obligated to stay by his side.

The wind tossed my hair around until I was sure a bird would land on my head, mistaking my tangles for its nest. I brushed strands from my face and looked at my surroundings. The way of life here wasn't bad. In fact, I envied their slow pace and strict schedules. Everyone had a job and everyone belonged.

A man smiled at me as I walked beyond the castle. He'd paused his touch-up painting to the mural on the front of the building to acknowledge me, but returned to his task with focus and careful strokes.

This community would never suit my free-flying mother. I knew it took everything she had to come here and demand a divorce. She was always a woman of her word, a mother–for all her flaws–who inspired me to respect the truth in every situation. I'd never lie and since others didn't live by the same code, I learned how to tell the difference between deceit and truth.

I sucked in a breath of the salty scent mixed with fresh soil as I passed the massive garden behind the castle. Several people hoed the dirt while two others knelt on the ground and yanked at weeds between the strawberry patches. I kept walking until I ended up in the graveyard.

A bronzed plaque replaced the pyre where Tricia's body had burned. The simple plaque had been engraved with her name and the dates during which she lived.

I took a seat on the ground, ignoring the dampness of the grass that seeped into my pants. My investigation accounted for every single person on this island, and none of them could have murdered Tricia. Detective Wilhelm would wrap this up as a suicide–not because he was lazy, but because another violent crime in the city would have forced him to move on. *A case without suspects is a case that goes cold.*

I sighed and dropped my head into my hands. Who was I missing? The word itself triggered my memory of the case I'd told my boss I'd dig into. I flipped my notebook open to the list of suspects that included Heath, Delores, the late King Fable, and Frankenstein's monster.

"Ebenezer Scrooge," I cursed. I'd been asking the wrong questions. With everyone accounted for at the time of Tricia's death, could the suspect not be a person at all?

The pages bent and crinkled as I turned to the front of the notebook where I'd kept information on the monster. I'd listed that he strangled his victims, killed men, removed body parts, and seemed to murder at night. Tricia wasn't strangled, but the killer went for her throat just as the monster went for mine.

Was I stretching it? Did I invent a connection where one didn't exist so that I'd have something to bring back to my boss?

No. My heart thumped as my thoughts raced and tangled and tried to make sense of the sudden realization. I'd been doing the opposite of Detective Wilhelm's accusation. I *didn't* want to see a thread because that meant the monster had murdered again and I'd made a huge mistake by ignoring his story.

The thought of Frankenstein triggered a memory of the book. I'd forgotten about the piece of paper I'd found inside Mary Shelley's novel.

I shoved my hand into my pocket where I'd stuffed the scrap of paper. After smoothing it out, I could see the chicken scratch handwriting. Once the paper was flat enough, the marks looked like words. Instructions were listed on the page, but most of the words looked ineligible, as if written in a hurry or maybe by a doctor. I snorted at that last thought knowing how impossible my allergy prescriptions looked after my Ear, Nose, and Throat doc scribbled on them.

I squinted to make out the last phrase.

"Head transplant?" I breathed.

Did someone on Cygnus Island toy with the instructions from the scrap of paper? Did the monster undergo a head transplant? The thought sounded insane considering how little technology this community used. Doctors with the most complex equipment couldn't even accomplish such a feat. But with story protection. . .

I flipped through the pages to find my old notes about Travis Young and the mechanic's disappearance. Along the edges of the paper, I'd scribbled Detective Wilhelm's theories, but I'd underlined that I suspected both men vanished under the same causes.

If only my phone hadn't shattered, I'd access the picture I'd snapped of Henry's sketched portrait and see if it matched the face of the monster.

Kai would tell me to forget everything else that nagged at my brain and look at the case. And only the case. I needed that reminder since becoming a mother. Thoughts of Wendy's pinching at daycare, work deadlines, and my underwear showing through yoga pants, all distracted me from that focus I'd once had. Kai had unraveled a roll of toilet paper, plopped the cardboard tube down on the Coffee Table of Evidence, and insisted I look at my notes through it. The tube made it so that I couldn't see the mess around the house, Wendy crawling instead of walking, or my phone lighting up with another scheduled reminder.

I didn't have a toilet paper tube. Instead, I closed my eyes and called back to the file in my brain where I kept case information. My mind's eye retraced the drawing of Henry. It was vague, like in a dream —or a nightmare if my suspicions were correct.

My eyes shot open.

"That's why I recognized him," I said, confirming my theory aloud. I scrambled to my feet and gathered my notebook under my arm. *And that's why the murders don't match up.* Doctor Frankenstein or someone else must have killed Henry and Travis Young to create the monster. My gaze dropped to Tricia's plaque. "I know who killed you. Or, *what* killed you." The wind swept my voice away, but it couldn't take my excitement.

My heart raced as I ran up the hill toward the castle. The back of my sneaker rubbed my sockless heel raw, but I didn't slow down.

By the time I made it inside the castle and reached the top of the staircase, I gasped for breath. I definitely needed to get into better shape for when Wendy learned to run. Scarlet greeted me with a lazy hello until she saw the look on my face.

"What is it, Rudolph?" she asked, teasing.

I glanced in the mirror over the room's single sink and spotted my red-streaked cheeks and nose. The wind had done a number on my skin. Wendy stirred, blinking sleepy eyes up at the ceiling.

"Did the other reindeer leave you out of their games?" Scarlet laughed.

"You know what? You're inconsistent. How is it you don't know the word 'coincidence' but you're all over the Christmas classics?"

She raised both eyebrows at the last word. As it came from my mouth, I shook my head.

"No, Rudolph too?" I asked.

"No," she said, trying to stop laughing. "Have you lost your mind? I watched the fake movie—"

"Cartoon."

"I watched the cartoon with Wendy when I watched her last Christmas," she explained. "I forget words or shifts at work." Her face crinkled into a look of cringe until she brightened again. "But I never forget a story."

"Good," I said, taking a seat on the edge of the bed. Wendy crawled out of the blankets and into my lap as I reached for her. "Tell me everything you know about Frankenstein."

"The doctor or the monster?" Scarlet said. She stood and checked her hair in the mirror.

"The story, the plot, everything. I need to know why the monster killed Tricia."

The delicious scent of fresh bread drifted from downstairs. Spurts of noise came from the kitchen as people walked in and out. The castle had filled with people who busied themselves with cooking, cleaning, and preparing for their king's coronation. It served as an unwelcome reminder that I had one afternoon left to solve this murder and free my mother before she felt obligated to stand by Heath's side and stay on Cygnus Island and in her marriage.

Scarlet tucked her curls into her shirt so they wouldn't fall into her face as she spoke, then turned to face me and lean against the sink.

"I told you he'd kill people," she said. As much as I didn't appreciate the *I told you so* moment, I didn't have time to dwell on my mistake.

"All this time I thought the monster killed Henry and Travis Young and I didn't consider him in Tricia's death because the murder patterns don't match," I explained, scooting to the edge of the bed in my excitement. Scarlet's eyebrows lifted higher than I'd thought possible, but she listened with careful attention. "But the monster didn't kill the men, the men were killed to create the monster. And the patterns don't match because the monster murdered Tricia."

"Ah, a foregone conclusion," Scarlet said with a nod.

"A what?" I asked as I smoothed the tangles in Wendy's hair down. Naps always left her with a nest of bedhead in the back.

"It's a phrase from Shakespeare's Othello," she said, turning back to the mirror and meeting my gaze through the reflection. "It means that a result was expected."

Wendy tugged at the hood's strings that dangled over my collarbone. I didn't bother worrying if she'd untie them, since I'd knotted it tight enough to deter me from wanting to throw it off easily. But it tickled, so I sank to the floor and lifted Wendy to stand. I scooted away from her and beckoned her to walk toward me.

"Anyway," I said, moving on from Scarlet's second reminder that I'd made a mistake. She was right. I should have expected the monster would kill. But all I could do was move forward from here. "Henry's face is on the monster. Their copy of *Frankenstein* had this scrap inside it." Wendy grabbed for my arm, almost knocking the paper pinched between my fingers as I held it out to Scarlet. She turned and took it. "I knew I'd seen him before, but I didn't know where and this note mentions a head transplant. Since I know the story is real, I can connect the two."

The tilt of Scarlet's head and slight pinch between her brows told me she didn't buy it. "According to the novel, the monster kills because he's lonely. He's jealous of those with a family because Doctor Frankenstein refused to build him a mate. I think you're wrong."

"What?" My mouth dropped along with Wendy as she plopped on her butt. She gave up trying to take an unsteady step and crawled across the floor to stand with the help of the bed frame.

Scarlet twisted a curl around her finger and let her gaze fall to Wendy. I shifted from watching my daughter to Scarlet's face. Wendy tried to take her first step after releasing her grip on the bed, but promptly dropped to her knees and reached for the diaper bag on the floor. The wipes bag crinkled as she snapped it open and pulled the sheets out one at a time.

White wipes floated to the floor like giant, moist pieces of confetti.

"But modern society disturbs the stories, so maybe I'm wrong too," she said with a sigh that told me she missed the hood and the life that came with it. "I just think there's something you're missing."

I pulled my notebook off the bed and turned the pages, careful to acknowledge each piece of information and evidence I'd gathered. I refused to be like Detective Wilhelm and rush to a conclusion just to make myself feel better. And Scarlet had been right before, so I needed to listen to her consideration.

At the top of the next page, I'd scribbled the words the monster had first said to me.

You will not stop her, Keeper. Her?

"Maybe the monster is working with someone else," I said.

Scarlet stopped twisting her curls and tucked her hair behind her ears. When she met my gaze, she tilted her head. "Like partners?"

My eyes dropped to the floor where white wipes looked like snow-fall around Wendy. I frowned, but not at the mess.

"Like a hitman."

Chapter 14

Cry Havoc

A scream stopped our conversation short. Theories would have to wait. The piercing wail came from the entry. Scarlet and I burst from the bedroom to find the source of the panic. I scrambled down the stairs and nearly collided with Vivian.

The thick wrap of her braid smacked me in the face as she spun to grab hold of me.

"He, he—" Vivian's hand shot to her throat. A thick red line wrapped around the flesh of her neck. Tears poured from her glistening eyes and she sputtered and gasped for breath between sobs.

"He tried to kill me!" Vivian finally spit the words out.

I glanced at Scarlet who'd retrieved Wdny from the top of the stairs. My daughter had crawled out of the room to follow us. Scar held Wendy on her hip and we exchanged knowing looks before I turned back to Vivian.

I held her arms and kept her upright as her weight sunk into me. The stink of body odor masked the honeyed scent from her hair. The short sleeve of her simple dress revealed a red mark, matching the placement of Tricia's bruise. My quick evaluation confirmed Frankenstein's creation had attacked Vivian. Who had sent the Henry-headed monster to attack this woman, and why?

"Come sit," I said. I guided Vivian to the staircase, where I gently eased her to the step and sat beside her.

Footsteps closed in on us. Heath marched from the ballroom, the door swinging shut behind him. "What is the meaning of this?"

A look of concern twisted his ageless features. The excitement drew him toward the stairs. The queen followed in her son's wake with the thump of her cane echoing in the open space beneath the cells-turned-bedrooms.

"I found a note from Tricia," Vivian said. "She'd written it on the back of a ribbon and I found it when I went to decorate the ballroom for your coronation."

I didn't mean to be harsh or careless of Vivian's trauma, but I snatched the ribbon from her trembling hands before Heath could stoop to reach it.

Fable is killing us.

Years of a practiced poker face had me pinching my lips and resisting the rise of my hand to my mouth. I didn't gasp or widen my eyes. My heart skipped beats despite my outward calm. The note insisted I face the truth—my father was a murderer. How could I prove it in a domain where he claimed all control?

The word echoed in my head, reminding me what he'd said. He'd lost control, and he wasn't even the king yet. And he didn't even have complete control, not yet. But another Fable did.

Plus, the monster referred to 'her,' not 'him'.

My eyes flickered to the queen. Delores stood with a heavy lean on her cane. The chandelier sent spikey shadows in every direction beneath her like thorns had grown from her trunk and snaked in cracks across the polished floor. Thick white hair looped in a firm bun behind her head the threads knitted together in my brain. Queen Fable commanded the room with the look of a stern librarian, and I finally understood Johnson. He'd wanted to lead me to information about her, not my father.

The giddy sensation of solving another murder crept into my chest and limbs. The adrenaline made me want to get up and run. If I didn't respect rules and laws and know that following them led to better, long-term results, in the end, I'd run to solitary confinement and use the new self-defense moves I'd learned from YouTube against the guard to bust Mom out. Instead, I forced myself to stay still. The memory of the monster's words confirmed it.

You will not stop her. Her. Delores.

Heath reached for the paper, but Vivian's cough and sob startled him. My father's face pinched, and he knelt in front of his decorator. Once he took her hands in his, she calmed and met his gaze. The moment felt too intimate like I needed to take my scrap of treason and leave them alone. I folded the paper and slipped it into my pocket.

"He was an enormous man. When he came up behind me, he grabbed my throat," Vivian said without gulping breaths in between her words. She'd straightened and spoke smoother. "And he smelled horrible."

Yep, definitely Frankenstein's friend.

Did that make Delores Doctor Frankenstein himself? If only I knew the book better.

"We will do everything we can to track him down and make this right," Heath said. When he let go, I didn't miss Vivian's lingering hold. She squeezed his hands before he pulled away.

"Did you see if he had a weapon?" I asked. After a moment, Vivian broke her gaze on my father and blinked at me.

"His hands," she said once the question seemed to register. "But he dropped something. I saw something shiny, like a knife on the ground when I ran."

"May I ask how you escaped?"

"This is enough," Delores said. The thump of her cane drew near, but I didn't give her the satisfaction. I held Vivian's attention and refused to stop my mini-interview with another suspect in the case to prove my mother's innocence.

"I—" Vivian glanced at the queen.

"Go on." My father nodded, encouraging Vivian.

"Heath," Delores snapped. "I said that is enough."

For all the bad that my father had done, I didn't dislike him at that moment. He brushed off the queen's demand and remained focused on the victim. It didn't excuse his possessiveness or desperate need to control my mother, but it did aid in my investigation.

"Anything to help us find who did this," he said.

"You don't know what you're doing," Delores said between her teeth.

It took everything I had not to stand and interject. I wanted to throw my mother's name into the conversation with a few demands. *Get her the hell out, or else*. But the evidence from Vivian's experience was too much to risk.

"Shane whacked him," Vivian said. Her huge eyes shifted between the three of us. I was glad I hadn't stood and towered over her with them. She didn't need the motivation of intimidation to share what she knew.

"We're done with this." The queen spat. When Vivian flinched, I scooted closer to her, hoping she'd feel safe enough to keep going. "Johnson!" Delores shouted. "Where is he? Find him for me, Heath. Now."

Vivian's delicate hands looked like leaves rattling from a gust of wind. The queen's sharp tone and the message on Tricia's note likely scared the decorator in a way I didn't understand. The remote community operated under its own laws despite the modern city around it. Though I'd called for backup, nobody came and I finally understood that we were alone here. Vivian's fate was tied to this *kingdom*, and she knew it.

"I will not," Heath said. "Since I'm to be king tonight, I must learn to deal with this. I'll not have a murderer running rampant under my rule."

"You don't know what you're saying," she spoke between gritted teeth as if they'd block her words from reaching us. The Fables engaged in a stare-down, and the thin balance of power seemed to snap. Delores was slipping, and though Heath wasn't exactly the most upstanding guy, I was grateful for their temporary distraction.

"Who is Shane?" I asked, trying to keep my voice low and directed only at Vivian.

"He's a gardener," she said. "I went to Tricia's grave to gather courage after I'd found the ribbon. The man who attacked me must have followed me there."

"And Shane hit him?" I confirmed.

Vivian nodded and wiped snot from her nose. "With the weeder." She made a hacking motion with her hands. "The weed whacker. Into his head."

Oh, like whacked-whacked. Shane is kick-butt. Got it.

"I ran," she said.

I nodded and thanked her for her bravery. All too well, I knew the place of the victim. Though my stalker stood behind me now, a friend and partner, I still recalled the fear that nearly paralyzed me when I'd watched her write my name in blood. And Jameson was gone. He couldn't hurt me or hunt me anymore.

I stood, my back straight and chin up. "Release my mother."

Heath and Delores broke their argument to glare at me. Four nearly identical eyes bore through me until my father's face softened. But it wasn't him I intended to break. After a few minutes with the queen, I hoped I'd draw a confession from her.

"You know Schwanna isn't the murderer now," I said, fixing my eyes on my father. "Let her go."

"Heath." Delores's hand shot out and grabbed his arm as he moved to head to the dungeon.

He pulled away. "Schwanna is still my wife. She won't leave. Not after she's come here and felt it again."

Felt it? A soft groan came from the steps. Vivian turned her head away when I glanced at her. My eyes trailed to the middle of the stair-case where Scarlet held Wendy's hand. What would make my father say such a thing? My mom had left many times before. All she did was leave him. Like a case file reopening, my brain accessed what she'd said.

It feels like I'm close to whatever is missing.

What did my father have that she wanted?

Scarlet's lips twitched, and I knew we shared the same thought. It was time I dug into my mom's fairy tale.

"We don't know that Schwanna isn't working with the monster!"

Delores's jaw shifted back and forth. Her flighty eyes bounced between us and nerves painted her face with every twitch and blink.

There it is. She called him the monster. Delores knew about *Frankenstein.*

My father shook his head and marched from us, his footsteps stomping across the polished floor. He headed for the door at the far end, where the hall led to my trapped mother.

This is my in.

"Prince Fable," I said, addressing his title to appease his ego. "Wait." White breath escaped my mouth.

It worked. Heath paused and turned back to us, his body tense but patient.

"I have concluded my investigation." I resisted the urge to smile. Everything I needed wrapped up so perfectly. It's like the queen handed me the answer with a bow tied on top. Cases never end this easily unless they're on TV. I channeled my inner Richard Castle and Kate Beckett, wishing Kai was here to relish in the perfect case conclusion with me. We could riff off of one another—if we were as witty as the characters in the hit crime drama *Castle*, that is.

"Scarlet." I nodded toward the stairs. "Will you grab my notebook, please?"

Scarlet arched an eyebrow but scooped to lift Wendy then disappeared into the bedroom. She returned with my favorite sight—my daughter smiling. Oh, and the notebook with the page ripped from Mary Shelley's novel with the list of instructions in the margins. It was a risk. I didn't know if the handwriting would match the queen's, but I had far more against her than Heath could pin on my mother. And I was running out of time. We needed to get Mom and get off this island before Heath could guilt her into staying.

"Why are you listening to her?" Delores said, her voice cracked and squeaked with desperation. Heath afforded her a mere glance. He *had* said he wanted my mother proven innocent, after all. Maybe I had more on my side than I'd thought.

I flipped the notebook open and produced the page from *Frankenstein.* "This is going to sound a little crazy," I said, but Heath gasped.

I expected incredulous looks. I expected to simplify the truth with an explanation that didn't involve the actual monster himself, but some kind of manipulation from the queen using motivation from Mary Shelley's novel. It would wrap up in a straightforward case with Delores sounding insane. And my sexist father would no doubt buy right into it the fact that the queen needed a monstrous man to do her bidding. What he didn't know was that it would have worked if I wasn't here to stop her.

While my finding produced a look of shock on my father's face, it didn't mix with disbelief.

"Vivian never called her attacker a monster," I said. "But Delores knew about him because she's controlling him. I'm willing to bet this is her handwriting." When I lifted my gaze from the page, I saw my scraps of evidence didn't interest Heath. I'd pointed to the list of instructions in the margins. The scribbled notes about head transplants and whatever else they'd used to take the missing mechanic's body parts and create a new being covered the edges of the page.

"Mother. . ." His voice trailed. "You didn't."

The breath between his words reminded me of an overacted soap opera. The heat against my back alerted me that the resident TV fan herself had stepped up behind me. Scarlet leaned toward my ear so only I could hear her words.

"What do you see?" she whispered. "Are they both part of the same story?"

I gently shushed my partner, ignoring the aura rippling around the Fables. My moment of achievement over the case vanished. The investigation would continue if I tied this to a fairy tale or classic novel. But if I didn't, it could end right here and right now with the suspect in custody.

Delores stopped her son with her cane. The stick pressed into the soft spot between his ribcage and stomach. Heath's pinched brow deepened and faint wrinkles became clear in his anger.

"Father didn't want this," he said.

I wouldn't let my evidence slip away into their family drama. I held up the page, stabbing my finger to the list, and matched it with Tricia's note in my other hand. Instead of pacing around the suspect while eyeing her up and down as an investigator might on a TV show, I stood my ground, half because I'm not an actress and half because Wendy had latched onto my leg.

"I suspect Tricia's note is referring to Queen Fable," I said. "You said so yourself, Heath. Your mother wanted the control longer, and she silenced anyone who didn't like it. The death prolonged her reign and put off your coronation."

"Preposterous!" Delores said with a huff.

"Mari, please," Heath said. He held his hand out as if to quiet me. Normally, I'd speak louder, insisting the evidence I presented be heard. But my father's plea wasn't unkind. Desperation tugged at his features, pulling his lips down into a disgusted grimace.

"Are you going to listen to someone you hardly know?" Delores said. The slight shake in her voice revealed her fear. She didn't afford me the respect of a glance.

"I know my father's handwriting when I see it," he said. "He regretted what he did, you know that."

Delores scoffed and pressed harder into Heath's chest. The cane wrinkled his white shirt and looked uncomfortably deep into his belly.

"Victor was just afraid to die," she said.

A soft nudge dug into my back. It startled a slight gasp from me. I quickly quieted and shot a look at my partner.

"Victor," Scarlet said, her voice seething with meaning.

I yanked the page back and stared at the scribbles. The name appeared several times throughout the text on the scrap of Mary Shelley's novel. Understanding dawned. *Soap opera confirmed. My grandfather is Doctor Frankenstein. What next?* I expected Vivian to faint or a talk show host to appear and tell us we'd been led here to fight over our family drama in front of a live studio audience.

"Father was sick and scared of what that meant for him," Heath said. "But he never condoned hurting others for the sake of surviving." With a sweep of his hand, he knocked the cane away. The wooden stick clattered against the polished floor and rolled away from us. Delores nearly toppled over.

Relentless, the queen straightened and cackled. The sound of it dissipated my talk show image. Instead, I swore I'd stepped right into a Magical Place movie where the evil villain had warts on her nose and a rotting snaggletooth.

White breath laced the air in front of Delores. "You cannot stand on this moral high ground when you had to steal to get a—"

"Stop!" Heath interrupted. His chest rose and fell with heaving breaths.

The volume of his voice didn't deter his mother. The queen merely raised her white eyebrows. I took the pause as my opportunity to seal the case. With a question or two, I intended to trip Delores into a blatant confession. Wendy released her fistful of my pants and sat back on the floor, happy to pull her slippered shoes off.

"How did you know who to tell the monster to kill?" I asked. I met her sharp gaze with one of my own. *Two can play this game.*

"I—" She snapped her jaw shut and licked her lips.

"Did Tricia know you wanted to keep Heath from the throne?" I dug, taking a step toward her, but never wavering with my eyes.

"I don't care who sits on the throne," she said with a curt laugh.

"But you care you stay in control," I said. Another step.

"No."

"You wanted the monster to eliminate anyone who didn't agree with you. If Tricia announced you were sabotaging Heath's coronation, your reign would end." My voice quieted so Delores would know I was speaking to her and only her. With the distance closed between us, I caught the scent of fruity wine on her breath.

"I want Heath on the throne," she said, refusing to back down from me. She didn't so much as lean away from me. Without the hunch of her reaching for the cane, she stood as tall as me.

"You killed Tricia and you want to kill Vivian because she knows you'll do whatever it takes to stay queen," I said. My white breath blew into her face. Adrenaline coursed through me and, for a moment, her face looked hairy, with a long snout and black nose. I blinked and shook the memory of the wolf. *I think I can. I think I can.*

Can I? The surrounding colors left me light-headed and dizzy. I didn't want to talk about the monster as an actual monster. I'd gotten past the story part of this, right?

I forced the next question before my resolve withered. "That's why you had my mother thrown in the dungeon. Isn't it?"

"Mother?" Heath said from behind me. "She is my wife."

Delores's eye twitched. "Think of it as a gift, Son," she said. "I only ensured she'd stay."

"You admit you framed Schwanna Fable for the murder of Tricia and attempted murder of Vivian?" I asked, ready to close this case. For once, I wished Detective Wilhelm stood by my side since I didn't carry handcuffs or have the authority to arrest the suspect upon confession. At least we had a dungeon nearby.

The queen didn't answer. The sharp turn of her head broke our stare-down and guilt flushed her cheeks.

"How could you?" Heath breathed, his voice gruff.

"What does it matter?" Delores said. "Schwanna's bound to find it and leave." Spit flung from her mouth. "You'll be left with nothing because you're a coward, just like Victor was, and you'll die as he did. We were going to be immortal."

Immortal? My hand shot to the hood's strings that tugged and twisted around my fingers. I knew of only one way to live forever and it involved messing with classic stories and fairy tales, so they never ended as written. They couldn't know about the story cycle. . .

"I don't know," Heath said.

"So we lose a character here and there." She waved her hand and her overgrown nails cemented the image of the evil witch.

"Not just characters—people!" My father seethed. "I don't want to end up dying in regret like Father."

"You wouldn't die at all if you just let me do this for you," the queen spoke between her teeth. Heath's throat rippled with a swallow and he nodded, a faint and silent agreement with her.

My heart thumped, and my brain scrambled to catch up with the conversation.

Do they know they're characters? No, it wasn't possible. But the facts added up, the portal door, the library of glowing books, and how desperately they guarded those books. Why would it matter if someone saw copies of classics? Libraries all over the world shelved *Frankenstein*, Mythologies, but. . . *the new books.*

A crash jolted me from my thoughts. The theory I'd pieced together scattered in my mind like a toddler knocking a puzzle off the table. My muscles stiffened as the ground shook beneath us. The page from *Frankenstein* slipped from my fingers and floated to the floor, where a massive shadow loomed and blocked the light from the chandelier.

The face of the mechanic appeared with a twisted grimace, and he lunged at Vivian. My daughter sat on the floor beside those steps and I'd die before I let the beast from Mary Shelley's imagination hurt Wendy. In a flash of Mama Bear strength, I barreled for the monster and knocked him two steps back with my hands shoving against his torso.

Vivian screamed and scrambled up the steps while Scarlet swooped in and snatched a wailing Wendy. Chaos descended as the monster recovered from the shock and took two massive steps up the staircase. In one easy hit, he knocked the wind from me as his palm landed against my collarbone. I stumbled and smacked my tailbone against the floor. Still bruised from falling outside the library, the pain snaked up my spine and I released a yelp.

The monster gripped his meaty hand around Vivian's ankle and yanked her toward him with little effort. She flailed and kicked while shrieking in a pitch that should have shattered the chandelier.

Heath might have been stupid, but he wasn't a coward. He placed himself in front of the monster and took a swing. Within seconds, the monster recovered and lifted Vivian by her throat.

"Mother," Heath shouted. "Stop him."

Delores's face revealed no emotion. She watched the scene unfold without apparent fear or disappointment or even interest.

A sick gurgling sound came from Vivian's throat, and I reacted. After scrambling to my feet, I readied to kick the back of the monster's knees and buckle him just enough to release his hold. Heath took another swing at the monster, but the monster reacted with a swipe of his free arm. My father slammed against the railing on the staircase and went limp, a mass of limbs and clothes on the steps.

"Heath!" Delores cried. "That's enough." It seemed to be her favorite phrase. This time, it changed everything. I didn't listen when she'd said it and neither did my father. But the monster obeyed. He opened his fist and dropped Vivian the way Wendy does when she tosses peaches or handfuls of cut strawberries on the floor over the side of her highchair.

Vivian dropped with a crack of bone against the hard steps on the staircase. Before any of us could react, the monster took to the entry. He stormed out of the castle, leaving destruction and pain in his wake.

Nobody spoke or dared move for one horrible moment of silence. Even Wendy had stopped crying. I hurried to scoop her into my arms and hold her face against the base of my neck.

Quiet fell, but it was long from over. *Frankenstein* only hit its midpoint and a new story had just begun. One where my father and grandmother were the authors.

Chapter 15

Couldn't Sleep a Wink

With the case closed, Delores locked in the dungeon, and my mother walking free, I should have celebrated. I deserved a banana cheesecake and a night in with my husband. I wanted nothing more than the comfort of my couch, an unwatched Netflix queue, and our daughter snoring in my lap. Of course, we couldn't watch the spicier or more intense shows with the threat of our toddler waking and seeing the TV, but I'd given up fantasy shows with sexy monster hunters anyway. Nobody looked that good while killing beasts. Nobody.

I craned my neck to peer in the mirror on the bedroom wall over the sink and rub the exhaustion from my eyes. It didn't work. Dark circles still plagued me and I didn't have time for a moment of satisfaction after solving Tricia's murder.

The celebration would have to wait. In all the chaos before Heath had Delores dragged to the dungeon, she'd mentioned immortality, and it opened Pandora's box inside my brain. Not only did I have my mother's fairy tale to identify and a monster to deal with, but now I knew they knew what I didn't want to know.

Stupid story cycle.

The edge of the mattress sank under my mom's weight. She

perched on the corner with graceful air even after spending two days dirty and cold in solitary confinement. Scarlet sat criss cross applesauce on the floor. I stood and paced the room slowly enough for Wendy to hold my finger and follow along. Whenever I pulled my finger from her grip, she froze and refused to take a step on her own.

"You worry too much," Mom said.

"We should leave right now," I said.

"I can't," she said. She shook her head. "I feel more whole than I have in years, Mari."

I pinched the bridge of my nose. "This doesn't make sense."

"Stories," Scarlet mumbled out of the side of her mouth.

"You actually want to stay with Heath?" I asked in disbelief.

"Of course not," my mother said. "The man doesn't love me. He wants to own me."

"Exactly, so let's go. We have one day until his coronation, and you know he's going to force you to stand by his side."

"Stories," Scarlet said again, louder this time.

I shot her a look. When I crouched, I could have sworn Wendy shuffled her foot forward. But she only reached for me, then dropped to a crawl. I sighed and hung my head.

"I need to stay here until I figure out what I've been missing," Mom said.

"I'm not leaving without you," I said, determined to convince both her and Scarlet to pack up and skedaddle as soon as I'd changed Wendy's diaper. The back of my toddler's stretchy pants sagged from the weight of the wetness. I stood and swooped her onto the bed where I dumped the diaper bag and dug for a fresh size three.

"I'm grateful you solved the murder and cleared my name, Mari," Mom said. "But I've been searching for something for a long time and suddenly it feels so close."

I paused and studied my mom's features. She thought she'd find peace in her nose job and boob job and Botox or a bunch of wealthy gentlemen that wined and dined her. But she never seemed satisfied.

Half naked, Wendy tried to crawl away, reaching for the wipes and wasting them sheet by sheet. My attention snapped back to my feisty, diaperless daughter. I let her entertain herself with the mess long enough to wrestle a fresh diaper around her waist. The powdery smell masked Mom's scent of a two-day unwashed body.

"Stories." Scarlet coughed in a sound about as fake as people look in cartoons.

"Okay," I said. "I get it." I looked back at my mom and nodded toward the claw-footed tub near the sink. Since the room offered no privacy for a separate washroom, I offered to leave. "You can get washed up while we look into something."

"No, thank you." Mom shook her head. "But I'd rather like a nap on an actual bed."

"Are you sure you don't want to wash up?" I knew I didn't smell great in my same-day clothes either, but it wasn't like my mother to be anything less than pristine.

A strange heaviness came over her face. Her eyes dropped to her lap, and she scratched at her fingernail. "I'm recalling more from my younger years since I've been here."

I took a seat on the bed next to her, ready to listen. Scarlet's nagging could wait. I asked her to take Wendy for a 'nack' in the kitchen so Mom might feel comfortable enough to share her memories with me.

Wendy squealed at the familiar word and started babbling about Goldfish. Once Scarlet picked her up, they left in search of a cracker-like snack.

Mom feigned extreme interest in her fingernails while she allowed her vulnerable side to show. "I think I lost something while I was bathing a very long time ago."

"Like what?"

"I don't know, it's just a muddled memory," she said, touching her fingertips to her forehead. "I need to rest. It has been a very long couple of days."

I nodded and stood so she could lie back on the bed. When I descended the staircase, I turned and pushed through the kitchen door.

The room was empty of food and the ice chest had been moved into the ballroom, where tables were set for dining. Cooks left a mess in

their hurry to prepare the food for the celebration after Heath's coronation. Knives and dirty wooden cutting boards covered the counter. The
table had been stripped of the running cloth and half the candles were
taken.

The notebook fell open as I dropped it on the table in front of Scarlet. Wendy stood with her palms slapping the seat of a tall oak chair at
the end of the table. Fleshy blobs covered the seat of the chair and the
thin blueberry peels dotted the surrounding floor.

"I told you she won't eat anything juicy," I said, plopping into the
chair. With the world's worst manners, I propped my elbows on the
table and dropped my chin into my upturned palms.

Scarlet reviewed the list I'd scribbled between the walk from the
bedroom and the kitchen. It was hit or miss whether she'd decipher my
hurried handwriting.

- *Evidence the Fables know about the story cycle:*
- *The portal door.*
- *Delores's mention of immortality.*
- *They know who created Frankenstein's monster.*

A low humming sound came from my partner's throat. Red curls
bounced about her face as she nodded. Finally, her lashes ticked
upward, and she narrowed her eyes at me.

"Have you lost your mind?" Scarlet asked. And here I thought it
would be more pleasant working with her than Detective Wilhelm. So
much for that.

I popped a blueberry into my mouth and smiled at Wendy. She
mimicked me but instantly spit it back out. The ball of fruit fell on the
chair and rolled across the seat. Before it could slip over the edge,
Wendy's hand came down on it with a splat.

And so much for *that*, too.

"How would they know about the story cycle?" she asked. "I've
lived for hundreds of years and never met another person who believed
it."

"You're also not an investigator," I said between munches. I'd miss the flavor of fruit right from the garden when we left Cygnus Island. And only the fruit. Though maybe my father wasn't so bad. *At least he locked his mother away.* The question was–would he keep her there?

"Right." Scarlet flicked her fair back from her face. "I'm just the babysitter."

"No, we're friends and—" Before the words could slip out, I bit my lip. I didn't want to call Scarlet my partner out loud. If I acknowledged it, she'd take it as an opportunity to push me over the edge and into the story world. Unfortunately for her, I'd never abandon my life in the real world and live for the hunt of villains. If motherhood had taught me anything, I could do both. *Right?* Right.

"You're not completely wrong," she said, tracing her finger down the list. She stopped in the middle and stabbed Delores's name. "If she mentioned immortality, that means she's trying to repeat the story loop."

"Which only happens when the story doesn't end," I said. The way it all worked reminded me of a math equation. And I hated math. "Cruel queen plus knowledge of the cycle equals killing main characters in stories so that they don't end correctly and she gets to live forever."

"That would make sense why the story aura still showed on Tricia after she was dead."

"How do you figure?" I stuffed several more blueberries from the basket into my mouth. I felt like a squirrel stocking up for a long winter, or tomorrow's long day full of investigating, a coronation, and figuring out what in the wonderland my mom wanted here before we left the island.

"That means her purpose in the story was to die," Scarlet said with a thoughtful look. "If she died by the wrong means, it could throw the other characters from the same story back into the loop." Her clear eyes trailed to the candles in the middle of the table and she pursed her lips.

"Like a red shirt?" I asked.

"It's a red hood and you cannot die. Remember?" She nodded toward the strings hanging over my collarbone.

"Never mind," I said. Of course, the show I referenced wasn't one of the many she'd watched in her quest to understand modern society. Though, the original Star Trek probably wouldn't teach a lot about life in California in the twenty-first century.

Scarlet flipped the notebook shut and slid it across the table, bumping it into my elbows. "I think you're trying to find a new case to distract you from the real fairy tale that your mother is wrapped up in."

"Psh, no," I said.

"I'm proud of you for considering the story cycle at all," she said. "But you need to close Frankenstein and your mother's plot."

"I'm not a killer," I muttered.

"The monster is."

Wendy reached for the basket and yanked it off the table. Blueberries flew around the room as she flung the basket on the floor.

"Bad," she said.

"I know you don't like fruit, but it's good for you," I said.

"Even your toddler can see it," Scarlet said. "The monster is bad, and he's supposed to die at the end of the story."

"Ah." I stuck my finger in the air. "Actually, I looked up the Spark-Notes version of the novel, and the monster says he's going to kill himself, but that's not a scene in the book."

"Mari." She glared at me, unimpressed by my internet research on the book.

"The Fables know about the story cycle and I'm going to prove it to you," I said.

"Why?"

"Why? Because innocent people are being killed so that the cruel queen never dies. You said so yourself when you first described the story cycle to me. Remember? Something about people clamoring to become characters so they could twist the endings and keep living."

Scarlet nodded and wiped a smashed blueberry off the table near her arm.

"I just cannot fathom how they'd know about the story world spilling into our world," she said. I stood and guided Wendy around the room, pointing and instructing her to pick up each piece of fruit. She could learn to clean and practice walking at the same time. It spun into a game where she led me around and hurried to get the blueberries back into the basket.

"I don't know how they know but they do and the multiple colors show that Heath and Delores are characters in a lot of stories," I said. After the blueberries filled the basket, I continued walking with her and turned our little jaunt around the kitchen into some bounces and dance moves.

"You're certainly in high spirits suddenly," she said.

"I always get a little giddy when a case is solved. If I don't celebrate the little wins, I *will* lose my mind."

Wendy reached for me when I let go of her hand. Instead of walking, she crouched and scooped a fistful of blueberries to drop one by one and squish between her bare toes. If it'd been grapes, we'd have wine. The squelching sound delighted her and she responded with a squeal.

"Anyway." Scarlet sighed. "I'm sorry to burp your bubble, but a person can't be more than one character. It just doesn't work that way," she said.

"Burst my bubble," I said. A gasp escaped me and startled Wendy. She fell back into the basket and her face pinched, readying for a scream of the century. After I scooped her up and tried to distract her from the fall, I took a seat across from Scarlet.

"Hear me out," I said while picking smashed blueberries off of the back of Wendy's pants. "I think you hit the nail on the head."

Scarlet raised her eyebrow.

"It doesn't work that way because they're messing with it."

"I guess—"

"Those books we didn't know could be the key," I said, excited to dive into another investigation. The pages in my notebook bent and crinkled as I hurried to the most recent list. I uncapped the pen with my mouth to avoid Wendy's grabbing hands and scribbled another item on the bottom.

New books = new stories in the cycle. Are Heath and Delores the authors?

"Maybe that's why we can't figure out which story my mother belongs to, because the book is brand new and there's only one copy of it in this guarded library." What I didn't say was how desperately I needed my theory to be true. Something about my father's coronation tethered my mother here, and I only had one day to find out what it was before I lost her. The thought of returning to my routine knowing Mom wouldn't be around, cut off from even a phone call under the community's no-technology rule, left my stomach spoiled.

First, my mom would leave, and then Kai. Then. . . Wendy, when she grew old without me. If the Fables had found an answer to mortality, I wanted it. But not at the expense of innocent lives. I capped the pen and looked at Scarlet. She shoved the red curls from her face, but they fell forward again, framing her cheeks with wisps of hair floating in front of her eyes.

"Is it possible—" I said, my voice cracking with unexpected emotion. With a cough, I cleared the pain away and focused on getting answers. If we were all immortal, I wouldn't have to say goodbye someday. "Is it possible for the Fables to write happy stories?"

Scarlet tilted her head. The thick curls blocked her eyes, and she blew a puff of breath to get them out of her face.

"I mean," I continued. "Could happy stories be twisted and keep people immortal?"

"Ah," she said. "No."

The momentary lift of hope dropped like a thousand-pound brick to the pit of my stomach. I swallowed and sucked in a tight breath. "Why?"

Whether or not she noticed the distress on my face, she didn't acknowledge it. Scarlet scooped her hair into one hand and held it to the side of her head before looking me straight in the eyes. "Because the stories always end one way or another. The Keeper's job is to make sure it ends correctly. If happy stories end, the people return to mortals, the only way to subvert this is by chipping away the story protection and removing a character from the story through death. If a character is dead, the story can never end correctly. So the other characters live on, though the story protection is gone."

I'd never considered immortality and the story protection to be separate powers before, but it made sense now. Once this situation ended, I'd note the distinction in my journal for future reference. The story protection meant characters could not die by any means until the story played out, but immortality kept you alive at the same age, forever.

"But they can't force new stories into the cycle unless you take off the hood," Scarlet said with a twitch of her brow. The equation unraveled. Or had I never solved it?

"You said you don't know why some stories are part of the cycle and others aren't. Like Shakespeare's plays," I said. "Shouldn't they all be real? Who decides what's a classic and what's not?"

"I suppose you're right. I'm not an investigator." Scarlet didn't look sad, but she sighed anyway. I wondered if she kept failing at flipping burgers because she wanted a job like mine. "Instead of researching and trying to understand it all, I just learned as I went and tried to help the stories find their correct endings."

"Tomorrow we'll go to the library and you can investigate with me." *We'll find the new story Delores or Dad wrote Mom into and we'll twist it so she can come home.* The plan was flimsy, and we had little time left on the clock to pull it off, but at least I had a plan. And I loved deadlines.

"What about the monster?" Scarlet asked as we climbed the stairs. Wendy went limp in my arms from the excitement of the day. Though it was my toddler's bedtime, I was ready to turn in too. Brainstorming took it out of me, not to mention the monster's attack.

"I'm only one person," I said, standing and tucking the notebook under my arm and pen in my pocket. "I'll get to that"

"Make it so," she said, following me out of the kitchen, up the stairs, and into the first room.

"Oh, come on!" I shook my head. "You know Picard's catchphrase but not about the red shirts? We're binging The Next Generation when this is all over."

"I don't know what that means," Scarlet said.

Carefully, I laid Wendy onto the bed beside my mother and turned to Scarlet with a finger over my lips. If I knew anything about toddlers, it was that they did the opposite of what you expect. Carrying her up the stairs and arguing over Star Trek didn't wake her but the soft mattress and whispers between Scar and I did.

Wendy groaned and yanked on the blanket to pull it off of my mother. My daughter's eyes blinked open, and she tapped her lips with her thumb. The gesture was her own made-up signal, saying she needed a drink—which meant she wanted to avoid bedtime. Mom's exhaustion kept her peacefully snoozing while Wendy shuffled around in the bed.

I filled a sippy cup from the sink in the room and let her sip it until she slipped into snoring again. Scarlet left for the next room over. Though Scar's constant excitable energy followed her from the room, I couldn't relax.

I sank to the floor, where I crossed my legs and opened the notebook in my lap. The dim light of the single bulb over the sink offered enough light to see the handwriting on the page, but my eyes strained. Or was it my brain?

With a sigh, I leaned my head back against the bed and closed my eyes. How did solving the murder only bring more questions and a new mystery? I'd thought the biggest issue would be to free my mother from Heath's possessive nature, yet I'd stumbled deeper into a complex web of story aura. If the Fables created new stories for the cycle, making themselves immortal by continuing to avoid the story's endings, then I had a much bigger twist coming.

The edge of the mattress dug into the back of my neck. I pulled up my heavy head and opened my eyes. Though tired, I didn't plan on sleeping. If I could survive raising a newborn, I'd make it through tonight.

Chapter 16

Tell the Truth and Shame the Devil

I stood and tiptoed from the room, leaving Wendy and Mom to snore side-by-side. The door clicked shut as I eased it into place. The castle felt larger at night with the lights dimmed and the silence of sleep. My footsteps echoed with each step I took down the stairs.

The only other sound came from the throne room and it was the voice of the man I needed to speak with. I pushed through the door to see my father leaning forward. He sat on the steps beneath the throne with his elbows on his knees and head in his hands.

Johnson stood over him, hands in his jacket pocket and a toothpick jutting from his mouth. Neither noticed me enter, but I didn't intend on eavesdropping. I marched toward them and inserted myself into the conversation.

"Mari," Johnson said with a nod. The toothpick shifted to the other side of his mouth after his mumbled version of my name.

Heath looked up from his palms and it seemed he'd aged half a decade in a couple of hours.

"I need to speak with you privately," I said. My glance at Johnson signaled I wanted him to leave. If Johnson didn't know about the story cycle, I wanted to keep it that way. No sense in adding more immortal-hungry people into the mix. Though I intended to speak alone with

Johnson soon, too. What *did* he know about the Fables? Was it that queen Fable had people killed when they discovered her secret?

Heath agreed and Johnson left. The door slammed shut on his way out, but I didn't flinch. I'd grown used to Johnson's rough behavior. Victims mixed into the schemes of killers often built tough exteriors to deal with the situation. I couldn't blame him for having a chip on his unhygienic shoulder after years of serving a cruel queen.

A long sigh escaped Heath's mouth in a puff of misty white. Speaking of growing used to something, the cold in the castle didn't bother me anymore. Though I couldn't claim Elsa of Arendelle status. At least I didn't shiver like a chihuahua without a sweater.

"I suppose an investigator like you wants to know how my father created the monster," he said, more to his hands than me. Was he ashamed of his family? What kept him from meeting my eye?

"Science I'm guessing?" I said, taking a seat on the bench in the front row. I wanted him to tell me how much they knew about the story cycle rather than coach him into saying it. Detective Wilhelm didn't always agree with my method of digging for truth over producing results, but I stuck to my guns.

Surprised, he looked up. "Um. Yes, science."

"King Fable was a doctor?" I asked, keeping the word *Franken-stein* out of it.

"Of a sort."

"And you understand Delores will need to be officially arrested for first-degree murder and tried in a court of law?"

"Mari, she's the queen—"

"So you do intend to release her," I confirmed.

He uncrossed his legs then crossed them again before finally meeting my gaze. "I need her experience with running the communi-ty," he said.

Running the community or staying immortal? I shifted my jaw back and forth and resisted the urge to come out with it. Emotions rarely left me this impatient, but past interviews didn't involve my family trying to become immortal, either. Heath was stressed but stoic. He let nothing new slip as our conversation continued. After questions about how he planned to hold Delores accountable, I paused.

Silence fell between us and reminded me I'd turn into a pumpkin right about now. I swallowed a yawn and cursed my brain for failing to direct the conversation toward the story cycle. What was my father's weakness?

Control. He needed to control my mother, and it seemed he'd inherited that from Delores and her control of the monster. So if he thought he would lose it. . .

"You should know I have officers of the law on their way to the island right now," I lied. I'd seen Detective Wilhelm employ the same method to trick criminals into confessions. And it wasn't entirely untrue. They simply didn't have the time or resources to send officers across the bay. "They'll investigate Delores and the illegal distribution of copyrighted material in your library." *Doggone that sounded good.* I silently praised myself for slipping the library into the legal lie to see how he'd react.

And react he did.

Heath stood and ran his hand through his sandy hair. "Mari, you don't know what you're getting yourself involved in."

"This isn't my first investigation," I said as I watched his muscles stiffen. If he believed I could take away both Delores and the books, did that threaten his immortality? Or could he simply write more? "They'll also need to monitor your library from here on out."

The curling and uncurling of his fists told me he believed me. Not to mention that he clung to the idea of immortality despite the argument he'd had with Delores. My instincts were right, my father wasn't innocent.

Heath crouched in front of me and met my gaze. I didn't expect him to appeal to my human side—to place himself physically beneath me and allow his vulnerability to show.

"Mari, please call it off," he begged.

"They're just books," I said.

"No!" he huffed, emotion cracking his voice.

"Oh?" I pretended to be confused. He'd like that he'd need to explain it to me. I gave him a moment of control back. "What does that mean?"

"It is very complex," he said, raking his fingers over his skull again. "And a long story."

"Consider me The Keeper of stories." The title sent a course of energy rippling through me. When he didn't answer, the rush of adrenaline encouraged me to be more direct.

"You won't believe it."

"Try me," I said.

"Then you promise you'll call off the law enforcement?"

I nodded and laid my palm over my heart as confirmation of my word. It seemed to ease him as his crinkled forehead smoothed and he breathed easier.

"King Fable was a big fan of the classics," he said. "He collected all his favorites and turned that old building into a library. He took a fancy to writing stories, too. That is until he found out they came true." Heath's gaze flickered. I tried to repress any reaction to show him I was listening. But it felt weird to talk about this to someone who wasn't Kai or Scarlet. Nobody else was supposed to know about the story aura. How did they figure it out? And, more importantly, could the past king's stories really join the next cycle? The questions appeared in different colors in my mind's eye.

"I might need to explain this to the officers," I said, pressuring him to keep going. "Unless I understand it better." A sheen of sweat on his forehead caught the glow of the fairy lights that decorated the crown molding for tomorrow's coronation.

"Right." He nodded. "King Fable, uh, he realized he was a lot like Doctor Frankenstein in Mary Shelley's novel." My father chuckled nervously, and I knew I'd gained control of the situation. "He became obsessed with the idea of creating life as well as extending it. But his creation turned into a monster."

"And the stories that came true?" I prodded.

"My mother wanted the stories to save him from his sickness. But he stopped writing and he—" my father paused. Was he afraid to say the word? His eyes shifted around the room as if he expected a reaper to burst in and take him away.

"I'm sorry about your father," I said, relieving the tension just enough to let Heath know he could trust me. Exhaustion pulled on my limbs, a physical reminder that it was way past my bedtime and any sense of schedule had gotten away from me. I needed to get the conversation moving. "But he was right," I said.

Too soon. My impatience got to me. Heath's brow furrowed and eyes darkened. He stood and towered over me.

"I will not create monsters," he said.

"But the stories are hurting innocent people—"

"That's enough," he said, no longer threatened by my lie. Did he see through me? It was too late. I'd lost my hold over him and revealed what I knew. "People die every day. There is no proof it is from the stories."

I stood. Though tired, my brain organized my thoughts and filed each one away in the appropriate section. Blue for my mother's fairy tale under *unsolved*. And red for the potential that the throne, or crown, or something else here, gave my father similar powers that the hood gave The Keeper.

Which was me. And I still had no clue how to use said powers. *Crap.*

"No proof yet," I said. With that, I marched from the room. I needed a moment to myself to create a plan of attack. In less than twenty-four hours, my father would somehow gain the power to create new stories, which was likely the reason he decided not to care about the threat of law enforcement. He could simply write them into a book and send them on their merry way through the plot.

The heavy door slammed shut behind me and echoed through the open space below the bedrooms.

We were in a race now. I had to find proof the stories killed people and convince my father of the cruelty behind it despite what he wanted to believe. Even fairy tales were violent because, as Scar said, all stories must have conflict or they're not stories at all.

"Hey," a gruff voice said behind me.

I spun around to see Johnson in the shadows. He emerged, like the cliche character in a seedy bar, ready to share some undercover information.

"Remember that gift your father intended to give your daughter?" he asked. It was clear he didn't share my distaste for eavesdropping, since he'd been hiding right outside the throne room's door.

The memory sent me back almost two years when I'd first met Johnson. He came to our condo while I was in the middle of solving the Red Riding Hood case. I'd brushed him off as a nuisance and my father's lackey. I had no interest in the apparent gift Johnson had claimed Heath wanted to give to Wendy.

"I remember," I said.

"It's immortality," he said. Air left my lungs as my chest tightened. I couldn't let emotions cloud my thoughts. Immorality was the answer I needed for Kai and Wendy, so they wouldn't grow old without me.

Johnson didn't notice the pained look on my face. Or he did, and he wanted to capitalize on it. "Immortality for all the Fables," he continued. "But it comes with a price, of course."

I didn't doubt that. My father's 'price' couldn't have been clearer. He wanted control over everything, and he'd have it if he truly gained the power to make stories come true once he became king. My stomach twisted, but I didn't let that show on my face.

"Trapping us here, I assume," I spoke as emotionlessly as possible, which proved difficult late at night in a strange place that threatened the freedom of my mother, myself, my friend, and, worst of all, my daughter.

Johnson dipped his head in a faint nod and leaned closer into my face. "If I were you, I'd get myself and my mommy out quick before King Fable writes another story that keeps me here." The pause between his words hung in a stale breath between us. I didn't know whether to hold my breath or punch the guy in the face for trying to tell me what to do.

"Forever," he finished. The knot in his throat bobbed, but his expression steeled and revealed nothing more than the twitch of his lip. When he folded his arms across his chest, I swore I saw dust puff into the air. At least I knew why he always wore the jacket. The icy castle and freezing library belonged in my daughter's favorite movie, with Olaf and Elsa and snow magic.

"Is that why you let me into the library?" I asked, drawing from what little fuel I had left in my investigator's tank. Even a few hours of sleep would afford me the recharge I needed, though I hated to give up that precious time.

"What Schwanna's looking for," he said, pointing in the general direction of the library. "It's in there."

"Why would you help us? You threw her into the dungeon the first chance you got." I mirrored his crossed arms. Gruff men didn't intimidate me, not even at midnight in a strange place where a monster ran free. I had Detective Wilhelm to thank for that.

"Let's just say I do my duty around here so I don't become one of the royal's puppets," he said, followed by a wet cough. "Or rather, a character." The twinkle in his eye told me he knew just as much as Heath and Delores.

My hand found the hood's string. It twirled and tangled around my fingers as I toyed with it. Johnson didn't break his intense gaze into my eyes. It seemed he could see my soul and the guilt I carried for procrastinating the hood's responsibilities for so long. If only I'd focused on the fairy tale instead of the murder investigation, I might have convinced my mother to leave.

"The library will be unguarded during Prince Fable's coronation," Johnson said. He dipped back into the shadow and sauntered off without giving me a chance to respond.

I didn't intend to wait that long. In the morning, I'd hatch a plan with Scar to break into the library. The long climb up the stairs left me barely awake as I crawled into the bed. Curling up on the edge with Wendy sandwiched between me and Mom, didn't bring sleep. Instead, I squinted in the dim light of the moon from the small window and cracked open my notebook.

The pages rustled as I flipped to the back and scribbled a schedule.

- In yellow, *Morning: visit the library and find the story that killed Tricia.*
- In orange, *Afternoon: decide on a twist ending to Mom's fairy tale and/or find what she's missing so she'll agree to leave.*
- Red for highest priority, *Evening: use Tricia's story to convince Heath the story cycle kills innocent people.*

Then get the hell off this island. I didn't write the last part because I wouldn't forget it. It was time to close this case once and for all, and that included leading the monster to his death. The story threads all tangled together and, in one weird lucid dream, I was a cat with a ball of yarn tangled in my claws but the claws were covered in blood.

The thud of the notebook falling from my hands was the last thing I remembered before full, restless sleep took over.

Chapter 17

As Bad Luck Would Have It

A series of nightmares left me haggard and in serious need of a coffee the next morning. The kitchen stocked the caffeine beans, but no sugary creamer was to be found. I sighed and settled for an orange. I was brave enough to interview serial killers, but I put my foot down on bitter coffee.

Over breakfast, we hatched a ridiculous plan to sneak past the guards and into the library. It helped that the coronation would begin soon and most of the kingdom busied themselves preparing. Some mingled inside and around the castle while others trickled in slowly.

Of course, the plan only felt ridiculous because it involved using my knowledge of the stories against the people. Plus, it took us all morning to secure a Plan B and C in case I slipped past the guard but the door was locked, or if I ran into another guard once I got inside. We were already running behind schedule and I nearly hyperventilated on our power walk to the library.

Wendy stayed with Mom. Though it took a bit of convincing to keep Mom inside, she'd confirmed Johnson's statement. The pull she felt came from the library, which meant whatever treasure she'd lost was hidden somewhere inside that building. I didn't want to risk getting her into trouble after the kingdom had already suspected her of murder. Though it meant whatever she needed would be harder to find.

We approached the library and Scar put on her best flirtatious face. She asked the guard a series of questions, not unlike the ones with which she'd interrogated innocent San Francisco pedestrians only days before. It felt like a lifetime ago that I'd gotten the phone call from my mother, not a mere week.

My heart ached to see Kai. He'd no doubt been sent into a panic. In fact, I wouldn't be surprised if he'd dragged Detective Wilhelm or another cop to the island to find us. But the walls kept us separated—a problem for later after I convinced Heath to let go of the story cycle.

After a slight shake of Scar's head, I knew she'd failed to identify the guard's fairy tale. If we didn't know what story he'd come from, we wouldn't be able to encourage him to look for his mermaid lover or trick him into rushing off to chop down a beanstalk.

Scarlet's flirty words drifted into interrogation. From several yards away, I could see the man's brow furrow and his voice raised. He didn't like whatever she'd accused him of, but the argument distracted him long enough for me to slip past.

To my relief, the knob turned easily, and I closed the door behind me. The overwhelming story aura sent my head spinning worse than it did after the first hangover I'd suffered in my thirties.

I squinted and started thumbing through the books. Thousands of texts would take me hours, days even. I quickly pivoted plans, proud of myself for deviating from the schedule even if it made my stomach a little sick.

I retraced the steps Scar and I had discovered by first pulling out the fake copy of Shel Silverstein's *A Light in the Attic*. The skylight rolled open and let a bright beam of sunshine into the middle of the room.

With the extra light, I spied the dark cover of the block painted to look like *Doors to the Unknown*. After a pull, it triggered a mechanism that pushed another book from its place. I swiveled, expecting to see the history of Little Red Riding Hood halfway out of its place on the shelf on the wall to my right.

Instead, the book—an actual book, not a block—titled *A Collection of Fairy Tales* stuck out. I hurried to pull it from the shelf. The book looked like nothing special, no new fairy tales or stories I hadn't heard before. As I flipped through the pages, illustrations caught my eye. The Beast and his Beauty stared back at me. Could my mother's treasure be the rose? No, that belonged to the Beast and his curse. I shuffled to the next page to see Rapunzel looking over the ledge of the stair-less tower that trapped her. So many fairy tales involved kidnapping. I wrinkled my nose and moved on.

The painting in the next image depicted a naked woman turned away with her butt covered by water. She stood in a pond and a heap of feathered wings lay on the shore behind her. The caption underneath told of a shape-shifting woman who'd removed her robe of feathers to bathe her human skin.

The Swan Maiden.

My breath caught in my throat. Finally, one of the many threads became untangled. Mom's desire to change her looks, her impossible grace, and desperation to run from the man who'd forced her to marry him fit the maiden's fairy tale. *Heath stole her robe.*

If Scarlet knew my mom better this would have been solved a long time ago. Or if I'd studied fairy tales like she'd said.

I skimmed the story to confirm the bits and pieces I knew about it but didn't have time to read to the end. Our late start to the day pushed me to hurry through the schedule. Even if I found Mom's robe and freed her, I might trap Wendy, Scar, and me. I still needed to find Tricia's story and convince my father to change his mind before the coronation.

First things first. And I needed to hurry. Too many books glowed with the same faint shade of white that had surrounded Tricia. Good thing I was fast at reading. I hurried and pulled the different texts off the shelves around the room and started skimming.

Texts melted into one another after too much reading and the angle of the sunbeam from the skylight shifted. How long had I been stuck here mulling over dozens of books? I couldn't read them all, I couldn't even skim them all. But I also couldn't skip the order of the schedule. I needed to bring my proof to my father, just like the evidence I'd produced to have Delores arrested.

My watch read half-past five. *No, no, no!*

I'd tried to identify pieces of what I knew about Delores, Tricia, and my father in each of the books I pulled. I even refreshed myself on the events of *Frankenstein* and tried to fit Tricia into the role of Henry and Elizabeth from the novel. But a square peg didn't match a round hole. Tricia wasn't the late king's best friend, nor his betrothed. Besides, her aura didn't match the yellow that surrounded the monster.

I sighed and dropped my head into my hands. Scarlet needed to be here. Someone who knew story structure and characters and fairy tale morals would have found Tricia's book. It was arrogant of me to assume my investigative experience put me at an advantage.

The click of a lock startled me from my pity party.

Ebenezer Scrooge.

Talk about trapped.

Chapter 18

The Way Madness Lies

The guard's footsteps faded before I gathered the wherewithal to call out. My voice died in my throat and I yanked on the handle. It wouldn't budge. After several shouts, I gave up, knowing the entire community had made their way to the castle for the coronation.

The stupid schedule I'd followed left me in the wrong place at the wrong time.

I roundhouse kicked at the crack between the doors but only stumbled back with a bruised foot and black and blue ego.

Brute force wouldn't work. I needed to approach my escape from a different angle. After scanning the room, I decided tinkering with the mechanisms in the wall would be my best bet. If the robe was hidden somewhere inside the walls, it could lead to another exit.

With the thick fairy tale book as my stool, I peered at the empty spot on the shelf. I only saw a small wooden slab built into the shelf and darkness beyond that. On my tiptoes, I angled my hand over the slab of wood and felt around in the darkness. On second thought, I should have been more cautious, but I was already there, feeling the lever.

This is all too convenient. If I had a moment of extra time, I'd stop to consider the situation before pulling the lever. But it was too late for that. The mechanism released a loud thunk as I yanked on it. Wood groaned as the shelves on the back wall shifted. The doggone bookshelf was a door and the block of *Doors to the Unknown*, the handle.

I hopped off the fairy tale collection and hurried to the crack in the bookshelf. Tugging on the block pulled the bookshelf door toward me. The open shelf revealed a small room with a skylight of its own.

Instead of books, this room only stored one object, the white-feathered robe. Even though I'd fought a man-turned-wolf, seen Frankenstein's monster with my own eyes, and wore an invisible hood twenty-four-seven, I still didn't expect the robe to be actual swan feathered wings.

Maybe in another year I'd get used to this Keeper and story stuff. It took me about that long to get used to seeing dead bodies when I'd become an investigative journalist.

I stepped into the small, stuffy room. The hook on the back wall, only a few steps from me, held the robe in place. The wings hung folded over one another. A less observant person might have ripped the robe from its hook and skedaddled, happy to save the day. Fortunately, I saw the crack in the wall behind it and smelled the wooden walls soaked with gasoline. The hook was weighted by the robe and connected to a gas power line with a knob on the ceiling that reminded me of a stove.

They designed the entire room into a furnace, ready to ignite into flames if the robe was removed. But what about the books? Whoever had designed the trap either didn't care for the stories, or didn't expect anyone to have the guts to remove the robe.

Was this what the guards and locks protected? It made sense since the king supposedly could write any new story he wanted and replace whatever they'd lost in the library. Once they had a king, that is.

A loud bang startled a yelp from me. Wood cracked and splintered before clattering across the floor. Cool evening light flooded in from behind me. I turned to see a hulking figure.

Frankenstein's monster closed the distance between us in only a few sweeping steps. Caught between the library and the robe room, I had nowhere to run but backward. It didn't matter. My heart crashed against my ribcage as the monster's huge hand closed around my neck. I didn't have a moment to think. Strategy, schedules, psychology—none of my skills could save me now.

But I tried anyway. With what little air I had left in my lungs, I forced out the words. "What do you want?" I asked. "Don't hurt me and I'll help you." Whether he could understand my choking voice, I didn't know. Not until his eyes shifted and met mine.

My chest burned, aching for fresh air, but I did my best to hold his gaze. His eyes flickered behind me. For a moment, he focused on the wall and the pulley system. The width of his nostrils expanded and understanding flushed his face.

"Fire," he muttered.

"What do you want?" I repeated, begging for his attention before he strangled me in his distraction.

"I don't know," he said, as his gaze snapped back to me. His breath smelled like death, worse even, but I didn't have any air to cough away the stench. "My master died."

Victor, the king. My thoughts blurred, but I blinked and sucked in a small gasp of air when his grip loosened.

The monster's lip twitched, and I realized how surreal and sick it was to see the mechanic's head stitched onto someone else's body. Though I didn't know the mechanic, his face clearly didn't match the rest of the monster. His grasp tightened again and black stars dotted my vision.

"I'll help." I tried again, appealing to his needs.

"You can't." He breathed. "I hate your perfect family. Your sister and mother and baby. I should have a family. He should have made me a mate, so I wouldn't be alone. I hate him and I hate you."

"Victor—" I tried to ask who he hated, but the monster squeezed tighter, and I nearly went limp. If it weren't for him holding me in place, I'd collapse.

"Hate," he repeated. The mention of his creator's name pushed him over the edge.

Grief flickered in his gaze. The dim, natural light of the evening caught the wetness in his eyes. A tear slipped down the mechanic's, or the monster's, cheek.

Everything I'd planned went wrong, and I'd pay the price with my life. Once again, I needed Scarlet or Detective Wilhelm, or anyone else to attack this case. I'd failed.

The worst part was, I didn't care. In the end, the only thing that mattered wasn't color-coded files or the satisfaction of a well-kept schedule. Nobody would remember me for staying on task or talk about how well I controlled the chaos of my life as a mother, journalist, and villain hunter within the bounds of a calendar's box.

Let go, please. I didn't know whether my mind begged the monster or myself. The crush of my windpipe left me dizzy as consciousness slipped away.

In one terrible moment, I mirrored the monster. Before blackness covered my wide-open eyes, we stared at one another, tears streaking my face and his. Only one thought rolled over and over in my mind, stuck in a loop of horrible grief. The hood was supposed to make me immortal, invincible. But if I'd learned anything on Cygnus Island, I'd learned even Scarlet didn't fully understand the hood and the story cycle.

I'll never get to see Wendy walk. I'll never see my daughter walk. . .

"I'm sorry," he said. The look on his face had shifted from rage to a broken expression mixed with shame and sadness. His grip relaxed.

Blood rushed to my head, and my legs buckled underneath me. I registered the faint knock of my temple against wood but the numbness in my head temporarily blocked pain.

In the distance, horns burst into a fanfare. The bright, forceful sound had caused the monster to drop me. He stormed from the library; the floor shaking beneath my body.

The instruments carried a lively tune that echoed from the castle. Heath's coronation had ended, and the celebration began. Even though I didn't save my mother or myself from a new classic–a classic written by the new king where he had to kidnap his family to keep them here, I didn't care. For now, I'd survived. Knowing I'd see my mother, friend, and daughter again was all that mattered.

Chapter 19

Out of the Jaws of Death

The horns blared a new tune. This melody rose and fell at a slower pace. I didn't know how much time I'd lost while unconscious, but a twist of my head told me the robe still waited on its hook. It hung like a white ghost, a haunting reminder that I didn't know what to do with it. If I returned the wings to my mother, could she overpower my father? Or was this a trick that Heath's lackey had led me into?

Surely, I'd need to twist whatever horrible fate waited for my mother in her fairy tale. But I couldn't twist what I didn't know. My focus shifted from using Tricia's story to convince my father to free my mother. I couldn't do everything, but I could try to do that.

I hobbled across the library and folded my legs beneath me beside the book I'd used as a stool. The pages curled over as I shuffled to find *The Swan Maiden*. Maybe my mother had dormant powers as a shapeshifting swan and the robe would bring them out. Maybe she'd be able to fly with the wings and get us help.

If I knew the end of her fairy tale, I could help the story complete and maybe it'd throw my father from the loop before he wrote a new one. With his story protection stripped, he couldn't risk testing his mortality with new stories. There was too much Scarlet, and I still didn't understand about the fairy tales come to life. Like who'd created the portal and how did the crown of Cygnus Island make new stories come true?

Instead of skimming, I read each word. My head throbbed from the attack, but I finished the story despite the pressure of time.

You're late, you're late.

I spoke over the nagging thoughts and muttered the key points of the story. "The prince steals the maiden's robe. Without it, she's stuck marrying him. Their children ask why their mother always cries. . ." My voice cracked. Though I was one of the unnamed children in the story, I'd never seen her weep. But now I recognized her cold behavior had been inspired by grief, not paranoia.

My finger traced the wings in the picture. I wasn't meant to twist this story at all. Returning the feathers would free my mother, just as the children in the tale did.

Carefully, I folded the page over to mark the spot and set the book on top of the stack I'd collected earlier. The gentle, patient motion gave me a bit of practice. I'd need a soft hand when I replaced the robe with another weighted object to keep the room from igniting.

Like Indiana Jones and the holy grail, I gingerly approached the treasure. The soft feathers gave under my touch. When I started to lift it from the hook, sure enough, the pulley inside the wall raised the hook and the knob ticked. The smell of gasoline permeated the room with a heavier scent that left me nauseated.

I pulled the robe down but kept my hold on the hook. Tossing the feathered robe in a heap on the floor felt wrong, but I needed my hand free to remove my shoe. I lifted my foot to my free hand and slipped it off.

The shoe balanced on the hook easily enough, but when I eased the weight of my hand from the hook; it rose. The shoe didn't weigh enough. Neither did two shoes.

I tried shimmying out of my pants but even jeans couldn't match the weight of the thick, down feathers. Half-naked, and barefoot on one side, I almost wanted to give up.

Patience. Forcing a slow inhale, I considered my options. The moment of calm brought clarity. I could return the robe, keeping myself and the entire room from going up in flames, then return later with something else of equal weight to hang on the hook. The plan was simple, but normally I'd write it down just to feel the satisfaction of the checkmark to come later. It was solid, except that it'd give Heath time to write a new story and the snowball could roll out of control—or under the king's control. I wasn't willing to risk that.

But I had another option. The hood's strings tangled around my fingers, and I hadn't realized I'd been playing with it again. Bile rose in my throat and burned on the back of my tongue. I hated the thought of letting my plan go. While Wendy had inherited a splash of Heath's hair color, maybe I'd gotten his need for control.

I untangled the string from my fingers.

"No," I whispered.

Yes. If returning this robe to my mother gave us even a chance to stop my father from a looping immortal existence where he'd continue to sacrifice innocent lives, I'd take it. A knot tightened in my stomach and the weight of the world felt a lot heavier than Humpty Dumpty sitting on my chest.

Ebenezer Scrooge. I tugged the strings loose and the knot unraveled easily, as the hood knew my intent. Removing the hood, as I knew it, meant all the stories ever written could become part of the story cycle. Indiana Jones himself would be a real person. Someone else would turn into Godzilla, and—oh, no—Star Wars' Jar Jar Binks would come to life.

Or would they? If it didn't happen when I tore the hood from Scarlet the first time, maybe the magic had died.

I slipped the hood off of one shoulder. The ground's sudden and violent shake knocked me sideways and I yelped. My body crashed into the wall, with the back of my head smacking hard too. Books fell with rhythmic thumps in the other room as the earth rocked side to side beneath me. My head throbbed, but I had the clarity of mind to yank the hood back over my shoulder.

The quaking ceased as quickly as it had started.

No way. I'd caused the earthquake, or rather the story world did, as it spilled into our world.

I couldn't take the hood off. Could I? Godzilla and Indiana Jones wouldn't enter the cycle for another ninety-eight years. If Scarlet's timeline was correct, I had nearly a century to prepare. I'd deal with it then. My mother deserved freedom and to return to her true self. Once Heath controlled the kingdom, who knew if I, or anyone else, could make it back here and get the robe.

With my palm firmly pressed against the wall, I straightened. A sick rush of fear shuddered through me, but I sucked in a calming breath. Once I reminded myself that this was my first real decision as The Keeper, I gathered a slice of courage.

I released the strings and let the hood fall from my shoulders. The earth shook again, angry that I'd released more of the story aura into the natural world. I kept my hand against the wall, but this quake raged more intensely than the last. Once it finally quieted, I breathed again.

The hood had materialized in my hands. It felt heavy and thick with velvety, red fabric the way I'd first seen it and looked the way I imagined it was designed in *The Little Cloak Girl* fairy tale.

Gently, I hung it on the hook and the hood balanced the pulley perfectly. A sigh escaped my lips, and I coughed from the choking stench of gasoline. I stooped to pull my pants back on, slip my feet into my shoes, then gather the thick robe into my arms.

Fresh air filled my lungs when I left the robe room behind. Though I never felt the weight or fabric of the surrounding hood, the absence of it left me chilled as I stepped from the library and into the salty breeze. Remnants of the sun's glow dotted the partially cloudy sky with blood orange.

With a huff, I hefted the winged robe up higher. The more I piled it into my arms, the more it seemed to slip from my hold. If I couldn't fold a fitted sheet, I definitely couldn't carry the slippery feathers with any grace. At least Wendy's refusal to walk left my arms strong enough to hold the heavy garment.

It dragged on the ground with every step I took. Hopefully, a little dirt wouldn't hurt it. The wings were too large and even thrown over my shoulder, the tips still reached past my feet.

The weight of them pushed my neck and head forward, but I forced it up when I drew closer to the castle. The people of Cygnus had taken to the street. They lined the walkway as if waiting for a parade of Disneyland floats or dancing characters. Well, they'd get one character, anyway.

I didn't want to think too carefully about what would happen to my mom when she got her wings again. Despite my effort to redirect my thoughts, the worries plagued me anyway. I could pretend to be tough and strong, but my heart ached. What if freedom pulled her away before I could say goodbye? She'd wanted this for so long. Would she turn into a swan and forget me? Would she fly away and leave us behind?

Yes. I knew the story now. I'd read it. According to the fairy tale, the Swan Maiden vanishes, never to return.

One or two heads turned at the sight of me huffing and puffing along. I'd blow my father's house down if it meant he couldn't play with people's lives through stories any longer. Instead of three little pigs, however, I caught sight of Heath exiting the castle with the crown on his head and my mother on his arm.

Those in the crowd who noticed me didn't let their gazes linger. Apparently, a crazed-looking woman carrying giant wings couldn't compete with the king for attention. Rage and allergy-induced asthma burned in my chest. I picked up the pace, running now with all the strength I had left.

In the corner of my eye, I saw Scar with Wendy. What had happened to her after I went into the library? Scar's mouth hung open. Perhaps she couldn't believe I'd figured out Mom's fairy tale, or found the robe, or considered the story cycle at all. Or she saw the strings' absence from my neck and knew I'd temporarily abandoned the hood. What she didn't know was the tiny, last little plan that hovered over my thoughts—end *The Swan Maiden* and strip Heath of his story protection.

The density of the crowd blocked the path between me and my

mother. The press of bodies in the walkway forced me to stop and angle around them, pushing past elbows and around shoulders.

Even buried in the white feathers, Wendy recognized me.

"Mama!" Her tiny hand reached out. Unlike me, she wasn't scared of what came next. My daughter simply wanted her mother after the long day's separation. She squealed for me with the same smile she'd have when I picked her up from Ruby Slippers daycare once the workday had ended.

The sound of Wendy's voice alerted my mother. Schwanna's gaze scanned the crowd and landed on the hunk of white feathers moving through the sea of cheering faces. The people of Cygnus whistled and waved and clapped at the sight of their new royal leaders.

Nothing in my mother's expression matched their delight. Regret curved her mouth and the wrinkle between her brow sunk deep into her forehead. Until she recognized what I carried, that is. Her lips parted and eyes fixed on the robe, her lost skin, the piece of herself she'd been searching for my whole life. The breeze swept hair into her face and I wondered if she'd remember how to fly.

My heart cracked in two at the sound of Wendy's voice. This time, she called for Gramma Sammy.

The story says the Swan Maiden never returns. Who would I call if I failed to potty train my daughter? What about when Wendy got into trouble at school for the first time? Could I survive her teen years without Mom's advice?

Salt mixed with the smell of people. Cheers rang in my ears and reminded me of my own teen years crowded in clubs and concerts. If only my mother's story was as happy as a Jane Austen novel or as simple as the Magical Place's version of fairy tales.

When Schwanna let go of my father's arm, he turned and snapped his attention toward me.

"No!" The shout slipped from his mouth as his eyes widened. He pointed at me, his arm shaking with fury or fear or that icky, sinking feeling one gets when control slips through your fingers. "Stop her!"

I pushed through the crowd, but bodies crushed tighter together, confused by the king's demand and the approaching guards. The linked gaze between my mother and I broke as she twisted her head in the opposite direction. Heath's crown fell from his head and, before I knew what had happened, cheers turned into screams.

Arms whacked my face and people trampled on one another's feet as they rushed to clear the pathway. They pushed into one another as panic took hold. The ground shook and the fairy lights that decorated the outside of the castle fell when the monster ripped them down. The pathway fell into the dim light of evening when the sun had descended but left a hazy orange behind. The glow of the decorative lights came from the ground, but the bulbs cracked and crushed underfoot.

Wendy! I craned my neck to see behind me. Arms and heads and bodies blocked my view of my daughter's face, but I could see red curls running away from us, to safety. Scar carried Wendy around the corner and behind the castle.

The hulking figure of Frankenstein's creation stormed through the crowd, ignoring the innocent bodies he knocked aside in his rampage. The face of the mechanic curdled with pain, not unlike the expression I'd just recognized in my mother.

Regret.

Instead of anger, the monster's eyes shone with tears. His loping steps closed the distance quickly as he crashed toward me. If he'd come to finish the job, I'd die knowing I'd stopped my father and freed my mother. But I also wasn't a complete idiot.

I dodged to the side to clear a way for the monster. Though where he intended to go or what he planned to do, I couldn't guess. I didn't stop to read Mary Shelley's novel as I should have. How did I ignore my responsibility for so long?

Speaking of idiots, Heath pushed my mother back toward the castle doors. She stumbled but didn't fall, always the graceful, balanced woman—just like a bird, her true self. The rough castle wall dug into my back. My mother's robe nearly spilled from my arms.

Instead of moving from the monster's path, my father stepped onto the walkway. He held out his hand the way a superhero might stop a car from hitting a child in the road. And, of course, that was exactly what he thought of himself. The glow of story protection rippled around him.

The monster didn't so much as slow. The scars where the mechanic's head had been stitched onto someone else's torso burned red with infection. Pink veins streaked his neck and disappeared down his chest beneath his dirty, sweat-stained shirt. Story protection kept the creation alive until. . . until what?

I'd planned for everything except this story.

Frankenstein's monster swung his thick trunk of an arm into Heath. The king's body bashed into the stone castle wall and crumpled to the ground. Screams pierced the chaos as their new leader collapsed. Heath hadn't learned from the last attack. Or did he believe himself stronger, incapable of even injury now that he controlled the creation of stories and lives?

The answer didn't matter. I saw my opportunity. Two guards ran to my father while the others dealt with the crushing chaos of the crowd. They'd stopped their pursuit of me.

A stunned boy stood in the walkway, but his mother hurried to snatch him from the monster's path. Frankenstein's creation turned his head and fixed his eyes on me. A slice of fear struck through my heart at the memory of his hand around my throat. He stopped. His dead gaze left everyone it passed over paled and frozen, or screaming. It shifted from me and back toward the castle doors. I followed his line of sight and hoped he hadn't fixed his attention on my mother.

I hadn't noticed Delores near the front steps.

"Her," the former queen said with a flick of her head. The monster followed the direction of her glance, right at me.

"No," he said in a deep, rumbling voice that could only belong to a monster. But the words that followed didn't match his unfortunate title. "I won't hurt people anymore."

She yanked her head away, refusing to meet the monster's gaze. Delores had lost control of her husband's creation. As such, her plan to skirt mortality crumbled.

"I killed," the monster said. A thick, crystal clear tear rolled down the cheek that had once belonged to a mechanic in San Francisco. "So I must be killed."

"What the hell?" I caught the sound of my father's voice cutting through the chaos. Heath dabbed at his nose and stared at the blood on his hands while guards lifted him to his feet.

The monster didn't intend to hurt me or anyone else. Confusion swam in his eyes as he turned and ran from the castle. Somehow, I could relate to the monster created by the late king. I knew the feeling of wondering who you are, of not recognizing yourself, and regretting decisions you'd made.

I refused to regret this moment. Before my father could gather himself to send his guards after me, I'd let go.

Everyone held their breaths and watched the monster. He'd said his piece and continued onward. While they watched him disappear into the library's wide-open doors, I turned and stumbled toward my mother.

Mom stumbled backward, and the distance between us grew. My brain caught up with the scene as Delores brought down her cane from where it had jabbed into my mother's side. The former queen blocked Schwanna and reached out, ready to tear the robe from my arms as a guard seized me from behind. His thick arm wrapped around my collarbone. Delores dug her fingers into the feathers and pulled, proving her wiry strength in her old age.

A flash of panic had me gasping for breath as the guard's thick forearm dug into my neck. For one terrible moment, I thought the monster lifted me in a chokehold again where access to oxygen and blood would be cut from my head and I'd collapse at my grandmother's feet.

Delores yanked at the robe in my hands, while Heath clutched my mother's shoulders and held her back from reaching for the robe.

I cursed in the name of *A Christmas Carol*, and I wished Kai or even Detective Wilhelm were here to help.

"Go to Mama, Wednesday." My daughter's nickname caught my attention. I turned my head to see Scarlet had emerged from the crowd and set Wendy on her feet.

My daughter lifted her foot and set it down, then followed with another. She'd taken her first step, and I almost sobbed and laughed at the same time. Wendy took proper steps, walking for the first time in the middle of complete chaos.

Before I could blink the tears away, Scar skirted around my daughter and dealt a blow to Delores' face. Her fist landed with a crack against my grandmother's nose. With the cane, Delores stayed steady but released her grasp on the robe.

One down, two to go. The guard pulled back, but I reacted with a swift kick to the groin—my favorite self-defense move against unsuspecting jerks. The moment he released me, I gathered the heavy robe as high as I could and lunged past a bloody-nosed Delores.

I dumped, rather than threw, the robe into my mother's arms. After freeing up my hands, I turned and scooped up my daughter who'd walked the four or five steps toward me.

Heath tried to shove the robe from Mom's arms but she looked stronger with her original swan skin in her hands. She ducked away from him with ease after he'd let go to steal it away. It looked neither heavy nor bulking in her delicate grasp. Her eyes flicked to me. A mixture of sadness and hope left her brow pinched and lips parted.

The weight of Mom's gaze suddenly made me aware of the tears streaking my face and tightening the skin on my cheeks. The wind dried the wetness and left salt behind on my face. I nodded—an answer to her unspoken question.

I'll be okay.

Delores shouted for her son, but Heath had frozen, likely shocked by his wife's newfound strength and how easily she'd slipped away from him. The guards pushed past him, coming for the wings.

My mother moved like water, fluid and unstoppable. She draped the robe over her shoulders and transformed.

A thousand schedules or carefully laid plans couldn't have prepared me to watch my mother shape-shift into a swan. Her flesh and hair and even the whites of her eyes vanished.

White wings spread into the space and forced the guards back. In the blink of an eye, she'd lifted over our heads. The slow beat of her wings carried her higher, out of the guards' and my father's reach.

Graceful and mesmerizing, Schwanna slipped away. The stark white of her feathers stuck out against dark clouds as an uncommon threat of summer rain moved over the bay. Wendy lifted her tiny hand, and I thought she'd wave. Instead, she pointed at the swan in the sky and babbled a new word, *bird*.

My mother flew with her long neck outstretched, but she never turned to look back.

Chapter 20

Be All and End All

Mom escaped, but I remained stuck in my father's fiery gaze. The guards seized my arms, digging their fingernails into my flesh. I didn't let that intimidate me. After years of dealing with Detective Wilhelm's gruff behavior and grumpy attitude, Heath and his lackeys couldn't shake me.

"How could you?" Heath shouted. The roar of his voice burped my bubble, as Scar would say. "Are you insane? You've destroyed my marriage!"

The entire kingdom watched. Hundreds of eyes fixed on my father as they waited for his decision. What would he do with me? Confusion covered their faces as they tried to make sense of the monster, their king's outburst, and the Swan Maiden herself.

So I did what I do best. I informed the public of the danger. Investigating was in my blood, but the journalism part of it thrilled me the most. They deserved to know.

"Your leaders are liars," I said. Emotion cracked my voice, but I cleared it away, pushing aside the goodbye I never got with Mom and filled my lungs with air. "Heath and Delores act as though they keep the community running, but they're using you."

"Shut up!" Delores screeched. "You don't know—"

"Queen Fable killed Tricia to silence her, but I will tell you the truth," I said. Adrenaline pumped in my veins and I could no longer feel the iron grip of the guard's hold. "Delores tried to extend her own life at the risk of yours. They protect the library because you've all been written into real-life stories. You're a character, a subject in a greater plan."

"Mari," my father growled. I looked from the people to him.

"Don't you see how wrong this is?" I asked as my face pulled tight.

"You don't understand it," he said. "We can write stories without death."

"No," I said, glancing at Delores. She still stood in the doorway as unmoving as a cold, hard statue. "You can't. A story isn't a story without conflict and those that end happily end completely. Immortality gone. You'll become villains, writing characters and forcing the story to loop again by killing them in ways the story doesn't say when it plays out, and the protection has chipped away."

Heath finally broke his glare to look at Delores. His eyes searched her steely expression, but she gave no sign I'd convinced her otherwise. My father flicked his head. The guards understood the gesture and released their bruising grip on my biceps. I rubbed my arm, and it felt the entire community waited for his response. Did they believe it? After the monster and my mother's shape-shifting, it wouldn't be hard to accept the king and former queen's quest for immortality.

And I almost couldn't blame the Fables for their desire. If they made it possible, I'd want a slice of that pie for my husband and my daughter. But my own immortality was a problem for another time.

"You told me the stories would keep us alive," Heath said to the former queen.

"They will," she confirmed. The harsh line of her thin lips broke into a laugh without joy. "In your story, you kidnapped your wife," she said. "What makes you think others will be happier? You know stories are lessons and warnings—"

"And means of hope," Scarlet said. Her voice inspired a flinch from Delores, whose nose looked a little crooked and fit her evil witch persona perfectly.

"So it's true," my father said, his face contorted with shock. "You had Tricia murdered and tried to kill Vivian."

"I tried to protect our family since Victor was too much of a coward!" Delores spat.

Heath raked his hand through his hair. The sky was empty, devoid of my mother's presence in only minutes. Though it felt hours passed as the people of the Cygnus community watched and waited for the next unbelievable event. Mom had disappeared from our sights, but Heath still narrowed his gaze toward the sky, forever searching for the woman he wanted to control.

Do the right thing. Why in the wonderland didn't I say it aloud?

I cleared my throat. "Look, King Fable." I appealed to his ego, a reminder that he had control of his title. I used it to ease the blow of what I had to say. "I don't know how you know about the story cycle, but you cannot manipulate—"

He shook his head. "It doesn't matter. Many of the stories are already written. I was to distribute them to be read as a gift to my people tonight. It was all Johnson's plan. He brought the magic to us."

A scream erupted from the crowd. Mutters and gasps rippled like waves of realization throughout the community. They didn't listen to their king but pointed toward the library. I craned my neck to follow the excitement.

The sunset finally pulled its last bits of orange beneath the horizon, but the night lit up with another fiery glow. The library roared into flames. A hollow scream echoed between the cracks of fire as it ate away the wood.

"The monster's vow," Scarlet said.

"What?" I blinked at her.

"He vows to kill himself. You really need to read the books," she said.

The monster cried out in pain, his last breaths a witness to the world about the dangers of tinkering with mortality.

Sea wind stoked the flames that engulfed the library. The fire lifted higher in its radiant glow of white and yellow, orange and red. Air caught in my throat as emotions spilled over one another. The sight of the crumbling building should have distressed me, but I found relief in the end. *Frankenstein* came to a close, and the monster brought the new books down with him. Fire would consume whatever Delores and Heath had written. And Johnson. . .

"Scar." I breathed. "Did you hear what Heath said?"

Speak of the devil. My father interrupted with a command. "Guards!" His voice was taut and strained, but more than loud enough. "Save what you can from the building."

My blood ran cold. Despite the wind whipping around us and the cool night air, the icy chill came from within my veins. *The hood is going to burn.*

What had I done? Did it end the story cycle? It couldn't be that easy or Scarlet would have destroyed it long ago. *Or could it?*

"The hood is inside." The whisper slipped from my mouth. Scar snapped her attention to me with her mouth agape.

"You took it off?" she asked. Her eyes flicked to my collarbone.

I closed my eyes and nodded. I couldn't fathom how I'd wrecked with the magic. What fate did this mean for me? When I removed it, I'd intended to return to the library, put it back on, and attack the duties that came with the power. I never expected to lose it.

"Will I have to wear the ashes?" I asked. It sounded idiotic coming from my mouth, but I didn't know what else to say.

"You took it off," she repeated.

"Yes," I said. I turned to her. "I needed to get Heath out of the story loop."

"But all the other stories—"

"I'll deal with them in ninety-whatever years," I said.

The twitch of a smile betrayed her. Scarlet raised an eyebrow and her lips followed. The sudden shift in her expression jarred me. "You're going to be The Keeper. For real?" Excitement laced her words and Wendy followed suit, smiling and babbling for Mama and Dada and 'Let' as she called Scar. It took me a moment to register that Scarlet had used a common slang phrase. She'd likely learned to say 'for real' from a TV show, but it was the using it correctly part that impressed me.

"The hood is burning," I said. I nodded toward the library and confusion swirled in my brain.

Scarlet laughed, and I almost smiled from sheer relief at her reaction. "The library isn't Mordor," she said. "The hood is indestructible."

My half-smile faded. It was indestructible, but like the One Ring, it could still get lost. *And fall into the wrong hands. No, no, no!* Suddenly, Johnson's encouragement to look in the library made sense. Only he and the Fables had access, and Delores wanted to keep us out, preserving her secret quest for immortality. But Johnson led me right into it. Right to the robe. All those creepy stares hadn't been because he wanted to leer at my breasts. Could Johnson see the hood?

I hefted Wendy higher on my hip and spun around. My father had turned to address the community, but I interjected before he could get whatever announcement he had out.

"Where is Johnson?" I asked.

"I think you've done enough, Mari," he said, affording me only a quick glance. I shifted Wendy to my other hip and marched over to my father. The fairy lights glowed at everyone's feet while the story aura stripped away around Heath. Color by color, the glow of his character sloughed off and disintegrated, leaving him plain. Without the brightness, the lines of his wrinkles became apparent, digging in around his eyes and mouth.

"I believe Johnson is stealing something extremely important," I said. How else could I describe it? My father and Delores, with her eavesdropping ears, couldn't know about the hood. I didn't trust them as far as I could throw them and, considering how I struggled to toss the robe, I didn't have the strength to fight immortality seekers over the hood.

Heath frowned. It was an expression that aged him. His glare sliced through me. "You stole my wife!" Spit flung from his mouth and I resisted the urge to wipe it off my face. Like mother, like son.

The wind picked up, twisting and tangling my hair. Strands caught in my mouth as I opened it to push my father over the edge.

"She never loved you," I said. Heath flinched in another twitch that resembled his mother. The curve of his lips mirrored the former queen's frown. "You stole her robe and forced her into this."

He finally flicked his eyes toward me, but I spoke before he could get an argument out.

"I have some good friends in law enforcement," I said with as much stoicism as I could muster. Detective Wilhelm didn't openly detest me anymore, but I wouldn't call us friends. "And Schwanna had a presence, and s driver's license, the whole shebang—what do you think the police are going to do if I tell them you made her disappear?"

Apparently, my father loved his garlic bread. With his sudden exhale, came the stink of the spice into my face.

"Nack," Wendy said. *Oh, gross.* Did my toddler take after her grandfather in more ways than hair color? She rubbed her belly with her palm and I could only imagine she'd smelled his breath.

Heath glanced at his granddaughter, then back at me. He might be family in blood, but Schwanna raised me while he was busy chasing both her and immortality. I owed him nothing, but I couldn't deny the twinge of disappointment.

Focus, Mari.

"Where. Is. Johnson?" I asked again.

"I don't know," he finally said after his throat rippled with an honest swallow.

I groaned, then searched my father's eyes. He hadn't promised to give up on new stories yet, which meant my job here wasn't finished.

"I'll be back," I said.

"Hey, I know that quote!" Scarlet said. "From The Terminator film, right?" When I turned, she met me with a smile. Temporary pride beamed in her face until she recognized the strain on mine. If she knew what I knew, she definitely wouldn't be smiling or thinking about movies. Of course, since our night out, she'd been free of the responsibilities and swung so far in the other direction I wondered if her lazy phase would end soon.

"I need your help," I said.

My father's voice boomed as he spoke to the community. Now I knew why he said he didn't have the talent for speeches. His minced words and pitchy voice botched the invitation.

The people had pressed in again, closer together to hear their king's words while the library burned behind them. Occupied guards weren't there to keep them in order or back from crowding up to the king. It would take them forever to douse the fire with the buckets of saltwater saved for filtration.

The crowd of people pushed against us, filing into the castle. Heath promised them an explanation and asked them inside to enjoy the food. I'd return to be sure he detained Delores while I alerted San Francisco cops again.

Scarlet and I shoved through. My lungs burned as we speed-walked like the old ladies do in Pioneer Park. Except the old ladies were faster than me.

"I have no clue how he knew about the hood, but I think Johnson tricked me into taking it off," I said.

The squeak that came from Scarlet reminded me of Cinderella's mouse friends. Did that make me Cinderella as I ran from the castle and the kingdom's ball? Not really Cinderella, of course, but I wouldn't be surprised if I turned into a pumpkin for losing the hood. What did Johnson want with it?

"Are you thinking what I'm thinking?" Scarlet asked between breaths. The crack of the flames ripped through the night. Wind carried smoke and ash into the sky.

"Johnson made the portal," I said, nodding. "Could he be a Keeper too?"

We finally broke from the crowd, and Scarlet suddenly halted. Heavy breaths left her chest rising, then caving. Her usual rosy, freckled cheeks paled to a sickening white.

"What?" I asked.

She pulled Wendy from my arms and glanced at the library. "Get the hood, Mari. Run!"

I blinked. The silliness, the jokes, the 'hey, this is your responsibility now' nudges vanished as blinding fear washed over Scarlet's face.

For the first time, I wanted the hood back. I wanted the strings dangling over my collarbone. This *was* my responsibility and I couldn't lose it now.

I took Scarlet's words to heart—something I should have done a long time ago—and ran.

Chapter 21

Once More Unto the Breach

Stories came to life, so why couldn't a cliche be real too? The sky joined in on a classic story cliche with a few tears of its own. The Northern California coast rarely got rain in June. *But this doesn't feel like San Francisco anymore, Toto.*

The guards paid me no attention as I danced around outside the library. *Where are you?* What *are you?* I saw no sight of the icky leather jacket and greasy hair. Everything smelled like smoke, so I couldn't sniff him out either. Not that I was a bloodhound. But since becoming a mother, I had a particular talent for noticing the stink of a dirty diaper and other smells before anyone else.

Rain droplets helped curb the flames and allowed me to draw closer to the building without the radiating heat that threatened to melt my face. I darted around the back of the building, where the hidden room had been. It was the first to fall, crumbling in on itself as the fire ate away the walls.

For a moment, I was back in Pioneer Park, stunned and too stupid to move at the sight of a figure in the brush. Then, I'd witnessed a man turn into a wolf and charge me. Now, I recognized the man who'd dragged my mother across the ocean and dumped her in front of her possessive husband. Though I suspected Johnson didn't care whether my father lived happily ever after. Had he been luring me here all this time?

"Hey!" I shouted. My voice died in the fire's roar, but Johnson's shadow moved. The cover of the trees blocked most of my view of him.

I ran from the library to follow him. Did he already have the hood? Was he waiting for the fire to calm down before reaching for it?

I jumped on a rock and stumbled off, following him. The memory of the look on Scar's face kept me going when my burning lungs almost had me convinced the fire had moved from the library to the inside of my body. My ankle twisted on uneven ground, but Johnson wasn't exactly in shape. I might skip yoga here and there, or always, but at least I carried Wendy and walked to work every morning.

Our short chase ended when I reached for the back of his jacket. My fingers closed around the fabric. He tried to turn sideways and jar my grip, but he stumbled. In a flash, we both went down, me refusing to let go of him, and him losing balance over a rock.

Pain shot through my elbow as the not-so-funny bone landed against said rock. Johnson scrambled away, but I reached out and grabbed for whatever I could reach. My fingers found velvet, smooth velvet that definitely didn't belong in Johnson's wardrobe. He had the hood in his hands.

Like two dogs playing in the woods, we engaged in a battle of tug-of-war. Johnson's wheezing descended into a wracking cough that weakened his grip. Thankfully, I had practice yanking a stubborn stroller from its folded position when the lock had gotten stuck from jelly. One of these days I'd clean the jelly off, but today was not that day.

I tumbled backward as the hood fell into my full grasp. Johnson struggled to breathe while the cough wracked his lungs.

If this were one of Scarlet's movies, I might have said a witty line about that being the reason smoking was bad, with a point in Johnson's direction. Despite the lie Scarlet and I had concocted for the queen about directors and documentaries, this was a grove of trees on Cygnus Island, not a filming sight.

I pushed to my feet. My elbow screamed while the pain snaked up my arm and into my shoulder, but I refused to let the hood go.

I'd never be as graceful as my shape-shifting mother, but I copied the way she slipped into the robe. With the hood over my shoulders, it sensed my intent and allowed me to tighten the strings into an impossible knot. And for once, it fit. Well, it always fit since it conformed to my will, but it fit *me*.

Johnson looked up, eyes wide. The sight of the hood withered away, and I felt nothing but the tickle of the tie hanging on my collarbone. Though the trees blocked most of the wind, the sea air still lifted the strings and swung them in one direction.

Pride would have me shouting at him that I was The Keeper, and I owned this hood now. Nobody would steal it from me unless they pried it from my warm, dead hands. Warm because if they chased me down to steal it, my body wouldn't be cold yet. The phrase always bothered me since I'd seen plenty of dead bodies and knew they take a full day to cool completely.

I pushed pride aside and dug for information instead. "How much do you know?"

The dirty rag he pulled from the pocket inside his jacket covered his mouth. He coughed another round as he struggled to his feet.

"You led me to the library and moved the book of fairy tales into Little Red Riding Hood's spot, didn't you?"

Only several yards behind us, the guards shouted at one another. They cheered for the rain that started pattering the ground with increased speed. The clouds offered their help, fighting the fire along with the guards. Leaves and tree branches only partially blocked the rain from slowly soaking us.

"You wanted me to find my mother's robe," I said, pulling the pieces together as I did with any investigation. Except for this one involved eternity and an endless cycle of life and death and sealed fates. "Didn't you?"

Johnson only scoffed. Or perhaps he coughed while attempting to grunt.

"This means you never served the Fables at all, did you? You betrayed my father when you led me to the robe," I said.

"As if you know anything," he growled. The curl of his lip reminded me of an angry dog. *He's not the wolf. He's not the wolf.* Instead of slowing after the chase ended, my heart rate picked up, pounding in my chest from the flashback.

He's not the wolf. But who is he?

Scarlet might have known something, and I hadn't had the time to investigate.

"You've been The Keeper for, what, a year?" he asked. After another cough, he hocked phlegm onto his tongue and spat it on the rock that'd tripped him.

"Tell me who you are or I'll tell King Fable you betrayed him," I said, taking a step toward him. Johnson backed up as if afraid of me.

"I don't care about him." He laughed, but the shine in his eyes called his bluff. My father had once said he saw Johnson like a brother. I suspected the feelings went both ways. Together, they were going to be immortal, a family forever stuck in the story loop by their own intentions.

"Then who are you?"

"Why don't you ask the Little Cloak Girl?" he said. Dark eyes met my gaze, and I knew he'd finished talking. His poker face rivaled mine as the shine vanished from his eyes and he took control of his emotions again.

Scarlet.

"Come with me," I said as I reached for the sleeve of his dirty jacket. I could sanitize my hands later. A gasp escaped him and he yanked his arm away.

"Don't touch that!" Johnson almost tripped on the rock a second time as he stepped back. The reaction startled me. Once I blinked confusion away, I reached for him again, not willing to let him out of my sight. We'd have a long interview together where I'd investigate his role in the story world and what danger he posed to the people who became characters.

"Wait," I said, but my hand missed his arm. He backed up to a tree and turned. Before my brain could catch up, Johnson had traced his finger in a crude rectangle, just large enough for his body to fit through. Tree bark opened in a window to the other side, a place I didn't recognize. The door glowed, but not as bright as the portals Scarlet could create.

The impossibly bright houses looked pixelated. A city hummed with life, but the people milling about didn't all resemble people. A woman wore what looked like fake, pointed ears and a man, too tall to be human, walked up to her.

I blinked, trying to make sense of what I saw. When Johnson stepped through, the glow on the tree vanished behind him, taking the portal with him.

"Ebenezer Scrooge." I breathed.

The splash of the rain against thousands of tree leaves mixed with the distant crash of waves on the shore. Both sounds melted into one another and sounded the same. The hood didn't keep me dry since it nearly disappeared once on me. All except the strings.

I reached up and twisted the tie around my finger, letting the rain soak my hair and clothes. I was The Keeper of Stories, but I couldn't do *that*.

The tree returned to its ordinary tree-ness, and the night struck me. With the flames tamed and the glow of the door gone, I stood in darkness. The irony of my mirrored physical and mental state wasn't lost on me. As a journalist, I looked for and pulled the symbolism from situations. If I were to report on my experience here, I'd say the answers I found only created more questions.

At least I wore the hood. I turned and hiked back toward the library. Though the rain helped, flames still clung to the walls. The roof had entirely caved in and left the building looking skeletal with its frame withering.

Did Frankenstein's monster intend to destroy the new books? Scarlet said he killed in revenge. I couldn't help but wonder if this was his revenge against the queen for forcing him to do her dirty work. Much like Johnson, did the monster believe he was part of the Fable family? From what I remembered about the pieces of movies and shows adapted from Mary Shelley's novel, the monster grieved his creator's death. Maybe he'd thought of Victor as his father.

My head hung heavy on the short pathway back to the castle. The rain had driven everyone inside, including Scarlet and Wendy. Or so I assumed since I saw not a soul on the walk back other than the guards tending to the fire.

With the sense of urgency that I had to free my mother then fetch the hood gone, exhaustion pulled at my limbs. Both my biceps and forearms felt sore from the weight of the robe, and my elbow still throbbed with my pulse.

I reached to pull the door open, but something caught the corner of my eye. A white, wet feather lay on the ground. The rain soaked it and nearly buried it in mud, but I crouched to pluck it from the earth.

The feather's smooth edges shined. I tucked it inside the front pocket of my pants and opened the castle doors.

Scar sat with her legs crossed and her back against the hallway wall in the entry. Wendy carried a peach with a bite taken out of it and strolled in a circle with her head tilted. The toddler version of dancing, plus fighting sleep, left her looking like a tiny zombie.

I bent and scooped her up, ignoring the ache in my arms and elbow. Before I knew it, she'd shoved the peach against my mouth.

"Mama. Nack," she said.

"Thank you." I took the peach and looked at Scar, who'd stood and dusted off her pants. Her incessant cleanliness was a stark contrast to Johnson. "You got her to eat fruit now, too?"

Scar shook her head. "I didn't get her to do anything. If you give her a little space, she'll make the decisions on her own."

Wendy had already found the strings and tugged on them before taking another bite of peach. She scrunched her nose as juice dripped down the fruit's flesh, but chewed and swallowed the food, anyway.

"I see you got the hood," Scar said.

"Yeah," I said. "I have a lot to tell you. But first things first." I lifted my chin toward the ballroom.

As much as I wanted to climb the staircase, snuggle up with my daughter, and crash on the bed for a long sleep, the night wasn't over. My father would give up immortality and I knew exactly which strings to pull to get him to do it.

Chapter 22

Heavy Is the Head That Wears the Crown

The chandelier glittered across the polished floor. Somehow, the mud from people's feet only added to the beauty inside the castle. The simple reminder of earth and reality left the entry and open space feeling cozier.

Conversation and laughter drifted from the ballroom where people enjoyed their meal of fresh vegetables and plenty of bread with garlic butter melted into it. Scarlet followed as I stepped inside the room. Like a wedding, my father sat at a grand table at one end of the massive room while the two hundred-odd other people enjoyed their meals at a round table spread along the walls. Vivian had designed the setup with the middle of the room open for dancing.

A man played the violin in the corner. I had to admit, the smell of fresh food and the light yet elegant decorations made me long for a simpler lifestyle. I survived San Francisco on too much caffeine, an unhealthy obsession with my day planner, and mobile food ordering. Something about growing and cooking my food interested me in a way it never did before. Of course, I'd return to the city where I'd be expected to answer emails, fight for my daughter's spot in crowded preschools, and pay for my car registration on time. If I could remember.

For a moment, I wanted to trade it all in. I'd take a small spot on Cygnus Island over the Department of Motor Vehicles any day. But the charm would quickly wear off for someone like me who craved to expose the darker sides of humanity. It was simple here, safe now that we'd arrived and put Delores and Dad in their places.

Almost.

Soaking wet, muddy, and all, I marched across the room. People stopped dancing and those eating looked up from their plates to watch me. I plopped Wendy on the grand table and she happily dangled her feet over the edge. She twisted around and offered the peach to Heath, but his eyes fixed on me.

"I know what you're going to say." He raised his palm to stop me before I started. "I locked my mother away."

The momentary shock left me speechless.

"I didn't want to believe it before, but now I know she killed Tricia and tried to kill—" His voice broke and he swallowed. With a shift of his gaze, my suspicions were confirmed. I followed his line of sight to Vivian, who stood on her tiptoes to fix a string of fairy lights that had lagged along the wall.

Whether he deserved a happily ever after wasn't my focus. I couldn't let my personal feelings stop me from using the situation to my advantage. Heath needed to promise to abandon the idea of new stories and leave people's lives alone.

"Good," I said. "I'll have law enforcement come and take her to a real prison as soon as I can."

"I can deal with her." He looked at me again.

"I have no reason to trust that after what you did to my mother."

He dropped his eyes and became suddenly interested in the peach Wendy had discarded on the table.

"But I know the story aura probably pushed you over the edge," I said, my voice softening. The plot of *Little Red Riding Hood* took a sexually harassing jerk with a temper problem and twisted him into a full-blown serial killer. My father's need for control sucked him into *The Swan Maiden* and deepened his possessiveness into a form of abuse. I could only hope that the absence of the auras would return him to a halfway normal human being.

"I will make sure Delores is arrested for first-degree murder," I said, not an ounce of leniency in my voice. My father's nostrils flared as he inhaled sharply. With his frustration apparent and me standing over him, I felt like a mother scolding a reckless teenager. "And you are going to swear on your life that you will never write a new story and mess with innocent people's lives." I lowered my head and forced him to look at me. It worked and he looked to be listening respectfully. Maybe I wouldn't totally fail at parenthood when Wendy hit puberty.

Heath frowned, but he nodded. "I don't," he paused. "I don't want to hurt anyone."

"So you'll swear it?" I prodded.

"Some stories are good—"

"I never said they're not good. I said they have a conflict. Look at the bruises on Vivian's neck. Frankenstein's monster almost killed her right in front of you. Do you want to risk that again? Once the story aura takes hold, you have no control."

He gnawed on his lip and stared at me. The added bit of control was the perfect bonus, an easy pull to remind him what he really wanted—authority, a wife, and a queen on the throne beside him.

"What if you made a mistake in the story? You might not use a lot of technology here, but I've seen some with the electricity and weed whackers. Those mess with the story cycle." I might have embellished the truth, but the lie was for a good cause. And this wasn't an article I intended to write; I reserved these words for my father only.

"Yes," he said with a sigh. "Johnson mentioned that."

"How much did you know about him?" I lowered my voice. This pull for information didn't require a harsh tone or demands.

"He had what the late King Fable called magic," Heath said. "He joined our community when we moved here from Arizona. Johnson helped us create the stories and gave us a way in and out of these walls. That's all I know."

I nodded. "Thank you. So you swear?"

"I don't need to," he said.

"Heath—"

My father held up his hand again, not letting me interrupt him this time. "After today, I realize the crown and throne have nothing to do with the magic. It all belonged to Johnson."

The violinist ended a song with a fast rhythm, like a bumblebee zooming around. The energy in the room slowed as the musician dipped the bow along the string with ease and a calming tune rolled out.

Absentmindedly, I reached to block Wendy from tipping head first over the side of the table as she reached for a spoon that she'd dropped on the floor. I didn't take my eyes off my father, who raked his fingers through his hair and took a deep breath.

Heath had nothing left. With Johnson's disappearance, the books burned, and *The Swan Maiden* over, he'd lost everything that he'd once controlled. Everything except the community itself. Wendy rolled onto her stomach and grabbed a jelly biscuit off Heath's plate. She stuffed it into her mouth, leaving crumbs and streaks of purple jelly across her chin and fingertips.

"And you won't try to become a story character?" I asked.

Silence fell between us. My father picked up the peach, then turned it around to scrutinize the full, unbitten side. When he turned it back, he frowned at the fleshy orange inside that had dried and brown.

"Depending on how you see things, stories are good. You said fairy tales are often warnings, but what is a warning if not something to teach us?"

I didn't deal with vague words and riddles. Maybe Scarlet did when she was The Keeper and I hated to admit I could be more like Johnson, who spoke simply and directly, but I refused to beat around the book bush.

"Does that mean yes or no?"

"No." He set the peach down on his plate where the jelly biscuit had been stolen by my toddler's hands. "It means no. I've had my warning." His gaze flickered to Vivian again. "Besides, if my father had insisted on immortality, I'd never have become the king I was raised to be." With a sigh, Heath stood and walked around the long table. Before I knew what was happening, he took me into his arms and offered an awkward hug that smelled too much like garlic. "Tell your mother I'm sorry."

With that, he released me and walked toward Vivian. I turned to watch him invite the decorator to dance and the entire scene looked straight out of a Magical Place movie with dresses and kings and fairy lights.

As pretty as it was, I ached for Kai and our little messy home.

Tell your mother I'm sorry? I'd never see Mom again, and I might have slugged my father for suggesting otherwise. But after how long Delores got away with everything under his nose, and how easily Johnson led him to believe he'd have the power to control lives once he became king, Heath didn't strike me as the most observant bulb in the strawberry patch. Or however the phrase went. Maybe Scarlet's confused quotes had gotten to me. Or sheer exhaustion.

I helped Wendy slide over the edge of the table and she walked beside me, slowly but surely, without holding onto my hand.

I'd had enough of the Fable family for one day and needed to return home to a Rowan. The thought of seeing Kai again after what felt like a lifetime inspired a rush of energy. If I had to track down Rapunzel and insist she let us use her hair to scale over the wall, I'd do it. Of course, finding fairy tale characters was my *job* now, my second —no, third—job after motherhood and investigative journalism.

No matter what, we'd make it home tonight.

Chapter 23

A Fool's Paradise

A year and a half ago, I killed a man. First, I shot him, then I sliced through his belly with a blade and gagged when his entrails had spilled out—me along with them.

My daughter walked over to the spot where he'd died. Though the space was open, the line of trees below us blocked the wind rushing up from off the shore. Scarlet, Wendy, and I took refuge from the whipping air while we waited for Kai to hike to the other side of the island to get better service.

The summer storm didn't help. As suspected, my husband knew where we were. Yesterday, he'd arrived with Detective Wilhelm, the only cop who believed Kai when he claimed his wife and child were missing. But after the detective found nothing unusual on the island, he'd returned to the city, insisting he didn't have time to spare over 'Rowan's drama'.

Apparently, my boss made the situation worse. When questioned, Pam had informed the police that I was undercover on an investigation and would no doubt resurface once I'd gathered vital information. Sure, I was dedicated to my job, but not that obsessive.

My husband had persisted until he'd found the small gate hidden by shrubs on a rocky area of the island. The gate led to a small cliff that dropped off directly into where the water crashed against jagged rocks below. Thankfully, Kai wasn't as clumsy as me and had climbed over the rocks and kicked through the gate's lock.

I closed my notebook since the wind flipped the pages and made it difficult to write. My list wasn't a to-do record or items of investigation. It was another journal entry. Someday I'd collect all the scribble entries across used notebooks and compile them. Maybe Wendy would read them when she grew up. She could enjoy this entry about how her daddy found her mommy trapped inside the walls of Cygnus Island. Kai had saved both of his princesses. Well, we'd saved ourselves then he'd helped us find the way out.

The purple pen ran dry, but I capped it anyway and tucked it back into the organizer with its colorful friends.

"Maybe I should have gone with him," Scarlet shouted over the howling wind. Between that and the waves crashing against the rocks below, I almost didn't hear the suggestion in her voice.

"Kai is perfectly capable," I said. "He's the one that found the entrance through the walls and got us out."

"I'm saying." She paused as she took a seat on the rock next to me. Wendy sat in the dirt and reached into the diaper bag. Somehow, in the dark recesses of a pocket full of crumbs and crumpled snack bags, she'd found a juice box. She struggled to her feet, the wind trying to topple her, and held the apple juice up like a prized trophy.

"Maybe I should have gone with him because I want to help," Scarlet continued.

I leaned forward and took the juice box from Wendy to open the straw and situate it inside the opening. After she grabbed it back, I pulled her into my lap and smoothed down her hair.

"He'll be right back," I said.

"I'm still useless, aren't I?" Her question came out with a sob. No tears shined in her eyes, but the emotion choked her voice all the same.

"No, Scar, why would you say that?"

Now sitting still, Wendy finally crashed. She polished off the juice box and her eyelids drooped as she curled up against me. I scooted closer to Scarlet and put my arm around her while Wendy cuddled my other arm. The bruise on my elbow had deepened to a colorful black and purple and, of course, my toddler wanted to snuggle up to that arm with her hand wrapped around my elbow.

"We're going back to the city and I don't know where I belong there," Scarlet said.

"You skipped the whole growing up and having to find yourself phase," I said. "Maybe that's what you're doing now."

"I know who I am," she clarified. "But who I am doesn't fit into twenty-first-century San Francisco. I'm only good at two things."

"Misquoting phrases and watching TV?" I joked, hoping to lighten the mood. Exhaustion mixed with chilly wind and a restless toddler does a number on a lady's mood.

"Classic literature and hunting villains."

I licked my lips to defend against the drying wind, but it only made my hair stick to my mouth. One strand at a time, I peeled the hair off.

"So you can be an English professor or—"

"I got it!" Kai's voice stopped me.

We both turned to see my husband dodging rocks as he made his way back toward us. The uneven ground demanded he watch where he stepped to avoid spraining an ankle or slipping and bruising his tail-bone as I did too often.

Kai offered his hand to help me up, then slung the diaper bag over his shoulder. "A ferry will be here in twenty minutes. We need to make it over to the shore on the other side."

I stood and adjusted Wendy in my arms. Her head snuggled into my neck and her arms draped over my shoulders.

Once we made it around to the other side, the light from the ferry greeted us. In approximately five minutes, it would pull close enough for us to board and we'd be off Cygnus Island. Which meant in another thirty minutes, we'd be home.

"I thought the ferry to Alcatraz only ran once in the morning and once at night?" I said. My watch battery had died long ago and, without the charger and my phone, I didn't have an exact time, but the last I looked at Kai's phone, it was well past midnight.

"I may have called in a favor with the captain," he said.

Wendy snorted and adjusted her head, turning in the other direction, then settling back to drool on the base of my neck. We climbed down the side of the island, one careful step at a time, and made it to the wooden pier.

"You have the boat captain on speed dial?" I asked.

"Close," Kai said. "When he took me out here the first time, I bribed him to let me contact him. He may or may not be under the impression that the amazing investigative journalist I'm married to will write an article on ferry captains."

"Kai!" I tried to swat at him, but it wasn't worth the risk of waking Wendy. The wooden pier creaked under our footsteps.

"What?" he said. "I figured you could use something simple and mundane to report on after this wild adventure." He waved his hand in the general direction of the island as we stepped onto the ferry.

The captain didn't waste a second before setting off toward Pier 99. I plopped into a chair and let my head fall toward my husband's shoulder. He wasn't wrong. Researching and reporting on something simple, like the life of a ferry captain, sounded like the perfect escape from murders and monsters. Plus, it'd be a nice nod to the people of Cygnus. But that part was just for me to know.

Despite the howling wind and my groaning stomach, I drifted. One minute I was lying on Kai's shoulder, the next falling from the wolf's stomach. Blood and guts surrounded me and the horrible twist of fear knotted in my belly. My elbow crashed into the rocky ground and sent a jolt of pain up through my shoulder and neck.

"I killed, so I must be killed." The monster's voice sounded clear as it cut through the roaring wind.

I looked up from where I lay in the shadow of Frankenstein's creation. The beat of white swan wings caught my eye, and I tore my gaze from the face of the missing mechanic. The monster reached up impossibly high and ripped my mother from the sky.

He threw her at my feet and crouched, forcing me to look into his dead eyes. The monster wasn't alive, not really. He was an amalgamation of other people risen and kept alive by the power of the story aura so *Frankenstein* could cycle into the real world for the second time in history.

"You will not stop, Keeper."

I heard his voice in my head, but his lips didn't move. The vision of his face blurred, and I barely recognized where the sound came from.

"You will never stop. The cycle never ends and you're The Keeper now. You're immortal."

A gasp startled me. I jolted pin-straight in my seat. The ferry pulled into Pier 99. Scarlet was slumped across from me, curled with her face tucked into the hood of her sweatshirt to block the wind.

"What's wrong?" Kai asked. "You're sweating. Was it a nightmare?"

"Something like that," I said between breaths. Wendy moved to get comfortable again. In the fifteen minutes it took to sail to San Francisco, I'd slipped into a restless sleep. The hollowness in my stomach ached and my heart joined it.

I couldn't look at Wendy or Kai right now, not when the realities of immortality slapped me in the face. They'd grow up and grow old while I looped. Realistically, it was my hair that slapped my cheeks and eyes. I shook the dark locks from my face and stared at the pier. My chest constricted, and a lump thickened in my throat. I didn't have the energy to cry. I considered my father's quest, my grandmother and grandfather's desperation for a life that never ends.

If I could find that for Wendy and Kai, I would take it in a heartbeat. But I'd never send innocent people to their death to get it. So it was just me. I'd enter the next century to fight all the hundreds of thousands of villains over countless stories, alone.

"Mari," Kai said. He'd offered his hand to help me up. "Are you okay?"

I grunted and shifted Wendy to my hip and allowed my husband to pull us up with my free hand.

"I don't know," I said.

"The bad dream?"

"A never-ending bad dream," I corrected.

Kai's brow twitched in concern. He put his arm around me and pulled me in for a kiss on the temple as we exited the boat with Scarlet in tow behind us.

The sight of our car parked at the meter along the road soothed me. It was the first thing of home I'd seen in three days but it came with a pile of tickets for overparking.

The familiar smell of stale coffee and old potato chips welcomed me as I lifted Wendy into her car seat. I climbed in and collapsed on the passenger seat.

Like with all the new stories I'd maybe, possibly added to the story cycle, my immortality was a problem for tomorrow. Tonight, I'd sleep and when I woke, I'd do what I do best—investigate. Except for this time, I didn't have a dead body. I had dozens of stories with characters come to life, a missing Johnson, and one big question.

Who or what determines which stories are classics and become real?

Chapter 24

All's Well That Ends Well

In the wee hours of the morning, I snuck out to the porch. Waking Kai or Wendy after the long night wasn't a risk I was willing to take. Despite my lack of rest, I couldn't sleep knowing I had information about the missing persons case. The other line trilled and trilled until Detective Wilhelm answered with a grumpy greeting.

"What is it, Rowan?" he asked.

I paced the short length of the porch and dove into the details. The phrase 'mad scientist' may have slipped into my explanation. The detective complained about another boat trip to the island after Kai had dragged him out there, but he was silenced when I told him where to find most of the mechanic's missing body and Travis Young's limbs.

Below the porch, car engines roared as the city woke. Traffic picked up on Main street as the sun lifted and brought its glow to the horizon. I leaned my bruise-less elbow against the porch wall and watched the cars honk at one another on their rush to work or the gym or wherever they headed before seven in the morning. The smell of exhaust made me miss the mixture of fresh soil and baked bread on Cygnus Island.

"Delores Fable is detained by Heath Fable and awaiting retrieval from law enforcement," I said.

Silence on the other line told me the look on the detective's face. I guessed it was a combination of shock and confusion with a dash of disgust. My foot tapped for a physical release of the tension.

"Their names are Fable?" he asked. "Did I hear that right?"

"Yes, unfortunately. And another man named Johnson, but he got away."

The worst part was, the detective likely didn't believe me. Maybe I'd lost my mind or was desperate for attention. I knew those thoughts crossed his mind and I couldn't blame him. But he needed to believe me. I needed the detective's help. Despite Johnson's claim, Scarlet, or the Little Cloak Girl, didn't know who he was. When I'd asked, she'd insisted she didn't recognize him.

A driver beeped at another car for not using their blinker before shifting lanes. Pedestrians took to the sidewalks and carried their disposable cups of coffee to their destinations. The cup would later be discarded on the ground or fall from overfilled trash cans.

"Will you go to the island?" I asked.

A rush of air blew into the speaker and I almost thought I could hear the crash of waves from our condo. The detective had sighed into the phone and followed it with a groan.

"Yes," he said. "I'll go. You were right about Travis Young's girl-friend. She was a pain, but definitely not a killer. We caught her and her brother on a security camera buying booze at a drugstore at the approximate time of Young's death."

I wanted to add to the detail of the unlikeliness that a tiny girl like her could chop off her boyfriend's limbs and drag his body across the ocean even with the help of her brother. But I stayed quiet and relished in the detective's unspoken words. *You haven't steered me wrong yet, Rowan.*

Lucky for him, I did most of his job. This meant I might need to hire an assistant soon, someone I could train to become my partner with since Kai was busy with a passion of his own. Even with the extra help, my husband would still be the best brainstormer to bounce theories off of.

With the sun higher now, I could see the rim of the beige sky hovering over the city. Pollution sealed around us like the glass of a dirty snow globe. But San Francisco had beauty too if you knew where to look.

"Is Johnson a first name or last name?" he asked. I could hear the scratch of lead against paper. That was one habit the detective and I had in common: old-fashioned, handwritten note-taking. I watched two women hug on the sidewalk below. Their laughs echoed and mixed with the echo of sirens in the distance. An elderly man greeted a mother who jogged with her baby stroller. The good mixed with the bad. The city didn't try to be anything other than what it was. Maybe I'd vow to slow down and acknowledge that once in a while.

"Unclear," I said. "But I can give a description to the sketch artist at the station."

With a sketch, I'd have more eyes watching for Johnson's whereabouts than only myself and my prospective partner.

The doorbell rang, and I jumped, not from the sound but that it might wake Wendy.

"Call me when you get the body to the medical examiner," I said. "Please."

The detective grumbled in agreement, and I tapped the red circle on my screen. I slid the glass door on its track and hurried inside. Plastic toys, board books, baby butt wipe bags, and unused diapers were scattered across the floor. I dodged them and almost made it to the front door without triggering a toddler alarm, AKA the chime of a toy or rustle of a snack bag.

My foot came down on something spiky and I jumped forward, crashing into a pile of toys. I glanced back to see the doll brush laying in my path with the bristles up. A stuffed dog barked as I tripped and knocked it with my foot. Why couldn't Wendy like quiet animals like stuffed bunnies? I froze and waited for the sound of her cry or the call of 'Mama' from her crib.

My heart leaped into my throat as the doorbell rang throughout the house again.

"Ebenezer Scrooge, don't you know I have a child sleeping in here?" I muttered and yanked the door open. I expected to see our older neighbor Tala, ready to offer a cup of tea for an answer about where I'd been the past few days. She put her nose where it didn't belong, but at least she'd bring a warm beverage when she did it.

Instead, a mess of red curls pushed past me and into the living room. Scarlet slumped on the chair beside the couch and ruffled both hands through her hair. The movement only thickened the mess with tangles and frizz.

I closed the door and furrowed my brow. "Scar. . . Are you okay?"

She huffed and tossed her head back, throwing the hair from her face. "I can't do a horse's tail."

"Excuse me?" I asked as I hopped from open floor space to open floor space like my living room was a forest and the piles of mess a river.

"The hairstyle," Scarlet said.

Once I'd successfully made it to the couch, déjà vu hit me. Nearly two years ago, we sat in these exact spots—my butt on the imprint of the couch's left side and Scarlet in the chair. We'd come to the end of *Little Red Riding Hood* then and now we successfully navigated *The Swan Maiden* and *Frankenstein*. I couldn't help but wonder what three stories we'd be tackling in another year.

And, for the first time, the thought of a future as The Keeper didn't make me want to wet my pants. Of course, I had plenty of diapers laying around just in case.

"Umm," I said, settling into the worn couch cushions. It felt good to know Detective Wilhelm had my information on the investigation and would close the case. I could finally relax. And focus. My scattered brain forgot the topic of our conversation.

"Are you awake, Mari?" Scar asked.

"What?" I sat up. "Yeah. The horse carriage."

"Hairstyle!" She corrected me. Oh, how the tables had turned. Or twirled or twisted, according to Scar's misquoted attempts at the phrase. She needed me now.

"Oh," I said, my mind catching up. "Right. A ponytail."

Scar nodded and shook her hands through her hair. The curls

doubled in volume from frizz and static electricity. At this rate, her head could power half of San Francisco's grid. "My hair is broken."

"Wait, my husband is a history buff," I said with narrowed eyes. "I happen to know ponytails have existed since ancient Greece. How do you not know the name of it or how to wear it?"

The question earned me a death glare that curled into the hint of a pout. I didn't know whether Scarlet had taught Wendy the look or the other way around. Either way, I knew the disappointment went deeper than broken hair. With Wendy, pouting often meant she needed sleep or a snack. Unfortunately, Scar was a bit more complex.

"I spent centuries going from story to story. I barely had time to eat or sleep, much less learn hair or fashion or anything. And with the hood, I didn't need to. I wore the same thing and my hair never changed." Her gaze dropped to her hands in her lap. The mismatched clothes reminded me of some of the older kids at Wendy's daycare who clearly went through independence-flexing phases and insisted on dressing themselves.

I still wasn't buying it. The hair looked a mess and likely drove her bananas when it hung in her face, but it was a symptom of a bigger problem.

Kai's snores from the bedroom came through the closed door in muffled sounds. I resisted the urge to make a joke to lighten the mood. But Scarlet came to me with a concern, and not everybody dealt with stress through sarcasm as I did.

I scooted to the edge of the cushion and gave her my full attention. Despite the surrounding mess, I didn't need to look at her through a toilet paper tube. She had my full attention.

"What's going on, Scar?"

She shook her head and tried to smooth her hair. "I told you." A thick rubber band fell limply in her fingers. "Also, this hurts."

I stood and walked around behind the chair, picked up the doll brush, and told Scarlet to sit up. Her large loopy curls had loosened with length, but her lack of hair care left them tangled. I started from the bottom and moved up to avoid any pull on her scalp.

"First," I said. "This looks more like a tourniquet than a rubber band. You need a hair tie." I slipped off the one I wore on my wrist for emergency half-ponytails when I changed a diaper or inspected a dead body. After carefully brushing, I pulled her hair in a bunch and wrangled the hair tie around it. "There."

Scarlet twisted in the chair to look at me. "Thank you," she said. "The truth is, I'm panicking."

Hey, that's my job. But I stayed quiet, only furrowing my brow.

"You took the hood off and now the monsters on TV will spill over into our world."

"Hey, you actually called it TV," I said."

"Do you realize how bad this is?" she asked. Her frown told me she didn't appreciate that I wasn't ready to face the consequences of the decision I'd made. This century's cycle was set. I had ninety-eight years to prepare for all the stories in the next cycle.

I twirled my finger above her head. "Turn back around. Your ponytail is sideways."

"Mari, you're not listening!" she snapped but did as I said. I gently untwisted the hair tie and raked the brush through her hair again.

"I know," I said. "I messed up. But it's already done."

"Messed up?" She laughed without joy. The movement of her head caused me to brush a little too hard, and the bristles caught in another tangle. "I don't think you understand. These past two years have been quiet. The story aura doesn't always space characters out. Sometimes you'll have dozens or hundreds to deal with in just a few years."

"I'll make it work," I said, pulling on the brush.

"I hadn't taken it off since the eighteen hundreds when Jane Austen was writing romances. You didn't even want to deal with Frankenstein's monster. Are you really ready to fight aliens and that horrible creature with eyeballs in his hands?" Her shoulders shuddered.

"Did you watch Pan's Labyrinth?" I asked.

"I mistook it for Peter Pan," she said with a shrug. The simple gesture quickly turned tense when she turned and narrowed her eyes at me. "The point is, this is a disaster. You *messed up* worse than you can even imagine."

I grit my teeth and continued brushing. If I yanked harder now, I didn't notice. Or maybe I did. For the first time in a long time, I wasn't worried because I'd finally come to terms with the hood. But Scar seemed determined to change that with her harsh words and sharp tone.

"The stories are only getting more confusing and intense with modern society," she said. I kept brushing and tugging the hair back until I snapped the hair tie around it. Tangles still plagued the back of the ponytail, so I wrapped my hand around the hair tie to keep the style in place while I brushed the tail.

"Think about how invasive technology will become ninety-eight years from now. Classic stories don't stand a chance," she said. "You don't read literature and look where that got you with your mother's fairy tale. It took you forever to piece it together when it should have gone much quicker since you knew your mother so well. Now it won't be possible to read all the books because there are too many. You'll definitely fail–"

"You won't even be there, so what do you care?" I interrupted. The brush came free from her tangles with a swift pull. Scarlet yelped and slapped her palm against her scalp. The look of shock melted and her gaze dropped to a pile of books on the floor. Even in a ponytail, her long hair tumbled down her back. I secured the tie lower on the back of her head so the thick hair wouldn't pull heavy against her scalp.

"Mama." Wendy's voice echoed from her bedroom. "Mama." The second call came louder. I dropped the brush in Scarlet's lap and hurried to Wendy's room. She stood against the railing in her crib and reached grabby hands for me. I lifted her over the railing and carried her into the kitchen.

"Down," she said. "Down, Mama."

Surprised, I smiled. After bending and placing her on the floor, Wendy noticed Scarlet. My daughter squealed and toddled into the living room on her own. The maze of toys and mess didn't help with her unsteady gait, but she made it to the Coffee Table of Evidence and reached for Scar to lift her into her lap. A few days ago I was paranoid Wendy didn't develop on time. Now it felt she was growing too fast. And I didn't have an eternity with Kai and Wendy, only with the hood, and myself.

"I'm sorry," I said from across the room. Scarlet had pulled the ponytail over her shoulder and smoothed it between her hands. It hung low like the effortless messy bun that had become popular. "I let stress get to me, but that's no excuse to take it out on a friend."

A small smile twitched at the edges of Scar's mouth. She nodded her acceptance of my apology and tossed the bunch of hair behind her. "You've never called me your friend before."

I shook my head and headed to the coffeemaker. "It may or may not have taken me about two years to get over the fact that you tried to lure me to my death."

The machine whirred to life, and I pulled a mug down from the cabinet. I selected decaf today, no need for jitters, and I'd put the to-do lists on hold. For now. The aromatic smell filled the condo. Over the counter, I caught Scar's wrinkled nose and guessed it had something to do with the memory of coffee's bitter taste.

"No cup for you?" I asked.

Scar scooped Wendy into her lap and started brushing her wispy hair with the doll's toy. The brush easily passed through my daughter's hair which hadn't filled in with thickness yet.

"Do I have to like that stuff to be, you know, a modern person?" Scarlet asked. I laughed, and she continued in defense of her perspective. "Everybody seems to drink it. There are entire stores dedicated to it. And they're everywhere!"

I dumped creamer and sugar in the cup, treating myself after the long week on the not-so-abandoned Alcatraz. After swirling the beverage to mix the ingredients, I took a long sniff, then carefully carried the cup to the living room.

"So, am I going to fail at being the Keeper?" I asked, after taking a sip.

"Not if I can teach you," Scarlet said. "But you have to read the books." Speaking of which, the pile of books caught Wendy's interest. She grew bored with the hair brushing and slid from Scar's lap. Her uneven walk stopped in front of the pile where she crouched to pick up the books one at a time and stack them in a tower.

Maybe I'd teach Wendy to clean up while Scarlet taught me Keeper. . . things.

"I still think you'll be utterly destroyed in the next cycle," she said. "Stories are everywhere in this day and age and now they'll all come true."

"You don't know for sure," I said. "Not all the stories from the past have come to life." The coffee gave me the courage to address the topic. No, that was a lie. The coffee did nothing. After surviving the monster's grip on my throat, I didn't feel the fight-or-flight response. A sense of hope for what I could accomplish replaced it. "Who even decides what's a classic and what's not?"

Scarlet raised her eyebrows, and her gaze drifted to watch Wendy build the tower of books. It threatened to topple with each book she added. "I never had time to research it."

"Let," Wendy said. Her pudgy finger jabbed at the cartoon picture on the book at the top of the stack. I craned my neck to see she pointed to *Little Red Riding Hood*. She couldn't possibly remember Scarlet when she wore the hood, right? "Let," she repeated. Maybe Scar's blood-red hair reminded Wendy of the hood.

"I think I'd like researching though," Scarlet said.

Wendy returned to stacking with *Peter Pan* balanced on top. The tower teetered but stayed standing.

I resisted the urge to bust out my planner and go to town. If I could find out what determined the classics in the story cycle, maybe I could reverse the process. I had ninety-eight years to find out, but that didn't mean I should wait. Besides, my planner needed a break. I'd vowed to slow down, maybe even be a little spontaneous.

"Perfect timing," Kai said as he emerged from the bedroom. Even in sweatpants and with his thick hair in a mess, I wanted to tackle him. His side smile beamed from me to Wendy. "I know my wife will want the afternoon to write her article." He looked at Scarlet. "But after that, I've planned an early dinner date right here in this living room for us, which means Wendy will need a trip to the park. Are you in?" He rested an elbow on the tall counter that separated the living room from the kitchen, and his hair flopped to one side.

"Kai," I said. "Scar won't have time for babysitting anymore."

"No, I'd love to," she said, then glanced back at me with wide eyes. "Wait, what do you mean?"

The drink warmed my throat and chest. I smiled and shrugged. "I was thinking about a trade. You teach me fairy tales and I'll teach you investigative journalism."

"For real?" If it were possible, her eyebrows raised even higher. They nearly disappeared into her hairline—a hairline that looked pretty good in a ponytail. And if I could do Scarlet's hair, I'd manage with Wendy's too.

"I have to get it approved with Pam," I said. "We've been short-staffed since Jameson. . . you know. But I still need to run it by her."

Kai gasped from the kitchen, where he dumped pre-workout powder into a mixer cup. The shake of the mixer ball danced around, knocking into the plastic as he walked toward us. "You're going to replace me?"

"Never." I patted the couch cushion next to me for him to come and sit. He obliged, taking a seat and wrapping his free hand into mine. "I'll need an entire team to help me survive being The Keeper." *Especially since I'll be alone next century. . .* I shook the thought away and focused on the present.

Enough of planning. Right now, that very moment needed my attention.

Chapter 25

Come What May

Buffy slew another vampire with a stake stabbed through his heart. A cheesy but lovable one-liner followed the violence, and I grabbed the remote to flick the subtitles on. Maybe I'd learn a thing or two from her hunting skills and I hoped to pick up a few cheeky phrases since I knew it'd make Scar's day.

Kai returned fresh from his shower after our alone time had left us both a little sweaty. I'd jumped from the shower early to make sure we didn't miss our food order. I'd pulled comfy PJ pants back on after the quick shower and had returned to the couch to wait for the knock on the door. Penguin pants didn't work for an on-the-job outfit, but they did the trick for seduction, mostly because they slipped off quickly— no zippers or buttons.

The smell of vanilla and almonds wafted into the room with Kai's wet hair. He scuffed his fingers through to dry it before reaching for the cup in my hand. Droplets of water dotted my face.

Kai carried the cup to the kitchen for a flavored water refill. "Are you okay?" he asked with a glance back at me from the kitchen.

I offered a sad smile and nodded. "I just miss my mom."

Ice clinked into the glass cups, and Kai carefully brought them back to the coffee table. "I know. It makes sense that she's a swan, though." He sat beside me and pulled me into his chest.

"Now that we know, it seems like it should have been obvious," I said. "Our family feels so small now." I sighed and dropped my head against his shoulder. "Your family is so far away. My mom's gone, and I don't have any siblings."

"I don't know what I would have done growing up without my sister," Kai said. "Grace and I got through some hard times together."

I gnawed on my lip and turned to look at my husband. A small smile quirked on his mouth and his eyebrows raised.

"Are you thinking what I'm thinking?" I asked.

"We can't replace your mom's presence," he said.

"Of course not, but if it's a girl or a boy, we can still name it after her." Giddiness sped up my words. They spilled from my mouth with excited fervor.

"I like the name Sammy," he agreed. "Are you sure you wouldn't be too stressed? I know you're an amazing mother, but you don't always remember that."

Scarlet and Mom's words came to mind. Both of them had told me to give Wendy a little space. A new baby would force me to do that. A week ago, the idea of adding to our chaos would have traumatized me, but with the chaos and mess came love too, and I had plenty of that to give.

"I'll be okay," I said with a nod. I cupped Kai's cheeks in my palms and squished his face together. "A little Kai would be adorable."

He laughed and pulled my hands from his face to wrap them around his neck.

At the precise moment our lips touched, the doorbell rang. Kai sighed, but when I scooted forward to stand, he insisted I relax. I snuggled back into my spot, pulling the blanket from the back of the couch across my lap. With his final testing week over and my case coming to a close, I felt good. Not perfect, since Mom had gone. But good. And I almost relaxed, as Kai had hoped. Plus, the view of watching my husband walk away in sweatpants was a bonus.

"Thanks, man," Kai said to the delivery driver.

The driver apologized for the late order. He explained the line to wait for tables at The Cheesecake Factory, went out the door and the mobile orders took longer than estimated. Something about the guy's voice sounded familiar, so I scooted to the edge of the cushion and craned my neck.

"No worries," my husband assured him. "Hey, do I know you from somewhere?"

The guy tilted his head. A faint brown aura glowed around him. His enormous nose and goofy expression reminded me of a cartoon character and he looked barely old enough to drive a car, much less pioneer an invention. *Wait! I know him.*

I stood and walked to the door. "You're the guy who built a sentient robot," I said. I paraphrased the title of the news article I'd seen about him.

He nodded and beamed a toothy grin. "That's me. Unfortunately, it only looked good on paper. Would you believe selling that invention didn't get me enough to buy a house here in the city?"

Kids bought houses now? Apparently, he was older than he looked. The guy scoffed and shook his bald head. The remaining fuzz coated his scalp from his uneven shave.

"Oh yeah, Creator Carlo, right?" Kai snapped his fingers. "I read about you in the news a couple of months ago."

I bit back a gasp with a chomp on my bottom lip. The name and glow combination sparked a memory. I glanced behind us at Wendy's tower of books that had stayed upright all day. The spine of *The Adventures of Pinocchio* showed in the middle with red and twirly font. Below the title read Carlo Collodi, the author's name. I turned back and stared at him, maybe a little too wide-eyed.

"I prefer CarloGM1881. It's my IGN," Carlo said, shoving his hands into his sweatshirt pocket. His oversized tie-dye sweatshirt was mismatched with the reddish pants and it reminded me of Scarlet's modern style.

"You go by your in-game name?" Kai asked, clarifying the acronym.

"Sure do," CarloGM-whatever-numbers said. "I've moved on from sentient robots, though. It's all about virtual reality now."

"Huh." Kai nodded, and I knew he'd want to dive into an hours-long conversation over the change in technology and how it affects humans. Something he liked to track in historical patterns. My husband was one of those old guys who'd talk your ear off without being old. "Is that like that new movie where the non-player video game character learns how to have his own personality?"

Carlo squinted his eyes. "Not quite. More like an alternate universe where people can hide and live. Like the SIMS on steroids. Of course, that'll be taken from me too. . . " His voice trailed and his eyes moistened. I'd seen emotion in enough interviews with victims' loved ones to know our delivery driver was about to cry. He coughed and cleared his throat.

Kai elbowed me, then nodded toward Carlo. "If you get bored with ferry captains, maybe you can write about SIMS on steroids." My husband raised his eyebrows with a knowing look. My expression likely revealed my mixture of shock, excitement, and 'oh crap'. Kai knew me well enough to know I could see the story aura on Carlo. As far as I could remember, nobody poisoned or ate or killed anyone in Pinocchio's adventures, and that left me with a twinge of hope. Carlo Collodi's stories would be the perfect practice to dig deeper into my role as The Keeper. And maybe I'd even help my yoga teacher find Mr. Darcy in *Pride and Prejudice* instead of actively avoiding it—and exercise.

The delivery driver swiped his sweatshirt sleeve under his nose and sniffed. "Do you write books?" he asked, looking wide-eyed and naïve. Another resemblance to Scarlet.

"I'm a journalist," I said. "Let me get you my card if you're ever interested in getting your virtual reality world in the news."

"Hey, wait," he said before I could turn around. "I think I have your card. Yeah, I remember delivering here before. You write articles and junk."

"And junk," I muttered.

The smell of Alfredo sauce and warm bread left my stomach groaning, but I didn't want to ignore the story character standing at my front door.

"Yeah." Carlo nodded, his head bobbing like a doll on a car's dashboard. "It'd be totally epic if you got my story out there."

I shivered at the word. The late afternoon breeze blowing down the open hallway didn't help either. I was really going to go all in. . .

Carlo shrugged and kicked at nothing on the ground. "A big tech company stole my robot design. They're gunning for my virtual reality world now too. Could an article, like, help get people on my side?"

"Um, I guess?" I said. What did any of this have to do with Pinocchio?

His eyes moistened again. The plastic bags full of styrofoam dropped to the ground, and he threw himself against me into a hug. His head only came up to my collarbone, and he'd wrapped his arms around me with my own arms pinned to my sides. I exchanged bugged-out eyeballs with Kai. The hood's strings dangled over Carlo's head, brushing against the fuzz.

"Thank you," he said. "Thank you." His sniffles broke the words into small bursts. I couldn't tell if he was crying or not, but something felt wet on my sleeve. "This is exactly what I needed. I'm so screwed."

"What—" I peeled him off of me and backed up to create a personal bubble around myself. Kai retrieved the abandoned food order from the outside of our front door. "What do you mean?"

It wasn't a question I'd ask any stranger or delivery driver or even someone I knew well when I needed my introvert time. But Carlo was both a story character and now a potential subject for an article which meant my introvert time would have to wait.

He stepped back and shoved his hands into the pocket again. The giant sweatshirt swallowed his neck and made his head look too small for his body.

"It's a long story," he said.

"I'm kind of a story buff," I said. *Lie.* But I would be, after some research, reading, and more time spent with Scarlet.

Kai squeezed past him with the discarded food and made for the coffee table. The pasta's smell almost intoxicated me as he walked by. I sighed. The background noise of another Buffy the Vampire Slayer one-liner reminded me of the night I was giving up—the night I'd planned on.

But life throws curveballs—or Pinocchios—and I couldn't exist inside the parameters of scheduling all the time.

"Why don't you come in?" I said. I nodded my head toward the couch. "You can tell me more about it."

Carlo perked up and nodded eagerly. Kai pivoted his aim for the coffee table and placed the mobile food containers on the floor instead. We'd need the space for note-taking. My smile offered gratitude to my husband for reading my mind. Date night disappeared, but at least we'd enjoy some investigating together. Maybe Kai could pull in the author's history and how that affected his writing of Pinocchio while I jotted down Carlo's modern details.

"There isn't enough food to share," Kai said. "I'm going to order more." He snorted a laugh and held up his phone with the screen facing me. "Look at me, ordering food for the guy who delivered our ordered food. Meta, right?"

I smiled and shook my head at the attempted cheesy dad-joke, considering a metaverse was basically what Carlo had created. Or so it seemed.

By the time the second delivery driver arrived, I'd concocted a few theories. I kept them to myself for now. Pinocchio didn't know about himself and didn't need to know that I knew. *Talk about meta.* So I took down the details about his case and the threat the big tech company posed to his design.

Carlo explained that people hid from reality in the world he'd created. It sounded as simple as a video game until he claimed people could create simulated bodies for the avatar version of themselves outside the virtual reality. The terms went over our heads, but I wrote them down for later research.

We said goodbye to our new friend Carlo and curled up on the couch together. Rows of colorful sticky notes organized the details, blue for the tech company's threats, red for Carlo's investment, and yellow for the situation's relation to the original Pinocchio story.

When date night finally began, Scarlet would be returning with Wendy. We had ten minutes to ourselves. But it didn't matter because I'd already buried the Coffee Table of Evidence in Wendy's copy of *The Adventures of Pinocchio*, a laptop I'd borrowed from Kai, my notebook, and dozens of sticky notes. A new investigation had begun.

"Hey, why do you think I could see the story aura at the island but not on Carlo?" Kai asked.

"I wish I knew," I said. "Scarlet's best guess about the new story glow was in relation to Johnson. We don't know what he's capable of."

The soothing circles Kai rubbed over my back helped my brain focus. It slowed me down and narrowed my thoughts to the situation at hand. Pinocchio had arrived on my doorstep with a story and a problem and I had every intention to solve it. After a quick cuddle.

I sighed and leaned into the couch, letting Kai wrap his arm around me. Still, my eyes didn't break from the notes.

"There are enough differences here to prove technology has changed the story. What was once a classic adventure about a wooden boy has turned into a science-fiction horror," I said as I sat up again to mull over the sticky notes' contents.

Kai reached for another piece of bread from the containers on the floor and nodded. "Who even decides what makes a story a classic?"

"Johnson? Aliens? My nightmares?" I joked without joy. "Who knows?" The lingering scent of Kai's soap distracted me from the sticky notes. "But it's only five minutes until Scarlet and Wendy come back. . ."

Alone again, I turned to my husband and pulled his face in for a kiss. He tasted like butter and we melted into one another. Before I knew it, I'd accidentally kicked my planner off the coffee table while climbing on top of him.

Our passionate kissing came to an abrupt halt with a thought.

"Ebenezer Scrooge," I said. "I know where Johnson is hiding."

Epilogue

Dear Journal,

I've come to terms with addressing you. We're friends now. Haven't I always been friends with pen and paper?

Let's get to the point. I've decided I'm going to kick butt at being The Keeper of Stories or die trying. Except that I can't die. Can I? Immortality is an issue for another time.

There's still too much both Scarlet and I don't understand. Johnson being one of them. The portal creation tells me he's another Keeper. Scar swears she's the first and only one but can't explain how she even came into the role. I vow to research this.

Every story has an origin.

I LOOK FORWARD TO SHARING THE NEXT INSTALLMENT OF THE SERIES, RELEASING JULY 5, 2022.

THE MARI FABLE MYSTERIES: THE PINOCCHIO PROJECT!

Emily Fluke

*IF YOU ENJOYED THIS STORY, PLEASE CONSIDER LEAVING A REVIEW AT YOUR FAVORITE PLACE TO PURCHASE BOOKS! MY QUEST AS AN AUTHOR IS TO MAKE OTHERS FEEL SEEN THROUGH THE ADVENTURE OF FICTION. PLEASE REACH OUT TO ME AND LET ME KNOW IF MY STORIES HAVE TOUCHED YOU. YOU, DEAR READER, ARE WHO THIS BOOK WAS WRITTEN FOR.

About the Author

Congenital Heart Defect survivor, Emily Fluke, finds joy and peace through the expression of writing. She is a strong believer that all stories need a little magic and a lot of excitement. Emily and her husband spend their free time wrangling two children and playing video games in their busy California lifestyle. Otherwise, you'll find Emily solving an escape room, running, or writing Magic the Gathering-based poetry.

To stay up to date on new releases and connect with me, visit my website at Emilyfluke.com or follow me on social media under Author Emily Fluke, or @emilyflukefairytales

with questions for Sandro. "You're in middle school, yes? University plans?"

"Fachmittelschule. I don't know what you say in English."

Sarah jumped in. She had been through this conversation with him. "It's kinda like high school, but for students who are going to be a teacher or lawyer or something like that. Sandro's an incredible artist!"

"Not so, Sarah, not at all!" Sandro, proving he was Swiss, was embarrassed by the compliment.

Unbidden, Gabriella swung by their table and set a Caffè Freddo in a take-out cup in front of Sandro. He thanked her and explained to the others, "I work today. Gabriella knows my schedule."

Federica picked up the disconnect, "But not delivering pizza?"

"No, painting."

"Painting?"

"Sort of."

Jenny explained, "He paints stuff at the skatepark."

Stonecrop understood now, why Sandro knew where the Naegeli was. "Tagger?" he borrowed Sarah's word.

"For work, yes. I'm not . . . you know, I don't *tag*."

"Graffiti, then. Like Naegeli?"

"Art."

"Well, now-a-days, in Zürich and elsewhere there's little difference, right? No fines and no jail," Stonecrop said, believing he was defending Sandro's interest.

"Not really. People don't like taggers. Come to the skatepark. I'm working on the sidewalls for the largest ramp. I don't do buildings or people's houses. Unless they ask. That would be wrong."

"And Naegeli's graffiti? Was he doing something wrong?" Stonecrop prodded, curious about Sandro's opinion, and what that opinion might say about Sandro.

"Yes." Sandro was unequivocal.

"And if one night a perfect piece of art were painted on the side of the Rathaus, should the artist be fined?" Stonecrop continued.

"Yes, of course," Sandro laughed. "But for perfection, maybe just a very, very little fine." Sandro laughed, pinching his finger and thumb together and squeezing his eyes. A natural charmer.

"And thrown in jail?" Stonecrop baited him.

Federica answered for Sandro, "Yup. Throw the key in the damned Limmat!"

"Ah, the artist would like the Giacometti murals," Sandro said and earned respectful grins from both Stonecrop and Federica.

Located in the Schipfe and near where the family had been hunting for the Naegeli was the Waisenhaus—a former orphanage dating back to the late 1700s, a portion of which had been redesigned in the 1920s by Augusto Giacometti. The dark and gloomy vault ceiling and walls had been transformed by Giacometti, who had smothered them with bright, cheery floral patterns. The entry hall was designated a national treasure. Today, the building was used by the Zürich *Stadtpolizei*—the City Police.

"The issue, my artsy-fartsy friend," Federica turned toward Stonecrop and had a sip of water before speaking further, "is not about the work in question being *art*. That's a moving target. The issue is about some idiot defacing another's property, about stepping on *their* rights. Artists are not angels, and they are not above the law."

Jenny yawned. "Sandro, will you draw me?"

"Ja sure, but I have to go. Sorry. I'm being late already."

Federica turned to Sandro, once more touching his forearm. "Would you like a private tour of *Blüemlihalle*—hall of little flowers? A friend, Vittore Vormittag, works there. I've known him since I was a child. He can give you *and* the girls a private tour. He's a police Kommissar, and he's a kind man. I promise he won't arrest you!"

"Yes, thank you," Sandro smiled. "I'd like that very much. Sorry, I have to go." He rose and made the round of goodbyes. The caffè freddo levitated off the table. The drink was weightless in Sandro's long fingers. On the way out he picked up the pizza at the counter.

"Show Federica," Jenny ordered her sister.

All eyes turned to Sarah. After a condemning glance at Jenny, she reached into her pack and pulled out a journal. She opened the book to a line drawing, done in a confident hand and picturing Sarah, easily recognizable as Sarah, slouched against a graffiti covered wall at the park. Her skateboard leaned against her leg; her helmet dangled from the tips of her fingers.

Stonecrop was floored. The quality and sensitivity of the drawing had the irrational effect of easing concerns he had about his daughter's relationship with Sandro. The boy had real talent.

A plaintive mooing emanated from Stonecrop's phone. The unkind ringtone announced a text from his ex, nee Matina Holstein-Scherer.

<<MHS: Stuck in Paris. A week; maybe more. Sorry! Girls ok? You ok? I worry about them in a strange city!>>

Stonecrop replied with a thumbs-up emoji, adding <<MS: No

problem. Zürich safest city in the world!>>

As Sarah's journal made its way around the table, Federica's phone chattered to life. Federica read the message and rose from her chair.

"Max. Shit. I gotta go. Vormittag's been shot!"

Käse

Stonecrop's concern for Vormittag was obvious. His daughters didn't know the man but knew their father was unusually tense.

He said little after Federica left the table and urged the girls to eat quickly. After he paid the bill, the three of them walked up Münstergasse to the Central and hopped on the Polybahn. The tram, a red parallelogram, was slanted so passengers could sit horizontally as they ascended the twenty-three percent grade. They rode to the top and walked the short distance to the hospital.

Additional security personnel had been posted at the entrance. Federica, in scrubs and with her pass at the ready, would have been admitted with a nod from the front desk. Stonecrop and his daughters remained in the visitors' area and flipped through magazines in German, French, and English. Stonecrop perused *Zwanzig Minuten*, Zürich's gossipy tabloid.

Three-quarters of an hour passed before a nurse retrieved them and guided the group to the emergency department's patient holding area. Vormittag was the only patient. His avuncular appearance defused the tension the girls felt from being in a foreign hospital and meeting a stranger who had just been the victim of a shooting.

Federica could not hold back; she laughed a goofy-from-too-many-hours-of-work laugh, and the patient laughed with her. Stonecrop watched as she read through the resident physician's notes. She smiled and coughed up the words in Zürcher German: "Käse! Wirklich! They were arguing about cheese? Why is that even *in* the medical notes?"

"Basta, stop!" Vormittag said, the English word sounding like "Schtop." "It hurts if I laugh. That is confidential information! I shall have to arrest your student doctor!" He had switched to English when Stonecrop and his daughters walked in. As a rule, he and Federica spoke Italian with each other. He had been born in Ticino—the Italian region of Switzerland; his wife and her family were from Palermo. After thirty years with the Zürich *Stadtpolizei* and *Kantonspolizei*, the man now passed as a Züri local and spoke the raspy local dialect.

The out-of-place festivity was Vittore Vormittag's doing. Even propped up on the bed and with blood seeping through the dressing on his left shoulder, there was a comic aspect to him: The pudgy penguin shape, the so utterly un-Italian habit of leaving his arms glued to his sides as he spoke, and a disarming moustache that bobbed up and down to a tune of its own.

Vormittag was every child's favorite uncle. Certainly, that was how Federica felt toward him. They had known each other since she was a pig-tailed teen, a time when she had been traipsing around the world with her father and bouncing between home in Firenze, Italy, and years-long stints in East Africa, Russia, and Japan. From Firenze, she accompanied her father on a weekly pilgrimage to Zürich where he would spend a day or two sorting out financial matters. At some point in this routine, a deeper connection arose between the pre-Kommissar Vittore Vormittag and her father.

To Federica, Vormittag's Santa-like eyes were gentle. Not so, to Stonecrop. To him those same eyes read your mind like a book and took your measure; they expressed intelligence and unambiguous authority.

Jenny spoke up, "Cheese! Käse is cheese."

"Ja, stimmt! Quiet right. Very good!" he rejoined.

Stonecrop looked to Federica for an explanation.

"The Kommissar's nephew lives close to the station. When the Kommissar went there, when he got to the door, he heard his nephew and a friend shouting and arguing, then fighting. He entered the room and was shot." To confirm the authenticity of the report, Vormittag's moustache rose and fell.

"Fortunately, the bullet did little damage." Federica put her hand on his good shoulder. She leaned over and faced him. "You'll be home tomorrow."

"Will you see if I might be released today?" Vormittag asked. "You can text me."

He was giving his personal handy number to Federica when Jenny tugged at the sleeve of his gown, the sleeve for the arm not in a sling.

"Can I see?" Jenny asked and pointed at his injury.

Vormittag motioned for her to come closer. Taking care, he used two fingers to lift the bottom of the gauze wrap that bound his arm and shoulder. He winced and then nodded for her to peek under the gauze. His expression implied that the opportunity was for her and her only.

Jenny shivered once, then asked, "Does it hurt?"

The moustache pinched against his nose as he nodded yes.

"That's so lame, you know, to argue about cheese. Seriously!" Sarah said.

"Ma certo," he agreed, but in a way that invited questioning looks. "You see, here, in der Schweiz, cheese is *very* important. I love cheese!" He looked at the girls. "You too, yes?" They nodded back. "Ja, and so do lots of people. But I am telling you a secret." For the punchline, he lowered his voice and made to look under the bed, a movement that, for him, was impossible. "Ten per cent of our own Swiss Emmentaler is fake! There are criminals who make counterfeit cheese! They pretend the cheese is Swiss. And there are thieves who steal cheese! The situation is worse in Italy. A kilo of Parmesan costs thirty-five Swiss Francs. In the last two years, thieves in Reggio Emilia stole over two thousand wheels!"

"What's a wheel?" Jenny asked.

"It is a thick block cheese that looks like a wheel for an automobile." He waved his good arm over the bed to inscribe the dimensions in the air. "A wheel weighs about thirty-eight kilos. They age in warehouses, for a year or two. Even banks keep them as collateral for loans to cheese producers!"

"That's two million, six hundred sixty-thousand Swiss Francs!"

To Vormittag's amazement, and no one else's, Jenny, without hesitation, made the calculation.

Jenny wasn't going to miss a chance to show off to her new friend. She was the class smarty pants, already taking online courses at Brigham Young University. Everyone back home accommodated her insatiable curiosity for all things mathematic. Three times a week, New Roaring Fork Middle School excused her from two hours of mid-day classes, at which times Jenny became the ward and darling of the coffee shop two blocks from the school. The owners gave her cocoa and kept an eye on her as she watched and listened to lectures on her laptop. Perfect scores on college entrance exams had already precipitated scholarship offers.

Stonecrop had majored in math out of laziness, as the shortest path to a credible degree. Doing so gave him time for climbing and his real academic interest—ancient philosophy. For him, raising Jenny was an intellectual adventure. He had switched from reading children's books to her at bedtime to giving her problems in number theory. Anything to stop her chattering and asking questions. The ritual was straightforward: they'd talk about a problem for a half-hour, she'd go to sleep, and at breakfast the next day she'd give him the proof or solution. If she got stuck, they'd warehouse the problem until the weekend. The arrangement wasn't ideal and more than once resulted in Jenny missing school because she had been up all night wrestling with a problem. The Stonecrop family never made a fuss over her extraordinary skills; Jenny was just being Jenny.

"Were they stealing cheese? Is that why they shot you?" Jenny was relentless.

"I don't know."

"Why not?"

"A neighbor called Stadtpolizei about the argument. The receptionist recognized my nephew's address and passed the line to me. The caller said my nephew and his friend were arguing—something crazy, the caller said, an argument about cheese. That's all I know."

"Who shot you?"

"No one." To avoid Jenny's follow-up questions, Vormittag elaborated, "When I entered the apartment the front door was unlocked. I heard but did not see the men in the kitchen. Through the doorway to the kitchen I saw gun on top of the table, and the men's hands. Two men. They were standing, yelling at each other, but stopped when I walked in. One of them reached for the gun, the other tried to stop him. The gun was knocked to the floor and discharged. My nephew brought me to the Spital. The other man ran off."

"Max has a gun. He lets me shoot it." Jenny announced.

The statement got Vormittag's attention.

"I know he has a rifle, a very specialized rifle, for biathlon competitions," he stated. He was familiar with Stonecrop's reputation as a biathlete and had heard from other Polizei who had seen him at the Schützenhaus shooting range in Albisrieder. The Kommissar had grilled Stonecrop about the subject during his investigation of a "terrorist" explosion at a farmhouse near the Schützenhaus. "Your father is a trained athlete and shooter," Vormittag explained matter-of-factly, an adult-to-adult tone.

"No. I mean, I can shoot a rifle. I'm a certified Junior Biathlete. So's Sarah." Jenny paused before continuing, as if what she was about to say would betray a confidence. "But I shot a gun, too—an HK. That stands for Heckler and Koch. The HK is hard to hold. You sort of squeeze the handle."

"Ah, I believe that's right. There is a model HK made with an unusual grip, ja? Probably too big for your hand?" Jenny shook her head, no. After Jenny's response, Vormittag turned to Stonecrop, delivering a wordless admonishment. *What in the hell is your twelve-year-old daughter doing with an HK service pistol?* And then, speaking to no one, "I don't understand Americans and guns!"

"I don't believe you," Jenny protested. Her voice flipped the direction of the conversation. The impertinent tone earned a sharp look from Stonecrop. Federica hid a smile.

"Enough," Stonecrop said.

"But he's not telling the truth!"

Vormittag let out a grimaced laugh—the wound annoying him. "I think, young lady, we have a place for you at the Stadtpolizei!"

"In jail," Sarah suggested.

"Quite the contrary—on my interrogation team!"

"That would be so fun!" Jenny was raring to go to work. She crossed her arms, ready for her first assignment.

Stonecrop had known Kommissar Vormittag for a little over a year, and during that time Vormittag had always been the predator, the formidable Kommissar making his victims sweat. Jenny had turned the tables.

A penguin like arm, the uninjured one, rose from the bed. A hand took a firm hold of Jenny's shoulder. "You are correct," he said as he leaned forward with difficulty. His voice was soft; they were face-to-face. "But in this case the truth is something which is inappropriate for someone your age. Is that acceptable?"

"Yes," she replied, and used Vormittag's words, even imitating his accent, "that is acceptable. Because it's the truth."

Favors

"Max, can we talk. Not long, five minutes."

"Of course." To give Vormittag the time he needed, Stonecrop asked Federica if she could walk the girls to the tram stop. They knew which tram to take and how to get to Frau Ott's from the last stop at the Zoo. He kissed each of the girls on the forehead. Sarah greeted the "I won't be long" by pulling back slightly, resenting the little kid treatment. Jenny blew a kiss. Federica said nothing. She looked at him over her left shoulder. The message: I'm not the nanny and I'm bloody working. Then, turning to look over her right shoulder and accenting the expression with a subtle bob of shoulder, she delivered a different message: it's been a while.

Stonecrop breathed in and audibly exhaled, resigned to the present course. He moved the chair closer to the hospital bed and sat, elbows forward and resting on his knees. He looked out the window and thought about lies, about how they corrode and eat away at people, about how they destroy relationships. Not a happy topic, and one that he'd done his best to avoid while his children were visiting.

The coverup he and the others had fabricated concerning the dramatic events eight months prior was full of holes. Proverbial swiss cheese. Half the truth could put him behind bars for years. And here he was, sitting in room with all those lies, sharing the room with the man whose job was to know the truth. *Breathe.*

Even worse, were an investigation to deepen and dredge up what had transpired in Mozambique, well, *that* would justify extradition. Max had hunted down, shot, and burned alive Alves and Henrique "Hennie" Couto. Well, the burning alive part had not been his doing. But he had been there and had been unable to control the blaze. They were both murderers, he rationalized, responsible for the deaths of scores of innocent people, people who had thought that the brothers had been dispensing quality pharmaceuticals from a trusted source, specifically—and that was his personal cross to bear—a venture capital portfolio company that Max had advised.

After exhausting multiple legal means—none of which were successful—to right the wrong his employers had abetted, he had gone underground to find the people behind the scam. That folly had cost two years of his life, destroyed his career, and contributed to the demise of his marriage. And then there were the unrecoverable hours without his children. In those two long years, he had done things that would have been, in his prior life, inconceivable. Against the odds, he'd gotten away with a litany of "crimes." On paper, at any rate, not in his heart.

The third person he had killed in Mozambique, his jailor, a vicious man, had attacked a house servant and charged at Stonecrop. Stonecrop had been armed, and let the man live long enough to know that death was imminent, two shots to the chest, then one in the head —*the Mozambique Drill. What kind of crazy fuck does something like that?* He knew the answer and the answer disturbed him. He was not pleased with himself. Nor would any authority in the U.S. or Switzerland or Mozambique regard the extra-judicial actions and executions as justifiable, even if, technically, he could argue that they had been in self-defense. There were no witnesses; the dead don't speak.

"Max?" Vormittag tried to get Stonecrop's attention. Getting no response, he spoke his name again, but louder: "Max."

Stonecrop jumped. "Sorry. Distracted."

"Your younger daughter, what is her name?"

"Jenny."

"Is she always so curious?"

"Always."

"Precocious, that's the English word, I think, with numbers?"

Stonecrop nodded. Vormittag was softening him up. May as well fall down the well. The room was growing smaller; Vormittag becoming a dark pool of water at the bottom. "What can I do for you, Kommissar?"

"Yes." Vormittag leaned this way and that, failing to escape the discomfort of the bed. He scanned the room and hallway and looked out the window. Stonecrop followed his gaze. They both ended up staring at the mosaic of windows in the office building across the street, witnessing the same comings and goings of people, but from different angles, and no doubt ascribing different interpretations to what they saw.

"Yes," he repeated, the conversation more with himself than with Stonecrop. "The department will let the cheese case . . . ripen." That got smiles. "My nephew and his friend are not important."

"The friend took the shot, right? Your nephew stopped him."

"Lorenzo didn't know about the gun. His friend—no name, Lorenzo wouldn't give me his name—was high. Lorenzo tried to stop him but was too late."

"Lousy shot?"

"Sì, lousy shot." Stonecrop felt like he could hear the smile. "Not like you, thank god."

They were still facing the window, not each other. Their special *lying* window. Why wouldn't Vormittag get to the point? Was he waiting for Stonecrop to say something self-incriminating? Was that an interrogation technique? *Fine,* Stonecrop said to himself, *I'll just shut up.*

Going elsewhere, Vormittag spoke first: "The problem is money, you see."

"Often is," Stonecrop relaxed with the cliché. "From bootleg cheese?"

"Yes. Lorenzo needed the cash for something else."

"And do you know what?"

"He wouldn't tell me, but I believe a woman. He is coming to dinner tomorrow."

"That leaves a lot of options, Kommissar."

"Yes, quite true."

"You inquired, of course."

"Certo. Lorenzo had little to say. His mamma is worried; she was present when we spoke."

Funny how even one Italian word personalizes a conversation.

Stonecrop, much relieved that their chat so far had had nothing to do with him or his past, mustered the courage to face Vormittag, turning sideways in the chair and putting one arm over the back and letting his hand dangle, at ease, in space.

"So," Stonecrop nudged the conversation forward, "there's something that he can't or won't talk about with the Polizei . . . or in front of his mother."

"Genau. Exactly, he is afraid." Vormittag had shifted back to

Kommissar mode, back to German.

"And you want to understand more before taking any official steps you can't back out of, steps that might get you or Lorenzo in trouble?"

"As you say, something like that." It was Vormittag's turn to look Stonecrop in the face. "Would you consider—"

Stonecrop interrupted, "You've spoken to Gregor and Claudia?"

"No." Vormittag offered no explanation. By implication, neither should Stonecrop speak to them. "Nor—"

Vormittag's handy—as mobile phones are called in much of Europe —rattled on the tray on the stand next to his bed. Stonecrop looked to the window again, as if by doing so he would not overhear the conversation, and then he realized Vormittag might not be able to reach the phone with his good arm. He picked up the phone, tapped answer, and handed it to Vormittag.

"Herr Chum . . . No, I'm fine . . . thank you . . . I have a minute, of course . . ."

Stonecrop pointed to himself and then put a finger to his lips to indicate that he did not want Vormittag to mention that he was here.

"Yes, I have. He is right here, with me."

The Kommissar gave the phone back to Stonecrop, having realized too late what Stonecrop's intention had been. His moustache descended in apology. He started to raise his shoulders but caught himself. To do so would hurt.

"Mr. Chum." Stonecrop made no effort to sound pleased to be speaking to the man.

"So thrilled to have tracked you down. Why haven't you returned my calls? You don't like me, do you? You hurt my feelings, Max!"

Stonecrop let him prattle on. This man was, according to Federica's father, the U.S embassy's in-house CIA representative. From his overt behavior, one could believe that Chum was nothing more than the bird-brained *Community Liaison Officer* his title suggested.

"Big party tomorrow night. I would so, so love you to attend. I'll send along an email with a list of the other attendees. Julius Baer will be there in force and, I hear, and looking for deals."

"Harry, I don't do deals anymore. That was years ago, my past life."

"So you say. Says here in the bio, though, Max Stonecrop, once a venture capitalist, always a venture capitalist. I refuse to believe a man like you is ever truly out of the game. Don't be coy!"

When Stonecrop didn't respond, Chum continued, "A minor request —then I do need to finish up with Kommissar Vormittag. Relieved he's okay. Ah, relatives do keep us on our toes!"

"Your request?" Stonecrop was keen to end their conversation, and keen for people to stop asking for favors. With Chum, he knew, any favor would have strings attached.

"Just this. Do you know anything about blockchain?"

The question broad-sided Stonecrop. "Some. Why?"

"Your old firm led on two blockchain investments here in Switzerland, correct?"

Stonecrop didn't bother to answer. The embassy commercial people kept track of all U.S. investments activities in Swiss firms. He knew that and so did Chum. Both countries openly promoted such deals.

"I need the teensiest bit of tech support—really, all I know to do is re-start my computer." The man audibly sighed. "That is, only if you have the time."

"Try the NSA."

"Very funny! No, the humiliation would undo me! We can pay, you know. If that's an issue. This is official embassy business."

"Can you be a little more specific?"

"If you're willing, I'd like the briefest tutorial on blockchain. A layman's recap, tomorrow, at the affair? Which is, I failed to mention, only a five-minute walk from your friend's . . . what's the name?"

"You're referring to Federica? Or the street, Susenbergstrasse?"

"Yes, exactly. Both."

The thought was not a comfortable one, that Chum knew where Federica lived and that she and Stonecrop were, as he said, *friends*.

"That lovely thing must join you; I insist!"

If you said 'lovely thing' to her face, that lovely thing would bust your balls. That was if Stonecrop didn't do it first. But Chum had said that intentionally. *To rile me, so I wouldn't brood over why you always seem to know where the fuck I am and who I'm with.*

Harry wasn't finished: "It'll be such fun! The Ambassador will be there, city fathers, and—ich drücke dir die Daumen—maybe a local celebrity or two. I'm doing my best!"

He must have just learned the German version of "crossing one's fingers," and had to show off. *Press those thumbs in your tiny little fists,* Stonecrop thought. He was weary of their conversation and offered a tepid, "We'll try." Fede, most likely, would be stuck at work and he could call Chum later and apologize.

"Dinner at six, then. Nineteen-hundred hours! I'll do my homework before I see you. Networking, cocktails on the terrace, we'll catch up after dinner!"

"Harry, wait! Six or seven?"

"My bad, goodness! Yes, *seven*. Seventeen hundred Zulu. That's easier, to use Greenwich Mean Time in La Suisse."

I can't socialize, Harry. I'll freak out. "We'll pass on dinner. If we show, it'll be for a drink only, at nine or so."

Stonecrop passed the phone back to Vormittag although he could hear Chum going on about something else.

"Kommissar Vormittag here. . . I know how important this is . . . We are, as you Americans say, 'good to go' . . . Tomorrow, yes, that will be fine. Tschüss."

"That man is an idiot," Stonecrop spoke as though he were addressing someone behind Vormittag. He instantly regretted having revealed his animosity toward Chum. And what, he asked himself, warranted the common interest of both the Minister of Fiestas and the *Stadtpolizei* officer? The more Stonecrop thought, the more he feared that what they had in common was him . . . or Gregor.

The phone made its way from Vormittag to Stonecrop to the table. The Kommissar reengaged from where he had left off, "I don't intend to . . ."

Still in his own thoughts, Stonecrop gave Vormittag a puzzled look, causing the Kommissar to hesitate.

". . . to speak with Claudia and Gregor, about Lorenzo."

"Ah, yes." Stonecrop had no choice but to support his friend, the injured penguin. "Of course I'll help, Kommissar. If I can."

"Thank you, Max. Day after tomorrow, eleven, at Stehli?"

Stonecrop nodded okay and repeated the time and place, regretting his sudden popularity.

Vormittag looked both relieved and as exhausted as he exclaimed, "Sono stanco morto."

"Did you mention the incident with Lorenzo to Harry?"

"No. Not a word."

"Harry mentioned 'relatives,' implying that he already knew something about the affair. He said something like 'relatives are trouble' or something like that."

"Yes," he replied with fading enthusiasm for further discussion of the matter. "Often the case, I suppose."

The allusion to Chum knowing more than he should have about Vormittag's personal affairs seemed to not bother Vormittag.

With stubby, wing-like arms pressed to his sides, the Kommissar leaned back. His eyes closed and his head sank into the embrace of the casket-like pillow, as if seeking eternal rest. Max looked out the window one last time before he left the room, seeking something as well, something he was sure he had missed.

Deposition

Why he felt rested the next morning was unclear. As usual, the nightmares had done a number on him. Then Federica's friend, Alicia Gilli, had knocked on the door after the he and girls had gone to bed. She had let herself in and stepped into the bedroom to wake him for a hello and goodnight bone-crushing hug—reminding him why her colleagues at the U.S. Treasury's Defense Criminal Investigative Service had dubbed her *la compactadora*. She had settled in in the spare bedroom and then, just as he was falling asleep, Federica had arrived home from work. It was one a.m. He heard her rummaging around the fridge for leftovers he had prepared. And then showering. He fell asleep a third time, only to wake up anew when Federica plopped down on the bed and tossed a heavy leg over him. She'd fallen asleep almost immediately. He had lain there, dreading another interruption and his nightmares on rewind.

Nevertheless, he felt rested. Moreover, he had awoken determined to take steps to get his life in order. He dressed quickly and was out the door, on to a meeting that was to be a step in the right direction.

Within minutes, he settled into the chair and let the cold wrought iron rest against his back. Recent conversations with Chum and Vormittag replayed in his head; his chest tightened. Either man had the power to put him behind bars.

Deal with it, he scolded himself.

"Some water, Hamdi?" The words came out parched like his throat.

Hamdi, his friend and the owner of Café Stehli, caught the eye of one of his two sons and motioned as if he were drinking something. Johan, sharp as the soccer player he was, picked up the signal and filled a glass with Hahnewasser. He knew Stonecrop preferred tapwater. Zürich's city water was better than anything that came in a bottle. Hamdi took the seat across from Stonecrop. He was frowning at an article in the Neue Zürcher Zeitung. The *NZZ*, Stonecrop knew, was one of the longest published papers in Europe.

Johan arrived with the water.

"Merci vilmal, Johan," Stonecrop thanked Johan and turned back to Hamdi. "I want to talk to you about something, a document I'm having drawn up. Can we do that?"

"I am listening." Hamdi Habibi put down the paper and leaned forward, the embodiment of patience.

"I . . ." Stonecrop faltered. His wish was that if he wrote down what had transpired two years ago, when he had been in Maputo, Mozambique, that the articulation of those events would put an end to that caged panther pacing back and forth in his mind. That wish had not been granted. There was another desire, a purpose, that was equally important. He sighed an involuntary sigh. "Hamdi, if something happens to me . . . well, anything can happen to anybody, right?"

The attempt to soften the antecedent fell flat.

"You are getting ready to confess but I am not a priest!"

"I've written a deposition," Stonecrop pressed on, "a deposition which I am going to leave with a trustee at UBS, the bank's branch at Paradeplatz. The bank managers know me well. I will give them your name and arrange permission to give you access to the document."

"I know the bank. I don't know what that thing is, though—a *deposition*."

"It's a sworn testimony, dated and signed by me, and notarized by bank attorneys to assure the world that I am the document's true author. Hamdi, this is a factual record of things I did."

"A story?"

"Yeah, about stuff that happened in Mozambique. Things that, if Fede knew about them, she would feel obliged to report to the authorities. I don't want to force a difficult choice on her, not now. And if I even mention the deposition, she'll insist on reading it. But I do want her and my daughters to know the truth. Especially if something happens to me. See the problem?"

"I will do as you ask. You are a good man," Hamdi tapped a finger on the table, "and a coward."

They both laughed, Stonecrop a little too loudly, then sat in silence.

"I am a man of faith, Max—in Allah, and in you. I am sure you had good reason or little choice to do whatever you did. My wise wife says that our regrets swallow us if we don't as well accept the good in our hearts."

The comment disquieted Stonecrop on multiple levels. He didn't want to rethink the decision he had made. Too-glib, goody-goody generalizations always grated on him.

"Is there more in this . . .deposition?" Hamdi asked. "What about that unpleasantness last November?"

Stonecrop shook his head, no. He didn't want to discuss the events that had unfolded soon after his arrival in Zürich. He'd escaped Mozambique and weathered an unexpected divorce. Then came a life-threatening ice climbing accident on the Sustenhorn and a heli-ride to the hospital in Zürich where he'd crossed paths with Federica for a second time. The first had been years earlier on the overnight train to Venezia. She had been eighteen; he had never forgotten her. Reacquainted in Zürich, Federica had helped him land a menial job with her father, a supposedly reformed Bulgarian thug named Gregor Ratzow. Within months of his resettlement, Federica had been abducted and there had been a brutal assault on Federica's friend and retired nanny.

That's when Stonecrop first met Harry Chum, then as now, a representative from the U.S. embassy. The nanny was a U.S. citizen and ostensibly the reason for Chum's engagement. The truth was that Chum had showed more interest in him and Federica's Bulgarian father than the welfare of the nanny. The complex affair had escalated to a deadly crescendo and was still an open case—and a potential source of trouble for Stonecrop if Chum or Vormittag were to discover details of Stonecrop's inculpatory involvement.

Of the two men, Chum was the greater worry. CIA resources obviously stretched to Africa and beyond. No doubt their database contained a file on Mr. Gregor Ratzow, and now, by association, a page or two about Stonecrop.

Stonecrop's mood darkened, a shift that his perceptive friend didn't miss.

Hamdi took his hand. The backs of their hands were crisscrossed with histories. Hamdi's smooth, the skin thin from age and the veins a deep blue; Stonecrop's deeply veined as well, but splotched with scar-tissue from years of climbing.

"I have all day," the patient man said. "That was the same time when the terrorist thing happened, yes?" He waved to his son and this time mimed sipping tea, his baby finger up in the air. Stonecrop disliked the affectation. Two minutes later, Johan appeared with a tray bearing a silver pot of mint tea and two Moroccan etched-glass tea glasses, warm milk, and sugar. Stonecrop said nothing. He nursed his latte and debated whether to switch to tea.

"The bombing," Hamdi prompted, "it was not far from where you go to practice shooting that rifle with the shoulder straps, like in the Olympics. What is the sport?"

"Biathlon," Stonecrop answered. "Skiing and shooting. I train at the Schützenhaus in Albisrieder."

"The terrorist attack, your deposition says nothing about that?"

The tactful Hamdi had pushed enough. His instinct that that incident might be worthy of inclusion was not amiss. *Plenty of incriminating shit happened.* But there was no need for *that* story to go into a deposition because Fede had had firsthand experience. She knew, and would accept the consequences, should there be any.

"No, really, I was as shocked as anybody," Stonecrop, taking his time, said. He wondered if the lie were as transparent and hollow as the words had felt. He was a poor liar and Hamdi was hard to lie to.

"I accept this responsibility," Hamdi announced with solemnity.

"Thank you, Hamdi."

The men shook hands and with their free hands reached across the small table and held each other's shoulders.

"Ah, the boss is calling!" Hamdi released Stonecrop's shoulder and his grip and waved to Sofia, his wife. He tidied up things on the tea tray, pouring and leaving a glass for Stonecrop, and rose from the table.

"She works me to death!" He made his good-bye: "Beslama, my friend."

Stonecrop drained his drink and stood, stiff from sitting in the iron chair. He twisted to one side, then the other, stretching his torso. He smirked at his own haggard visage staring back at him from the café's window. Then froze. He caught only the shadow of the man who had passed by behind him. He swallowed, unable to breathe, but didn't turn around.

No, it can't be . . . By the time he turned around, the man had darted into an alleyway and out of view. Max took in a long, slow, breath. He expelled all the air out at once, emitting an uncharacteristic, bitter laugh.

He's dead. And as for Chum, fuck him.

His phone buzzed against his hip. Tugging it free from the zipped pocket, Stonecrop started. A message from Chum: <<HC: Don't forget our date, buddy!!!>>

Ugh. I throw his name into the universe and the shithead hears me.

Zürichberg

More Alpine in appearance than urban, the Sorell Hotel Zürichberg is a 1900s candy-striped Art Nouveau affair with a contrasting, modern, drum-shaped appendage affixed to its west flank. The mix of old and new should have clashed but didn't. The newer structure's spiral walkway, floating closets, and naturally lit bathrooms placed against an exterior wall (a rare hotel-room configuration) were, and still are, exciting innovations. The slatted exterior was a nod to the Swiss haybarn and evoked the relationship of the barn to the manor. The Hotel borders Zürichberg Park and is, as Chum had noted, only a five-minute walk from Federica's apartment.

This summer Federica and Stonecrop had become Zürichberg regulars. They enjoyed an occasional Sunday brunch, usually with Frau Ott, or, when work schedules allowed, a quick mid-week snack on the terrace. The panorama of the lake and city rose above a flowered alpine meadow adjacent to and below the terrace. The view was as advertised, one of the best in all of Zürich.

Tonight, bellows from calves at the Zoo's Kaeng Krachan Elephant Park, white canvas umbrellaed tables with glass lanterns, and the orderly array of tiki torches—like fireflies in a marching band—gave the terrace a festive, safari-esque air.

Stonecrop's attempt to blow off the hotel gathering had not gone well. Tagging Federica with a label had been a fatal mistake: "You're antisocial," he had announced. "Watch me!" she had thrown back at him. And like that, Stonecrop had to scramble.

He had long ago given away his closet-full of custom suits. Not wanting to give them to just anybody, he had spent a weekend cruising homeless camps. He looked for settlements where the grounds were clean and needle free, inquiring at tent flaps and cardboard doors and

29

seeking occupants that could put the clothes to use—both men and women. He wrote it off and his CPA gave him shit for not having receipts. *Get real!*

The solution to his current wardrobe dilemma was a last-minute inspiration in the form of a suit from Herr Bachman. The owner of the gallery where Stonecrop did a little part-time work was in his late 60s and several inches shorter than Stonecrop; he didn't look like a good match. The difference in stature, however, was due to osteoarthritis of the hip, a condition which forced the man to bend over a cane as he walked. Bachman, when Stonecrop explained his situation, offered up a twenty-year old, light-weight wool suit, that he assured, with his gallery owner's eye, would be a perfect fit. He gave Stonecrop a key to his house, instructions about where to find the suit, and in a snap, Stonecrop was clad for dinner.

The suit was a classic piece made by a friend of Bachman's in Biella, who, in his seventies, had won the *Forbici d'Oro*, the Golden Scissors Award from the Italian Tailoring Academy in Rome.

"At his home, one day after a fabulous, family lunch—I think we ate pheasant and cabbage," Bachman had recounted. "Guido showed me to a large room with bolts of fabric, mostly wool, piled to the ceiling. Many were one-of-a-kind fabrics. Being in the Golden Scissors, one couldn't buy a suit from Guido. If he liked you, or thought you worthy, he would offer to make a suit for you. The timeframe was up to him. The price was up to you. Naturally, I paid him as much at the time as I could and that I thought was fair."

As handsome as Stonecrop looked, Federica looked better. Her dress, which had been a gift from her father, had been purchased in Japan when she was twenty. The under-layer was a handmade floral print, rust orange and rose with splotches of jungle green and was softened by a gossamer, grey overlay. A narrow silk ribbon ran over each shoulder and supported an archipelago of strung jade hung across the triangle of bare flesh on her back. Her hair, worn high, and, as ever with Fede, a loose tress or two, left bare the lean muscle, sinew, and bone in her neck. Wafer thin flats separated her from the earth; from a few feet distant she appeared barefoot. She wore no jewelry save a white Apple watch. Stonecrop was reminded of Degas' *Young Woman Dressing Herself* and the feeling one had that model's gown had just fallen into place and that the Kirlian negative of her nakedness remained. He considered Federica, at that instant, as Degas might have.

"You're allowed to walk around alone in public like that?" Chum asked. His eyes were reddened from drink or lack of sleep. He tried to look elsewhere but failed.

"I'm *not* alone," she flirted and lifted Stonecrop's hand to her breasts. The act drew the fabric tight against them and revealed a becoming form.

The three of them stood framed in place by French doors opened to the sunset and the terrace: Stonecrop in black wool; Chum in white linen, and Federica, between them, a floral shoot nurtured by the last wash of daylight.

Chum turned to Stonecrop. "Don't ever take this woman for granted."

"Highly unlikely," he replied.

"You missed a great dinner . . . and opening remarks by the Ambassador."

"Witty, were they?" Federica asked.

"As a slug!" Chum came back.

That got a round of smiles.

He could not have possibly heard the remark or seen the round of smiles, but on cue the American Ambassador pivoted and looked their direction; wine sloshed over the rim of his glass with the turn.

"Ah, the slug advances!" Chum whispered.

"You're a cheery group, what did I miss?" the Ambassador interjected with no need of introduction. Having finished his remarks and likely an excellent meal, he'd been basking in banter and white wine. Stonecrop saw and smelled the Chardonnay that has spilled on the French cuff of the Ambassador's shirt and his hand. That the man could have cared less about the mishap was refreshing and unexpected.

Chum did his social director thing, and made polite introductions, adding the perfect sound bite about everyone present. He was good at his job and though he seemed to be drinking constantly from something sufficiently poisonous, not wine, he was on his game.

"Tell me, Mr. Ambassador," Federica asked, threading an arm through the Ambassador's, "you were a biologist, a geneticist. Is that right?"

"I still am, young lady. Left the board, but—between us—my old firm is selling more GMO seed to the third world than ever. Keep folks from starving's what we do. God's work, and if nothin' else, I try."

"So I've heard. Well, I need your advice on two matters." Her attention focused entirely on the Ambassador. He was hanging on her every word. "Neither have much to do with religion, Mr. Ambassador."

"First," she said, "a girl needs a drink . . ."

The Ambassador looked around the room. Was he scanning for a server or his wife? His gaze rose upward, contemplating forgiveness for his thoughts?

"And second, I've got slugs in my garden, and I don't know what to do!"

"Oh my God!" the Ambassador played along, oblivious now to anything but this angelic apparition with needs that he was uniquely qualified to address.

"C'mon, girl! Them's both serious matters. Yer Ambassador's comin' to the rescue."

The man presumed Federica was a U.S. ex-pat—though he would be, Stonecrop was certain, equally "chivalrous" to any lovely woman. The pair marched arm-in-arm off to the bar, leaving Stonecrop and Chum.

"Harry, I'll give you a half-hour." Stonecrop nodded to an empty table in less lit corner of the patio. "Over there."

With little enthusiasm and in a monotone voice, Stonecrop delivered a thirty-minute tutorial on blockchain. His student, either having feigned inebriation or simply having an extraordinary capacity for alcohol—certainly,, a good quality for a social director— had excellent questions and seemed to remember and comprehend what he had been taught. To test him, at the end of their session, Stonecrop hit him an oral pop-quiz. Done, he thought, *Our man Harry has passed with flying colors*—again, a surprise. Chum absorbed information like a sponge. The skill reminded him of Federica and her effortless command of languages, medicine, whatever.

Federica arrived as they finished up and set three glasses of wine on the table.

"Thanks, love. You know, I'd like something stronger. Be right back." Stonecrop left for the bar. Not expecting to meet anyone he knew, he bumped into a Reto Müller, a colleague from his VC days and now a partner at HBH Partners. HBH offices on Lowenstrasse were right behind those of Fede's non-profit, Aide Direct. The men talked shop some, but mostly Stonecrop danced around questions about why he had dropped off the radar the last two years. By the time they had finished, Stonecrop was one drink in. He ordered a second vodka and headed back to the table.

"May I join you," the Ambassador resurfaced from his rounds, all smiles. "Amazing woman, that gal of yours."

Stonecrop sensed there was something he wanted to ask.

"She is. Of course, please," Stonecrop answered, and the Ambassador fell in behind him.

Chum rose from his chair as if to leave the table. He was facing away from Stonecrop and anyone else who happened to be on the terrace. What happened next was unclear. He stepped behind Federica's chair, put his hands on her shoulders, pressing down, and leaned forward as if to speak with her. His hand slid forward, and Stonecrop heard her growl, "Behave, Harry!"

"Well now, you know what's up . . ." Chum said, and slid his other hand down the front of his pants.

Stonecrop silently set his drink on the nearest table. In three long steps he was behind Chum. He grabbed the man's shoulder and spun him around. One of Chum's hands was still tucked in his pants, the other had brusquely retreated from Federica's breast. He grinned, put that hand to his face, and touched the tips of his fingers to his lips. A defiant and bizarre gesture of male authority.

"Whoa, Max! Assault will get you ten. Just having a little fun's all. C'mon, the woman's a Siren, I mean, shit . . . look at her!"

"Want fun, Harry? I'll give you fun."

Stonecrop was prepared to drag Chum off to the bushes and have a word. He backed off after remembering the Ambassador at his heels and noticing a group of people walking toward their table. The ensemble was listening to and laughing about something else, oblivious to Chum's misdeed.

Federica rose. She straightened the top of her dress and retrieved something from her clutch.

"It's not worth it," she said. "He's drunk. Fucking Schafsseckel. Let's go."

"Fucking *what?*" Chum laughed and then slurred his way through the Swiss German word. The candlelight illuminated bits of spit coming from of his mouth.

Stonecrop had made up his mind. *I don't give a fuck, you're going down.*

Federica stepped between the two men, facing Chum. "Asshole. It means asshole, you prick."

"Well, make up your mind, woman! Am I to be an asshole or a

prick? Can't have it both ways, now, can we? Or could we, technically speaking? Regardless, dear, we shall be in *touch*. And thanks to you both! I mean that, really do. An educational and *entertaining* evening! Mañana, Max."

Stonecrop stepped toward Chum but felt the Ambassador's hand take his arm, restraining him.

"Gentlemen, please," the diplomat said. "Harry, I didn't see what all just transpired, but I think you owe the pretty lady an apology." In a sterner tone he continued, "And tomorrow you're gonna owe me an explanation."

"No need." Federica, suddenly all charm and sunshine, smiled at the Ambassador.

A smug grin settled across Chum's face. He didn't see it coming. Neither did Stonecrop or the Ambassador. Federica whirled around. Her fist clenched something. She delivered a blow hard enough to knock Chum off his feet. He fell across the table, toppling it and becoming tangled in the tablecloth, silverware, and broken glass. The candle lit lantern landed on the ground and burned dangerously close to the fabric. Chum quickly moved the tablecloth away from the flame and then used the fabric to staunch the bleeding from his lip and nose.

"Shall we go?" Federica said. She was positively perky.

The Ambassador moved to help Chum. He peeled the tablecloth off the man and stomped out the candle. Shards of glass sparkled in Chum's hair and on his bloodied face.

"Tomorrow. Don't forget!" Chum laughed as made an impromptu inspection of his front teeth with his thumb. "Your ass is on the line. And Gregor's!"

The Ambassador gave a quick *I got this* glance to Federica. Federica nodded back and she and Stonecrop walked away.

"What's he talking about?" Federica asked.

"He's ranting." Stonecrop escorted her across the patio.

"I know the difference between a threat and a rant, Max!"

"Yeah," he conceded. "You do. That was a threat. He knows something about Mozambique. I don't know how much. Maybe just what was in the papers, you know, about the company. Maybe more."

"Well, I don't know shit about Mozambique. And why Papà?"

"Same. I mean he had alluded to Gregor's sketchy past. Again, it was all inuendo. But shit, he's CIA, I'm sure, *does* have a lot on your father."

"I think Papà's got a lot on *them*. Let's go off piste."

They exited the patio and marked sidewalk and made an unlit path that cut diagonally across the field in front of the terrace. Federica's flats dangled from the fingers of one hand. In the other hand she loosely held her clutch and the thing she had wrapped her fist around. Stonecrop took the shoes so he could hold her hand.

"What the hell is that?"

"A present from Papà—a Kubotan. It's Japanese and made of a hard rubber molded to fit my grip." She showed him her hand, palm up, and opened and closed the fingers around the Kubotan. The weapon nestled perfectly into her fist. "Does double duty as my keychain."

"Where are the keys?"

"Just my access card for the Spital."

"The hand okay?"

"Needs a little TLC, sore metacarpal-phalangeal joint . . . the knuckle."

"And a whiskey?"

"Yes, that too, Herr Doktor Stonecrop."

The unfortunate encounter with Chum, though ugly, left the night sky untarnished and, miraculously, Federica's mood had much improved. She paused several times, saying nothing, but searching the stars. The unpleasantness, Stonecrop reflected, if anything, had reminded them of how much they cared for each other. That unwelcomed wall, the disquiet that had accompanied them to the event, had fallen as suddenly as Chum had at the table on the terrace.

Stonecrop looked up. He might have been talking to the stars.

"And how was the Ambassador? Was he the pompous ass?"

"Oh, maybe a little," Fede laughed and recanted, "but no, that would be unfair."

"Meaning?"

"For one," she laughed heartily this time, "he really does know a lot about botany and slugs! Can you believe I got a fifteen-minute lecture? He brought up Aristotle's work on clams. The assertion that clams are an example of a minimal life form."

"Clams?"

"Aristotle knew his clams. I'm serious, Max!" She poked him in the ribs.

Stonecrop, of course, knew his clams as well. He'd read Aristotle's *De Anima,* in Greek no less. He said nothing, though, preferring to let their thoughts, like the stars, drift where they may. Clams defecated, ate, and moved. Criteria for the observant Aristotle.

Holding hands, they walked in silence along Susenbergstrasse until they reached Frau Ott's home.

"The Ambassador asked me why I lived here instead of America—*the* best, most exceptional place in world, *sure as shootin'*."

"Absolutely," Stonecrop replied. They laughed together.

"I enlightened him."

"Uh oh."

"Well, I'm fucking Bulgarian and Italian, for Christ's sake. *Not* a U.S. citizen. That's a starter."

"And?"

"And fucking America—he always says *America*, like the U.S. owns the word. Jesus!"

"And?"

"And I told him the U.S. didn't own the word, or the world. And that I had zero interest in ever living there. The States is a toxic olio of power and money and racism."

"You two still on talking terms?"

"He said, 'Ain't that the truth, honey. Ain't that the sorry truth. We need gals like you, gals that outta run for office.' "

"Maybe there's hope," Stonecrop said.

They had arrived at the gate.

"There's hope for something, my love." She tossed her arms over his shoulders and pressed against him. "Come bed your woman."

"You know how proud I am of you?" he said.

"Show me . . ."

Kommissar Vormittag was as wrought in place as the chair in which he sat. One might mistake him for a mannequin or, a better comparison, a mime who earn his or her living via immobility. He sat at the same table where a month ago Stonecrop had met with Hamdi about his deposition. Placed upon the ground beside Kommissar Vormittag was a black briefcase, equally motionless and bond to the earth.

The Kommissar's eyes betrayed his fear that the slightest movement would have scalding consequences. Hamdi Habibi continued unperturbed by the Kommissar's trepidations and placed the glass on the table and poured the steaming tea, beginning with the spout close to the glass and then drawing the teapot upward until the spout hovered a good eighteen inches above the table. The Kommissar cradled his left arm in its black wing-like sling to avoid the stream of frothing liquid. The process ended abruptly when the blue, etched glass receptacle was filled to within a finger's width of the brim.

Even as Stonecrop took hold of his chair, Vormittag's eyes stayed on the glass. Hamdi had completed the pour without spilling a drop. Stonecrop knew this would be the case. The man leaned over and put a free arm around Stonecrop shoulders. "My friend, good to see you. Your usual?"

"You as well, Hamdi," Stonecrop said in a warm voice, replying as he sat. "Yes please."

"Let me bring you a scone. Sofia made fig scones! They're warm."

"Thank you, Hamdi. Perfect. Hi to Sofia."

The Kommissar observed, as was his nature.

"Morgan, Kommissar, you look better, rested. How's the shoulder?"

"Much improved, thank you." The tense moment had passed, and Vormittag rearranged himself on his chair. "Max, this man, the manager, insisted I take this tea." Vormittag looked down. "I've forgotten the name already. He said the tea would be good for the inflammation in my shoulder."

"Hamdi knows best. A few days ago, I'd had a tea he'd recommended to help me sleep. It did."

"You come here often? Of course, you do," he answered his own question, "it's so close."

"The tea Hamdi gave you is made with verbena leaves and lemon." The aroma was distinct. "And yes, often. When I'm not at Federica's." Stonecrop raised his hand and pointed to his apartment across the way. "I've gotten to know the family. Johan, one of the sons, helped me move in. They are, I think, the kindest people, the kindest family, I've ever known."

"Unusual that a Muslim family manages a venerable Swiss establishment like Stehli."

"Actually, they're the owners. Five-years, maybe six now. Hard work, kindness, generosity, humility. Those are qualities the Swiss respect and reward. The coffee and tea are terrific. So are their dried fruits. I'm sure the business is doing well."

Vormittag stared at his glass of tea, like he was waiting for it to speak. The tea said nothing, but the Kommissar's phone jumped to life, a ring tone Stonecrop had never heard before. He struggled to remove the handy from the coat pocket under the sling.

"Need a hand?" Stonecrop said, not intending to make a joke, but getting a smile anyway.

The Kommissar managed to extract the phone and answer the call unaided. Over the course of the two-minute conversation, which had begun and ended in a monotonic, monosyllabic, "Ja," the good demeanor he had had was gone; the moustache drooped.

"I don't have long," Stonecrop said, to move things along. "The girls are at Federica's and she's left for work. I need to pick them up."

"We won't be long. And thank you again."

"Kommissar, I haven't said *yes* to anything." In his mind, however, the only answer was yes.

"For listening."

"So tell me, what can I do for you?"

Whatever the thing was that Vormittag wanted, the thing was having a hard time getting out. Then finally it came, "I've agreed to loan thirty thousand Swiss to my nephew, Lorenzo. The funds are . . . for a business venture."

"Is this money for the cheese deal, or money he should have made but didn't because the deal cratered and now he owes someone?"

"I see why Gregor hired you."

"I'm a courier, Kommissar, a glorified delivery boy."

"Yes, of course," Vormittag said. He took the temperature of the tea glass with the hand poking out the black carapace. "It's the latter."

"But to do with a woman?" Stonecrop guessed, feeling on a roll.

"A woman, yes." With his good arm and with great care, Vormittag raised the cup and sipped the tea. "Excellent, very tasty."

"Her debt, then?"

"In a way. Lorenzo, he is young . . . and, I assume, in love. Who am I to say? I know nothing about the woman in question other than that she is an illegal immigrant and that she has to pay money to the people who brought her here."

"A prostitute?"

"I presume. Technically, prostitution is legal, that is, if the woman is not coerced into sex work. Sex trafficking, of course, is illegal. With Lorenzo, I expect the worst."

"Nationality?" He was curious. "Will she be sent back?"

Vormittag shook his head, no. Like a bobble-head doll, the rest of his body remained motionless. "In some cases, trafficked persons can be granted permits, even long-term permits, if that's what you're asking. She'll not be repatriated. Not immediately. She is, I believe, Nigerian."

"The cheese?"

"Ah, Lorenzo and friend—"

"—the friend who shot you."

"Yes, that friend. I should stop calling him *friend*." Vormittag grinned, drank some tea, and continued. "He and Lorenzo were going to buy the cheese rounds and resell them, making, I was told, a sixty-thousand profit. His share would have given Lorenzo enough money to buy the woman's contract with the traffickers. He has, if Lorenzo is to be believed, paid thirty thousand Swiss already. If my nephew fails to come up with the remaining money, that first thirty will be lost. I don't know much more, although Lorenzo swears they've broken no laws."

Vormittag appeared to reconsider his thoughts. "The correct thing to say is that the few details I do have, I don't trust. And I've lost count of the laws they've broken."

"Sixty thousand Swiss francs! That's a serious chunk of change."

"The madam, pimp, or trafficker enters into a contract with the victim, who is obliged to pay off the debt in three or four years. Fifty to sixty thousand is not unusual."

"Why not arrest the traffickers?"

"Ah, that things were that simple. And, personally, that would be my choice. The difficulty, you see, is a separate ongoing investigation. The girl is connected. You understand, as a Kommissar of the Kantonspolizei and special officer of the Stadtpolizei, I cannot let a personal affair interfere with an ongoing investigation."

"Can't you use Gregor?"

"I considered speaking to Gregor. He has never engaged in trafficking. And he hates the people who do. But he can't—" Vormittag hesitated. He could not find the words he needed.

"Gregor could handle this in his sleep." Stonecrop opined.

"I must ask you to not speak of this loan, nor of what I'm about to tell you, to anyone." The anyone, of course, meant Gregor. The request had come out more like a sigh. Vormittag, Stonecrop observed, had resigned himself to doing two things that made him uncomfortable: asking a favor and disclosing a confidence. "Agreed?"

Stonecrop bent forward so Vormittag could speak without being overheard by passersby. "Agreed."

"Gregor is assisting our office and Interpol in a separate matter. There is some overlap, we believe, in the players and the parties. Any pre-mature action in one area, could compromise the other."

"You want to keep him on a tight leash."

"The perfect expression, yes, *a tight leash*. English, American English, is so good with these expressions. *A tight leash*." He said the words slowly, like he had failed to give them the attention they deserved the first time. "I respect Gregor. However," the moustache rose and fell several times, weighing what came next, "he is unpredictable and impatient."

"You left off violent," Stonecrop added, not kidding in the least about Gregor's predilection for violence.

Vormittag was slow to concur. "Yes, there is that. And this situation is not without its share of risk . . . and potential for violence."

Stonecrop felt not dread but immense relief. There, at last, was an explanation for why Vormittag and the powers that be had been so hands-off with Ratzow and reluctant to confront him about the affair eight months prior. Though Ratzow's cooperation still didn't justify the entirety of what the authorities, and notably Vormittag, had ignored.

The remaining laxity, the willful ignorance by Vormittag et al., Stonecrop suspected, was more personal, dating back to Ratzow once having arranged transport of Vormittag's wife and children out of Palermo and, most importantly, out of harm's way. If Claudia's report of the affair was accurate, Ratzow had assassinated a major Palermo capo who had threatened Vormittag's family. In utter defiance of the rules of the game, Ratzow then made a blatant threat of brutal retaliation if any harm ever came to Vormittag's family. The form of the threat was a white flower that he had sent to every member of the dead capo's relatives and mafioso friends. Each flower had been accompanied with a card personally signed by Ratzow. That had been twenty years ago. He had to hand it to Gregor, he knew how to step up to the plate.

"What do I do?" This was the third time Stonecrop had asked.

"I don't trust Lorenzo with the money."

"Would he steal it?"

"No, no," Vormittag chuckled. "He might lose the money! Or someone might steal it from him. He is careless and not so clever."

"And you don't think he's being played?"

"I hope not. If so, then I'm the fool."

"So, I'm to baby sit?" Stonecrop asked as he moved his black, Patagonia daypack from his lap to the table.

"Essentially, yes. Please understand that if this exchange does not go as planned or if the personal risk . . . is unacceptable, you must walk away. I will not be upset with you. These traffickers, from what I know, are not people that one . . . toys with. Can you do this?" The words were difficult for Vormittag, he seemed to want to rescind them as he spoke. "Now that I think, you shouldn't . . . too much to ask. But I've been told there's little time—"

Stonecrop saved his tablemate from the uncomfortable back-peddling. He was grateful for the Kommissar's constancy and kindness with Federica. But there was something else that made him say yes: the woman from the compound in Maputo had been a victim of trafficking. She had helped him escape and probably had lost her life in the process. He'd dropped her off at clinic in Maputo. She had been barely breathing, unconscious, and bleeding from a vicious blow that had cracked her skull.

"When and where?" he said.

Vormittag reached into the old-school open-top briefcase beside his chair, extracted a bulky envelope.

"At nine tomorrow morning, Zürich-Bürkliplatz landing. Lorenzo will be there fifteen minutes early. He is to hand over the money and they hand over the woman." He gave Stonecrop a photo of Lorenzo. "Are you free tomorrow?"

"Straightforward enough. Sure."

"Max, nothing like this is ever straightforward."

Briefcase in hand, Vormittag rose. He exhaled from the effort, clearly relieved to be done with the unpleasantness of having to ask a favor. Stonecrop stood as well. Realizing he needed a free hand to shake Stonecrop's hand, the Kommissar set the briefcase on the chair. As he did so his handy rang, the same peculiar tone, and Vormittag struggled a second time to extract the handy from the jacket pocket. He listened carefully to the speaker for several minutes before replying.

"Ein Unglück kommt selten allein."

"Bad luck seldom comes alone," Stonecrop translated the words literally, speaking as he slipped the envelope into his much-used daypack.

The Kommissar expression darkened, prompting Stonecrop to look to him for an explanation.

"A body," Vormittag spoke as he covered the mic of the phone with the hand in the black sling. He seemed to be debating with himself about whether to say more.

"Student divers doing something called an 'open water checkout' found the body of a man. The upper half of a decomposed body was dangling out of the broken windshield of a vehicle submerged in the Marmorerasee reservoir. The car, a Ferrari no less, had been purchased in Zürich." Vormittag, a Geiger counter with its needle ready to jump, stared at Stonecrop. Self-aware and wildly radioactive, Stonecrop froze.

The Kommissar started to walk away, handy to his ear, then did an about face like a soldier or penguin drawing to attention. He saluted Stonecrop with the phone.

Both men knew the car's unfortunate occupant—or rather, had known him—and both had spoken with the man the afternoon he had died. There had been no direct evidence linking Stonecrop to the accident. Vormittag had had plenty of time to link the two. He had chosen to wait.

Are you done waiting, Kommissar?

"Thank you," said the Kommissar.

That's it? Stonecrop had little choice but to do everything he could to help Vormittag with his family problem. A risk that had not been mentioned was that if Stonecrop were to reveal the coverup of Lorenzo's affair to the authorities, then the Kommissar could lose his job or worse. That was leverage Stonecrop could not afford to squander. If he was lucky, Vormittag would downplay the Marmorerasee discovery as quid pro quo for Stonecrop's silence.

Vormittag took a few steps before Stonecrop ran up to him and placed the battered and forgotten briefcase at the Kommissar's feet. Vormittag looked at him and waited before speaking, as if he were expecting Stonecrop to utter a consoling word about the dead man. He returned the handy to the troublesome pocket, getting better at the motion, but the act still requiring some attention.

"Ah, I meant to ask, how did your conversation with Mr. Chum go? And the event? I heard the fete was well-attended."

"He's a good student. And a pig. Do you know him well, Kommissar?"

Vormittag had no physical reaction to Stonecrop's comments.

"I have little choice but to work with him . . ." he stated and paused as though he were going to say more, then didn't. "That's all. Again, thank you Max."

Bürklimäärt

At nine a.m. Bürkliplatz shoppers, tourists, and gawkers crowded the plaza to buy cut flowers and farm-fresh fruit and vegetables. The day sparkled and, though mid-week, city workers had fabricated reasons to avoid work. They wove through the stalls, one moment sampling the sun's warmth and next the temperate umbra of chestnut and maple trees.

Stonecrop texted Vormittag that he was about to meet Lorenzo at the base of the statue of Ganymede, the most prominent point of the lakeshore terrace and promenade and a stone's throw from the dock for the *Zürichsee-Schiffahrtsgesellschaft*. The Lake Zürich Navigation Company, known more commonly as the "ZSG," was a waterborne bus and taxi service for lakeside towns ringing the twenty-four mile long Zürisee.

Of the many representations of Ganymede's abduction by either an eagle or Zeus transformed into an eagle, the Hermann Hubacher statue was, as a piece of public art, a lousy choice. Even worse than the uninspiring execution was the story line: God abducts handsome adolescent to be immortal wine-pouring sex slave. How could Zürich's sober city fathers have believed that this statue exemplified Swiss life or values? Possibly it was the cheapest option. Even that, Stonecrop reflected, would be un-Swiss.

Lorenzo appeared five minutes before ten. An older version of the photo Vormittag had provided, he looked about the same age as Stonecrop, though shorter and thinner. Where Stonecrop had muscle, Lorenzo had concavities; instead of a thick fury of brown with sun-bleached streaks, his hair was a black widow-peaked, anti-slip floor-mat glued to the skull. The hard, almost cruel edge in Stonecrop's visage had nothing in common with Lorenzo's delicate-to-the-point-of-being-dainty features. Lorenzo's left hand death-gripped the stems of a half-dozen wildflowers. He held them the euro way, stem side up and blossoms down. He extended a nervous hand to Stonecrop. His entire body, like the flowers in his hand, quivered.

A timid voice choked out a name. "Lorenzo."

Stonecrop tilted his head closer as a way of asking the man to repeat what he had said.

"Lorenzo." The voice spouted the name, this time too clear and too loud. Several people turned their heads.

The man was nothing like what Stonecrop had imagined.

"Mornin'. Sorry, bit nervous. See, I was after buying flowers."

Stonecrop heard him clearly but was caught off-guard by the Irish-accented English.

"Do you need to use the bathroom?" Lorenzo was so fidgety; Stonecrop had felt obliged to ask.

"The loo. No. Good to go. Be done 'ere any minute."

"What's her name?" Stonecrop asked.

"Who?" Lorenzo asked.

After a pause, the nervous Lorenzo looked over one shoulder and then the other before responding. "Lomi." Another pause. "You're the tough mug, right?" Lorenzo asked.

"I'm not exactly a tough mug." Stonecrop laughed, and then nodded toward the pink, blue, and white flowers. "Nice. From the market?"

Lorenzo nodded. "You don't look tough," Lorenzo assessed Stonecrop, top to bottom and then back to the top again. "Except the crooked tooth maybe. One in front's off to the side, you know. The nose, too." He shuffled his feet, then raised the flowers close to Stonecrop's face. "They said to bring 'em. She'll be 'aving blooms too, you see. A code, 'at's what it is."

The chit-chat was interrupted by the approach of a heavy-set woman. She was fiftyish, if gauged by her body movement. Her face was older, the skin like pebble-grained leather. She wore a floral print sundress with matching flats and carried one of those large white and blue canvas bags used by sailors and shoppers. A clump of flowers poked out of the top of the bag. Stonecrop had noticed her earlier but had not given her a second thought. She had overheard them speaking English and addressed them accordingly. "Lorenzo, who is your friend?"

Lorenzo started the quivering again and seemed paralyzed by the question. His breathing was audible. Stonecrop stepped in front of him and faced the woman.

"I'm Max. Helping out my friend here. I am not Polizei, and not a reporter, and I'm not going to make trouble." He stepped closer to the woman. "Assuming we get the girl."

She looked straight at him, telegraphing neither her reaction to his introduction nor her intentions. "Very well," the throaty, though more cheerful than expected voice responded. "Money, please."

Stonecrop was sure she had backup milling about the stalls. He retrieved and gave the envelope from his pack to the woman who, in turn, slipped the packet into her canvas bag. If she had an accomplice, she did nothing to signal that she had received the payment. The backup must be close by.

"Merci vilmal," came the polite response.

He gauged the weight of her bag by the indentation the strap made in her shoulder. Rutabagas, he thought, or a handgun. He felt she was doing the same. Hell of a public place for a row.

In his case it was a Glock 19M. The weapon was compact and ergonomic, and, like Stonecrop, semi-ambidextrous. The U.S. Marine Corps had dubbed the automatic the "M007" in honor of James Bond.

Stonecrop was not ex-military. He did, however, compete in biathlons, a sport which entailed cross-country skiing and shooting. He had been selected for the U.S. Olympic trials as a young man. However, in the end, he did not participate due to a family tragedy— his teenage brother had committed suicide. As part of his biathlon training, Stonecrop had competed in combat pistol, and had had further shooting instruction from biathlon buddies who were members of a Special Forces winter combat unit stationed at Ft. Carson, Colorado. Stonecrop had traded winter survival know-how, in which he had considerable skill as a result of years of alpine climbing, for basic sniper training. The training had led to the discovery that he was at best a mediocre sniper, too distracted and bored by the waiting and tedium. On the other hand, no one could touch him at high-pressure, high pulse shooting. That, he discovered, was his métier.

Stonecrop scanned the market scene behind the woman, expecting to see the woman Lomi approach, or someone escort a woman toward Lorenzo. The swap was to happen simultaneously.

The woman addressed Lorenzo's concern and Stonecrop's darkening expression. "She's not here. The ferry is leaving in a few minutes. Get off at Halbinsel Au. She'll be there, alone, at the landing stage, flowers in hand. She's a lucky girl." The woman paused and smiled, "We're both lucky girls."

"That's it?" Stonecrop said, not happy with the terms.

"Voilà," she replied. Same cheerful lilt, like this was all a big lark.

Stonecrop took out his phone. "Smile!"

"Was zum Teufel!"

The snapshot both upset and surprised her. The "What the devil" was not native; her English was—a mental replay provided the answer —a Midwesterner.

"Relax, lady. If she's at Halbinsel Au, I'll delete the photo. If not," Stonecrop cracked a false smile, "we'll see." He took a minute to make a panoramic video of the crowd behind her, hoping to capture a photo of any cohorts.

Lorenzo turned to the south. His breathing was heavy. He fixed on the horizon of the lake, as if he might catch sight of Lomi if only he stared hard enough and long enough.

Stonecrop's threat, though weak and unspecified, got a reaction. The woman's light-hearted assurance cracked. She stared at the ground, then glared at him.

"She's there," she snapped. "Adieu." With that, she turned and walked away.

Stonecrop considered following her and then changed his mind. He faced Lorenzo and was about to suggest that Lorenzo remain at the dock and that he, Stonecrop, go to Halbinsel Au. But Lorenzo's shaking and wheezing grew more intense and made Stonecrop reconsider. He took hold of the thin shoulders, trying to calm him.

"I'm fine," Lorenzo said, but the nervous behavior continued. Stonecrop surmised that the condition was medical, something Lorenzo lived with. He would ask Fede if Vormittag should, on behalf of his nephew, encourage Lorenzo to see someone. When he looked back at the market, the woman was gone, swallowed up in the bags and sun hats and vendors with gayly colored carts.

"They said she would be here!" Lorenzo squealed the words, on the edge of panic. "What now?"

Stonecrop, speaking calmly, quoted Vormittag: "Nothing like this is ever straightforward."

Halbinsel Au

Lorenzo and Stonecrop sat in white perforated-plastic deck chairs in the second row of seats on the starboard side of the Helvetia's bow. Five minutes into the ferry ride, Lorenzo stopped shaking. Stonecrop, too, felt the calming effect of being on the water. The fresh air and the rocking of the boat brought up thoughts of *Zaca*. A remnant of his past life as a venture capital type, the Swan 44 lay on the hard in Formentera, the smallest of Spain's Balearic islands. The thought of the black-hulled beast on dry land and wrapped in tarps and bracing saddened him. He hadn't sailed her in several years. The sloop very well could have been confiscated for overdue decommission and storage fees. He made a mental note to make an inquiry. Maybe the time had come, the time to stop avoiding the world where people have goals, careers, and relationships.

On the prow-mounted pole the blue and white Zürich canton flag flapped in the apparent wind. Water slapped at the sides of the bow as the Helvetia made headway toward Halbinsel Au.

"Anxiety attacks. I git anxiety attacks 's all."

"It's okay," Stonecrop said in the voice of an adult distracting his child by going for a boat ride on the lake. "About ten minutes more, not far."

Halbinsel Au—Au Peninsula in English—lies on the southwestern shore of the Zürisee. Au was old German for "inland island" and referred to the lake south of the peninsula. To the west the slope rose over seven hundred meters to the wooded summit of Zimmerberg, a local foothill. A month earlier, Federica and Stonecrop had toured the Schloss Au, the 1650s Venetian style chateau that was the most prominent local structure. They had lunched at the Landgasthof Halbinsel Au and visited the wine museum and vineyard.

Stonecrop had forgotten most of what Fede had told him about the chateau other than a mention of Mentona Moser, a 1900s author from Au, a one-time resident at the Schloss, and, for a time, one of the wealthiest women in Europe. Federica had hung an old photo of Moser on the wall of Aide Direct's offices. She described Moser as a "force," who, at a time when women had few rights in conservative Switzerland, founded a service organization in Zürich for the blind, another for tubercular patients, a women's school, several workers' cooperatives, and a birth control and maternal and infant care clinic. Until her death in 1971, Moser had been a steadfast communist and humanitarian. In the end, penniless from the innumerable causes she had supported, and actions taken during the war by the anti-communist Nazi regime, she had resorted to writing to sustain herself and family. With few financial alternatives, Moser eventually accepted a pension and honorary citizenship in East Germany.

Federica, as they had walked the grounds at the chateau, had made the claim that smart people, given the opportunity, studied biology or mathematics. Moser, she pointed out, had been a zoology student at University of Zürich. Stonecrop thought the generalization was just that, a toothless generalization. Fede then barraged him with examples and skewered him for good with the fact that one of his classics' heroes, Aristotle, had been a zoologist first, and philosopher second.

The ferry bumped against the modest, unremarkable dock at Halbinsel Au and brought Stonecrop back from his daydreaming. The dock extended about forty feet into the lake.

"I don't see 'er," Lorenzo rose from his chair at the bow. "She'll 'ave a white scarf, long. 'er mark, you see. Always wearin' 'er white scarf. Bragged she's got a draw' full."

Heat radiated off the deck of the boat. The motion induced breeze had ceased.

"She'll show," Stonecrop said, guessing the odds were even and hoping Vormittag wouldn't lose his hard-earned francs. Then he saw her, about ten feet inland of the shoreline, a small, dark form, her black skin lost in the shade of a horse chestnut tree. She stood alone. Thin arms dangled to her sides. In one hand she gripped a mix of hand-picked wild flowers. The flowers lay parallel to the ground and suspended by two middle fingers curled about the mid-point of the stems. Her index and pinky fingers pointed to the ground. Cheap, rubber flip-flops, jeans from the Swiss *Coop* and a white tee completed the girl's frill-less attire. No other passengers exited or waited for the boat; the bouquet identifier had been unnecessary.

With Lorenzo breathing at his heels, Stonecrop approached. When they reached her, Lorenzo tried and failed to step around Stonecrop, who had with force grabbed him by the upper arm to hold him back.

"How old are you?" Stonecrop asked the girl.

The girl's arms went limp, her expression sad. She looked downward and answered in a voice that, though not at all loud, cut the air like a meadowlark's song. "Eighteen."

Stonecrop smiled. He looked left and right, then did his best to not appear threatening or condescending. "Try again."

After a pause, she re-engaged. "Sixteen," the bird-like voice said.

"I'm Max, a friend of Lorenzo's uncle."

She turned just enough to face Lorenzo. "Ciao, Lorenzo."

Stonecrop tightened his grip on Lorenzo's arm. His bouquet fell to the ground. The blooms scattered. A veil of desperation dropped over the would-be suitor's face.

Stonecrop's words to Lorenzo were sharp. "She's sixteen, Lorenzo, for Christ's sake!"

"She's not 'ere. I knew it. I knew it would go bad!"

Stonecrop, confused, let go the arm. The man dropped to the ground. Seated amid the flowers and with elbows resting on his knees, he covered his face. The hollow chest emitted a series of short gasps.

"Lomi left," the girl said. "She is sorry. She gave the woman some money. Then left."

Lorenzo looked up, eyes on the girl. "She comin' back?"

"No. Maybe, someday. I don't know. She said to say she's sorry."

It was clear now what had transpired. Lorenzo had been conned, thinking he had paid to free Lomi from bondage.

Lorenzo and the girl had lost Lomi. The loss hung over the two of them like the sagging branches of the chestnut tree.

The air was suffocating. Stonecrop longed for a breeze.

"And you are?" Stonecrop asked. He tried to put the young woman —girl, really—at ease.

"Destiny. Lomi is my sister."

On the ferry back to Bürkliplatz, Stonecrop learned that over the last six months, Destiny had journeyed with and been cared for by her older sister, Lomi. The two of them had been in the Zürich area for three months. Lomi went out each evening and returned before morning. They shared an apartment with three other girls, all older, and all with stories like Lomi's. The women had cared for Destiny and implored their madam to delay putting the underage girl on the street. The madam had complained, saying that in the not-so-old days, meaning 2013, sixteen had been the legal age for prostitution in Switzerland.

More than just a Lomi regular, Lorenzo, during off hours and against house rules, had spent time with Lomi and had met Destiny. There had been a conversation about running off or buying out Lomi's contract—an instrument which she referred to as a "bonding." Destiny had listened, and, she revealed to Stonecrop, pretended to not understand English.

Lorenzo had assumed that she spoke Yoruba and nothing else, ignorant of the fact that English was the official language of Nigeria, and that, like almost all Africans, Destiny spoke and understood the official language, her native one, which was Yoruba, and the lingua franca of her village. Her father, a Kenyan, had spoken Swahili with her. Thus came Lorenzo's second shock of the day, when Destiny spoke to Stonecrop in English, English that was in fact far better than his own Italian Irish mish-mash of the language.

The discovery prompted him to bombard Destiny with questions about Lomi. Her response, an empty stare, hardened as he repeated himself or raised his voice. Exasperated, angry, and pouting, he gave up and retreated to a deck chair at the stern of the boat, mumbling to himself. The words lost in the turbulent water and emotions.

Stonecrop and Destiny stood with backs against the railing at the bow of the Helvetia. They braced their feet, hands behind and holding the railing as they looked toward the cabin and stern of the ship. Music, Destiny said, had been her savior and her downfall. Supported by her family and the local church, she had attended music school and sung at social gatherings and in the church choir. What had been unknown to her was that the respected Christian pastor brokered girls from the church to sex traffickers. He held forth with glowing promises of jobs and educational opportunities in Europe.

Sex trafficking to Europe countries has a long history in Nigeria. So prevalent was the practice, Destiny reported, that high school girls who misbehave are called "Italians," as if their eventual disposition were pre-ordained. Making an already unjust situation even more unjust, families in some areas of Nigeria pray in Church or Juju ceremonies to have daughters, not sons, so that the girls could be sold abroad and eventually send money back to the families.

Destiny's parents loved her, she said. They had been reluctant to let her go. But the pastor had reassured them. "Switzerland is no Italy," he had said.

Potage Parmentier

"Speaking of sex, it's been forever . . ." Federica whispered in Stonecrop's ear.

"A week, ten days. C'mon."

"Exactly. Like I said, forever."

"Isn't that supposed to be the guy's line?" He didn't want to admit to Fede, or to himself, that his nightmares were getting worse and, obviously, taking a toll on his love life.

Sarah stood and chopped watercress at the table. Sandro sat next to her. His sketchbook was open, and Jenny sat in the chair on the other side of Sandro. She was the one doing the drawing. The two of them looked back and forth between what she was drawing and a Bonne Maman jar filled with water and flowers. Sandro had a pencil as well. He would step in when Jenny scrunched up her face in frustration. He'd add shading or thicken a line, or at times look puzzled or scrunch up his nose with her and make her laugh.

"I'm still really pissed about Chum," Stonecrop said.

"He was drunk. And he's so jealous of you. Plain as day on that false face of his."

"He's not much of a spy. At least not like the few I know, who are damned respectable people."

Federica put her arms around his waist. "Maybe he's not a spy, just acting like one."

"Doubt it, but why? What's to gain?"

"Or maybe he's like so virile and I'm so hot he couldn't help himself. And *you* just take me for granted."

She handed him a wooden spoon but not before a gentle poke in the ribs. Federica held back her pigtail as she leaned over his shoulder to watch him stir and to smell the soup cooking on the two-burner stovetop in Stonecrop's minuscule Niederdorf apartment. Not unintentionally, she let her breasts rest against his upper arm as he stirred. In a soft voice, she added, "Did you know Zwanzig Minuten says the Swiss have sex one-and-a-half times a week? Even more on the other side of the Röstigraben."

It took Stonecrop a moment to remember what the term referred to; the "hash-brown trench" was a slangy reference to the border between the German and French regions of Switzerland.

"Ouais," he exaggerated the yes. "Proving that the French are bigger liars than the Germans."

"And the Ticinesi think about sex all the time. Swiss-Italian men are the longest lived in Europe. I'm sure it's because *they* have the most sex. That's been proven with baboons!"

"You want to talk about this now? Sex with baboons?" he whispered. His eyes surveyed the gang of teenagers in the room. An aroma of spring onions filled the air in the crowded kitchen, mixed with eau de adolescence. The cook put the spoon down and picked up a Breville immersion blender. In a slow, circular motion, he pureed the potatoes and onions. Stonecrop had always enjoyed cooking, and lately the ritual had taken on fresh significance and become an important distraction from violent nightmares and flashbacks.

"Let me," Jenny walked up the stove and took the blender from Stonecrop. They managed the swap like kitchen pros. The blender never left the pot as Jenny, though much shorter than her father and needing to extend her arms, kept the same smooth motion with the blender.

"Ready for the watercress?" Stonecrop asked. Jenny nodded yes, and he swept the chopped watercress off the cutting board and into the pot. The fresh ingredients were from Bürklimäärt, after the misadventure with Lorenzo.

Post docking, he and Lorenzo had agreed that Lorenzo would go home. Stonecrop would update him as need be and break the news to Vormittag that his thirty-thousand Swiss was gone. Lomi was nowhere to be found and that they now had to do something with Lomi's undocumented, immigrant, younger sister.

What a cluster, Stonecrop said to himself.

Jenny let go the trigger on the Breville and turned to address Destiny who, like Sarah, rested her elbows on the table and used her hands as a prop for her chin.

"Sarah said you came to Zürich for sex."

The question silenced the room. Before the adults found their way, Destiny responded. The question had not put her off or embarrassed her. She smiled warmly at Jenny.

"Pepper," Stonecrop announced. "Does it need pepper?"

"No. I thought I was coming here for music school," Destiny ignored Stonecrop, "but that was a lie."

"Like, did you have to sleep with lots of men when you got here? Or do things with them?"

"Salt?" he asked. "What do think, Jenny?"

"No." The room quieted after the flat, emotionless response. "Thank god. But my sister did. And the other girls. They're older."

"Why—" Jenny let fly her favorite word.

"Jenny—" Stonecrop gave her the same look he had used when she had grilled Vormittag.

"I don't mind, Mr. Stonecrop," Destiny addressed the reprimand on Jenny's behalf. "That is, if you don't. We are not children." She gave him a moment to answer, got silence, and then faced Jenny. "We do sex for money, to buy our freedom and to help our families."

"You can't own a person."

Destiny pressed her lips together. The expression said, *Yes, one would think that*. "The people who brought me here from Nigeria *owned* me. Lorenzo must have given some money to Lomi. But then she gave that money and the money from Mr. Stonecrop to the madam. To pay for me."

"How much?"

"I owed sixty-thousand Swiss francs to the madam and her man. To pay for documents and travel from Nigeria to here."

"How much do the men pay?" Jenny asked, as though the question were the most normal thing in the world for a fourteen-year-old girl to ask a sixteen-year-old girl.

"Who want's soup?" Stonecrop announced; no one paid attention. Federica and Sandro were glued to the girls' exchange.

"About twenty a turn. That's a time with a man. Six or eight times a night. More money for some special things. There's a lot of standing between the times when they, you know, when they do it. But—the girls all say this—that when you're with the man, he doesn't take long. The men are very, very fast. There are tricks to make them faster."

A repressed smile escaped from Federica's face. She turned away. Stonecrop saw her but no one else could.

"That makes fourteen months to make what you owe." Jenny, as she was want to do, had run the numbers, or more likely, the numbers had run themselves in her brain.

"I don't know. But no, I'm told twice that. Because, Lomi says, you have to pay a lot, maybe two-thousand five-hundred Swiss Francs every month for expenses. And they keep your documents, even some of the fake ones, so you can't work. If you leave, they hurt you. Or worse, they hurt your family at home."

"That's not fair," Jenny added. Then, once again, doing the calculation in her head, Jenny blurted out the time required after expenses. "Thirty-six months!"

"Yes, that's about right. It is not fair," Destiny repeated. "And it is not right. We are not cattle."

"Sarah, bowls please, and water glasses," Stonecrop ordered. Then he addressed Jenny, "Enough, okay. Destiny might not want to talk about what she and her sister have been through." Stonecrop reflected that when he was fourteen a conversation as mature as this one would have been unthinkable.

Sarah moved a stack of five bowls from the open shelf to the counter next to Stonecrop. He ladled out the soup, added fresh sprigs of watercress, and put the steaming bowls on the table. Stonecrop had made enough soup for a second meal. Tomorrow the soup would be served chilled; more appropriate for the summer weather, and maybe with a dollop of crème fraîche. Federica added silverware, paper napkins, a cutting board with baguette, Tilsiter-caraway cheese, and prosciutto di Parma. Using everyday water glasses, she poured two glasses of Pinot Gris for the adults and sparkling water for the teens.

"I don't eat meat," Destiny announced. The inflection in her voice transformed the sentence into a song.

"Me neither!" Jenny was thrilled to discover a fellow vegetarian. "The soup is potatoes, onions, and water and watercress. Suuuuuper yummy. We make it all the time at home. I mean, we used to, before Max left."

The "Max left" hurt.

"Julia Child, right, Pops?" Sarah said. She, like Stonecrop, wanted to shift the conversation to food. Or, another possibility was that she sensed Jenny was on the verge of violating a promise that she and Jenny had made to Max, a promise to let him pick the time and place to explain why he had abandoned his family for almost two years. Sarah was always a step ahead.

"Exactly, Julia's Potage Parmentier."

Reading the underlying tension but likely missing the real source, Federica spoke: "Awkward conversations about awkward topics are important. If Destiny and her sister had had hard conversations, if they had challenged their pastor and learned from the experiences of other girls he had sent off for education or work in Europe, then the two of them might still be home with their family."

"Per—haps," Destiny said, keeping the two intoned syllables quite distinct. "We knew an 'Italian' girl. She sent home fifty euros a month. That's more than my father makes in a month. And we are not poor—"

Stonecrop heard a mobile buzz. He had not expected Destiny to have a phone.

Her eyes grew wide as she read the text. "It's Lomi! Excuse me."

"Where is she?" Federica asked.

"She's here! Outside. On the street."

"You told her where we were?" Stonecrop asked.

Her expression said that she had. "I didn't think she would come."

Stonecrop turned off the burner warming the soup. "I'll bring her up —"

"No. Lomi says only you, alone. On Ankengasse, the side door for a club." A tear ran down her cheek. A second followed the first. "She said I am to stay here."

Le Miroir

Le Miroir was a strip club that fronted the Limmatquai. The back door of the club was on Ankengasse, a short, steep alleyway that connected Münstergasse where Stonecrop's apartment was located to the Limmatquai, the main thoroughfare on his side of the river.

Stonecrop had never been in the club, but one time he had chatted with three women who worked there. It had been two a.m. and they had been on a smoke break. The trio wore matching red and black tutus, white fishnet stockings, and high heels. The glitter on their eyelids sparkled through the smoky haze. He'd been clomping and jingling down the alleyway in his plastic boots and carrying an enormous pack bedecked with ice-climbing regalia—helmet, twin Cobra ice tools, ice screws, single-point crampons, and rope coiled and tied to the top. He had just left his apartment to meet a fellow climber who was picking him up where Ankengasse intersected Limmatquai. Both Stonecrop and the women appreciated the humor of the situation. They'd joked about a group photo but there hadn't been time because his ride had been at the curb with the motor idling.

In three minutes, he was at the side door to Le Miroir. A darkened shape opened and held the door ajar. As he neared, she turned away and guided him into a narrow non-descript hallway. The door fell shut and took the light with it. Piecemeal images emerged as his eyes adjusted to the darkness: an oval head and an eye orbiting above a white scarf that double-wound round her neck and hung body-less in space. A silver hoop earring traced the same orbital path as the eye. He could see now that her teeth were bloodied and that they protruded fiercely from her mouth. He sensed he was being watched but saw no one, nothing but that lone eye.

Stonecrop started when she grasped his forearm. She pulled him close and steadied the two of them. He smelled orange on her breath, hair in need of a wash, and mostly he smelled the fear suspended in her sweat. The grip was firm; the hand holding him had done manual labor, real work, like gardeners do. The hand stayed on his arm. He didn't pull away.

"Destiny is at my apartment and with my family and friends," he began softly. "She's terribly worried about you." Stonecrop sought to reassure, to not threaten and to not judge.

"Yes, so she said—a text. I won't have her see me. Not like this, no." The *no* harbored a sigh of regret and sadness.

He made out the swollen cheekbone, a cut on the lip near where a tooth should have been, a tear on an earlobe where there should have been a place for a hoop. The contusion and swelling hid much of her right eye. There could easily be an orbital fracture.

"My girlfriend is with Destiny," he continued. "She's an emergency physician. Please, come back with me. You need to see a doctor."

"Yes, but I can't."

"Lomi, tell me what's going on." There was something familiar about her. The crowd at the market. He'd look back over the panorama he'd shot. Could be nothing more than the resemblance to Destiny.

"You don't know this . . ." She hesitated and then seemed relieved to continue. "No one knows this but there is a second 'Lorenzo.' He is not so stupid as Lorenzo. I never told Destiny. He paid, too, the same sum."

"Lorenzo told me that *he* had paid the first thirty thousand."

Her response was a grunt of incredulity. "Really? No, the only money from him was the money you brought. No more." She looked at the floor and the words fell into the darkness at their feet. "Lorenzo can be sweet. He tries but he is a helpless piece of shit. I used him. It was not Christian, the thing I did."

She held that pose for most of a minute, head down, before lifting her chin high and speaking again. "This other man, he loved me, too. He still loves me. But he will be angry with me because I used the money for my sister."

"You said *will*. So, he didn't do this to you. But are you afraid that he's going to hurt you as well?"

"No," she scoffed at the thought. "I am not at all afraid of him."

Stonecrop didn't trust her judgement or self-assessment. "You don't seem to be afraid of me, a stranger. Why?"

"Destiny's text said you are a man I can trust."

"She hardly knows me. Look Lomi, I'm no angel."

"I'm not looking for an angel. Human kindness is all," Lomi said, and squeezed his arm. Again, he was surprised at her strength. And her composure. She was strong, big-boned, a powerful woman. He was able to see better now. She was the antithesis of the self-anointed paramour Lorenzo. To imagine them as an item was almost comical.

"The two men provided money to pay your contract but you used the money to pay off Destiny's obligation, not your own. I would think the lover you duped would want his money back or the goods he paid for—namely you. And I assume you must still be under contract with the same jerks who conned you into coming here in the first place. Or was that voluntary?" That last part was mean, he knew, but he wanted to know.

The anger in her eyes preceded the words, "It was not, I swear to God!"

She knew her mind. He should listen. "What's next?"

Lomi paused. The hand that held him was damp. Her fingers moved as she spoke. There were beads of perspiration above her upper lip. The odor of sweat intensified, whether from tension or the heat of bodies in the confined space. His now blended with hers.

"It is so. I paid her bonding. But I'm not going back," she said.

"Back to Nigeria? Or back to work in Zürich?"

"Back to work. My employers will be angry."

"Won't they be back?"

"They will not, I believe they will not."

His look questioned and she responded:

"I said I would talk to the police." Her tone didn't convey the threat that the words should have implied.

"Would you? We can speak with Lorenzo's uncle. He loaned the money to Lorenzo. And he works for both Stadtpolizei and the Kantonspolizei. He can arrange for someplace safe, a place for you and for Destiny."

"Ha!" The derisive laugh was like a punch. "Look at my face! Do you see how 'safe' I am!"

"Wait. I'm confused. You just said they won't attack you again, but you're still not safe."

"My madam and her man, they will do nothing."

"I'm confused. Who did this to you?"

"I don't know. A stranger."

"From where you worked? A crazy customer?"

"I don't think so. I was fighting with the Japanese man, my madam's husband. Not the first time. He wasn't strong enough to really hurt me. But this time I truly hurt him. But then a stranger, he attacked me. A homeless man . . . but he wasn't. I could tell."

"Wasn't *how*?"

"Cologne. Teeth, white as snow. Soft hands, but evil. I thought he would kill both of us, even though I am strong. He had a friend. A big man with a beard. He was far away, but watched."

"What did you do?"

"I ran. He didn't catch me." Here she laughed and even cracked a smile. The smile must have hurt. "I run, every day. Even now. I ran track in my school at home. I am a fast runner!"

"You have got to speak to the Polizei," he insisted, aware of the fact that doing so would cost him any leverage he had over Vormittag and further that the revelations would hurt Vormittag's career.

"Listen to my words, Mr. Stonecrop—"

"Max, just Max," he interrupted. The 'mister' treatment reminded him of Frau Ott.

"Max, then," she said. "I am going someplace safe, you hear. Tell Destiny, and tell her to call our parents. They need to leave."

"Leave?"

"Go anywhere, away from that bastard. Away from the Pastor, away from his evil church, and away from our village. They must not wait. You understand. Now."

"Have you spoken with your parents?"

Lomi shook her head from side to side, obviously despondent. "They are so, so angry with me. They blame me. And they are right to blame me. They won't talk to me. If Destiny talks to them, I pray they will listen to her."

Lomi's handy buzzed. She turned away from him and withdrew the handy from the top of her blouse. Stonecrop leaned over her shoulder to read the text.

< . . . estou aqui . . .> was all he could make out.

Lomi faced him. "Tell Destiny I love her. She is always in my heart. I beg her forgive her bad, bad sister."

Stonecrop was at a loss. Lomi easily could have phoned Destiny and asked her to warn their parents. So that wasn't the reason. "Why did you want to see me?"

The half-smile on her face caused her some pain. Her eyes, well, the one that wasn't swollen shut, had an almost flirtatious glint. "I wanted to see you and to touch you. She told me, but I had to make *sure* for myself that you are a good man. I can tell about a man right away—good or bad—when I touch him. She will be safe with you."

An interior door cracked open. A woman, one of the dancers, said something Stonecrop didn't understand.

He was desperate to not lose her. "I can get the money to purchase your bonding. Soon, tomorrow even. You can stay with Destiny tonight." He rushed to say the words as Lomi backed him to the door and shoved him into the alleyway. He feared he might hurt her if he resisted.

"Care for her, Mr. Max. Good-bye. May God bless you." She squeezed his arm, taking his measure one last time before she pushed him away. He stumbled backward.

The door-bolt slide into place. Stonecrop waited and hoped Lomi might re-emerge. The abrupt end to their conversation befitted its unexpected initiation. Realizing she wasn't going to exit the alleyway door, he loped downhill to Limmatquai and the gaudy, neoned, streetside entrance to Le Miroir. He stepped between parked cars and into the street seconds too late.

She must have come out front door or another exit. From the passenger seat of a departing car, Lomi looked back, connected with him, and then turned away. She had pulled her white scarf over much of her head and face, a makeshift hajib. He couldn't see the driver. The traffic swallowed up the car, a late-model black VW Golf. Lomi was gone.

He walked uphill, feeling the cobblestones underfoot and rubbing his upper arm, sore from where Lomi had held him. For no reason, he memorized where the steps and doorway landings were and he thought about Zürich—the Zürich that most people imagined—a city where society was fair, ordered, and peaceful; a society that put education ahead of politics and where one could live in safety; a city with authorities beyond corruption and venality. No such place exists, of course. But Zürich, he had thought, was better than most. *And it was,* he coldly reflected, *if you had enough money and were born in Switzerland.*

Wasserschutzpolizei

The men had pre-arranged a time and place to meet. Stonecrop had squeezed in a half-hour morning jog along the river front. Vormittag was waiting for him when he loped up to the Zürich Limmatquai, a concrete landing point for small watercraft on the Niederdorf side of the Limmat River. The location was equidistant from Stonecrop's apartment and the *Stadtpolizei* office on Bahnhofquai, where Kommissar Vormittag kept an office. From the office one had to cross the Rudolf-Brun-Brücke and walk few hundred meters upriver in the direction of the lake and the Glarner Alpen to reach the riverbank landing, which was shroud in a sound-deadening ground fog.

The Kommissar acted as though he were short on time and then confirmed that that was indeed the case by asking Stonecrop for a brief recap. Stonecrop complied, relaying the events with Lorenzo in a few sentences. The Kommissar took the news better than expected. He seemed to not care so much about whose freedom he had bought, since Destiny was deserving, and the mishap would keep the mortified Lorenzo out of his hair, at least for a while. Nor did he press Stonecrop about how or why the switch occurred. Either he didn't care, or another more immediate concern had trumped this one. Stonecrop suspected the latter. He said nothing about his meeting with Lomi at Le Miroir, fearful that her beating was something that a city Kommissar could not ignore, and realizing that he, Stonecrop, would be drawn into the affair if there were an investigation. Any serious inquiry into his own background might turn up dead bodies. That, he reflected, was something he didn't want to explain, not yet, not ever, and not *briefly*.

"Ah, there." Vormittag pointed toward the lake. The six-meter long *Wasserschutzpolizei* launch emerged from the gloom downriver and made a U-turn to sidle up next to the platform. Several swans awaiting handouts and insulted by the intrusion dispersed. Two tourists, this time a young couple, disgruntled honeymooners whose intimate conversation had been interrupted, ascended the ten or so steps up to the Limmatquai sidewalk.

"They shouldn't feed them, you know," Vormittag said to no one. "Old bread, that is. The mold is deadly."

Stonecrop did not confess that when he had first visited Zürich, years ago and not knowing better, he had fed the swans.

"Where to?" Stonecrop asked, thinking that Kommissare rarely travel by boat.

"Halbinsel Au."

The mention of Halbinsel Au rattled Stonecrop. He had said nothing to the Kommissar about the exchange with Lorenzo having been at Halbinsel Au. Had Vormittag reached inside Stonecrop's mind, opened drawers, and rummaged about the contents?

"Another body," Vormittag continued. "First Marmorerasee, today Zürisee. Beh, what's next?

"Boating accident?" Stonecrop asked. He hoped he didn't appear too eager for the right answer.

"Tell me. You like boats. Do boaters often strangle each other?"

"If the fish is big enough," he smiled.

"Ja, this must be a very big fish," Vormittag said over his shoulder as he stepped aboard. The launch pilot supported the Kommissar's good arm to help with the step down from the landing to the deck. The bound arm flapped in the air to counterbalance the rocking from the waves created when the boat double-backed across its own wake.

"Mr. Chum," Vormittag looked over his shoulder, "has he spoken with you?"

"No." Stonecrop had not heard a word since the incident at Hotel Zürichberg. He had assumed Chum would be too embarrassed to contact him.

Once Vormittag had been settled onto a bench, the pilot set course for Halbinsel Au and sailed into the horizonless haze. The boat disappeared. Shortly after, the fog swallowed the rumble of its motor.

A Hungry Bear Doesn't Dance

Zürich was a cadaver. The wan, featureless surface of the water and the too-still air stuck like dead flesh to the bones of the city. Guild flags along the Limmatquai languished. The Hotel Storchen flagpoles, instead of giving a jaunty salute to the river, were burdened by their colors. Even the banners atop the twin towers of the Grossmünster, which, being higher, always flirted with the breeze, had gone silent. The city had lost its pulse.

On the other side of the river, in the foreground and below the tower of St. Peter, the pink façade of the Storchen Hotel fought the gloom. Though a pre-lunch hour, guests occupied several tables. There was only one table that interested Stonecrop. From the Niederdorf side and through the river haze, he saw that it was taken. Placed beyond the hotel's tacky outdoor fountain and out of earshot of the other tables, this table was always tagged with a gold script "Reserved" placard, and the man for whom the table was reserved was "In" and holding court. He had two guests: a woman Stonecrop recognized and a tall, well-dressed black man he did not.

In less than five minutes, Stonecrop stood behind Gregor Ratzow, who was going on about something, a something that was no doubt dripping with hyperbole. Perched opposite Ratzow sat Claudia Knight, Ratzow's fixer-in-chief. Through horn-rimmed glasses with bottle-thick lenses, those frog-eyes of hers missed little. Unlike Ratzow, a man immersed in a world of his own fantasies, Claudia was rooted in tooth-and-claw reality. Her firm, G24/7, provided strategic consulting services to less than lily-white clients. The four chairs arranged around Ratzow's table differed from the armless, prissy, uprights at other tables. Ratzow's table sported steel-framed captain's chairs with double-padded seats.

Claudia had made eye contact with Stonecrop ten meters earlier and with the flick of a smile at the corners of her U-shaped lips communicated to him that he was welcomed to interrupt. Similarly, she announced his arrival to Ratzow by shifting her gaze back forth between the two men.

"Da, my Transport Specialist, the best in all of Switzerland, shows up for work!" Ratzow spoke without facing Stonecrop.

Here comes the bullshit.

Ratzow hosted. "Max Stonecrop," he said, "meet Mr. Ibrahim Adewole."

"I have been told you are exceptional at your work, Mr. Stonecrop," Adewole said. He slouched in his seat as he extended a drooped hand, bent downward at the angle of a heron's beak. Stonecrop took the appendage, feeling like he was being asked to dance.

"And, I'm sure," Adewole rose from his chair and clung to Stonecrop's hand, "you have much to do. So, I shall leave you to your work."

Adewole released the hand from his tender hold and thanked Claudia, then Ratzow. Stonecrop received a parting nod.

Claudia motioned for Stonecrop to take the vacated, still-warm seat, which he did not do, preferring, for no good reason, the other open chair.

"That was quick. Did I interrupt?"

"Right on cue, darling!" Claudia answered.

"Since when am I a 'Transport Specialist?' I'm the guy who hand-delivers scraps of paper for you and helps Bachmann shuffle art around."

Ratzow harrumphed and popped a few almonds in his mouth before he spoke, declaring to Claudia, "They are not grateful, these young people," and turning to Stonecrop, "not papers or paintings, you ninny!"

"How are we, dearie? I haven't seen much of you lately. Feeling the harried father?"

"Sarah and Jenny are keeping me busy. Mattie is stuck in Paris, so I'm still on duty."

"Da, I pay for work while you play papa," Ratzow grumped.

"I can quit, Gregor?"

"Does not help. Swiss make me pay benefits! Maybe if you dr-r-rown I don't pay so much." Ratzow opened a hand toward the Limmat River, only meters from where they sat.

Stonecrop turned to Claudia and mimicked Ratzow, "Da, better-r-r I go."

"Boys, behave," Claudia intervened. "Gregor, Max cooks. He cooks lovely meals for your lovely daughter. Be grateful."

The claim was true: On her own, Federica would live on power-bars and smoothies. To Fede, food was fuel.

Ratzow reached across the table and patted Stonecrop's shoulder. "Keep cooking. She is not so skinny like before."

That was true. Stonecrop's resurrected obsession with cooking, his go-to therapy, had been good for Federica. Was it too good? Would she be transformed into a chubby babushka? *No way.* Though he'd love her whatever the hell she looked like.

Ratzow was overweight. The man never gave it a second thought. And he was scary strong. Ratzow's forearm was about the girth of his thigh. Even at his charming best, Ratzow's hands, his too massive and too powerful wrestler's hands, intimidated.

"Something's off, love, yes? Tell mother Claudia?" She sensed that he had been holding back. "We tried to reach you last night. Wanted you to cozy up to Mr. Adewole."

"Sorry, Claudia. Dead phone." The lame explanation seemed enough. He wondered what was up with this new acquaintance, Mr. Ibrahim Adewole.

"You'll have another chance; two, actually. He's expecting to meet with you tonight. A dinner, your choice of place, before a late flight out of Flughafen Zürich. Can you manage that?"

"I can," Stonecrop said. This was, after all, work. It was clear his daughters' presence couldn't be an excuse forever. "And the second?"

"At Therme Tavate, time TBD, but in a month or so."

The Therme was one of Group's properties. Fede had had been there a number of times. Stonecrop had not. Ratzow, himself, rarely visited. However, his imprimatur, Fede had recounted, gave the place a kind of criminal cachet, a bad-guy je ne sais quoi. Thugs felt at ease there among their fellow thugs. There were no interior surveillance cameras, supposedly no picture-taking. The internet and hotel mail were encrypted. The walls and doors had been sound-proofed and, though unadvertised in the spa's brochures but well-known among the clientele, the windows were made of bullet-proof glass. That feature, Federica had once commented, had been a brilliant guerrilla marketing move. Housekeeping made a fuss over doing a daily sweep for listening devices. Also a sales gimmick.

In the foyer, as visitors walked through the metal detectors, they were greeted by a gilt-framed photo of a young, bare-chested Gregor Ratzow in a boxing ring and holding a bizarre trophy made from a stuffed wolf's paw. Another photo, at the reception desk, portrayed the present-day Ratzow in a double-stitched three-piece that struggled to contain the squat, three-hundred-pound, barrel-chested Bulgarian with steak-thick hands. In Bulgaria, thugs called themselves *borets*—wrestlers. Ratzow was the quintessential boret.

"Sure. That too, I suppose I can do."

"You're entirely too agreeable, my dear. So, what's new and exciting? Been dull around here with you know who." Claudia rolled a thumb at Ratzow.

The waiter picked up the gesture and took it as a summons.

"Sir, ma'am?"

"I like being ma'amed," she flirted with him and then faced Stonecrop, asking if he wanted anything.

"Steak frites, please. Can you do a half-order?"

The waiter nodded, "Of course."

"And a glass of house red, a Pinot if you've got one open. Dijon on the side, please." He turned toward Gregor and Claudia. "Meeting Fede at the climbing gym in an hour."

"Water, sir? Sparkling or still?" the waiter enjoyed using his English.

"Hahnewasser, bitte," Stonecrop answered, enjoying using his German.

Though before the lunch hour, any guest of Ratzow's would be taken care of. The food was exceptional, particularly since Storchen was now a recognized farm-to-table establishment.

A sparrow landed on their table, lingered, and listened.

"Halo, little friend! Every day if I am here, he comes. See, he wants frite. Tell me, Max: What do *you* want?"

"Frites too," Stonecrop joked, "like your friend. No, I'm good."

That got a smile from Gregor. He repeated the question, "No, what do you want? No one is just *good*," he replied. He downed the remainder of his drink, no doubt the coarsest vodka Hotel Storchen could find, a drink that bonded Ratzow with any number of low-rank hotel employees. He never thought of himself as better than the next guy. That attitude made that next guy loyal as hell to Ratzow, Stonecrop included.

The "good," however, bothered him. Ratzow had trespassed on a word owned by Federica. Gregor's "good" was chopped wood. Her "good," the first time he had heard her say the word, had triggered his attraction to her. She spoke the word with a soft, but clear Chicago accent. Without using her lips, the puff of air, with a little click, escaped the hollow at the upper back of her throat as her tongue arched and grazed the roof of her mouth. Federica was right, they hadn't had much sex recently. Why the fuck was that?

"You called *me*, right?" Stonecrop asked, the question sounding grumpier than he had intended.

Claudia answered for Ratzow. "We did, darling, about your promotion!"

Before he could respond, her ring-bedecked forefinger rose to his lips to cut him off. "First, I want to know what's troubling you. A lover's spat? I certainly understand, the kids and all, no privacy."

Stonecrop said nothing, which never stopped Claudia from saying what was on her mind.

"Let's put this to bed, shall we, before we charge into your new employ— about which, love, I have to say, I am very excited," she turned to face Ratzow. "We all are!" She winked. Ratzow said nothing.

Stonecrop gave in. "Okay, here goes. Do you know anything about sex trafficking?" He looked back and forth between Claudia and Ratzow.

Ratzow spit on the sidewalk, an offense in Zürich. Had he been someone less than Gregor Ratzow, the act could have cost him his "residence" status at Storchen in addition to the fine from the *Stadtpolizei*.

Claudia responded. "Well, we hadn't considered sex, especially not that kind." She took a sip of wine, a white of some sort, and held the glass in the air, pinky aroused and aimed at him. "Please, elaborate."

Aware that Vormittag had stated that he didn't want to bring Gregor into the Lorenzo affair, and further aware that Claudia had a way of knowing everything about everybody, Stonecrop figured he'd just screwed up.

"I helped a friend pay off a bonding, a contract with a pimp. The payment was supposed to be for a Nigerian woman whose name was Lomi. But Lomi took the money. Instead of buying her own freedom she used the money for her younger sister, Destiny."

"Your money?" Ratzow asked and took a drink of water. He kept his eyes on Stonecrop as he drank. "The price?" he said as a water flowed down his gullet.

"Not mine. Sixty thousand Swiss. That's the total amount."

Ratzow pursed his lips and slowly rocked his head to one side, then the other. The gesture implied the price was about right.

"They took Swiss?" Ratzow asked.

After Stonecrop lowered and raised his eyes, indicating a yes, Ratzow added, "Is normal to pay dollars or euros. This one takes Swiss francs, so local business cleans money. Good practice to clean money close to source."

"A Swiss lover," Claudia jumped in. "So romantic! It's always the lover, a fool eager to share his citizenship!" She looked at Ratzow and touched his shoulder. "Our boy here got the job for the swap because he's so good at these sorts of things, right dearie, handing off the cash? Moonlighting, as it were. Names?"

Right again, he thought. *You are so annoying, Claudia.* When he nodded in agreement, he saw a shiver of delight. Claudia got off on being right. *And no, you are not getting the name.*

"Does the lover—you're not going to tell me who, are you?—does he not like the generic goods and want his money back? No, that's a little too obvious. Something more's afoot. Tell your sweet Claudia, what's the twist."

"I don't know. But the sister, the older one, got beat up bad."

"Bad, as in her face bad?" Claudia asked, two steps ahead.

"Yup."

"The perp is not the pimp. Can't float damaged property on the street. Kill the goose and all."

"She mentioned something about another lover, an ill-tempered one."

"Bingo! And that lover-boy is *not* Swiss. A Swiss man with that kind of money doesn't run around beating up women. That's more like a Russian or Georgian. And the pimp, I promise you, is going to break *his* fucking face." Claudia took another sip of wine. The waiter arrived and set the table for Stonecrop as a second waiter placed the Steak Frites and accoutrements on the table. Stonecrop dug in; he'd not eaten breakfast and was starved. The hiatus gave Claudia an opportunity to further speculate about nationality and cruelty.

"The next scene of this sordid little soap is the young sister—a virgin would be best—begging for you, the rich American—because you're all rich, you Americans—to save dear older sister. How could you say no? And you want money from Gregor, asap, because you don't have a war chest and are afraid of getting Federica involved. She would demand justice, and that's a headache for all of us. How am I doing, dearie?" The last bit of wine went down. She raised her glass for the waiter to bring another.

Stonecrop continued eating.

"You don't have to answer," Claudia said. "I know I'm right."

"Close, Claudia. But the sister, Destiny, didn't ask."

"You know, don't you love, how easily a young girl might manipulate *you*. It's happened before. Do you need reminding?"

Stonecrop smiled. "Touché." A day hadn't gone by since he met Federica that he hadn't thought about her. And his daughters. And Mattie. Women ruled his life, no doubt about it!

"Lomi says she quit the business," he added.

That statement got Ratzow's attention, as did the frites on Stonecrop's plate. Like his daughter, he couldn't resist pinching a few. Ratzow and Claudia looked at each other.

Claudia spoke first. "One can't just quit."

"Da, Claudia, is right. Russian beater has choice. Buy Lomi or pay medical expense for two. If lucky. Use girl to get sucker like you!"

The waiter arrived with Claudia's wine and a refresh for Ratzow, although he had not asked for one.

"So?" Stonecrop asked.

"So," Gregor, now affable, pronounced, "a hungry bear doesn't dance!"

"Meaning?"

"No loan," Gregor stated. "But I dance. Look, I *give* you money. Hiring bonus to Transport Specialist. First, you work." Vodka in hand, eyes grinning under bushy brows, he toasted Stonecrop.

Ratzow put down his glass and took a few more frites off Stonecrop's plate. The sparrow, the size of Ratzow's thumb, took one from his fingers and flew off. The act, for no reason, reminded Stonecrop that in the last thirty years bird species and populations had declined dramatically—*what was the number, thirty percent?*

Stonecrop finished chewing and washed the steak down with a swig of Pinot, swishing the wine around to clean his palette. The tannins washed away the residual fat, and he had a moment to think. Since he was climbing later, he would leave most of his wine at the table.

Ratzow lowered his voice. The tone shifted to conspiratorial. "Another hundred thousand in Malta. No tax, da!"

"And," Claudia delivered another bonus, "not my cup of tea, but you will get complimentary spa time at Tavate."

"You guys are making me nervous. And just *what* do I feed the bear?"

"I am wolf, not bear," Ratzow proclaimed for no reason that made sense to Stonecrop. "We do favor for our friends, Kommissar Vormittag and Harry Chum. Is little favor," Ratzow said, "mostly for Chum."

"Chum is a dick," Stonecrop asserted.

"Well, of course he is! So?" Claudia said. "Now, to business: this *little* favor, Max, successful or not, means your beloved employer," she paused and nodded in Ratzow's direction, "will remain a welcomed guest in Switzerland and the EU."

"Da, we both feed the bear, Max." A fatalistic Ratzow exhaled loudly.

Tired of the mystery, Stonecrop flattened his hands on the tabletop. "Enough with the bear or wolf or whatever the fuck it is bullshit! What's going down?"

"A *sting*, love!" For dramatic effect, Claudia aspirated the word "sting" and reached out and mimicked a bee attacking Stonecrop's forearm. "Like in the movies, you even get to wear a wire! In a manner of speaking. Times have changed since the Sopranos. Nobody really does that."

"I am not fucking—"

Claudia brushed aside whatever he was about to say with a wave of the hand, "Hear me out—"

Ratzow, equally impatient to make a point, welcomed or not, interrupted, "E-garbage is good business."

"It's e-waste, dear, not e-garbage. Technically, WEEE: wasted electrons, or something like that—"

"Waste Electrical and Electronic Equipment," Stonecrop finished for her. He was familiar with the term.

That morning had read an online article with a photo that depicted a boy, ten or eleven years old, pushing a shopping cart amid smoldering electronics equipment and appliances at an e-waste disposal site in Nigeria. The author described children exposed to neurotoxins and carcinogens, children who, kilo for kilo, drink and eat and breathe significantly more toxins than adults.

Ratzow ignored Stonecrop's clarification. "This e-shit, fifty-million metric tons of screens, laptops, microwaves, refrigerators, phones . . . is worth sixty, seventy billion U.S. You tell me. How much is recycled?" He grabbed the last of the frites on Stonecrop's plate and stared at Stonecrop, expecting, and awaiting an answer to his question.

"I don't know, maybe half?"

"Twenty."

"And?"

"Eighty percent, eighty percent of sixty billion. Is almost fifty-billion dollars for someone."

"Close enough. But the price per ton is—"

"Twice as good as gold ore!" Ratzow chewed cold frites as he made the point.

"Switzerland recycles everything. Leave the old handy at the store when you get a new one."

"Stimmt. Die Schweiz is better-r-r than most, seventy-five percent," he laughed, "but these Swiss materialists produce twice as much garbage as anyone else! Maybe Japanese are worse."

One never knew whether to trust Ratzow's numbers. But the man's net worth was over a hundred million, so he was doing something right, and he'd been doing something right for a long time.

"Now, smart venture capitalist man, now tell me how I make money?"

"Get a piece of the fifty billion," Stonecrop said, playing the game.

"Where is it, do you think?" Ratzow spread his arms wide, waiting for Stonecrop's answer to fill them.

"Landfills, the ocean, incinerated, third world—"

Ratzow finished his drink. "Da, some. Export?"

"Sure, but no one in E.U. can export e-waste except to another E.U. country. A closed system, in theory."

"Basel Convention. Only can export in E.U., and other Europe members. Da, E.U. did test. Put sensors on garbage. Guess what?" Ratzow stared at him.

"I'm enjoying the education, Gregor. What?"

"Twenty percent . . . poof!" Gregor tossed his arms up, like he was freeing a captive pigeon. "You see, is like laundering money, but is called *leakage*."

"And what on Earth does any of this have to do with me?"

Ratzow had had his fun. Now Claudia took a turn. "Group, I should say a subsidiary of Group, has a line on WEEE sourcing. The goods are containerized, and, like bad money, sanitized with clean documentation."

"Destination?" Stonecrop asked. He already felt like a co-conspirator.

"Lagos, Nigeria, where the product is treated, disposed of, or remarketed. We are, technically—there is a word for this, too—an *aggregator*. Adewole is the *grease*. He arranges customs and border security in Lagos. Group makes a boatload of money, no pun intended, and yours truly," she not-so-tenderly patted Gregor hand several times, "—and this is the real reason for playing the game—gets a pass regarding certain indiscretions."

"Uh-huh. And you've *aggregated* this stuff?" He had not seen one iota of evidence that Group had been engaged in collecting e-waste.

"In a box and tied with a bow!" she explained. "Our Swiss and Interpol associates, being our partners in crime, have been squirreling away e-waste for some months. They're terribly industrious!"

"Why Group?"

"Because Gregor, as they know and we know, is a logistics genius and credible, in a nasty way, with the right nasty people—the bigger fish, so to speak." She gave Ratzow an affectionate smile and again put her stubby little fingers over his stubby big ones.

He, Stonecrop, was not as sanguine about the "WEEE sting" as his tablemates, and not at all happy about doing anything with Chum. His expression said as much as he sagged back in his chair, leaning away from them and emotionally wanting to escape. He scanned people, regular people, milling about Weinplatz. *Is there any such thing as a regular person?* Was someone watching the three them, here, having lunch? *If I were Interpol, I'd keep tabs on Gregor 24-7.* He picked out a likely watcher. Gregor was a man of habits and routines. His watchers probably had a permanent room overlooking the plaza and long-installed listening devices in his apartment. Stonecrop felt around the rim and then looked under the table.

"Really." Claudia grinned her little U-grin. She had read his thoughts.

Ratzow stepped in for the close.

"Max, before you threaten to throw me in the river again—remember! Is when I know Fede has good man, man with balls!" Gregor laughed, and took a drink, this time from his water glass, and bent forward and lowered his voice. "Here is deal . . ."

He counted on his fingers, like a lawyer in a courtroom. "One: I give you money for this Lomi, and more, enough money to get your boat back. I let you keep *Zaca* in my Marina, best in Greece, for free, forever."

Where had that come from? Stonecrop asked himself. Federica must have said something to him about *Zaca*.

"Two." A second stubby finger stood up. "You do this, you make Fede very happy because now her Papà lives in Storchen and not 'hotel' with steel bars and bad men who might kill him.

"Three," he took another drink, already becoming a ritual for each point, "I talk to Harry Chum and Kommissar Vormittag for you, about things maybe you did or didn't do. Is easier for you to keep residence in Zürich. Sleep at night, da. We both sleep good.

"Four," another drink and another finger, "we do this one time only. No more after. Is like Claudia says, is sting, not business. You meet Adewole here one time, once in Violencia, and once more for meeting at Therme Tavate. Therme is good break, you spa with Fede. Is fun vacation, da."

"Violencia?"

Claudia answered for Gregor, "València, dear, he means València. On the Med, Costa Blanca."

"Violencia or València? Who cares?" Gregor, testy about the correction.

"Aren't you mixing things up?" Stonecrop asked.

Gregor didn't react. He'd rattle off a few specifics, but it was all in the abstract. The real world was fuzzy gray. Was he waiting for an answer, or maybe a question? Did he, Stonecrop, have a choice? *Of course, he had a choice.* Gregor had one thing right: Stonecrop's past could catch up with him at any point. Gregor's support would provide enormous leverage with the authorities, with any authorities. And the man was always good for his word.

"Why me? Why not the man himself, Gregor Ratzow?"

"I am boss. And I don't know shit. If *you* meet these people and don't know shit, who cares? They still believe someone in charge is smart. You are businessman. Why don't you know that!"

Ratzow tapped Stonecrop on the head with the knuckle of one finger. The tap smarted, but Stonecrop ignored the pain and agreed with the point.

"Besides, I am busy. I will be busy and can't go to Tavate party."

"Or València," Claudia added. "Gregor's too long of tooth for València. Operational work is best suited for a young, dashing, handsome man like you, darling."

Stonecrop had questions but questioned the value of knowing the answers. He might be less culpable knowing less than more.

"Okay, I'm in," he agreed, and made the response sound cheerier than he felt. He was not at all convinced he had made the right decision.

Claudia beamed. She placed a phone on the table and invited the men to huddle up. The handy looked used and had the usual array of apps. Claudia scrolled through the contacts. She had obviously cloned them from his phone. Or maybe Fede's. One app he didn't recognize.

"Tap this just before your meeting. Even if you turn off the phone, the recorder will stay on for the next two hours. If you restart the phone at less than two hours, recording goes until you double tap the app. Easy-peasy. The reception is a hundred times better than a normal phone. You can leave the thing in your pocket. Three meetings. Three recordings. That's all."

She slipped the phone under his hand and Stonecrop dropped the handy in his black daypack, a surreptitious act that accorded with the sunless gloom hanging over the city. The air had grown chilly. She also handed him a sheaf of paper, about ten pages. "Homework before your meeting tonight. Call me if you have any questions."

"Like I was saying . . ." He took the papers and pushed his still nearly full glass of wine away from his place setting. Claudia and Ratzow looked the happy couple. "I've always wanted to be a Transport Specialist."

One Planet's owners were a young couple from Oslo; one was trans, the other gay. Somebody in the organization had money. A climbing gym this size—about thirty-thousand square feet, with the walls with adjustable cracks, a route-setting cherry picker, fitness studios for yoga and dance, weights, and aerobic machines—had to cost north of ten million USD.

"Fuck, is that what we save them for?" Federica's tone was both angry and sad.

"You're on," Stonecrop said, meaning that she was 'on belay.' He clipped the Petzl GRIGRI belay device to his climbing harness, tugged the rope to make sure the brake-assisted cam would engage and that the rope was threaded properly, and then squeezed the carabiner connecting his harness to the GRIGRI to ensure that the gate was in the locked position.

Federica put her foot on the first foothold before Stonecrop flagged her for an additional safety check. "Hang on," he said, and faced her to make sure she had tied in the way Zürich's One Planet climbing gym required.

"Good to go. Have fun."

The route, a fifteen-meter "pitch" that started vertically, had a five-meter somewhat overhanging section in the middle, and delicate though less than vertical finish. This day was an enduro exercise. Twenty laps in an hour.

By the third lap, she had worked out the moves and figured out how to get her hip into the wall on the overhang, to optimize counterpressure with her feet and a dropped knee, and to set and use her lats. She climbed through the steep section quickly and recovered on the finish. Each time she topped out, she let go the holds and let

Stonecrop take her weight on the rope. He lightly pulled back on the lever on the GRIGRI to ease pressure on the cam, thus allowing the rope with all of Federica's weight on it to pass through the device at a safe rate of descent. The controlled lower took ten seconds; Federica would have a thirty-to-sixty second rest and a sip of water before the next lap.

"You give them choices they otherwise wouldn't have. And you save lives," he said.

The broken conversation started and stopped during half-minute breaks. She squirted hydration drink into her mouth and then wiped her chin and mouth with the front of her tank top.

"The stoves give them a few extra hours a day. They get basic health care. But for what? So they can go to church, sing in a choir, and end up as goddamned sex slaves!"

He smelled the orange drink on her breath. Her reference had been to Aide Direct, the non-profit she founded four years ago. Repurposing Papà's money, she had said. The organization provided medical and other services to women in a handful of needy communities in Africa, one outside of Maputo. Fede had worked in the field with her volunteers and had braved natural disasters, disease, entrenched bigotry and sexism, and warlords.

Music blared in the background. The climbers used hand signals when Federica reached the top of the wall or needed tension or slack.

Whenever she climbed, or worked, or tackled any task that required concentration, she did so with extraordinary directness and clarity. Stonecrop couldn't take his eyes off of her. No one could. He'd witnessed the same reaction in others when Federica, without trying, owned center stage.

And what am I? Stonecrop asked himself. *An over-educated jock, a failed venture capitalist. Oh yeah, I forgot MIA father and husband. On the bright side, I survived a string of violent encounters over the last two years. Max 'Hard To Kill' Stonecrop. That's something, I guess.*

"Ready, Max?"

"Can you add sex-trade warnings to your team's educational program?" Stonecrop suggested.

Federica delayed her start. "Not easy," she responded and took a few seconds more to catch her breath. "My volunteers are doctors and aid workers, not social workers. There'd be backlash from priests, from Juju men. Christ, even vaccinations are a major challenge. We're already disrupting the norms and economics of village life. If we overreach, we won't be invited back."

"Yeah, I get it," Stonecrop conceded. Her tank top had gone from aqua to dark blue, the entire shirt was soaked with sweat. Her arms and shoulders, thighs and calves, glistened in the mix of natural and artificial light. The music switched to an indie set streamed from, of all places, Portland, Oregon.

"Last one," he said, and leaned over to kiss her damp forehead. Wet hair clung to his lips. The smell of her body did something to him. Not arousal per se, something more complex, maybe the familiarity, the message more like when you're with this person you're safe. She brushed closer to him. "Got one more?" he asked.

"Kiss?" she kidded.

"No! One more pitch."

"Uh huh, I feel good. Strong." Federica flirted with him, and then turned away to reach up for the first hold.

The session wrapped up in under an hour, a solid session. Federica was too pooped to shower. Stonecrop held her hair back as she washed up and splashed cold water on her face. The bathrooms were co-ed. No one was near them, and he leaned against her from behind.

"We've got some time, you know, before I pick up the kiddos."

She wiggled her bottom against him and laughed, "Perfect timing." The way she said it, meant, of course, the exact opposite. She explained anyway, likely figuring Max was like most guys and would need it spelled out for him.

"Note: This girl is stinky, exhausted, and hungry!"

Another climber, a woman, walked up to sink and winked at Federica.

Climbers, you gotta love 'em.

An added amenity at One Planet was the small but inviting K-2 Café. The health-bar/restaurant served coffee, tea, power drinks, organic hausgemacht soups, farmers' market bio-salads, plates of fresh pastries, and local beer and wines. Posters of local rock-jocks hung from the walls, some signed, a few framed. Stonecrop was acquainted with and had climbed with a few of the local celebs.

Climber cuisine, as a rule, fell into either end of the health spectrum. Either vegan supreme, or mostly sugar and caffeine. Stonecrop, skinny and fit though he was, didn't fit the stereotype. His second lunch of the day was a latte and open-faced sandwich: cream cheese and salmon with dill on dark, seedy, Norwegian bread. He liked vodka with salmon, but he'd already had a splash of wine with lunch number one.

Plus, *his* enduro workout was coming up. And there was his first official meeting with Adewole later that night.

"Any luck with Lomi?" Federica asked, a continuation of an earlier discussion when Stonecrop had described his new "title" at GR Group and the sixty-thousand Swiss that Claudia would, post-sting, transfer to his account to pay for Lomi's bonding. That was if he could find her.

He checked for messages. "Nothing. I wasn't going to, but I did text Kommissar Vormittag about Lomi. Not about her being beaten, but just that I would have the cash and, as a favor to Destiny, I wanted to find Lomi. Just to help."

"And Lorenzo?"

"Leaving him out of the equation. For now."

Federica took several spoonfuls of cold celery soup, breaking up the center dollop of sour cream and fresh marjoram with each pass.

"More?"

"Not really. But what's creepy is that when I saw Vormittag this morning, he was going to Halbinsel Au . . . another body."

She lifted her spoon and pointed at the large format TV screen behind Stonecrop. "You mean that one?"

He twisted around in his chair to watch. An amateur video showed the Wasserschutzpolizei craft, and then panned three officers manhandling an uncooperative and very dead body over the transom. A long, water-soaked scarf dangled from the neck of the corpse. *Another lifeless flag.* The video zoomed in for a close-up of the face of the victim. Scattered images followed and then a last shot of the grey featureless sky before the screen went dark as an officer's hand grew large and covered the increasingly intrusive camera lens.

"He's Japanese," Federica said. "The white bandana, that's like something the kamikaze pilots wore."

Stonecrop used his fingers to wipe off a spot of soup that had dripped from her spoon onto her forearm. "You're pumped."

"That workout was a toughie."

He felt the muscles in her forearm. "Yup, you got worked. I'm still kinda hungry. Nachtisch?" Stonecrop asked if she wanted dessert. He rose, walked up to the service counter, keeping his focus on the TV, and ordered a *tuorta da nusch,* an Engadine dessert made with pastry dough and a caramelized walnut filling.

"I wonder," Stonecrop said when he returned, "if I could get a job here. You know, part-time."

"Teaching climbing?" she asked.

"No, cooking."

"No way! You'd never cook at home and your girl would starve to death."

"Still—"

"Poor Kommissar Vormittag," Federica interrupted. "First, he's shot, then Andreas turns up—that's bound to be on the news soon—and now this, the Japanese man."

"A shock about Andreas," he said. Again, self-conscious about the fact that he was a poor liar. He asked himself if it was the onslaught of news that made him want to escape to the comfort of the kitchen.

"I'm over him," she said. "Mostly."

"Trouble comes in threes," Stonecrop announced. He was uncomfortable with the finality of the words and dug into his *tuorta da nusch*, which he found to be excellent.

Body Count

After lunch number two for Stonecrop, the two climbers switched roles. Federica belayed as Stonecrop did back-to-back laps. He was, as always when he climbed, at ease and having fun. They were about an hour into the routine when one of the phones in Federica's back pocket vibrated. The handy was Stonecrop's; there was a text from Vormittag. He had returned from Halbinsel Au and wanted to meet as soon as possible. Stonecrop read the message after Federica lowered him to the ground. He fired off a brief reply.

"Twice in the same day," he said. "I'm dreading the popularity."

"Where?" Federica asked.

"He's coming here. Be here in a half-hour."

Stonecrop pushed through a half-dozen more laps before the *Stadtpolizei* vehicle drove up and parked in front of One Planet. The driver waited in the car as the Kommissar, arm in sling, exited and walked toward the open garage door that served as the entrance of the K-2 Café. Federica and Stonecrop watched as he approached.

No one bothered with hellos. With a few gestures, they found a table in a quiet corner far enough from the kitchen to dull the headbanging music.

"We saw the news." Federica opened the conversation.

"Sad, lately the news is always sad," Vormittag said. "I don't like my job. Not on days like today."

"Depressing weather," Stonecrop contributed to the gloom.

Vormittag nodded. "Ja, trübes Wetter. Men go mad—"

"Women, too," Federica spoke sharply. Stonecrop knew she regretted the tone of her interjection before she had finished speaking. Vormittag was no misogynist. She tempered her reaction by supplying a word he had missed. "*Gloomy* in English."

Federica plunged into the tragedy du jour: "Is he Japanese, the man in the lake?"

"I believe so. Swiss citizen though. Owned a car wash. 'Kar-Moppa.' Something funny like that. A well-established business and in good-standing."

Good standing in Zürich mostly meant that he had paid his taxes.

"I know the place!" Stonecrop's reaction was overly cheerful given their sober mood. "Love the name. The place is ten minutes from here. There's a funky billboard on Bernerstrasse, a Buddha with a bucket and an arrow that points to a side road."

Federica shook her head, the tips of her fingers at her forehead and elbows on the table, smiling as she spoke. "Karmapa *is* an enlightened teacher of Buddhism. The Karmapa's lineage goes back to the eleven-hundreds in Tibet. The current Karmapa, he's—I don't know—the seventeenth or eighteen in the line, lives in exile, in Dharamsala, India. I recently saw a TED talk he gave."

Vormittag was quiet. Had the unexpected levity upset him? Both Federica and Stonecrop were on an endorphin and sugar high. And as always, a certain gallows humor pervaded the climbing community, like some fear-masking essence. Take the K-2 Café, named after one of the deadliest mountains in the world.

"Suppose he likes being the poster child for a car wash?" Stonecrop asked.

"Yes, he would be honored!" Federica came back. "He'd grab a sponge and scrub away!"

Vormittag ordered an espresso. Stonecrop followed suit by holding up three fingers to the waiter.

The Kommissar brought them back on topic. "I am, as has been the case all day, pressed for time."

"Me, too," said Stonecrop. "Dinner with Ibrahim Adewole tonight."

He'd tossed out the name intentionally, to test whether or not what Claudia and Gregor had claimed was the case. Namely, that Chum and Vormittag were both a party to the WEEE-sting. Claudia had thought the name clever.

"Ah, good. Yes, I'd almost forgotten," Vormittag said, and then repeated, "*Almost* forgotten," the clarification averring there was no way he had forgotten. Using his good arm, he put his hand on Federica's wrist. "I apologize for revisiting a bad memory, but I have a question for Max." He turned to face Stonecrop.

"Do you want me to leave?" Federica offered.

"No, not necessary. I'd rather you stay," he replied to her and turned to face Stonecrop.

Always on tenterhooks in Vormittag's company, Stonecrop assumed that the Kommissar wanted Federica to remain so that he could assess their combined reaction to his inquiries, a methodology used to detect falsehoods.

"Max, back in November after you, Andreas Castro, and Federica left the Dolder Hotel, where did you go? We now know that Castro took off, driving to Saint Moritz where his pilot and plane were waiting for him. Federica, you," he faced her now, "I recall that you returned to Frau Ott's."

"I followed Castro," Stonecrop opted for a partial truth, "to make sure he wasn't going back to Fede's. Lost him just after Albula. Figured he was well on his way by then. Turned around and came home. Disrespectful to say now, but I kind of enjoyed the chase. He drove fast, maybe too fast for conditions. Summer tires and all. There were patches of ice on the road. The weather got nasty."

"Rather a long way to pursue him, just to see if he was not returning to Zürich, to Frau Ott's?"

"Yeah. I was making a point. Kind of in-your-face driving. Or rear-view mirror driving, as it were."

"And you didn't confront him personally? I want the truth, Max."

"Nope. I swear. Not a word," Stonecrop tried to not look away from Vormittag. At least what he had said was literally true, though he could not shake the feeling that Vormittag saw right through him.

"A web cam in Albula, the last one before Julier Pass, recorded your Audi a minute or so behind Castro. The same cam records your return . . . an hour later. You understand . . ."

"Yes, of course. I slid off the road at one point. Had to dig the car out and then decided it was too dangerous to go on. I'd lost Castro. I was exhausted. Then I drove home."

Months before, Stonecrop had told Federica and family the same lie he just told Vormittag. If enough people believe something, the belief will become the truth. He felt his blood pressure rise and sweat at his brow. *I so suck at lying!*

Vormittag won the stare down with Stonecrop, who made the rookie mistake of continuing to talk.

"What did his pilot say?" The interest was feigned and transparent.

Of course, Vormittag didn't have to answer the question; he could have squeezed Stonecrop. But he chose not to. Instead, he reported that the pilot had waited for his client. The pilot had commented later that Mr. Castro had missed reserved flights in the past. His absence, in other words, had not been a cause of concern. The plane had another charter opportunity and left without him.

Their coffees arrived and they sat in silence, savoring the espresso and the hiatus in the interrogation. Stonecrop wondered if the Kommissar was sorting out the facts and weighing his desire for the truth with realpolitik pressure from Chum and others to use Gregor and his transport specialist for the upcoming sting operation. He rotated in his chair to speak to Federica and winced, clearly having forgotten about his injury.

"Federica," Vormittag asked, "how do feel about Andreas, and his death?"

The question was unusual in that the poser could be either the avuncular and sympathetic family friend or the public investigator looking for motive or a cover-up. She responded immediately and with no disguise in her voice.

"Sad, of course. We'd broken off the engagement. As you know, he abused me. But he didn't deserve to die for it."

"And *did* he die for it? Do you think that?"

"In a way, yes. We were through. But now I feel guilty. He was so emotionally unstable and would get insanely angry over nothing. Andreas had little self-control." Bemused, she continued, "You know he was a terrible driver."

"Terrible in the sense of competency or risk-taking? Was he suicidal?"

"Suicidal? I don't think so. I rejected him. He took it hard, because he was so used to having his way with everything . . . and everybody. I suppose deeply selfish people can be suicidal if they don't get what they want. I'm no therapist, but, well, he was narcissistic. Extremely so."

Hell yeah, thought Stonecrop. He didn't say a word out of fear of revealing his enthusiasm about her characterization of Andreas.

"There was . . . that unpleasantness between you?" Vormittag was referencing a traumatic event that Fede had rarely discussed, not in any detail, with Stonecrop. "At least once, that time you called the Stadtpolizei."

Federica's measured the words. "We had been engaged, not for very long. He'd hurt me. Tio Vittore, you know I'd rather not talk about it. I'm sad about his death." With her thumb and middle finger she rotated her empty espresso cup, a quarter turn at a time. The familial term reset the course of the conversation.

"Perdonami. I am going to close the file on Castro. Is there anything more you'd like to tell me?"

"No. Well, yes. Two things . . . first, it was a matter of 'competence.' He was a very distracted driver."

"The other thing?"

"Yes. Have you contacted Lupita? His cousin. She's a friend. I don't want to be the one to break the news."

"In Dardin. No, but someone from my office has. His immediate family in Mexico has been notified. They have been worried and had filed a missing person's report in Mexico. That was some months ago. Our desk never saw the request. I shall have to look into why."

Even though Federica had implored Vormittag to end the Andreas Castro discussion, the Kommissar wasn't quite ready to drop the questioning: "It's odd, don't you think, that so much time had passed since the incident at Susenbergstrasse with no communication from Andreas, absolutely nothing. Castro had not contacted you, or Lupita, or any of his family. I find that strange. Impossible, really."

"Yes and no. With Andreas, months could go by without a word. As far as Lupita goes, well, you'll have to ask her. She'd had an unpleasant experience as well, only once—"

"With Castro?" Vormittag interjected.

"Yes," Federica answered, her gaze found its target again, into the espresso cup.

"When was that?"

"Years ago, she was young. Twelve, in fact. She never spoke a word to him, after that. I'd rather—"

"Yes, of course. That's between us. Do you want to see the family? I can let you know when they arrive to claim the body."

Federica acknowledged his statement by looking up, though not at him. She stopped rotating her cup and then resumed rotating it as she spoke. "Not really. What's done is done, Vittore. For me, emotionally, he died that day he drove off . . ."

"And likely physically died," Vormittag said. He quickly supplemented the response, aware that his comment had been unnecessarily harsh. "I'm sorry."

Her use again of the Kommissar's first name clearly implied that this conversation had shifted to the personal.

"Ah." The Kommissar had something more: "Harry Chum is

assisting the Mexican Consulate with some of the paperwork. They've not had to deal with the death of a Mexican national in Switzerland for some time."

Blood rushed to Stonecrop's head. He felt like he had frozen in place and that both Vormittag and Federica were able to move but he could not and soon they would discover his immobility. Deflection, that's all he had left in his quiver of deception.

"A carwash," Stonecrop announced, too brightly and out of context. "Why would someone murder a guy who owned a car wash?"

"Did I mention murder?" Vormittag rejoined.

"The news did," Stonecrop spoke calmly. He was trying—hopefully not too hard—to regain his composure. "Unless I misunderstood the German."

"The cause of death has not been determined," Vormittag added, appearing miffed about the news having made the unsupported claim. "Did the commentator mention prostitution?"

"No," Stonecrop said, now curious about why Vormittag had brought that up. "Was he a pimp or a customer?"

"Possibly. One of our men recognized the victim."

"Work," Federica held up her handy, rose from the table, and walked a few steps away. She was preoccupied with texting as Vormittag checked his phone as well, and then hurriedly made his goodbye to Stonecrop and walked to his car. Stonecrop watched as Vormittag roused the driver whose head and arms were slumped over the steering wheel. His hat lay askew on the dash.

"Shoji Jado," she announced to Max after Vormittag had left the building. "That's the guy in the lake."

"And how on Earth do you know that?"

"Japanese friend. I sent him the news link. He's very upset."

Federica stood next to Stonecrop. She leaned over, hands on the table. Stonecrop looked at her, noticing where her sweat-stained sleeveless T stuck to her breasts. He wanted to discard every thought in his mind and be with her, lost.

She spoke so they would not be overheard. "Shoji's death is connected to Lomi and Destiny. I know it."

She had not said the name of her Japanese friend. Stonecrop knew immediately that that had not been an unintentional omission. The "friend" was a person they had agreed to not talk about. Federica's capacity for forgiveness was something Stonecrop struggled to understand. *Listen to the woman,* he told himself. She walked the talk.

"We'll find out soon enough," he rallied. "The car's filthy."

"We'll find out soon enough," he rallied. "The car's filthy."

Kar-Moppa

They turned off Bernerstrasse and drove down a paved road in need of repair. Golden arrows on the billboard directed them to the Kar-Moppa Kar Wash.

"Reminds me of those 50s road signs in the States for Burma Shave."

Federica looked like she had no idea what he was talking about.

Stonecrop dodged potholes. He felt constrained and clumsy in his "dress" clothes—at the gym he had changed into a polo shirt, slacks, blazer, and loafers. The phone Claudia had given him felt too big for the pants pocket.

Federica read off the signs.

"Happy Finish! . . . Hot Suds Rubs! . . . Wax-on Wax-off! . . . Nirvana! . . . The Quickie! . . . Rim Trim!"

"The Quickie. Really!" he said.

"Rim Trim's got me wondering," she laughed.

The industrial neighborhood was non-descript. Chain-link fences overgrown by brush, warehouse walls, and stacks of containers barricaded offices and factories while signage, some new, some faded beyond readability identified businesses: Zahlinger Group Recycling und Rohstoffe; Willy & Sohn Hydraulik AG; Haas Speditions AG . . .

They made their way past warehoused pipes, steel transport containers of various sizes and colors, power company transformers, and rail equipment. Goods were stored outdoors, either in the open with the massive cement drainage tubes, or they were protected by expansive sheet-metal roofs. Invariably, firms with open inventory on the grounds topped the surrounding walls or chain-link fence with intimidating coils of razor-wire.

The road dead-ended at a turn-around and Kar-Moppa proper. Ivy had overgrown the entry gate and had been trimmed to create sunken skull-like pockets out of which snake-eyed security cameras surveilled the surroundings. A parking area, two drive-through wash stations, an adjacent office, and a road labeled "Exit Only" bordered the far end of an inner circular drive. Two cars were queued up at each of the wash stations; another, cleaning completed, pulled of the exit. Several attendants busied themselves with taking orders. Others were vacuuming vehicles, taping down windshield wipers, and spraying soiled areas on vehicles ahead of the pre-wash station.

Stonecrop and Federica joined the queue. Their car, one of Gregor's fleet, a black Audi S7, didn't stand out. As he approached the entrance, a uniformed attendant took the key fob and order, then ran the credit card on a phone sensor.

"Textilwäsche Staubsaugen Felgen-Spezial," Stonecrop repeated, to make sure the attendant got the order correct. In addition to the basic wash, he and Fede opted for interior cleaning, vacuuming, and the wheels special.

"Papà will be surprised," Fede said. Into the role, the schoolgirl on a date squeezed his arm.

The attendant overheard the English and grinned. He was missing half a tooth. "We do extra-good job for Papà!"

"Merci vilmal," Federica thanked him. Stonecrop noticed that she had resisted the temptation to respond in kind in his own language. Maybe, for once, she had not recognized it.

"North African," she said.

So much for that.

The two of them exited the Audi and strolled down a path paved with multi-colored, tinted-concrete steppingstones. At the end, they arrived at the waiting room and patio at the back of the front office and facing the interior yard of the facility. The Stations were neatly labeled and color coded. Station One was staffed by three men—also immigrants?—in charge of interior cleaning. Station Two workers chaperoned the vehicle through a stall with no-touch automatic sprayers and dryers. At the third station, another team oversaw drying. Arms with rags fluttered around the vehicle like a giant insect grooming itself. After polishing and waxing, the sparkling vehicle was then deposited at pick-up Platz, a parking area adjacent to the waiting room and with a landscaped patio and a fountain with four pissing cherubs. The interior waiting room offered ceiling windows, deep-cushioned sofas, a television, Wi-Fi, and Gratis-Kaffee, Wein, Käse & Butterbrezel.

"I meet Adewole in an hour. I hope the Quickie's quick." Stonecrop squirmed in his chair. He hadn't taken time to stretch after climbing and had to massage a calf muscle on the verge of cramping.

Federica leaned closer and pointed. "See, look, over there. After you pick up your car, you can go left to the exit or take the street on the right. A little farther along the exit road, the right one loops back. The trees block whatever's back there."

"First time?" a voice behind them asked. The English was good, though not native. The overweight and well-dressed man could easily be a manager at KPMG. The firm had a major office nearby in a nondescript building where the grunt work was done by hundreds of support staff and accountants.

"Yes. We were in Schlieren at the climbing gym and saw the sign," Federica said.

"Don't let the oddball signs deter you. This is the best carwash in Zürich."

"Do you come here often?"

"Every Tuesday. I bring lunch." The man took a moment to finish chewing. He took a drink from his water bottle. "Usually sit in the garden. Nice escape from the office."

Federica pointed to a wall of beech trees. "What's over there?"

"Ja, well," he winked and paused before speaking. He had just taken another bite of his sandwich and spoke as he chewed. "Ja, that costs more than washing the car!" He winked again, "It's not for me." He showed the back of his left hand and the wedding ring.

One of the uniformed workers parked the newly cleaned S7 in a parking slot a few meters away. He raised an arm and circled the drying cloth in the air—a universal gesture. Stonecrop approached him, took the key fob, and gave him a tip. Something about having a spotless, clean car inspired him to open the door for Federica. He followed her reflection on the hood as she neared the vehicle and climbed inside.

"Got that new car smell. The wash stall is touchless. Ironic, don't you think?" Federica ran her fingers over the dash, cleaned but without the residue or shininess that a cheap conditioner would leave. "Would my Alfa survive Kar-Moppa?"

"Fede, I'll wash that little old Alfa for you. And no, the auto wash would trash the top." He fired up the S7. "What's say a short tour?"

Like a Japanese garden—which it was—the compound revealed itself in layers. The road surface turned to white crushed gravel. The circuitous path wrapped around a series of stalls unrelated to washing cars. Each stall was unique, open on one side and harbored a place to park that was both private and uncramped. The facility was not unlike the city's legally sanctioned "sex boxes" with similar three-walled stalls.

There were differences, however. Kar-Moppa's cameras were somewhat camouflaged and there was no signage instructing both customers and workers about safe sex practices. And more, Stonecrop noted, the feel was different. The place wasn't the least tawdry. Not a scrap of garbage, wastepaper, or a cigarette butt. The gardens were as lovely as anything he'd seen in the city parks: vine maples, shore pines, a cacophony of flowering bushes, a small pond with koi and cattails and red-winged blackbirds, a ring of plane trees, and several shaded, tucked away, bowers.

Women lolled about: a group of three, and others of two or three on their own. One sat in a swing hanging off a branch of an ancient oak that the landscape architect had managed to preserve and integrate into the layout.

The women, poised and attractive, were a cross-section of race and nationality.

After the drive through, Federica directed them back to the front office. "I know your late to your appointment, but I gotta ask. I mean, we're here."

"Adewole's not going anywhere; he can wait. Divide and conquer?" he asked.

"Not on your life." Federica shook a finger at him. "You stay away from those women!"

"I'm really not in *that* much of hurry," he grinned back. Federica punched him in the shoulder.

The office receptionist pushed back on Stonecrop's request to speak with the owner and busied herself with stocking a display of auto cleaning supplies. When he asked about Lomi, the door to the manager's office swung open. The madam, a saddened, hollowed version of the same woman he had met at Bürkliplatz landing, stood by the door and showed them in.

"Sit," she said. There was none of the arrogance and confidence from their first meeting. She didn't bother to re-introduce herself.

Her dress was a drab, gray, cotton print; her hair rose in a frizzy briar. She took a seat at her desk and indicated they should use the two unpadded wooden chairs opposite her desk. The office was plain by comparison to the extraordinary grounds. One would say that the office looked like a car wash office should: a bulletin board cluttered with notes and photos that were attached with stickpins; a train of flat-screen displays linked to grounds cameras hung on the wall. "No Smoking" signs were posted throughout; nevertheless, there was an open pack on the desk. The madam extracted and lit a cigarette. She inhaled deeply through the fag. When she exhaled, the smoke curled around her face and further dried flesh already brittle, scored, and prematurely aged.

"I can get the money to pay her bonding. Lomi's bonding," Stonecrop said. He had taken direction from his subject and skipped the pleasantries.

"You know my husband just died. I can't even see his goddamned body until they finish their bullshit autopsy."

"I'm sorry," Federica said.

The older woman nodded, inhaled again. Smoke came out of her mouth as she spoke. "You're a big spender, big-boy. Destiny not do it for you?"

The sadness in her voice had been expelled with the smoke out of her nostrils.

"Where is she? Where is Lomi?"

The madam inhaled deeply and released another lungful before she spoke. Her voice hardened. "Damned if I know. You tell me."

"I know the price. I can't pay more." He had assumed she was negotiating.

"I'd love to separate you from your money, honey, but I don't have the goods."

"Where do you *think* she is?"

"Maybe the bottom of the fucking lake!" she screamed at him. The self-restraint slipped away. "You don't know shit, do you? When a girl takes off, I tell my people. They find her. I'm still out the money. But they settle the score."

The conversation was going nowhere. They stared at each other. Federica gave it a go.

"Was he your husband? Shoji? Was he from the States, too?"

The woman laughed, a smoker's throaty laugh. She used her hand to remove a piece of tobacco from her mouth, a smoker gesture to stall a conversation. Empty and at the same time watery eyes stared at the ceiling.

"Osaka, as a matter of fact. Sure as fuck not St. Louis. He was my gardener. Gardened the shit out of me like there was no tomorrow. Not that that's any of your goddamned business.

"Everyone *sort of* loved him. The girls, the marks, the servicemen . . . the goddamned plants, they loved the little shit. And, like I said, me. Everything he touched he made prettier . . . and poorer. He squeezed the money out 'til there was nothin' more to squeeze."

A tear formed and fled across the desert flesh before spotting the cotton shirr rimming the bosom of her blouse. "The greedy, green thumb. That's what he was. That's Shoji."

"Was he Buddhist?" Federica asked.

The madam let out an untethered hysterical laugh. More tears followed.

"Of course he was fucking Buddhist! Endless buddha bullshit poured out of his mouth. The goddamned trees at the gate," she lowered her voice and laid on a Japanese accent, " 'they are, Kar-Moppa, female and male. *Led* pine has delicate bark and slender needles—' " she laughed at her intentional mispronunciation of *red*— " 'like woman.' He'd wink. 'Black pine needle is thick and stiff. Dark, has white bud.' He'd grab his balls. Got a real bonsai dick, I'll tell you. 'Woman has *led* bud,' he'd say, and wink again. Like that was supposed to be funny or smart or somethin'. Fucking moron never could say *red*."

"I think that's lovely," Federica said.

"Then you're a moron, too."

"How'd he die?" Stonecrop asked.

"She killed him, you fucking simpleton."

"Who killed him?"

"Watch the news."

"We did." Stonecrop and Federica answered in unison.

"The scarf, you see that white scarf around his neck?"

"I noticed, yes," Federica said, her voice attentive.

"That's Lomi's. Never saw her without one, a white scarf—had a dozen. Her *signature* piece, she said. Helps clients remembered her. A pussy is just a pussy; but a white scarf, well that's somethin' a john remembers."

"That proves nothing," Stonecrop said.

"I have proof, real proof." The disgust with which she said the words gave the claim credibility.

"I don't believe you."

The madam hovered over the keyboard of the laptop on her desk.

Red, tear-weary eyes jumped from image to image as she scanned through a series of videos, spending second or two on each one. She knew what she was looking for. When she found the video, she spun the laptop around so they could see the display.

"See for yourself."

The video was from one of Kar-Moppa's security cameras. The black and white images were blurred but clear enough to show ten seconds or so of Lomi pommeling Shoji with her fists. She was bigger than he was. And stronger.

"Did you report to the Polizei?"

"You live in the fucking ozone, right?" The string of remarks had rekindled her confidence. Disconsolate no more, she took a drag and leaned to the side to blow smoke out of a contorted corner of her mouth.

"Why not?" Stonecrop pressed her.

"'cause I'm going to kill the bitch myself. I'm gonna wind one of them white scarves around her neck and twist it 'til her eyes pop out of her pretty little head. Goddamned ungrateful cunt."

A reasonable reaction. Stonecrop got vengeance. "Why would she murder your husband?"

"She broke the rules. Shoji didn't like people breaking the rules."

"Maybe I can find her," he offered, not knowing how she would interpret the offer.

The madam seemed to be in her own world and didn't respond.

"Dodo, you asked *me* where she was? Remember?" He didn't respond. Without prompting, she continued. "After the Lorenzo fling, Shoji warned her. No more. Business is business. Lorenzo fucks you, I get paid, he said. She didn't stop. Dumb bitch carried on with some other john, too. You see, Shoji figured he paid for that money-maker between her legs. They fought a lot. I don't blame him. We were both pissed. But she's a big woman. And she's a mean woman."

"Was he a violent man?"

"Bonsai's about control, not kindness. Make those plants suffer in tight little pots. What do *you* think, bright boy?"

"What I think is I can give you sixty-thousand francs to forget about her." Despite the video, Stonecrop didn't believe Lomi killed Shoji. He'd seen her. She wasn't a killer. Or did he *want* to believe that? The few killers Stonecrop had known had something that set them apart. Though his was not a reliable universe. Would Vormittag figure out who had murdered the husband? Would the traffickers get to Lomi first?

The madam's face hardened; it could have been lava rock. "That your car?" She looked out the office window. The Audi was parked a few feet away, next to several other cars waiting to be claimed by their owners.

A long ash dangled off the end of her cigarette and then landed on her dress. She brushed it off with the back of her hand, slapping uncaringly at her bosom, as if she were punishing her breasts.

The madam rotated the laptop and was staring at the screen, re-watching the footage. "Car's done. Get the fuck out of here."

Stonecrop looked away. He and Federica left her to grieve or rant, whatever gave her solace, and drove Ratzow's gleaming Audi into the gloomy brume.

Adewole

There had been just enough time to drop off Federica, grab a shower, and make the meeting with Adewole at UBS. It being the tail-end of the bank's "cafeteria" dining hours the UBS private client dining area —refurbished and upgraded since Stonecrop's venture capital days— was almost empty. Their table, a discrete distance from another table with two diners, overlooked Paradeplatz. Were it not for the fog, the view would have been grand. Dampened sounds of trams and traffic and an occasional siren propagated through the mist and reverberated against the bank's narrow paned windows.

He'd chosen UBS as his firm's bank when he, on behalf of his employer, had opened their Swiss branch. The rationale for the choice was that UBS had already paid $780 million in fines and provided select account access to the U.S. Department of Justice's Tax Division. In other words, they were over the hump of the U.S. Treasury's effort to recover lost revenue resulting from elaborate tax-avoidance schemes and the concomitant clash with Swiss bank-client-secrecy regulations. UBS had paid their dues, followed the rules, and would not be targeted in the future. The new atmosphere of relative transparency forced the bank to offer something in addition to discretion, something which came naturally to the Swiss—namely, no-airs great service.

Stonecrop kept a small personal account at UBS, but the bank treated him as they had in the past, as one of the select, a VC who might someday use the bank's investment banking services for major fee-generating transactions. His personal banker had kept in touch through the years and had never missed a birthday card to his client.

"Sorry I'm late. Traffic," Stonecrop lied. Good to get in the swing of things and start off with a lie. In truth, he'd been in a private office at UBS where he'd skimmed through the materials from Claudia. It felt like VC days when he'd prep for a meeting or presentation. Stonecrop's short-term memory was killer.

"They know you here," Adewole opined.

"Mr. Stonecrop," the waiter validated Adewole's observation as he smiled at Stonecrop and approached to take their dinner orders. "It is good to see you again."

Two years, in fact, had gone by since Stonecrop had dined at the bank. Nkassa, discrete to the core, knew better than to reveal such information to Stonecrop's guest. He continued, "The sole is good today. I recall you like the sole."

"Good to see you, Nkassa. I've been traveling. How are you? And your family?"

"I am fine. They are still in DRC. My wife says Zürich is too cold!"

Stonecrop didn't press him. The real reason, as they both knew, is that getting a permit and visa for Switzerland was a years-long process.

"I see that's the menu today. The sole, please." Stonecrop caught a nod from Adewole indicating Stonecrop should do the ordering. "The same for my guest."

"Wine?" Stonecrop asked.

"Coffee," Adewole responded.

"Coffee. And a Stoli on the rocks, for me. Thank you, Nkassa."

"I have a ten o'clock flight," Adewole announced, saving Stonecrop from having to ask.

"Do you have your bags with you?"

"I do."

"A bank driver can run you out to Flughafen Zürich. Traffic will be light."

"Before we start, let me apologize. Your València contact was in Zürich yesterday; but, he had to leave today. An urgent personal matter. I had hoped you would meet each other."

It would have been better, Stonecrop agreed, to have had that first meeting here rather than someplace unfamiliar. Working with someone new in a new location compounds the risks. As in any business, the chemistry of the participants was important.

"Not a problem. We'll make it work," Stonecrop said, not knowing what else to say.

"Shall we begin? What do you propose?"

Stonecrop pulled out his new handy and turned it off. He put it back in his pack. "Phones."

Adewole followed suit and turned off and put away his phone.

Since he knew little about transport logistics, Claudia had given Stonecrop a crash course specific to the transaction with Adewole. The first objective of the operation was to become a trusted, albeit minor participant. The degree of participation was unimportant; Gregor's reputation was such that he would be welcomed at any level. Everyone knew Gregor's GR Group could go big at the drop of a hat.

The second part of Stonecrop's assignment required no coaching, nor could Claudia and Gregor provide any. The implementation of blockchain technology by legitimate logistics companies was cutting into Adewole's and his colleague's profits. Adewole's people wanted to learn about blockchain and strategies to mitigate blockchain's impact on their illegal WEEE business in Lagos. At a later date, Stonecrop was to school them on the basics.

"Our aggregators source product in Italy and Spain," Stonecrop explained and then elaborated: "Lecco, Bergamo, Vicenza, and Reggio Emilia. And major industrial areas outside of Barcelona, Catalonia, and northern Asturias, and the Basque provinces. The first container of product is en route to València."

It was mostly bullshit but the container was real. The words felt like a fabrication. They were a fabrication.

"Nothing from Switzerland?" Adewole asked.

"Not much. E-waste is tightly regulated here."

"I see. And how many containers are we to expect?"

"Not much to start, I'm afraid. Two per month. One now. Toe in the water."

Disappointment as thick as the fog outside floated across Adewole's face. He made no attempt to hide his displeasure. "I am sorry, but that is . . . nothing. Perhaps six or seven tonnes."

"Assuming things go smoothly, three times that by year-end."

"Better. A token shipment like this, we'll do for Gregor. Normally not, you understand?" Adewole's voice was even, none of the arrogance Stonecrop had expected. "We may have to bundle your shipment with another order. If we do, there will be additional handling charges."

Stonecrop gestured that he expected as much.

And so it went for the better part of an hour, a tit-for-tat negotiation detailing the e-waste product categories, shipping, processing, re-marketing strategies, and fees.

A break in the conversation followed as Nkassa refilled Adewole's coffee and put a second vodka on the table. Stonecrop reminded himself about the perils of mixing drink and work, and then polished off the vodka. Fuck it. He'd eaten too much, drunk too much, and needed a nap. And he was bored with the charade and weary of Adewole.

Adewole marched onward. "C.I.F. Lagos, fifteen percent of our net; a third to be credited to the next delivery, two-thirds to an account you will provide within ten days of our taking delivery and inspecting the container."

"Cap the dumping charges. I trust you, but if you get squeezed in Lagos, we're not going to pay."

Stonecrop had perked up for a moment. In a best-case scenario, transport from València took sixteen days, plus a minimum of a week in port on either side. That meant a month-plus in transport if everything went smoothly. A lot of commodity price movement can happen in a month.

"I will ask, but I don't think I can give a cap."

"That's the deal. And we'd like twenty."

"Mr. Stonecrop," Adewole grinned. His lips peeled back. The bared teeth appeared oversized for his mouth. "Nice try, but no. You understand, I hope, how small your transaction is." He squeezed his eyes and squinted at a tiny gap between his thumb and finger. "Nigeria accepts, no one knows for certain, at least a hundred-thousand tonnes a year!"

"So I'll buy dinner." Stonecrop smiled back.

Adewole's answer had been the one he had expected. He didn't really care. The next part of their discussion—bogus values on the bill of lading and insurance—really put him sleep. He stared out the window, finding the fog far more interesting than the conversation.

"Exactly." Adewole said.

Stonecrop tried to remember what it was that the *exactly* had referred to. For the life of him, he couldn't remember a word of what either of them had said in the last ten minutes. Or maybe fifteen or twenty.

Adewole sipped his coffee and relaxed his tone of voice, no doubt sensing Stonecrop's drifting off. "Tell me, Mr. Stonecrop. Have you done this sort of thing before?"

"Never," he answered. "First time in e-waste. Did pharma, in Africa. Don't take advantage of me!"

"I suspected as much. And, of course, I won't take advantage of you.

We want to build a relationship. Group enjoys an excellent reputation in the pharma trade. Though now, I've heard, it has closed up shop—at least in Africa. Why is that?"

"Above my pay grade, Mr. Adewole." *And well below my interest grade. Like a give a shit about Gregor's criminal past. Fuck it, I hope he has to pay through the nose for his goddamned garbage.*

"You are being cycled out of pharma to e-waste, yes?"

"That's the plan," Stonecrop duly replied, worried that he would pass out and his head would drop forward and crash on the table.

"A more common story than one would think. Several of my people are . You might have crossed paths with them. Today, WEEE is *the* big opportunity. You won't regret the transition."

Adewole added an aside, "We are look forward to the blockchain session you will be leading in St. Moritz. We are so, so old school. You will have to be patient with your students! And one day you must tell me how you came to be an expert in this sort of thing—Gregor assures me you are."

Somewhere in Zürich, Claudia was listening to and recording their conversation and sharing or planning to share the evidence with Harry Chum, who, no doubt, was eagerly gearing up for the transaction in València and gathering in St. Moritz.

A sober concern voiced itself in the back of his mind. Nkassa had spoken relatively candidly of his family. Was that information, given how Chum could twist things around, something that could be used against their server, or as leverage for some other purpose? The worry, Stonecrop realized, reflected his total erosion of confidence in the embassy's Minister of Fiestas since the episode at Hotel Zürichberg. And further reminded him that he had to find out what Chum had learned about Andreas' death, specifically if anything led to him or Gregor.

The work-talk had exhausted itself. They wrapped up the meeting with chatter about soccer and the inspirational U.S. women's team. Stonecrop welcomed the change of topic. Claudia—likely glued to her headphones—was probably bored and irritated. The unkind thought elicited a moment of schadenfreude.

Zaca

He could swim like this all night, lost in a hypnotic vision and rhythm of his own making. Stroke after stroke broke the surface of the water, each a beacon, a swirling vortex of moonlight.

A line attached to his waist tugged in fits-and-starts. In sync, the inflatable raft laden with two waterproof duffles jerked forward, glided, and went slack. He followed the wake and cadence of Federica's six-beat flutter kick.

The sound of an electronic bass from a shoreline nightclub rumbled across the water like some oceanic indigestion as much felt as heard. Stonecrop glanced at his watch—three a.m., an hour that belonged to both night or morning. Hearing the music and moving soundlessly, they breast-stroked the last ten meters to the boat.

Federica peeled off her swim goggles. "What if someone's onboard?"

He couldn't see her; her disembodied whisper had come from the shadow under the hull.

"We'll know soon enough," Stonecrop said. "Wait here."

He lowered his swim-goggles to around his neck and then untied and handed Federica the cord for the raft. The swim platform at the stern of the boat made it easy to climb aboard. Stonecrop reached in his pocket, found and unsheathed his rigging knife. The tip of the blade was a stubby, the edge serrated. The marlin's spike and shackle key were built into the handle. The stainless-steel blade was beefy enough to cut thick lines or shuck an oyster and, in this case, sufficiently stiff to jimmy open a hatch.

The boat's helm was placed at the back of the cockpit and consisted of a forty-seven-inch spoked wheel, a weatherized display panel, compass, and throttle controls. The wheel, controls, and instruments were mounted on the binnacle post and protected from the sun and salt air by a canvas cover. The hatch, his objective, was two meters forward and covered the entry to the companionway that descended into the cabin.

He inspected the hatch by feel more than sight. It was unlocked, though there was evidence that the hatch had been forced open before. The plexiglass cover slid back smoothly. The door configuration was a typical two-piece affair. He lifted the two slats out of their slots and placed them aside, one on each of the teak bench settees. He'd secure them later to the wall mounts behind the ladder-like steps that led down the companionway. Moonlight poured through narrow rectangular portholes in the cabin walls. The shades were half-drawn. Stonecrop felt his way around the familiar layout. He checked the forward and aft berths, listening for breathing and movement before touching the berths to confirm that they were indeed empty.

He poked his head out the companionway. "No one home."

Federica had made her way to the swim platform and set the duffles in the cockpit. She'd also removed the canvas helm cover.

"Is there an alarm?" she asked.

"I never had one. Doubt the charter folks bothered to install an alarm. On Ibiza, maybe it makes sense. Formentera's dead quiet."

"Are you having fun, Max?" she asked as she loosened a set pin on the binnacle that had locked the wheel in place while the boat was moored.

"I am having *so* much fun!" Truth was, he was giddy.

"Are you worried about Jenny and Sarah?"

"Not at all. Mattie's coming. Frau Ott can handle them until she arrives."

"Alicia might come, too. I never know her schedule."

His girls were becoming more self-reliant. And, of course, they adored Frau Ott. No one had objected when he had announced that he needed to leave Zürich for a couple days in his new role as Gregor's Transport Specialist.

"What's next, Cap'n?"

"We ghost outta here; no motor, no lights." He stood still, feeling the breeze and its direction. "It's light, just enough to take us out of the harbor."

Stonecrop moved by memory across the deck and worked his way to the bow. After making sure the boathook was handy, he freed the mooring line from the bow cleat and quietly lowered the line into the water. He cradled the forestay drum for the roller furling line and felt no obstructions. Leaning into the forestay and headstay, he determined that the steel cables were slightly slack, as they should be if the boat were moored for any lengthy period. He'd stiffen the mast later with a minor adjustment to the backstays.

Back in the cockpit, Federica released the locking lever of the Lewmar block and kept some tension on the furling line as Stonecrop eased out the jib sheet by hand. He let the breeze fill about half the sail, then let it flutter. Federica locked the block and took the helm. Stonecrop put three wraps of the jib sheet on the cockpit's forward starboard self-tailing winch and trimmed the sheet, pulling in enough of the sheet to fill, but still let air spill from the sail.

Zaca, back in his hands after a three-year absence, eased forward. The boat felt perky, eager to grab the wind.

"This *is* the right boat?"

"Oh yeah."

"You chartered *Zaca*? I remember you called them."

"Not exactly," he said as he moved their duffles forward and over to the starboard settee. "I reserved the boat, under a false name."

"Why?"

"Sorry, I should have explained. After I found out Mattie had been paying the storage fees, I checked the company's web site. My boat was supposed to be on the hard, decommissioned, and wrapped—that is, protected from the weather and out of the water. Instead, the marina used *Zaca* for rental charters, which I figure they did since they hadn't heard from me. They're making money off wear and tear on *Zaca*. I didn't want a confrontation, so I figured we'd not make a fuss and just slip out of here."

"And steal your boat back!"

"How's that?" He was nose-to-nose with her. "Never stolen a boat before?"

"Can't say that I have," she laughed with him. "Kinda fun being your partner in crime!"

"I'll text the marina tomorrow. A no harm, no foul message."

Federica bussed him on the cheek, a noisy smack.

"The tack is good—280 or so." His head stretched high like a dog sniffing the breeze and looking side-to-side. "Eight-to-twelve out of the south. Perfect wind."

Stonecrop arranged the sheets and furling lines in loose coils. They'd let out the rest of the jib—a number one genoa—and raise the mainsail after they cleared the harbor and coast of Formentera.

"Charter guys took the offshore life-raft. See the mounting brackets there," he pointed, "in front of the mast." The raft certification was expired anyway. The life-raft, unnecessary for day-sailing, had probably been sold. "We don't have a dingy, either. I'm gonna run a safety check: through-hulls, fuel, battery, safety stuff for two-day run."

"I packed a spare radio, but I didn't pack much food," he added. "Cheese, salami, butter, jam. Got some fresh rolls, St. Galler Ruchbrot. From the Coop. Doubles of boxed chai, coffee, and juice. And eight liters of water."

"Enough for two days?" Federica wasn't sure.

"Barely. But if the weather holds, we'll be there in a day. Should be a reach all the way to València."

"And *I* brought chocolate from Sprüngli!" she added.

"Brilliant!" Stonecrop said, hungry after the swim.

Stonecrop didn't want to think about food. But then, he thought, he should think about food. He should think about everything. Safe sailing was an exercise in preparation. Food, fuel, rigging, weather knowledge, man overboard drills—all of it—mattered. His boat, he knew well. He also suspected the vessel had been cannibalized but to what extent was unknown. And inexperienced hands had been hard on her. Hopefully, she had not been damaged in any way that would make an offshore cruise unsafe. His crew, Fede, was solid. She'd sailed before and had made a few longer passages, mostly in the Med.

He opened the locker under the port settee and found two once-new suspender style life-vest/harnesses. The harness strap contained a charge that would inflate in the water and transform the garment into a full-fledged life vest. He handed one to Federica, along with a monkey line—an extendable safety tether with a carabiner style clip. Federica eased her arms out of the straps of her one-piece bathing suit, the kind real swimmers wear for pool workouts, and let the suit drop to the deck. She pulled a floral cover-up from the duffle, tied two corners together, and wrapped material around her back. She gave the knotted section a half-twist and dropped the bundle of fabric over her head. Voilà, instant dress. Stonecrop slipped into a baggy, oxford button-down dress shirt. White and wrinkled, stained with coffee, wine, and motor oil; the shirt had weathered multiple trans-Atlantic crossings.

"You can wait until we're clear of the islands. For the harness." He disappeared below.

Twenty minutes later, Stonecrop re-emerged from the red-light lit cabin. He carried two lengths of flat, one-inch-wide nylon webbing, which he strung from bow to stern and secured at both ends. One ran down the port side and the other the starboard side of the deck.

"Jacklines," he said.

They were entering open water, so he toggled on running lights, GPS, radar and other electronics they would use for the crossing. The battery had been fully charged for his supposed charter. He removed the second hood covering the domed, pedestal-mounted compass and the adjacent weatherized computer screen. After a few taps on the display, the full-color chart-plotter was set for night viewing and showed their position. He activated the radar's collision avoidance system. As if by magic, coastal features, fishing boats, merchant and recreational vessels, and navigational markers populated the display as bright, color-coded icons or patterns. An overlay showed their range and bearing. *Zaca* had indeed come to life.

So had Stonecrop.

The air had cooled; Federica shivered. He stepped behind her and leaned against her.

"Cold?"

She pressed back and rubbed against him. "Warmer now."

Stonecrop became aroused but restrained himself.

"Been awhile, my love," she said.

"No, c'mon, a week," he responded with faux incredulity.

"Like I said, been awhile . . ."

"Well, a lot of important stuff going on," he whispered close to her ear. Salty strands of her hair brushed against his face and mouth.

Keeping one hand on the wheel to steady herself, Federica reached down with the other and parted the slit at the front of her cover-up. She leaned forward, letting her breasts brush the wheel's suede leather cover, reacting to the sway of the boat and Stonecrop's minute course corrections. Still pressed against Stonecrop, her fingers traced a path from her breast to her stomach, and then settled on her sex. She touched herself and shivered. This time, it wasn't the cold.

With his free hand, Stonecrop pulled down the front of his trunks. He reached under her wrap and braced his thumb against her tailbone, then slid a splayed hand under her crouch. His fingers touched her own. He gently tilted her up and back against the palm of his hand. She arched and spread her buttocks into him, shuddered and came. The intensity and suddenness surprised him.

Her left leg and foot reached behind and wrapped around the outside of his calf and knee. She drew him in and used the wheel to brace against the action of the waves and roll of the boat. Stonecrop let go the helm and guided his cock between her legs. She rose as he took her. Fede looked upward and let the back of her head fall, cradled into Stonecrop's shoulder. A swell of air escaped her lungs, a groan as deep as the sea below them.

"Don't hold back. Rough . . . is good." The words rode clumsily on her breath.

Stonecrop wanted to devour her.

"Fede, I—"

"Shhh . . ." She twisted her head to half-face him and pressed her cheek against his. Her breaths, short and quick, traversed his face. Stonecrop felt her fist around his cock, guiding it in short, fierce jabs until, shaking uncontrollably, he did as she had wished, ravaging her with abandon. The duet at the helm resolved into a single arrhythmic spasm of a two-headed organism with four legs and four arms celebrating its union. A gush of warm liquid lay a path down their legs and cooled as it evaporated.

Open mouths, lips missed their mark in clumsy delight.

"Golly." Stonecrop felt like a teen-ager when the 'Golly' came out. "Never—"

The jib snapped loudly, and a gust bloated the sail. *Zaca* had drifted well off course. The breeze freshened again, and second violent puff jerked the bow to port. They careened in an awkward arc against the starboard settee. The boat heeled further, broaching, though not enough for water to flood the cabin. Stonecrop grabbed the jib sheet and with one flick of the wrist freed it from the self-tailing winch. The untethered clew of the sail whipped the wind as the seven-tonne keel did its job and *Zaca* self-righted. Water captured in the belly of the sail emptied into the sea.

Federica had clung to the wheel for support. She waited for the rudder to re-submerge, for there to be sufficient purchase to steer. She pointed *Zaca* into the wind, the easiest point of sail from which to trim sails. By then Stonecrop had started the engine. He gave *Zaca* a touch of throttle to keep the flapping sails amidship.

"That was really fucking dangerous. Sorry, I should've been paying attention."

"That was really fucking incredible fucking," Fede laughed. "You paid attention alright: the *Lioness and the Cheese-Grater!*"

"Come again?"

"Sharpen up Max, remember Aristophanes' *Lysistrata* and "shredding the cheese.""

She had brushed aside the knockdown.

"You are one fearless woman," he said. Uncertain himself whether he was referring to the broaching or the sex.

Stonecrop observed her, in awe. He willed himself to remember what he was seeing. The light from the compass binnacle illuminated the fine, linear angles of her face. Behind gossamer wisps of red-lit hair, a few stars glimmered like diamonds. He closed his eyes to make the image an indelible memory.

"Max, you alright?" Fede reeled him in.

"The wind's clocking again," he said, though that hadn't been the source of his distraction.

A puff hammered *Zaca*. The rigging shuddered for second, unfazed and resilient, ready. With only one sail up, the jenny, she was unbalanced.

"Harnesses," he commanded. "That was my fuckup, you know. Us not being strapped in."

Federica reached back and pressed him against her backside. "No problem with harnesses here!"

A second gust induced a second list to starboard. They disengaged, feeling clumsy and awkward, and tried to steady each other. Fede kept the helm as Stonecrop pulled on his shorts. He pressed a knee against the wheel and helped Federica into her harness and tether. She clipped into the port jackline.

"Anytime we're on deck tonight and in open water, we're in harnesses and clipped in. Okay?"

"Aye, aye, Cap'n!" Federica put a hand on either side of his head and brought him close so their foreheads touched. She pressed her head against his.

"I love you," she said as he adjusted to her harness.

"I love you, too." The response was not quite perfunctory, but close. He was preoccupied with the weather and having to balance sail set. "Let's pop the mains'l. The wind'll figure where it's coming from when we're free of the islands."

"I'm freezing." Federica dug around her duffle and found shorts and a Patagonia jacket. "Chai?" she asked as she slipped on the coat.

"Mains'l first. Can you undo the sail ties, please? I'm on the halyard."

Stonecrop uncoiled the main sheet and brought the boom amidships to limit travel. He kept *Zaca* pointed into the wind. There would be little effect on the sails as Federica undid the sashes that in intervals bound the mainsail, like some elongated mummy within the trough-shaped boom. As she undid each tie the sailcloth came alive with the breeze. Like a white apparition, it rose from the dead one segment at a time. The mains'l halyard wound round the self-tailing winch. The gears ceased their work when the head of the sail reached the halfway point to the top of the sixty-foot carbon fiber mast. Both sails luffed in the wind, lusting for air. He cut the engine.

Federica slid the carabiner on the monkey line along the jack-line, carefully stepping over and around cars, blocks, and stays. A few feet back from the forestay, she manually backwinded the jib by holding the clew of the sail, the corner of the jib to which the jib sheet was attached, against the wind coming over the port side. The bow nudged to starboard, and Stonecrop eased the helm to starboard to let the sails fill with air. Federica rejoined him in the cockpit and they worked in unison to trim the sails.

The course for València was a reach, a fast point of sail if the wind held. Fede dug out a thermos of chai. The air freshened, both cooler and stronger, as they finally entered open water.

Stonecrop keyed in the course on the display and pressed the auto-pilot switch. Below deck, a motor whirled, then died. He tried a second time with the same outcome. There was a fix, but not one they could do on the fly, not in the next few hours.

"Auto's dead. No surprise, damned thing sucks. Always has. Two-hour shifts?"

"Works for me."

"She's a piece of cake to sail. We'll sleep on deck."

"Your girl wants food, Max."

"So demanding!"

"I am." She played the vamp. "Sex, food, then sleep."

"Comin' up." He turned over the helm and went to work making sandwiches; a simple fare of salami, cheese, cornichons, and *Ruchbrot*. He topped off the picnic menu with a big bag of paprika chips. His eyes had adjusted to the dark and he was able to complete the task under the red glow of the compass and starlight.

They ate in silence. Stonecrop placed his foot on the bottom of the wheel to steer.

"You know the Khoisan myth about the Milky Way?" Fede asked.

"I know the Greek one, or maybe it's Roman, the one that says Hera was suckling a child and then she rejected the child. When she pushed it away, her breast milk spilled across the night sky."

"The Khoisans say a dancing girl threw embers into the night to give us a path through the darkness."

Rosy-fingered Dawn

Even rosy-fingered Dawn wanted to sleep in. Stonecrop thought about *The Odyssey*, the memory of reading to Fede that first night they had met, and how that encounter had shaped their lives. He was happy, being here, watching Federica drift in and out of sleep. Usually, she slept like the dead and could fall asleep as if on demand—a not uncommon skill for sleep-deprived physicians—but this morning she slept fitfully. He thought about stroking her head, as one would a child, but with the motion of the boat his touch would have the opposite effect and startle her. So he watched, wanting to care for her. He noted the markers of her discontent, the tightened brow, the lines radiating from her eyes, the twitches around the mouth, and wondered if that when she dreamt—there was little doubt she *was* dreaming—did she do so in words, and, if so, then in what languages were those words?

They'd had a brief exchange some hours ago, after Federica had ended her watch. He had encouraged her to go back to sleep. He knew he wouldn't be able to sleep, being her opposite regarding sleep, especially on a boat. Something in the back of his head tracked and cataloged every creak and tick and splosh. Anything unusual propelled him from pseudo-slumber to a state of alert.

A yoga teacher had once said that Stonecrop was ruled by his sympathetic nervous system and in a constant state of fight-or-flight. Maybe she was right. Except for extreme climbing and shooting, where the activity demanded unwavering attention, he was constantly aware of and attentive to his surroundings. It was fear, of course. Fear in a variety of favors and colors. Fear of outright failure, fear of others being hurt, and there was an unhealthy and underlying pride that feared being judged unworthy for even the smallest infractions. He accepted this heightened state and the unhappiness or dissatisfaction that at times accompanied it.

He had, however, stumbled onto an antidote of sorts. She was sleeping a few feet from him. Not that he needed her to be *his* to be happy—though he couldn't imagine life without her—but that he needed her as an example of how full one's life, lived without second thoughts, lived without pride and fear of failure, lived in commitment and clarity of purpose, could be. He wanted to be a better man, a man without fear and regrets, a better man for her.

Federica pulled the sleeping bag higher over her neck. She was reclining on an improvised bed on the cockpit settee where she and Stonecrop had been hot bunking in two-hour shifts. Her head and shoulders rested on cushions piled up against the bulkhead. She opened her eyes, greeted him but said nothing, and gazed at the eastern horizon. With each wave, the line of horizon rose and fell between the aft deck and the lower tier of the cable rail. The ensign snapped at the air—*The day's afoot*, it shouted! And no one listened.

Stonecrop scanned the surface of the water and paused to focus on a set of lights from a distant freighter on the still-dark western horizon. Three whites and a green meant the boat was to port and would pass them to port. *Zaca* was still on a starboard tack. Plenty of seaway and room to fall off.

Get on with it, he repeated. That's where Fede landed. She didn't want to hear his stories and he didn't want to tell them. She could be a very unsympathetic woman and for that he was grateful. Self-pity's for narcissists and fools, she had said. That had been a conversation after the Chum episode at Sorel Zürichberg. Then she had gone on about the Ambassador. There's a man with gumption, she said. He knew his snails, did what he loved. Do that, Max. Get on with it.

Stonecrop listened. He had acted—spending time with his kids, retrieving *Zaca*, admitting to his love for Federica. He was thinking about these things and others as he watched her and as she awoke.

"Ugh, my back," Federica groaned at the day. She squirmed and stretched against the confines of the sleeping bag.

"That was okay, last night?" She faced the east and soaked in the warming light.

The memory aroused him. "If the autopilot worked, I'd show you."

"Whoa cowboy! I was talking about the shifts. You did extra—" Federica interrupted herself. "Gotta hit the head."

"I tried," he winked.

"Next trip, we'll bring Alicia. She's a morning person."

"She scares me."

"You know . . . I don't care," Federica stretched and yawned, "if you sleep with her, but no sex after seven. After seven, you're mine." She stretched again: head, arms, and shoulders, one body part after another poked out of the top of the bag, the butterfly emerging from its chrysalis. Feet and legs popped out the bottom. The middle of the bag, zipped like a corset, wrapped her torso.

Stonecrop laughed, "Yeah, well, I'll keep that in mind."

Federica extended a foot and tried to kick him.

"Not interested, I promise," he said.

"What if Alicia were here right now . . . I wish she were!"

Stonecrop was happy for their friendship. And if he was honest with himself, maybe a little aroused by the idea of the two women together. He looked to the side, then at her. Smiling.

"In your dreams, cowboy." She'd read his mind. "Men are so predictable."

A playful wink was followed by a somewhat sterner expression. "Look, there is something I want to talk about."

"The autopilot?" He was too tired to be clever.

"Kind of. Sometimes I feel like our relationship is on autopilot. And we're accommodating all these people around us. Let's change that dynamic."

"Before or after you pee?" Stonecrop was exhausted from the long night and the weight of his own thoughts to hold up his end of the conversation.

"You're a silly ass. I so don't ever want to see you in the Spital again. I want you in *my* bed!"

She was not fully awake, he realized, and flipping topics and moods like morning pancakes.

"Gotcha, and I promise we'll talk. The objective today is a cozy slip at Real Club Náutico de València. And real food and plenty of sangria. If the wind holds, we'll easily make dinner—no one eats until eleven —"

"I wish you hadn't mentioned food. I'm hungry, but I gotta poop."

"Yeah, good to know." He wasn't being cute. "No, really. Check the 'Y' valve in the head. The waste goes in the holding tank; no solid discharge overboard until the MSD's refurbished. Anywhere in the Med, we use the tank."

"I know." Federica's tone became solemn. "Tell that to the thousands of people risking their lives to reach Europe's shores."

"In that regard, Destiny and Lomi were lucky." Stonecrop trimmed the mains'l as he spoke.

Federica drank out of her water bottle and glanced around the cockpit for a snack. She found a chip on the settee, inspected it, and ate it.

"I'm sorry about the provisions," Stonecrop went on, "we should've brought more. Look, tomorrow morning I inspect a couple containers of e-crap, check the manifests, hand this key to Adewole's rep—he buys off the powers-that-be at the commercial marina and customs—and we hop on a plane home. Two-hour flight."

"What key?"

Stonecrop opened the flap of the Patagonia backpack at his feet. He pulled out a small stuff sack.

"Directions and key. The Clerk left a package for Adewole's team in a locker at La Marina de València. That's the big marina on the north side of the harbor."

"Why couldn't the Clerk do this exchange?"

Stonecrop had had the same question. Francis de Bruyn, otherwise known as "the Clerk," headed up a team of a dozen or so at GR Group's office in Valleta, Malta. Stonecrop met with de Bruyn bi-monthly in Valleta to hand-carry documents. Officially, the Clerk was a pencil pusher; one sensed, however, that he was more a rocket-propelled-grenade kind of guy.

"I asked Claudia. She said Chum thought he was too familiar a face. Anyway, Gregor needed him in Malta. What I don't know is the name of the guy we contact, or woman, when we get to València. Claudia said I'd get a text on the burner tomorrow. Speaking of which, I gotta charge the damned thing. Don't let me forget."

Federica snuggled up to him for a quick hug and kiss before she dropped down the companionway.

"Poop time. I'll think about the threesome!"

"Really!"

"No, you perve!" That earned him another peck on the cheek.

Ambushed

The harbor master had directed them to an open slip at the yacht club or—as the locals called the club—the "Real" or the "CRN." As at many marinas in the Mediterranean, one docked stern-to. The drill was easy enough under ideal conditions. But *Zaca* was short-handed, and a fifteen-to-twenty knot breeze blew across their beam. Lastly, the slip lay between two multi-million-dollar behemoths with only a meter and change on either side of *Zaca*.

They were saved from potential disaster by a crew member of the thirty-meter power yacht *Juliette*, who, though the hour was late, was still on watch. He'd seen *Zaca* approach and had tossed Federica a docking line to hold the bow fast as *Zaca's* stern backed into the slip and the protected lee of *Juliette*.

València was jumping. The cold and hungry crew of *Zaca* spent as little time as possible securing the boat before heading off to Restaurante Mediterráneo, a cozy, casual place and just across the channel from where they had docked.

The crewman and new friend aboard *Juliette*—a New Zealander, based upon his accent—was named Freddy. He had informed them that he had called the restaurant to reserve a table. To top off the courtesies, he had pre-ordered meals. Whoever Freddy's captain was—presumably, the owner of the *Juliette*—he had pull at Mediterráneo. Freddy had mentioned the owner's name, but Stonecrop had missed it. Freddy also commented that the owner was "not famous, just rich."

Federica and Stonecrop killed a carafe of sangria before their meal arrived; also, the plates were not what they had expected. The specialty of Spanish port cities was typically paella mariscos: a medley of squid, prawns, clams, and mussels cooked with rice in a fish broth. What arrived at their table was a paella, but this one was rabbit and chicken, runner beans, garlic, and tomato. Zing and color came from paprika and saffron. The one pan affair had a welcoming, home-cooked aroma. The dish was, the waiter said, Freddy's boss's favorite.

Both Federica and Stonecrop were bushed and relieved to be eating "comfort" food, noting that everyone around them was doing battle with shellfish, a process that took overly much effort and enthusiasm. A second carafe of Sangria, unbidden, appeared at their table.

They ate without talking. The rabbit was tender and delicious. Stonecrop used a piece of bread to wipe up the last of the sauce on his plate.

"Unbelievable, this sauce. Love, can I abandon you for a sec?"

Federica shushed him away with her fork and continued eating. Stonecrop, napkin in hand, disappeared into the kitchen. The grunts on the line in the kitchen looked surprised, but the minute he started asking questions and raving about the sauce—albeit in English and needing some translation—they took him by the arm and introduced him to the chef who then, delighted by his customer's accolades, unscrewed the cap of an herb-filled jug and let Stonecrop smell the contents. Still cooking with one arm, he used the other to slap two glasses on the work counter, filled each with a finger of the flowery local drink. He handed one to Stonecrop. A happy Stonecrop rattled off a few of the flavors he smelled—orange, chamomile, sage, marjoram, rosemary, basil, thyme, juniper, and anise—and downed the drink.

The cook toasted Stonecrop and smiled—he was missing a front bottom tooth. All this transpired while he had been shifting flaming dishes around burners on the stove and ordering around sous-chefs. He gave Stonecrop his number. Stonecrop punched it into his phone.

"Text. I give you recipe for rabbit sauce." He poured brandy into a pan on the stove and swirled the pan and contents over the burner. "Now work."

Buzzed and smelling like anise, Stonecrop returned to his table. Before sitting, he dug two phones out of the pack: his own and the phone to be used for recording the conversation with his contact.

"Were you a pain in the ass?" Fede kidded. She had finished her plate while he had been gone. "Did they throw you out of kitchen?"

"Super pain! No. The chef couldn't have been nicer. I gotta make this dish."

"Phew . . . I smell anise." She waved her hand in front of her nose but didn't frown.

"Homemade drink. Something called Herbero de Joaquín!"

"I am going to burst . . ." Federica patted her tummy, drank some water, and let out a very un-ladylike burp.

"I should see if there's anything from the kids. And this guy we're meeting tomorrow."

There were few messages. Sarah had sent photos from a picnic at Zürich's mini beach at Strandbad Mythenquai. Sandro was with the group, as was Alicia. Seems she had become the de facto chaperon. Still no explanation from Mattie. This time she had called Sarah to announce another delay. His ex-wife's absence didn't concern Stonecrop as much as the fact that she had offered no explanation for it. He didn't want to pry, thinking that the reason might be something she didn't want to share. On the other hand, there was always the possibility that his past actions might have in some way put her in danger. He texted Mattie's hotel and phone number to Claudia to see if her people could confirm Mattie's well-being.

Federica waited for him to finish, then spoke: "Sandro's become a regular. I like him."

"Me too. He's a good kid—I think."

Stonecrop put the personal phone away. Family was okay; that was good. He fired up the burner.

"You know, Chum should use an undercover pro for this stuff, not me."

"I don't think Papà would—"

"Crap!"

He showed the message to Federica.

<<HC: Change of plans. Where the fuck are you? Need key tonight.>>

"Damnit! We were supposed to meet tomorrow. Shit."

Stonecrop texted back to HC, the person he was supposed to meet.

<<Max: Just arrived. Missed flight.>>

<<HC: BS. Where r u?>>

<<Max: Mediterráneo>>

<<HC: close by be there in 5 black jacket cap funny face.>>

<<Max: ok>>

"He's coming, here, in five minutes."

He showed her the text.

"What's 'funny face?' "

"No clue—" He replied, having the same question.

"Got the key?"

"Yeah." He fished around in his pack, found and placed the small waterproof stuff sack on the table. In the locker was a payment to their expected guest for services to be provided; namely, bribing customs and paying off lackeys in the port authority's office to guarantee that the containers Ratzow had shipped to València would be loaded and forwarded without delay to Lagos, Nigeria.

Stonecrop set the record feature on the burner and put the phone in his pocket. "Chum wanted to catch the drop. I don't know if there's enough charge. Or if it's too noisy."

"Should I leave," Federica asked.

"Shit, I didn't want you mixed up in this."

"A little late for that," Federica said. She seemed unperturbed at the prospect of being present at the exchange. The wine, Stonecrop decided, had calmed her, or lack of sleep, or both.

The waiter came by and cleared the table. Federica, in near-native Castilian Spanish, ordered an espresso and asked for the check. A crowd had gathered at the door and was waiting for tables.

"Gotta hit the head," Stonecrop said. "Back in a sec."

"I'll watch for Mr. Funny Face."

The tension that had been building in him turned tactile and struck like a sucker punch the moment he stepped into the restroom and locked the door. He stood, dizzy as if he were seasick—though he wasn't—and pissing at the fly marker in the toilet bowl. His mind flooded with concerns about their passage, this meeting, being Ratzow's fake Transit Specialist, and now an overarching fear of Fede being dragged into Chum's danger-ridden scheme.

"What the *fuck* are you doing?" He berated himself out loud, splashed cold water on his face, and rubbed the bristly skin dry with a paper towel. Bits of towel, like snowflakes, stuck to his chin. The face in the mirror looked back at him and hardened. That face had no tolerance for self-pity.

"C'mon mother-fucker. You're gonna do this thing."

The pounding in his heart subsided. He exhaled compressed his diaphragm to empty his lungs, then slowly inhaled. His personal phone vibrated.

<<FR: he's here>>

Stonecrop filled a cupped hand with water, swished the water around in his mouth and spit it out. The odor of Herbero de Joaquín filled the cramped bathroom. A shirtsleeve dried and cleaned mouth and chin. When he cracked open the door, he immediately picked out Funny Face.

Except there was nothing funny about the face under that black baseball cap. It belonged to Henrique Couto, a man whose brother Stonecrop had shot and killed in front of Henrique's own eyes. As for Henrique Couto himself, Stonecrop had put two rounds into his chest and then left him to burn to death. The man had risen from the dead. Evil had reincarnated from the flaming hell that he, Stonecrop, had once sent him to.

Memories came in a deluge: the compound in Maputo where he had been imprisoned and tortured; the Coutos, pharma distributors extraordinaire, dumping bad or expired drugs; and Stonecrop's own firm, a source of some of those drugs. The victims had been communities in Mozambique and other regions of southeast Africa where the Coutos, expanding their mini empire, had hawked imperfect drugs.

Couto wore a leather coat that was too long and too warm for the weather. Probably he was hiding a weapon. Stonecrop turned out the light in the restroom and left the door slightly ajar. Couto was scanning the room as Stonecrop texted Federica.

<<MS: he can't know I'm here ignore him armed.>>

<<FR: too late. I waved.>>

His phone rang. She had dialed him and put in an earpiece and brushed her hair over the ear. Stonecrop could now hear the conversation around the table. He could hear her breathing. Calmly breathing.

"Who the fuck are you?" Henrique "Hennie" Couto started off the introductions.

"You're new best friend." The jaunty greeting surprised everyone.

"That so? You're *Max*? They send a cona, I don't believe it!"

"Maxine, cabrão." After calling him an asshole and doing so in the same breezy tone, she piled on a sexy smile. She was clearly proud of dishing out the Portuguese insult. She'd instantly pegged him as a Portuguese speaker. Couto returned a sort of half-smile himself; the effect was disarming and comic as the corner of the mouth that had not been fused to the surrounding skin rose and reached toward his eye. The right side of face was a plane of scar tissue. One could see, however, that he had once been a handsome man.

"Believe this," she said. As cool as could be, Federica slid the stuff sack across the table.

"*Max* is an unfortunate name." Couto didn't elaborate.

The waiter approached the table. "Your bill has been taken care of."

He set down the receipt, her espresso, and two elegant, stem crystals of anise liqueur. "Cumprimentos." He ignored the stranger in black. Having dealt with the public for many years, he knew trouble when he saw it.

As Couto looked in the bag and examined the contents, Stonecrop looked for a weapon. He could grab a knife from another table. He had no doubt that Couto, given the chance and blind with rage at seeing Stonecrop, would shoot him on the spot and then go after Fede.

"Thoughtful that. Adewole said you worked Africa. Ya sure look like a newbie to me . . ." He checked his phone. "Merda, I have to go." Couto looked her over, "Next time, I show you around."

He picked up one of the drinks the waiter had brought—he had assumed that Federica had ordered for the two of them—and downed the contents in one swallow. To avoid dribbling, he had to tilt his head to one side as he drank. The difficulty eating and drinking, Stonecrop imagined, must be a constant reminder and source of bitterness.

Federica stared at Couto. Stonecrop surmised that she was neither upset nor frightened by the disfigured face; she had worked in the burn ward and intensive care unit long enough to feel compassion for him, whatever he had done. Couto seemed to relax.

"You're a funny one, you know that," he said. He was holding the empty glass in the air, inspecting the crystal glass, then Federica, back and forth. "Sweet things like you see a mug like mine and duck out the door."

Federica and Couto continued looking at each other and saying nothing. Despite the restaurant bustle surrounding them, Stonecrop felt the silence.

"You don't. You don't look away," he said. The statement was a statement of fact, lacking innuendo.

"No," Federica replied in the same tone of voice, "I don't."

"Next time," Couto said. He put the empty glass on the table, doing so without making a sound. There was no trace of anger or suspicion in his words.

Fede looked genuinely sad that Funny Face, the man she had just met, was leaving.

Hennie tipped the brim of his black baseball cap, a cordial thanks for the drink, and merged into the crowd at the door and then the shadows beyond.

Juliette

The tap on *Zaca's* hatch cover half-woke Stonecrop. He crawled from the thick of sleep, exhausted. The new day's light framed the rectangular perimeter of the porthole shades, becoming brighter as the Couto encounter had countlessly replayed in his dreams. Variations of the scenario wove together like a Bach fugue and left him tangled in his sweaty bedsheets and with patches of damp on the bench settee in the main cabin, his berth for the night.

Similarly entwined, Federica was sleeping face down and flopped across the bench settee opposite him. One arm and one leg dangled over the side of the narrow berth and lay against the cool floorboards.

"Anyone home?" A too-cheerful-for-the-hour Freddy chippered and knocked again on the hatch. A third rapping was followed by a now concerned voice. "You 'right, mates?"

Stonecrop gave in and complied with the rising, not so much the shining. He stumbled toward the hatch. With some fumbling, it slid open. The freshly shaved, crisply attired, and lively Freddy peered down at him. A square of blue sky framed his head. Fresh air flowed in the open hatch as stale air escaped. Stonecrop had been too bushed last night to find and install screens on the portholes and companionway entry.

"Apologize for the O-Dark whatever it is. Well, now, it's not really O-Dark anything, is it! Almost eight! Day's half-done, mates. You two are invited next door. Breakfast with the neighbor, el Capitán, in fifteen. Brush the fuzz out of your teeth. The best coffee in all València awaits, lovingly prepared by your truly."

"Yours truly is a Kiwi," said a froggy-voiced Federica. Her fingers traced indentations left on her face from the rumpled sheets her head had pressed against. No doubt she thought of Couto, and that unlike

Couto's scars, her etchings would be gone in minutes. "A Kiwi coffee's gonna suck."

"Suspend all judgement!" he commanded. "Yours truly did ten years in Napoli."

"Ah! Pray, Archangel, deliver us from Nescafé!" A punchy Federica rolled the other foot to the floor and sat on the settee. Her back stiffened; hands braced themselves on knees. She pretended to be awake, though she was at her disheveled best: hair a rat's-nest and flopped to one shoulder, an oversized tee leaving the other shoulder bare, and the twisted-open borrowed boxers that reached to her knees.

"Snappy outfit," Freddy observed appreciatively. "In fifteen. He's not a stickler for dress. An understatement that—skivvies 'll do."

They beat the clock and were ready in ten. When they egressed from the hatch, Freddy was dockside to meet them. He reached out to help with the jump from the stern of *Zaca* to the dock, and then guided them across the railed gangway leading up to the rear deck on *Juliette*.

"The skipper knows you," Freddy announced.

The first thought stopped Stonecrop in his tracks. Could the skipper of *Juliette* and Hennie be one and the same? No, impossible.

"Name?" Stonecrop curtly asked.

"Wesley, goes by Wes."

"Hennie?" Stonecrop said, fearing he had misheard.

"No, Wes, Wes Waterman," Freddy repeated.

Stonecrop continued the grilling as they stepped aboard.

"How does he know me?"

"I dug up the registry for *Zaca*."

This act, too, was worrisome. If Freddy could find his identity that easily, so could Couto. Federica must have come to the same conclusion. She started checking over her shoulder. When she caught Stonecrop's attention, she shook her head, no. He understood: no sign of Couto.

A white table with matching white-cushioned, white chairs was set for three and covered with a blue-and-white checkered tablecloth, fresh from the laundry. A Navy-blue canvas bimini protected them from the direct morning sun and the light reflecting off of the surrounding gleaming-white surfaces.

Waterman was a handsome man of indeterminate age, anywhere between early-sixties and mid-seventies, an imposing six-five tall, and trim. He greeted them warmly. Grey patches fought for space on the thatch of tan hair, the lot swept to the back as if the man were facing to windward. The hair had no part and exposed a not unbecoming widow's peak. The skivvies remark had been a misdirect. He wore white linen pants, a tasteful print shirt with a dark-hued Tahitian pattern, and sandals with non-scuff deck soles.

"Pardon my prying. I asked Freddy for background data about my new neighbors. We've had docking *incidents* in the past, you see." The English was North American, a New Englander. A Mainer.

They shook hands. The meet and greet was relaxed. Stonecrop's concerns about Couto abated. He let himself be as tired as he felt.

"Not that I was worried about *Zaca* in your hands," Waterman added. "Lovely boat, though I saw she had been under charter recently."

Stonecrop finished the thought for Waterman, ". . . meaning any idiot could be at the helm."

"I knew that was not the case, however."

"Because—"

"Because no catastrophic crashes interrupted a perfect night's sleep," he laughed. "And you introduced yourselves to Freddy last night."

"I don't remember—"

Federica nodded in the affirmative. Stonecrop had forgotten, but she had remembered, of course. She forgets nothing.

"Freddy said you know me. Have we met? I don't think so," Stonecrop queried.

"Yes and no. In the flesh, no."

Stonecrop's eyes had adjusted to the shade under the bimini. He could see through the glass doors into the rear salon. Hanging on the wall in the salon was a copy, a good one, of Gustave Courbet's *The Bathers*.

Waterman saw him eyeing the painting. "You recognize the Courbet?"

"Yup, *The Bathers*. Can't see from here but seems like a quality copy." As he said the words, the recollection came together in a flash.

"I have you to thank," Waterman said, "you saved me a good million in sales tax. Never had a chance to thank you in person, so Voilà!"

"Not for the Courbet reproduction?"

"No, no. Another work."

He aimed a nod of thanks in Stonecrop's direction. He seemed disinclined to mention the specific piece he'd referred to.

Waterman continued speaking, saving Stonecrop the effort. "I read about the divorce. Sorry about that. Been down that road—twice, in fact." Then he looked at Federica, with obvious admiration. "Seems you've landed on your feet."

The aside would not sit well with Fede. And she hadn't had coffee yet. One more slip by Waterman and Federica would take off his head.

Waterman, to his credit, realized he'd poked the dragon. He pulled out a chair for her at the table and ramped up the charm: "Please; Miss Ratzow—that's correct, I hope—I'm honored to have you aboard. You must be an artist? This man, I suspect, orbits beauty like a planet the sun."

"Good save," she forgave him. He wasn't fully off the hook but the drakaina's ire had been partially discharged by the cheesy compliment. "Not an artist, but I do live in a museum."

"And where might that museum be?" Waterman played along.

"Zürich. My landlady has a museum's worth of art; she has so many paintings and sculptures. She stores a bunch in my basement apartment."

"What fun! A fellow collector. Her name?"

"Frau Ott. Frau Marthe Ott, née Meyer."

Surprised looks appeared on the faces of both of Federica's breakfast companions. In Stonecrop's case because he had had no idea that Frau Ott had once been married. The surprise on Waterman's face was greater; he seemed genuinely moved. "My God! Frau Ott. My dear, indeed you *do* live in a gallery. I've offered her a ransom and a half, several *Juliettes'* worth, for that monster *art brut* Jean Dubuffet in her collection. Does she still have that magnificent piece?"

"Jean and me, we're like this." Federica lifted two fingers in the air and then wrapped her other hand around them. "That painting leans against the wall in my bedroom which, by the way, is not very big. So you can imagine, even unframed the piece takes up the entire wall."

"Guards? She must have security?"

"She's got me," Stonecrop jumped in unnecessarily, in case Waterman wasn't the gentleman he appeared to be. "And a ferocious guard dog!"

He smiled to himself at the thought of Rosie, Frau Ott's dachshund. He missed Rosie.

Freddy set a round of cappuccini on the table, along with freshly squeezed blood-orange juice, assorted fruits and meats, hard-boiled eggs, and warm rolls and jam.

"Ah, I believe you. Please, give her my regards . . . and remind her that I'm still interested in the painting. Now, dig in. And, after some sustenance, tell me what brings you to València."

They followed captain's orders and enjoyed the spread Freddy had laid out before them.

His coffee finished, a revived Stonecrop addressed Waterman's question. "A temporary new home for *Zaca*. We stole her back from the outfit that, without my permission, was putting her out for charter in Formentera."

Waterman roared, "You stole her! Bravo! Tell me how; I'm sure there's a good story."

The next minutes were consumed with the tale: the night swim, ghosting out of the harbor, the freshening breeze, and eventual arrival in València. They left out the bit about the knock-down—too embarrassing on multiple fronts.

"You are aware . . ." Waterman said, "Oh, probably not, that I was once involved in all manner of thievery, all at the behest of our beloved CIA. I had been in line to head up the Operations Directorate. They get to do the fun stuff. Got passed over. Hence, retirement."

"You must miss the service?" Federica stated, openly curious how a man immersed in the mayhem of the clandestine world would adjust to retirement. She had often told Stonecrop that she loved what she did and would never stop working as an emergency physician. Waterman's career, given his means, had clearly been a choice and something he had loved.

"Yes and no," Waterman said, rotating his cup the same way that Fede did when she was thinking about something. "The scope of what we did takes one's breath away. The agency does much good work for which it receives no public recognition, and, I'm sorry to say, often times, little political support. As to the muck ups we've made over the last twenty years, some of which have gone public, that was my job. Not to blunder, that is! I was the clean-up man. An inglorious role, and one which I deeply enjoyed.

"Your question, I should say, was not off the mark. I *had* considered hurling myself off a cliff when I retired. You know, pin a note on the shirt—*sorry for the mess*. True to my calling, I'd even picked out the cliff, one where the cleanup would be little trouble."

"When you contemplate your own death in such detail," Federica spoke in earnest and with some concern, "they say, that is the medical community says, that the threat of self-harm is a real one, in contrast to someone trying to get attention."

"Quite so, yes. I am detail oriented. And never keen on getting attention," he laughed. "But, I was fortunate. I did have all this family money. None of it was money I had earned—I like to be clear about that. And then I became deeply involved in art, collecting mostly. I'd say that art was my salvation, all those crucifixes at the Uffizi spared me. And here we are: I'm pouring out confidences to my new friends. You must think me loony and a terrible bore!"

"Not at all." Federica took a firm hold of his wrist. "I am so grateful that we are together, this moment; and I'm grateful for your generosity *and* your candor about your life." She looked down at her cup, which she was cradling in the palm of her other hand, and smiled warmly. "And for this yummy cappuccino."

"The rabbit, too. The Med dinner was fabulous. Thank you." Stonecrop added. He had searched for a way to complement what Federica had said and realized after the fact how flat his words sounded.

The next hour passed in conversation about how sailing had changed over the years, the rise of piracy at sea, and the challenges and responsibilities one has when encountering immigrants under sail in open waters and in un-provisioned and unsafe vessels.

"What's next? You rent a car, take a drive through the Pyrénées-Orientales. Yes, I'd recommend that route back to Zürich. Or will you train? Both are quite scenic."

"Not a bad idea," Stonecrop agreed, "renting a car. We were planning to fly back—ought to get back for work. Right now, though, we'd rather avoid the airport in València—something personal. I suppose we'll get a rental, drive to Barcelona, and catch a flight from there."

Waterman didn't' press Stonecrop about the personal matter. "Nonsense! Let me take you to Barcelona. A lark, four or five hours. What say, Freddy?"

"Yessir! Fine day for a run north," Freddy answered. He was obviously eager to do something more exciting than serving coffee.

"It's done, then. No arguing!"

Stonecrop looked at Federica, who had been won over by the cappuccino, the connection with Frau Ott, and Waterman's open and friendly demeanor.

"We have two duffels. Thank you. We're truly grateful," she said.

Waterman couldn't have misread the relief on their faces.

Federica leaned over to Stonecrop. "The containers," she reminded him quietly. He was to make a final inspection of the two containers of e-waste going to Lagos.

"Fuck it," Stonecrop said.

"Come again?" Waterman asked.

"I'd like to see the Courbet," Stonecrop said. He suspected Waterman had overheard them but was politely ignoring the exchange.

"Yes, of course, as soon as we're underway. I'll give you the tour, and—I'll take a minute—show you a lovely watercolor of Rosie! I couldn't agree more, a ferocious animal!"

Claudia's Mantra

"Not good, love, not good at all."

They walked side-by-side as if they were looking for something on the ground in front of them. There was no urgency to Claudia's steps, nor to her words. A few meters later and at the same monotonous pace she aired the same monotonous words. By then the monotone utterance had given up semantic value and become an invocation for intervention.

"Does anyone else know?" Stonecrop asked.

"No. Let's sit." Claudia's feet were bothering her. "That's the store, right."

"Yes, just over there," he pointed. "Nothing to be afraid of, Claudia."

"Easy for you to say!" she exclaimed and then went on to answer his question. "No, just the doctor. Appointment was yesterday. 'Exercise or die!' he yelled in my ear, like I was some addled, hard-of-hearing piece-of-shit. The bastard!"

Stonecrop had been asking after Henrique "Hennie" Couto, not her recent exam. He did care about her health issues, of course.

He tried again, more specific this time. "Who else knows about Hennie?"

"No one that I'm aware of," she said. "In València, obviously, he's a familiar face. Not that you can forget that face!" She had debriefed Stonecrop last night at the Hauptbahnhof soon after he and Fede had landed at the Zürich Flughafen and trained back to the city.

Stonecrop took her arm and helped her settle onto the park bench. He sat beside her, enjoyed the crisp morning air, fresh though they were in the middle of the city along the Bahnhofstrasse. People were getting on and off trams, heading to work, school, shopping, whatever.

128

Pestalozzianlage hosted a smattering of tourists, workers on break, and students. In one corner of the park, a group of ex-pats from a class at the Coop were holding an urban picnic and practiced their German. Stonecrop, though without Federica's perfect ear, had picked up her habit of identifying languages and drawing distinctions between regional dialects. Among the ex-pat group, he detected U.S., Ukrainian, Arabic, and one with an origin he couldn't pin down. Turkish, there were a lot of Turks in Zürich.

"They're not open yet." She looked across the park to the shuttered Ochs Sports storefront.

"No, we have a few minutes."

"I'm fucked, dear boy."

Uncertain as to what she was referencing this time, he asked for clarification.

"You mean the doctor insisting you exercise, or the fact that Couto is alive and well?"

"Pick your poison!" She laughed heartily, a nervous laugh, but a real one. Stonecrop laughed with her. The gallows humor faced off with the glorious day. For Stonecrop, the day triumphed.

The tram clanged a warning to a pedestrian. One would think Zürchers, being Swiss, would be cautious pedestrians. But no, they were unapologetic jaywalkers. Hell, no one could blame them for having a spring in their step on this beautiful day. He'd try to get in a run.

" 'You exercise or you die,' that's what the bugger said. That, from Federica's boss at the Spital! The S.O.B. has no bedside manner."

"Fede swears by Herr Doktor Weller. She said he trained as a cardiologist before heading up the E.D."

Fede, Stonecrop knew, had prepared Weller and informed him that Claudia would be a handful. Claudia, overweight and always under stress, exhibited a host of symptoms associated with heart disease: chest discomfort, swollen feet, irregular heartbeat, shortness of breath, and so forth. What she rarely was, despite all the huffing and groaning, was mentally fatigued. In her brain, there existed an everlasting plutonium core of nervous energy. As to health, she blew off warnings by friends and physicians and her own body.

"I thought you were imagining things, dearie," she said, changing to Side B of their conversation. "So, I checked with Adewole. Flicked a line over the top of water, nothing direct. He said enough to confirm that his boy was a Mozambique vet, an ex-pharma guy, doing e-waste out of València. Adewole thought you two would really hit it off."

"Not a bad guess at what would happen—literally."

"You know precious Mr. Couto how again?" she asked.

"Shot him," Stonecrop said.

"You shot him?" Her bottle-thick eyeglasses slipped an inch down her nose when she jerked her head up. "Huh," she said, and pushed them back in place.

"Yup. And then I left him to burn to death."

Claudia took a minute to let that settle in. Beads of sweat formed on her upper lip.

"That's what you meant when you said you'd gotten *mixed up* down there. I knew you'd confronted Couto's boss and beat the living daylights out of him. These were Gregor's people . . . Christ Almighty. How 'bout we confess to Mother Claudia, love, the whole sordid little story?"

Stonecrop didn't bite. Everything was in his deposition. That the Coutos were Gregor's minions was irrelevant. Stonecrop had put two rounds in Hennie's chest and watched him fly backwards over a chair. Then he shot the brother. They had both been armed. By then Chloë, the housekeeper, had started the fire and Hennie got trapped in the flames. Stonecrop had been certain that both brothers had died.

"Nope," he replied.

"My sweet, you're a dead man if Hennie sees you. I never told Gregor, you know, that you'd tangled with any of his people. You implied there had been a scuffle."

"And I appreciate that you didn't out me. I've told no one else, Claudia. I did write up a deposition about what I'd seen and done. Left the document with a trustee at UBS."

"That's rich. The guilt get to you? Burn the fucking document; not kidding. Don't flatter yourself. If Gregor found out, he'd be on you like a rabid dog. And if you, my vengeful bunny, butchered your lover's Papà, well, that'd be fucking Shakespearean! The other consideration, of course, is that sweet Gregor pays my bills. And I do have an affection for the man. This is ugly, child."

She looked at Ochs Sports again. "Are they fucking open yet?"

"I think so."

"What the fuck are these things called again?"

"Nordic Walking Poles."

"Just for walking?"

"For walking, yes. I'll give you a lesson."

"Good grief. I fucking know how to fucking walk!"

"You can do this, Claudia."

"Go fuck yourself."

"You're really swearing a lot. When's the last time you exercised?"

"My mother's womb, you . . . ninny."

Claudia groaned as they rose and headed toward the store.

"I don't want Fede mixed up in this," Stonecrop said.

"Ah, Frau 'Maxine,' the secret agent! Tell me something I don't already know. More to the point, I shall tell *you* what *you* don't know.

"First, Couto is *the* most dangerous men I've ever come across. Note well, I didn't say 'one of.' Not to me personally, but the dossier we compiled when we vetted the guy for Gregor would make you piss your pants. Second, in my little chit-chat with Adewole, he confirmed that the containers are now en route to Lagos—your fucked-up, non-inspection notwithstanding.

"I've informed butterballs at the embassy."

"Harry—" Stonecrop started to speak, but this was her show.

"The peripatetic Harry Chum, yes. And," Claudia continued, "I passed on the approved watered-down update to Kommissar Vormittag.

"The e-waste, barring delays, will be in transit three weeks. Chum is tracking all the players and giggling like a schoolboy with his hand in the cookie jar. They're such goddamned amateurs. Not Gregor or Group; but Stadtpolizei and CIA, Interpol, or whatever the fuck team Chum plays for. I do wonder at all this bullshit just to keep Gregor dear out of the slammer."

"Claudia, was that the 'what I don't know'?"

"Nothing much else dearie. Only that your soon to be BFF, the one you perforated and barbequed in Maputo, adores Zürich. No proof of why he's a frequent flyer. Maybe he loves raclette. Jesus, I hate raclette."

That data point hit like a brain freeze. He stopped walking.

Claudia saw his reaction and decided to add to what she had already revealed. "The lad flits about, between here, Lagos, and València. He's got a hottie here. That's the rumor, mind. Been going on a for a while; bloody miracle you haven't run into each other. Zürich is such a gossipy little burg. And he's not exactly someone you don't notice."

Claudia kept eye contact with him. He offered nothing because he had nothing. The news had stunned him. He thought about the inexplicable fear that had arisen from the reflection in the window at Stehli. Had that been Couto?

She took his arm, dropped her head, and shuffled toward Ochs Sports, tugging Stonecrop along and syncing their steps to her mantra: "Not good, love, not good at all."

Maxine Unmasked

The door to Ratzow's Storchen apartment flew open at the first knock. Come by Gregor's for a drink, Claudia had said. She had said nothing about Stonecrop being accosted and lifted off his feet. He was a head taller than Ratzow. But now, pinned against the door with his toes grazing the floor, he was more like two-heads taller. What was meant to be a threatening gesture—Ratzow's massive hands holding him aloft and ripping the collars of his Patagonia jacket—devolved into a comic antic. Stonecrop tried to not laugh. Ratzow panted, buffeting Stonecrop's face with odors of vodka and cigar. Don't fight, he told himself. And don't smile or else Ratzow might do something truly regrettable, like a knee to the groin or hand to the trachea. Patience, Stonecrop told himself, Ratzow will poop out and come to his senses.

As expected, Gregor flagged. They were soon nose-to-nose and now Stonecrop's legs bowed like a scarecrows.

"What the fuck you thinking! You r-r-r-risk my Fede's life." Ratzow belched, then continued. "Bah, you no think! Why should I think, he says! You I give too much credit."

Claudia's voice was even: "Gregor, for Christ's sake settle down." Her new Nordic walking poles leaned against the chair.

Thank you, Claudia! Her presence made both men temper their tempers. If he reacted to Ratzow, if he hurt him, Federica would never forgive him. The right thing to do—was nothing.

Claudia rose from her chair. The bottom cushion, relieved of its burden, struggled to regain its original dimensions. She went to the bar, plucked two glasses from the shelf, and poured three fingers of vodka in each. One neat; the second got a handful of ice from the ice-chest and a slice of lime from the mini-fridge. She handed their respective drinks to the men.

"Kiss and make up!"

Ratzow released Stonecrop, who rose to his normal height and inspected his coat and shirt.

"You know, Gregor, for a guy—"

"Shut up," Ratzow cut him off, turned to Claudia, and reached for his drink.

"Blagodarya. I need, da." He tossed out a brusque, Bulgarian thank you.

"Max, darling." She paused to give him a sympathetic look. "An update: Gregor had a worrisome chat with Adewole." Claudia continued as if Ratzow were not in the room. "You know, dearie, I never told him. Does Fede know?"

She was referring, of course, to Stonecrop's African history, the unspoken parts.

"Some, not much, yeah," Stonecrop responded.

"Some! Yeah! What!" The words exploded one at a time from Ratzow's mouth.

"Sit, gentlemen. I will explain, if, Gregor sweet, you promise to not kill anyone in this room."

The men sat beside each other on the cushy sofa that matched the chair Claudia was en route to. Despite the mutual antagonism, they sat right next to each other, thigh to thigh in the middle of the sofa. Each man, stubborn in his own way, had staked out his turf and wouldn't give an inch. Claudia appreciated the humor of the situation. She struggled with a smile.

Ratzow spoke first. "Tell me why my daughter was in València with Transport Specialist, da? And why Adewole's man said he met with a *Maxine* who was her and not you?" He looked at Stonecrop like he was an object about to go out with the trash.

Claudia was not going to hand over the meeting to Ratzow. She spun around and brought the bottle of Stoli with her to her chair, stopped to add to the men's drinks and wagged a pinky finger at them. "Promise, love. First you must promise."

"Da . . . but is bullshit." He lifted his drink to toast her pinky.

"You know, our dear boy," this time the "boy" in question was Stonecrop, "was mixed up with bad players in Mozambique . . ."

Ratzow didn't speak but acknowledged her statement with a glance.

She paused to give Ratzow time to cool off and appreciate that she was answering his question, "What you don't know is that Max, our Max, crossed paths with your team in East Africa. Apparently, it was a not particularly pleasant encounter. There are few details, but he killed Alves Couto, and he shot and roasted his brother. Both were your men."

Ratzow remained silent. His eyes widened and his fingers twitched. Ripples formed on the surface of his drink.

"Max had already beaten the daylights out of their boss; I think you knew him better than the Coutos."

"Boss quit, no reason," Ratzow added and glared at Stonecrop. "You wreck business, kill my people, and then my daughter—"

"Be fair, dearie."

"Be fair! Da, Claudia, I am thinking is fair to—"

"Max had no idea," Claudia said, arguing for the defense.

"Listen to you!" Ratzow faced off with Stonecrop as he spoke. "So, tough guy, am I on list? You cook me?!"

"Gregor, I wasn't trying to *cook* anybody. I wanted to stop my company's bad drugs from being resold. People were dying. I couldn't let that continue. Anyway, the Coutos were about to kill me."

"Stupid, Max. You are stupid! Now is cheap Chinese shit, everything is from China or India, boatloads of fentanyl and diet pills, every day from thousands of pill factories no one knows where. Da, from Hong Kong, Guangzhou, Shanghai; thousands of agents in some shithole office in some shithole warehouse." Ratzow shook a fist at Stonecrop. "Why not fuck them, da. But no, you fuck me." He beat his chest. Both men started to get up, but Claudia motioned with a flopping fishtail hand that they remain seated.

The peacekeeper addressed Stonecrop. "Gregor didn't know the pharmaceuticals the bothers distributed were deadly. Most were expired, but still good. Or so he thought. Okay?"

Ratzow had moved on. He spat the next words at Stonecrop: "Fede? Why is she *Maxine*?"

"Gregor, I am truly sorry. Hennie appearance was a complete surprise. So was changing the meetup time and place. I had no intention of involving Fede in any of this."

"And pretending to be Maxine. That's on her. I was in the head when Hennie walked in the door," Stonecrop explained. "When I did see him I was afraid of what he would do if he saw me. That he'd come unhinged and hurt Federica. I hid and told Fede to ignore him."

"Da, you are number one asshole in world he wants to murder."

"Fede had already waved him over. She improvised when Hennie approached. He got the key. The containers made it through. And Fede and I got the hell out of there. We didn't set foot back in València. Hitched a ride on a neighbor's yacht to avoid an accidental meeting at the airport or in the city.

"Look, Gregor," Stonecrop continued, "don't forget this whole fucking charade is to keep you from doing time. I was in the head when Couto showed. I'm just as upset as you are about Fede confronting Hennie."

Ratzow gave Claudia one of those looks, one eyebrow up, the other down, that was meant to intimidate but failed.

This time Ratzow's voice was quieter and for that reason more threatening. "You think for one second I give shit about this thing—Harry Chum's little sting—if one hair on Federica head is hurt?"

"No one's going to hurt Fede," Claudia interceded, "because they know what my Gregor dear would do to them and *that* is not going change no matter what Max did or didn't do."

The mention of Chum bothered Stonecrop. He decided, after little reflection, the Federica must not have said anything to her father about the incident with Chum. Doing so would have been a deal-breaker for her father, and Fede would never want to ruin his one chance for exculpation.

"What did you tell Adewole?" Stonecrop asked Ratzow.

"I told him you shit your pants, eat bad fish. My daughter was being too cute for her own good."

"Damned near the truth, Gregor."

"Get the fuck out," he said to Stonecrop, "before I forget she likes you still with balls."

"Is Hennie in Zürich?" Stonecrop asked.

Claudia tilted her head and shrugged her shoulders.

"I'm going to find out."

Stonecrop said nothing as he left. Maybe, he hoped, Gregor could control Hennie. Fear can do wonders.

Skatepark Sketch

"I don't know what the deal is with your mom. I'm sure you guys are bored of hanging out with me. Do you want to go back to Paris? You can hop on a train tomorrow."

"Pops, chill," Jenny spoke first. "We *want* to stay here with you. We told Mom. And she said it's cool."

Sarah worked on her *cono gelato*, a mid-afternoon treat and break from the midday heat that like a hot flash had struck without warning. *Capricious weather for capricious times.*

They were standing outside of Gelateria Dieci, the one on Niederdorfstrasse and two minutes from Stonecrop's place. The kids were already regulars. Sandro leaned against the wall, sketchbook balanced on his thigh and held in place by the same hand holding his gelato. He did lightning-fast caricatures of passersby. He didn't have time or body position for a complete drawing, so he would detail only a single interesting feature of his subject and fill in the rest with a few quick gestures.

"Federica told us about stealing back *Zaca*! That's so cool!" Sarah knew the boat well and enjoyed sailing. Jenny, not so much.

"Won't you get in trouble?" Jenny asked. She turned her head sideways to lick a dribble of gelato on the back of her hand. A wisp of hair dragged across the *cono*, reminding him of Federica's braid's uncanny knack for always being in the wrong place at the wrong time. How the hell did she manage in the Emergency Room? Tied it up, he supposed.

"No." Stonecrop said, then reconsidered. "Well, yes. I might be arrested any moment now!" The authorities could pick up Stonecrop on any number of charges, all of which were more serious than stealing back his boat. If he were arrested, he'd rather the girls think the crime was theft, not murder.

He waited for more questions, but nobody seemed to care.

"Sandro," Jenny said. "Show Max my picture."

"Which one?"

"From the Skatepark, the one with Rosy!"

Sandro stepped next to Stonecrop and held his sketchbook open for Stonecrop to view. He flipped through a few pages. His spidery fingers managed the task without disturbing his gelato. The drawings were deft, mature, and in a distinct hand. Line thickness and intensity was that of a seasoned professional. Sandro possessed skills that couldn't be taught. Stonecrop made a mental note to introduce Sandro to Herr Bachman.

When Sandro found the sketches from the previous night, he handed the book to Stonecrop. There were several quick drawings of Jenny and Sarah. One was of Sarah seated at the base of a ramp post-crash and with head held between her hands. There was a well-composed picture of Jenny, helmet askew, sitting on her board and with Rosy in her lap.

"Fuck!"

Stonecrop's outburst surprised and frightened Jenny and earned a condemning look from a man and woman holding hands and looking in the windows of nearby shops.

"Um . . . that was awkward, Pops," Sarah said, her eyes smiling, wide and focused on him—a gotcha look.

Sandro's reaction was the opposite, one of real concern. Jenny stared at her father, wanting to question him, but this time she waited.

"Sorry, guys, I apologize." Stonecrop slowed his breathing. He willed his hands to steady, and they did. He had that ability. He did not want to share his terror with the kids. He looked up and down Niederdorfstrasse and assessed everyone in his range of sight, even scanning nearby windows, balconies, and rooftops.

His gaze returned to Sandro's notebook and fixed on a drawing of three figures standing behind a chest high, wood rail fence. Two figures, a man and woman, stood together. They were probably parents watching and encouraging a son or daughter. A few feet from the couple, arms relaxed and resting on the top rail, was a man with a baseball cap pulled low to cover his eyes and part of his face. As Sandro did in other works, he focused on a detail of the subject. In this drawing, the feature was the fused flesh along the ear on right side of a once handsome face.

"Earth to Dad," Sarah stepped closer, her face inches from her father's. "Pops?" She put an arm around him and pulled him close. Jenny was the one who always asked questions. Sarah never had to. She knew what he was feeling.

Stonecrop responded after he'd completed a second scan of the street. He pointed at the figure in the drawing and addressed Sandro.

"This guy. Describe him."

"Sad. His face is sad. But he didn't behave like he was sad."

"Describe him, please."

"Disfigured. Half his face, the right side. At first, I thought he had tats on his face and neck; but they were scars, more one long twisted scar. From a burn or acid, I think. His head too. He wore a cap. But I could see the hairless skin went under the cap. Black leather jacket, long. Baggy pockets. He moved quietly, *graziös*—gracefully. When I'm there, at the Park, I watch *how* people move. I must, to draw someone who moves. Even his fingers. I wanted to draw how they rested on the wood, the railing. But didn't have time."

"Did he see you?"

"I suppose. Where he was is a good place to see everything. He saw that I was drawing him. He smiled and didn't seem to care."

Sandro's confusion showed on his face. Stonecrop felt Sandro staring at him and eager to understand what was going on.

"Max?" Sandro was adult enough, or concerned enough, to address Stonecrop as Max. "Was ist?"

The German was Sandro, intentionally or not, showing his maturity, surmising that whatever had upset Stonecrop was something that he might not want discuss in front of his daughters and indicating that if he wanted to, they could speak German.

"You can't go back to the skatepark." Stonecrop reached out and held Sandro's elbow.

"I work there. In two days, I must go back."

"I mean the girls."

Stonecrop was still holding Sandro's arm: "You know, it might not be a bad idea for you to take a little time off, a week maybe. Yeah. Can you get a week off?"

"Sure." Sandro smiled back, confused. "But why should I want to do that?"

"It's not safe."

He couldn't think of a way to soften what he would have to say. He had not meant to frighten them but there was no way to sugarcoat the danger.

"You joke, yes?" Sandro said. He didn't get what was going on.

"No, not at all. This man," Stonecrop said, "has tried to kill me. He would think nothing of harming my family, and now by extension, you. I know this is frightening. I promise I'm not kidding."

Jenny had settled down; now questions rolled out. "Why?"

Stonecrop gently put his hands on either side of her face. "Jenny, sweet Jenny, I can't go into it."

"You mean you won't talk, like Mr. Vormittag wouldn't talk about what happened to him."

"The same, yes."

"It's bad to hide things." The words sounded so innocent.

"Yes, it is. But . . ." Stonecrop was again at a loss for what to say. "Sometimes, that's what adults have to do."

"Adults have too many secrets. That's what I think."

"Think what you will." Stonecrop had no patience for a debate.

"So if the man with the weird face said I shouldn't say anything to you—because you wouldn't understand—then I shouldn't."

Stonecrop froze, looked around once more, and then seized Jenny by both arms.

"He spoke to you!"

"I don't know if you'd understand." Defiant, she pulled back, crossed her arms, and looked away from him.

"Jenny, just tell me what happened. Please, this is serious."

"Tell a secret?"

Stonecrop was angry. Jenny reddened; she knew she was being a smartass.

"He asked me my name and where I was from. And if I skated at home, too."

"What did you say?"

"I told my name was Jenny and that I didn't skate at home. But I skied."

Stonecrop sensed there was more. He waited.

"He said, 'I bet you're a good skier!' I told him I was, and he smiled —sort of. It's hard for him to smile."

"Anything else?"

"That's all. Sarah, like, grabbed my arm and dragged me away. She said I shouldn't talk to strangers, especially creepy ones."

"That was it," Sarah added. "The guy weirded me out. Like the guy wasn't there with anyone else and he watched us for a while. I wasn't rude to him, Max. He's the bad guy, isn't he?"

Stonecrop said nothing.

"Dad?"

The rarely used "Dad" got his attention.

"He's the bad guy, Sarah, as bad as they get."

Bern

"Look at it this way, pet . . ." Claudia took him by the arm and wove a shuffler's path through the mid-day crowd in Zürich Hauptbahnhof's subterranean shopping mall. Her Nordic walking poles were tucked under the other arm. People came at them and flew by, others passed from behind. Everyone seemed to be moving faster than they were, though people were on guard when they were threatened by or bumped into the rubber-tipped poles. "Hennie's had plenty of opportunity to do you in or threaten your family, and . . ." she paused to catch her breath, ". . . he's done nothing. Zilch."

"That is true," Stonecrop weighed each word, noticing that the three words matched Claudia's maddeningly slow pace. Federica, from conversations with her *boss*, had learned that Claudia might need hip surgery. The news made Stonecrop more sympathetic. Sympathetic or not, though, the snail-pace was annoying. "But that doesn't mean he's *not* going to do something. Have you considered that if he knows so much about me and about my family, then he might very well know about this whole cockamamie plan to nail Adewole's gang?"

"A good point, yes. Who's to say? But we don't think that's the case."

"*We* being?"

"Me and my wannabe bestie, Harry Chum."

"Asshole wants to be everyone's bestie. Yup. Butted in on the investigation into Andreas' accident. Not his turf at all, but he found a back door through the Mexican consulate."

"Not good."

"And he pawed Federica at the Zürichberg affair." Stonecrop slipped up, a mistake.

"Did he!? The pig. Is she okay? Or did she rip off the little prick's head?"

"The latter," he said as he gave off one of those emotional and not funny laughs. "She called him prick to his face. And something else in Swiss German that I can't pronounce."

"Unpronounceable is good; the jerk deserves unpronounceable. And you, love?"

"I asked permission to break him in two. Fede said no." Stonecrop couldn't hold back his smile.

"Please tell your Claudia why you are grinning ear-to-ear?"

"I didn't really expect this. And the Ambassador was standing right next to us. But Fede clocked him, clocked him real good."

"I presume, love, you mean Harry, not the dear Ambassador. I adore Mr. Ambassador. By the way, did you know he's an expert on snails!"

What is with this man and snails?

"She nailed Chum. Decked him on the spot."

"Well, brava girl!"

"That punch, you know who the punch was really for?"

"Was it tits, ass, or pussy? Sounds like a fucking multiple-choice quiz."

"Fede did it for every woman who's had to go through that kind of shit. For the Lomi's and Destiny's, and of course for herself. She didn't hold back. I was worried as hell about her hand."

"And how did the Mr. Ambassador react?"

"He patted her on the shoulder . . . gingerly, like a hot kettle."

Claudia stopped walking and turned so her face was opposite his.

"The humiliation women endure is unconscionable, and it fucking goes on and on and on. Doesn't matter a rat's ass if you're accomplished like Fede and your Claudia here, or a hapless victim like Destiny."

The unexpected soliloquy had come from the heart and endeared her to Stonecrop. The two pressed on. Stonecrop fended off commuters.

"He's gonna pay, Claudia."

"Can you stuff the incident in a box until we're done with Chum's caper? I get how you feel. I feel the same. But I don't want to muck things up."

"I'll put on a professional face, Claudia, I promise. As phony as Chum's."

They had come to a stop again. Stonecrop looked ahead and took Claudia's arm.

"We should keep moving," Claudia said.

They resumed walking. Stonecrop had another question: "Is Vormittag in the loop?"

Although Kommissar Vormittag was Chum's liaison with the *Stadtpolizei* and *Kantonspolizei*, Stonecrop figured that Zürich based officer would have limited access to and knowledge of Chum's grander scheme.

"He's responsible for hand-holding Gregor and keeping tabs on Adewole when he's in Zürich. To my knowledge—which is far from omniscient on this matter—the Kommissar is in the dark regarding your Hennie Couto."

"Can you tell me again where we're going?"

"A quick sortie to Bern, dearie, for a promenade with that pig you'd love to roast on a spit."

"Chum? You're fucking kidding me."

"Harry the Merry in the flesh, yes. Not to worry. I was afraid to tell you. Thought my dear Max would ditch me."

"I *am* fucking worried. What if Couto walks in the door at Ott's and slaughtered my family while I'm off playing spy games with the asshole who mauled my girlfriend."

"Rosie's got your back," Claudia said, too cheerfully.

"Brave as she is, it wouldn't be a fair fight. I'm worried, Claudia."

"We've got people watching the house. They are following Fede and the girls twenty-four seven. You have forgotten, haven't you? I do this for living. Trust me, sweet, they'll be fine."

Stonecrop flashed back to Sandro's drawing of the skatepark and the "hockey parents" from where Hennie had been standing.

"Did you know Hennie was here before I told you?"

"Rumors, only rumors, which, by the way, we assumed were true and acted upon. In my business, you always assume the worst. Seldom fails to pay off." She paused to check departures on an overhead LED screen. The split-flap display had been phased out. Stonecrop missed the familiar clickety-clack. Claudia qualified her statement: "Now, the last few days. Now we know."

"Yeah. Well, I would have appreciated a heads up."

"We connected the dots, dearest, after your din-din in València. Didn't want to give our hand away. S.O.P. Sorry, love."

Claudia flashed an 'I'm sorry' expression, the lips an upside-down *U*. She took the lead as they rode the escalator to the train platforms below the underground mall. The lowest platforms were used for commuter routes to major Swiss cities.

"Gleis 32. Over there." She pointed with the handle of her pole, as if Stonecrop needed a guide.

Track 32 was a through platform, not a dead end, making for efficient travel between terminals. A train for Bern departed every half-hour.

"Tickets?" Stonecrop said. He was offering to get them.

Claudia released his arm, dug two first class tickets out of her pocket, and handed one to Stonecrop. The Bern train awaited them. The few free seats in the first-class car were not side-by-side, thus giving Stonecrop an uninterrupted hour to rest and to prepare for his meeting with Harry Chum: Spy, groper, and Community Liaison Officer and self-anointed "Minister of Fiestas" at the U.S. Embassy in Bern.

He'd first ran into Chum last November, when the man, dressed head-to-toe in insulated motorcycle garb, had dropped by to visit with Ratzow about a consular matter—specifically, the assault on Candi Cook, Federica's friend and pensioned nanny. Chum had been out for one last ride before the weather turned wintry. A big surprise was that Chum had recognized Stonecrop's name, recalling that Stonecrop had been selected for the U.S. Olympic Biathlon trials, and also recalling that he had dropped out because of a family tragedy.

The Harry Chum that greeted Stonecrop at the Bern station was neither the Kevlar clad Hell's Angel nor the Brooks Brothers diplomat he'd confronted at Hotel Zürichberg. This one was dressed top-to-toe in designer togs, could have been a salesperson on lunchbreak from Boutique Roma. Chum 2.0 sported a stylish coif, a well-trimmed fake beard, and pricey oversized Armani glasses. That the occasion was surreal would be an understatement. Without the garrulous greeting and introduction, Stonecrop would not have recognized him. The man exhibited not a shred of memory or animosity from their previous encounter. Stonecrop stared at him. Close inspection revealed the make-up covering facial scratches and a line of stitches that looked like a caterpillar wandered across his lower lip and disappeared into the false beard. Something about the nose was off—swollen on one side? The swelling could have been from the blow from Federica. But not the rest.

Chum supplied air kisses to Claudia and slapped Stonecrop on the back. He chattered non-stop, treating them like relatives from afar arriving for his daughter's wedding. The greeter quickly became the guide and whisked them out of the train station and into a sprinter van with a driver and dark-tinted windows.

The physicality of the engagements with Claudia and Chum, the way they were always touching him or taking his arm, instantiated the word "handlers." He felt oppressed and claustrophobic. The more time that past, the more unnerving was the fact that Chum did nothing and said nothing about Zürichberg.

"Where are we going?" Stonecrop asked.

"Reichenbachwald, a few kilometers north. Can't use Tierpark, our lovely city park. Unfortunately, the park surrounded by foreign embassies. Diplomats are a colorful lot, great fun, and far more dangerous than anything at the zoo. I know them all, and they all know me . . . and you, Claudia.

"Ah, tell me. Do you like the outfit? I think I might keep the sunglasses." He removed them, examining them as he spoke. "These curious consuls keep tabs on me, my comings and goings to and from Zürich. No free time this week—busy, busy, busy—you see.

"Yes, don't let me forget: After we finish, you'll be dropped off at the Kunsthalle, to see the Christo exhibit. So sad he's passed. Easy cover, given your art background. And I thought you would enjoy the exhibit."

"You know his work?" Stonecrop asked, non-plussed at the normality of the conversation and oddly relieved to speak to a familiar topic.

"Yes, of course," Chum replied.

"Favorite piece?" Stonecrop asked, honestly curious.

"None that I can name. Sorry. You?"

"*Running Fence*, twenty-four-miles-long, in the hills around Bodega Bay. Brilliant piece."

"Lovely," Chum responded immediately.

"And *Migrating Goats*, I really liked that one. Follows their entire route."

"Lovely as well." Right after he said the words, Chum realized he'd been snookered. "You made that one up, didn't you?"

Stonecrop grinned, "You're so full of shit, Harry. You're worse than Gregor."

Chum laughed and shrugged. "I *am* familiar with the *Running Fence!*"

"You know I'm an art guy?" Stonecrop asked. "How's that?"

"Max," his interlocutor turned his swivel-seat sideways to face

Stonecrop, "did you know there's a file on you?" His finger and thumb spread a few inches apart. "This thick. I'm not kidding! Between us, my bosses had talked about recruiting you for a full-time gig. I gathered you had been approached before."

"Yeah, could be. A so-called work-study, in Tbilisi. That was years ago."

"The Agency has a memory like an elephant." He laughed. "Moves like one, too."

Stonecrop remembered being pressed by his Ancient Greek professor to consider a research position in Georgia. The same professor taught Arabic and Middle East studies. In retrospect, he must have been recruiting.

A career working for a U.S. intelligence agency had had its appeal. The handful of people he had known in the intelligence field were people he respected and admired. What didn't work for him, was that during much of his life and his father's—a Vietnam vet and anti-war activist—the country had been engaged in questionable wars. His father had argued that in Southeast Asia the U.S. had been on the wrong side and that there had been no justification for the endless engagements in Middle East. The atrocities had piled up. His Dad wasn't a pacifist and he wasn't a radical. His words, his convictions, and his uncertainties had been neither wasted nor forgotten.

That said, and contrary to these obvious negatives, Stonecrop had the deepest respect for those who served and the fundamental values they honored. An ex-girlfriend and fellow biathlete had gone to work for the CIA right after graduation. He'd tried to keep in touch, but she had gone totally off his radar and everybody else's. He made a mental note to try again. Jenny was named after her.

"You got the chops," Chum interrupted Stonecrop's reflections. "Proven language skills, clean record, you were fresh out of college, competitive athlete."

"I liked that professor; he was my favorite, actually."

"He's retired from academia—or, I should say, mostly retired."

Chum was older than Stonecrop, but not by much. He could have been a couple years ahead at University of Colorado. That would explain why, at their first encounter, he had heard of Stonecrop the biathlete. The news had been all over the alumni newsletters.

Stonecrop put on his game hat. "I presume we're here to talk about Adewole."

"Indeed, we are," Chum answered.

A Walk in the Park

The van came to a stop. Chum slid open the side door. The three of them exited and set off down the dirt path that wound around the marsh-like pond and then followed the arc of the Aare river. The place was a perfect bird habitat. Stones crunched underfoot. As they walked a bubble of silence traveled with them. Songs of insects and birds ceased as the group approached and restarted as they departed. And when the three of them were passed by someone on the path, like the birds around them, their own conversation ceased.

"He must be a bigger fish than I thought," Stonecrop opined. "Big enough for you to play dress-up and drag us to the outskirts of Bern. And big enough for your agency to overlook my patchy background. I'm far from the squeaky-clean recruit your agency once considered."

"Quite right on both counts, Max." Chum smiled a friendly aren't we so-lucky-to-be-comrades smile. The happy act was getting on Stonecrop's nerves.

"I'm not saying *yes* to anything, you understand," Stonecrop asserted.

"Of course."

"Harry, talk to me about our person of interest."

"With pleasure. He is a long-time, major player in e-waste. Operates out of Lagos, and almost never leaves the place. The man is royalty; lives in a palace. Seen it myself. If I were him, I'd never leave. Adewole is cautious. And paranoid. As a rule, he works only with locals he's vetted. We've never been able to get anyone to turn on him and we can't out-maneuver him on his own turf in Nigeria. The Agency and Interpol tried for years."

"How thick is the file on him?"

"Like yours on steroids," Chum answered.

"Why move now?"

For a change, Chum was direct. "Pressure at home and Europe and coming from skyrocketing liabilities related to environment irresponsibility—deserved or not—by major hardware manufacturers. A mountain of recycled product is masquerading as original equipment.

"Because it's a lot easier for the courts to go after legitimate companies than the Adewoles of the world, Big Tech is feeling the heat. In turn, they put pressure on the Pols—the ones whose campaigns they finance—to rein in big, bad e-waste players. And the Pols make us do the dirty work. Simple."

"Simple? Yeah, an oversimplification." Stonecrop was skeptical. Usually, a specific and egregious offense precipitated real action. "I don't buy it."

Chum ignored the dissent. "He's here, in Switzerland. Not sure how long, but we know why. He has people here, but nothing like Lagos. We have a window, a rare opportunity, to learn more."

"Since my ass is on the line, I assume I get to learn more about the *why*."

"Oh, you will. Full dossiers on Adewole and old friends. The old friends gadabout quite regularly on the Continent. That's how we triangulated on the upcoming meeting in St. Moritz. The group, there are four members, a fifth if they accept Gregor, is facing a crisis of sorts. Legitimate traders, using blockchain, have cut into their shady WEEE operations. They call themselves *Clave*. One of the gang, when she was a young woman, played in an Afro-Cuban salsa band. She tagged them with Clave and the name stuck. Kind of clever really, bit of a play on the U.S. Harmonized Tariff Schedule, *the* reference for customs duties on imports and classifications of exports. Shall I sing a clave rhythm for you? There are several."

Chum started clapping the rhythm with hands, humming something to himself, ready to burst into song, at least until Claudia reached out and clumsily took hold of his hands.

"Stop it," she ordered.

"Why Gregor?" Stonecrop asked. "And why me?"

"Mr. Gregor Ratzow, as you can imagine," Chum's manner changed, a jester turned conspirator, "has been in and out of our radar for-ever." He elongated the *for* and *ever*.

Chum pointed to a bench beside the water. "He's an interesting man. I rather like Gregor Ratzow, I do—"

"However?" Stonecrop interjected. He kept walking. He'd blow up if he had to fucking sit still. Claudia was making do, using her poles for support.

"He's made a lot of money, that man: legally, some not so legally. His African pharma trade blew up on him. He'd had a solid organization until someone started skimming from the top, at which time, my sources say, he'd found better things to do with his money."

Could be Harry here doesn't know the real story . . .

"But you know, I am ever the optimist about my fellow man. Those brothers who worked for him—long records, those two—were too heavy-handed for Gregor. Speculation is that you roughed up their boss-man and he turned tail and ran. There was a price on your head, did you know that?" Chum looked at his feet, and then Claudia did the same, looking at her feet. Stonecrop felt like he should look at his, just to fit in.

Shit, he knows.

"Someone," Chum interrupted his own discourse with a stitches-limited grin, "graciously pulled the bounty and called off the hunt." Finding no gesture too trite, Chum blew on the fingernails on his right hand and then polished them briefly on his left shoulder.

Stonecrop suspected that the report that the agency bailed him out was pure bullshit. Agency guesswork mixed with hogwash he'd been spoon fed by Claudia. Knowing Ratzow's bloody history, he didn't buy for a second the "too heavy-handed" explanation for Ratzow's exit from Africa. Gregor was a two-fisted sledgehammer.

"If Adewole's done his homework," Stonecrop added, "he knows I was in Mozambique to *stop* shitty drugs from being distributing. Why on Earth would he trust me?"

"Because, he said, *you* took out the Coutos."

Stonecrop hid his surprise. There was only one witness, as far as he knew, to what had transpired.

"In addition," Chum went on, "even after that, you were still cozy with Gregor. You see, from Adewole's perspective you wouldn't be alive today if you had not been working *for* Gregor in the first place. Adewole and others are convinced that you were Gregor's inside guy with orders to tie up loose ends in Mozambique when Gregor wanted out. You performed the task with deadly effect. *That* is what gives *you*, my new friend, all the credibility in the world with all the right people."

"Harry, that's all speculation based on coincidence, not fact. There's a long history, a trail of my exploiting legitimate means—"

"Ah, Mr. Stonecrop, let me interrupt. There's an alternative narrative, a different trail entirely and one that suggests those legitimate activities were cover fabricated by you and your current employer."

"That's a crock and you know it."

"Oh, I resent that! Far from a crock, your new past is a finely crafted piece of intelligence work. Lies and a cheap wig turn the world, my naïve friend. Don't worry, Max. Your wig's gonna itch but the scene is short."

Asshole.

Stonecrop was incensed. He was also curious about the mechanics of altering someone's past. What right did these bastards have to re-invent his past? None, of course. But there was no question of rights, not to them. He would play along with the farce. He had to do so, he told himself, to protect his family and Fede. Furthermore, he promised himself that he wouldn't think about payback. Evening the score hadn't gone so well in the past. That didn't mean, however, that he couldn't be mad as hell.

This gay-spirited and heretofore unremarkable man, Harry Chum, was a despicable human being. His unveiling was a warning to Stonecrop to not underestimate the man. Gregor had dismissed him as run-of-the-mill CIA type working his way up the agency food-chain and using the embassy position as official cover. However, Chum had crossed the line now; he'd used *nonofficial* cover. That practice, Stonecrop knew from his CIA friends, was more than *not* Agency policy. It was strictly prohibited. And it raised the question: Was Chum's rogue behavior a mere indiscretion, or indicative of something more?

"To be clear: I didn't want to play with your kind before, Harry. If I do now, I do so with great reluctance. For the record, I don't give a damn about a bunch of loaded tech companies sweating pollution fines or competition from counterfeit products. And you get that I'm living in Switzerland, a neutral country? Beyond the moral objection to working on behalf of an agency and government I don't particularly trust, I'm a lousy liar and your line of work entails shitloads of lying."

"Max, Max," Chum cajoled, "dismount the high horse. You're right. Maybe the pollution stateside isn't horrific, but the people—many of them children—who work at these e-waste recovery and disposal sites in Nigeria, Ghana, and other places do die from handling toxic contaminants. To use your word, the working conditions are atrocious, no limit to them really.

"Now, to the latter point." Chum's somewhat impaired grin widened. "You've been living a lie for a quite some time and seem just dandy. I believe you're in denial."

"Speak for yourself—"

"And your new family here, in Switzerland," Chum pressed him, "certainly you would prefer that the Ratzow family remain united? Federica lost her mother—that was so sad. She doesn't want to lose her father. Even if he is a monster."

Mentioning Federica set him off again. Stonecrop snapped and started to reach for Chum's throat.

Claudia, who had been between them, read his intent and toppled into Chum. One of her Nordic poles slipped between his ankles. He hit the ground knees first. A hard hit. Through cockeyed glasses she glared at Stonecrop. Chum either didn't see or chose to not acknowledge Stonecrop's attempted assault. He remained on hands and knees staring at the Nordic pole between his legs. He didn't move at first. He was collecting his thoughts or maybe waiting for the pain to subside.

"Terribly sorry, Harry dear! Oh, so clumsy of me," Claudia apologized profusely. She tsked as she took his arm.

His glowing smile had dimmed. "Be careful with those—"

"Nordic walking poles," she supplied the name. "Useful, actually."

The intervention and Claudia's quip quelled Stonecrop's anger.

"Harry, we need to have a different conversation." Stonecrop roughly pulled Chum to his feet. The gesture bordered on threat.

"Max." Claudia adjusted crooked glasses and lowered her squeaky pitched voice. "Max, time out. Please."

He got the message: your day will come. He released Chum with a light push.

"Gregor's untouchable in Zürich," Stonecrop said.

"Come, come." Chum rubbed his neck like he was letting Stonecrop's threat roll off to the side. "We know better. The U.S. and U.K. authorities can, at a minimum, decimate his business empire. That will hurt, and impact Ms. Ratzow. She an easy target you know, laundering money through her non-profit."

Undaunted, Chum had conjured up another provocation, another prevarication. For a second time, Claudia anticipated trouble and stepped between the two men. Stonecrop marched, eyes forward and drilling into the ground before him. His gaze shifted to the river.

Claudia took over: "Harry, that's a load of crap and you know it. The only thing Aide Direct ever laundered was socks and undies. Let's move on to the incentives, shall we!"

"Right, the big carrot!" Chum clasped his hands in front of his chest. Was that glee, or a plea? The man's demeanor could flip in a heartbeat.

The pitchman spoke: "Not only will your potential father-in-law's misdeeds from the past be expunged, so will *yours*."

"You mean the ones you guys trumped up? Gosh, thanks." Stonecrop faced Claudia. "What jurisdictions are we talking about? By whom specifically?" He turned on Chum. "Harry, you're all hot air. A clean slate for a man or an organization with as much history as Gregor's is a stretch. And, frankly, I think you'll be hard pressed to pin anything on me."

"Maybe not in Mozambique—for you. Switzerland, however, is not a sanctuary for murderers. Unless you have money, a great deal of money. And you murder a great many people." He made the usual gesture, rubbing the fingertips together, and added, "Which you don't, but we do. The money, not the slaughter!"

"That's not *carrot* talk, Harry." Claudia narrowed her eyes, to express her displeasure and to focus better. The thick lenses of her glasses distorted the size and shape of her eyes and revealed the pores of her skin and thick makeup. Beads of sweat grew to the size of raindrops. The walk was too much for her. The tension was too much for the both of them.

Chum settled into smugness like it was a well-worn Lazy-Boy but Claudia wouldn't have it.

Claudia re-engaged. "My compassionate social director, when will you learn? Unbeknownst to you," she looked briefly at Stonecrop and then returned to face Chum, "and *your* little band of conspirators, I do have coverage—in writing, my sweets—from certain Swiss authorities."

"He can be extradited—"

"Also," Claudia interrupted, "a few muckety-mucks in the U.S., U.K. and, believe it or not, Japan. *Dear little spy-man*," she drew out the words, confidently returning the ace he thought he had served, "you don't have an exclusive on money or friends in high places."

Stonecrop had abandoned the game, mentally and physically. He walked ahead, barely within earshot.

Chum ignored her challenge and changed the subject. "This

negotiation among Adewole and his colleagues has been going on for some time. We thought we'd have to make a low-percentage play in Lagos; but here we are, with an unforeseen opportunity right in our lap. A chance to make a move, right here in Switzerland."

Stonecrop stopped and turned around to face them. "You two know everything there is to know," he said. "I want to get the hell out of here. I'll take my chances with Couto."

"They're not going to touch you," Chum responded. "I know these crooks, Alves and Henrique Couto."

Stonecrop reflected that Chum didn't know the Coutos well enough to pronounce their name correctly. Chum had the vowel's backwards: the *ou* wasn't like the English *oo* in spook, it was a long *o* sound like joke; and the *o* at the end of their name, that was the vowel like the English *oo* in spook. Chum knew the brothers on paper, not in the flesh. And he spoke as if Alves was alive. Stonecrop was certain he had died. As far as he knew, the only living witnesses were Hennie and himself.

"Yeah, how's that?" Stonecrop demanded.

"For one," Chum began, "Henrique—his nickname is Hennie—is more attached to money than revenge. Adewole got Hennie to join his team—did you know that?—even though Hennie believed that Gregor had sent you to take him out. Hennie is willing to work with Gregor again and, by extension, with you. You see, the money is what matters. Not loyalty, not revenge. And there's big money at stake. Hundreds of millions."

"Harry, do you live in the fucking Twilight Zone?! The real numbers are pissant. The deal with Adewole is a few containers a month. It'll be years—"

"Granted, we're not there yet. But Adewole's about to graduate. Gregor's name carries weight. The other players know Gregor can go big. Adewole thinks he's using Gregor for leverage. Truth is, that's backwards. Gregor—hence, we—are using Adewole to get a major seat at the table. Adewole claims the time to strike is now. We agree and we'll strike with him."

Claudia added a clarification. "For what it's worth, Adewole is not in the CIA's pocket, Max. And he *is* a rising star in the illegal e-waste sector; my sources have confirmed that assertion."

Stonecrop trusted Claudia somewhat. At any rate, he trusted her more than Chum. And Chum's argument maybe, just maybe, made sense for Couto. It wouldn't work for Stonecrop, not in his DNA to let his brother's killer off the hook no matter how much money was involved. That was a projection on his part.

"You're assuming I did try to kill them."

"Yes, of course, and that Hennie miraculously survived you and some damned fire. What can I say," Chum showed a toothy grin and cocked his head to the side, "forgive and forget—for the right price."

Chum's teeth, Stonecrop noted, at least those weren't non-descript. Too perfect, too white. The fact made him glad for his own irregular teeth, the top one in front that had always been crooked, and there was a small gap.

"Why the hell *is* Hennie in Zürich?" Stonecrop asked.

This time Claudia responded. "Two explanations, love. One rumor, one fact."

The rumor got Chum's attention. Curiosity was so apparent that Stonecrop recalibrated his earlier assessment of Chum as the consummate actor. Or was his reaction an act within an act?

Claudia continued, "Like Harry implied, Couto wants back in Gregor's good graces. In Hennie's mind, you're a threat to him, love, but not as big a threat as Gregor, if indeed Gregor was still inclined to eliminate him."

"Is that the fact or the rumor?"

"Fact." She tilted her head at him and then continued, "I've also heard that Hennie is involved in a torrid affair. Juicy Rom-Com, more news to follow. The object of his affection—though these days we shouldn't say *object*—is a Zürcher immigrant."

Stonecrop immediately had further questions, but Chum spoke first.

"You asked how a few containers can mean so much to Adewole." He seemed to have ignored the hot gossip that a minute ago had him at rapt attention and now refocused on the upcoming transaction, which, as Stonecrop had correctly noted, was a rounding error in the world of illegal e-waste.

Chum continued, "Sources in Lagos suggest that a palace coup is in the offing. The port is where the money is and Adewole is making a move to control more of the port action. The number of containers isn't the endgame. There's little doubt that with Gregor as a potential ally, Adewole will have more sway."

The group's circumnavigation of the river trail had come to an end and they climbed back into the van, taking the same seats as before. Chum peeled off the fake beard, careful to not pop the stitches on his jaw. Next came the wig. He ran his fingers through thin, flattened hair, removing hairpins and rubbing his scalp as if he were giving himself a vigorous shampooing. A silent Claudia gazed out the window of the van and focused on something in the distance. The distraction seemed to quash her innate compulsion to rehash Chum's claims. Unfettered, she could beat a dead horse to death and then some.

"Hot and itchy, these things." Chum addressed the wig in his hands. He looked for all the world a crazed madman. "That's why I quit theatre." He tilted his head back and put his hands in the air. An appropriately theatrical expression crossed his face.

"Harry, I'm not a wig kind of guy," Stonecrop said.

"You forget about it," he shoved the costume items in a briefcase as he spoke, "as soon as you step on stage."

Mansplaining

Stonecrop and Federica had never seriously argued until that day. Federica had been led to believe that the trip with Claudia to Bern three days ago had been the end of the "Chump" affair, her most recent pet name for the sting. Their disagreement arose when Stonecrop had told her that he, rather than Gregor, had to go to Saint Moritz tomorrow to attend a second meeting related to the sting, one that was "high level." At first, Federica had pouted. Then, with no explanation given but with a determined look on her face, she picked up her phone and texted Herr Doktor Weller, her boss. His response was immediate and elicited a look of satisfaction in the caller. She double-checked the dates on her handy, fired off a few more texts, and a minute later announced how much fun it was going to be for Stonecrop that "the girls"—meaning Alicia, and Lupita—would join her at Therme Tavate after Stonecrop's meeting, and that Weller had let her off her shift tomorrow, so she could ride up with him!

Stonecrop wasn't quite sure how to respond and lost the chance when Federica jumped up from the table, "Gotta pee," and moved on to the shower, leaving him to clear the table and wash the dinner dishes.

Compartmentalization deferred the matter until post-shower. Federica, naked except for a white turban wrapping her wet hair, tossed a duffle on the bed to pack for the trip.

"We're gonna spa," she half-sang. She couldn't sing worth a damn and couldn't care less.

Stonecrop joined her in the bedroom. "It's not gonna happen. Sorry, Fede."

"Says who? Papà? Babbo's not some dictator."

She only used the term "Babbo" for Gregor when she was in a good mood, which meant this discussion was going to be awkward.

"I work for him, Fede. He *is* my personal dictator," Stonecrop replied, assuming that would end the discussion.

She was not persuaded. Socks, bras, and underwear flew in a flat arc from the armoire to the bed, aiming for, and mostly missing, the open duffle. Stonecrop slipped off his socks to get ready for a shower.

"This is not your world," Stonecrop stated. "You know what happened at Mediterráneo. Do you have any idea—."

"No mansplaining!" Federica struck a defiant pose: legs spread, knuckles to her hips.

"Fede, I mean it," he asserted.

"Me too, mister. Look, Frau Ott will be here, and Sandro can help. Lupita's still on the fence. God, I'd love to see her. Weller can juggle schedules at the Spital."

Federica threw her slippers toward the bed. Stonecrop ducked; they slippers just missed him.

"These are dangerous people, Fede."

"Who's dangerous? What people? You haven't even told me who's going to be there!"

"I don't know, actually. All of them are dangerous. What if Couto's there? You should have told me about your—"

"I did tell you," she interrupted, "last week. And the last time Alicia was here, we talked about Tavate. Why don't you remember?"

"I'm not like you. I forgot things."

"You're whining and it's not very attractive."

"I'm not bloody whining." Stonecrop's words failed to carry the intended conviction.

"Anyway, Alicia will be there—an armed deterrent."

"Fede, I need two days da solo. Give me that, then drive up with Alicia."

"You sure? You know I happen to be Gregor Ratzow's daughter. That tells you who's fucking dangerous. Me! Maybe *you* should stay at home. Bake some of those—whatever they are you love to bake—"

"Spitzbuben. Look, I don't have a choice—"

"Horseshit! Choices scare the fuck out of you. Oh, the drama of it all!" She threw her arms up in the air. "Max Stonecrop, you're boring your girl!"

Stonecrop sat on the bed. Three camisoles, like doves in flight, landed beside him.

Since becoming Gregor's Transport Specialist, Stonecrop had been on an emotional roller-coaster, one minute disconsolate and testy when he was doing Chum's bidding, and then elated when feeling his old self, taking initiative, and being with Fede. His mood swings made him angry with himself, and Fede rubbing it in didn't help.

A handful of movers and shakers in e-waste, all Adewole associates, were slated to attend the meeting at Therme Tavate. Per Claudia, Harry Chum had coaxed a reluctant Gregor Ratzow to insist to Adewole that Stonecrop be point. Adewole seemed not to object. With that, Stonecrop had become Ratzow's major-domo, the favorite, the man whose reputation was based on the false perception that he had been the man assigned to run clean-up in Maputo, among other things.

"Max, my truly wise but acting like an idiot boyfriend Max. Whatever the fuck is bothering you, deal with it. No handwringing. Am I clear?"

"Lecture over?" He wasn't in the mood for this.

Stonecrop bent down to pick up a sock that had missed the duffle and lay on the floor.

"Ow! Fuck!" An airborne clog had caught him behind the ear.

"You're toast," he threatened and charged Federica. He wrapped his arms around her waist and flung her over his shoulder and carried her to the bed. With Federica squirming in his arms, Stonecrop fell backwards on the bed. The slats supporting the mattress strained, one cracked. Federica lay across his lap, buttocks up. She pulled his sweatpants downward and bit into the muscle tissue of his obliques. Her teeth locked on to him and she pretend growled. Saliva oozed out of the corner of her mouth. An arm shot up under his shirt for a no-quarter-given tickle. Stonecrop grimaced and laughed, and then slapped her bottom harder than intended. The crack of flesh-on-flesh froze the actors mid-grapple. The she-dog released her bite and howled. Above them in Frau Ott's living room, Rosie howled with her.

"I give, uncle, whatever—" Stonecrop shouted. He was out of breath from laughing and put a hand over the red marks on his hip. "That frickin' hurt!"

Federica rolled, then swung around to straddle him. She didn't bother to wipe her lips or chin.

"I told you," she pressed the words against the fleshy nook of his neck, and then reached down between his legs, "I'm dangerous."

"Cancel, Fede. Please, I'm begging—"

Fede pulled him closer. "Make me."

Julier Pass

They had compromised: Federica would not make the drive with him, but when his meetings were concluded, Stonecrop promised to stick around and wait for Federica and company.

Of course, the heart of their argument and the underlying source of tension had been Federica's observation—and that it was true hurt—that Stonecrop had not yet taken control of his life. He leaned on Federica, her authenticity and her raw spirit. Stonecrop vowed to right things. He was smart enough to know change wouldn't happen overnight, and dumb enough to believe that driving two-hundred-kilometers-per-hour would help.

The Taycan devoured kilometers en route to St. Moritz. He passed the Marmorerasee reservoir where a month ago Kanton Polizei had fished out a Ferrari with the decomposed remains of the driver, Andreas Castro. Stonecrop avoided staring at the section of the berm cordoned off with red and white barricade tape. A divot in the road made the wheel shudder and turn toward the barrier. He grinned and jerked the Taycan back on track. *Fuck,* he told himself. *Be you, she says. Well, I'm no angel!*

He downshifted, tapped the console to turn off the artificial purring sound of the "engine." Watching for pedestrians, bicyclers, and wandering cows, he threaded the car through the winding cobblestone streets of Bivio. The town was a pastel pastiche of stucco and stone. Buildings were decorated with *sgraffiti,* a technique in which a layer of plaster was etched to reveal a contrasting underlayer; walls were painted with geometric patterns or Romanesque figures, elaborate vines, and wild animals. Green and brown wood-slatted shutters and flower boxes stuffed with geraniums framed windows deep-set in thick walls designed to temper seasonal extremes.

Gregor Ratzow, aware of his Transport Specialist's reluctance to join the party at Therme Tavate, had handed him the keys to the green, all-electric Porsche Taycan Turbo S, a recent addition to Ratzow's rotating stable of cars. Though Ratzow had no interest in exotic automobiles, his tax attorney did. Every six-months, one or two vehicles would matriculate and be replaced by new ones. The sales and replacement purchases were timed with a biannual income bump in one of Ratzow's companies. Stonecrop must have said something about the Porsche. Ratzow had overheard and, just like that, the car had made the roster.

Ratzow's bribe sort of worked. Despite fear of imminent death at the hands of Henrique "Hennie" Couto and relationship pressure from Fede, Stonecrop felt happier than he'd been in a while. *Be you: drive fast.*

He led the green beast through its paces. Over seven-hundred horsepower, zero-to-sixty in under three seconds, balanced-handling even on less-than-ideal road surfaces, wet or dry. He loved the car. The Taycan was no Tesla, for which he was relieved. Under the designer lines, a Tesla was vulnerable; a Porsche was not. This car had the pedigree and the soul of a genuine race machine, and driving this Porsche was, well, as lovely as driving every other Porsche he had driven.

The five-hundred-meter tour of Julier Pass began at Bivio and ended equidistant from the summit and five-hundred meters lower, at Silvaplana. The pass formed the saddle point: The maximum elevation between the Rhine drainage to the West and, to the East, the Danube drainage; and the minimum elevation between the northern feature, Piz Julier, and Piz Lagrev to the South.

In less than twenty minutes, the green beast had traversed the *tornanti* from Bivio to the summit and taken the plunge into the shadows darkening Silvaplana and stretching across the mile-wide expanse of the Upper Engadine. In a few stretches, he had pushed the car toward two-hundred kilometers per hour—it took less than ten seconds—and then buried the nose to avoid flying off a curve. A relaxing twenty minutes southeast and upstream along the Inn river— *En* in Romansh—took Stonecrop to the tree and shrub bordered approach to the garage and reception area of Therme Tavate. Twenty-five meters short of the garage entry and under cover of a shaded bight in the road and hidden from Tavate's cameras, Stonecrop pulled onto the berm. He opened the sunroof, stood on driver's seat, and tossed a black Patagonia daypack over the perimeter fence. He stared at the pack. *Be you: do your job well.*

The pack landed in the underbrush behind a tennis shed on the other side. The arc of the pack flying through the air would only be visible from the tree foliage to the thicket, thus the risk of exposure was nominal. In the dim light of dusk, security cameras, if they noticed anything at all, would assume a bird had dropped to the ground. The pack was identical to the one he routinely carried. The contents were not: a taser; a folding knife like those carried by Navy Seals, and a Glock 19M with an extra clip. If the others found a weapon on him, then fine. That would be an acceptable level of distrust and something you'd expect from someone with Stonecrop's hyped-up bad-ass reputation, but you did have to leave it at the door.

Tavate posted armed guards at the entry and required guests to go through a metal detector. Ingress and egress points to the compound were few and were guarded either by personnel or by cameras that provided real-time feedback. Nothing was recorded for more than a day. At Therme Tavate, there was no stigma associated with walking in the door with a weapon. No big deal: *leave the Uzi with the valet, here's your chit, enjoy the spa.* The tennis court was considered part of the secure compound. Stonecrop would retrieve his pack after he checked into his room.

Clave

Therme Tavate overlooked the Silsersee. The largest natural lake in the Alps at over one-thousand meters elevation, Silsersee was tucked in the valley under Piz Corvatsch, Piz Grefasalva, and Piz da la Margna. Stonecrop knew the area well from having competed in the Engadine Ski Marathon, an annual forty-two-kilometer cross-country ski race that starts from the Neo-Renaissance styled Maloja Palace Hotel at the southwestern end of the lake, passes through Saint Moritz, and ends at S-chanf. The course is an easy one, as ski-marathons go, a gentle downhill run with one mid-tour climb.

From the air, the Tavate hotel and spa facility resembled a random array of eight squares of various sizes that had fallen and landed at irregular angles and elevations. Six of the square structures had roofs covered with alpine grasses; one square was the open-air thermal pool, blue or gray as the sky demanded; another was a red clay tennis court. The structures were surrounded by patches of stone pine and larch. Abutting the northernmost corner was an abandoned quartzite quarry, an open wound where remnants of excavators, hole drillers, and conveyors, poised like giant insects.

The walls and floors of Therme Tavate were quartzite. A token amount was in situ, while most came from the Soglio Quartzite Quarry in Dogana, on the Mera river and an hour to the southwest.

The pool complex faced the dawn and was walled in panels of bullet-proof glass that floated between Frank Stella-like stelae a meter-square and three-meters tall. Federica named the place "The Keep." Three thigh-thick columns of water gushed out of paw-shaped copper spouts. Earth-toned mineral residue stained the stone beneath the spouts. The surface of patio floor was warmed by geo-thermal piping. The radiant heat dried the feet of frost-coated skeletons of outdoor furniture, sans cushions and waiting for the sun. A few rough-hewn wood planters lay against the west wall, some with the brittle remains of fall plantings and others, in the sun, with red geraniums.

The visual symmetry of the outdoor patio and the dining room, intentional or not, was disorienting. Not so much during the day or night, but at this hour when the sun was at the brink of extinction. The LED track-lighting meandered and snaked across the ceiling of the dining area and presented so realistic a reflection in the glass bordering the patio that an observer could easily be convinced that he or she were viewing an extension of the fixture on the other side of glass and suspended in space with no visible means of support.

"Apologize for being late." It felt like he was always late and always apologizing for it. Stonecrop looked around the dinner table as he spoke. Of the eight place-settings, two were empty: one next to the Clerk, and another across from the Clerk and next to Ibrahim Adewole. He chose the place next to the Clerk and slipped the Patagonia daypack off and put it on floor on his right side. That meant the guest entry door was behind him. He could see the door to the kitchen, but his potential killer wouldn't enter from the kitchen.

He was surprised and relieved to see Francis de Bruyn, the Clerk. He saw de Bruyn on his bi-monthly courier runs to Valleta, Malta. De Bruyn's presence meant Stonecrop would have back up and then some; the man was ex-South African military, knew Africa well, and was trusted enough by Ratzow to manage Group's logistics operation in Malta.

The three new faces at the table had been in Chum's briefings: Oghenefejiro "Ode" Ikande; Jamila Oparei, the only woman in group; and Kabili Prince. Their bios had been full of holes, with long periods unaccounted for, and the mug shots were dated but adequate.

Two of them, Ikande and Oparei, were Nigerian. Prince had been described as East African. The Clerk made introductions and did Stonecrop a much-appreciated favor by introducing him as being new to the business, naïve in some ways, but having a few fresh thoughts to contribute. The pre-qualification didn't really matter; he was Gregor Ratzow's designated stand-in. The Clerk also mentioned that Stonecrop had worked in pharma in Africa, as had Adewole's yet to arrive associate.

"Can you please tell me your name again? I didn't quite get it," Stonecrop asked Oghenefejiro "Ode" Ikande.

"Just call me Ode." He laughed one of those deep, sonorous laughs.

Others at the table joined in.

Stonecrop repeated the name, "Ode. *That* I can pronounce, thank you."

Kabili, the woman, lowered her head and touched her forehead to her hand. She tried to hold back a smile. Stonecrop asked the question without speaking, raising an eyebrow. *Am I picking up Ratzow's habits?*

"Dumb," Kabili said aloud. "Ode means *dumb* . . ."

". . . but I never let it go to my head!" Deep-voiced Ode launched another round of laughter.

"Nice to meet you, Ode," Stonecrop reached across and shook Ode's hand a second time. He was grateful for Ode's good humor, and for his setting a casual tone to a gathering that Stonecrop had envisioned as being a stiff affair. Ode's hands were calloused like a bricklayer's, though his grip was measured, appropriate for the circumstances. He was a big man, but he moved lightly.

Treating Stonecrop in the same, warm manner as Ode, the woman of the group, Jamila Oparei, asked him to address her as Jami.

"Jami means *beautiful!*" She slapped Ode's shoulder as she spoke. The good-humored man smiled back at her.

"And call me Prince." Kabili Prince's voice, a good octave higher than Ode's, could have been a woman's. "I *am* a singer," he added, and widened his eyes as if he were about to begin singing. "But not *the* Prince singer!"

Again, the group laughed, Stonecrop with them. They were a charming and disarming group. He was beginning to feel foolish for having smuggled the Glock into the meeting. Still, no sign of Couto.

A waiter came in, asked for everyone's attention, and announced that he would be serving a half-dozen dishes, small portions, each a separate course. A dessert tray would follow, along with coffee and aperitifs. He further announced that he would be their server, the only server, and that the dining room was private and secure. He took drink orders and then returned to the kitchen. Stonecrop recognized the waiter as the cook from Therme Tavate's bar, reputed to be a long-time friend of Gregor Ratzow. More backup. *I'll take that, too,* Stonecrop thought to himself.

"I don't know why my associate is delayed," Adewole announced. "Let us begin without him."

For the next hour—in between tapas derived from Graubünden specialties and accompanied by local wines served in earthenware pitchers—Adewole, Ode, Prince, and Jami gave updates on operations at the Lagos Port complex, including adjacent Apapa and Tin Can Island Port. Infrastructure, personnel training, and technology improvements by mega-importers like Fouani, professional terminal managers like APM, part of A.P.Moller-Maersk, and logistics firms like TradeLens, with help from IBM, had modernized much of the complex. For import-export consortiums like Clave, a group that took advantage of market inefficiencies to smuggle e-waste, modernization, more specifically, blockchain, was perceived as the biggest single threat to the bottom line.

Adewole took the floor. "Our businesses do not adjust to changes in the industry. The market is growing, but we are losing ground. If our ports and terminals become fully integrated, we are dead. Recent improvements in supply chain efficiency, flexibility and tracking have forced us to disperse goods over multiple carriers. We survive by getting smaller and smaller. This is not a viable business model."

The others nodded in agreement. Jami spoke for them: "What Ibrahim says is true. We lose two container last month! They say, 'Not in system, sorry.' Apapa Port put our containers in the Graveyard."

Stonecrop looked for a clarification.

"Apapa's holding facility," Jami explained. "Revenue is good, but this is because, like Ibrahim said, the local business in Africa grows." Jami paused and shook a finger at the group. "*Not* because we are clever."

Ode pointed a finger away from the table. He seemed to know where south was, a fact which impressed Stonecrop. "They are the clever ones. These blockchain people down there."

"Yes. This is true," said Jama.

Stonecrop loved Jama's voice; the lilt and intonation reminded him of Destiny. Had Jama too been a choir girl? And if so, then how does a choir girl become a major WEEE smuggler? Or, like Lomi, possibly a murderer?

The thought reinforced his desire to be done with his role for Chum and resume the search for Lomi. Originally, he had taken on the ordeal with Lomi to gain leverage with Vormittag. But at this point, looking after Lomi and Destiny had become personal.

This gathering, Stonecrop reflected, was the same as any other board meeting or strategy session. He enjoyed the Swiss tapas, asked intelligent questions, and learned about the business. His colleagues were helpful and good-natured, so much so, that he felt guilty over his duplicity. Chum, Gregor reported, had wanted this session recorded.

Gregor had agreed, but then told Stonecrop to do the opposite. The policy at Therme Tavate was no recordings, no bugs. Gregor would lie to Chum and lay the blame on Stonecrop for the fuck-up. *Whatever*, Stonecrop said to himself.

Compared to well-run start-ups and life science companies he'd worked with, the Port and the Clave consortium were both disorganized and undisciplined. Even after the modernization effort at the Apapa and Lagos complex, trucks lined up for miles and clogged access and exit points; holding lots overflowed; and rogue vessels docked wherever, their berths chosen by availability and how much water a ship drew and needed to dock and unload. The result was containers stacked upon containers willy-nilly throughout the entire complex. Importers still used gangs of children to search for their containers. And once found, there remained the challenge of accessing the container by ground transport. Drivers slept in their trucks, sometimes waiting a week in the queue at a particular depot. Vessels waited at sea, again sometimes for weeks, until they were given a berth at which to unload.

All of that was changing, he learned. Not overnight, but steadily. The reason was blockchain. The situation was as Chum had predicted. And that was what had driven this unprecedented meeting and brought Adewole out of his lair in Lagos.

Stonecrop, being an ex-VC, understood blockchain. All venture capital types did, and some years ago blockchain deals had been all the rage. As expected, a lot of deals failed. The reason wasn't so much the technology per se, although well-known limitations dog blockchain, but its implementation. Blockchain was a glorified ledger and if the setup was sloppy the output was sloppy. Reversing an error or malfunction was a nightmare.

Stonecrop's task, on behalf of GR Group and Gregor, was to run through blockchain basics with Clave so they would understand what they were up against. The participants here were about to join the twenty-first century and brainstorm ideas about how to launder WEEE within the burgeoning blockchain eco-system. Theoretically, they would share best practices in WEEE leakage and laundry mechanics by letting each participant present one real-life case study. As a business move, Stonecrop decided, the approach was sound.

He was thinking about his own talking points when the hand dropped onto his shoulder. Stonecrop had not seen or heard Couto approach. He reacted instantly, dropping his right hand into the pack on floor.

The Clerk's arm moved with Stonecrop's and caught his wrist as Stonecrop's fingers wrapped the butt of the Glock. De Bruyn, the unflappable Clerk, faced Stonecrop. His lips were inches from Stonecrop's eyes. Stonecrop read those lips loud and clear. Without breaking the smile, the Clerk whispered, "Play nice, Max." Some trick, Stonecrop mused, to do both at once, to whisper and grin like that.

"Hello, Maxine!" The feisty voice attached to the man behind him spoke, raspier than he had remembered. In València, he had only heard the voice through Fede's handy. "You look worried? Don't be."

Stonecrop didn't turn around. He relaxed his grip on the automatic and withdrew his hand. De Bruyn draped the top flap back over the pack.

"Sorry we missed at Mediterráneo."

"Yes, sad that," Stonecrop replied, assuming the "missed" referred to Couto's not having killed him when he had had the chance. He still hadn't turned to face Couto. What would that be like, to look at this man's disfigured face, into his eyes, and know that he, Stonecrop, had been responsible.

"Lovely, that honey of yours. And the boat too! Trying to impress her, were you! Well, certainly impressed me. I mean both, you know, the girl and the boat. One's a little skinny. The other's short, shy of being a real yacht. No mind that, you take what you get. Or get what you take! Right, Maxine? Accept fate and move on. That's what I say."

The worst nightmare he could imagine was Couto, standing there, holding a gun to his head, and this group witnessing an execution they had sanctioned in advance. But the Clerk was here; he'd never turn on Ratzow. Unless Ratzow wanted Stonecrop out. Had the Porsche been his goodbye ride?

"Say something, lad. Here, let's be friends, shall we?"

The others at the table watched the two of them. Did they sense how this encounter could explode? He had no idea. Stonecrop felt blood pumping through the veins in his scalp and neck and wondered if it showed.

Couto stepped beside Stonecrop, released the shoulder, and offered his hand. Stonecrop rose slowly, easing back the chair and in the process brushing the man's leather coat open to see if he was armed. The holster was empty. That didn't necessarily mean he was unarmed.

He shook Couto's hand, an ordinary enough handshake. The men followed the handshake with a nod of acknowledgement, and then

Couto walked around the table, chatting with everyone and saving Adewole for last. He and Ode exchanged man-hugs and appeared genuinely pleased to see each other. There was some whispered chatter between them, which Stonecrop and others at the table couldn't hear. Adewole rose, pulled back the empty chair, and invited Couto to sit beside him. Couto's cap never left his head. The tension in Stonecrop, and in the room, subsided.

Until Death Do Us Part

The remainder of the meeting had gone without a hitch. There had been no handouts, notes, or PowerPoint presentations. The group, each one of them, had done their homework and Stonecrop was both surprised and pleased. Ode had even worked on one IBM blockchain implementation and had a hands-on understanding of its application, in fact, more real-world experience than Stonecrop. Both Ode and Stonecrop agreed that if Clave wanted to improved growth, then a percentage of the business would have to be re-directed through a parallel blockchain protocol wherein the end nodes would be synchronized and goods run through inspection and verification points under Clave's control.

The Clerk had an IT team at the ready, cleared and groomed by GR Group and, behind the scenes, there was Chum, whose goal was nothing short of tracking every bit of e-waste that Clave would divert or camouflage.

Stonecrop found Chum's expectations naïve, unless of course they were backed with significant resources from an organization like the CIA. Somehow, he had a feeling that wasn't the case. In fact, the whole affair felt like a local operation. *Is Gregor being set up? Am I being set up?* Something smelled fishy.

The group followed up the session with coffees and cordials at the bar. Jami and Prince had departed for Samedan Airport, the St. Moritz regional airport. They had chosen to spend the night at the Hotel Terminus next to airport, an easier option for a first light departure on Prince's Lear. Samedan had one major runway, no night operations and was not equipped for instrument landings.

After plunges and massages, Ode and Adewole took up the Clerk on an offer to drive the three of them to Zürich. As De Bruyn waved good-bye and drove off, Stonecrop wanted to run after him and scream, "Don't leave me!" His adversary, Couto, had not made his move. If and when he did, Stonecrop assumed, the strike would be unexpected, fast, and deadly.

The bartender, the same man who had served their dinner, was still at work. Though past midnight, but the man gave no indication that he was tired or unwilling to keep the bar open for as long as customers wanted. A boisterous group of Georgians occupied a table nearby, oblivious to the hour. The group's stereotypes were reversed: the women dominated, and the handsome young men were the arm-candy.

"Funny, ain't it," Couto remarked when he looked at the group. "Times are changing."

"Yes indeedy."

"Did you put away that toy of yours? I gave mine up fair and square at the door, you sneaky bastard! Shove it up your arse, did you?"

"Over the fence, by the tennis court."

"Christ, that easy?" Couto drank from his Stange. "Post it online, I would. Get Gregor's hackles all fuzzy and stiff! Like a fuckin' Rottweiler, he'll be!"

"He would," Stonecrop laughed with him. "It's a marketing gimmick, all the security, I'm told."

"You're right there."

Another long drink from his beer. Stonecrop did the same with his vodka.

"Talk about the elephant, shall we?"

"Talk away," Stonecrop answered. "Talk's better than the alternative."

"Done a bit of poaching. You know that. But look, you're Gregor's pet. You're fucking his daughter, for fuck's sake! Maybe you're fucking him, for what I know—" Couto interrupted himself to take a drink. "And your guardian angel, the goddamned Clerk, was clear: I mess with you, I'm a dead man. So's anybody and anything I ever cared about. That's Gregor's M.O, you know. One nasty Bulgarian, that bugger Gregor."

"I didn't want the fire, or for you to be disfigured. That was not intentional."

"Kind of you. Two tidy holes in the chest. Neatness freak. More your style, I see that. I'm the one ought to be nervous, here. Gregor sic'd you on me once already."

"I lost my brother," Stonecrop added, trying to be empathetic, and not state the words: I killed your brother.

"Well, *I* didn't fucking shoot him, now, did I?" Couto set the mug on the bar, banging loud enough to be heard over the Georgians.

The bartender nodded and started another draw. Stonecrop put his glass next to the empty beer stein and got a second nod.

They sat in silence, watching the other tables until the fresh drinks arrived.

"That's Gregor's boy." Couto threw his chin at the bartender. "A dirty secret. I'll bet my life on it."

Never, had Stonecrop considered that the present and thoughtful bartender, waiter, and night clerk could be Ratzow's son. His manner suggested he was something more than an employee. If one looked closely, there was a resemblance—the stocky build, the thick hands.

"Shall we ask?" Couto asked.

"No."

"I wouldn't, you know. If you want to keep fucking the daughter."

That didn't require a response.

"The elephant—" Couto whispered conspiratorially. The whisper triggered the Georgians' interest. But he continued. "I know, I know. Look, I'm pissed, don't get me wrong." Couto removed his cap as he spoke. The act humanized the man. The right side of his face, the ear, much of the right side of skull was a shining surface of stretched and scarred skin, thin in places, like a map with streets and avenues of veins and arteries. Stonecrop looked and thought about the people who had died by Couto's hand.

"Truly pissed, and I ought to put a bullet in your fucking head. More than once I almost put one in my own, I'll have you know. I would have, had the right woman not come along." The remark suggested an improbable analogy to Stonecrop's experience with Federica after the encounter with Couto.

Couto bent forward and pointed to the right side of his face. "Pissed about this, but not about the brother, you see." He went on and looked upward, talking at the ceiling. "Did me a favor there, you did. Cabrão was stealing, taking *my* share of the blood money. Didn't know how much 'til you popped him off and I got a looky-look at the books. I trusted Alves! A shame, that. Got it back, most of it. You made me a richer man, Massimo! Funds are stuck in a bank right now, a few months. Some kinda estate law, if you can believe."

Couto faced Stonecrop and raised his glass for a toast. "Can you believe it? My own brother robbin' me blind. Burn in hell, asshole!" he roared. "Seems a thing these days, stiffing yours truly."

As if there were more that he wanted to say, Couto paused, and then let the thought hang. Putting both hands to his chest and with some drama, he unbuttoned two buttons of his shirt. Stonecrop jumped. Then Couto showed him two scarred-over bullet wounds. Both shots had been from Stonecrop's weapon. Judging by the holes' locations, it was hard to believe the shots had not been fatal. They were just below the heart. Stonecrop's expression said as much.

His tablemate pointed to the scars. "Nice group, asshole!"

They clinked glasses. Stonecrop's participation was automatic. The Georgians joined in the toast from across the room and yelled "asshole!" Stonecrop debated with himself about this twist. Couto was not the first man for whom greed trumped family. *What a depressing thought*, he said to himself, drunk but nonetheless still worried about Couto killing him.

"Call it night, shall we," Couto looked into Stonecrop's eyes. The eyes neither threatened nor feared. Couto was impossible to read. Stonecrop hadn't believed until this evening that Couto might be one who had been afraid, afraid that Stonecrop would finish the job he'd started in Maputo. Didn't matter, he told himself. A sober thought surfaced: scared dogs bite.

Couto rose and nodded to the cheering crowd that was waving them over and imploring them to join the party.

"Nighty-night, assholes!" Couto yelled to the table as he exited the room.

"Assholes!" the chorus sang back in thick Georgian accents, genuinely sad over the man's departure.

The next morning, Stonecrop awoke refreshed and relaxed. He had expected a fitful night and that he would have been tormented with nightmares of Couto flinging Sarah and Jenny into a bonfire. Instead, he slept like a baby.

He'd not slept in his room. After Couto had retired, he asked the bartender if there were an extra room, a room that no one at Tavate would expect to be occupied, and if he could sleep there. The barman —he went by Fritz, no last name offered—had taken Stonecrop to his personal quarters.

The accommodations were luxurious and gave credibility to the suggestion that Fritz, if not Ratzow's son, was at a minimum someone very important to him. Fritz's quarters were separated from Therme

Tavate guest rooms. The apartment had a spacious studio living room and kitchen; two bedrooms, each with a full bath; and a den of sorts. Several animal mounts, including one he recognized by the heart-shaped antlers, an African Springbok, hung on the walls in the den; an over-sized desk built of solid-stock rosewood took up a quarter of the floor space; a glass-faced locked case displayed a half-dozen hunting rifles. Glass spanned the width of one wall of the studio and presented a panoramic view of the Engadine valley. The furniture was Italian, all classic pieces, including a set of 70s Mario Bellini Tentazione chairs. These were not pieces that one could afford on a bartender's salary. A chef's salary? Maybe a very, very well-paid chef.

It was past noon before Stonecrop caught up with Fritz again. The man was back at work and brought a pot of coffee to Stonecrop and Couto, who were seated together again on Tavate's outdoor patio, enjoying the mountain air and talking about Clave. Fritz, when he saw Stonecrop, made no reference to the previous night. Stonecrop didn't have to declare that Couto was the reason for his guest's reluctance to stay in his own room. So far, Couto had behaved. Nevertheless, Stonecrop kept the Glock handy and did not hide the fact from Couto.

When he had last spoken with Federica, she had told Stonecrop to expect her and her pals, Alicia and Lupita, to arrive at Tavate before dinner. He had steeled himself for the deluge, and he hoped that Couto would depart as soon as possible and avoid an overlap.

His phone vibrated with a text from Federica.

<FR: Canceled trip. Lupita sick. Alicia jammed with work in Zürich. Girls with me. A full house. Motherhood! I didn't ask for this!>

"We done here?" Couto asked.

Stonecrop put down the phone. "Done. I need to get back to the kids."

"Lovely children," Couto said. His voice gave no indication whether or not the statement was intended as a threat.

"If you touch them, I'll kill you."

"I can see that; you'd at least have a good go at it," Couto laughed. "I don't go down easy, mate. Got lucky that first time. Ought to know that by now!"

"That makes two of us," Stonecrop responded. The tone was as cold as he had intended.

"No worries," he continued. "See, now we both got bigger fish to fry."

They didn't shake hands. Couto rose, stretched, and headed off.

Without turning to look at Stonecrop he added, "Give the cona a squeeze, I like her . . ."

Yes, Stonecrop thought, *I'll give the cona a squeeze.* He tried to remember what Fede had called Couto but had forgotten.

Stonecrop took in the view. He would return to Zürich and his children. He was flummoxed about Mattie, their mother, who still had not responded to his texts and emails.

Fritz approached the table. "Everything in order, Mr. Stonecrop?"

"Max, just Max. And thank you again. For last night."

"Shall I ask them to bring the car around?"

"That would be great," Stonecrop said and thanked him one more time.

It was four. He texted Fede that he'd be home for dinner.

Less burdened by the dread and uncertainty about a confrontation with Couto, Stonecrop was comparatively at peace on the drive back to Zürich. With that tension gone, he gave in to uneasy reflections, specifically moral concerns about supporting the work of Clave, even though in theory the reason for that support was to undermine the organization's activities. These sorts of ethical questions were invariably framed as matters of degree rather than being simply right or wrong.

He mentally ran through the catalog the raw materials extracted from WEEE: lead, gold, silver, mercury, cadmium, arsenic, beryllium, PCBs, flame retardants. There had to be more. The process entailed exposure to burning plastics, batteries, acid baths for metal recovery, open dumps, melting circuit boards. Handling these toxic materials and processes without personal protective equipment were children, pregnant women, and poor people with no better work options. They worked like slaves and contracted a host of ailments: skin disease, under-development of the brain in children, endocrine aberrations, respiratory damage, poor natal outcomes, blood contamination . . .

Blockchain, Stonecrop knew, could put a real dent in the underground WEEE business. When manufacturers were forced to track every component of every piece of electronic equipment from beginning to end, and that was the key, the "end" part of the equation, then transport logistics would become transparent and smuggling increasingly complex and expensive. Maybe.

Of course, without the political will to back up good policy, the effort would devolve into so much talk, or worse, systemic corruption that was more efficient than its predecessor. *My fellow man,* Stonecrop reflected, *when given the opportunity to do good, seldom failed to disappoint.*

Zürich City was too wired from the workday to settle down for the night. Streetlights came on, retailers and restauranteurs lit signs to prepare for the night crowd. The Number 6 tram clawed up Krähbühlstrasse en route to the Zoo. At the curve at Susenbergstrasse the metal-on-metal squeal grated on the ears. The sun hid behind a low layer of clouds but managed to illuminate the Glarner Alps to the South. A thin haze, humidity not smog, hung in the air.

Frau Ott, with the assistance of her long-time housekeeper and the enthusiastic Stonecrop girls and Destiny, had prepared and was serving an al fresco *cena* in the backyard garden. Japanese lanterns and tiki torches defended the diners against the shadow rising from the Zürisee to Frau Ott's home.

In the kitchen, Frau Ott handed out dishes and silverware to Destiny and Sarah. They then joined the cook in carrying items to a table set for six and covered with a festive tablecloth, a print of cracker-sized, blue-white, Kanton Zürich flags.

At the table were Frau Ott, Federica, Destiny, Sarah, and Jenny. What a capable, confident lot. They were purposeful people—even the teens—grounded and sensible. He, by contrast, felt like a scatterbrained imposter, and tonight was filled with self-doubt. Fede told him to drop the self-examination: *Be yourself and—oh, yeah—cook for me*.

"Pops." Jenny poked his leg. "You're talking to yourself. What are you thinking about?"

"Sunset," Stonecrop said, an easy out. "Have we ever taken the tram to Uetliberg? And gone up the tower?"

"The tower, there." She pointed to the girded structure atop the foothill on the opposite side of the lake. "Yes, remember the metal stairs, the dragons on the lamps, and the planets and sun along the path, and—"

"That's right. I remember now."

"You told me you run there from the Schützenhaus in Albisrieden. Can we go shooting?"

"I'll have to check. I'm doing a little coaching, junior biathletes—like you!"

"Can I clean your Glock?" Jenny put her arm through his, putting most of her weight on the arm so he was pulled down on one side.

"Yeah, sure."

"Max," Vormittag's voice leapt out of the shadows behind him and startled the still adrift-in-his-thoughts Stonecrop.

"Is she in earnest?" Vormittag asked.

"Kommissar Vormittag, good evening." Stonecrop regained his composure and overcompensated for the interruption with excessive formality. He offered a hand to the man, acting before noticing that Vormittag's left arm was still in a sling and his right hand was gripping his open-top briefcase.

Vormittag spoke as though he were addressing Stonecrop's extended hand. "I apologize. I asked Frau Ott if I might speak with you for a minute. No more than a minute."

"Kommissar, you are welcome to join us."

"Well, it is quite a party. No, but thank you. I promised my wife to be home, and I'm late."

"Let's not keep you. What's so important to delay your dinner and ours?" The statement not so politely informed the Kommissar that this was not the time or place for a chat.

"The younger sister, Destiny. Has she been in touch with Lomi?" Vormittag asked.

"Destiny is hiding from you. In fact, right behind that door," he nodded in the direction of the kitchen, "with Sarah and ready to bolt. She's afraid of being taken into custody. Can't blame her. I'd do the same. She doesn't want to talk to you, Kommissar."

"Yes, I'd expect as much. I'll leave directly. Unless Lomi is there as well, hiding behind the door?"

Stonecrop shook his head no. Judging by the resignation in the Kommissar's face, he had expected as much. So why *was* he here?

"Is she a suspect in the Halbinsel Au incident?" Stonecrop asked. He assumed Vormittag would hesitate or hedge his answer.

He didn't. "Yes, she is a suspect, as are others."

"You've questioned the madam at Kar-Moppa and seen the video, the altercation between Shoji and Lomi?"

Vormittag nodded that he had. The weak nod implied that this was information he should not have shared.

"Helpful woman, isn't she?"

"Max, please, who is supposed to be asking questions?" Vormittag was irritated. Both men would rather be having dinner with their families.

Jenny had been silent, an unusual state for her. She wriggled against Stonecrop's arm. She was, he suspected, fighting the urge to speak.

"Max promised to protect Destiny." The take-charge-of-the-situation Jenny couldn't wait any longer. "You can't arrest her."

"Ah, my inquisitoressa! Come stai?"

The Kommissar, with some effort, squatted down so his head, once above Jenny's, was now below. His good arm leaned on the briefcase for balance, one knee dropped to the ground. Federica had ignored the group until she saw the one-armed Vormittag squat on the ground and then teeter as he tried to get up.

"Good," Jenny answered.

"I could use your help," Vormittag asserted again, as he had at the Spital.

Federica arrived and slid an arm under Vormittag's good arm to help him rise. Once he was up, she leaned over and brushed grass and dirt off his pantleg where his knee had rested upon the ground. "Rimani per cena, caro," she invited him to stay for dinner.

In a warmer and more voluble manner, Vormittag gave the same answer, this time in Italian, that he had given to Stonecrop. The Italian, like a nice Chianti, had washed away his irritable demeanor.

Stonecrop was ravenous. He'd been too nervous to eat much at lunch and he had driven non-stop from St. Moritz to Frau Ott's and then spent the last hour in a frenzied cook-a-thon in the kitchen. The Porsche Taycan had been a lovely escape. Instead of returning the car to Ratzow's garage to gather dust with other vehicles in his collection, he had parked the car at Frau Ott's.

"Cara," Vormittag addressed Jenny. "I don't intend to arrest anybody. I want to help her. You see, her sister is in trouble. If Sarah were in trouble, you would want to help her, yes?"

Jenny scrunched her nose and tilted her head. "I don't know. It depends."

"I heard that!" Sarah yelled and laughed as she marched by with a serving plate of antipasti, the first course for the evening. The aroma of salami, olives, peppers, anchovies, artichokes, and taleggio cheese tortured the senses. The housekeeper set pitchers of Chianti on table. The wine had been a gift from friends of Federica's in Firenze.

"Kommissar," Stonecrop addressed Vormittag and shelved the pleasantries, "let me give you my report. Then you should leave."

"Agreed." Vormittag, too, must have smelled the antipasti and, like any good Italian, was willing to be late for anything except food or opera.

"Lomi called once. She asked Destiny to warn her parents that she had left Kar-Mappa. She implied that there would be repercussions in Nigeria. She also said she wasn't going back. She had met Shoji at Halbinsel Au. They argued. Then someone she didn't know, a homeless man, assaulted them. Another man watched from a distance. She had been beaten, badly beaten, but was able to run off. She's gone. I have no idea where she is. She wouldn't tell Destiny."

"You are not hiding her?"

"I am *not* hiding her. Destiny wants to find her. Me, too. By now she could be halfway to Lagos."

Vormittag looked at Jenny. "Does Lomi look like Destiny?"

Jenny just smiled back him.

Federica lingered on Vormittag's arm, though she too was impatient for dinner. "Is this necessary, Kommissar? I mean now, is this necessary right now?"

"Count the places at the table," Jenny blurted out.

Vormittag did as she asked, then looked around the yard.

"You see," Jenny announced in her professorial best, "one-to-one mapping of places and people. If Lomi was here, she'd have a place."

Stonecrop put an arm around Jenny. "An isomorphism, right kiddo?"

Jenny nodded back. Stonecrop half expected her to fold her arms across her chest and stamp her foot down. She didn't.

"Ora di cena!" Federica announced.

"My wife . . ." Vormittag's phone signaled an incoming call or message. He understood at that point there was nothing more that he would learn. "I apologize for the intrusion. And," he turned to Jenny, "I apologize for the presumption."

"You're not a very clever inspector," Jenny announced. The ball was still in her court and very much under her control.

Turning first to Jenny and then to Stonecrop, Vormittag answered, "I am not. If Lomi calls again . . .well, you know what to say. I'd like to help her. Good Evening."

He paused before leaving.

"Ah," Vormittag looked over his shoulder. The eyebrows dropped. "Is Jenny really going to clean your Glock?"

"Absolutely!" Stonecrop answered. Jenny went along with the act, pointed her finger and thumb like a pistol and aimed at the sky.

Vormittag looked at Jenny, shook his head, and then directed his attention to Frau Ott. He made polite goodbyes and snooped about Frau Ott's upstairs kitchen as he left. Stonecrop saw him through the window. He imagined Vormittag counting soup bowls warming for the *secondi*. The Kommissar observed the group below. He watched as Destiny joined Jenny and Sarah at the table, and then vanished.

Tiramisu

"Why the fuck didn't you tell me?" Federica slouched in her chair. One leg dangled over the side, the other was tucked up under her. Impolite as both the language and the posture were, no one took offense. Frau Ott let it slide. Then, testing social limits, one of the girls farted. The group traded looks. Federica downed a hearty slug of wine and the girls giggled. Again, Frau Ott either didn't notice or pretended not to notice. Or maybe she loved it, loved all of it, being with a gaggle of women and girls, and the devil-may-care freshness of youth.

Be yourself, be happy. The girl does walk-the-talk.

The air had cooled. Stonecrop took in the stars and was reminded of their recent sail on *Zaca*. He looked at Fede, wanting her.

The *contorni* had carried them through dusk. This night, there had been two: the cannellini beans with lemon and oil plus fresh asparagus, pine nuts, and tomatoes, also drizzled in olive oil. The *secondi* had been slices of *bistecca alla Fiorentina* with parsley garnish. Stonecrop had been starved and had put too much meat on his plate. Some monstrous Tuscan *chianina* had given its life for Stonecrop's dinner. He felt obligated to not waste the beef. The food coma settled in just as the housekeeper deposited a mountain of tiramisu in front of him. The girls had made the dessert. Jenny was in high gear, even though the hour was late. He dreaded the impact of the "pick-me-up."

Federica grabbed his sleeve. "Max, we can fix this. It's so easy." Farting aside, offender or not, her command presence demanded attention.

"How so?" Max asked as others wound down conversations.

"I'll give you the sixty-K. I can't believe Papà is making you wait until this thing with Adewole is over. Dumb. Why not make the madam happy? Destiny gets her sister back and the traffickers leave their Nigerian family alone."

"That's generous, Fede. I had considered asking Gregor for the cash sooner rather than later, for the same reasons. But—"

Stonecrop stopped mid-sentence. He needed a coffee. He remembered Hamdi's gesture to his son and got Sarah's attention and then raised a pinched thumb and first finger to his lips as if he were drinking an espresso. She winked back, rose from the table and disappeared in the kitchen.

"Well, first. Gregor would say no. Although you or Claudia could talk to him. The other thing is that the madam and our Vittore Vormittag are both convinced that Lomi murdered the pimp. What was his name?"

"Shoji."

Her eyes locked onto him as she sipped her wine. "Yeah. And maybe she did. Either way, at this point, Shoji's wife—I think she's a whacko and a drunk—might let the traffickers think Lomi bolted even if I paid her."

"Why?"

"Pure meanness. Vormittag will give Lomi the benefit of a trial. The madam's convicted her. She's thinking screw her *and* her family."

"You think she'll keep the money and lie to the traffickers."

"I don't know, but yeah, I could see that."

Federica swung her legs around to meet his own, leaned toward him and put her hands on his knees. Her scarf came untied. The ends fell in pile over her hands. He felt the warmth from her hands and scarf, and from her knees as she pressed them against his own.

"Let's talk to her again," she said.

"Her listening skills aren't the best."

"She might listen to me. I've treated some of the women. Nobody gets turned down at the Spital, even if they don't have ID or insurance. We're not Polizei."

"I'd rather talk to Lomi. But I have no idea where she is or how to reach her. Destiny said Lomi ditched her phone. Lomi told her that if she called again, it would be from a different number."

"The Miroir? We should check there again."

Sarah placed an espresso on the table in front of him and asked, "Max, are you going to eat that?" She was looking at the tiramisu.

"Grazie . . . è il tuo," he said.

"Thanks, Pops!" She leaned over and kissed his forehead, scooped up the plate and spoon, and ferried the dessert to a bench shared by

Jenny and Destiny. Sarah squeezed between them. They took turns eating bites. Jenny pointed out stars and constellations that, in the mounting moonlight, were vanishing as fast as the tiramisu. Destiny, he observed, acted younger when she was around Sarah and Jenny.

Brasilera

"The Beast needs a wash." Stonecrop was happy with any excuse to drive the Taycan. He followed the rules of the road as he drove. One would never attempt spirited driving within Zürich proper. Photo-radar crisscrossed every street and intersection.

The thought reminded him of Lomi's departure from the Miroir and of his reluctance to share that information with Vormittag. The Kommissar's office could request traffic photo logs of the Golf and its driver. If he were unsuccessful in his own inquiries, he would make the ask, even if doing so presented problems for Vormittag.

"You know," Stonecrop was thinking aloud, "if I were Kommissar Vormittag, I wouldn't be so keen about finding Lomi."

"He has to try, that is if he believes she may have murdered Shoji."

"Shoji was a scumbag," Stonecrop said.

"Swiss Polizei are not mafia and losing a scumbag is not a rounding error to justice."

"He's in a tough spot, though," Stonecrop continued. "If he brings in Lomi, the incident with Lorenzo, a personal problem that because of his position with Polizei he was able to make go away, suddenly becomes public, disgracing him and the Stadtpolizei. Vormittag put up cash to buy a prostitute, who also happens to be an illegal immigrant, a trafficked woman—and all on behalf of his deadbeat nephew who was involved in a bogus cheese scam. The Stadtpolizei will question Lorenzo. Poor guy will freak out."

"*Stadtpolizei Kommissar in Spektakularen Käsenraub!* I can see the headline in *Zwanzig Minuten*. I'd hate for Vittore get in trouble. He's been a revered figure with the Stadtpolizei and with my family for much of my life."

"Maybe there's an alternative."

"Meaning?" Federica asked.

"Your buddy, Alicia. Her associates here have nothing to do with Vormittag. Could she request the data from the Verkehrsamt?"

"I can ask." Federica agreed but didn't sound confident. "They'll probably want to know why."

"True. And any exposé would drag in Gregor and me, and maybe compromise the arrangement with Chum. A can of worms, so maybe not such a great idea."

"Do you think the madam will be there?" Federica asked as they approached the turnoff.

"No clue. Make sense though, for her to at least have a room for late nights when she doesn't want to make the schlep home."

Once again, they turned at the golden arrows past the billboard advertising the Kar-Moppa Kar Wash, drove by fences and walls topped with razor wire, and at the end of the road passed under the snake-eyed gaze of cams nestled in the vine-covered entryway.

"Not much business today," Stonecrop observed.

There were no cars in the queue. The attendant perked up when saw the Porsche. Federica and Stonecrop both lowered their windows but remained in the car.

"Same guy who took care of us last time," Stonecrop said.

Federica, with her flawless memory, confirmed, "It is. The North African man with the chipped tooth." Federica reached into a drawer in her brainbox and pulled out the language that felt right.

"Salam."

The attendant brightened. A string of consonants ensued between the two of them, sounding somewhat like what Hamdi and his sons spoke.

"Moroccan?" Stonecrop asked.

"Well done, Max! Street Moroccan, Darija. Like Arabic spiced with Berber. Classical Arabic, I know. Berber, very little. Darija has a lot of French and Spanish words, which helps." She looked back and forth between Max and the attendant and introduced them to each other.

Abdella bowed briefly and, in decent English, asked, "Did your Papà like the clean car? The black Audi?"

"He did, thank you, Abdella. I'm surprised you remember."

"I am a good rememberer!"

"Do you remember Lomi and Destiny?"

He blinked. "Lomi, yes. Destiny, I was told to not remember. She is not a worker. No customer go with her."

"That what she says, too. You know she's living with me."

Abdella's eyes, a second time, lit up, brown and bright, forming tears. "She is safe? We have all been worried."

"Safe. And free."

"No more money?"

"No more money," Federica confirmed.

Abdella put one hand on the car over the passenger window and the other on the sill by Federica. "Praise to Allah," he said, with a broad smile that advertised the toothy gap. "That is good. But they say Lomi ran away. Very bad, for her and her family."

"Lomi is gone. We're trying to find her, to help her. Does she have friends here?"

"Yes." Abdella's eyes narrowed. Questions about Lomi's whereabouts made him suspicious.

Federica placed her hand on Abdella's and turned toward Stonecrop. "Lomi's text, Max. Her friend said: 'estoy aqui.' "

"I just caught part of it."

"Spanish, anyway."

She faced Abdella. "Does Madam have any Spanish speaking women?"

"Several. But home tongue, two maybe."

"Max," Federica said, "you just saw the text. Lomi didn't *say* it, right?"

"Right."

"Spell what you saw."

"Something *e-u*, and *a-q-u-i*."

"That's Portuguese, not Spanish!"

Federica squeezed Abdella's hand. Her physician's touch never threatened. "Portuguese? Any Portuguese?"

"Beatriz. Not from Portugal, she is Brasilera. But she is not here. Two weeks now, she too, paid the money. She was not here a longtime."

"Is she a dancer?" Stonecrop asked.

Abdella looked at Stonecrop as if he were crazy. "She is Brasilera! Of course, she is a dancer."

"Does she dance at the Miroir?"

They looked for confirmation but got shrugged shoulders.

Another car had joined the line for service. Abdella looked back and forth between Federica and new customer. He waved to them, holding up a finger to indicate that he would be there momentarily.

Stonecrop exited the car. "Bitte, touchless spray, water only."

"Shokran bezzaf," Federica thanked Abdella as she and Stonecrop made their way to the madam's office.

She must have seen them arrive and, just as in their last visit, she held the office door open for them, invited them to sit down, and then retreated to the vintage Aero chair behind the desk. She flopped down and lit a cigarette. He had not noticed last visit, either the chair was lopsided, or that was her habit, to sit in a crooked manner. Her right leg was extended like she was driving a car.

"Just can't stay away, can you?" The madam squinted. Could be bad vision, or simply smoke. The effort tightened parched skin, the crow's feet extended and deepened. She picked something off her lip and flicked it away.

"Needed a wash," Stonecrop said.

"Fancy wheels. Not yours. Belong to this hot thing?" She looked at Federica and then addressed her. "He's taking you for a ride, honey. Don't waste your money."

Federica laughed, "You got that right." She punched Stonecrop in the shoulder.

The madam didn't wait for the question. "I still don't know where the hell Lomi is. Wish I did. I'd strangle the bitch with one of her precious white scarves."

"Did you get to see Shoji?" Federica remembered that the Polizei had not let her see him until the autopsy had been completed.

"Yeah, she beat him bad. Wasn't pretty."

"Did you tell them who it was?"

"My husband, sure."

"No, that you think Lomi was responsible."

"What do *you* think? I showed them the video, dodo." She inhaled deeply, holding the smoke, then exhaled through her nostrils.

Stonecrop found he was taking shallow breaths to minimize the impact of the secondary smoke. "I thought you were going to wait and deal with Lomi yourself?"

"Well, big-boy, I didn't, did I?"

"You couldn't find her," he stated, and hoped for a reaction or some additional information as to Lomi's whereabouts.

"Like I'd fucking tell you shit. Why do you care so much?"

"What happens to Lomi's family?"

"They get burned. Literally. Maybe skinned alive. Like I know? Or care? That's the arrangement. I get burned. They get burned. Sounds fair to me."

"If we pay the sixty for her, can you call off the dogs?"

"Sure, honey. If you're dumb enough to drop sixty thou Swiss on a lost cause."

Stonecrop had her interest. Federica meanwhile placed a small bag on the desk with the cash for Lomi's bonding. Given that Lomi by now must have worked off some of what she owed, the money would be a windfall for the madam.

Federica kept her fingers on the bag as she slid it across the desk. When the madam's fingers reached out and touched the bag, Federica spoke.

"The Brazilian woman who worked here. Where is she?"

"You writing for some shit magazine?"

"Her name is Beatriz."

"Mulatta. We called the Brazilian 'Mulatta.' " The madam turned to Stonecrop. "Honey, you like those mulatta girls? Used to have a pair of them. Premium package, booked 'em as sisters."

Federica brought her back, getting her attention by tapping the bag with her fingers. "Beatriz?"

"You talked to my little Abdella? Do that again and I'll fire his ass." She snuffed out the remains of the cigarette, then buried the butt among others in the ashtray.

She lit another, took another deep drag and blew smoke, intentionally or not, in Stonecrop's face. He coughed and stood up. The act was a threat. Her hand came off the bag as she leaned sideways on her chair.

"Take it easy. The Mulatta left a couple weeks ago. She made good money here, and on the side. Paid what she owed way ahead. No forwarding address. It's not like the woman wants these fucking jackasses coming after her."

"The extra money," Federica asked. "She danced at Miroir, right?"

"Don't you know all the answers."

"Last name, phone, address? How do we find her?"

"You got all I got. Ain't nothin' more."

"There is *somethin'* more. Passports." Federica looked at Stonecrop and spoke as if the madam were not present. "She's holding their passports."

A squinty acquiescence by the madam was followed by a groan, precipitated, Stonecrop presumed, by either the mention of or the effort required to find and hand over passports for Lomi and Destiny. The madam put both hands on the edge of her desk and pushed her chair back. She rummaged around in the top drawer of the desk for a set of keys, found them, and then bent forward to unlock a separate file drawer. There appeared to be no order to the binders in the drawer except that the rubber bands around the binders were in different colors. After examining the contents of several folders with red rubber bands, she found the one she had been looking for.   She groaned deeply as she extracted the passports for Lomi and Destiny, thus confirming the effort the task had required. She placed them onto the desk one at a time, like a dealer at a blackjack table.

Federica took a minute and flipped through the pages of each one. She rose and nodded to Stonecrop. "They look good. They entered the E.U. together."

"To be clear: anything that happens to Lomi's family, happens to you." Stonecrop threw a phrase back at her: "Sounds fair to me!"

The madam was trying hard to not look intimidated. She drew upon what bravado remained after their first meeting at Bürklimäärt. "I'm as Swiss as raclette, honey."

"Well, honey, I'm not and I hate raclette."

The words were as cold as he could muster. He leaned toward the desk. Federica took his arm to lead him away, but Stonecrop didn't move.

"Call off the dogs or no money. And no yapping about our little visit?"

"Fuck off," she looked at him.

Stonecrop stepped forward and with one arm sent everything on the top of the desk flying across the room.

"Got it! For Christ's sake, leave me the fuck alone."

Fede pulled him by the other arm and headed for the door. Stonecrop went along, but backed away, eyes menacing and locked on the madam.

"Shit!" the madam swore.

She rolled her chair back and bent forward. The effort forced stale air from her lungs, or from what remained of them. The cigarette butt had singed her fingers and she had dropped it somewhere on the floor under the desk.

Federica tossed the bag of cash on the table.

There were no good-byes as they left the office. Outside, Abdella twirled a red mechanics rag in the air. He stood beside the green Porsche Taycan. Beads of water covered the car.

Lomi

"She wants to speak with you," Destiny's voice, as fresh as a morning lark, sang words as sweet as Juliet's soliloquy. To the groggy Stonecrop, they announced *Night is over, and day is come.* He crawled out of a thick dream and found himself a set piece in the kitchen. Destiny opened his fingers and placed her phone in his hand. Federica, as groggy as Stonecrop, stood transfixed before the spasms of the six-cup Bialetti macchina. Her hand gripped a blood-red pitcher of orange juice. On the table, brioche fell over each other in a wicker basket missing the napkin to capture the crumbs. Beside the basket a ceramic cup overflowed with marmalade packets.

God, I'm tired.

"Lomi, where are you?" Stonecrop fumbled with the phone as he scrounged for a cup.

"Destiny loves your daughters, yes. Sarah and Jenny are their names," the husky voice said. "They are lovely names."

Stonecrop pretended to rally. "And we adore Destiny, although I don't know how much longer we can protect her. From the authorities. They know she's here they but haven't done anything about it."

"Yes, well. It is for the best . . . for her to be close to you. She is in danger." Lomi's voice was even more stressed than the last time they spoke.

"Her bonding is paid. Why is she in danger?"

"From the man who tried to kill me. Pimps don't kill their women or boys. Not the first time they leave their madam. That's not how this system works, you see. This business has rules."

"I get that. Look, Lomi, I'm putting you on speaker so Fede and Destiny can hear."

There was silence on the other end, but the connection wasn't broken. She was listening.

Federica set down the Bialetti. "Lomi, hi. My name is Federica. I'm an emergency medicine doctor at the Spital. I've treated a few women from Kar-Moppa. Can we take a minute to talk about your injuries?"

Stonecrop took over coffee duty, poured a double espresso for himself and another for Federica. Destiny declined and put water on for tea. Jenny, half-asleep, shuffled out of the bedroom and joined Destiny at the teapot.

Federica moved to her bedroom so she could speak privately with Lomi. Over the next twenty minutes, she conducted a virtual medical exam, including reviewing photos of some of Lomi's injuries. At the end of the exam, Federica returned to the kitchen and passed the phone back to Stonecrop.

"She'll be okay." Federica nursed an empty cup. "I told her we paid the madam and have their passports. She thanked me, then covered the phone. I heard her sobbing. When she came back on, she said that the assault wasn't a warning. Someone had tried to really kill her." Federica put her arm around Destiny and held her. "I'm sorry, Destiny."

Before speaking to Lomi, Stonecrop questioned Federica and Destiny.

"Does Lomi know who it was?"

Federica looked down and shook her head no.

He turned his attention to the phone and Lomi. "Why were you at Halbinsel Au?"

"I was supposed to meet Herr Shoji. He and his wife live nearby, in Wädenswil. I asked a friend to be there because I knew Shoji would be angry when I told him I wasn't coming back to Kar-Moppa. I told Shoji we would pay the bonding soon, in sixty days, maybe ninety at most. My friend would have the money and would pay him what was owed, even more if he would wait."

"Is this the same person who paid the other half of Destiny's bonding?"

"Yes."

"Why would he be willing to help you again, to trust you?"

"He loves me. And he has a lot of money. Or he will have. His money is tied up in something now, but he is going to get a lot of money, soon. He promised me."

"Does boyfriend have a name?"

"He said he would get in trouble if I told anyone his name. That is a promise I made to him. I will not say his name."

"You're in trouble."

"He is not. And I . . ."

Destiny stood near Stonecrop and overheard the conversation, even though the phone was no longer on speaker.

"She loves him," Destiny interrupted. "I've never seen him. But I know they love each other." The soprano quivered, "Lomi told me he's suffered, even more than she has."

"Not Lorenzo?" Stonecrop asked, reminding himself that love is fickle.

"No, not Lorenzo," Destiny confirmed.

"I presume your friend didn't show at Halbinsel Au?" Stonecrop continued with Lomi. She seemed willing to talk after the conversation with Federica.

"Yes. That is, yes, he did not meet me, if that is what you mean. At the last minute, he had to work. Something important, he said. Something important for us." Lomi spoke the words like anyone who would have deferred to a spouse's work summons.

"Who else knew about the meeting?"

"No one else," she replied.

"The Polizei found your scarf around Shoji's neck."

"I saw on the news. We had a . . . a very physical argument. But I didn't kill him."

"Can you tell me what happened? Or describe the man who assaulted you?"

"A white man, like a homeless man. Heavy, a little, not fat. I smelled oil or petrol on his clothes. His beard—he had a beard—was short and gray, and a baseball cap and dark glasses. The man was sleeping on the bench. I didn't see him at first, you know. It was dark. The bench was in a shadow.

"I was fighting with Shoji. Then the homeless man—I thought he was going to help me—I heard him come up behind me. He grabbed me from behind with one hand and used something to hit Shoji on the head, very hard, and Shoji fell. I never really saw the man's face, only a little. He wore gloves. They were dirty, too, dirty with grease on them. I smelled them when he tried to choke me. He grabbed my scarf. I could not believe that I would die like this, here, in Switzerland."

"How did you get away from him?" Stonecrop asked.

"I stepped as hard as I could on the top of his foot—I saw that on TV once—and then I scratched his face with my nails. My nails are strong.

I knew I had hurt him because he backed away. But then he used this piece of metal to hit me, what you use for a tire."

Her words were a contralto to Destiny's soprano. He imagined the sisters in church, singing together. Stonecrop wished she had spoken to the Polizei right after the incident. They could have collected a DNA sample from her fingernails. Too late now. Metal even left outside in the elements could retain fingerprints for a couple of years. The assailant would have to have been careless about handling the tire iron before or after wearing gloves, and he would have to have been careless about discarding potential evidence. An unlikely confluence. The man who assaulted her was no down-on-his-luck homeless guy.

"Did he have a gun?"

"I don't think so. There were people up the hill by a streetlight, not very far away, who could hear. They weren't *that* close or watching us, but if they heard a gunshot, they would look and call for help."

"You didn't yell for help?"

"I didn't. Everything happened just like that." Stonecrop heard her snap her fingers.

"I didn't turn to look at him. I ran as fast as I could toward the people and the light." She continued, "It was uphill, and I am a very fast runner. He didn't chase me. I didn't look back, but I know I hurt his foot."

"Did you talk to any of the people? Did they see you running from the man?"

"One did. But he didn't say anything. He was with the people but left them and started walking down toward the dock. I don't know why but I was afraid of him."

"Could you see him, his face?"

"No. It was too dark and too far. He wore one of those American baseball hats and big coat. He was big and he took big clumsy steps. My eye, one of my eyes was hurt bad."

"How did you get away from them?"

"I ran by the parking lot—it's before where the people were. I saw Shoji's car and I knew he leaves the keys under the floormat. I took his car."

"Where's the car now?"

"On Limmatquai. Not far from the Miroir."

The vehicle, if parked anywhere on the Limmatquai, would have been towed.

"Are you with Beatriz?"

"No, she is home, in Brazil. Her mother is sick."

"Did she drive you from the Miroir after we spoke?"

"No. My friend did. He will find the man who attacked me."

During their conversation, Federica had tossed on a pair of Levi's and a Tee. She bussed Stonecrop on the cheek and hugged Destiny and Jenny.

"Work meetings," she said, and grabbed a brioche and her white Muji thermos of green tea with honey. The thermos was a constant companion at work. "Should wrap up early, three at the latest. I'll text."

She paused half-way out the door and turned, seeing the same thing as Stonecrop: a half-asleep Sandro exit the door to the extra bedroom. The black mane covered his face. He wore his signature shirt, the black-meshed T. His hair was trapped under the neck opening. The long-fingered hands with their dramatic black nails reached up and freed the hair in a single flick; one back and forth swoosh of the head set the hair in place for the day. Sarah followed behind him, one finger hanging onto the back pocket of Sandro's baggy black pants.

Stonecrop, having never dealt with this sort of thing before, looked to Federica for help. She tried and failed to hold back the smile. Eyes half open, she turned toward Sandro. "Good morning, Sandro. Can you make your own coffee . . ."

The next bit of their exchange was hidden within rapid-fire Romansh. Neither Sandro nor Federica offered to translate. Fede winked and was out the door. Her parting glance at Stonecrop said, *Good luck, you asked for this!*

"Sandro!" Stonecrop said, much louder than intended. Everyone jumped, Sandro the most.

He responded in a controlled voice, referring to Federica, "She is . . . very direct—"

"It's the Bernina Massif," Stonecrop proclaimed, "the ridgeline of the Bernina Massif!"

The visibly relieved Sandro raised his shirt to display the tattooed line across his young, lightly muscled, and hairless chest. "I got it after I completed the Tour Bernina."

Jenny and Sarah stared, confused.

"You did the entire Bernina Tour! How was it?" Stonecrop reached for the Bialetti.

"The Biancograt on Piz Bernina." A relieved Sandro let the shirt fall and raised both arms as if he were about hallelujah the heavens. "The most beautiful place I have been, ever, ever in my whole life."

The drama subsided and Stonecrop realized that he was still on the line with Lomi.

"I'm sorry, Lomi. Are you still there?"

"This is Max who is speaking, yes?" she said.

"It is," he answered. "Can I call you on this number?"

"Yes, for now. I would like to speak to my sister, please."

Destiny overheard and took the handy from Stonecrop. Like Fede, she took the phone to the bedroom for privacy. Stonecrop was curious about how the kids had managed the sleeping arrangements, and about how and when Sandro had arrived.

Sarah flopped down in a chair at the table. The half-shut eyes rolled open and looked up at her father. "Somethin' against sex, Max?"

Jenny snapped at her, "Don't be snarky, Sarah. You know—"

Sarah reached up and not-so-gently put her hand over Jenny's mouth.

Stonecrop said the first thing that came to mind: "Pancakes?!"

All hands in the room went up except Sarah's. One hand remained on Jenny's mouth; the other was under the table. Sandro raised his toward the ceiling. Destiny's head poked out from behind the door to the bedroom where she had been speaking with Lomi. She waved her hand, the one holding the phone, like a shipboard passenger arriving at home port and trying to get the attention of relatives standing at the dock and waiting for her.

"Lomi?" Stonecrop asked, thinking she was flagging him over because Lomi wanted to speak to him again.

"No," the playful voice sang to the room. "I want pancakes!"

Blueberry Pancakes

"We're hitting the good stuff."

He ferreted through the cupboard at Federica's where he had stashed a bottle of Maine Gold maple syrup.

"World's best maple syrup!"

I've been spending too much time with Gregor.

He tried to unwind the hyperbole: "Well, I mean I like this syrup."

A suddenly cheerful Sarah squeezed Sandro's hand. "It comes from where we sail in Penobscot Bay. The islands are so beautiful. Sandro, you have to come visit."

Sarah and Jenny took on the task of mentoring their respective sous-chefs—Sandro and Destiny—in the all-American, very messy tradition of making blueberry pancakes. Frying pans sizzled and butter and batter splattered everywhere. Globules of pancake mix hung like tree ornaments in Jenny's hair. Casualties were few. Only Sarah got a minor burn. Interesting, at least to Stonecrop, was the care and attention both Sandro and Destiny gave to the task. They were used to doing things with their hands, things that required close attention. The coordination of his own children, by comparison, seemed clumsy, and with Jenny, positively whimsical. He adored them of course, but the observation brought him back to Vormittag's comment about Jenny and handguns and made him question his blind trust in his children. Was he, Stonecrop, in this respect, any different than Gregor, whose faith in Federica was unassailable? Trust was a two-edged sword. Trust entails risk and vulnerability.

"Earth. To. Max. No more batter," Sarah intoned.

The blueberries and the syrup had been a gift from Mattie, who, even after their divorce, surprised Stonecrop with random presents. Two five-pound boxes of frozen, organic blueberries had been shipped by DHL from Whiting, Maine, a small community near the Canadian border, to Zürich. With only a minifridge at Münstergasse, he had had to store the lot in Frau Ott's basement freezer.

"Pops," Jenny sounded, "help!"

In the oven, flapjacks had flopped over the edges of the platter. Stonecrop grabbed two dishtowels and moved the platter to the kitchen island. He rescued pancakes that had gone overboard. On the stovetop, the dark, golden syrup was the same color as the copper pot in which it had been warmed.

"That's plenty!" Stonecrop turned off the oven and burners.

At the sink, Jenny made a half-hearted effort to remove the blueberry stains from her fingers.

With food, spirits brightened, Stonecrop's included, especially after Fede had texted him from the hospital:

<<FR: nothing bad happened btw the kiddos>>

She provided no further details about her thirty-second conversation in Romansh with Sandro.

At the end of the meal, Stonecrop made himself an americano, moved to the bench in Frau Ott's backyard, and watched the city below awaken. The too-clear air distorted distance. One could touch the tips of peaks in the Berner Oberland a hundred-fifty kilometers to the southwest. Between the call with Lomi, the shocker that his daughter had in some manner spent the night with Sandro, and the gung-ho cooking session, Stonecrop was bushed. *A mid-morning nap? Why not.*

He downed the dregs of his coffee in a last-ditch effort to revive. The caffeine did nothing, so he made his way to the hammock beside the Buddha and under the plane tree. The Buddha's lichenous, reassuring hands took his cup. Stonecrop approached the hammock with care not to shock-load the weathered braiding. He gently lowered into the cocoon-like embrace. Eyes closed on their own. Non-sensical chatter from inside the house lulled him into a delicious, half-sleep.

The blissful respite, his and that of the nearby Buddha, was interrupted by an incoming text message that had cardioverted his handy. Stonecrop peeled open heavy eyelids and noted the quiet. The swarm of noise from the kitchen had moved on. For no reason at all, that made him smile. He rolled his head to the side and bathed in the gentle traction on his neck muscles. A few minutes passed, and a second text pinged. This time he fished out the phone.

<<IA: Meet now? Zurich.>>

Shit.

The message from Ibrahim Adewole could not have been more unwelcome. Stonecrop had hoped, in retrospect naively, that he was done with Chum's grand plan. He'd survived his gig at the Tavate gathering, and he had been assured by Claudia that nothing more would be required on his part. It was the Clerk's turn to run point for Gregor.

<<MS: Where?>>

<<IA: Someplace private, near you.>>

<<MS: ASVZ track bench by turnstile where you enter. Across Klosterweg from Zürich Zoo. Give me 15>>

<<IA: in 30>>

Stonecrop tapped a thumbs up. He felt refreshed though he had no idea how long he had slept. When he checked his phone, the refreshed feeling made sense; out for over two hours. He would quickly dispatch whatever Adewole wanted. He was done with Chum. And tonight, after Fede returned, he would have a heart-to-heart with Lomi and Destiny and try to convince them to accept protective custody from Kommissar Vormittag and Zürich Kantonspolizei. *That* would take some convincing. Lomi distrusted the authorities and still feared arrest and prison for the murder of Shoji Jado.

Amazing what a little rest could do.

Turnstile

Stonecrop had an electronic pass to use the University's track facilities and was doing warm-up laps when the silver BMW sedan driven by Adewole pulled into a parking slot near the turnstile and entry gate to the athletic field. Adewole was alone. Adewole exited the vehicle and stood next to the open door, blocking the sun with his hand as he scanned the grounds and picked up Stonecrop jogging toward the car. He waved him over, then retook his seat behind the wheel, closed his own door, and opened the passenger door. The BMW was a rental.

"Mr. Adewole. I'm surprised to see you. I thought you had gone back to Lagos."

"No rest for the wicked," he said as he extended a hand to Stonecrop.

Wicked he was, Stonecrop reflected, but his handshake was about as wicked as a limp noodle.

"Allow me to get to the point."

"Yeah, sure." The dead tone implied that whenever someone said that, they probably would do the opposite.

"I have known Hennie, who you know as Henrique Couto, for some time. We are, one would say, close, although not friends; I don't think he truly has *any* friends."

It was going to take him forever to get it out. Stonecrop settled in for the long-haul, trying to relax his legs and stretch them in the cramped passenger's seat. He fumbled around to slide the seat back and recline the backrest. "Yeah," he said more addressing the seat controls than Adewole.

"You have quite the reputation. Though not once have I heard from your lips, one word, about your work in Africa."

The comment was concerning. Had Adewole seen through the

bogus background Chum had fabricated, or Gregor's impossible to pin down bullshit? A dark thought surfaced: *Never be far from the Glock when you're with these assholes.*

"Humor me, please. Tell me about when Gregor ordered you to eliminate the Couto brothers—"

"I not going to tell you anything, Mr. Adewole," Stonecrop shut him down. "That's Gregor's business, not yours."

Undeterred, Adewole continued. "This man, Couto, works for me now. Why did Gregor want to get rid of him? So much so, that he sent you to do the job. You are, I gather, not so experienced in logistics, but you are certainly a specialist at other things . . ."

Was this supposed to be the point? Stonecrop asked himself. *My curriculum vitae as an agent of death.* He rearranged himself, finding the contoured features of the bucket seat about as comfortable as the grilling from Adewole.

"Couto is a good man. The best. You can trust him." Stonecrop groaned as he again repositioned himself. He hoped that his response would be enough to end the conversation.

"Why? Tell me, why did you have to kill them?"

"Mr. Adewole," Stonecrop put his hand on the door handle, "I'm telling you and you're not listening. *Why* is not my business. I'm the help. Pretty low guy on the totem pole. Do you understand that?"

Unexpectantly, the clarification made Adewole smile and show off a blinding white set of teeth.

"I'm pleased to hear that." He brushed Stonecrop's shoulder with the tips of his fingers. The touch was tentative, as if he were dealing with an animal who could turn on him in a flash.

"I'm told that you walked in the front door of their home at the compound in Maputo. The brothers were sitting there and minding their own business. Just like that. Poof! You shot them. Point blank— two bullets apiece. And then you torched the place!"

"Something like that," Stonecrop said, at a loss over how to derail the conversation. He felt like vomiting. *Well, vomiting might do the trick.*

"And the guard, two in the chest and one in the head. Hennie told me that's called the Mozambique Drill. Quite impressive, that sort of panache." He paused here, put his fingers into a steeple, and stared at his squirmy passenger. "You have to excuse the observation, but you just don't seem like that kind of man."

"You're right there, I'm not. The whole thing went down before I knew what had happened."

"I see." Adewole took some time before he continued. "The yardman tried to stop you. And what did you do? You drove right over him! You and that old maid. My god, what an escapade!" He laughed a deep from the bowels of hell laugh. "Is that what happened? I looked for her by the way. The old maid. But she vanished. Or did you make her vanish? A ditch on the side of the road? Did you *enjoy* making a woman vanish?" Adewole seemed convinced by his own narrative.

Never very good at concealing his feelings or lying, Stonecrop figured his best course of action would be to get the hell out of the car as soon as possible. Adewole's comments disgusted him. But something kept him riveted to the contoured seat and riveted upon the words from the mouth of this venal man. Adewole's eyes sparkled. He was aroused and sufficiently emboldened to let his hand wrap over Stonecrop's shoulder.

"I, too . . ." Adewole saying the words, closed the distance between them and confirmed that the teeth had been stained white. His breath reeked of dead fish and decay behind the white porcelain patina.

Stonecrop had no intention of revealing what had transpired. Chloë had been a sex slave and when she no longer served that purpose had taken work as a household servant for the brothers. Right after Stonecrop had escaped from his cell and minutes before the conflagration at the house, she had told him about a handgun in the glovebox in the guard's truck, thus providing the weapon he had used on the brothers and the guard. He owed her his life but had no idea if she was dead or alive. The woman—crazy Chloë, as Stonecrop thought of her—had been viciously attacked by the goon that had been guarding Stonecrop's cell. The guard had cracked her skull open with a baseball bat as she was splashing petrol around the room. That had been after Stonecrop had shot the brothers. After the brutal assault on the maid, the guard had come at him. In an insane fugue over what had been done to Chloë, Stonecrop had methodically executed the guard. With bare hands he had repacked the woman's dislodged brain matter into her skull in an utterly desperate attempt to keep her alive. Using an old EMT trick, he tied her bloodied hair in a knot to stabilize fragments of her skull. She was waif thin. He had carried her to the guard's truck and strapped her into the passenger's seat. As they drove out of compound, a man had tried to stop them and shooting wildly at the vehicle had put a round into Stonecrop's side. Cause enough to run over the bastard, Stonecrop had thought. Once out of the gates and in the city proper he had dropped off Chloë at a clinic where, he suspected, she had died.

"You are a brilliant marksman, or so I'm told." Adewole, still dancing around his point, changed the topic.

Stonecrop was so lost in his memories that he forgot where he was or what they had been talking about.

"The shots in Alvis were an inch apart, in the heart. Same with the guard." Adewole removed his other hand from the steering wheel and put two over his heart, finding the place where the rounds would have struck Stonecrop's victims.

Some perverse corner of Stonecrop's mind memorized the points on Adewole's chest for future reference.

"Tell me one thing," Adewole continued. "Only this, and I will stop pestering you with questions. The rounds were like this with Hennie." This time he used a thumb and index finger, finding two hypothetical points of penetration, an inch apart, but lower, under the heart. "That's why Hennie survived. Why did you miss?"

Stonecrop opted for the truth. Hennie had obviously been interrogated by Adewole. The stories had to jibe. "He was sitting at the table, holding up a map that hid his torso. I only saw the top of his head and his hands on the map."

"You shot him through the map?"

"Yes."

"Brilliant. But he was alive. Why not finish him off!"

"Got distracted . . . I'm getting distracted a lot, I mean really a lot. Like right fucking now. Anyway, he was on fire."

Adewole ignored the threat. "And you knowingly left him to burn to death. So cruel, Mr. Stonecrop, so very cruel."

"Yes." Stonecrop let the clock run as if he were thinking about Adewole's question. "I suppose." He aimed the words to the hand he wanted to wrench off his shoulder.

Adewole read his thoughts and put his hands in his lap and intertwined the fingers. Stonecrop followed the hands—the man was likely righthanded—and slightly twisted right and then left to see if anyone were nearby. Some panicking animal within him was preparing to kill Adewole.

"The only people alive who know you shot through the map are you and Henrique Couto. Hennie told me he'd been surprised, to be shot like that, totally surprised. The bullets pierced Congo on the map. Funny he remembered that. Said that at first, he felt nothing. Wasn't there a dog?"

"Killed the fucking dog. I like dogs. Just not that one. Are we done?" Stonecrop put on a pissy attitude. " 'cause I'm done. I got shit to do."

The white porcelain flashed again. *He had a face that would frighten children,* Stonecrop thought, *maybe more than Couto.* The bulging white of the eyes and the teeth. The lips peeled back like some shape-shifting organism and revealed an arcade of inflamed gums.

"You work for Gregor for money, yes?"

That question didn't deserve an answer. Stonecrop's gaze drifted to the door handle.

"I want to hire you, Mr. Stonecrop. A freelance job for a man of your unique skills. The job . . ." He took a breath, searched for the right word, failed, and restarted. "This is between us. No one else." Adewole waited. Not getting a response, he delivered the answer to the question he had expected his interviewee to ask. "I'll tell you who in a second."

Let him talk, Stonecrop told himself. *Hear him out and report to Claudia.* Stonecrop had had enough of Adewole, enough of Chum and his games. He would tell Claudia that going forward he wanted the Clerk, anybody else, to be the go-between.

Stonecrop put his hands together, intertwining the fingers, and placed them on his lap, mocking and mimicking Adewole.

"I'm the one with the money, let's not forget that."

"I thought you were in fucking hurry. So, big shot, be in a fucking hurry." Stonecrop raised his hands as though he were about to do something with them.

"Yes, I expected this reaction. My point is this: I want to get rid of a woman. I want her to vanish like the one in Maputo. No trace."

Adewole must have mistakenly assumed that Stonecrop had departed with a healthy Chloë and subsequently murdered and disposed of her body. That meant Couto must have not seen the guard attack her. His clothes had caught fire and he had been crawling away from Stonecrop.

Adewole's calculated desire to end a person's life sickened Stonecrop. He thought of Chloë and felt anger at the world, a world that had stacked the deck against any chance for her, for so many women like her, to have a normal life. He made a mental note to contact the clinic where he had left her. That is, if he could remember enough to find it.

"*This* woman is a whore." Adewole's fingers tightened and pressed against his crotch. Was he aroused? *What a sick fuck.* "Like the woman in Mozambique. An African whore. She is a risk to Clave, a loose mouth, maybe even an informer. She has threatened to go to the authorities."

"What's her connection to Clave?"

"I used her services."

Stonecrop did not have to pretend to be surprised. "For?" he asked.

"To gather intelligence about our competitors."

"Do you mean Ode or Prince? Jama? Someone else?"

"Let's leave it at that," Adewole answered.

"Easy, pay her. Problem solved," Stonecrop replied, the solution being the most obvious if he were in Adewole's position.

"I tried, very hard—I am a generous man—but without success."

"Try again. I'm not your fucking hit man, Jesus Christ. Use Hennie." He brushed back hair that had fallen to the side of his face, aware suddenly that he was sweating. The suggestion he had just made was a mistake, a big mistake. Whoever she was, Stonecrop wouldn't harm her.

"You know—" Stonecrop started to backpedal.

Adewole interrupted, "I considered Hennie. But he is . . . preoccupied. I still might, though, if I knew where she was."

Adewole was lying. The conversation felt surreal.

Without thinking, Stonecrop decided to take the job. It was the only way to protect the woman. "Not sure I can help."

He made to get out of the vehicle. Adewole gently stopped him.

"I think you can." The words oozed out.

"Name?"

"Lomi. Like me, she is a Nigerian."

Adewole was so eager he looked comic rather than threatening. He peered into Stonecrop's eyes. Would those eyes detect a reaction that would make Stonecrop out for the treasonous imposter he was?

So emotive was Adewole's look that Stonecrop flashed back to college days and visualized himself in improv class. Few paths made sense if Lomi was to live. He could end Adewole's life—here and now —or play along. He opted to utter the line the last act of the play required: "How much?"

"Twenty-five thousand, U.S."

Stonecrop put up both thumbs.

"You accept, then. Splendid—"

"Think again," Stonecrop threw back his head, swishing the mop to the side, just like he did in college days in the quad when his professor had given the class a skit to perform.

"You don't *surprise* me, Mr. Stonecrop."

Adewole patted Stonecrop on the knee. Stonecrop took no offense this time, the touchy-feely was part of the schtick. *I need to get through the final act,* he told himself, *and get the fuck out of here. Chum is right. It's all theater.*

"Thirty-five, Mr. Stonecrop," the offer made as Adewole turned away from him. "I do have less expensive alternatives."

Not as good as me. Stonecrop had Destiny and through Destiny he had access to Lomi. He knew it and Adewole knew it or he wouldn't be here. Had Adewole spoken with the madam? Refusing to accept the hit would put Destiny in danger as well as Lomi.

Had Stonecrop's threat been enough to keep the madam from talking to the traffickers but maybe not Adewole? She received the bonding payment. But might she not simply want retribution for her husband's murder?

Adewole had finished. Stonecrop shrugged, bored of the affair, and exited the vehicle. Before shutting the door, he planted both hands on the roof and leaned in, lowering his head between his arms, as if stretching.

"My way. My schedule." Stonecrop rolled his shoulders and took a second stretch that elongated his oversized climber lats and shoulders.

To see Stonecrop, Adewole lowered his head and lengthened his neck, a heron peeking up at a tiger.

"A week, no more," Adewole said.

On a roll and in the role, Stonecrop found the appropriate monosyllabic closer: "Done."

Turning toward the track, longing for it in fact, he spoke to the air, "Gotta Run."

He closed the door as one normally would and then used his ASVZ fob to pass through the turnstile to enter the track area. A few more laps, he needed a few more laps . . . to work off the fear, to work off the loathing.

His handy vibrated. A one-hour alert for an appointment at the Schützenhaus in Albisrieder and a training session for a group of young shooters with the Zürich biathlon club. After the surreal experience with Adewole, the normality of coaching a few kids about rifle safety and competitive shooting would be a welcomed break, even fun.

Jenny was in the hammock under the plane tree and reading a book about knot theory. Rosie lay beside her. The pair of them worked their way through a not particularly healthy bag of Sweifel Paprika potato chips.

"I'm going to the range. Want to come?"

He knew the answer. She loved shooting. The club's policy was strict: she could not fire a weapon until she had completed formal training and local certification. *The Swiss love their certifications.* But she could watch and help. Jenny tumbled out of the hammock. Rosie leapt to the ground. A cloud of crumbs followed.

"Wash up, okay," and then to Rosie, "You stay, girl."

It took ten minutes to load the car and twenty more before they passed the wooded picnic area with a view back across the lake toward Zürichberg. He parked the attention-grabbing Porsche at the stucco-walled clubhouse. An old wooden sign hung on the wall outside of the structure: *Häxehuusli.*

"What's 'hacks-eh-usely'?"

"Not sure; I think it's 'little witch house.' At Sprüngli, I saw a gingerbread house made with two square cookies that leaned together in the shape of a tent. And inside the tent there was a ceramic witch statue, like something out of a Grimm's fairy tale."

"Cool!"

The first thing on Stonecrop's agenda was to get Jenny settled in. He found a stool for her to stand on and set her up at the tall wooden bench behind the shooter's stations. He gave her his shooting scope and tripod. The scope, once calibrated for a selected distance, could swivel on the horizontal plane and smoothly move from target to target.

"You up for calling where the rounds land? Remember, like a clock, and in or out of the outer ring," he instructed.

Jenny was eager to help. "Totally got this!"

Next was the lesson. Stonecrop introduced everybody and announced that they would be working on standing, or as shooters said, the off-hand position, where the stock of the rifle gently rested atop a hand that was supported by an elbow on the hip or arm nestled against the rib cage.

For the next hour, Stonecrop drilled his students. He stood beside each student and would breathe with them to balance the inhale and exhale. His goal was to eliminate the obsessive anxiety associated with aiming. From long experience, he knew that if the set up was right and the shooter relaxed, the round would find the target, the sensation being like a stone dropping to the center of a well.

When they had finished, he took them aside and as a group they talked about the experience. He needed to give Jenny something to do, so, without attracting attention, he took the Glock out of his daypack, removed the magazine, and racked the slide to make sure the chamber was clear. He set her up at the table with the Glock, a desk mat that identified all the parts of the gun, and a few basic cleaning supplies. With no questions asked, she went to work.

"Weird how there's no safety," she said. Her hands could be clumsy, but there was nothing clumsy about her understanding of mechanics. Like her grandfather, she was a fearless mechanic.

"The safety is built into the trigger, see. You can throw this thing against the wall and it won't fire. But the trigger can snag at the same time as the release. Never had it happen, but I've heard about incidents. To be safe, never leave a round in the chamber."

"The slide release is on both sides, left and right. That's neat. I mean, for lefties like me."

Stonecrop gave her his phone and opened a Glock website.

By the time he had finished with the group, Jenny had broken down the top of the weapon, wiped it clean, and reassembled the pieces. Stonecrop was proud of her.

He still didn't have a plan for Lomi and Destiny and needed to talk to Fede.

Driving back to Frau Ott's, he received a text and handed the phone to Jenny.

"Federica's going to be late. She's done with work but had to do something," Jenny reported.

"Where is she?" Stonecrop asked. He was approaching Central in downtown Zürich and he could pick her up if her errands had taken her to the Coop for groceries. Or if she were close to work, he would be driving right by Universitäts-Spital.

"I asked. She said she had to go."

"Can you find her phone?"

Jenny's response was immediate. "She's on Reitergasse, by the Hauptbahnhof."

Stonecrop knew the street and corrected Jenny's pronunciation, "The *ei* is like the English *eye*. I think the cross-street is Militärstrasse? Opposite Transa."

"Lagerstrasse and Militärstrasse. Between them," she confirmed.

Reitergasse was across the Sihl canal and a few blocks from Aide Direct. She could be seeing a colleague. Stonecrop wound around the circle at Central, backtracked on the Bahnhofbrücke and Postbrücke, passed Hiltl Sihlpost, and turned up Lagerstrasse. A hundred meters later, he was in front of Reitergasse 3, a shaded alleyway. He waited for a car to vacate a parking space, then tried Fede again.

He texted. And waited. Then he tried her work number and left a message. Fede always answered her work phone. Still nothing. A police vehicle crawled down Reitergasse. The driver eyed Stonecrop and Jenny as he drove by. When he reached the end of the street he turned up Lagerstrasse, still driving slowly and watchfully. Stonecrop spooked. He double-checked the location of Federica's mobile. *Ready or not, here I come.*

"No answer. Wait here," Stonecrop exited the Taycan.

He walked up to the glass door to the apartment building and pushed the button for the ground floor buzzer. When there was no response, he did the same for apartments on the first and second floors. Again, no response. A man descending the stairs inside exited the door and let Stonecrop slip in. Once inside, he turned the latch to prevent the door from auto-locking. Jenny could join him if need be.

There were only four apartments listed, so Fede had to be in the third-floor apartment. The stairwell received enough outside light make one's way. The wooden stairs had seen better days. The treads were shallow and sagged from use; the noses dipped downward at an awkward angle that created a hazard if one were descending. The risers varied in height between the floors, a fact which irked Stonecrop's mathematical sense of order. Steps creaked. The wooden handrail, warped and oval in shape, wobbled loosely in ill-fitting circular iron brackets.

Wanting to not startle Fede, he tapped on the door and quietly spoke her name. From within, her voice asked who was there. This time he spoke in a normal tone of voice.

"It's me, Fede. Max."

The double-lock mechanism clicked twice and Federica's face appeared in the inch-wide opening. He saw enough of her face to see that she was upset.

"Were you following me?"

"No, not at all," Stonecrop answered. He felt somewhat embarrassed at arriving unannounced. "I sent a text and tried to call. Figured I'd give you ride home. Jenny tracked your phone. Thought you might have an armful of groceries."

Fede said something in Portuguese, not to him. He saw her hands, one of them in a light blue exam glove. Then she turned to him. "You alone, Max?"

"Jenny's in the car. We miraculously found a parking spot right in front."

"Go home, please," she said.

From inside came a husky voice, a familiar contralto: "It is all right, Federica. Now he knows where I am living. No sense to hide the fact, sim."

The Portuguese *sim* for yes colored her voice, made it warmer.

Lomi lay on the bed, wearing only a bathrobe, a fluffy, hotel souvenir sort of bathrobe. Her face was patched with butterfly bandages and near her ear, in what must have been a painful procedure, a dozen or so stitches zig-zagged across a bared patch of scalp. Her elbow was wrapped in gauze and one finger had been splinted and taped to a buddy finger. A syringe and bottle of anesthetic, gauze pads and tape, disinfectant and other medical supplies were strewn across a blue and white sterile pad atop the bedstand. The bloodied gauze pads accumulated in a clear-plastic bag beside the bed. Her lip was swollen and the missing tooth was still AWOL. One eye was covered with a gauze patch. The other, the good eye, followed him as he stepped in the room.

"Thank you. For Destiny." She struggled to form the words, like someone who had just been to the dentist.

"How's the eye?" he asked. From what little he had seen at the Miroir, the injury to her eye had been serious. Of course, there may have been internal injuries. Those, he had had no means to assess.

"I think it's going to be fine," Federica answered for her. "I'm more worried about possible kidney damage and the concussion."

"Lomi, it sounds like you should go to the Spital," he said, knowing before he had finished the words that Lomi must have heard the same from Federica.

Stonecrop's handy vibrated: <<JS: creepy guy with black hat just went in>>

He called Jenny. She didn't answer.

"Answer, damnit!"

"Max?" Federica stepped close to see the text. "Shit."

<<MS: stay in the car>>

"I'm gonna take a look," Stonecrop ordered. "Lock the door. If I don't come right back, call 117."

The man ascending the stairs made no attempt to hide his approach. He stepped lightly and paused briefly at the landing between the ground level and the first floor, where the stairs reversed direction. With no place to hide, Stonecrop descended to the landing between the second and third floors. He had moved quietly, though still making some noise. From the landing below, he retreated a few steps up and back to be out of view.

I should have grabbed a knife.

The man below must have heard something. His steps had become quieter and deliberate. A hand fiddled with something. Keys, a weapon?

Stonecrop waited. The brim of a baseball cap appeared as the man made to turn the corner at the landing. Stonecrop lunged at him, trying to get in close to bind or block any arm with a weapon.

The intruder had anticipated the attack and used Stonecrop's own momentum to hurl him downward and into the corner of the landing. The man dropped the keys in his hand, faced Stonecrop, and withdrew a knife.

"*You!*" they said the same word at the same moment.

"Jinx." Couto, the more composed of the two men, laughed. He locked his gaze on Stonecrop's eyes. "Wouldn't jump about, no sir, not a good idea. I know you. You're a bloody pussycat."

"You're working for Adewole," Stonecrop half-asked, half-stated, believing now that in spite of what Adewole had told him this morning, he had hired Couto to kill Lomi. Made sense; Couto was a murderer.

"Right, short memory, have we?" The tone of voice conveyed his confusion at Stonecrop's statement.

"I'm going to stop you," Stonecrop announced and pulled his feet closer, so he could get up.

Without taking his eyes off Stonecrop, Couto reached under his coat and unholstered an old school Beretta. He rolled the slide-mounted safety to the off position. "Nah-nah, move that tootsie again and you'll lose it."

"Don't move!" came a small voice, one that should have been tremulous but was not.

Couto smiled at the preposterous threat issued by this short, curly-haired cutie. His smile evaporated when she racked the slide to arm the Glock. Having just spent a good hour cleaning and working with the Glock, Jenny handled the weapon with ease and familiarity. Couto's expression recalibrated, realizing that Jenny meant what she had said and that she had the wherewithal to follow through on the threat.

"You Yanks start'em young," Couto remarked. His tone was light. There was even a hint of admiration.

A voice from the third floor screamed down to them, "Hennie! No!"

Stonecrop heard them hobble down the stairs. The irregular rattle of the railing rattled marked their progress. Federica appeared backside first to protect Lomi from tumbling down the stairwell. At the landing, Lomi left Federica's support and wrapped her arms around Couto. Her robe hung open as she pressed her naked body against him.

"My love, por favor. Put the gun down. I am begging you."

"You sure about that?" Couto broke his fix on Stonecrop and faced Lomi.

"Sim, I am sure," Lomi replied with even an edge even of sweetness. The words and tone had the desired effect.

"Ah." Couto turned to Federica and smiled his half-smile. "Cona Maxine! The whole bloody family's here. Where's the other little shit, skate-boarding on the roof?"

"Watch your mouth!" Lomi did the best she could to scold him for the vulgarity. Her good eye shuttled back and forth between Couto and Jenny.

He flipped on the safety and holstered the Beretta. With a flick of the wrist, the blade caught the light and the knife disappeared into a dark pocket as magically as when it had been extracted.

Jenny disarmed the Glock without having to look at the weapon. She had not dropped the bead on Couto. Her target followed her actions, clearly impressed.

"I like this little girl, Max. Knows her stuff."

Stonecrop felt like an idiot. He got to his feet and took the Glock from Jenny. He lifted his daypack off her back and stowed the handgun.

"I thought you were coming after Lomi," Stonecrop explained to Couto.

"I was. To see if she was alright and all," Couto responded. "What'd you think I was doing?"

"I thought you were coming to kill her . . ." The words had an unwarranted normality about them, so much so even Jenny didn't react.

"Now why would I do a crazy-fuck thing like that?" he asked, genuinely perplexed. He turned to Jenny, "Sorry. Need to watch that mouth of mine."

"It's okay," she said, "Max swears a lot too."

"Why are *you* here?" Stonecrop asked. "I thought you were that crazy . . . from Halbinsel Au."

Federica noticed that Jenny was not missing a word of their conversation. She removed the exam glove from her hand and took Jenny by the arm. "Upstairs, Jenny. Let's go; I need a hand cleaning up."

Stonecrop waited to speak until Jenny and Federica were back in Lomi's room.

"Your boss, Adewole, hired me . . ." he turned to Lomi, "to make her disappear."

Couto's looked confused. "Well, fuck me!"

Stonecrop explained, "He said she knew too much about Clave and was about to speak to the Polizei."

"That is not true, not a word. I swear!" Lomi trembled. The reaction was a mix of anger and fear.

Couto pulled her closer and with cold control, added: "Lomi, I own this. You understand, my fault. I told Adewole about you. He was suspicious about me comin' and goin' to Zürich. I told him I thought you might be able to help with Clave. One big fuck-up that was. Never thought he'd go this far."

The smooth plain of dead flesh on Couto's face was an emotion-free desert. The regret over having been the cause of Lomi's suffering was left to his eyes to express. The story they told was clear: he loved Lomi. That she cared for him was equally self-evident. Until this moment, Stonecrop had felt little sympathy for the man. He did now, though, as surely as the hatred they both shared for Adewole.

"I can't take care of the son-of-a-bitch. Not yet. As soon as we have our money," Couto assured her. "That'll be the end of him."

Stonecrop nodded a *you and me both* back to him.

Federica returned from the apartment. "Lomi, upstairs," she ordered. "You need to rest." She took Lomi by the arm and, aided by Couto, helped her manage the stairs and return to bed. Stonecrop, ego and body bruised and sore from the collision with the wall, followed.

Jenny was busy packing medical odds and ends into Federica's red and white stuffed wilderness emergency medicine kit. Given the energetic focus on the task, Stonecrop suspected she had been listening at the doorway until she heard Federica et al. start back up the stairs.

He wasn't upset with her. How could he be, after she had shown such grit and—though embarrassing for him—come to his rescue. He worried that she had been traumatized by the talk of murder, her own threat to take another's life, and seeing her father, helpless, with a gun to his head. Would Couto haunt her dreams as he had haunted Stonecrop's?

The answer to Stonecrop's concerns, to some degree, was answered as the group gathered to leave. Couto and Lomi needed time together.

"Thank you, little girl," Couto looked directly at Jenny as he spoke to her.

"Why?" she answered. "I was going to shoot you. I wasn't pretending."

"Sim, true. But you didn't!" He laughed and reached out to tousle her hair. She started, and his hand stopped just over her head. Then something between them softened, and she leaned forward into his hand and let him. "And you stopped me from hurting a good man." He looked up at Stonecrop and then back at Jenny. "That would have been wrong—to hurt a good man—wouldn't it?"

"Yes," she answered.

A truce had been reached.

As they were leaving the room, Jenny, holding Stonecrop's hand, turned back to look at Couto: "My name is Jenny. I'm *not* a little girl."

He beamed his half-smile back at her. "I am corrected! You are *not* a little girl." There was a brief pause before he spoke again, "Good-bye, Miss Jenny."

"Good-bye . . ."

"Hennie, my name is Hennie. Rhymes with yours."

Subito

The parking lot clung to the wall of the Dolder Grand Hotel like a giant shelf-mushroom. The arc of tarmac was dotted with humps of dark limos and gaudy blooms of autodom: a Pride pink Porsche; an iridescent McLaren; a posy of Ferraris; the obligatory Bugatti; and a lime-green Lamborghini. Amid such royalty, the Taycan was just another ride. At the far end of the lot, a ten-year-old, unwashed VW Golf came off as special. The Golf's driver half-sat, half-leaned on the front fender with his cap pulled down, eyes open or closed—one couldn't tell—like a cat napping in the sun. He came to life without fanfare when he noticed Stonecrop's approach. The preternatural awareness was well in advance of his actual arrival.

"Couto," Stonecrop's voice was calm. He had never imagined he could do that, say *Couto* without a shimmer of fear.

"This is how you make people *disappear*? Sign me up, will ya!"

Stonecrop looked at and confirmed the grandeur of the view and the hotel behind him.

"What did you tell Adewole?" Couto asked.

"That the job was done. She's gone and no fucking further questions."

"Did he believe you? He's sick in the head, gets off on the gory bits."

"I had the same reaction when I met with him at the track. Anyway, I think so. Besides, she *is* gone. That is, the old Lomi. Have you been able to see her?"

"I have. She's grateful as hell. Me, too. You're guy here, the concierge, he's a solid." Couto looked squarely at Stonecrop. "Thank you. And I'll square up with you when I have the dinero. The sixty."

"So, I take it you're *not* gonna kill me?" Stonecrop half-joked.

Couto's hand came out of his pocket, knife at the ready. The motion was too quick to follow. It was crystal clear to Stonecrop now, that whenever the hell he wanted, Couto could make *him* disappear. "I'm on the fence," Couto kidded. "Not today, anyway. Too nice a day. And I always pay what I owe."

"Then take your time with the money!" Stonecrop put his hands up in surrender.

The blade had flashed once in the sun as he put it away. The fear had come and gone as quickly. *No*, Stonecrop told himself, *Couto is not going to kill me*. He joined Couto at the fender. The car yielded to his weight.

"Ready for the latest from Harry?" Stonecrop announced.

"Lay it on me."

"There's been a change of plans. I'm to go back to València." He paused, then added, "You know that wasn't part of the original deal."

"To do what in València?"

"Move a couple of crates from Adewole's container to a different container. Fix some fuck-up of Harry's. He didn't—I should say, wouldn't—give me an explanation. Some security guy Harry knows is gonna walk me around. All hush-hush, he says. Not a word to anyone, including Gregor."

"Is this supposed to be a solo gig?"

"Yup."

"Want company?"

"Yup."

"Text the details. I'll be there. I don't trust these bastards. And I want my cut. Plus, you'll probably muck it up on your own."

"Yeah, probably so," Stonecrop laughed. "Is Adewole still around? He shocked me the other day. Chum keeps telling me Adewole never leaves his hole in Lagos, but I can't get rid of the son-of-a-bitch."

"He's gone."

"You didn't make him *gone* gone?"

"Clock's ticking, but no. I don't get paid until the containers land in Lagos. Adewole controls the money. That's his pass for now."

The men made their good-byes without fanfare. Stonecrop watched Couto drive off. On foot, he slalomed though the limos back to the front door to the hotel.

"Lenz, good to see you!"

"Max," the concierge gave Stonecrop a hearty hug and held his shoulders. "Look at you! Fit as a fiddle. Not like me!"

Lenz patted his tummy and sighed. He'd been at the Dolder for ten years, a concierge for twenty, and knew Stonecrop from the Schützenhaus and from cross-country skiing at Einsiedeln, a cozy ski area a half-hour south of Zürich. Lenz kept an old-school Airstream trailer on a family farm adjacent to the ski trails where he, along with his wife and two children, traded the trappings of city life for a simpler existence in Einsiedeln.

"Our Lucas loved the training session last week, the shooting without sights! He practices in front of the mirror. And he wears a headband like a Samurai. One motion, swoosh!" Lenz did a clumsy imitation of the routine Stonecrop had been working on with Lucas.

"He got the idea. He really looks great," Stonecrop answered, pleased that Lucas was training on his own.

"Did he shoot well? He was on the paper, I hope."

"I don't track it," Stonecrop avoided the specifics. "All the kids had fun."

He knew, of course, exactly how Lucas had shot, but that hadn't been the point of the exercise. Regardless, he rarely discussed the kids' performance with the parents. He wanted the kids to have fun, no matter what level they were at.

"The women settled in?"

"They've adjusted quite well and are making friends among the rich and famous."

Lenz managed the needs of visiting film stars, rock artists, business bigwigs, and diplomats. These guests, as one might expect, demanded discretion and anonymity. He had been delighted when Stonecrop had asked him to care for the sisters. He had found a quiet room in the Spa wing for them. From their deck, one could see the city below and, on the horizon, the Mönch, Sustenhorn, and the Tödi.

"Ah," Lenz added, "Herr Ratzow and guests await you."

Lenz guided Stonecrop to an outdoor table in a quiet corner of the patio and under a white canvas umbrella that protected the group from the midday sun.

Two weeks had passed since Stonecrop last saw Ratzow. The man had quite simply gone off the map. Being unable to consult with him about the decision, Federica and Stonecrop had moved the girls to the Dolder. The last place anyone hunting down two impoverished immigrants would look was a five-star hotel.

Lenz put the charges on Gregor's account, which was why Stonecrop expected the worst and then was pleasantly surprised as he approached the table and found Ratzow, Claudia, and Federica all in good spirits. Must be the weather: a few cotton puffs on the horizon and a cooling upslope breeze.

Gregor was drinking Champagne and holding court. His dark skin color advertised time spent someplace sunnier than Zürich. Claudia sat erect in her chair; the Nordic walking was working. Federica had tossed a light sweater across her shoulders, the arms of which were tied and draped across her breasts. Instead of avoiding the direct sun, she had moved her chair away from the table and thrown her head back to feel the sun's warmth on her face. The blouse grew transparent in the intense light. She wore blue denims and, in a most unladylike posture. slouched in the chair and opened her legs to the sun's caress. Stonecrop imagined the heat on her body and quickly took a seat.

". . . the Minister, do you remember him, Federica, he is so fat now that he can't get out of chair without help!" Ratzow laughed, and continued, "Da, I send him sticks like those—"

"They're not just sticks, dear, they're Nordic walking poles," Claudia chirped. Clearly, she had drunk the Kool-Aid.

"His butt . . ." Ratzow spread his hands apart like he was describing a fish. "Remember, we did safari with him. On foot, we walked, slept in tents, at night the lions make big noise! Good time, Fede, da!"

"Yes, a good time, Papà. I'm sad Baba is so overweight. Has he ever mentioned diabetes?"

That made Ratzow roar, "Diabetes, no!" He took a drink and went on, "He is ox. Problem is wives. Too many: young, old, pretty, ugly. I lose count. He says they all cook and if he doesn't eat what they cook they are jealous, so he has to eat everything!"

"I'd forgotten about Baba's wives. Funny how something can be so normal there and so awkward here. I'd never given it a second thought. I feel sorry for them." Federica said the words as she leaned forward and hopped her chair up to the table and back under the shade.

"Sorry! You should be sorry for him! He takes care of them, good, and their families. All of them. And they can leave whenever they want. Not like here, they are not slaves, not like at carwash—"

Ratzow looked for the names.

"Lomi and Destiny," Federica supplied them for him.

"Is good here for them," he waved a hand in the direction of the hotel. "Smart. Safer than Polizei. Better food."

Apparently, Gregor *wasn't* upset that Lomi and Destiny were costing him a mint.

In the first wave of a pincer movement, two waiters placed lobster and melon salads around the table; the second wave brought a second bottle of blanc de blanc Champagne and bread rolls and butter.

"Is like water," Ratzow announced as the waiter poured a glass for Max.

"Babbo?" Max had not heard the name before and confused name with the Bulgarian term of affection Federica sometimes used for her father.

"No, *Baba*," she corrected. "Papà and I met Baba—Nicky Mbaba is his real name—when we lived in Mozambique. He's from Walvis, Namibia. He was working in a U.N. program on the cause and prevention of violent extremism. He's smart—well, maybe not so with women." She smiled and sipped her drink. Her gaze traversed the trough-like water feature that spanned the length of the patio, as if its reflections were recollections from years lived in Africa. "Max, the Khoisan myth, about the Milky Way I told you about on *Zaca*, that's from Baba, from Baba's people."

Claudia went back and forth between wanting a bite of salad and giving in to her compulsion to speak. She opted for an unattractive combination of both: "Let me fill you in," she chewed a moment, "lovie. Gregor saw Minister Mbaba last week. Where did you meet him?" Her fork skewered a piece of lobster that subsequently vanished in her mouth. Her erect little finger directed the event like a traffic cop.

Gregor waved away her question. Too busy eating.

"Well," she continued, "some rustic island next to Malta—"

"Gozo," Federica interrupted. "The local name is Ghawdex."

"Yes, sweetie, that's it," Claudia thanked her. "Anyway, Gregor had some astonishingly good news and some not-so-good news to report. He asked Mbaba to factcheck claims made by our friend in Bern. I don't know how, but Mbaba was able to confirm that the Southern African Development Community and Interpol have, within their joint Protocol on Politics, Defense and Security Co-operation, been informed that all Red Notices concerning Gregor, his company, and those in his employ—including Max darling—have been deleted from the Commission for the Control of Interpol's Files. As of the date deleted, you two gentlemen face no detention, arrest, restriction of movement, or extradition threats from government agencies in, roughly, the southern half of Africa."

"Whoa, Chum actually did this!" Stonecrop was incredulous.

"Appears so. The flake unflaked, promises made and delivered.

Don't know whose boot—or worse—he's licking, but there we have it."

The right reaction to news that was too good to be true was to challenge the source. Stonecrop had no way to do so and had little choice but to take Claudia at her word.

"I'm not a believer, not yet." Stonecrop shifted from Claudia to Fede, "Do you think Alicia could verify what Mbaba said?"

Fede nodded, picked up phone and walked to a quiet spot at the end of the patio and leaned against the glass railing. The group ate in silence as she completed the call. She returned directly.

"Left a message."

Claudia continued, "Let me repeat, dearies, all is not roses."

Bracing herself for her next act, Claudia skewered another piece of lobster. She stabbed repeatedly and with gusto, as if she were wary that the poor beast, had survived having been boiled alive—though maybe, mercifully, it had been pithed first. A swill of Champagne washed the morsel down her throat and to oblivion.

Maybe Jenny was right: eating meat was barbaric. He had never asked *why* she was vegetarian—ethics, environment, the taste? Did it matter how one ate meat? Did rituals matter? Or what of domestic animals and so-called Humane Slaughter Act? What an oxymoron.

Claudia carried on, "First: A low-life ex-agency chap I know told me that he and Harry the Chump did a little unofficial side-work some years back. Our man lost his job and swears he was set up whilst Chum got a promotion. We don't know if the boy's actions were run-of-the-mill political backstabbing or something more nefarious."

More skewering attempts implied a strategy. She was avoiding the nüssli lettuce.

"I assume there's a second point?" Stonecrop asked.

A speck of meat clung to bottom of her chin. Fede put her finger to her own chin. Claudia got the hint, lifted her face upward, and scraped off the barnacle of meat with her napkin.

"Point Two: The African association's rulings are regional. The prudent approach is to assume Gregor is still at risk in Europe, at least until we get an independent read on his status. We can't ask our poor Kommissar."

"Why 'poor' Kommissar?" Federica asked.

"Ah, you haven't heard!" Her expression matched the tone. "Dear Vittore has been asked to take holiday." Fork in hand, *holiday* still got air quotes. She leaned over and put a hand on Gregor's knee. "You know, you should have taken him with you."

Federica leaned into the word and the table. "Holiday?" she repeated. "No way. After god knows how many years, the Polizei can't do that. Kanton or Stadt?"

"Kanton. But he's taking a leave of absence from Stadt as well. Too much overlap of responsibilities."

Ratzow added to what Claudia had said. "Da, last night. I see Vittore at Reithalle. We drink. He did not tell wife."

"Did he say why he was put on leave?" Stonecrop asked.

Claudia answered again, "Omission. He omitted relevant information in his report about the incident with Lorenzo. Internally, they're calling the inquiry the *Käseskandal*."

"It's the resident physician," Federica scoffed. "He medicated Vittore and the Kommissar might have said more than he had intended and the resident scribble notes about cheese incident in the medical record. A joke, I thought. But I guess not. The records are digitized daily and word somehow reached his superiors."

"Do they know about the payment for Lomi?" Stonecrop asked.

Ratzow's lower lip protruded; he nodded up-and-down but said, "Ne."

It took Stonecrop a moment to remind himself that yes and no head gestures in Bulgarian are opposite the norm, at least the norm for much of the western world.

"Then, without confirmation from Vittore, we take Chum at his word." Federica added, "Or reach Alicia."

Ratzow shook his head side-to-side, meaning Yes.

"What will Vittore do?" Federica asked aloud, then quickly answered her own question. "Of course," she said with school-girl cheeriness, "he'll do what he always does. Work."

As if Vormittag himself, though not present, were responding to her question, Stonecrop's handy vibrated with a message from him. Instead of texting, Stonecrop called him, put the phone on speaker, and placed it in the center of the table.

"Were your ears burning?"

A laugh leapt out of the handy's speaker. "I've not heard that expression for some time. So, Gregor told you?"

"You're on speaker, Kommissar," Stonecrop answered. "Gregor, Claudia, and Fede are here. We're at the Dolder."

Vormittag, forgetting that he was not on duty made a demand as if he were: "I still want to speak with Destiny's sister, Lomi."

"What hat are you wearing, Kommissar?" Stonecrop asked.

"Since I am on leave, I am not officially required to report my actions or for that matter wear a hat. I still want to speak with her. Is she in Zürich?"

"Where are you?"

"At Kantonspolizei. I needed to turn in my pistol, but . . ."

"Yes?"

" I can't find it. That is, the pistol must be *somewhere*. At home, or the Stadtpolizei safe. Been years since . . ." Vormittag muttered something unintelligible. The rare moment of befuddlement made everyone smile, especially from Gregor.

Curious, Stonecrop asked, "Aren't all Polizei required to do monthly target practice?"

"Yes, ah, sometimes I go. Well, that is, I have gone. Really, after twenty years, who cares."

Federica had a different line of questions for the embarrassed Kommissar. "Vittore, how's your shoulder?"

"Better, yes. Much better. Grazie, Federica."

Stonecrop tapped the mute button. "I, for one, would value the Kommissar's opinion. Especially now that he doesn't have to report what he's doing."

All present signed agreement.

He unmuted: "Vittore. Come join us. There's someone here you'd like to meet."

"Sì, sì, subito!"

València Redux

The view through the galley portholes was a familiar one. *Zaca* lay side-by-side with *Juliette*, whose gleaming white hull playfully caught and released shards of light from the choppy surface of the water. For two days now, there had been no sign of Captain Wes Waterman or Freddy, his first mate.

With naval regularity, port personnel had been making the rounds to check *Juliette's* dock lines, water hose, and electrical power extensions. Twice a night, a port security officer boarded the vessel to patrol the perimeter and run a torch across *Zaca's* deck and hull. He appeared familiar with the *Juliette* and diligently tested doors and inspected portals and hatches. That level of security, Stonecrop noted, was unusual.

Any worries about the yacht or its crew dissipated the moment Stonecrop heard the quick, light-footed step of Freddy on *Juliette's* gantry. The sound brought with it a gratifying normality.

He debated about whether to hail Freddy and be neighborly. Of course, he'd be asked why he was in València and would probably fumble the explanation. Though maybe not. He realized the simplest explanation could be a genuine one: *Zaca* did need an overhaul. He'd call the marina in a few hours, arrange for a mechanic to check the engine, repair the impossible to repair autopilot, and install a new offshore life raft. Might as well have a rigger run up the mast to inspect attachment points for stays and pulleys and perform cleaning and calibration of mast mounted instruments. If the topsides clean up didn't break the bank, he'd ask a diver to inspect the hull, rudder, and prop for damage. Boat maintenance was never-ending and expensive. He would have to budget time as well to visit the marine supply shop for a suitable life raft. And if he were to do any cruising, *Zaca* would need a new tender, probably a relatively inexpensive, inflatable PVC dinghy with a rigid floor and a small outboard. Something sturdier would be better for the tropics; but for the near-term, Stonecrop had zero plans for extended cruising.

In part to keep expenses to a minimum and in part to feel comfortable with the various onboard systems, Stonecrop usually did much of the maintenance work himself. This day and the next, however, there were more pressing commitments. Specifically, he had a second rendezvous with Hennie Couto—one that would be infinitely less terrifying than the first—for an undertaking that he hoped would be the end of his obligations to Chum and company.

Couto had taken a taxi and was waiting in the vehicle at the marina's gated entry. He had arrived on time, armed with a briefcase, a sheaf of papers, and in uniform: black baseball cap and leather jacket with baggy side pockets, Levi's, black Polo shirt, and olive-colored canvas deck shoes. The deck shoes were a surprise. Stonecrop had not taken Couto for a boat-guy. Of course, the slit-bottomed soles were good on wet surfaces, and they were quiet. To be attired in dark clothes was a night-time advantage. Midday, the uniform would come across as too black, too hot. The weather, however, had accommodated Couto's dress regimen. It had been overcast, stormy, and unseasonably cool. Even under the punishing sun, Hennie Couto was a man who could get away with a non-standard wardrobe. The scarring on his face and reaching up the side of his scalp distracted from his attire. The poor man, people assumed, had been through hell; he could wear whatever.

His coat fit clung tightly to the right armpit; he had long past brushed aside the consequences of running around with a concealed weapon. He had told Stonecrop that wherever he traveled on the Continent, his first stop was to gather essentials: medications, a Beretta, spare magazines, knife, a few tools, burner phones and cash, and a change of clothes. In València, he had obtained a spare Glock with waist-belt holster for Stonecrop.

One would think Couto a man with few friends, but Stonecrop had learned otherwise. In València, as an example, a couple in their 70s, people of modest means, kept a spare bedroom and a car for him. Couto paid for the car's upkeep and for extra space in the garage for a safe with his arsenal and other essentials.

The *Project*, as Couto was fond of referring to Stonecrop's current assignment, was a two-part affair. Part one, this afternoon, was routine.

They would show up at the container yard identified by Adewole, show their IDs to the yard supervisor, be approved to enter the secure, outdoor in-transit zone, and then be conducted by an authorized port employee to two forty-foot containers, one registered to a shell company controlled by Ode Ikande, and another registered to a shell company owned by Gregor. Both containers had been scheduled to be loaded aboard the Binnur D, a Panama-registered vessel docked nearby and preparing to sail to the container terminal at Tin Can Island in Lagos, Nigeria. It was part two of the Project that scared the crap out of Stonecrop.

A taxi deposited them at the container terminal. Part one went by swimmingly.

"So far, a lark," Couto leaned close to Stonecrop so that the guard, a man who also doubled as their guide, wouldn't overhear. Their visitor-labeled helmets tapped together.

The security guard, once he checked his paperwork and found Stonecrop's name, had agreed to let Stonecrop's "assistant," Hennie Couto, join the party even though his name had not been on the visitors list. Couto had scrawled a half-legible "Jack Rabbit" on the sign-in sheet, not so subtly letting the guard know that he knew the formalities were a farce.

Speaking as softly as Couto had, Stonecrop whispered back, "Why are we fucking armed to the teeth?"

"Precaution. Should be a piece of cake, but you never know," Couto said, and then, with a quick flick of his hand in the air like a pistol, added, "Brought you an extra mag."

"Roger, one extra. You?"

"Two. One on the strap, another taped to my dick."

Stonecrop raised his eyebrows and smiled.

"Inner thigh, Max, the thigh! Wanna see?" Couto made to lift his pants leg up slightly.

"I'll pass."

They walked four or five minutes through the labyrinth of stacked containers and beneath the underbellies of Godzilla-scale, bow-legged, quadrupedal cranes, all the while hanging on the heels of their coveralled guide with his official Port Security cap, clipboard, and bolt cutter.

En route to their destination, the guard pointed to a sign-less gate in the chain link fence. "You leave that way," he said. Stonecrop marked the waypoint on his phone and memorized the location.

Though the air was cool, Couto sweated. He handed the overlarge briefcase to Stonecrop, who had not expected the ten-plus kilos and nearly dropped the case on the spot. Okay, sweat explained.

"Earn your money, Maxie." Couto whispered.

"Gentlemen." Their leader didn't bother to turn around when he spoke. He came to a halt and with feigned formality inspected the clipboard. An eighteen-inch bolt cutter dangled like an extra limb from his other hand. The three men stood before the travel-worn and bleached by sea and sun forty-foot container. A bystander would wonder what demanded the shared moment of silence. And Stonecrop wondered if the guard, who was conducting an unsanctioned container break-in, was having second thoughts. Opening a container for redistribution or inspection was generally done at a station specifically designated for the task. The guard broke the spell and tapped the container with the bolt cutter the way one might kick a tire to check the air pressure.

Couto checked the eleven-digit alpha-numeric tag that identified the owner, equipment category, serial number, and check digit. He pointed to the three-digit owner-code which, as expected, referred to the shell company owned by Ode Ikande.

While Couto was looking over the contents on the manifest, Stonecrop glanced at the locking hardware used to secure the container: A single, four-inch-long "bolt seal" ran through a hasp on the lower handle of the right door, locking the handle in place. A flange on the right door prevented the left from opening. The two pieces of the barbell-shaped seal, once the top pin was inserted into the slot in the barrel below, could not be opened. Any attempt to break the seal would leave traces of tampering and indicate that the contents of the container might have been violated. At the final destination, the owner would take possession of the container and would use bolt cutters to break the seal. The simple system was used on three-quarters of all ocean-going containers.

A seal's brand and serial number was recorded on the shipping manifest and was unique. *That is, unless you were Harry Chum.* Mr. Chum had bragged to Stonecrop that the replacement seal for Ode Ikande's container bore laser-engraved carrier and seal numbers on the barrel and pin of the bolt that matched those on Ode's container. The replacement seals were in Stonecrop's pocket.

"That's one of them," the guard tapped the metal again, as if had he not done so they would have not been able to see the massive steel box a few feet in front of them.

"Righto. And this is in the same shipping lot as the other one." Couto mimicked the guard's gesture by tapping the steel door with his knuckles. The guard nodded back.

"And this baby's sailing on the Binnur D, correct?" Couto demanded.

The guard checked the manifest and showed the document to Couto, who seemed satisfied.

"One down, one to go," Couto announced.

Stonecrop marked the waypoint on his phone. He had good sense of direction, but at night in the poorly lit yard, the stacks—some four-or-five high—of Lego-bright containers could morph into mostly uniform bricks of gray and black, making them difficult to identify.

Leaning into Stonecrop as they walked a few yards behind their guide, Couto whispered, "Thank god the fucker's on ground level. A major cock-up that would be if it wasn't!"

Couto was right. The transfer would be all but impossible if the containers were not at ground level. They would need a forklift. Stonecrop had by now become the sweater-in-chief. The "briefcase" weighed more with every step. He wanted to ask Couto about the contents, but they were rarely out of earshot from the third man.

A few minutes more and they stood before their second objective. That fucker too was at ground level.

Again, Couto checked the markings and the manifest. Stonecrop was grateful for Couto at his side. This was Couto's turf. He was comfortable and confident whereas Stonecrop felt like the poseur that he was.

The identity numbers on the container were the ones registered to Gregor's company. The bins of e-waste within had been collected by Chum's people and delivered so as to appear as though GR Group had been the aggregator. Group in turn had sold the contents, FOB Lagos, to Adewole per the agreement he and Stonecrop had negotiated. This was the first shipment of the elaborate sting Chum had orchestrated.

In the container, and in addition to the e-waste contents, were four sealed plastic boxes that Chum had asked Stonecrop to transfer to Ode Ikande's container. Chum had refused to give any explanation other than that it was imperative to transfer the boxes before the containers were loaded aboard the Binnur D.

Failure to do so, he had stated, would jeopardize the entire operation and would have consequences for Ratzow. Stonecrop had no idea if the threat had teeth. He and Gregor, he thought, had been "deleted" from the Red List. Could they be relisted? Can those sorts of things happen on a whim, on Chum's whim? Chum had said nothing about the Red List and Stonecrop hadn't asked.

Stonecrop *had* raised the point that since Chum's people were the ones who had provided the contents in the first place, then they should be the ones to move the goods. The appeal fell flat. "Those idiots would just make things worse," Chum had said. "Nope, this is not your problem, but you're the guy who's got to take care of it."

Couto turned to the guard. "Open sesame!"

The three men were about to open and reseal a container, an act which typically requires a time stamp, signatures, and an annotation to the manifest. With one hand holding both the arm of the bolt cutters and the clipboard, and the other hand on the remaining arm of the bolt cutters, the guard had enough leverage to snap the steel shaft of the seal. The separated pin and barrel fell to the ground. He then tucked the bolt cutters under his arm and held the clipboard for Stonecrop and Couto to initial, and then checked the seal's number against what was on the manifest, as well as that of the replacement seal Chum had given Stonecrop.

The men initialed the form. Catching the others by surprise, Stonecrop snapped a photo of the document and pocketed the remains of the broken seal. He left a hand in his pocket, twirling the broken-off barrel. Something nagged at him, but he couldn't pin it down.

Couto abruptly thanked the guard and held out an envelope full of cash.

The recipient's eyes, lifeless until that moment, shot a furtive look right and left before he accepted the envelop. Had that not been part of the plan? Couto's action seemed to have caught him unaware. Or maybe their guard had hoped they would huddle-up someplace out of sight to finalize the payoff. The message conveyed by Couto was clear. *Get moving*, there would be no huddle, no bro moment. The guard had his orders and did a sharp about-face and marched off.

The briefcase—which seemed to have doubled in size and weight over the last half-hour—lay on the ground. Couto flipped up the clasps and extracted a Maglite flashlight. Inside the briefcase, Stonecrop saw a jaws mechanism for a bolt cutter and pieces of tubing to extent its handles to leverage the applied force; a hammer head, which, similarly, could be attached to the one of the tubes; and lastly, a file, a chisel, miscellaneous bolts and nuts, glue, and a battery-powered drill. It was a box of tools with a purpose.

Stonecrop gave Couto an inquiring look.

"Plan B," Couto replied without elaborating.

The men unlatched the right door, thus freeing the left as well, and stepped inside. They closed the doors behind them and wound through several waist-high wooden crates three-quarters full of e-waste. Mid-container, they found four plastic boxes as Chum had foretold, each roughly three-feet long by a foot-and-a-half tall and wide.

"This it?"

"I presume. He said four plastic boxes," Stonecrop responded.

"I presume . . ." Couto repeated as he crouched down over the container. He ran the light along the edges, looking at various markings on the container. His expression changed, shifting from inquiring to certainty. "I presume, Max, you're gonna get fucked big-time." He snorted and said dryly, "Hungarian. Decent quality."

"Decent quality what?" Stonecrop asked, although he had a sudden suspicion of what the answer was going to be.

"Guns, mate. A couple of ten-packs. AK-47s. And these two," he pushed against the boxes to test their weight, "are ammo."

"Why on earth did Chum's people cache weapons in Gregor's e-waste container? And why transfer the stuff to Ode's? Chum said it was a mistake."

"Good questions. Mistake? Mistake my ass!" Couto stood up and exhaled the words, "What a shithead. What a fucking A-1 bastard."

"Are the rifles something Ode's guys wanted?"

Couto laughed. "Not exactly. Ode's not an arms guy. And he's not an idiot. The smartest of the lot of them, and the most trustworthy." Couto immediately back-pedaled, "Not that you should trust any of those buggers."

Couto sat on the ammo box. "You see, Ode's never sold an AK in his life. That's one reason his stuff is conveniently overlooked at Lagos Port. And as far as I know, Adewole's never been a gun pusher either. What's even weirder is that this pissant shipment is not what real arms dealers do. You see, the risk don't justify it. Arms are really moved through bogus military contracts and the numbers are huge, like really fucking astronomic. We're talking thousands of pieces, millions of rounds."

"A gift, or what?"

"It's a gift alright, like a Trojan horse right up your arse. Penalties for e-waste are a slap on the wrist. The penalty for any military grade arms transfer, even something this pissy, are horrific. Way out of proportion to the crime, 'cause the judge rightly figures it's the tip of the iceberg."

"So, this is a set up?" Stonecrop asked.

"Bright boy, Maxie." Couto smiled his half-smile. Stonecrop realized that he no longer noticed the man's disfigured features. "Chum's about to take out one of the competition—and it's not Adewole. Someone's gonna rat on comrade Ode when this shit hits Tin Can Island Port. I'd bet my dear sweet mother on it.

"Lad's gonna carve out a chunk of Clave's business. See, it bumps Gregor and Adewole up the food chain. Unless Gregor's behind this? You know him better than me, Maxie. What say you?"

"Doubt it. Sneaky is not his style. If he doesn't want you around, he'll tell you to your face and pull the trigger himself."

Couto patted the ammo box a few times, thinking. "Did Chum ever say anything like, like maybe he was working *with* Adewole?"

"The contrary," Stonecrop replied. "Chum's story all along was that Adewole was the target. Gregor, per Chum, is his inside man. Gregor's supposed to get a seat at the table and get enough to hang Adewole. And then get the hell out."

"Why wouldn't he leave a couple crates here, to take down Adewole? Or say, leave a couple here and a couple with Ode? Nail them both. Gregor doesn't matter. He's getting out anyway."

"I can see him first removing Ode. Consolidate Clave around Adewole and Gregor. Then go after Adewole when he has a bigger piece of the pie."

"Or he's got other plans for Adewole. Did you look at the stuff here? For e-waste, it's primo."

"What do we do?" Stonecrop asked.

"Fucking clear as day. Adewole owes me and I need the asshole to succeed or I don't get paid. Not much choice for yours truly. And Chum's got you and Gregor by the short ones. But, if Ode is put away, don't think that's the end of the story. Ode has friends and payback is in order. And, Maxie, you're the fall guy. There'll be a fucking target on your back, is what. Gregor, too. I think Chum's takin' you down, Maxie."

"Houston, we got a problem," Stonecrop quipped. He was staring at Gregor's replacement seal in his hand.

"Maxie, that's not a problem. You signed in fair and square; you can change the seal on your own container if it's on the manifest. The stiff wrote the new number on the manifest."

"But it's not a new number. Same number, same type. This is an exact duplicate."

Couto reacted with a further question. "What's the number on the other one, on Ode's?"

Stonecrop brought out his phone. When he'd marked the waypoint, he had also photographed the other seal. He showed the photo to Couto and held up Ode's replacement seal. They were different models. That's what had been nagging at him. From the photo, he couldn't tell if the numbers were the same or not.

"Number doesn't matter," Couto said. "If the seals don't match, you're screwed."

"So, what happens then?"

"Customs catches the coverup. Then Ode screams to high heaven that someone—and that someone is us, right here, right now—planted the weapons. He's right, of course. He's also screwed. Just like you!

"And if customs doesn't notice, Ode sure as fuck will, and he'll figure we doctored his container. He'll check visitors at València no matter what, and guess whose name pops up—you and your sidekick, Jack Rabbit. That is, if the manifest the guard had isn't bogus."

"If there's a duplicate seal on Gregor's container, what does *that* mean?"

"It means," Couto explained, "that as far as the official record is concerned, we were here, but didn't touch Gregor's container."

"If we do what Chum wants, what will Ode do?"

"Skin us alive, I reckon. Unless he can come up with something worse."

"But we can talk to him."

"And risk blowing up Gregor's delivery and me not getting paid? No thanks, Maxie. I got a better idea." He grinned. "What's that Yank expression, 'this ain't my first rodeo'?"

Rodeo

After three long, cold hours huddled in an unlit steel box with a man he had once tried to kill, Stonecrop realized that he had begun to accept and trust Couto. Like a wildfire out of fuel to burn, the fear had run its course. Yes, the man had done despicable things: pushing bogus drugs, arms dealing, god knows what else; and certainly, he had killed people. Somewhere in that dark CV, were years of military and mercenary service. Stonecrop had blamed him for Chloë; however, that accusation Couto had resisted, adamant that he had never harmed her and had taken her in and treated her kindly after she had been written off as "used goods." He said that was not the case with his brother to whom, he said, she was chattel. Chloë, he guessed, had hated Alves as much as Couto had. Couto put a period to a discussion they had had about the matter: "Who the fuck are you to judge anybody!"

Stonecrop cracked open the door of their container and stepped into an alien world. A reddish sea-fog hugged the ground. Droplets hung in the air and glowed from overhead yard-lights that were shapeless and more suggested than seen. In every direction, greyed-out stacks of containers and the allées they defined converged to vanishing points that were at one and the same time infinite and claustrophobic. The color warmed; the cold cut to the bone.

Limb by limb, Couto rose from the floor. He moved at ease in the darkness like a jaguar across the tangled growth of the jungle floor, though in this case the path wove through crates of discarded electronics. In retrospect, it was no surprise that he had gotten the drop on Stonecrop at the Brasilera's apartment.

"Have we a schedule of security patrols?" Couto asked.

"Harry Chum promised they'd be on holiday tonight."

"Naturally, no worries then." The sarcasm matched the bite of the air. "You realize, amigo, that the AKs up the ante. New game now."

Stonecrop jammed his hands into the pockets of his Patagonia hoody and stamped his feet up and down, pumping blood and warmth through a body stiff from hours of immobility in a corner of the container.

"Are we still in agreement?" Couto asked.

They had hashed over the options and had decided to not make an enemy out of Ode Ikande. Couto had declared, simply enough, "You like him; I like him. Let's not fuck the guy."

Couto had explained that half the money he had invested alongside Adewole would be automatically wired, along with a percentage of the profit, as soon as the containers left for Lagos Port. The goods were being shipped FOB—Free on Board. The remainder would be wired when Gregor's container cleared customs at Tan Can Island Port.

"And what *do* we do with the arms?" Stonecrop asked.

"Carry the shit as little as possible," Couto responded, and looked at the container next to them. "We can't leave the stuff laying about or Chum will know it didn't make it to Ode's container."

"Do you recognize the carrier?" Stonecrop asked as he inspected the neighboring container.

"Nope. And I don't care."

"They'll be in a shitload of trouble if they're inspected."

"Let me clarify, Maxie: I don't care. As in I don't give a fuck."

Stonecrop had assumed Couto would snip the seal, as the security guard had. He was mistaken.

"We'll be nice—and I got all this crap with me." He held up his briefcase. "May as well use it and give 'em a fighting chance." Couto removed his hardhat and replace it with his signature black baseball cap. He flung the hardhat into a black gap between the containers. Stonecrop did the same. While immobilized in the container, they had worn the helmets for warmth. Now they were able to move around.

Couto put the briefcase on the ground and opened and assembled the hammer by attaching the hammer head and one of the metal tubes. He placed the edge of the chisel in the seam between the round-headed bolt and hasp that secured the seal. With one blow the head of the bolt fell to the ground. A second tap with a punch pushed the shaft of the bolt through and out of its hole. With the hasp rotated and seal still intact, the unlatched door gently swung open. The entire process had taken seconds.

The adjacent container was half-empty. Crates wrapped with metal straps were secured by nylon belts to floor pallets; the markings were in Chinese. In a quarter-hour, they muscled the four one-hundred-pound-plus boxes of arms into the container.

The latch reassembly was executed almost as fast as the break-in. Couto glued a new nut to the inner wall of the container and around the existing through-hole. Then, closing the door and putting the hasp and seal back in place, he threaded a new round-headed bolt into the nut. He tapped the head of the bolt lightly with the hammer. The deformation sealed the bolt and added a modicum of wear and tear.

"How did you know?" Stonecrop asked, handing tools for Couto like an RN in the OR.

"Plan B. If Chum's replacement seals weren't right, this would be about the only option. Like I said, Max, been here before."

He bypassed Stonecrop and tossed the hammer tube in the briefcase himself, saying "Let's get out of here."

In the minutes that had passed, few as they were, the fog had thickened. Even if the container facility had security cameras blanketing the facility, there would be no record of the break-in.

Using his phone for directions, Stonecrop followed a zig-zag path through the grid of containers. Couto moved without making a sound, prompting Stonecrop to look over his shoulder every so often to make sure he was still there.

He stopped to check their position on his phone and turned to report to Couto. When he looked back, he saw Couto, crouched and with weapon drawn and aimed at Stonecrop's head. The briefcase lay on the ground.

Had Couto been waiting for the perfect moment. Just the two them, Couto's money assured, Lomi safe? Was it payback time and had Stonecrop been naïve, foolishly trusting and charmed by Couto's camaraderie, his inexplicable connection to Jenny, and his extraordinary skills?

The shot passed within inches of Stonecrop's head. He turned to the side and crouched, having decided to not charge Couto, who he knew would be faster. Maybe he could get a hand on the Glock. Maybe if Couto's second round struck him it wouldn't kill him. Maybe Stonecrop would get one return shot.

Couto fired again. The same point of aim! Couto was shooting at something behind Stonecrop.

"Down, amigo . . ." Couto calmly ordered.

Stonecrop ducked and rotated to see what Couto had been firing at. He saw nothing.

Couto took the phone from Stonecrop and put a finger over the waypoint for the gate.

"Avoid," he said. "They'll assume we'll run for it. We don't; we sit tight. Somebody's cleaning up loose ends. They had to, you see, assume we'd eventually explain the set up to Ode and Gregor."

"Why did you wait—"

"Wasn't sure. Didn't want to worry you." Couto smiled, "Pretty sure now!"

"Fuck you, Hennie. How many?"

"I don't know. Three if I had to guess. One was limping. Could be more."

"Why fire?"

"They mean business, Maxie. I can tell when a man means business. Just like I can tell there's more than three of them. It's the way they moved, over-confident, like they had backup. Two are ex-military, well-armed. Carrying weight—weapons, could have body armor. About to take us out, Maxie. Sure as hell wasn't some out-of-form security guys."

"We gave away our position."

"Maxie, they knew *exactly* where we were. They'll call their mates. We'll let 'em come to us. Then we'll know exactly where *they* are."

"Hennie, I don't think—"

A hand cupped Stonecrop's mouth. Couto's eyes darted left and right, the message obvious. He removed the hand and then turned his baseball cap around, bill to the back to clear his peripheral vision, and pointed to gap between two stacks of containers at the opposite side of their ten-foot-wide alleyway. The fog thickened.

"Stay," Couto ordered—he might as well of been talking to Rosie— and then scurried like a sand crab across the aisle and into a two-foot gap between two containers. From the covered position, he executed a sequence of hand signals that completely baffled Stonecrop. He had never been drilled in combat communications, and for that matter, had never been in real combat.

Another round of hand-waving from Couto and he sort of understood. Stonecrop was to cover one approach on the alley, Couto would cover the other. The bet was that whoever was looking for them wouldn't risk the narrower gaps between containers, some of which a man could squeeze through, some of which were too narrow.

As if Couto had both foreseen and scripted the choreography, three shadows armed with handguns approached and walked toward them. They seemed familiar with the terrain and moved in concert: one would advance to a gap while covered by the other two. Then a second would leap-frog to the next gap, always with backup.

Couto signaled Stonecrop, indicating that he should point the barrel of the Glock downward. He didn't want Stonecrop to reveal their position. Stonecrop got the message. He repositioned his body and feet to match Couto's—forty-five degrees, feet about eighteen inches apart so one could quickly step forward, fire, and equally important, quickly retreat. Again, copying Couto, he dropped the angle of his entire arm until he was ready to expose his position and fire. Couto's eyes were fixed on the corner edge of the container. When the target crossed the edge, he would make his move.

The only way to gauge the progress of their assailants was by sound. Three men moving on dirt make noise even when the sound is dampened by fog. Not having seen or heard anything for several minutes, the men had grown impatient and sloppy. More noise, then voices. Whispers in Spanish and the grit of gravel underfoot.

Stonecrop watched Couto. The man was the picture of calm,

listening intently, eyes glued to the container's edge, prepared to shoot at anything that violated that vertical tripwire. Stonecrop did the same, waiting and listening.

In his peripheral vision, he saw Couto's hand move, trying to get his attention. Couto poked the barrel of the Beretta back and forth a few times in the direction of the side he was covering. A change in strategy. They would take advantage of their stalkers' expectation that the intruders had fled for the gate. *Showtime*, Stonecrop thought. Couto pointed to Stonecrop and then himself, made a motion like his fingers were taking only a single step. He raised three fingers for the countdown.

Stonecrop stood motionless and tense. He could see his breath and feared giving away his position. He waited. Couto was measuring his adversaries' advances, attuned to each footfall, and no doubt counting them to determine exactly how many targets would be exposed when he and Stonecrop engaged them. The goal was to do as much damage as possible in the shortest possible time. The voices were now clear enough to make out a few words.

Couto started the countdown: Three, two, one—

Stonecrop aped Couto's movement. He realized now why Couto had wanted to be across from him. Couto shot lefthanded. They could each shoot while exposing almost no target area. And their adversaries would be confused by the source of fire coming from locations on both sides of the alley.

On *three* the defilade caught one man fully exposed. Their shooting was perfectly synchronized. The four shots were indistinguishable from two. The shadow, now with a face and features—a thin moustache and dock hat—stretched out in space, pinned in the air by the impacts of four bullets that had crisscrossed his torso. Like a modern dancer giving the performance of a lifetime, the body rocked back on its heels and arms shot skyward. There was a brief and hollow silence in the aftermath of the gunfire and, as hearing returned, a muffled thud that induced an involuntary exhalation as the man, recast as a corpse, gave its last breath.

Their emotional states were anything but in sync. Couto had acted with the sangfroid of a professional doing his job: he had exposed himself long enough to look up and down the alley, his eyes checked high for snipers and low for trip wires or whatever. One glance revealed tell-tale movements from the remaining assailants who had dived for cover when their point man had been cut down.

Stonecrop had felt the life drain from the man's eyes and couldn't shake the image. He accepted, as he had in the past and in similar situations, that he was not cut out for this sort of thing.

The shooters had immediately retreated behind containers for cover. Another sound broke the silence. A man had jumped into the alley and fired wildly. Several rounds ricocheted off the steel-walled containers, some distant, some nearby. Stonecrop heard one or two footsteps as the man advanced. Before he had a chance to coordinate his response with Couto, Couto jumped around the corner a second time and fired. The two rounds had found home and the man crumpled face down in the dirt. No one would have a chance against Couto, Stonecrop reflected. He was unpredictable, insanely quick, and deadly.

Couto's take-down was followed by a swarm of bullets pinballing through the alleyway. Even in the thick air and at this late hour, someone must have heard the racket and called the *Policía*. The volley clearly made the point that he and Couto were outgunned. Well-armed backup must have moved from the exit gate to rejoin the first team.

Couto, without exposing his head or torso, emptied the rest of his magazine in the general direction of the source of the automatic fire.

"Sig MPX," he yelled across the gap between them. "Good choice. I mean, for them it's a good choice."

Couto peeked around the corner. Once again, a finger went to his lips and ordered silence. *Why is he grinning?* He loved this shit, Stonecrop realized. *He enjoys this as much as I hate it.*

Couto switched hands and inserted a fresh magazine. An ambidextrous shooter. *Like me.* They set up as before, but this time lacked the element of surprise. Couto's strategy appeared to have changed. He once again conveyed his thoughts in a flurry of hand signals that Stonecrop failed to understand. Stonecrop unsuccessfully tried to convey that fact to Couto. Finally, in a mad inspiration, he put the Glock on the ground, stared at Couto, and did the Macarena. The antic shattered Couto's composure. The eyes sparkled and let down their guard. He had to cover his mouth to hold back the laugh.

"Wait to fire, barrel down and out of sight, stand at forty-five degrees, same as before!" he got out the words in a loud whisper.

Stonecrop now knew the drill. If someone approached and the two of them were viewing the target at the same angle, they would see the target at the same time and not be caught in each other's fire. A second consideration was that they would be out of sight of the backup shooters. At such close range, if the point had an automatic weapon and if he moved faster than Couto and Stonecrop, he would slice them to ribbons.

Pick'em off, one by one—was that Couto's plan?

Exactly as predicted, the blunt nose of a Sig MPX appeared. Stonecrop didn't wait for Couto to move. Their success depended upon their creating a momentary confusion and delay in their assailant's response, a delay that marked the difference between life and death. Four rounds hit the man. Stonecrop had shot for the torso. The rounds were on target but the man had been wearing a Kevlar vest. Stonecrop recognized him as their guide.

Couto, reading in advance what Stonecrop would do and trusting him to do his part, put two rounds in the man's face. Couto was smiling his funny half-smile. He wore the expression of a teacher who was pleased that his student had done well. Couto was a natural hunter, instinctual, and never the prey. Without having to think, he knew when to wait and when to strike. What a fluke that he, Stonecrop, had caught Couto by surprise in Maputo. Plain dumb luck. They both knew that.

Dropping team two's point man led to another lull in the action. After losing three men, their attackers would be wary. If they had the numbers, they could fan out and start spraying into the narrow gaps between the containers. Stonecrop doubted they had the manpower, time, or desire to make that kind of ruckus. If they did, then the only way out, Stonecrop reasoned, was up. Someplace where they could wait and hope that the commotion would rouse the *Policía Municipal*. Stonecrop looked at Couto and pointed overhead. Couto tilted his head, pointed a finger, and made circles: *you're crazy*.

Instead of responding, Stonecrop put one foot against the container in front of him and braced the other, along with his back, against the container behind. He holstered the Glock and put a hand on each wall. Couto did the same. Chimneying between the damp sidewalls of the containers took concentration. As a climber, Stonecrop had the muscle memory and had been through this exercise a thousand times, on surfaces wet and dry, in the Alps, the Dolomites, Yosemite, and the Rockies.

The technique for Couto was relatively new. He was steady but slow. His shoes, though the soles were excellent, fit loosely. He moved carefully. Halfway up the third container—his column was three high —he slipped and caught himself by grabbing the rim of the roof of the container. He hung there, vulnerable and struggling to reposition himself.

Stonecrop had reached the top of his stack of four containers. He risked a look from the top. Two men were inching forward and ten meters or so from where they would be able to see Couto. Without hesitation, Stonecrop backed up, crouched like he was about to run a hundred-meter dash, and ran toward Couto's column. With legs spinning like an air runner in a ninja movie, he flew across the alleyway and crash landed on the wet top of the three-stack. He tripped over one of the support brackets, rolled onto his backside, and slid, splayed and out of control for another few feet. The impact knocked the Glock out from its holster and into the black void below. An enfilade of gunfire combed the air behind him. He leaned over the side of the container and clasped Couto's wrist. Couto pushed off a fitting on the side of the container and with a hoist from Stonecrop flopped over the top.

"What, no cape?" Couto joked.

"You okay?"

"Promise, amigo," was Couto's thanks. He put an arm around Stonecrop's shoulder.

Stonecrop thought about the *amigo*, nodded back, and returned the cheer. Then admitted, "I lost the Glock."

"I saw; we'll make do."

Without a weapon, Stonecrop felt helpless.

Couto must have sensed it. "You're not gonna get hysterical on me?"

Stonecrop laughed, gallows humor again. No, there'd be no hysteria. Stonecrop was never hysterical and, senses permitting, would be acutely conscious of everything right up to the last instant of his existence.

A voice from below echoed between the container walls and emerged from where the light met the shadows. The men had not risked stepping into the dark abyss from which Stonecrop had extracted Couto.

"Max. Do you hear me? Max Stonecrop. You know who I am."

He did indeed recognize the voice: Harry Chum.

"A nasty mix-up," the familiar voice announced. "Terrible. So terribly sorry," the voice pleaded. "We botched things, you see. Security didn't know it was you, you and your buddy. You really shouldn't have brought him."

Stonecrop ordered, "Put your weapons on the ground."

Couto scrunched a face at Stonecrop, disapproving the polite talk.

He slipped his hand down the front of his pants, pursed his lips, squinted, and emitted a mousy squeak as he ripped off the tape securing the extra magazine to his inner thigh. Stonecrop grinned, shook his head and looked down. Couto inserted the fresh magazine into the hand grip of the Beretta and stowed the near-empty one in the now-free carrier on his shoulder strap. He tested the weight of the gun. The extra rounds were for weight as much as firepower, to make the handgun more stable.

Surprising Stonecrop, Couto handed over the Beretta. He didn't know why, but Couto wanted him to take the shot. Couto answered by holding a finger to his right eye. The take down would be better for a right-handed shooter who could hug the edge of the container and minimize exposure. Couto was ambidextrous, but apparently his right eye—was it from the fire in Maputo?—wasn't his best.

"Mozambique the mother-fucker," Couto hissed the words and pointed to the dark edge of the container along the alley from where Stonecrop should take the shot.

"Harry, what's going on?" Stonecrop took the weapon and spoke to stall Chum. He intentionally projected his voice from the top of the container right above the alleyway so that whoever was below would assume that was his location.

"Listen, Max. I swear. It's all a big mix-up. You're safe, now. Forklift's on the way, along with a crew to clean up the mess. I can whisk you two out of here, no questions asked. How about dinner at Mediterráneo? The three of us, nice and cozy. Sort things out over a glass. What d' you say?"

The forklift's mechanical march was audible. It was muffled by the fog but grew louder as the machine approached. They didn't risk a look.

"All straightened out," Chum continued. "I swear to god. Called an ambulance. Policía Municipal—hear the sirens! Listen, I'd like to get you out of here. Back to your Federica. She's home right now. I know she is, this very minute, sleeping like a baby. Got someone watching her."

Stonecrop opened his phone. The Find My Phone app showed Federica at home on Susenbergstrasse. He sent her a text.

<<MS: you ok?>>

The response was unnerving.

<<FR: Until you called. Sleeping. Work at 7. What's up? Shit the>>

<<MS: Lock door call Gregor>>

He waited for a response. Getting none, texted again: <<MS: you there?>>

<<FR: To late to bad by>>

"Illiterate cocksucker! Someone's got Fede's phone," Stonecrop's brain was panicking.

When Stonecrop showed him the text, Couto's expression hardened.

"Henrique, I know that's you," Chum yelled. "I'm on your side too, and Ibrahim Adewole's. I spoke to him tonight. No worries, truly. Neither one of you need to worry."

"Adewole," Couto voiced the word so softly that Stonecrop had to replay the word. "Of course! He's in Chum's pocket. You get it lad, their bedfellows. Fucking perverted, that is."

"Seems Chum's not out to nail Adewole. They're after something else . . ." Stonecrop responded, though frantic inside and eager to contact Gregor to protect Fede and his children.

"Adewole knew I wouldn't touch Lomi," Stonecrop said. "That's why he tagged you for the job. But Chum was who told Adewole to keep me away from Halbinsel Au. And Chum's the jerk who attacked her. He's limping I bet. Lomi stomped the guy's foot. I want to see his face, see if it's torn up."

Couto crept toward the edge of the container. Stonecrop grabbed him. They'd pick him off.

"I'm texting Gregor."

"Max, Henrique," Chum yelled. "Not much time, my friends. You are my friends."

The text went to both Vormittag and Gregor: <<MS: Fede in danger now armed intruder at Ott. Chum attacked Lomi.>>

Again, he showed the text to Couto.

"You there, Max? Time's a-wasting my friends."

"Move," Couto ordered and pointed to a spot midway and along the side edge of the container. Stonecrop made his way there. If anybody from the alleyway looked in the shadows, their eyes would take time to adjust. For Stonecrop, being in the dark and shooting into the light would be an advantage. The big unknown was whether or not Chum and his cohorts would be in the firing line from the gap between the containers.

Stonecrop leaned over the side of container and lay splayed out like he was back on the biathlon range, Beretta at the ready. Couto removed and eased his hat over the edge of the container. A volley of bullets sprayed the ridge of container.

Stonecrop had hoped to have a clear shot at Chum, but one of his goons was in the way. Even so, Chum and company were foolish to be standing in the light and in line with the space between the containers where they had last scene Couto.

Work with what you got. Stonecrop visualized himself at the range, totally focused and relaxed; a mental place he had been at a thousand times in biathlon training and competitions. As he exhaled, he squeezed the trigger and put a round through the front of the neck of the goon standing next to Chum. He intentionally aimed forward of the man's spine so the bullet would be minimally deflected and would retain enough force to strike Chum.

"Brilliant," Couto shouted at him and pumped a fist.

He risked a peek after the commotion. The shot had struck home.

The man hit in the neck was on his knees, hands at his throat, and making gurgling noises. Chum had yelped and was holding his shoulder. Stonecrop tossed the Beretta to Couto. He caught it in both hands, but when he eased to the edge of the container, a burst of gunfire from below made him back off. Chum was wounded and one more assailant was down, but Stonecrop and Couto were still trapped.

The forklift approached. The outstretched silver tines were perched high on the yellow mast.

"That'll do, gents," a Kiwi accented voice ordered.

A short exchange of gunfire ensued, followed by a shot-gun blast that punctuated the end of the armed dialogue.

A second voice, this one also familiar. "Harry, behave yourself."

"Wes, thank god it's you!" Chum whined. "They had me cornered. Two more up there. I tried to stop them."

Stonecrop and Couto eased forward.

Freddy from the yacht raised his weapon but lowered it when he recognized Stonecrop. Couto understood the man was no enemy, so he and Stonecrop dropped their legs over the side of the container. From their balcony seats, they watched the scene below play out.

Wes Waterman looked up from his seat on the forklift and nodded to them. He kept the shotgun leveled at Chum. On one side of Chum, a pile of flesh lay in a growing puddle of blood, the recipient of a near point-blank shotgun blast. On the other side of Chum, a second black pool grew around the man Stonecrop had shot through the neck.

"This'll be interesting." Couto smiled and twirled his hat around in hands, jabbing a finger in and out of a fresh hole.

"Stop them from what, Harry?" Waterman asked.

"E-waste, they're shipping WEEE and weapons to Nigeria. I've got all the players. I wanted to make sure before—"

"Before what? Harry, did you get a promotion? Operations Officer, are we?" Waterman asked.

"Not officially, Wes. But you know how that goes. Swim first, then they teach you to swim." Chum still seemed hopeful that he could talk his way out of the mess he had created.

"Ah, so that's how it works? Always wondered." Waterman turned to Freddy, confirming that Freddy had Chum covered.

"Gentlemen," he shouted, "a lift?" Waterman swung the forklift tines around and skimmed the top of their container. Each man stepped on a blade and held the mast as it descended in a series of short, clumsy jerks to ground level.

Hennie hopped off first. Quite cheery, he addressed Waterman and Freddy, "Good timing, and all." He practically skipped as he retrieved his briefcase, extracted the Maglite, and headed toward the dark slot where Stonecrop had lost the Glock. He didn't step into the shadows, however, having doubts or a last-minute thought.

"The vest, Harry. Be a good lad and give me the vest."

Chum was in no condition to take off the Kevlar vest himself. Couto had really been asking Waterman if he could approach Chum and take it. Waterman gave the okay and Couto removed the garment and ignored the pain the act inflicted on Chum's shoulder.

He faced Chum as he donned the vest. Like a photographer posing his subject, his hand took Chum's chin and turned his face to one side and then the other, examining the fresh scars. Twice, he lightly slapped Chum's cheek over a tender place where Lomi's nails had raked the skin. Chum winced but otherwise stood still.

Couto's message was clear enough. *You're a dead man.*

"If I was them, I'd a sent one more around the side. You see anything?" Couto was speaking to Waterman. His eyes, however, were locked on Chum.

"Which side, Harry?" he continued.

Chum didn't speak, but his body language gave him away. He was for once transparent.

Couto placed the Beretta under Chum's chin and closed the gap between the two of them, their faces an inch apart. Chum's eyes darted to the passage where Couto had tried to climb up between the containers.

"Be right back," he said, and then slipped into the dark slot, Beretta drawn.

"Should I give him a hand?" Freddy spoke as he pulled Chum's arms behind his back and secured them with a zip-tie around the wrists.

Waterman shook his head no and then looked at Chum.

"How many more, Harry? I count one. I assure you, *I* have backup."

"Wouldn't know," Chum lied. He'd lost the audience. Everyone knew it was a lie.

And everyone ducked as the sound of three shots reverberated from within the black canyon into which Couto had disappeared.

Stonecrop stared at the ground. Vacant, malodorous death lay at his feet. He eased the bloodied Sig MPX from under the man without a throat. Though nauseous and sick with fear, he decided he should follow Couto, to help the man he'd once tried to kill and now accepted as a friend. He gagged and swallowed bile in his throat.

Freddy and Waterman watched. The silence was broken by heaving breaths originating from the black void that had whale-like swallowed Couto.

"A hand, mates," Couto hollered.

Stonecrop put down the Sig and ran toward the sound. He collided with Couto before his eyes had adjusted to the dark.

"You okay?"

"Better than this bastard!" Couto grunted.

The man Couto supported was gasping in deep, uneasy breaths. Couto had holstered the Beretta. Stonecrop's Glock and another nine-millimeter handgun flopped around in Couto's baggy coat pockets. Once in the light, the man's wounds were obvious. Couto's knife-work had been enough to disable but not kill him.

"Hay otros?" Couto leaned over his victim: "Verdad o navaja?" He brought out and flashed the knife in front the man's terror-filled face. No translation was required. Couto had offered the man a choice: truth or the blade.

"No," the face answered to the knife. "No más! No más!"

"Gentlemen," Waterman addressed Couto and Stonecrop, "can you find your way to Gate Eight? It's cleared and you're free to go. I'll tidy up here."

"Retired, huh?" Stonecrop addressed Waterman.

"Obviously not entirely. My apologies for the misdirection."

"You knew all along what Chum was up to?" Stonecrop asked.

"We thought so. But we did didn't truly see the entire picture until today."

"When I first called the harbor master and was directed to a slip next to *Juliette,* that was your doing?"

"It was."

"And Hennie?" Stonecrop wanted to know if Hennie had been part Waterman's plan.

"A wild card, Mr. Couto was . . . and is. We were concerned, assuming at first that since he was working for Adewole that he was also working with Chum. That was clearly not the case. Caught us by surprise. We also assumed that at some point we would have to . . . restrain Mr. Couto."

"Hence the dinner reservation at Mediterráneo. You had people there."

"We did," Waterman said. "But everybody played nice-nice."

Stonecrop shook his head. "That would've gone south fast if your people would have tried anything." He had learned that one ought never take Henrique Couto for granted. Another realization came to Stonecrop, namely that Couto was not only good at his work, but that he was loyal to those he worked with. He must have felt deeply betrayed by Gregor. Couto deserved the truth; Stonecrop vowed that he would have it.

"I'm inclined to agree." Waterman offered an obvious nod of respect toward Couto. "We underestimated him," Waterman said to Stonecrop and then turned to face Couto. "In a number of ways. Won't happen again, Henrique!"

Couto looked up and winked at Waterman. "Guy and gal, corner table, north side, best view of the exits, big purple purse on the table. Best seats to cover the action." He had fingered Waterman's people the second he had walked in the door.

Couto returned to busying himself with hardware. First order of business was wiping down his knife. He ejected the magazine from the gun that had belonged to his assailant and tossed the weapon and magazine to the ground between the two corpses. The retrieved Glock was returned to Stonecrop.

"Outside the gate," Waterman directed with a hand gesture, "is an old Audi, a black S3." He handed the key fob to Stonecrop. "It's mine. Leave the key with the attendant at the marina. Freddy provisioned *Zaca*. Lie low a few days, maybe a nice sail to Collioure. You know it?"

Stonecrop indicated that he did not.

"Castle of the Templars, nice replicas of works painted in Collioure by Matisse and Derain. And good moorings."

"I can't," Stonecrop replied. "I think one of Chum's men is threatening Fede—now. I sent a text to Gregor and Vormittag."

Chum had been silent until that moment. Probably he had been debating whether to play the diplomat or play the thug and threaten that if he were arrested, then Federica would be harmed.

"I can't guarantee her safety," Chum piped in. When they looked at him, he added, "Unless you guarantee mine." If that was an attempt to find a middle ground, it failed.

"My, my, Harry!" Waterman seemed pleased by the threat. "Acting career over? Too late for an Oscar, I fear."

Stonecrop dialed Ratzow, who picked up immediately.

Ratzow didn't bother with a greeting. "She is good," he laughed. "Da, wait, you wait . . ."

Stonecrop heard an excited Gregor Ratzow giving orders, "Is good, Vittore? Like this, I like this . . . smile when I fart, asshole! . . . Da, beautiful. Is for Tavate."

"Gregor, what is going on?"

"Wait. Vittore, hurry, send picture!"

A message from Ratzow's phone appeared on Stonecrop's handy and displayed a photo of Gregor illuminated by auto headlamps and curbside at Susenbergstrasse. He was standing like a big game hunter with one foot resting on the butt of a man, a big mean-looking man, a very unhappy man, whose head had been pressed against the asphalt. The brim of his cap hip-hopped to one side. Jenny stood beside Gregor. She was all smiles and waving at the photographer. Rosie licked their captive's face.

"Christ, Gregor!"

"You want me to fry fish or see if swim in cement?"

Waterman asked for the phone and then asked to speak with Kommissar Vormittag. He put the handy on speaker.

"Kommissar, this is Wes Waterman. We spoke a few days ago. Is everything under control there?"

"Ja," Vormittag answered before switching to English. "Everything is in order."

"Have you been reinstated?" Waterman asked.

"Not officially. However, that does not prevent me from detaining this man for the Kanton Polizei. They are en route and will be here in one moment."

Stonecrop was beginning to relax, enough so that he detected Vormittag's disquiet and awkward, literal English.

"We have taken care of things on our end," Waterman said. He looked at the surrounding scene of death and mayhem before continuing. "I want to apologize again, for the deception promulgated by our erstwhile colleague Mr. Harry Chum. He is under arrest. I plan to speak with your chief to commend and recognize your role in this operation."

"Thank you, Herr Waterman. Now that I think over that," Vormittag bumbled along, "in fact, I would prefer that we—help me with the English expression—'let the dirt settle' before you speak to either Kanton or Stadt authorities."

"How much time do you need?"

"A week, perhaps. I . . . since I was on leave, I promised my wife some days someplace warm and with sunshine."

"As you wish, Kommissar. Let's give that *dust* plenty of time to settle." Waterman went on, his tone of voice somewhat apologetic, "This has been an unfortunate affair. I will do my best to set things right."

"Thank you, Herr Waterman." The gracious Vormittag sounded relieved.

"One more thing," Waterman added. Vormittag waited for

Waterman to finish. "Just as you and I, and Kantonpolizei, were taken in by this charlatan, so were Messrs. Ratzow, Stonecrop, and Couto. I would not want them to be treated unfairly."

"I understand," Vormittag slipped into Kommissar speak. "There are two matters that require attention. If Mr. Chum is, as it appears, responsible for the assault on Lomi, he must answer for that. I mean answer to local authorities. Second, there is the matter of aggregating the e-waste. Kantonpolizei will want names of companies and individuals who engaged in *illegal* disposal of e-waste. Ah, Ja. One more thing—a report concerning a vehicle owned by Group traveling at nearly two-hundred kilometers per hour on Julier Pass."

"Surely this is not a serious matter, Kommissar?"

"The penalties are . . . I don't know the actual penalties, but I assure you they are very serious."

Couto slapped Stonecrop on the back and let the hand rest on his shoulder. Stonecrop hung his head. "I'm screwed."

Waterman held up a finger to Stonecrop, indicating that he should be quiet. He continued with the Kommissar: "Herr Vormittag, if the vehicle had temporary OSCE plates, would that make a difference?"

"What is—"

"Organization for Security and Co-operation in Europe." Waterman winked at Stonecrop.

"Possibly. I don't know if OSCE is an affiliated organization in Switzerland," Vormittag replied. "Please ask Max to speak with me when he returns."

"And you will have our complete cooperation," Waterman answered and saw that Stonecrop, though grateful for Waterman's intervention, was eager to retrieve his handy. "I'm ringing off. Thank you, Kommissar."

The gate was unlocked as promised. Waterman's Audi was there as promised. Stonecrop drove with care through a parade of flashing lights and braying sirens from police vehicles and ambulances queueing up at an adjacent gate.

"We not going to marina, are we?" Couto asked.

"Hell no," Stonecrop confirmed and added with no lack of sarcasm, "A four-day cruise? You gotta be kidding. Waterman wants us out of his hair while he does damage control here and in Zürich, and wherever else Harry stirred the pot."

"Airport, is it?" Couto asked.

"Yup," Stonecrop handed his phone to Couto to check for flights.

There were usually several a day.

"Got to drop off the hardware and pick up my pass and few other things. Need an hour, maybe a little more." Couto read the phone display as he spoke. "Direct's not until two. It's what, five?"

"Hungry?" Stonecrop asked.

"Worked up an appetite, gotta admit."

"Change of plans. Freddy provisioned *Zaca*. We go to the marina. I cook. We eat, clean up, then hit the airport. How's that?"

"You're okay, Stonecrop. For a guy who tried to kill me, you're really okay. Max . . ." Couto paused.

"Yes."

"Slow down. I don't want a goddammed speeding ticket."

Couto exhaled and slouched in the seat, maybe the first time Stonecrop witnessed the man with his guard down. He removed his hat, twirled it around in his hands, occasionally wiggled a finger through the hole, and like a little kid chuckled to himself.

Stonecrop told his phone to call Federica.

Silvaplana

The breeze was fresh and full of mischief, gently luring one into complacency and the next moment snatching napkins off of laps. Mattie, Stonecrop's ex-wife, waved and then planted a hand atop her sun hat. Another wave and the breeze behaved, as if from its al fresca podium she and Café Sol's host were orchestrating the perfect outdoor Lake Silvaplana dining experience. She blew off the offer to be escorted to a table, removed her overlarge sunglasses, and strutted back into Stonecrop's life with the swagger of an A-list runway model. Unlike a runway model, Mattie never ran in circles. And she journeyed with purpose in her eyes, not vacuity.

Atypically for a European restaurant, whispers and phosphorescent glimpses trailed in her wake. Upon arrival she halted and let the busy-body turbulence exhaust itself. Customers young and old—tourist and locals here to sun, swim, and kiteboard—reengaged with drinks, meals, and tablemates. Stonecrop scanned the shore for his girls and Sandro and saw the triumvirate seated side-by-side-by-side on a paddleboard and talking and gesturing non-stop the way teens do.

Federica and Stonecrop were in bathing suits still damp from a two-kilometer swim. Over the Speedo, Stonecrop wore a loose cotton shirt and a pair of baggy Harlem capris. Federica had on a long-sleeve chemise to protected her from the sun and to hide twin bruises that ringed her upper arms. She had brushed aside questions about the encounter with her hirsute assailant. There was, Stonecrop noticed, additional discoloration around the neck. "Later," she had said to his inquiries, "I'll tell you later." Later had yet to arrive.

They were a pair, a bundle of violent blemishes, aches, and pains. The swim had loosened up the bruised muscle tissue. The sitting brought it back. València had been hard on him. *I'm soft*, he confessed to himself and then wondered how Couto was fairing.

Federica's gaze swung back and forth between Mattie and Stonecrop. She reached under the table, under Stonecrop's shirt and pants and into his speedo. He started and reached down for her hand. He quickly realized the hand wasn't going anywhere until she decided to let go.

"Nervous?" Federica asked, as feisty as he'd seen her in some time.

He was trapped. Both god-grade women, powerful in their own ways, commanded whatever turf they occupied. He, a lowly mortal—and a male at that—was ground zero.

A broad-rimmed hat more appropriate to the French Rivera than the sportif Engadina region protected Mattie's face from the sun. She thrust out her arm like a lance about to pierce the heart of an adversary and stepped up to their table.

Federica's hand left the damp sphagnum of Stonecrop's crotch and grasped the stick-fingered hand of her opposite. Once freed of Federica's grasp, Mattie picked up a napkin from the table, wiped the hand, and seated herself.

"I do miss that," she said by way of greeting, embarrassing Stonecrop but earning points with Federica. "At last, we meet in the flesh. Skype calls don't do you justice, Federica. You're much prettier in the flesh."

The barb, if that what it was, flew by its target unnoticed and unacknowledged.

"Sarah and Jenny have missed you. They are absolutely wonderful children. I wish I'd had more time with them."

Stonecrop flagged the waiter, ordered a glass of house white for Mattie and refills for himself and Fede. At least the waiter was aware that he was sitting at the table. *I drink, therefore I am*. He did drink and took in more wine than expected. He had mistaken the wine glass for a water glass and forced a hard swallow. He belched. The women continued to ignored him.

"I wish that, too," Mattie replied. Was that kind or not? A haughty tone clung to her voice. "I so do."

Mattie turned her body to face Stonecrop, offering perfection and wealth, giving him a moment to appreciate too late what he had lost. "Well, soldier. How's the battle going?"

She was referring to either to his recovery from Mozambique or the divorce. Hard to say. She had no knowledge of his recent entanglements, which, in their own way, had been equally violent and traumatizing. Speaking with her in person made him uncomfortable. The computer or phone screen had made their interactions antiseptic and safe.

"I am well, Mattie. You?"

"You look fit," she said, and as an aside to Federica, added, "He's always fit. It doesn't make you immortal, did you know that, Max?"

"Germans say 'in form'," Federica offered.

"You are quite the linguist, I hear."

"A regular polyglot . . . intermediate Spanish and German." Federica's reply was a beyond ludicrous understatement.

Stonecrop assumed she was weighing whether or not to recant what she had just said. She went with the latter. Mattie, more the talker than a listener, seemed not to care.

"Max, who is no longer *my* Max, what do you do with all these precocious women in your life?"

"I'm used to it," he chirped back, openly happy with his fate.

"And art? Do you miss art?"

"No," he paused and changed his response. "Yes, a little. I work parttime at a gallery in town. Small, but Herr Bachman, the owner, knows his stuff."

"I don't *get* art," Federica stepped into the batter's box.

"What don't you *get*?" Mattie said, well-intentioned this time, not catty. Stonecrop could read her tone like an open book.

"Art is ubiquitous and important to people, people everywhere. Always has been. Max really cares. But why? I know that's a stupid thing to ask. I'm sorry."

"Not at all, Federica." Mattie sipped wine to clear her throat. She swished it around her mouth and Stonecrop honestly thought that the wine would go the way of mouthwash.

"Everyone has a theory; a million people, a million theories."

"And yours?"

"My theory du jour—someone in my line must have something controversial to say to impress gallery owners and museum curators— is that Art is coeval with shame. Man's nature is to destroy everything he sees. Art has to atone for his base behavior. A pet theory. Happy to attempt a defense if you'd like to argue. That's how we come to understand, don't you agree?"

"I do. Thank you. I see that part of Max in you, Max the philosopher. Did you study philosophy . . ."

The conversation proceeded as if Max were not present. Stonecrop watched kite-boarders skimming above the lake, working the wind-stippled surface. The sport took technique more than strength. One boarder, who looked to be about the same age as his daughters, would go airborne, grab the front of her board, switch hands, and then grab the back of the board; a simple trick. He saw Sarah following the boarder's motions, mimicking the stunt. He felt himself doing the same. He and Sarah were, as they say, cut from the same cloth.

Mattie pushed Stonecrop's wine glass forward on the table's surface, an inch or two, allergic to the commonplace.

"Your father," she continued to address Federica, "is in trucking or transportation. Is that right?"

"Taught me to drive a semi when I was sixteen," Federica lied in her best 'merican accent.

"My, my. Spanish and semis. And—oh yes—medicine, there's that." Mattie wasn't fooled for a second. "Max is a lucky man."

"Sarah and Jenny," Federica started to speak, then stopped to rearrange herself. She was bored, even annoyed. Stonecrop could tell by the way she slouched and plunked her elbows on the table. Her wine glass tilted left then right, suspended on the tips of her fingers that presented an exacting display of fine motor control. "Sarah and Jenny are wonderful."

Aware that he had not even made an introduction, Stonecrop felt obligated to say something. "Matts, what kept you in Paris. Work?"

The question spawned a rueful grin. "*You* kept me in Paris, dear."

The wine arrived. With the flair and drama of a Hollywood actress from the 50s, Mattie thrust a stick-like arm upward. Her hand hovered in the air and waited for the glass to float off the tray and into the fingers of its new owner and commander. The tray tremored and re-steadied.

"*Me?*" Stonecrop replied.

"Are you playing dumb or are you truly that oblivious?" she prodded him with both words and the wine glass in her hand.

"He needed time," Federica saved Stonecrop from further embarrassment and Mattie from further explanation, "to be a dad again, the time you gave him."

"Well said! See, Max, Federica, who is not even a parent—as far as I know—understands," Mattie lectured, in the right and proud of it.

Stonecrop realized that he agreed with her and had nothing to add. Had he been asked to take the children for an extended period, he would have declined. His excuse would have been that he wasn't ready; whereas the truth was, one was never ready. Parenting was something one shows up for, ready or not.

"Speak of the devil . . ." Max said, as Jenny ran up and gave her mother a big hug.

"Hungry?" he asked to the table. Knowing the answer, he rose and left the three of them to continue without him.

Walking to the service buffet, he saw that Sandro and Sarah were holding hands and leaning against each other, tilting back and forth in unison, aware, he was sure, that these might be their last hours together for some time to come.

He returned in fifteen minutes with a platter of snacks.

"Tell me, Jenny," Mattie asked, "what was to most fun thing you did with your dad?"

Jenny looked first to Federica, who locked eyes with Jenny and challenged her without having to say a word—*how you gonna answer that one!* Then Jenny gave Stonecrop that look that precedes a volley of annoying questions. She walked behind Stonecrop, wrapped her arms around him and whispered in his ear. Though she whispered, she intended others at the table hear her request.

"Pops, can you walk me auf die Toilette?"

Before anyone else at the table could offer, Stonecrop stood up and took her hand. *A parenting moment*, he said to himself. *I can demonstrate a normal parenting moment. And, of course, his reaction notwithstanding, it was a parenting moment.*

They walked hand in hand, unhurried, winding through the tables, and found the restrooms at the back of the outdoor bar.

"You don't really have to go, do you?" he asked.

"No."

"So, what's up?"

"Well, I love Mom. But I don't think she'd understand. You know, like Kommissar Vormittag said, about someone not being ready for the truth."

"And that has to do with what?" he asked.

"Okay. So, the most *fun* I had was saving your life. That was like the coolest thing I ever, ever did. And making friends with Hennie, even though he's supposed to be this really bad guy. And making friends with Destiny too, and she's a prostitute—"

"She is not a prostitute!" Stonecrop interrupted and corrected her. "And Lomi was . . . Well, it's complicated. You know that."

"Yeah, I do. You know what I mean, okay."

"Okay." He agreed, but the way he said it admonished.

"And the next most *fun* thing was saving Federica—"

"Hold on here. Just how did you save Federica?" This claim, Stonecrop believed, was really a stretch. He had heard nothing about Jenny's actions the night of the intrusion at Frau Ott's. That said, Jenny had been in the staged photo of Ratzow with his foot on the butt of the man caught at Federica's. The big game hunter and his humiliated kill.

"Federica didn't tell you? Or Kommissar Vormittag, did he tell you?"

"No one said anything," he answered.

"Well, when you called to warn Federica about that guy—he was already there, inside the house and it was like four in the morning. Rosie was barking, but she's always barking at something and nothing ever wakes up Federica. Except your call did."

"What are you saying, Jenny?"

"Well, I heard the phone and saw the creep and called Kommissar Vormittag."

"You had his number?"

"He said it, remember, at the hospital. I remembered because it was like mostly perfect numbers. I mean, how cool *is* that, a phone number with perfect numbers! Anyway, he came right over. I think he'd been sleeping in the car next to the house."

"I didn't notice—" Stonecrop tried, unsuccessfully, to remember the Kommissar's number. He had dialed it many times.

"And I woke Alicia. She was there and she and Federica had been really drinking a lot—are they lovers, Max?—they said a bunch of silly stuff. I think sometimes they sleep in the same bed. But last night Fede had to work early so they were in separate beds. I had to like shove Alicia hard to wake her up. I put my hand over her mouth so she wouldn't make any noise and the creep wouldn't hear."

"Jesus, Jenny. I don't think they're lovers. They *are* close friends. Why do you—"

"I hide on the stairs and listen—"

He wanted to ask more, but Jenny pressed ahead. "And Alicia had her gun and—she was naked, Max, it was so rad! She walked up behind this guy—he was like hovering over Federica in the bed—and Alicia *clobbered him!* Right on the head. He was out but woke up pretty fast. She like kept guard—like she was this naked lady with a gun . . . so rad! Then Fede's dad and the Kommissar got there, one right after the other."

"Odd, no one told me about any of this. I was unaware that Alicia was there," Stonecrop said.

"Yeah, I think maybe that was the point. Destiny kind of explained it to me. Girls like to hang out, you know, without dumb guys around."

He doubted Jenny's explanation. What he didn't doubt was the likelihood of Claudia posting a guard or asking Vormittag to keep an eye on Frau Ott's while Stonecrop was away—even before he had made the call from València.

"Any more *fun stuff* you're considering sharing?" He dreaded the answer as he asked the question.

"Sure, I mean I learned all about human trafficking and being a sex worker—like how much money you make. And, you know, the skate-park and meeting Sandro and his drawing me."

"And just what *was* your question?" His head was swimming.

"What do I tell Mom?"

Jenny, after they had arrived at the toilets and had been standing there for a time, decided that she did indeed need to pee. Stonecrop waited outside the ladies' room, laughing to himself, at times shaking his head—a man in a conversation with himself—and smiling at the sky, the exquisite day, and marveling at his own ignorance about love and life, and his adoration for his children and Federica. He owed Alicia, and others. He was, indeed, rich in friends.

"Goodness," Mattie said when they returned to their table, "that took quite a while. Did Daddy help his little girl?"

Jenny bristled at the *little girl* talk.

"Yes. *Daddy*," she paused at the word 'Daddy,' testing the foreign feel of the word on her lips, "helped."

Jenny had been a smart-ass. She rallied to derail the 'Daddy' business.

"Fun," she announced the word as if it were a topic for a TED talk. Jenny was addressing Mattie's earlier question, though by now Mattie had probably forgotten.

"The skate-park, Mom. That was the most fun. And when Sandro drew me."

Clearly wanting to keep the momentum positive, she dove into her backpack, found her notebook, and displayed a sketch for Mattie to see. This clever shunt side-tracked her mother who, as everyone at the table sensed, was fishing for the appropriate reprimand for Jenny's disrespect.

"I want to meet this Sandro!" Mattie blurted out.

As if directed to enter the stage, Sandro and Sarah arrived and stood beside her. Stonecrop had accepted that the two were a teen item. He liked Sandro. Sarah was level-headed and he trusted her decisions.

As if I had a choice!

"At your service," Sandro said, making nice in his best English to the mother of the girl whose hand he had not let go of for the last hour.

Mattie swiveled around to look at them. She was openly puzzled by Sandro's tattoo. No one volunteered an explanation, so she swiveled back to Federica.

"Amor fati!" Federica said.

"Come again?"

"Love of fate," Federica explained. "Nietzsche wrote *Eternal Recurrence* right here, in Silvaplana. The theory is ancient; he recast it. The idea is that our lives cycle through, constantly repeating what's happened before. The take-away is to accept who you are and what comes your way; it's fate."

"So, that's what this is? Sounds a rather fatalistic and depressing philosophy, don't you think?" Mattie said.

"Not at all," Federica laughed. "Not at all," she repeated and, mimicked Sarah by taking Stonecrop's hand. "Liberating, in fact!" She squeezed his hand hard, climber-hard. Stonecrop returned the gesture. Sarah registered the support and said thank you by raising her fist and Sandro's a few inches higher and giving a little fist-bump in the air.

Federica, like Stonecrop a few minutes earlier, enjoyed a silent conversation with herself—he saw her lips moving. She too had found something in the clouds that made her happy.

"Alicia's coming," she directed the statement to Stonecrop. "She'll be here tonight. Spa day with the girls tomorrow?"

"Sure, why not!" he said.

She looked Stonecrop in the eyes and said, "Good."

At the utterance, the others at the table, once discussants, quieted like a proper audience.

This was the Federica "good," the word she had transformed and made her own the first night they had made love. Fede's *good* started in the back of throat, a uvular consonant delivered with a faint poof of air. The word ended as her tongue rose uncertain about whether to touch the roof of her mouth. The word was sexual from start to finish, expectant and conclusive, indefinite and direct, enticing and assured.

"Good," she repeated.

Therme Tavate

The male attendant, attired in white and as stiff and starchy in demeanor as dress, placed his hand on the door of the "Wellness Room." He prepared to open the door for Stonecrop, who was also attired in white, in his case, floppy spa slippers and a terry cloth robe embossed with a gold wolf's paw crest.

Stonecrop peeked through the diamond shaped window in the door but saw nothing beyond the fogged glass. He waited, thinking the glass might clear, and thought about the last few days. His daughters had departed with Mattie. Couto and Lomi were in Zürich where Kommissar Vormittag had been reinstated and put in charge of wrapping up the city and Kanton's role in the Chum affair. Waterman had quietly receded from the spotlight—though not before he confided that he, not Chum, had arranged the deletion of Ratzow and Stonecrop from the Red List. Unwinding Stonecrop's fabricated past, he had added, was a work in progress and he advised Max to not leave Switzerland. Cleansing their records was, Waterman had explained, a fair deal for their cooperation with the Agency's effort to nab Chum.

Stonecrop stepped into the Wellness room expecting to see overweight, Speedo-clad Georgian kleptocrats. Instead, two women greeted him with friendly, though disinterested smiles. Both were in their mid-thirties and naked. One woman held her hair out of her face as she rotated under a beaded wall of water from an overhead perforated, copper pipe; the second woman reclined in a chaise. A careless towel lay thrown across her belly along with a splayed-open copy of some fashion rag. A third woman appeared and vanished behind a door labeled "Sauna."

Stonecrop nodded and lowered his gaze, "Pardon." He turned and exited the room and found Jorge exactly where he'd left him.

"I believe this is the women's spa," Stonecrop said.

The attendant, on stage, pegged Stonecrop as a Swiss baths novitiate. "Yes, this is the women's spa . . ." He paused, with the timing of a stand-up comic, ". . . and the men's."

"Right," Stonecrop said, "Of course."

He was saved from further embarrassment by the arrival of his spa-mates: Federica Ratzow and Alicia Gilli.

They unleashed a white-robed flurry of hugs and Zürcher air-kisses. Alicia threaded her arm through Stonecrop's and leaned into him with just enough intimacy to make him uncomfortable.

"Reinforcements!" Jorge quipped and re-opened the door Stonecrop had just exited.

"Jorge, e aí, como cê tá?" Federica slipped into Brazilian slang to say hello and ask Jorge how he was doing. Stonecrop noted the "J," which was soft like the French *Je*.

"Was that better?" she asked.

"Perfeito," Jorge replied. "A pleasure to see you again. Is Herr Ratzow visiting? Shall I book a massage or . . ." Jorge's voiced faltered when he saw the bruises on Federica's neck.

"Papà, I think, is not coming," she answered, and then responded to his gaze: "Don't want to talk about it. Girl time, you know." The comment satisfied Jorge, who now honored Stonecrop as one of the girls.

"My man," Federica winked, looking at Stonecrop but addressing Jorge.

Alicia confirmed Stonecrop's membership-ness by squeezing his arm to her chest.

Federica conducted them to the far end of the spa's wellness area. They discarded slippers and hung robes over a fat, brass tube that could have doubled as a bicycle rack. Six wide steps descended into a shallow canal that was separated from the pool by strip curtain of transparent plastic.

Over the last twenty-four hours, weather had changed seasons. The memory of swimming at Silvaplana, though only yesterday, felt like it had been months ago. Air frost hovered over the pool.

At the lead and afloat in the mineralized thirty-two-degree-centigrade water, Federica dove and re-surfaced beyond the plastic as a ghostly vapor-shroud form.

Submerged dividers split the end of the pool into three booths with tiled bench seats. The women sat next to each other; Stonecrop sat across from them. He took in their nakedness. Federica's plait had been loosed and nested on the shelf of one shoulder. Federica's legs wrapped Stonecrop's calves.

"Happy?"

"Mostly, yeah," he smiled back.

"Miss them already?"

"I do. It's like I'm this . . ." He searched for the right expression. "After everything we've been through, it's like I'm this empty vessel."

"They'll be fine," Federica smiled. "You'll be fine, too!"

Stonecrop closed his eyes. It took too much effort to be heard over the cascades of water.

"C'mon. *Wach auf!*" She tickled him.

He grinned a fake grin and yawned a real yawn. He had no idea how long he had slept. "No Wagner, please!"

Federica laughed again, "C'mon sailor, time for food."

Stonecrop had half-forgotten where he was. Clouds crowded the sky. The air temperature was rising, but still, the sun was a no-show. Federica guided him to the plastic curtain. He dove under the curtain and, on the other side, Alicia took an arm and lifted him to his feet. She gathered up the robes and slippers and they walked arm-in-arm to the room they first entered. Stonecrop made minute adjustments of his body's position under the shower bar so that hot water wrapped as much surface area as possible. He shut his eyes and pretended that he was not standing next to two very lovely, very attractive, and very naked women.

A few minutes later, he led Federica to chair, helped her dry, and handed her a robe. He was dead tired but trying to rally.

She wasn't fooled. "You okay?"

"Just cratered. Better now."

"Food will help," she said. "And a stange."

Twenty minutes later, the group trouped through the door of the Taverna Tavate. The ristorante was busier than last time with Couto. A bevy of Russian men and women packed the tables. Most guests wore the same embossed bathrobes and floppy slippers. Some of the men, hair caked with pomade, were fresh arrivals yet to hit the baths. The women with them, had not visited the baths or steam. Their dos had puffed up like muffins in the humid air.

The three of them found seats at the horseshoe-shaped bar. The bartender wiped down the countertop and they oriented the chairs to face each other. Federica stepped behind the bar, gave the barman a hug, and planted a kiss on his cheek.

"Hi Fritz," she said, still holding him at the waist.

"Fede," Fritz replied. The use of her family nickname didn't surprise Stonecrop.

Fritz acknowledged Stonecrop but made no comment about the night shared in his apartment, when Stonecrop had feared that Couto might kill him. In retrospect, Stonecrop mused, Couto could have ended Stonecrop's life whenever the hell he wanted.

There was brief exchange in Italian. Federica had ordered *Pizzoccheri*. "It's fabulous, not on the menu today, but Fritz has enough for us."

The dish was the chef's version of a Graubünden specialty—tagliatelle noodles made with buckwheat flour. The Tavate chef, Federica announced, had history with Ratzow. She offered no specifics.

The bar faced the kitchen serving window. In silence, they watched Fritz and the kitchen staff work—boiling, straining, and then tossing grey, speckled, al dente pasta in an iron skillet, along with chard, Valtellina Casera cheese, garlic and a health-spa inappropriate chunk of alpine butter. Before serving, the cook tasted the pasta with his fingers and then fired the dishes for a minute under a fierce salamander.

"This counter is the same stone as the stove in Lupita's house," Stonecrop ran his hand over the green, honed soapstone.

The aroma of garlic brought Stonecrop to life. He picked up the menu, got Fritz's attention, and asked for a side of *Bündnerfleisch*—cured, air-dried beef. And he nixed Federica's *Stange* and ordered a bottle of pinot noir produced in *Quinten*, a hamlet—population three thousand—inset on the north shore of the Walensee and primarily accessed by boat or on foot. Walled in by hills and abutting the lake, the enclave's weather was kind to tender pinot noir grapes.

Alicia pulled out her phone and flipped through photos of Fede and Alicia's family. "Chicago days. We had fun," she said.

"Your parents . . ." Federica asked.

"Happy, healthy, and retired. Let's call them together tonight."

Stonecrop relaxed. The wine helped. He felt mesmerized as he watched and listened to Alicia and Federica reminisce. Their youth surprised him, as though he had noticed them for the first time, and their gay energy reminded him that soon his own daughters would be in college.

He was lost mid-thought when Alicia dropped her phone into her plate of pizzoccheri and toppled her chair as she jumped to her feet.

"That's the guy, right?" Alicia had recognized him from photos she had been given.

"Alicia, he's not a threat. I promise." Federica continued, "He's even kind of a friend."

"I know, I know" she answered, embarrassed by her reaction. "Sorry. It's just, well, I had this idea of him in my head, and then actually seeing him. I'm sorry."

Ratzow followed Couto through the door. Under his muscled arm and half-resting on his less-muscled belly he carried a large, framed photo, the very one he had texted when Stonecrop and Couto had been in València.

With thumb and trigger finger, Stonecrop plucked the handy out of the pasta. Federica shooed away Fritz, who was en route to gather and replace the dish with a fresh one. Alicia righted the toppled chair and grabbed extra napkins to wipe down the phone.

Every head in the room had eyes on them. Noise from the kitchen staff preparing food somehow normalized the situation and soon customers resumed dining. A Russian cleared his throat, a sink disposal clogged with twenty years of two-packs-a-day.

A half-smile crept over the left half of Couto's face. Stonecrop inadvertently mimicked the gesture, one corner of his mouth rising. Each man was happy to see the other.

Author Bio

Wayne and his wonderful wife share a modest home a block from the beach in Manzanita, Oregon. He writes, climbs, and skis. His background includes long stretches of work in venture capital and project finance, and equally long stretches of study in philosophy, ancient Greek, and mathematics. He enjoys reading Shakespeare before bed, dancing salsa, cooking, and playing congas. He dearly wishes he knew a dozen languages but struggles mightily with the few with which he is familiar.

Other works:

How I Learned French or Certain Events in the Life of Otto Pulaski

RED MONKEY

Website: wwgoss.com